Praise for the Last War series

'Likely the next *Game of Thrones*, and the best book I've read in several years'
Glen Cook, author of *The Black Company* on *We Are the Dead*

'Like Tarantino crossed with David Gemmell . . . Absolutely splendid'
Peter McLean, author of *Priest of Bones* on *We Are the Dead*

'Hooked from page one, *We Are the Dead* rattles along with the pace of a runaway bullet train . . . This is a powerful debut'
Gavin Smith, author of *The Bastard Legion*

'A masterpiece of a story about hope, resistance and fellowship'
The Book Bag on *We Are the Dead*

'An adventure that's rich in darkness and bloodshed'
SFX on *We Are the Dead*

'*We Are the Dead* is a staggering, marvellous and gripping fantasy debut'
Grimdark Magazine

'Fans of Joe Abercrombie and R. F. Kuang will find something to love here'
Fantasy Hive on *We Are the Dead*

'A barnstorming book of ordinary people dealing with extraordinary circumstances – great fun and very entertaining'
Tom Lloyd, author of *Stranger of Tempest* on *We Are the Dead*

'Gripping, grim and glorious'
  Mark Stay, author of *The End of Magic* on *We Are the Dead*

'An utter masterpiece'
  Where There's Ink There's Paper on *We Are the Dead*

'One of the best fantasy novels of the year . . . A heart-hammering sequel'
  Novel Notions on *A Fool's Hope*

'Dark, brutal, wonderful'
  Nick Martell, author of *The Kingdom of Liars*, on *A Fool's Hope*

'Epic and horrific, wonderful and depressing, exhilarating and distressing and truly a must-read for all fans of the genre'
  The Chronicler on *A Fool's Hope*

UNTIL
THE LAST

Also by Mike Shackle from Gollancz

We Are the Dead
A Fool's Hope

UNTIL THE LAST

BOOK THREE OF THE LAST WAR

MIKE SHACKLE

This edition first published in Great Britain in 2023 by Gollancz
an imprint of the Orion Publishing Group Ltd
Carmelite House, 50 Victoria Embankment
London EC4Y ODZ

An Hachette UK Company

1 3 5 7 9 10 8 6 4 2

A CIP catalogue record for this book
is available from the British Library.

ISBN (Paperback) 978 1 473 22530 5
ISBN (eBook) 978 1 473 22531 2
ISBN (Audio Download) 978 1 473 22851 1

Typeset by Deltatype Ltd, Birkenhead, Merseyside

Printed in Great Britain by Clays Ltd, Elcograf S.p.A.

www.gollancz.co.uk

For Mum

The Last Prayer

God or man,
Death calls for you.

Prologue

Raaku

Kagestan

His Imperial Majesty Raaku, son of the mighty Kage, the one true God, walked through the caverns beneath his castle. Four monstrous bodyguards followed in his step, but he was barely aware of them. After all, they'd been his shadows for nearly a century now, from the very first days after he took control of his tribe. He gave them strength and long lives; they gave him their eternal loyalty and protection. Not that he needed it here, in the heart of his kingdom, at the source of his power. Servants fell to their knees and bowed as he passed, but Raaku paid them no heed.

The caverns spread out under his castle in every direction. Each cave had its own pool of holy water, used by Raaku in a different way. The largest was dedicated to the Daijaku. In that chamber alone there were hundreds of cocoons, half-submerged in the water, at various stages of development. Veksters, his most skilled workers, waded amongst the shells, checking the growth of the inhabitants, looking for cracks, making sure no harm came to their charges until they were ready to hatch. It took six months to turn a man into a Daijaku. And then a few more to train them to be lethal.

He passed chamber after chamber, pausing only here and there to check on the Veksters' work, ensuring that they carried out their tasks meticulously.

Despite their trusted status, the Veksters heads were enclosed in

3

iron bascinets and their bodies barely clothed to ensure that none of them could drink or steal the holy waters. He also insisted their tongues were removed to prevent them from talking about what they witnessed beneath the castle. Each Vekster served for a maximum of five years before they gave their lives to Kage in the Red Lake, lest prolonged exposure to the waters gave them powers they did not deserve.

One waited outside the iron door that marked the last chamber in the caverns, a tray laden with food and water in her hands. She did not bow as Raaku approached, merely waited, still as stone – the way she had been taught.

His guardians moved to either side of the door, taking up their positions. They were not allowed to follow him inside. As much as he trusted them, some conversations were not meant for ears other than his own.

Raaku waited while the Vekster's key activated the runes engraved in the door. Red light danced across its surface as the locks slid free. The Vekster pushed the door open and stepped aside so Raaku could enter alone. Runes carved into the walls illuminated the interior, revealing the chamber's sole occupant.

The man stared at Raaku, his bravery borne out of madness as he bared his teeth in greeting. His hair was long and his beard in need of a trim, but no doubt the Veksters would see to that soon enough. Chains trailed from his wrists to the walls, just long enough to allow the man to move around his cell. The man's only comfort was a cot to sleep on. He was a heathen after all and deserved no more – not even after a hundred years of captivity.

The Emperor waited while the Vekster placed the tray to one side and retrieved the buckets filled with the prisoner's waste. She returned a moment later with two fresh buckets and placed them beside the cot. Only then did she leave and shut the door behind her.

'Hello, Laafien,' said Raaku.

The Jian bared his teeth and growled.

'I came to tell you it has begun.'

'It began long ago.' Laafien's voice was full of anger and hate.

Raaku smiled. 'When you found me.'

'A cursed day.' The man bared his teeth once more and rattled his chains.

'A blessed day. My father sent you to show me the way to eternal glory.'

'So you believe.'

'So I know. After all, Sekanowari is upon us and soon the False Gods will be no more.'

'If you believe that, why are you here?' The man jutted his chin towards Raaku, clicking his teeth. 'Even you have doubts. Fears. Victory is not certain.'

'What have you seen?'

'Of the future? Not enough. Never enough.' A flash of a smile. 'Otherwise I'd never have found you – and let you live.'

'That was my father's hand at work,' said Raaku. 'But you are also right. I want to know what you can see of the days ahead, the battles I must fight.' He reached down to his belt and the gourds that hung there. The man skittered back as he saw Raaku select one and uncork it.

'I won't drink it,' hissed Laafien with a shake of his head. 'I won't.'

'But you must,' said Raaku. 'You have to drink the holy water if you are to have your visions and to prolong your life.'

'I don't want to live!' screamed the man, but Raaku ignored him. After a hundred and twenty years together, the man was predictable.

He grasped the man's jaws, squeezed his mouth open and poured the holy water down his throat. The man spluttered, tried to spit the water out, but Raaku held his jaw until enough had been swallowed. He then stepped back and waited for the water to do its work.

'I hate you!' The man thrashed against his chains. 'I curse the day I met you. I curse you and all who follow you.'

Raaku smiled. 'We found out long ago that your words have no power to harm me.'

'Then why do you keep me here? Why don't you send me to your father in the Great Darkness?'

'Because you were his gift to me and I will always value you as such. You opened my eyes to my divine role in Sekanowari and helped guide me down the long road here. Now, you will help direct my victory.'

'No. Noo … urgh … n … aaargh!' The prisoner collapsed, convulsing as the holy water opened up his mind to the future.

Raaku watched him writhe on the ground, curious as ever regarding his father's choice of this man – this Jian – as his messenger. One hundred and twenty years ago, Raaku had watched the dark-skinned heathen – the brother of Aasgod, the Jian's Lord Mage – walk into his tribe's camp on the northern steppes, his face unmasked, on a quest to find holy water. For some reason he did not know, Raaku stopped his tribe from killing Laafien for his trespass and instead, the boy who would become Emperor gave the man a seat by his fire and his food to eat and listened to his tales of magic. He heard how the holy water gave Laafien the ability to see the future, and it was at that point that Raaku began to dream of the future, too.

Raaku spent years then, serving first as the man's guide and protector as they searched for the holy water, then as his assistant in exploring the caverns over which he later built his city. When Laafien drank the holy water for the first time, Raaku witnessed the Jian's vision and, by his reaction, he knew the man had seen Raaku's betrayal in his future. He'd tried to run but Raaku was a man by then and faster and stronger than some Jian mage. That was the first time Laafien had slept in this very chamber, his hands and feet bound, his legs broken, aware at last of who had walked beside him all those years. Aware of what Raaku would become.

The son of Kage.

The Emperor of an Egril Empire that stretched from north to south, east to west.

'They come,' gurgled the prisoner. 'The Four. The light. The dark. The land. The sea. From far and near. She will kill you and you will kill her and she will kill you and you will kill her. Life. Death. They come from the water to fight you for earth. The Four will come. You will go, or you will die. To Aisair. That is where Sekanowari will be won.'

Raaku listened. He knew better than to ask questions. The

6

man always spoke true and yet his words were never precise.

'The Great Darkness waits for death. Death calls all. All is death.' The man grew still, then sucked in air as if he'd never breathed before. His head shot up, his gleaming eyes fixed on Raaku, a mad smile slashed across his face. 'Victory can be yours if you can defeat death. Stop death. Then you will truly be a God.'

'If that is my father's will, it shall be done,' said Raaku. 'Thank you, Laafien.'

Raaku left the chamber and locked the door behind him. His guardians fell into step behind him as he made his way back through the caverns. He had much to do. He had the end of the world to plan.

Part I

The Best-Laid Plans

I

Tinnstra

Tinnstra stood at the window in the library at the Jian embassy and watched the sun rise over the harbour. Ten days had passed since the utter defeat of the Egril and the city was slowly recovering from the attack. The embassy itself was basically a ruin, but they'd managed to repair enough of it to make a small portion habitable once more.

Despite the early hour, a crowd had gathered outside the embassy grounds, kept back by a newly erected fence and a contingent of Meigorian soldiers. Some had been there since the morning after the victory over the Skulls, come to give thanks to Zorique for all she'd done, and their numbers had only swelled since then. They'd tied flowers to the railings and burned candles and incense in her honour. Some sat quietly, watching the embassy for signs of the queen, while others were more vocal, singing their praise or uttering prayers. But they all reacted the same when they saw Zorique: screaming, shouting, crying, all begging her to come and talk to them, to bless them. They thought her a God made flesh.

Tinnstra wasn't sure how that made her feel. On one hand, claiming divinity had done Raaku no harm. His army was more than ready to sacrifice itself for the son of Kage. However, Tinnstra knew Zorique only had her powers because Aasgod had force-fed her mother − her real mother − with Chikara water while Zorique and her brother were still in the womb. It had been a desperate gamble on the mage's part and something she hadn't forgiven the man for – even though the Aasgod with them now was his younger self, who she'd dragged kicking and screaming from the past, guilty of nothing.

In truth, Zorique was more a lucky experiment than a God. Tinnstra didn't want Zorique to pretend otherwise, to live any sort of lie.

Zorique doesn't need to cheat like I do. She has real power. It's the rest of us – it's me – who's faking it.

Still, Tinnstra had to admit it felt damn good to have stopped the Skulls from gaining a foothold in Meigore. If she closed her eyes, she could still see Zorique burning the Daijaku from the sky. She could still feel the rush of pleasure she'd enjoyed as the last Skull was executed. Belief burned in her heart that they could end this awful war once and for all.

She'd lived with Raaku's shadow hanging over her and Zorique for too long, losing friend after friend and ally after ally. Now she was the one sending souls to the Great Darkness. Meigore was free and Jia would be next.

Tinnstra just had to work out how to do it.

She turned back to the large table and the ancient map spread across it – the map she'd stolen from some Jian lord a thousand years in the past. It was unique in that it displayed not just the four nations of Meigore, Chongore, Dornway and Jia but also the Egril Empire to the north and the forgotten lands to the west. As far as Tinnstra was aware, it was the only map in existence that covered those territories. Whoever made it had explored further than anyone had thought possible before or since.

But it was Jia that occupied her attention now, as it had all night. How to invade? How to regain control? How to overcome the Skulls? And, more importantly, how to do it all without it costing countless lives?

She took a sip of tea and grimaced. It was cold and bitter from sitting too long and forgotten. Perhaps a fresh pot would help her think better.

Perhaps sleep would be best of all. Worry about this another day.

Tinnstra laughed. When had she ever done the sensible thing?

She stood up and, teapot in hand, left the library to head for the kitchens. A few more hours and then she'd sleep.

Tinnstra was halfway down the stairs when she heard the voices: a man talking to the maid provided by Tian Galrin, the new ruler of Meigore. They were laughing together – flirting, even – and Tinnstra felt a slight pang of ... what? Anger? Jealousy?

It was only Ralasis, after all. He flirted with everyone.

Tinnstra continued down the staircase, and as it curved towards the main hall she saw the sea captain and the maid, heads all but touching as she giggled at whatever joke he whispered.

'Good morning,' said Tinnstra before they were aware she was there. The maid jumped back, blushing, but Ralasis just turned his attention towards her, his smile broadening. He was wearing trousers tucked into high boots and a dark blue shirt open at the neck, a look that suited him better than the loose robes most Meigorian men chose to wear.

'It certainly is now,' he said, eyes twinkling with mischief.

'I was just explaining to Captain Ralasis that it was too early to call on you, ma'am,' said the maid. 'But he was insisting.'

'Is that what you call it?' said Tinnstra with a smile of her own. There was something about Ralasis that made it impossible for her to be annoyed with him.

'I was explaining that it wasn't too early as I knew a dedicated warrior like yourself would already be up and hard at work,' said Ralasis, a slight slur to his words.

'Are you drunk, Captain?' asked Tinnstra.

'Not drunk,' he replied. 'But I've been drinking. There is a significant difference. However, I'm not averse to trying to attain that state of inebriation. Perhaps you'd like to share a bottle of wine with me?'

'Who drinks in the morning?' Gods, he had her smiling even more.

'Well, I've not been to bed yet so it's still night as far as I'm concerned.' He raised an eyebrow, probably thinking it made him look attractive. 'What about you? Still last night or is it this morning?'

'I've not been to bed yet if that's what you're asking.'

'Yet!' said Ralasis. 'Then this is perfect timing.' He turned to the maid. 'Elise, if you please, fetch a bottle of your finest white wine.'

The maid looked to Tinnstra, horrified.

'Do as he asks,' said Tinnstra. 'We'll be upstairs.' Both of Ralasis' eyebrows shot up at hearing that and his grin ... Gods. Tinnstra shook her head and tried not to laugh. 'In the library.'

Ralasis gave her a sweeping bow as the maid scuttled off. 'Lead the way, my dear.'

'Call me "my dear" again and I'll break your arm,' said Tinnstra, heading back up the stairs.

'I'm sure you could do that quite easily,' said Ralasis, following behind. 'Ah, whatever happened to the nice young lady I rescued from a tiny boat in the Golden Channel?'

Tinnstra stopped on the stairs and turned to look down on Ralasis. 'Rescued? I seem to remember that *I* rescued *you* from the Daijaku.'

'That is true – so, in fact, we rescued each other.' Again, he flashed that damn smile of his.

'Stop that.'

'Stop what?'

'Your flirting. I heard you trying it on with the maid and now you're trying your luck with me. It won't work.'

'Flirting? I'd never do such a thing. I'm almost offended by the suggestion.'

'I doubt anything could offend you.' Tinnstra chuckled. 'Why are you here?'

'I wanted to make sure both you and Zorique were well and being cared for after the unpleasantries.'

'The unpleasantries?'

He waved a hand in the air. 'The scuffle with the Egril.'

'Ah, *those* unpleasantries. I'd almost forgotten.' Tinnstra entered the library, seeing the mess she'd made of the place; books lay sprawled all over the floor and stacked haphazardly upon the table. 'And that couldn't wait till later?'

But it was as if she'd never spoken. Ralasis' eyes had been drawn to the map. 'What's this?'

'A map. I thought that was obvious.'

'Is it real?' He ran his hand over the parchment with a surprising tenderness. 'Please tell me it's real.'

'The man I stole it from swore that it was.'

'Thank the Gods.' He bent down until he was all but sniffing the thing. 'It's extraordinary. I've never seen anything like it.'

'It's the only one of its kind, as far as I know.'

'It is – as far as I know. You said you stole it?' He looked up with a childish glint in his eye.

Tinnstra shrugged. 'From some Jian lord a long time ago.'

'He must've been furious.'

'He certainly wasn't happy – especially after I stuck a sword in his leg.'

Ralasis roared with laughter. 'Good girl.'

There was a knock at the door and Elise entered, eyes downcast, carrying a tray with a bottle of wine and two cups. Tinnstra moved some books from the corner of the table so she could place the tray there and gave her a nod of thanks. Elise all but ran from the room.

The wine at least made Ralasis look up from the map. 'Shall I pour or ...'

'I can do it.' Tinnstra filled the cups and passed one to Ralasis.

'Thank you, my ... Tinnstra.' He raised the cup to her before taking a sip. 'Delightful.'

'What am I doing?' Tinnstra muttered to herself before taking a sip herself. The wine was light and chilled, with a sweetness to it that was, as Ralasis said, quite delightful.

Not that the Meigorian seemed to care. The map had his total attention. 'The places I would explore if I owned this map.'

'It's yours, if you want it,' said Tinnstra. 'Once Jia is free.'

Ralasis looked up. 'I couldn't accept such a priceless gift. But perhaps I could have it copied?'

'I won't need it after the war. It's yours.'

'You have plans?'

'When we win? I'm going to find somewhere quiet, far from anyone, grow old and die in my bed of boredom.'

'By yourself?'

'Who knows?'

'That would be a shame. A woman like you needs someone to spoil her,' said Ralasis. 'However, I will accept your generous gift – because when this war is over, I'm going to get on my ship and sail until I run out of sea to explore.'

Tinnstra raised her cup once more. 'To your endless adventure.'

After taking another gulp of wine, Ralasis nodded at the map. 'What are you planning here?'

'I'm going over my strategy for retaking Jia. I have a meeting this afternoon with Tian Galrin's new military leader to discuss our options.'

'Which are?'

'We have two possible routes as far as I can see – one that gives us a chance of winning the war within five or six days and another that could take months.'

'Doesn't sound like much of a choice. When it comes to war, I prefer it to be over as quickly as possible. There's less chance of me getting killed that way.'

'The quick option depends on certain factors.'

'Tell me.'

'I thought you were more interested in the wine,' said Tinnstra.

Ralasis examined his cup and then held it out to be refilled. 'I can drink and listen.'

'Of course you can,' said Tinnstra, pouring more wine.

'So, tell me.'

Tinnstra moved beside the Meigorian. 'I've been told the only viable landing place for a fleet the size of ours is Omason Beach – here, near Kiyosun.' She placed her finger on the location marked on the map.

'That's right,' said Ralasis. 'If we sail further up the western coast, we risk running into storms this time of year and the fleet could wind up scattered over a hundred miles or sunk beneath the waves. Omason Beach is a good landing place for us.' As he tapped the map, his hand brushed hers.

'But we come ashore at the very southern tip of Jia,' said Tinnstra, ignoring the touch, 'and the key to victory is retaking Aisair.' She moved her finger up the map, tracing the route to Jia's capital along the Northern Road.

'That's a long way.'

'Three to four weeks if we're walking. Probably fighting all the way.'

'That doesn't sound particularly enticing. Are there other roads?'

'Only if we're prepared to take months reaching Aisair, weaving our way through the mountains or following the eastern coast.'

'But you said we could win in five or six days?'

'When I escaped from Aisair with the queen, we were taken to a temple in the Olyisius Mountains. It's three days from Aisair.' Again, Tinnstra pointed out the location. 'There's a gate that connects to a counterpart in the Ascalian Mountains, a day from Kiyosun.'

'A gate like the Tonin create?'

'Exactly.'

'That sounds better.'

'If we can use it, we might even take the Skulls by surprise. We can fight one decisive battle instead of only the Gods know how many taking the Northern Road.'

'I'd be happy not to have to walk that far.' Ralasis took another sip of wine, then looked Tinnstra in the eye. 'So, what's the problem?'

'I don't know if these gates still exist. When we escaped, a Chosen followed us through. If he told anyone about it, then it's either in Skull hands or destroyed.'

'And then we're walking.'

Tinnstra nodded. 'Then we're walking.'

'We have to assume he did. Why would he not?'

'He got his head cut off a day after he discovered it,' said Tinnstra, with a smile. 'So he might not have had time to pass the information on.'

Ralasis laughed. 'That would shut a man up. Did you do the cutting?'

'No. That honour fell to a great Shulka named Jax, but I was there. I saw it happen.'

The sea captain poured himself some more wine and topped up Tinnstra's cup. 'We need to send someone to Jia to find out if we still have access to the gates and, if we do, to guard them until we arrive.'

'I already have,' Tinnstra said.

'You have?'

'One of my people left yesterday. We'll have the information we need by the end of the week.'

'And did you clear this mission with the new Meigorian military leader?' Ralasis had his head tilted to one side in a way she found ... uncomfortable.

'I told you to stop the flirting.'

Ralasis laughed. 'I'm not flirting.'

Tinnstra shook her head. 'Gods. You probably don't even know you're doing it.' *That* made her feel special. 'Look, it's been a long night. I'm tired. Thank you for calling on me but it's best you go. I need to get some sleep before I see this great leader of yours – and no, I didn't tell him about sending Wenna to Jia. Why should I? He's probably another idiot in a dress like most of you Meigorians.'

'Harsh,' said Ralasis, 'but fair. I must admit I've never liked those robes. Very unflattering.'

'Have you met Tian Galrin's man?'

'I know him well – and you're right, he is an idiot.'

Tinnstra leaned forwards. 'Tell me more.'

Ralasis wagged a finger at her. 'That would ruin the surprise. And besides, you might like the man when you meet him. I wouldn't want to cloud your judgement any more than I have. Especially since I know he's already very impressed by you.' He stood up, downed his wine, glanced at the small amount left in the bottle and then smiled that smile. 'And you're right – we should both get some sleep. I want to be at my best later, too.'

'You'll be there?'

'Of course. Some, most notably my father, would say I'm the biggest idiot of them all. How could I miss such a gathering?'

'Well, I'll have at least one friend there.'

Ralasis picked up Tinnstra's hand and kissed the back of it. 'You certainly will. Good night or good morning – whatever it is.' He picked up the wine bottle and swaggered out of the library with a wave.

Immediately, the room felt like all the life had been sucked from it. She wasn't sure she'd trust Ralasis with more than getting a ship from one place to another, but he made her smile. Not many people had managed that for a long time.

Her eyes drifted to the map once more, moving from Kiyosun to Aisair to Egril and lingered there.

2

Vallia

Tolledheim

Commander Vallia rubbed her thumb up and down her sword hilt while she watched her men impale the last of the heathens. A long afternoon's work, but necessary. After all, rebellion against His Imperial Majesty could never be tolerated.

Now, three thousand Dorwanese were lined up on spikes along the streets of their capital, Tolledheim, as a warning to anyone else contemplating action against the Egril Empire.

'Were all of them rebels?' said Chancellor Astin, who had arrived a few minutes before from Kagestan. He wasn't a tall man, certainly no warrior, with his back hunched as if the weight of the world rested on his shoulders. His grey skin matched his grey mask. He wore no weapon. In a world where one's measure was weighed in lives taken, Vallia couldn't imagine this man had ever got his own hands bloody. His ink-stained fingers were testament to his tools. Vallia had never liked administrators but she could not deny the man's value to the Emperor.

'Yes – in heart if not in action,' replied Vallia. She looked over at the man. 'You disapprove?'

'No. You've sent heathen souls to Kage. What greater duty is there?' replied Astin, sounding far from convinced.

'Do you have a message for me?' said Vallia. She didn't have time for small talk.

'I've been asked to bring you back to Kagestan – to see the Emperor.'

She turned to one of her officers, General Wallan. He'd served with her from the beginning of the War of Unification. 'Take command here. The Emperor has summoned me.'

Wallan saluted in acknowledgement. There was no need to say more. He knew what to do.

Vallia gestured to the Great Hall where the Tonin was kept and began to walk, expecting Astin to keep up. If the Emperor wished to see her, Vallia wasn't going to keep him waiting. 'What's happened?'

'We have a few problems in Jia. Rebels managed to smuggle Princess Zorique, the last surviving member of the royal family other than *our* king, out of the country to Meigore. In the process, they left a trail of Egril dead from Aisair in the north to Kiyosun in the south. Two Chosen – Darus Monsuta and his sister Skara – were also killed,' said Astin. A few yards and he was already out of breath.

'I thought the princess was a child?'

'She was four years old.'

'Was?'

'Lord Bacas went with a force of over five thousand soldiers to Meigore with explicit orders to kill the child and seize the capital in the Emperor's name, after which we intended to invade and conquer the entire country.'

There was something in Astin's tone that gave Vallia a bad feeling. 'He was unsuccessful?'

'Yes,' said Astin. 'The whole invasion force was wiped out. Only six survivors returned to Kagestan. Lord Bacas was not amongst them.'

Vallia stopped at the impossibility of this news. 'Lord Bacas was killed?'

'According to the survivors, the city was all but won. Then three people appeared with magical powers and turned the tide of the battle in their favour.'

'Three people?' Vallia resumed walking. The Great Hall loomed ahead, a long, single-storey building. Dragons carved out of wood loitered on each corner of the roof, designed to protect the occupants from the powers of the Great Darkness. They made her smile every time she saw them. Only a child would believe in such nonsense. Against her army's swords, even the famed Dorwanese berserker warriors had fallen like wheat before the scythe. 'How was that possible?'

'One of the women possessed vast powers and almost single-handedly defeated our forces. His Imperial Majesty believes the woman to be Zorique.'

'I thought you said she was four years old?' Guards opened the doors to the Great Hall. Tables stretched the length of the room with fire pits in between. It was claimed most of the city could feast in this room at any one time, but Vallia doubted that. Then again, perhaps now that there were three thousand fewer citizens to seat ...

'The Emperor believes the heathens did something to age her, to bring her into her powers.' Astin puffed behind Vallia as she led him to the quarters at the rear of the hall. The Dorwanese king once lived there, back when there was a king. Vallia had the last person to hold that title spiked within days of the invasion. It'd seemed the simplest solution once he refused to cooperate.

The Tonin was kept in a cell at the far end of the hall. Two soldiers stood guard – two of Vallia's best. As mighty as the Imperial army was, the Tonin were the key to their success. They were precious commodities that had to be protected at all costs, for their numbers were finite.

The door to the cell was already open and when Vallia's aide saw them approach, she motioned to the Tonin to create a gate connected to the Tonin in Raaku's castle in Kagestan.

Vallia clenched her jaw as the creature began its magic. Even after all these years, she hated the shriek as they tore a hole in the very air, to connect one place to another. It set every nerve in her body on edge.

Vallia didn't bother continuing the conversation until they had stepped through the gate and into the Emperor's castle. As they left that Tonin's chambers, her ears still rang with the echo of the creature's screech. 'Where is the Emperor?'

'He waits for us in the caverns,' said Astin.

Vallia nodded. It was to be expected. Raaku spent a great deal of his time there, creating the resources the Empire required. She set a brisk pace through the castle, wasting no time, the chancellor on her heels. Down they went, into the depths of the building, to the red caves.

The stairs were winding and narrow. Astin was sweating by the time they reached the last few steps and even more out of breath. Too much time spent at his desk, battling paperwork. Getting weak. Unacceptable. If not for the trust Raaku placed in Astin, Vallia would have found a stake for him as well.

Egril could never be weak. Once, it was because life on the steppes would never have tolerated such a thing. There, one was either predator or prey. Now, it was because the Egril had an Empire to maintain. The weak could not conquer the world.

Stepping into His Majesty's caverns was as awe-inspiring as ever. To see his wonders with one's own eyes was a privilege few enjoyed. When the Emperor first showed her the caverns and what he was creating, her mind had raced with all the possible military applications the Daijaku alone would offer her. She'd always believed in Raaku, but it was only when she'd seen his children that Vallia knew the False Gods would be defeated.

Over the years, she'd come here to drink of the holy waters. They kept her young and strong. She might've been born some eighty winters ago but she looked like it had been only thirty.

As they walked through the chambers, Vallia watched the cocooned bodies twist and turn as they were transformed. It was an agonising experience, but those brave souls endured it for Kage's eternal glory. They personified the strength of the Egril and her heart swelled with pride.

So unlike the scribe next to her.

Torchlight danced across the cocoons' moist surfaces and mingled with the red of the holy waters as they passed the Tonin, the Kojins, the Kyoryu, past the Chosen's birthing pool and into the darker, smaller areas where Raaku conducted his experiments, creating creatures from his imagination, with inspiration sent by his father out of the Great Darkness.

A dozen soldiers from the First Legion stood guard outside one of the last chambers, mere shadows in their red armour and demon masks. Their captain nodded as Vallia and Astin approached, and doors were opened without the need for any words.

Astin went no further. 'I will leave you here. But see me afterwards and I will organise whatever you need to accomplish His Imperial Majesty's orders.'

Vallia nodded. She turned to walk into the darkness, but a guard held up a hand.

'Your sword,' he said.

Vallia unhooked the sheathed weapon from her belt. 'Take care of it. It's very precious to me. The Emperor himself gave it to me.'

'Of course, Commander,' the sentry replied.

A small pond lay in the centre of the chamber, steam dancing across its surface. Smoke from the few torches mounted on the walls further thickened the air. Raaku was submerged up to his waist as he worked his magic on a single large cocoon. Crackles of energy flickered across its surface as Raaku ran his palms over the shell, revealing a man-shaped creature inside who twitched with each burst of magic. Vallia couldn't see Raaku's four guardians, but she knew they lurked somewhere in the shadows, close at hand if needed.

Vallia knelt by the water's edge and bowed. The rock was warm to the touch and she could feel the faintest vibrations echoing out from the pool as Raaku worked his magic.

'Rise, Commander.' Raaku's voice rumbled like thunder. Remaining on her knees, Vallia straightened her back. Her master was still focused on the cocoon and hadn't even looked her way. Magic glistened across the muscles of his giant back, his skin like stone; a reminder that Raaku was no mortal. 'I'm grateful you have answered my summons.'

'I am yours to command, Master,' replied Vallia.

Raaku continued to work on the cocoon. The body within twitched and turned as the Emperor manipulated his magic through the shell, changing with each spark, becoming more than it once was – becoming what Raaku willed it to be. 'We fight Sekanowari, my loyal servant, as we knew we would. The Last War is finally here.'

'Yes, Master.'

'We have been waiting for the False Gods to show their hand and reveal their champions. I thought they would appear with each land we invaded, with each temple we burned. But they kept silent. Hidden. Scared.'

'Yes, Master.'

'But no longer. They are bolstered by this victory, thinking we are weak, and we must be ready to destroy them.'

'Yes, Master.' Vallia watched the body convulse inside the cocoon as Raaku poured more magic into it. It appeared to grow violently, pushing against the confines of the cocoon, then shrink back to normal size again and again until Raaku stepped away from the cocoon, his magic retreating into his hands.

Only then did her master turn to her. A simple mask covered the upper part of his face, old and cracked. Raaku had worn it when he travelled alone into the northern mountains as a child and spoke with his true father for the first time. It was the mask he'd worn during the War of Unification, and he'd worn it when he was crowned Emperor of all the tribes. A lesser man would have taken his rise to power as an opportunity to gather wealth, but not Raaku. That was not his way. Everything he did was to honour Kage and strengthen his people's place in the world. No more than that. A God had no ego.

'Three champions have shown themselves,' said Raaku. 'The first is Zorique, the younger woman who can fly, who has been aged by magic and brought into her powers. The second is the mage, Aasgod. We believed that the Monsutas had killed the Jians' Lord Mage, but he has returned. The third is a Shulka woman with tremendous strength. There will be a fourth.'

'I will go to Meigore immediately and destroy them,' said Vallia.

'No, not Meigore. The False Gods' champions will come to retake Jia and you will meet them there.' Raaku climbed out of the pool. He took a cloak from a Vekster and threw it over his shoulders.

'I will not fail you. Victory will be yours.'

'Walk with me, Vallia.'

She rose to her feet, still keeping her head bowed. She was a tall woman, almost six feet in height, but the Emperor towered over her. He headed out of the chamber and Vallia followed a step behind.

'How long have we fought together?' asked Raaku.

'A long time. Since you led our tribe from the steppes.'

'That was fifty winters ago.'

'Yes, Master.' It seemed longer and yet it could've been yesterday. Vallia had only been a soldier in Raaku's army back then. Eager to please her master. A lot of ground had been conquered since. A lot of blood spilled.

'In that time, you've never lost a battle.'

'No, Master.'

'Now, that will change. You will lose battles. Vast numbers of our forces will most likely be destroyed during each encounter with the False Gods' champions.'

'They will?' replied Vallia, trying to hide her confusion. The Emperor had given her an army strong enough to shatter the world. Surely the threat from three people wasn't really that great?

Raaku stared down at her as if reading her thoughts. 'This is Sekanowari, Commander. All that matters is that we win the war. To do that, you must weaken the heathens at every turn. Make them pay with a hundred lives for every step they take on Jian soil. Know that when others talk of defeats, it is a necessary part of my plan.'

'Yes, Master.'

'Believe in me, Vallia, and eternal glory will be yours.'

Vallia bowed once more, her heart swelling with the honour bestowed upon her. Her place in the Great Darkness would be assured.

3

Wenna

The Golden Channel

Wenna could see Jia up ahead, a shadow on the horizon. Her home. By the Four Gods, she never thought she'd make it back. How many times had she nearly died in Meigore? How many of her friends had she left back there, dead in ditches and alleyways and in that cursed prison?

Too Godsdamned many.

The small fishing boat bumped up and down with the waves, cold spray stinging Wenna's face, but she didn't care. After a day and a night at sea, she was going home.

She glanced back at the two Meigorian sailors with her. They'd barely spoken to each other since they left Layso, but that suited her fine. Just because they now shared an enemy in the Skulls didn't suddenly make them her friends. The majority of Meigorians had stood by silently when their king ordered every Jian, refugee or not, locked up in a prison. Even worse, a minority had applauded the action. That knowledge still cut Wenna. She wasn't going to make small talk with anyone who could support such actions. What sort of person turned their back on people in need?

It was all different now, of course. Now the Skulls had invaded their country, too, and the Meigorians had got a little taste of what Jia had been going through for so long. Now they understood what it was like to have your home turned to ash and to see your loved ones butchered.

The irony wasn't lost on Wenna that the only reason Meigore wasn't now an occupied country was because Jians had come to their rescue.

And what Jians they were.

Hard to believe that Zorique and Tinnstra were the same people she'd helped escape from the prison camp. They'd only been gone a couple of days and yet they'd come back full of magic and at least ten years older.

They'd slaughtered the Skulls. Burned them from the skies and carved them up on the streets. Like Gods.

And now it was Jia's turn to be freed.

She didn't want to think about the state the country must be in after nine months of occupation. Her family had been in Aisair when the Skulls invaded, but she'd not heard a word about them since then. Knowing the fate of most Shulka, she wasn't holding out much hope of finding them alive. Her brother, Darl, was all of ten. That was no age to die in a pointless war. No age at all.

She just hoped the Hanran hadn't been crushed by the Skulls, that there was still some resistance to the invaders. Winning the country back would be all the more difficult if there was no fight left within Jian hearts.

The waves calmed the closer to shore they came, the curve of the bay welcoming them in. Even the looming cliffs felt protective, hiding them from any Skull that might be watching, and when the boat bit into the shingle and juddered to a stop, relief rushed through Wenna. No matter what happened next, she was home.

'Good luck,' said one of the sailors in Meigorian.

Wenna nodded. 'I'll meet you here in two days with messages to take back.'

The sailor grunted in agreement.

Wenna shouldered her bag, checked her sword and jumped onto Jian soil. She waded ashore, not looking back. She heard the sailors push the boat off the shingle and the creak of the sail as it found the wind again. Let them go. She was home. That was all that mattered.

When she was ten yards from the sea and sure she was alone,

Wenna sank to her knees and buried both her hands in the sand. It was so good to feel her country again, to breathe its air, just to be one with it and praise the Four Gods for helping her stay alive.

Tears came suddenly, catching her off guard. She couldn't stop them – nor did she want to. Big, chest-heaving sobs, full of all the pain, sorrow and fear that she'd bottled up for so long. She grieved for all the lives lost, for her family, for a world gone so wrong, and she cried for everything they had yet to endure.

She fell forwards, until her head was touching the sand, and cried and cried.

She was home. She couldn't believe it. How many times had she dreamed of this moment? How many times had the thought of Jia given her strength in her darkest hours?

Wenna clenched clumps of sand in her fists. 'This is why I fight,' she whispered. 'Home.'

Whatever happened next, she'd never leave it again. She would live and die in Jia.

With a deep breath, Wenna sat up and dried her eyes. That would be the last tears she'd cry. It was time for the Skulls to weep instead. She rolled her neck, filling her lungs with Jian air, hardening her soul, finding the Shulka she'd once been.

She had a job to do.

She found the hidden stairs leading up from the beach where Tinnstra had said they would be. When she was halfway up, she turned around to gaze out over the ocean. The sailing boat was already out of sight and Meigore lost in the darkness. Soon, there would be over a hundred warships full of soldiers making the journey she'd just made, and what a glorious sight that would be.

When she reached the top of the cliffs, she found signs of battle: broken blades, used arrows and Egril armour rusting over rotted corpses. No Jians, though. If her countrymen had fallen, their bodies had been taken away for burning. A good sign that the Hanran were still active.

Wenna set off along the main road to Kiyosun. It wasn't a city she had visited before but Tinnstra had briefed her well on what to expect and who she had to find.

The Ascalian Mountains loomed high to the north, a shadow

against the night stars. Somewhere on their slopes lay a temple to Nasri, the God of the Sea, and the doorway to the rest of Jia and the key to Tinnstra's plan. All their hopes rested on that temple still being in Hanran hands.

Sunrise was still only a faint glow in the distance when Wenna got her first glimpse of the city, a spit of land jutting out into the ocean. There were no lights burning, though, and that worried her. A city like Kiyosun would always have signs of life, no matter what the time of day or night.

So why so dark?

Wenna took her time approaching the city, making sure she didn't kick over any loose rocks and sticking to the shadows as best she could. She kept a careful eye out for Daijaku above and any Skulls who might be lurking. But all was quiet.

Too quiet?

She loosened her sword in its sheath and rolled her shoulders, getting ready to fight an enemy she couldn't see. Her unease only grew the closer she got to the city.

Then she saw why no lights burned within its walls and her heart sank.

The Skulls had destroyed Kiyosun. Great stretches were completely flattened while other areas had been reduced to jagged shards of what used to be buildings.

'Not a pretty sight, is it?'

Wenna spun around at the sound of the voice, sword already drawn, as four human shapes loomed out of the rocks. Hoods covered their faces but there was no hiding the weapons in their hands.

'Who are you?' a woman asked.

'A friend.'

'Give us your name and then we'll be the judge of that,' the woman replied, stepping closer, her own sword pointed at Wenna's chest. Beneath their sand-coloured cloaks, they wore a mixture of armour; some had Shulka breastplates, while others had the Skull plated armour, only painted so it was no longer white. They were definitely not Egril.

Wenna smiled, lowering her sword, and held up her other

hand. 'I am Wenna of Clan Inaren. I come from Meigore with information for General Jax of Clan Huska.'

'Never heard of him.' She nodded to one of the others. 'Take her weapons.'

'Hold on a minute,' said Wenna. 'I'm not going to—'

The woman stepped even closer, moving the tip of her sword within an inch of Wenna's face. 'You will if you want to carry on breathing. Throwing a few names around of people we've never heard of doesn't mean shit. The only reason you're still alive is because you're Jian. No more than that.'

Wenna took a breath. 'I understand.'

With her weapons gone and her hands bound tight in front of her, the Hanran led her along a path through the rocks, taking her high up into the mountains, often turning this way and that without apparent reason onto twisting paths that doubled back on themselves before advancing, making it impossible for Wenna to remember the route, if that had been her intention.

No one spoke to her, but no one tried to kill her, either, so Wenna was happy to keep her thoughts to herself. Instead, she enjoyed the climb, watching the sun rise higher and higher, filling the sky with beautiful golden streaks. Proof that, no matter what else was happening in the world, the Gods still loved this land.

'Why do you keep smiling?' asked the woman suddenly as they walked along a narrow path, a hundred-foot drop to one side. 'Most people are scared senseless when they're taken along here for the first time.'

'I'm just happy to be home,' replied Wenna. 'Even the sun shines brighter here.'

'How long have you been away?'

'Two years. I was stationed at the embassy in Meigore.'

'A lot's happened since then,' said the man leading the group. 'Jia's not the place you remember.'

'Fucking Skulls.' The man behind her spat.

'It'll be ours again one day soon,' said Wenna. 'I promise you that.'

'We'll see,' said the woman. 'Stop here. We're going to blind-fold you.'

'Is that wise?' said Wenna, looking down at the drop to her left.

'Don't worry,' replied the woman. 'You'll only fall if we decide to push you off the path.'

Wenna glanced over her shoulder at the man behind her. She thought she could see a grin in the shadows of the hood. 'That's not very reassuring,' said Wenna.

'Suppose not,' replied the woman. 'We can always say goodbye here if you'd prefer.'

Wenna looked down at the drop again. 'Not particularly.'

The man behind her tied a cloth tight around her eyes and Wenna took a deep breath. All would be well.

He kept his hands on her shoulders, gently guiding her along the mountain path. Wind brushed her face, the sun warmed her skin and she could feel the light all around her. All she had to do was not think about what one wrong step would mean.

Wenna had no idea how much longer they walked as she allowed herself to be guided to the Hanran's base, trusting in her countrymen. After all, there were much easier ways to kill her than making her walk halfway up a mountain first.

Then everything changed. The light around Wenna disappeared. She could feel rock brush close on either side. At one point, the man behind her guided her head to one side with his hand before allowing her to straighten again.

'We're here,' said the woman, and someone removed Wenna's blindfold.

They were in a large cavern, at least a thousand feet across and some five hundred feet high. A fresh-water stream ran through its heart and light shone through holes spotted across the roof. Shelters and shacks had been built on either side of the riverbank and Wenna could see children running around amongst the adults. It wasn't just soldiers here, then, there were families, too. It was like a small town built underground.

'How many of you are there?' asked Wenna.

'Not enough,' said the woman. She lowered her hood. Her hair was cut short and her face was long and lean, with dark rings around her eyes. 'Keep her here,' she said to the others. 'I'll get Hasan.'

'I was told only to speak to General Jax,' said Wenna.

'Hasan's in charge now.' The woman turned and headed off into the cavern.

'Don't mind Royati,' said the man, lowering his hood. His beard was streaked with grey, but he had young eyes still. 'If she didn't like you, she would've thrown you off the ledge.'

'I'm glad she didn't,' replied Wenna. 'A lot of people are counting on me.'

'My name's Tavis,' said the man. He leaned forward and untied her hands.

'Thank you,' said Wenna, rubbing her wrists.

Tavis gave her a look. 'What was it like over there? We've been hoping the Meigorians would send some help, but we've not heard anything for a long time.'

'Pretty grim. Plenty died, and not just when the Skulls came.'

'I'm sorry.'

'Don't be. Things ended well.'

Something flashed across Tavis's face then. Something Wenna hadn't seen in a long time – was it hope? 'They did?'

Wenna smiled. 'Very much so.'

A whistle drew their attention. Royati waved them over from the other side of the cave.

'Looks like the chief will see you,' said Tavis. 'Come on.'

Leaving the other two, he led Wenna towards a small hut that had been built under an outcropping of rock. A group of children played off to one side while a man and a woman sat around a small fire. Armed guards formed a perimeter, ensuring no one got too close without an invitation.

As they approached, Wenna noticed the woman had tears tattooed on her cheek and her good cheer disappeared just like that. She stopped and looked closer at the guards. Some of them had tears inked on their faces as well. Dear Gods, they were Weeping Men – gangsters of the lowest order, smugglers, slavers and hired killers.

'What's wrong?' asked Tavis.

'I thought you were Hanran,' said Wenna, her hand going to an empty scabbard.

33

'We are,' said Tavis.

'Then why are Weeping Men amongst your number?'

'Because we're at war and they fight as well as the next Jian. Besides, Yas leads them now. They're not as bad as they were. They're on our side.'

'Who's Yas?'

Tavis pointed to the woman by the fire. 'And that's Hasan with her. Come on.'

They resumed walking, but Wenna still felt uneasy. She'd been in too many fights with Weeping Men ever to believe they were capable of doing good. She shouldn't have let them take her weapons. She'd been too happy to be back in Jia to think clearly.

'I thought you were about to turn around and make a run for Meigore just now,' said Royati when Wenna reached the hut.

'I still might,' said Wenna, not bothering to hide her unease.

'She's got a thing about tears,' said Tavis, touching a finger to his face.

'Get over it like the rest of us,' said Royati. She turned to the man by the fire. 'Chief, this is the woman I told you about.'

The man stood up. He was tall and good-looking with a warrior's body. His long hair was pulled back in a more relaxed version of a Shulka's topknot. 'I'm Hasan of Clan Huska. I hear you've come a long way to give me some news.'

'I was told to see General Jax,' said Wenna, her eyes drifting to the woman still sitting by the fire. 'My information is for his ears alone.'

'I'm afraid Jax died during the bombing of Kiyosun. Along with many others.' Hasan's smile was full of sadness. 'I'm afraid you're left with me.'

'And the Weeping Men,' said Wenna, despite herself.

The woman stood up quick, eyes blazing. 'You got a problem with that?' She was nearly as tall as Hasan, slender yet strong. Two tears on her cheek said she was dangerous, too.

'I do, actually.' Wenna glared at Hasan. 'Like all Shulka should.'

'Different times,' said Hasan. 'We're all friends here.'

The woman shook her head. 'I don't think our guest agrees, Hasan. Maybe she's come here to make trouble, not friends.'

Hasan held out a hand. 'Easy, Yas.'

Wenna took a deep breath. She had a mission. 'I'm sorry. I meant no offence.'

The woman snorted. 'I didn't ask to be put in charge of the Weeping Men, but life doesn't seem to care much about what any of us bloody well want. We just have to deal with what we're given.'

'A lot of people here owe their lives to Yas,' said Hasan. 'Myself included. Now please, tell me your news.'

'I was sent here to tell General Jax that an armada will be sailing from Meigore three months from now – with over forty thousand soldiers aboard,' said Wenna. 'Queen Zorique is coming back to reclaim her throne.'

'The girl is still alive?' said Hasan. 'Thank the Gods.'

The woman, Yas, was less excited. 'Queen Zorique? She's four years old. What good's she going to do us? Even if she does have an army with her.'

'She's not four years old anymore,' said Wenna, chest swelling with pride. 'And she could probably win back Jia on her own.'

'You'd better sit down,' said Hasan. 'It sounds like you have quite the tale to tell.'

4

Tinnstra

Layso

Elise knocked on Tinnstra's door. 'Ma'am, the queen asked me to make sure you were awake. You have to leave for the palace soon.'

Tinnstra's head hurt. Light streamed through the window. She'd hardly slept. Both Aasgod and Zorique were downstairs and their magic shone in her mind, making it hard to think. She'd gained the ability to see magic by drinking Chikara water and it had proven to be a blessing in battle, but now? She wanted to scream. 'I'll be there in a minute.' She sat up but immediately fell back onto the bed. Gods, why had she stayed up all night? She couldn't face anyone in this state.

Get up. Get up. Get up.

Tinnstra concentrated on the pain in her head, isolating it like Aasgod had taught her, packing it away so it was tolerable. It was becoming harder by the day. Even drinking more Chikara water didn't even help soften the pain like it once had.

Of course, Aasgod being in close proximity to Zorique made everything worse, as they amplified each other's auras. It didn't help either that Aasgod and his self-importance drove her mad.

With a groan, Tinnstra sat back up and swung her legs out of the bed. Elise had laid her Shulka dress uniform out for her. Just looking at it gave Tinnstra a pang of guilt. It felt wrong wearing it given she'd never actually taken her vows. In fact, she'd been expelled from the Shulka altogether for her cowardice.

That girl is long gone. I'm a different person now and I've earned the uniform the hard way – the bloody way.

Tinnstra dressed quickly, trying not to yawn. As she did so, her eyes drifted to the bag in the corner. Her supply of Chikara water was inside. If she drank a vial, she'd have the energy to get through the day.

But maybe it wasn't the best idea going to meet Tian Galrin and his new military head ramped up and in the mood to fight. But it might help if she was tired. She might keep her mouth shut. Not cause any problems.

She walked over to the bag and opened it. There were thirty vials left in the bag she'd brought back from the past. Enough to get her through a short campaign. Enough if they had control of the gates. At least, she'd not have to share her supply with the mage. He needed the water, after all, to power his own magic, but Aasgod had brought another bag of vials back with him when he'd returned from the past.

She'd drunk three vials since the victory over the Egril – with good reason, too; Bacas had hurt her and she'd needed to get back on her feet quickly. Even so, it was more than she was used to, and taking more now ...

She lifted a vial and held it up to the light. The sunlight glittered through the green liquid but there was no real sign of the power it contained.

Maybe if she didn't drink all of it ... just had a sip to wake herself up, clear her thoughts. That would be all right. In fact, that made sense. She'd be on an even keel then.

The knock at the door made her jump. 'Ma'am?' It was Elise. 'The coach is here.'

'One moment.'

Tinnstra uncorked the vial, took a slug of the green water. She winced at the bitterness but immediately felt its fire racing through her veins. Too fast. Too hot. Her body shook with it. So much. Too much. She clenched her teeth, fighting the rush. This wasn't what she'd wanted. Not now.

Gods, how much had she drunk?

Tinnstra looked down, saw the near-empty vial and cursed

herself. How could she face Zorique and Aasgod now? The mage would know. He always did. And Zorique? She hated Tinnstra drinking the water. She didn't understand how much Tinnstra needed it. How ordinary she'd be without it. How useless.

No. Breathe. Accept it. Don't fight it. Breathe. You can do this. Another minute and it'll be over. You'll be back to normal. No one will know. Just be calm.

Tinnstra sat down and tried to put her boots on. Gods, but that was difficult, with her hands shaking with the urge to rip them apart. Rip anything apart. It took three attempts to get her left foot into its boot and two for the right.

But she did it. And she looked smart. Like a Shulka. Especially when she strapped her sword on. No one would argue with her. She was Grim Dagen's daughter at last. She would destroy anyone that stood in her way. She just needed the rush to slow down. Get her thoughts in order.

Calm yourself. You can do this.

Tinnstra opened the door to her room, trying to ignore the trembling in her hands. She concentrated on her breathing as she went back down the stairs, pushing aside the pain in her mind, ignoring the colours she could see caused by Aasgod and Zorique's magic.

'There she is,' said Aasgod, as smug and self-important as ever. The man was certainly adapting well to his role as Zorique's advisor. Typically, he was wearing one of the Meigorian flowing robes that Tinnstra had been making fun of earlier. *Another idiot in a dress.*

'Tinn!' said Zorique.

The sight of her adopted daughter made Tinnstra stop in her tracks. It wasn't just the myriad colours floating around Zorique – Tinnstra was used to seeing that, after all. But Zorique ... Tinnstra's rough-and-tumble warrior of a daughter was dressed in a beautiful gown with her hair tied up. She looked stunning. She looked like ... a queen. 'Hello, my love.'

A surge of Chikara water hit Tinnstra and she had to look down, lest her legs go from under her. Gods, she could slaughter a squadron of Skulls after drinking a vial and yet tackling some stairs was too much for her.

She started walking again, aware they were watching her, and kept her head low. She had enough guilt already without their disapproving looks. 'Shall we go?'

'Are you feeling well?' asked Aasgod. She could tell by his tone that he *knew*.

'I'm fine,' Tinnstra replied through gritted teeth. 'I'm just tired. The carriage?' She looked up then, letting the mage see her fury, letting him know what she would do if he said something.

'It's waiting.'

'I was just saying to Aasgod that I'd rather fly,' said Zorique. 'Avoid the crowds.'

'I don't think you're dressed for flying,' said Tinnstra. She took a deep breath and turned her attention to her daughter. 'You look too beautiful.'

'I don't think so,' said Zorique. 'Why can't I wear a uniform like you? I look stupid in this dress.'

'You look like a queen,' said Aasgod. 'And a queen is who we need today.'

'Tinn?' Zorique looked to Tinnstra, hoping for help.

'He's not wrong.'

'Great,' said Zorique. 'Today had to be the day you two agreed on something.' She headed for the main doors. 'Let's get it over with.'

The crowds started screaming the moment she stepped outside, but Zorique kept her head down and headed straight for the carriage. Tinnstra followed with Aasgod on her heels.

Tinnstra took the seat next to Zorique, leaving the mage to sit on his own, opposite them. She didn't want him getting too comfortable always being by Zorique's side. After all, he was only there because Tinnstra had dragged him along by the scruff of his neck.

The screams got louder as they reached the gates and turned into a frenzy as they passed through them. People banged on the carriage sides, reaching for the windows, screaming Zorique's name.

'I wish they'd go away,' said her daughter.

'They're grateful that you saved them,' said Aasgod.

'*We* saved them,' said Zorique.

Tinnstra chuckled. 'You were the one flying through the sky, making all the Daijaku burst into flames.'

'I'm not a God.'

'We know,' said Tinnstra.

The carriage broke free of the press and the driver picked up speed, leaving the mob behind. They took the main road up to the palace, through the northern part of Layso. Ten days had not been long enough to repair the damage done by the Egril invasion, but life was starting to return to some semblance of normal. Tinnstra watched people going to and fro and couldn't help but think how lucky they'd been.

What would it be like in Jia after six or seven months of occupation? It had been bad enough when she'd left. Part of her wished she'd gone with Wenna, but she knew her place was with Zorique. She'd not leave her daughter's side.

Tinnstra was starting to feel normal again as the carriage crossed the causeway connecting the city to the mountaintop on which the palace perched. Well, as normal as she ever felt these days. Being so close to Aasgod and Zorique together was giving her a headache that would take days to overcome. Each of their magics flared against the other, sending a series of colourful waves through Tinnstra's mind over and over again.

She did everything she could to contain it as Aasgod had taught her, but it was like spitting into a fire.

The carriage took several minutes to travel from the main gates to the front of the palace, stopping in a courtyard where two hundred knights stood neatly in ranks, awaiting them. They stood like stone despite the heat of the day, a display of perfection in front of the building's scorched walls.

Even though the palace was magic-made, it had taken quite the battering during the failed Egril invasion and Tinnstra imagined it would need years of work to restore it to its former glory.

Servants appeared as the carriage stopped. One opened the carriage door while another placed steps in front of it to make it easier to climb down.

'I hate this formality,' whispered Zorique.

Tinnstra smiled. 'It's the least they can do for the Queen of Jia.'

'Don't you start,' said Zorique.

Tinnstra had to shield her eyes as she stepped out of the carriage. It was well after midday and the sun was blinding hot. She still wasn't sure why anyone would choose to live in a place that never seemed to get cool. Tinnstra's uniform already felt constrictive and sweat had started to run down her back. The Chikara water burning through her veins didn't help matters.

At least the servants led them inside quickly, which gave them an immediate respite from the sun.

Battle damage was everywhere, but there were plenty of men working to clear away rubble and shore up the walls. And even with the scars of war, the interior of the palace was breathtaking.

Beautiful paintings covered curved ceilings that were twice the height of any building Tinnstra had been in before, including the palace back in Jia's capital, Aisair. White pillars ran the length of the hall. Sheets of rice paper dangled between them. Some were little more than burned strips, whereas Tinnstra could see on others exquisite calligraphy detailing passages from the scriptures of the Four Gods.

The servants led them deeper into the palace. Their feet were hidden by their robes so that they appeared to glide along silently. Tinnstra and the others, however, moved with none of that Meigorian grace. Their footsteps echoed throughout the hall, announcing their presence to all.

Finally, they reached the white doors that led to the king's audience chamber. A servant gave their names to a clerk and then swiftly departed without another word. Zorique looked at Tinnstra and rolled her eyes. Neither of them liked ceremony – unlike Aasgod, whose chest seemed to swell with each step towards the Tian.

Tinnstra had been in the throne room before. In fact, she'd nearly died in it. This was where she'd fought Bacas. It had taken everything both she and Zorique had to defeat the man. Even so, they could've just as easily been the ones who'd died. It made her plan seem even more insane.

The king's old throne sat abandoned to one side, a chunk taken out of it by a Chosen's blast. In its place, a group of five men stood around a table with a map of Jia spread across it. Ralasis was there and he gave her a wink as the clerk announced them. He wore his dress uniform rather than the flowing robes of the others, looking quite different from the semi-drunk man who'd appeared at the embassy that morning.

Tian Galrin stepped forwards and gave Zorique a curt bow. 'It's good to see you once again, Your Majesty'

Zorique bowed in turn. 'And you, Tian.'

'May I introduce the man who will be leading the Meigorian forces in Jia?' Galrin stepped back. 'You've met Captain ... I mean Commander Ralasis before, haven't you?'

'We've met.' Ralasis bowed with a flourish. 'It is my pleasure to serve you once more.'

'It's *you*?' said Tinnstra. She couldn't believe it. He'd not said a word when they were ... talking earlier.

Ralasis grinned. 'At least I'm not an idiot in a dress.'

'But still an idiot?' she snapped, annoyed at him and even more annoyed at herself.

His smile grew wider. 'Of that, there's no doubt.'

5

Vallia

Aisair

Vallia watched the grey skies roll over Aisair, threatening rain.
Only two days had passed since she'd received Raaku's instruc-
tions but already it was obvious much had to be done. Astin had
travelled with her but he was due to return to Kagestan later that
evening. The chancellor lurked in a corner of the room, while
the leaders of the Egril armed forces in Jia were gathered around
a long table, where a map of the country had been laid as she'd
requested.

They waited now while she looked over the city. It was so
very different from Kagestan with its squat stone buildings, or
Tolledheim with its wooden houses and curved roofs. She'd been
told that the centre of Aisair, including the royal palace, had been
magic-made more than a thousand years ago, but she'd not believed it at the time. Now, she did. Now, she could see the power
the heathens once had. She could understand the arrogance they
still possessed. No wonder they thought themselves better than
the Egril. No wonder they'd yet to accept His Imperial Majesty's
rule.

'How strong are the rebel forces?' she asked.

'They are no more than an irritant, Commander,' said Rollio,
the most senior officer present. It had been his responsibility to
bring the country under effective control. His failure. 'A few
handfuls of troublemakers here and there. They present no real
threat.'

'Except they give people hope. They cost us soldiers,' replied Vallia. She hadn't yet decided what to do with the man, but there was a good chance he'd be with Kage by nightfall.

'Nothing we can't deal with,' said Rollio, shifting his chair as she approached the table.

Vallia sighed. She'd had enough of men and their false bravado to last a lifetime. She walked around the table, looking at the map of Jia from every angle. 'Do we know what sort of force we can expect from Meigore?'

'No,' said Astin from the far corner of the room. 'We've lost contact with all our spies in the country.'

'Dead, no doubt,' said a captain from the other side of the table.

Vallia stopped at the southern end of the map, pointed to a spot on the edge of Jia. 'And it's this city ... Kiyosun, that was overrun by the heathen rebels?'

'Yes,' said Rollio.

'The heathens that cause us no trouble?' Vallia looked up, watched Rollio ponder his answer. Good, that meant the man wasn't completely stupid. He realised on what thin ice he walked.

'They were lucky,' he said eventually, his voice full of resentment.

'And this is where the princess escaped from? This Zorique?'

'Yes.'

Her attention returned to the map. 'It's the closest port to Meigore.'

'Yes.'

'Is the city back under our control?'

'In a way. We sent the First Legion there and they met heavy resistance. Kiyosun wasn't worth the cost of retaking it so it was flattened to the ground instead, killing everyone inside and ending the rebel threat.'

Again, Vallia looked up at the man. 'Please, do not be so naive. The heathens will have scuttled away into their holes until they think it is safe to come out again. Unless you have seen their dead bodies, assume they are alive.'

Rollio bowed his head. 'I apologise.' He didn't sound like he meant it.

44

'I want an immediate crackdown on the rebels throughout the country,' said Vallia to the whole room. 'From now on, there is to be no shrugging of our shoulders at their activity. No more thinking that they are of no consequence. We must break them before their champions return, otherwise we will face an uprising in every corner of Jia.'

'It's impossible,' said Rollio. 'We're—'

'There will also be no more excuses,' Vallia interrupted. 'Three more legions will arrive today and more will follow. You will have enough men to make this happen. You will use lethal force on anyone you suspect of being a rebel. Is that understood?'

'Yes, Commander,' echoed the men like good soldiers at last.

'Astin, when will the spikes that I requested be ready?'

'They are in production as we speak,' said the chancellor. 'I had to reassign one of our armouries' forges to make the items. The first shipment will be ready by the end of the week.'

'Spikes?' asked Rollio.

She nodded. 'Spikes. I mean to make an example of the heathens. There will be no more hangings. Every rebel will be impaled and left for all to see. If any of our glorious warriors are killed, we will impale ten Jians for every one of them. If a city – like this Kiyosun – should try to rise up against us, then every man, woman and child will be put on spikes as a result. And all their nearest neighbours. Soon, the Jians will truly know fear. No one will dare take up arms against us.'

No one spoke. Good.

'And,' she continued, 'if anyone here fails to carry out my orders, they, too, will be impaled. Do I make myself clear?'

'Yes, Commander.'

'Now go. You all have much work to do.'

Everyone left except Astin. He joined her at the table as Vallia continued to stare at the map.

'I need intelligence, Astin. I need to know where the heathens will land and how many I will face.'

'I will speak to His Imperial Majesty.'

'I intend to meet the enemy with an overwhelming force, Astin.' She ran her finger along the southern coast. 'Kage willing, they will come at us as a single assault force and I can meet them head-on. Perhaps, with enough Daijaku, we can sink them before they even reach the coast.'

Astin nodded. 'I will see you have all you need.'

'Our worst case is if they come in small numbers, spread out along the coast. We can't defend too large an area. If they do that, they'd be able to move inland and regroup behind our lines.'

'What would you do in their position?' asked Astin.

Vallia was quite surprised by Astin's question. But, she reminded herself, he was a smart man. The Emperor wouldn't make a fool his chancellor. 'I would cross from Meigore in small numbers and be patient before I regrouped, perhaps even wait long enough for my enemy to think I wasn't coming at all. Then I would strike when our guard was down.

'But I don't think the Jians will do that. They've had a victory. They're feeling confident. They have something to prove. They'll come at us head-on and I will kill them in one devastating attack.'

'The Emperor would be pleased if you did. However, I will provide the resources you need to reinforce the defences here in Aisair.'

Vallia stared at the man. 'Am I not Vallia the Victorious? I have fought with Raaku for over fifty years and I have never lost a battle. I do not plan for that to change now – no matter how powerful these heathens think they are.'

'Praise be to Kage that it will be so,' said Astin.

Vallia nodded. 'It will be.'

And yet Raaku's words haunted her. He believed she would lose. She swallowed her pride. 'And I will turn Aisair into a fortress strong enough to stop a God.'

6

Wenna

The Ascalian Mountains

Hasan himself led Wenna up the mountain to show her the gate at the heart of all Tinnstra's plans. Royati and Tavis climbed with them. Tavis moved like a man a quarter of his age and as sure-footed as a mountain goat, leading the way without pause or compass as if he'd spent his whole life on the slopes of Ascalian.

Despite the hard climb, Wenna had to admit she was enjoying herself. It felt so good being amongst her fellow Shulka again – to be back in Jia. It had only been a few days but she felt reborn.

Hasan noticed. 'The smile suits you.'

'I must look mad,' said Wenna.

'No. Just happy.'

'I've been away so long, I'd forgotten how beautiful Jia is. Even the air smells wonderful. So ... clean. It's very different from what I've had to put up with in Meigore.'

'It might feel like that up here. But down there, in the cities? It's not been wonderful for a long time,' replied Hasan. 'Everyone's suffering.'

'I'm sorry. I didn't mean to ... I'm just glad to be back. Doing something to change things. Even last night, giving some good news to the sailors who brought me here, felt like a victory.'

Hasan held up a hand. 'It's okay. And you're right – it is a good country. Or it will be again one day.'

'It will be. When Zorique gets here, everything will change.'

Hasan shook his head. 'Is she really as powerful as you say?'

'Probably more so.'

'Gods, it doesn't sound possible. I just keep remembering the little four year old we rescued. Hard to imagine her grown up, let alone a mage.'

'I met her in the prison camp in Meigore,' said Wenna. 'A child, as you say. A lot of my friends died so she could escape and, if I'm being honest, I thought it a waste of good Shulka. They were skilled soldiers, after all. Zorique was a kid, and Tinnstra? Well, she knew how to use a sword, but she was no different from my friends. Why did they have to die so she could live, right?'

'Right.'

'We made it to the Jian embassy and I left them there while I tried to find us a ship to take us away from Meigore. Of course, things went wrong. The man who was supposed to help me had been arrested and troops – who would've been more than happy to arrest me, too – were crawling all over the city. I couldn't even get back to the embassy. Then the Skulls invaded.'

'From bad to worse, eh?' said Hasan.

'At least no one was trying to arrest me, and I had people to kill. But there were so many of them. Swarming everywhere. I thought I was going to die there, and I didn't want that. It wasn't the dying that bothered me, just dying over *there*, you know? I didn't think I'd ever see Jia again.'

'I can understand that.'

'Then, right in the thick of it, when I could barely stand any more, let alone swing a sword, Zorique appeared. Like a star, she was, and everything changed. I saw Daijaku fall from the sky, burning all the way down. I saw her pulverise a squad of Skulls with a shield of shining light as if they were ants. She was everywhere, flying so fast from one side of the city to the other. And the Skulls were all defeated by dawn.'

'Did you know it was Zorique?'

'Not then. Why should I? As you say, Zorique was a four year old as far as I knew. But after the fighting was over, I went to the embassy. Mainly because I didn't know where else to go. At the very least, I thought I'd see my friends' bodies and say a few words to Xin for them.'

'Not many of us will receive that honour,' said Hasan.

'Alas, no. But she was there. Zorique. Shining so bright I could barely look at her. And Tinnstra, too, but older than she'd been a day before, and bigger. Much bigger. She looked like she could take on all the Skulls by herself.'

'Tinnstra?'

'Yeah, Tinnstra. She's ... dangerous now. And when they get here, to Jia? The Skulls don't have a chance.'

'Gods, I hope so.'

'I know so,' said Wenna. She had no doubt.

They reached the temple just before midday. It wasn't quite at the mountain peak, but close enough for Wenna to have to catch her breath in the cold wind. At first, she didn't see the building. It was some twelve feet by six feet at most, made so long ago that its stone walls looked like part of the mountain now. The years had worn the rock smooth and bleached the colour from its surface, until it resembled a small hump in the mountainside rather than anything man-made. She could see the outline of a door, but it was hewn from the same stone as the building, with no obvious way of opening it.

'Is this it?' she asked, not hiding her disappointment.

'Doesn't look like much, does it?' said Hasan.

'No. No, it doesn't.' Wenna ran her hand over the side of the building, feeling the faintest of indentations.

'They're dedications to Nasri,' said Tavis. 'Sailors would leave offerings here, hoping for a safe and bountiful voyage, but it's been a long time since anyone has made the trek up the mountain from Kiyosun to do that.'

'Once, buildings like this provided gateways to all of Jia,' said Hasan, 'but most of the connecting temples fell into the hands of the Egril during the invasion and they destroyed them. Jax reckoned someone betrayed us, because their locations were well-kept secrets and the Skulls shouldn't have known about them. We never found out for sure, though.'

'The Skulls have creatures that sense magic,' said Wenna. 'They could've discovered the first gates by accident, and once they knew what they were looking for, the others would have been easier to locate.'

'I hope so. With all the ill that has befallen us, the last thing any of us needs are traitors still lurking around.'

'Show me the inside.'

'I can do that,' said Tavis, stepping forwards. 'Just have to find the right spot.' He ran his hand over the centre of the door, his brows knitted in concentration. Tavis must've found what he was looking for because his hand stopped and he turned his palm to the right. It was almost invisible to the eye but Wenna could've sworn she saw the stone move. There was no mistaking the clunk as a lock disengaged. Tavis pushed the door open. 'This way.'

Wenna and Hasan followed him inside. For a moment, it was too dark to see much by the light that leaked in from behind her, and Wenna felt a sudden wave of claustrophobia. She looked back at the entrance and thought about running outside to fresh air but, just as quickly, everything changed. A green light began to seep out of the very rocks themselves, riding a breeze until it floated like smoke in the air around them.

'Behold Nasri's majesty,' said Tavis, his voice cracking with awe.

As the light travelled deeper into the temple, Wenna realised the place was far larger inside than it appeared on the outside. 'How is this possible? The space ...'

'The temples were built by a magic long lost, when Jians were all but Gods walking the earth,' said Tavis. 'I don't know how they made them, just how they work. I was about ten when my father first brought me up here and showed me the ways of it all. Same as his father before him.'

'So, we can go anywhere in Jia from here?' asked Wenna.

'Not anywhere. You need a gate at the other end to connect to,' said Tavis. He walked to one of the alcoves that ran along the walls and passed his hand over the markings inside it. 'Each one has a unique set of wards that connect the gateway to another temple in Jia. This one used to link to a temple to Alo in Inaka, but it was destroyed by the Egril.' Green light danced between the wards like smoke, following Tavis around the interior and swirling about Wenna and Hasan's feet. 'My father taught me how to operate the gates, which markings have to be pressed.'

'How many gates are still in our control?' Wenna couldn't hide the awe in her voice. She knew about the gate in the basement of the Jian embassy in Layso, but she'd never been down there – never seen it work.

'There's the gate in the Olyisius Mountains that we told you about,' said Hasan. 'Plus another in Selto, one in Gambril and the last one in Chita.'

'The four corners of Jia,' said Wenna. 'And its heart.'

'Aye,' said the Shulka. 'We could transport an army across the country pretty damn fast when the time comes.'

Wenna grinned. 'We could take the country back faster than the Skulls took it. They won't know what hit them.'

Hasan nodded. 'It's a nice thought. And long overdue if we can pull it off.'

'If? We will. We bloody well will.' Wenna clapped her hands.

'Is it Aisair you're wanting to go to?' asked Tavis.

The question took some of the excitement out of Wenna. They hadn't climbed all that way just to do a bit of sightseeing. There was a reason. She glanced over at Royati. 'Yes. It is.'

'You sure about this?' asked Hasan. 'We've already sent people ahead to spread the word that Zorique is coming. There's no need for you to go yourself. You can stay here.'

Wenna shook her head. 'No. I have to go. There's something I need to do for Tinnstra.'

'What's that?'

'I just need to find out some things for her.'

Hasan held up his hands. 'Right. Royati knows the way down Olyisius and where to find help before you head into Aisair. Kos will meet you at the stables in Garret Street once you get into the city. Tell him to send people up to guard the gate and I'll do the same here. Make sure nothing happens to it before Zorique arrives.'

Wenna nodded. 'Thanks. Thanks for everything.'

'It was no trouble,' said Hasan. 'I'll see you after your friends arrive.'

'You do that.' Wenna turned to Royati. 'You ready?'

'Ready as I'll ever be.'

'If you'll step this way, ladies,' said Tavis. He beckoned them to join him at an alcove in the far corner. 'And hold on tight.'

Tavis's fingers danced over the wards, pressing one then another, and the green light grew brighter and brighter.

Wenna's stomach lurched as the floor fell away and the light blinded her. Up became down, life became lost, lost, lost. Lost in the light. She would've screamed. Maybe she did. Someone did.

Gods.

Gods help her.

A heartbeat later, it was over and the three of them were still standing in the temple, unmoved – except ... 'Where's Hasan?' she croaked.

'Back in Kiyosun,' said Tavis, with his hands on his knees. 'By the Gods, that never gets any easier.'

Royati staggered to the door, pulled it open and retched on the ground outside.

Wenna gasped – they were on a mountain, but the distant sandy lands of Kiyosun had been replaced by a green carpet rolling into the distance. Tavis took her arm, and together they followed Royati outside. Wenna sucked in the cold mountain air as her legs steadied. 'It works.'

Tavis slumped down on a rock and took a slug of water. 'Aye, it does. Feels like dying every time, but it works. Gods only know what it'll be like trying to move an army through the gates.'

'But we can do it,' said Wenna, eyes wide and mind racing.

'We should be on our way,' said Royati. 'The Hanran are waiting for us at the Kotege. We'll spend the night there before we head to Aisair.'

Tavis got to his feet. 'I'll be saying my goodbyes for now.'

'You heading back already?' asked Wenna. The man was still deathly pale from the trip there. 'Surely you can rest a while?'

'Hasan's waiting for me. He'll never find his way down the mountain if I'm not there to show him the way.' Tavis smiled. 'Besides, I might as well get it over with. No point feeling better only to feel worse again.'

Wenna grinned. 'True.'

'Just look after yourself, eh?' said Tavis. 'Plenty of Skulls out there that will be happy to kill you.'

'I won't forget,' said Wenna. She watched Tavis limp back into the temple and shut the door, then turned to Royati. 'Let's go and free Jia.'

7

Jax

Gundan

Jax stumbled and went sprawling. He hit the ground hard, blinked, looked around. There was a body at his feet. A Skull. Long dead. The flesh rotted away, leaving real bones under rusted white armour, grass growing around the skeleton.

He was outside. Not in the dungeon. He was in a valley, grass dancing in the wind, the scent of spring filling his nose. Free. How in the Four Gods' names had he got there?

He was filthy, barefoot, his skin covered in a thousand scratches and bruises. His clothes were no more than rags, but they weren't the same clothes he'd been wearing back in Kiyosun when he was captured.

'Jax! Hurry.' A man waved him on. Three others with him. They were familiar, as if remembered from a dream, but he couldn't recall any of their names. At least they spoke Jian. They were his countrymen.

The last thing he remembered was being dragged out of that cell in Kagestan, in Raaku's castle. Being taken to die.

'Come on,' shouted the man. 'We can't get captured now. Move!'

Jax forced his legs to work, headed towards the others, moving at a half-run. Every breath of the spring-cold air made him feel more awake, more alive. If only he knew where he was.

But he wasn't in prison – and for that he was bloody grateful.

How long since he'd been captured? He was thin from not

enough food but otherwise he felt strong. Not the mess he'd been in Kiyosun. Not burned up and half-mad. And no Darus Monsuta talking to him. Thank the Gods.

A glint of metal drew his eye to the ground once more. A scimitar, long and lean and still looking sharp. Jax picked it up. What was it they said? Better to have a sword and not need it than need a sword and not have one.

It still didn't feel comfortable in his left hand, but that was all he had so he'd better get used to it.

The others had stopped at the top of the rise. Four silhouettes against the horizon. Easy to spot from miles away. 'Don't stand there. Get over the ridge,' he called. But none of them moved, the fools.

'I thought you didn't want to get cap—' The words died in Jax's throat as he stumbled to a stop next to the others. His eyes tried to take in what he was seeing, but he was more confused than ever. It was impossible.

Another valley stretched out before them, and at the far end was Gundan.

The fortress of Gundan.

They were on the Egril side of the border, but there was no mistaking his last command, despite it being a broken shell of a thing now. The thirty-foot-high walls were more hole than stone and the watchtowers mere hints at what they'd once been. The Egril had done a good job destroying it.

His mind took him straight back to that night. He'd been the head of the Shulka, leading Gundan's defence. Except he'd not thought about defending anything. He'd been thinking about massacring Egril, like he had done every time he'd faced the old enemy. But this time the Egril had come with other ideas. They attacked with their troops, their magic and their monsters and it had been the Shulka who'd been put to the sword instead.

He lost his arm – for the first time – that night. His son had broken his back. So many of his Shulka died. It was the last place he wanted to be now. Too many memories. Too many ghosts.

What was he doing at Gundan?

'Are you all right?' asked the man, gaunt-faced, filthy, just like Jax. A southern accent.

'I ... I ...' Jax didn't know what to say. He didn't want to go anywhere near the fortress, but it was the crossing point between Egril and Jia. A way home.

'We need to move,' said a woman with matted red hair, her eyes darting everywhere. She was clutching a knife as if her life depended on it. Jax felt like he should know her name, but what was it?

There were two others. Women: one who looked like she'd had half her hair ripped out; the other smaller, younger, perhaps still a child, hiding behind everyone else. They felt familiar, too. He knew them. He knew that much, at least.

'Who are—' The barking stopped Jax from saying any more. More than one dog. A pack.

All heads turned back the way they'd come, towards Egril, and they all saw the dogs and the men with them, saw the glint of weapons already drawn. Too many for Jax to fight with his one arm.

He was running a second later. Towards Gundan, towards home. No time to think about what had happened before. All that mattered now was survival.

The sword was heavy in Jax's hand, but he was glad of the extra weight to carry. He'd need it if the dogs caught up with them.

They moved fast, running downhill, the slope helping their tired legs. Even so, the small woman fell hard, but the man hauled her up without breaking stride, and then she was running again.

They wove a path through the corpses littering the valley floor and avoided the arrows that jutted up here and there, memorials to his failed attempt to stop the enemy.

Gundan was a mile away. Once he could have run it in minutes without losing breath. Now it felt a hundred times too far. His chest burned and his legs threatened to give up at any moment. But he couldn't stop. Not now. The barking of the dogs urged them on, getting ever closer, but Jax dared not look back. At least he couldn't hear horses, but that meant nothing. Luck hadn't been on his side for a long time.

The others weren't in any better shape than Jax and gaps soon opened up between them.

'Come on,' huffed the man. Maybe to himself as much as the others. The name Remie came to Jax's mind all of a sudden. Was that who he was?

'I can't, Sarah,' cried the small woman, slowing down. 'I need to stop.'

'Don't give up, Esto,' said the red-haired woman. 'Not now. Not when we're so close.' She hooked an arm around Esto's waist and tried to keep her moving. 'Someone help us.'

Jax didn't have a spare hand and he wasn't going to drop the sword, but the woman with the half-head of hair answered the call. 'Jia's on the other side of that wall. We're nearly there. We can do it.'

They staggered on to Gundan again, half a mile away now, moving slowly when they should be running, towards a wall offering no protection, with holes big enough for an army to march through. Whether they were this side or that side of the wall would make no difference if they got caught.

The barking grew louder and finally Jax looked back – and wished he hadn't. The dogs were on the crest of the hill. A pack of them, with half a dozen men holding their leashes. A half-mile behind them. And he knew the dogs would reach them quicker than they could reach Gundan.

'Run!' roared Jax. 'Run for your very lives.'

It was everyone for themselves. They all knew it. A race that not all of them would finish.

Jax and Remie surged ahead. Jax knew it was wrong – not the Shulka thing to do – but he'd abandoned his vows long ago. He only had an urge to live now. Nothing more.

The women tried to carry Esto but she fell and dragged them down with her. Sarah and the half-haired woman got back to their feet and set off without Esto, despite her cries. They knew they had no hope if they stayed with her.

The rest of the world ceased to exist for Jax. There was just the sound of his feet, his heart, his ragged breath, and those dogs, their barks, their howls. Gundan ahead of him. Death behind. Maybe he would find other weapons there, walls to hide behind, a place to fight, to make a last stand. Maybe. He just had to run.

The wall was five hundred yards away when he heard Esto's screams, the ripping of flesh, the frenzy of the dogs. Jax would've prayed for her if he had the breath, but all his thoughts were for himself. *Get to the wall. Find somewhere safe. She's dead. Save yourself.*

Monsuta would've laughed at his cowardice, but that voice was silent. Hopefully he'd left it behind in Raaku's palace, back in Kagestan.

Gundan was three hundred yards away. So close. So far.

Esto still screamed, but her cries were fading. More whimpers than anything else.

Two hundred yards.

Remie was ahead, clearing the rubble. He turned, eyes wide with fear, and waved them towards him. 'Come on!'

Jax could see the two women out of the corner of his eye. They were almost level with him. Then the redhead was a yard in front. He tried to find an extra burst of speed and couldn't. He dropped the sword, hoping that would free some more energy, and tried not to think that this would be the moment he needed the weapon most.

The half-haired woman was by his shoulder, teeth gritted, arms pumping, white-faced. Gundan was one hundred yards away. They were going to make it. Then the woman was gone, just like that. Hauled down by the dogs. It could've just as easily been him.

She was screaming as he reached the wall and Remie hauled him over, into Gundan, into Jia. He looked back, saw the dogs mauling the half-haired woman, saw their handlers chasing after them, spears in hand.

'This way,' he said and set off in a limping run, ignoring the stone digging into his feet, past the decayed corpses of his Shulka, across the parade ground filled with craters. The main keep was ahead, where his office had been, where the armoury was, where

– if the Gods had any mercy – there would still be doors to lock and hide behind.

But the dogs had other ideas. They came bounding over the broken wall, full of fury, and one backward glance told Jax they'd not make the keep.

'Get weapons!' he shouted, bending down to scoop up a spear. He turned just as a dog leaped at him, smacked it down with the spear's shaft. It landed on its back, legs kicking in the air, and Jax thrust the spear into its belly before it could right itself.

Remie had found a spear of his own and Sarah had a Shulka sword. Jax stepped to the left of Sarah so they had the spears on their flanks when they faced the rest of the pack, jabbing at any dog that got too close.

'Walk backwards. We need to get to the keep,' said Jax. 'We'll have a chance there.'

The dogs snapped and snarled, fangs red with Jax's companions' blood, but the spears did their work as he and the others retreated.

But of course, their handlers had to appear. They climbed over the wall one by one, until all six could join their dogs. They wore masks shaped like their hounds' heads, with snouts and pointed ears, and each had a scimitar in their hand.

'How far to the keep?' said Remie.

'Don't worry about it,' said Jax. 'We'll make it. Just watch the dogs.'

'Hey!' shouted one of their pursuers in Egril. 'We've chased you far enough. Time to give up. Let us take you back to prison and you get to live.'

'Fuck off,' Jax snapped in that hated tongue.

'You speak their language?' asked Sarah. 'What did they say?'

'It doesn't matter,' replied Jax. 'It's all lies.' Perhaps sensing his distraction, a dog lunged, but Jax's spear was quicker and he cut a gash in its leg.

'You hurt the dogs, we hurt you,' said the Egril, his voice cold. 'Now drop your weapons.'

Jax didn't bother replying. What was the point? He and the others kept retreating slowly, making their way through the dead left by the Egril invasion. Judging by the state of the bodies, that night had been long ago. But how long? Jax remembered helping the queen escape and the madness that followed. He remembered being captured and taken to Kagestan and placed in the cells beneath Raaku's palace. He remembered the guards coming for him. But after that? Nothing.

He glanced back, saw the keep was close. The entrance had been blown apart but it was better than where they were, and if the stairs were still standing, maybe they could gain a position they could defend. Walls on either side and behind them would be good. They would have a chance.

The Egril must've realised that, too, because they began to spread out, moving around their dogs, trying to flank Jax and the others. Jax jabbed at a dog, as a warning to their handlers as much as to the animals themselves. 'Stay back.'

'You make me laugh, one-arm,' said the Egril. 'Too dumb to know you're already dead. Your soul belongs to Kage now. Why prolong things? Give up now. I want to see my wife, my family. I've chased you heathens halfway across the country and I've had enough.'

'How long have you been chasing us?' asked Jax, still moving backwards. He knocked a skull with his foot and tried not to think of whose it could've been.

'Too long.' The Egril looked around the ruins of Gundan and shook his head. 'We thought we had you so many times, but you kept slipping away. But, hey, you did it. You made it home. Congratulations. You can die amongst your friends.'

He whistled and the dogs attacked.

8

Wenna

It'd been years since Wenna was last in Aisair. Back in the days before the invasion, when the Shulka were invincible and the country was a place of peace and prosperity. Back when Aisair was the beating heart of the land.

But now? Wenna dreaded to think what the Egril had done to it.

After climbing down from the mountain gate, they'd met with the local Hanran at the Kotege. Their news had been pretty grim though. Apparently, things in the city were bad and getting worse, but when Wenna had pressed for more details, she'd been told that it was best she see for herself. They'd provided Wenna and Royati with a wagon and some livestock so they could pretend they were going to the capital to trade. A local lad named Sami had joined them as well to help with the ruse. He was only about twelve years old, but he was smart and knew the area well. It helped at the checkpoints to have a kid along. Made Wenna and Royati look less threatening.

Still, Wenna felt a sense of dread building as they approached the edge of Hascombe Woods. They'd have to be careful every step of the way now. A simple slip-up and they'd be hanged before nightfall – especially if the Skulls found the weapons hidden in the cart.

That queasy feeling got worse when they heard the felling of

61

trees, followed by shouted orders and the crack of whips. She exchanged looks with Royati but turning back wasn't an option.

Another half-mile and they saw the cause of all the noise. Work crews were clearing the forest under the supervision of Skull guards. There had to be hundreds of Jians cutting and sawing at trees and dragging the trunks away. The Skulls were working them mercilessly, too. Whips cracked in every direction, urging them on, allowing no rest.

'Bastards,' whispered Wenna. Every Jian she saw had red gashes on their body from the whips and a haunted expression on their face. Some didn't look strong enough to last another hour.

'Easy, girl,' said Royati. 'Remember what we're here to do. We can't help any of these unfortunates, but we can help stop any more of our people from joining them.'

Wenna nodded, a sour taste in her mouth, but she could see Aisair through the trees. They were close. They just had a check-point to get past first.

The four Skulls manning the post watched the cart approach.

'Are you sure our paperwork is good?' asked Wenna.

'Yes,' said Royati. 'Stop fretting.'

Sami was sitting in the back with a freshly butchered pig and two baskets of live chickens squawking away, given to them by the local Hanran the previous day. The pig had bled everywhere and the chickens were going crazy at the smell – just as Wenna wanted. Hopefully, the mess and the noise would stop the Skulls from looking too closely at the inside of the cart or noticing how low to the ground it was.

Wenna turned around in her seat. 'You doing okay, kid?'

Sami nodded, as eager as could be. 'I'm good.' The fact that Sami had survived this long in the war was testament enough to his endurance and quick wits. He hadn't complained, either, when they covered him in pig's blood and left guts all around his feet. 'Chickens ain't happy, though.'

'Keep them that way, eh?'

'I will. Promise.' And Sami gave one of the baskets a good kick that got the birds squawking some more.

Wenna smiled. 'Well done.'

She turned her attention back to the road and the Skulls who stepped out to meet them.

Royati flicked the reins and brought the cart to a stop. By the Gods, Wenna wanted to kill all the Skulls right there, right then, but Royati's hand slipped over hers and squeezed it just enough to calm her down.

'Papers,' said the Skull on Royati's side. She handed them over without looking at the man. Wenna felt her heart lurch as the Egril began to read.

'Where you go?' asked the Skull next to her.

Wenna pointed ahead. 'To the city.' Then she pointed over her shoulder with her thumb. 'Sell meat.'

The Skull peered in the back. 'Why kill pig?'

'Pigs don't walk fast,' said Wenna. 'Travel faster.'

The Skull wandered around to get a better look at the contents of the cart. 'It's mess.'

'Pigs bleed a lot,' said Royati.

The Skull at the back of the cart shouted something in Egril too quick for Wenna to understand. Two of his mates came running over to join him and she didn't like that. Not at all.

'Something wrong?' asked Royati.

'Shut up,' said the Skull with her papers.

Wenna heard a sword slip free of its sheath. She turned, wondering what she could do with no weapon, how she could fight so many Skulls and win if it came to it. Stupid thoughts. She'd be dead in an instant.

'Face front,' said the Skull who'd questioned her, his sword out and pointing.

Wenna did as she was ordered, heart hammering away, then flinched at the sound of steel hacking into flesh. Sami!

'Oi,' said the boy. 'Leave our pig alone.'

'Be quiet,' snapped a Skull.

'Do as he says,' said Wenna. 'Let them take whatever they want.'

What they wanted, it turned out, was a leg of pork and a chicken. Just as Wenna had hoped. It didn't matter what side anyone was on, everyone was hungry these days. Better to get the soldiers thinking about free food rather than what else could be in the wagon. Once the Skulls had enough for dinner, they waved Wenna and the others on.

Wenna did her best to keep her eyes on the road as they passed by the work crews, fearing she might cry if she were to look at their suffering more closely, and she'd sworn back at the beach that she'd cry no more.

The crews had been busy, clearing at least a couple of miles of forest, leaving only muddy stumps behind and a lot of open ground around the city.

They came to another checkpoint about five hundred yards from the city, flanked by more work crews. This time they were digging trenches that ran east to west. More Jians sat to one side, sharpening tree branches into spikes that would, no doubt, be stuck in the bottom of the trenches.

It cost Wenna three more chickens to continue onwards.

The last checkpoint was another two hundred yards ahead, where a barricade was being built around the city using the felled trees.

'Someone's expecting trouble,' said Royati.

'They are indeed,' replied Wenna. It worried her, seeing the Skulls hard at work like this, but it was to be expected. Zorique was no secret. She'd destroyed their army in Meigore and killed the head of the Emperor's Chosen. Raaku didn't have to be a genius to know she'd return to Jia next. Still, it would've made Wenna happy not to see the city's defences being bolstered like that.

By the time they were allowed through the city gates, their pig had lost another two limbs and they were down a whole basket of chickens. The gates were big and tall but nothing special. Certainly not too thick. They'd not been built to stop an invading army from entering the city, after all. That was good, at least. Unless the Skulls replaced them.

'Thieving bastards,' muttered Sami as the cart trundled into Aisair.

'Shush,' ordered Royati, with good reason. Ears listened everywhere. Eyes watched. Just because someone wasn't wearing

64

a Skull mask, it didn't mean they were any sort of friend. There was money to be earned or favour gained by giving someone up to the Skulls. Best to trust no one. Assume everyone was an enemy. Might be a shit way to live but forgetting those simple rules was a shit reason to die.

So they kept their mouths shut and eyes open.

Not that the Egril presence was in any way low-key. Red flags hung from nearly every building and Skulls filled the streets, and not just at the checkpoints. There had to be hundreds of the bastards. Thousands, even, if the whole city was like that. Jians, on the other hand, were few and far between. Anyone they did see kept their head down and moved quickly to wherever they were going. Most didn't look that much better off than the press-ganged workers outside the city. Tired, hungry, scared.

The king's castle loomed above the rooftops from the centre of the city. They said it was magic-made and Wenna could well believe that. Even with the damage done to it during the invasion, the building still clung to some of its old pride. 'And we'll bring it all back,' she whispered.

Royati knew the city well and they drove over to the stables on Garret Street.

A child sat outside – a young girl with thick, matted hair and a dirty face. She had a bowl in front of her, begging from anyone who passed. It was sad to see how asking for help made the girl invisible to the world, but it was perfect for the Hanran.

Royati gave a hand signal as they approached, and the girl knocked on the stable door. Two seconds later, the doors were open and Royati drove the cart straight in. A second after that, darkness fell over them as the doors were slid shut once more.

Safe.

A dozen men and women waited for them in the stables. Hanran one and all. Strangers to Wenna, but they were greeted by all like old friends, the bonds of resistance joining them tighter than family. They got to work, clearing out the back of the cart and removing the weapons from their hiding place. Wenna and Royati took their own swords, while the rest were placed inside two water barrels.

The stables were a decent size with a dozen empty horse stalls at the rear. To the right, a ladder led up to the loft, but judging by the dust swirling in the morning light, no one had climbed the ladder for a long time. There must be a window up there, too, but Wenna couldn't see it from where she stood.

The Hanran's leader was an old Shulka from Clan Inaren called Kos. Tall and wiry, his eyes were the colour of cold granite. 'Thank you for bringing us the weapons. They're much needed. The Skulls have been relentless in searching for all our hiding places.'

'Are there normally that many Skulls on the streets?' asked Wenna.

'A new general arrived this week. Since then they're more Skulls everywhere. They began arresting people for the work gangs the next day. Snatching folk just for breathing the wrong way.'

'That's when they started building the barricade and digging the trenches?' asked Royati. Her eyes met Wenna's.

Kos saw the glance. 'You know something we don't?'

Wenna nodded. 'That's why we're here.'

'With good news,' added Royati.

Kos sniffed. 'That's been in short supply for a long time.'

'Things are going to change,' said Wenna, 'but we'll need everyone's help.'

They gathered towards the back of the stables, near the stalls. Some sat on bales while others took up spots on the floor. Kos offered Wenna a stool and she gladly took it. Someone even gave Sami a bucket of water and a rag to wash the blood off his hands.

'The Meigorians are coming three months from now,' said Wenna when she had everyone's attention. 'Forty thousand of them. We're going to take back Jia.' And she told them of Zorique and all she could do, and she could see the hope start to shine in their eyes, just like it had in Tavis's. It was a beautiful sight, too long lost. It almost made up for the horrors she'd observed en route and she felt once more a surge of pride that Tinnstra had given her this mission.

'The main battle's going to be here in Aisair,' said Wenna.

'The Skulls know that, too, by the looks of things – that's why they're preparing the welcoming party outside the city.'

'What do you want us to do?' asked Kos.

'First of all,' said Wenna, 'we need to find out everything we can about the enemy – numbers and locations of the Skulls, which Chosen are here and their powers, what creatures they have hidden away and anything else that might help us kill them all when our army arrives.'

'We can do that,' said Kos. 'We've even got people in the king's castle.'

'Good,' said Wenna, 'because we also need to know where they keep the Tonin.'

Kos stared at her for a moment, chewing his lip. 'Why?'

'Best we keep that to ourselves for now,' said Royati.

Kos nodded. 'What else do you need?'

'We don't want the Skulls to have a city full of hostages to use against us.' Wenna leaned forwards. 'Get as many people out of the city as you can without alerting the Skulls to what's happening.'

Kos chewed on his lip. 'That's going to be difficult. At least people have roofs over their heads here and walls around them. Most won't want to leave.'

'Start with the ones who will go easily,' said Wenna. 'People you know you can trust. Get them somewhere safe, and then we can worry about those that don't want to leave.'

'We can do that.'

'Good. Then find shelters in the city where anyone who's left can hide from the fighting. Store what water and food you can spare so no one starves.'

'Enough of us are doing that already.'

'I'm not saying it'll be easy—'

There was a rap on the stable door. Everyone froze, listening. Then came another and another.

'Skulls are coming,' said Kos.

One of the Hanran opened the door and peeked out, before ducking back in as quick as he could. 'Skulls,' he confirmed, slamming the door shut. 'Loads of them.'

Kos looked for himself and didn't like what he saw. 'Too many of them to be a coincidence – they're coming for us. Everyone, grab a weapon. We're going to be fighting.'

Wenna put a hand on the man's arm. 'We can't be captured. Too many people are relying on us.'

'Fuck.' Kos looked from her to his people, then back again. 'Go up the ladder. You can get out onto the roof. I'll follow you up. Tomas, Emras – go with Wenna. Palix – move the cart so it blocks the front door. Trisk, find something to bar the back.'

'This way,' said a young woman to Wenna, not looking too happy to be leaving her friends.

'Everyone else,' said Kos as Wenna followed Emras up the ladder, 'fight hard, kill as many of those bastards as you can, then follow us. If you can't ... don't get captured.' She could hear the emotion in his voice, the pain. 'Remember – we are the dead.'

'We are the dead,' they chorused back.

Wenna helped Sami up into the loft. 'You okay?'

'I'm always okay,' said the boy, trying to sound brave.

'Just move fast and keep your head down,' said Royati, joining them.

A cold draught rushed into the loft as Emras opened the skylight to the roof. 'This way.'

A fist banged on the stable door below. 'Open up in the name of the Emperor.'

Wenna and the others climbed out onto the roof. Habit made her immediately check the skies, but there were no Daijaku to be seen. Not yet, anyway.

The Skulls in the street weren't waiting for an invitation to enter the stables. Something heavy smashed into the door, but whatever they were using didn't have enough power to move the cart. Even so, they kept going, hitting the door again and again. The sound echoed around the street, magnified even more when the Skulls at the rear of the stables started doing the same.

A small ledge ran along the edge of the roof, barely a foot wide, but it was enough to give them somewhere to stand. The next building over was an easy enough jump. Again, Emras went first, followed by Wenna, then Sami and Royati with Tomas taking the rear. There was no need to be quiet, not with the racket the Skulls were making down in the street. Even so, Wenna expected to hear a cry that said they'd been spotted.

Emras kept them moving, not willing to wait for anyone. The next building along required clambering up a six-foot wall and then scrambling up a steep slope of shifting tiles before sliding down to another ledge. Sami slipped on a tile as he followed Wenna and would've gone sailing off the roof if she hadn't snatched his collar at the last moment. His feet kicked out at open air before she managed to haul him back onto the ledge.

The kid lay against the roof, eyes wide and gasping for air.

'You okay?' Wenna asked.

The boy stared back, chest heaving. 'Think so.'

Wenna gave him a smile. 'On your feet, then, and let's be off.'

Sami, may the Gods bless him, did as he was told, still shaking and sweating, and the group set off once more.

Kos caught up with them two streets later, but still they didn't stop. Emras found an open door on a roof and led them down into the building. Once everyone was inside, she allowed them to catch their breath.

'Leave your weapons here,' said Kos.

'No way,' said Royati. 'I'm not fighting Skulls empty-handed.'

'The ones we left back at the stables are doing the fighting,' said Kos. 'We're doing the running and the swords will only give us away.'

Royati was going to protest some more, but Wenna shook her head. 'He's right.'

'I don't like this,' hissed Royati, but she put her sword with the others.

'Tomas, try and stash them on the roof somewhere,' said Kos, 'then come back later and pick them up – but only if it's safe.'

'You can count on me,' said the Hanran.

'We should split up when we hit the street,' said Emras. 'Easier to disappear that way.'

'Take Royati with you,' said Kos. 'Wenna and the lad can come with me. We'll meet at the old house before curfew tonight.'

They left Tomas with the weapons and hurried down the

stairs. Emras checked the street before signalling Kos, Wenna and Sami to leave.

'Stay alive, eh?' said Wenna to Royati.

'Don't worry about me,' replied her friend. 'Worry about yourself.'

Kos put his arm around Wenna's shoulders once they were out in the street and Wenna held on to Sami's hand good and tight. They walked quickly, heads down, not saying a word. Just like every beaten Jian in the city.

So much for bringing hope.

9

Jax

Gundan

The dogs lunged forwards, teeth bared.

Jax jabbed his spear at one but then arrows appeared from everywhere, stopping the dogs and peppering the Egril.

Each man was hit by at least a half-dozen; in the head, the chest, the back. More struck the dogs, stopping them from even getting close to Jax and the others.

For a moment, Jax just stared at the bodies, not believing his eyes, not believing the Egril were dead, not believing he was alive. But his heart was still beating and the blood on the floor was theirs, not his. Dear Gods, he was alive.

'Where ... where did those arrows come from?' said Remie.

The answer emerged from the ruins. Men and women, some in armour, others in rags, all carrying bows, all wearing swords.

'Hanran,' said Jax. Dozens of them.

Sarah fell to her knees, tears already streaking down her face.

Jax nearly did the same, so grateful was he to see soldiers once more, but no, he stayed upright on shaking legs and watched the new arrivals approach. They weren't just Hanran, they moved like Shulka, well spaced out, weapons ready despite the lack of any obvious threat, eyes never still. Trained, disciplined and looking damn near invincible, like he once had.

A woman walked at the group's head, older than the others, lean as a whip, a bandana keeping her grey hair from her face. 'Are any of you hurt?'

Dear Gods, Jax knew her. He really knew her, knew her name. 'Moiri? Moiri? Is that you?'

The woman stopped, her eyes narrowing. 'Who ... ?'

'It's me, Jax. Of Clan Huska.' He stepped forwards, grinning like a child, tears in his eyes. There was no hiding it. He'd thought Moiri had died when Gundan fell, along with her husband, Grim Dagen.

'General?' Recognition dawned on Moiri. 'Oh, Jax. It's so good to see you.' They embraced. 'I thought you were dead.'

Holding his friend was too much for Jax to bear. He wept. Wept for all they had lost together, wept for all the pain they both must've endured. 'I'm sorry. I shouldn't be like this.'

Moiri stepped back, looked at him with knowing eyes. 'Don't be sorry. If ever there was a time for tears, this is it.'

'I thought you died in the invasion.'

'I only survived by luck more than anything else. To be honest, I don't remember much.'

'You're not the only one,' said Jax.

'You saved us,' said Sarah, coming over. 'Thank you. Thank you.'

'We heard the dogs,' said Moiri. 'Got here as quick as we could.'

'Got here just in time,' said Remie. 'Another second and we would've been ...' He looked around at the dead Egril. He kicked one. 'Bastards would've fed us to their bloody animals.'

'Where did you come from?' asked one of Moiri's men.

'I ...' Jax stopped. He didn't know. Dear Gods, he had no memory of anything.

'We've run all the way from Kagestan,' said Remie. 'We escaped from Raaku's castle itself.'

'Been on the run for weeks,' said Sarah. 'There were more of us, but ...'

'At least they died free.' Moiri put her hand on Sarah's shoulder. 'And you made it.'

One of her soldiers leaned in. 'Commander, we should move. Get back to camp.'

Moiri's eyes drifted across the valley and then she smiled. 'Fin's right. Let's get you somewhere safe and warm and put some food in your stomachs.'

'That would be most welcome,' said Jax.

Moiri pointed to three of her soldiers. 'Bring the dogs. Let's not waste good meat.'

They walked for another hour, out of Gundan and up into the hills to the south-west. No one spoke. All stayed alert. Moiri had her troops well trained and, by the Gods, it felt good to be amongst them. Despite everything he'd been through, Jax felt himself grow stronger with every step he took alongside Moiri, as if he were finding his soul once more.

And there was only silence in his mind. No whispers. No taunts. No Darus Monsuta. He felt clean, as if the poison was gone. Whatever had happened to him in Kagestan, during the escape, it had actually done him good. Had he paid enough penance for his sins? For his failures? Dear Gods, let it be so.

For the first time in an age, he felt safe. He felt well.

The sky was blood-red by the time they reached the Hanran camp, high in the hills. The shelters had walls of loose rocks and canvas roofs scattered with rocks to disguise them from any Daijaku that might fly overhead.

There were more Hanran waiting for them as well. Lots more. Jax had spotted one or two as they weaved their way through the mountain passes towards the camp. They watched from a distance, making sure they were friendly, so he knew there must be others, but he'd not expected this. He turned to Moiri. 'How many ... ?'

'A couple of hundred at last count. Most of them are Shulka. A few waifs and strays we've picked up along the way. They're all good fighters.'

Jax's heart swelled. Most wore Shulka armour and carried swords and shields. They might only be a shadow of what the warriors once were, but it would do for now. More than do. They looked like an army. An army he could be a part of.

He straightened his back as he walked through the camp, remembering something of the Shulka he'd once been. He'd been a proud man before he'd become a broken man. Maybe it was time to regain some of that feeling. Eyes tracked him, and he could hear the whispers, the ripple of excitement that followed them.

One woman in particular started when she saw Jax and jumped to her feet. She rushed over, red-faced, a man following close behind. They were young, in their early twenties perhaps, but the war had hardened them both. Tiny scars criss-crossed their arms and faces. Despite their youth, both had seen a lot of combat. 'General?'

'Yes?'

The woman blushed. 'My name's Jen, from Clan Huska – though I only took my vows three years ago.' She pointed with her thumb at the man behind her. 'This is Cal, my cousin. We both served under you at Gundan.'

Jax flinched at the mention of Gundan, his greatest failure. 'It's good to see you both. Good that you survived.'

'It's not been easy, sir,' said Cal. 'Not easy at all.'

'But you're here now, General,' said Jen. 'Truly, we are blessed.'

The girl's eyes shone bright with admiration and Jax had to look away. 'I'm not that man anymore. I'm not a general. I ...' Dear Gods, what was he?

Moiri slipped her arm through his. 'Leave the poor man alone for a while, Jen. He's been through a lot. Jax needs some food and rest. You can tell him what a legend he is later.'

'Of course,' said Jen.

'It's good to meet you both,' said Jax.

The lad saluted Jax and then retreated with Jen to their lean-to.

On the far side of the camp, a fire pit had been built under a rocky overhang, hiding the flames from above. Moiri offered Jax and the others spots where they could sit and enjoy the warmth. Fin and another man set to work skinning and gutting the dogs and the meat was soon on spits over the fire.

Jax stretched out his legs, tears coming to his eyes. 'I can't remember the last time I could do this.'

Moiri smiled. 'It's good to have you back, old friend. We'll soon have you fighting fit again.'

Jax looked down at his bloody toes. 'That would be something.'

'We'll find you some boots in the morning. There's plenty of kit in Gundan still,' said Moiri as she sat down next to Jax.

'Boots, food, rest, safety.' Jax took a deep breath as Moiri settled. 'Am I dreaming?' He was only half-joking. He couldn't remember how he'd got to Gundan with the others. He didn't know why he wasn't still in that prison in Kagestan. He didn't know why he wasn't dead.

Moiri smiled. 'I can assure you, you're not.'

Her words didn't make Jax feel any better. How long had it been since he could trust his own mind? How long since Monsuta had consumed his every thought? Even the silence was disconcerting. 'Have you been here all this time?'

'No,' she replied. 'We were chased east after the invasion. We'd almost reached Myoshia before we lost them – or they gave up chasing us. We've spent the last nine months or so giving the Skulls a hard time. Doing what we could. The mountains were a good place to set up our camp so we came back here. You were lucky though. We were about to move out. Another day and we wouldn't have been around to save you.'

'Where are you going?'

'We got word a day or so ago that the Meigorians are going to invade Jia.'

'What?' The breath caught in Jax's throat. 'What did you say?'

'The Meigorians are coming. We're heading south to join them.'

'The Meigorians are invading ... So it worked,' said Jax, almost to himself. 'It worked.'

'What worked?'

'We helped Zorique, King Cariin's daughter, escape to Meigore. They promised to help us in the war effort if we got her free.' Jax paused as he dug through his memories. It was all so vague in his head. It all felt so long ago. And there was something else lurking in the shadows of his mind. He rubbed his face. Some information he had to tell Moiri. Something important.

His eyes drifted to the fire, watching the fat drip from the meat into the flames with a pop and a hiss. His mind was so dark. He couldn't remember anything about the recent past. Not their escape or the names of the people he'd run with or even what his last meal had been. But his time with Monsuta screwing up his mind? The death of his son? That felt like yesterday. So clear, so vivid, so raw. Suddenly, he sat upright as more memories returned. 'Your daughter. Of course. You don't know.'

'Tinnstra? What about her?'

'Yes, Tinnstra.' He laughed. 'Your daughter. She's alive – or she was. She was the one who got Zorique away. She went with her to Meigore.'

The happiness that filled Moiri's face touched Jax's heart. 'My Tinnstra?'

'She did you proud. She ... she ... killed the monster ... the Chosen who captured me.'

'Dear Gods, I can't tell you how happy that news makes me. I thought she was dead, along with Dagen and the rest of my children. If there's a chance she's still alive ...' She wiped a tear from her eye. 'No mother should outlive her children.'

The words cut deep into Jax's heart. 'No father, either.'

Moiri realised what she'd said. 'I'm sorry. Your son, Kaine ...'

'He's dead.' Jax didn't know what else he could say. His son had sacrificed himself in order to poison his father, to stop Jax from revealing the Hanran's plans to the Egril interrogator, to Darus Monsuta. But he'd died in vain. Monsuta had stopped the poison from working on Jax with his healing powers and Jax had then confessed everything under torture.

'I'm sorry,' said Moiri.

'So am I.'

Fin passed around cuts of meat and Jax took his time eating, sucking at the food as much as chewing it. It tasted glorious as his mouth came alive with flavour.

Across the fire, Fin whispered in a woman's ear while he kept his eyes on Jax, Remie and Sarah. She was also watching the runaways and Jax had to admit he didn't like their attention.

'Something bothering you both?' he asked.

'We were just talking about how you all escaped from Raaku's castle, from deep in Egril territory,' said Fin.

'How did you manage that?' said the woman, not hiding the scepticism in her voice.

Jax stared at them both, unable to reply. He had no idea.

'Take it easy, Dev,' said Moiri. 'Our guests have been through hell. They deserve a night without anyone hassling them.'

'She's just asking a simple question,' said Fin. 'For a simple story.'

'Now's not the—' Moiri stopped when Remie raised a hand.

'It's all right. I'll tell them the tale, if they want to know it,' said Remie, his voice full of emotion. 'I was a prisoner for four months in the dungeons of Raaku's castle, and you know what? The miracle wasn't that we escaped. It was the fact we survived that long in those cells.'

'You got that right,' said Sarah.

'Every morning before first light, the Skulls collected Jians from the cells,' continued Remie. 'They were taken up to the Red Lake. It surrounds the castle for a mile, maybe more, in every direction. Then, at sunrise, the drums would start, and by the time they stopped, those Jians were floating in the lake with their throats cut. Just like that.' He clicked his fingers.

'Now, everyone in those cells grew closer than family. Closer than any human can get to another, because we were rammed in there, shoulder to shoulder, sleeping standing up, pissing and shitting on our feet, the person next to you breathing in your ear, constantly on the edge of living and dying each and every day.' Remie glanced over at Sarah, then at Jax. 'I loved them all. I really did. But when morning came and we heard the Skulls approaching, I prayed one of them would die and not me. The door would open, and they would drag out my friends kicking and screaming, and it broke my heart to know I'd never see them again. I—'

Remie choked on his memories and Sarah squeezed his hand. 'It's all right. You don't need to say any more.'

Remie's eyes glistened with tears. 'May the Gods help me because I do. I need to say this – they need to know this – because every Godsdamned morning, I was fucking happy when it was them that got took and not me. I had another day of standing in everyone's piss and shit, breathing in that stinking, stale air, unable to sit down, unable to stretch out my arms, and I was so grateful.'

'You weren't the only one,' said Sarah. 'We all felt that way. Nothing to be ashamed of.'

Remie stared into the fire. 'Yeah, well, that might be so, but it don't make me feel any better for it. Anyway, it didn't matter in the end. One day my prayers went unanswered, my luck ran out. The Skulls grabbed me, Sarah, Jax, Esto, Caio and Wils along with maybe thirty others. Up the stairs we go. Time to get our throats cut and float in the lake. There were spears at our backs moving us on, but we weren't tied up or nothing. The Skulls probably thought we had no fight left in us and maybe they were right. But they hadn't counted on Jax.'

Jax looked up from the fire at the mention of his name. 'I didn't do anything.'

'Not until we were lined up on that bloodstained shoreline.' Remie paused, letting the moment play out. 'Then he grabbed a Skull's scimitar and ran it through the bastard. Got two more before they knew what was going on.'

Jax listened as rapt as the others, for it was all news to him. Even hearing Remie tell the story didn't stir any memories.

'He shouted at us to swim for it, he did,' added Sarah, 'and then he was off, jumping in that lake. I tell you, I didn't need telling twice. I followed him bloody damn quick.'

'You don't look like a swimmer,' said Fin. 'Very impressive.'

Jax ignored the sarcasm.

'It was a hard swim even with two arms, I can tell you,' continued Remie. 'After months in that hole, living on shit, all of us as weak as could be, but the Gods and Jax gave us a chance and we took it. He wasn't going to give in.' Remie fixed his eye on Fin. 'Even with one arm.'

'There were hundreds of Egril on the far shore watching us,' said Sarah. 'But they weren't fighters. Women and children mainly. A few old men. None of them could stop us. Once we were past them, we ran, heading south.'

'We hid where we could, moving at night,' said Remie. 'Out

into the countryside, living off the land or raiding farms, but always moving. Then those bastards with the dogs picked up our trail about a week ago and, if I'm being honest, I have no idea how we stayed ahead of them. Jax used every trick he knew but they kept coming.' His voice broke and the tears fell.

Sarah pulled his head against her shoulder, crying herself. 'We made it, love. We made it home.'

'Yeah, but only because of Jax. We owe him our lives, we do.'

The raw emotion on display affected them all. Some looked away. Others shed tears of their own. Even Fin and Dev appeared moved. They had no more questions, no barely hidden suspicions to voice.

As they cried, Moiri put her hand on Jax's shoulder. 'I'm glad you're here. After losing so many, it's a gift to have a good friend return. Gives me hope.'

'Hope,' said Jax. The word felt strange on his tongue but welcome all the same. 'It'd be good to have some of that again.'

He watched the fire burn, feeling better than he'd felt in only the Gods knew how long. The plan had worked. The Meigorians had joined the fight. Perhaps all their sacrifices had been worth it. Perhaps his failures were ... less catastrophic after all. 'Are you still planning on heading south, Moiri?'

'We were going to leave in the morning,' replied his old friend. 'We can wait another day or so if that would help you.'

'No. I don't need you to wait. In fact, I want to come with you. I want to fight. I want to be a part of the Hanran again. A Shulka.'

Moiri nodded, a smile on her lips. 'It would be an honour to have you.'

'Thank you.' Jax leaned back and closed his eyes. Yes, he had to go south. Find the others. Find Zorique.

He could see her so clearly in his mind, could see himself standing next to her with a sword in his hand. Her guardian. Her Shulka.

Winning the war.

10

Tinnstra

Layso

Tinnstra was grinning. She couldn't help herself. It was happening. It was really happening. The harbour was packed full of ships in various stages of completion that were going to make up her invasion armada.

She had to give the Meigorians credit. They'd made fast progress so far. She'd not believed it when they'd said they'd have the fleet ready to sail within three months but they'd damn well done it. In two weeks' time, they'd be on their way to Jia to send the Skulls running back to Egril. She couldn't wait.

In the meantime, it was a beautiful chaos; hammers and saws working away, men and women shouting and cursing, boys running from ship to ship with water to drink and girls singing about the quality of the dumplings they had to sell, all on top of a million other activities, not least of which was the growing crowd below their balcony. People had started gathering the moment word had got out that Zorique was there, with more arriving by the minute. They called out to her or sang prayers.

She and Zorique were watching from a balcony at the old harbour master's house. Ralasis had invited them down to see the armada's progress, but the captain – no, commander – had yet to appear. Aasgod had remained at the embassy, thank the Gods. The man really grated on Tinnstra's nerves. She wished more and more that the mage had stayed in the past.

'How many ships will set sail to Jia?' asked Zorique, her cheeks flushed. She was finding it harder than Tinnstra to ignore the people below them, judging by the way she shuffled her feet.

'One hundred and twenty of Meigore's finest, Your Majesty,' said Ralasis, suddenly in the doorway, 'carrying forty thousand men and women.' He had added a red sash to his uniform but looked no less the rogue, despite his new title.

'You sound impressed with yourself,' said Tinnstra.

'I've never been one to shy away from blowing my own trumpet,' replied Ralasis. 'But, in this case, I think my boasts have some merit.'

Tinnstra smiled. 'That's good. I'd hate to be disappointed.'

'I'd hate for you to be disappointed as well,' said Ralasis. 'Would you like to see for yourself?'

'I hope you're both still talking about the ships,' muttered Zorique.

'But of course, Your Majesty,' said Ralasis, grinning. 'If you'd like to follow me, I can take you on a tour of one near completion.' He bowed extravagantly, motioning back into the building.

Zorique glanced down at the dock. 'What about the ... er ... people outside?'

'Do they bother you?' asked Ralasis. 'I can have them removed.'

'No, you don't have to do that,' replied Zorique. 'It's just ... I'm not what they say I am.'

Ralasis arched an eyebrow. 'You're not a God?'

'No, I'm not.'

'I don't think it's a bad thing for others to think you are,' said Tinnstra. 'People will do anything for their God. Might be the edge we need.'

Zorique looked shocked. 'But I'm not.'

'I know. But we've seen what the Egril will do for Raaku because they believe in him.'

'It's hard enough being a queen,' said Zorique.

'Tinnstra does have a point,' said Ralasis. 'A bit of magic and mystery never did my reputation any harm.'

'Show us this ship,' said Tinnstra, 'before you start waving your ego around again.' She had to fight her smile. Whatever it was about Ralasis, he certainly didn't annoy her like Aasgod did.

'Then follow me.' Ralasis led them through the harbour master's house, down the stairs and out through the front door. A rush of noise hit them as the crowd surged forwards eagerly, shouting in excitement and calling Zorique's name. For a moment, Tinnstra worried that the trip wasn't such a good idea after all. An assassin could easily hide in the crowd and she started to scan faces, looking for anyone out of place.

'*Shirudan*,' said Zorique, and Tinnstra realised she needn't have been concerned. Zorique's shield formed around them, a glowing golden bubble just large enough to keep the crowd at arm's distance. It didn't deter anyone, though – far from it. They pressed up against her magic, desperate to touch it, happiness shining from their faces.

'Well, this is something,' said Ralasis, but he kept walking, leading them to a pier, as the shield made space for them. 'Can you teach me this trick? I can think of plenty of occasions where this would come in handy.'

'I'm afraid not, Commander,' said Zorique.

'That's a shame.' They passed through a sentry point, and Tinnstra was grateful that the soldiers there stopped the crowd from following them.

Zorique heard her breathe a sigh of relief. 'See? I told you it's not nice.'

'Yes, you did, Your Majesty. I beg your forgiveness.'

Zorique laughed, a sound that carried its own kind of magic, and this time Tinnstra didn't try to hide her smile.

Ralasis stopped by one of the ships. 'Here we are.' In many ways, it looked like the three-mast square-rigger that had rescued them from Jia, except the prow of this ship was different. It was wider than usual with a gentle curve, giving it a rounded appearance rather than the sharp, angular one typical of that type of boat.

Tinnstra looked around at the other ships moored nearby. They all had the same style of prow. 'Why have you altered the ships like this?'

'I'd like to claim the credit for this innovation but, alas, it was designed by someone slightly cleverer than me,' said Ralasis as he walked to the prow. 'When we arrive in Jia, it's very doubtful we'll find a nice pier like this one to dock at and take our time disembarking everyone.'

'I think that's a fair assumption,' said Tinnstra.

'These ships have been adapted to allow us to run them straight onto the beach at Omason,' said Ralasis. 'Inside are cables that will be cut and the prow will fall, creating a ramp for us to run down. We can get three hundred and fifty troops off this beast in a matter of minutes.'

'Have you actually tried this or is it all theory?' asked Tinnstra.

'Oh, we've tried it. On a smaller scale, of course, but it definitely works.'

'I'm impressed.'

'That's a first,' said Zorique.

'I'm honoured,' said Ralasis.

'So you should be,' said Tinnstra. 'Take us aboard.'

Ralasis was right to be proud of the vessel. In addition to the sails, oars ran along both sides of the ship, ensuring they could approach the beach at speed no matter the weather. There was also plenty of space onboard for stores and weaponry, and apparently some ships would be carrying horses for the cavalry.

Zorique was quiet, though, keeping her thoughts to herself during the tour.

'What's wrong?' asked Tinnstra, when Ralasis left them for a moment on the quarterdeck.

'Nothing,' replied Zorique.

'Tell me.'

Zorique shook her head. 'It's just ... these ships. They'll be carrying forty thousand people. Forty thousand! To fight for me.'

'For you and for Jia,' said Tinnstra.

'How many will die?'

'Some. Many.'

'I don't want their lives on my conscience.'

'War always has its price.'

'It's too much.'

'I know. But if we stay here – keep the forty thousand safe – then what of Jia? What of all those who have died there so far?

What about those who are yet to die because of the Skulls? We have to stop them, or the murders will continue for generations.'

'What if I just go on my own?'

'On your own?'

'Yes. I'm the one with powers, with a shield that will keep me safe. I can kill the Skulls and their demons. No one else need get hurt.'

Tinnstra smiled and pulled her daughter into a hug. 'Gods, you have a good soul.'

'I'm being serious,' said Zorique, pushing back. She looked Tinnstra in the eyes. 'I want to do it. I *can* do it.'

'Remember what happened here in Layso. We only just beat the Egril – and they'll have ten times the numbers in Jia.'

'I won't make the same mistakes again,' said Zorique. 'And I'm stronger now.'

'I know you are. But we caught them unawares before. You might be stronger, but they will be, too. The one thing I know for sure is that the Skulls never give up. They'll do everything they can to kill you.'

'They won't succeed.'

'Because we'll go with an army. This is Sekanowari. We take no chances. None of us is as strong as all of us. Wenna's told us we still have the gates, so we stick to the plan. The Egril won't even know we're coming. We'll be in Jia, through the gate and storming Aisair before the Skulls even know what's going on. The Gods willing, it'll all be over within a week.' Tinnstra smiled. 'Besides, you can't get rid of me that easily. I'm not leaving your side.'

'Thank you. Thank you for everything.'

'There's no need to say that, Your Majesty. I'm here to serve.'

Zorique slapped Tinnstra on the arm. 'Shut up.' Then she fell into Tinnstra's embrace and hugged her back, both of them laughing.

Tinnstra gazed out across the fleet once more. She was going to enjoy killing as many Skulls as she could on the way to victory. The Gods knew she deserved that pleasure.

II

Raaku

The prisoner looked up as Raaku entered his cell. 'Sekanowari draws near,' said the Emperor. 'I have need of your sight once more.'

Laafien smiled. 'What if I tell you news you do not wish to hear?'

'You once told me the future is but one of many possible paths to take,' said Raaku. 'To be chosen by those with the strongest will.'

'I should've taken the path that led me far from you. I should've stayed with my brother in Jia.'

'Your brother Aasgod was the one who sent you to find the holy waters.' Raaku smiled. 'He sent you to me.'

The prisoner dropped his head, then looked up so his eyes shone through the mess of his hair. 'Perhaps he will be the one who kills you.'

'Your brother has already died once. I do not fear the shadow that remains.'

'You should fear death, O mighty one. Even Gods can die.'

'So you warned me when last we spoke. "Victory can be yours if you can defeat death." Truly an apt challenge for the son of Kage.'

'Bah! You're the son of a hill farmer. I should know – I met the man.'

'He was but an instrument for Kage,' said Raaku. 'To give

85

my soul form. Just as you were necessary to show me the key to power. And I will be the one who sends the world into the Great Darkness.'

'Perhaps,' said the prisoner. 'Or because of your actions, the world will be rid of Kage once and for all.'

'Impossible.'

'Really? What will happen if you are defeated? If you lose Sekanowari? Do you think the world will go back to what it was before you dreamed of conquest? That the Egril will be able to carry on as before? No. If the Four Gods win, it will be the end of your sad religion.'

'I will not lose. I cannot lose.'

'You must fear that possibility,' said the prisoner. 'Otherwise you would not seek my counsel.'

'I do not fear it because it will not happen. You merely show me the shortest route to that destiny.'

'How can you trust me to show you the right way? I do not want your victory. I do not want your success.'

Raaku nodded. 'I know because you cannot lie when the water is in you.' He held up the gourd. 'And now I will hear your truth.'

The fight went from the prisoner. 'Don't do this. Please. I don't want to do this.' He retreated to the corner, but there was no escape. Raaku pushed him to his knees, forced his mouth open and poured the holy water in, only releasing the prisoner from his grip when he had swallowed everything.

He walked over to a stool on the far side of the cell and sat down.

The prisoner writhed on the floor as the holy water did its work. It was a shame that only the Jian had the ability of foresight. Despite his words to the contrary, it bothered Raaku that he did not have someone more loyal to seek guidance from. He'd tried to recreate the man's gift in his Chosen for decades, but he'd always been unsuccessful.

Laafien was, unfortunately, unique.

So, Raaku sat on a stool in the prisoner's cell, watching the man convulse, waiting for his words. One day, perhaps, he might put Laafien out of his misery and send him to Kage, but not yet. Not now.

'They come across the sea soon, soon, soon,' hissed the prisoner, foaming at the mouth, tears in his eyes. 'Returning to where they left. The dead city. The centre of hope. The beginning, the end. They seek gates to here, there, everywhere. Moving fast, or moving slow. Death's kiss. My brother so young. The queen so old. The Four. The light. The dark. The land. The sea. From far and near. Bleeding across the world.'

Already Raaku's mind worked, seeking meaning in the prisoner's rant. For one hundred and twenty years, he had used Laafien to guide his hand to build first a kingdom, then an empire. As much as the prisoner hated what his visions had enabled Raaku to achieve, he'd never lied to his master or guided him astray.

'Sekanowari. Sekanowari. It starts. It ends. Ends all. Blood for Kage. Souls for Kage. Your life for Kage.' The prisoner suddenly curled up in a ball, twitched once, twice, three times, then was still.

Still Raaku waited.

Slowly, the prisoner stretched out his long body before turning his head so he could see Raaku. He hissed through clenched teeth. 'How many people must you kill until you are satisfied?'

'The world is built on blood and bone. Every life is but a flash of light on its way to the Great Darkness,' replied Raaku. 'I will kill as many as it takes to reshape this world in my father's image. No more. No less.'

'You don't have to do this. You don't have to fight Sekanowari.'

'But I do. I will. You, of all people, know this to be true.'

The man nodded. 'The world will never know a killer like you again.'

'I am my father's son.' Raaku stood, a shadow filling the room. 'And I do his work.'

'You will destroy the world,' said the prisoner.

'If that is my destiny, then so be it. I will be rewarded in the Great Darkness.'

Raaku left him then, left him howling and screaming as he shut the iron door and the locks clunked into place.

His chancellor knelt by the entrance to the main Daijaku birthing pools, head bowed.

'Rise, Astin, there is much to do,' said Raaku.

'Yes, Master.' The man straightened but remained on his knees.

'How go the preparations in Jia?'

'Commander Vallia has fortified the capital over the last two months as well as carried out a purge of the rebel cells within the country.'

'Tell her to seek and destroy all the gates within the country at once. The False Gods' champions intend to use them to strike at us.'

'Yes, Master.'

A crack echoed around the cavern as an egg hatched. Veksters rushed through the waters to help with the birth and to calm the Daijaku as it emerged, reborn. Raaku watched for a moment, then turned back to the chancellor. 'The heathens will head to the dead city with their ships. Vallia will meet them there.'

'Yes, Master.'

There was a scream as the new Daijaku slashed out at a Vekster, opening his chest with a talon. The man fell, his blood blessing the holy water, as others tried to soothe the creature. The Daijaku's squawks grew louder as it smelled the blood, and it tried to take to the air on its fragile wings. 'My child calls me, Astin. Tell Vallia that Kage awaits the heathens' souls.'

'Yes, Master,' said Astin, bowing once more.

Raaku waded into the holy water. Other Daijaku, not yet hatched, reacted to his presence as he passed, feeding off his magic. Veksters stepped out of his way and bowed. When he reached the newborn, Raaku held out his hand to the creature as it frantically batted its wings. 'Calm yourself, little one. Your battle is not here.'

The Daijaku squawked, but its wings slowed and then stopped as its body slouched back down. Raaku beckoned the beautiful newborn over. The Daijaku were the first creatures he grew in the holy waters and they remained his most favoured.

The newborn waded to Raaku, its eyes fixed on its master. When it was close enough, the Emperor stroked its cheek. 'The things you will do will be remembered for eternity, little one.'

12

Ralasis

Layso

'Don't try and sleep with her,' muttered Ralasis. 'For once in your life, don't be an idiot.'

'Did you say something?' said Tinnstra. She'd stopped in the doorway of the carriage and turned back to look down on him, still standing in the street holding the door open for her. He'd suggested getting together to discuss the invasion and then, when he'd heard her only experience of Layso was slaughtering Skulls in the street, he'd insisted he take her out to show her the real city. Because, after all, that's how military leaders and their attractive allies bond.

It was her idea to get a drink. Not his. Not that he'd objected. No. In fact, he said yes to that suggestion pretty damn quick. Like a fool. A fool hoping to get himself into trouble. Like he always did.

Ralasis smiled. His default reaction to everything. 'Just talking to myself.'

'First sign of madness,' replied Tinnstra, before ducking into the carriage. She'd been wearing her full Shulka dress uniform earlier and wearing it well, but she'd taken off the jacket a short time ago because of the heat. Of course, that made it more comfortable for Tinnstra, but not for Ralasis. The woman had certainly changed from the girl he'd rescued.

Changed in all the best ways.

'Where to, Commander?' asked the driver as Ralasis climbed onto the carriage steps.

'Torenan Alley,' he replied.

The driver turned in his seat to look at Ralasis. 'Torenan Alley? You sure?'

'I'm sure.' He ducked inside and took the seat opposite Tinnstra. She still had her sword with her, but as far as Ralasis could see, that was her only weapon. Still, he had no doubt that Tinnstra could kill him without breaking a sweat. She might have become more beautiful, but she'd also become more dangerous while she'd been gone wherever she'd gone. Maybe that's why he liked her so much.

'Where are we going?' asked Tinnstra as the carriage lurched off. 'The driver didn't sound too sure about it.'

'I must admit that Torenan Alley is an acquired taste, but if you want to have a drink and be left alone, there's nowhere better,' said Ralasis. 'Of course, the last time I was there, Tian Kosa sent a squadron of soldiers to arrest me and I ended up starting a fire in the square. Might've killed someone as well.' He paused, enjoying the amused look Tinnstra gave him. 'I'm sure they'll have forgotten all about it by now.'

'You're not exactly the most forgettable person I've ever met.'

'Well, if anyone gives us any trouble, we'll just have to play the war hero act. We really shouldn't have to pay for another drink as long as we live.'

'We'll see.' Tinnstra turned her attention to Layso's streets, watching the world go past her window.

The fading sunlight honeyed her complexion, and Ralasis could just see the faintest trace of a scar running down her face. When he'd picked her up in the Golden Channel a few months ago, the wound had been freshly made, running from the top of her forehead to her jaw. Now it looked like it had happened a thousand years ago. Of course, Tinnstra had been nineteen then. He had no idea how old she was now. Closer to his age, that was for sure.

'You're staring,' she said without taking her eyes off the view outside.

'Guilty as charged.' He smiled, but she didn't see it. 'I was just thinking how much you've changed since we first met. It was only a few months ago—'

'Not for me, it wasn't.' Tinnstra's voice was quiet, almost as if she was talking to herself.

Ralasis might be a fool, but even he knew when someone didn't want to speak about something. Perhaps she'd tell him in her own time what had happened. Perhaps not. He, of all people, wasn't going to think any less of someone for keeping a secret or two. The Gods knew he had enough of his own. More than enough.

He followed Tinnstra's example and gazed out through the carriage window as they rattled along. There was still plenty of evidence of damage from the Egril's attack, but people were hard at work pretending life was back to normal.

It had been a close call when the Skulls attacked. If not for Zorique and Tinnstra's arrival, they'd all be speaking Egril – those who were still alive, that is. And to think the enemy had replaced the king with one of their own. The same shapeshifter that had taken Kosa's place.

'The Egril are something else, aren't they?'

That got Tinnstra's attention. 'What do you mean?'

'I was just thinking about the shapeshifter,' said Ralasis. 'Only the Gods know how long he'd been influencing the king, getting everyone worked up about the dangers of refugees, turning us against our natural allies, all the while preparing for his army to strike when we were at our weakest.'

'The Egril do war very well. Too well.'

'It makes me wonder if we can beat them.'

'Having second thoughts about the invasion, Commander?'

He shook his head. 'No, not second thoughts – just the same thoughts as usual. I'm going to be responsible for forty thousand lives. I know some will die, but I want as many as possible to return home with me. To do that, I want to understand my enemy as best I can.'

'Wise.'

'Not many would say that about me. Especially not my father. Perhaps I'm just sensible. Or a coward.'

'Believe me, *I* know you're not a coward.'

'You've met a few, have you?'

'Just one. That was enough.'

The carriage drew to a halt before Ralasis could say anything. 'Torenan Alley,' the driver called.

'Ah, you're in for a treat,' said Ralasis, opening the carriage door. 'After you.'

'Not going to help me down? I thought you were pretending to be a gentleman.' Tinnstra gave him a smile of her own.

'I don't think you need anyone's help – least of all mine.'

'You *are* wise.' She was laughing as she climbed out.

Ralasis followed, happy to be insulted. 'Wait here for us,' he told the driver before joining Tinnstra at the alley's entrance. It was strange not being welcomed by Druse and Dires, but neither had been seen since the attack. 'This way.'

The alley was narrow, leading to a cobblestone courtyard overlooked by town houses on either side. Meg's was open for business and a few of her ladies called out from a balcony when they saw Ralasis.

'Friends of yours?' asked Tinnstra, with an arched eyebrow.

'Would you believe me if I said I'd never seen them before?'

'No.'

'Ralasis! You paying us a visit?' asked one of Meg's girls before he could say anything else. He tried not to look, but he thought it was Seranina. She'd always had a cruel sense of humour.

'Ignore them,' he said. 'They like to tease men like me, who disapprove of what they do.'

'I imagine you must be horrified by such things,' said Tinnstra. The hardness of earlier had gone, thank the Gods, and she was enjoying herself – even if it was at his expense. Not that he cared in the slightest. He just wanted her to be happy.

He led her to the other side of the street, walking over cobblestones blackened by his home-made bombs, to the beaded curtain at the top of the stairs leading down to the tavern. 'This way.'

Nothing had changed since his last visit, not that anything had changed in the twenty years he'd been visiting, either. It was all so familiar; the buzzing of voices, the oh-so-familiar rattling of dice and the swishing of tiles, the smell of ... well, he was never sure what caused that particular smell. Probably for the best.

'Welcome to Layso's best tavern,' said Ralasis.

Tinnstra waved at the smoke that billowed in their faces and coughed. 'Very nice.'

Irnus was behind the bar, looking more sour than normal. 'You're not welcome here, Captain,' he called out. 'Be on your way.'

'Irnus, you old dog,' replied Ralasis, smiling wide and opening his arms as if to give the whole bar a hug. 'I've missed your jokes.'

'I'm not joking. I've just finished clearing up the mess from your last visit,' shouted the barman. 'You're trouble, and I don't want trouble.'

'Time to play the war hero?' Tinnstra whispered.

'Irnus, you're not going to embarrass me, are you?' Ralasis waved a hand towards Tinnstra. 'I have a war hero I'm trying to impress.'

'Shouldn't have brought her here, then,' grunted Irnus, but he gave Tinnstra another glance.

'Look fierce,' whispered Ralasis. 'If he's scared, he'll definitely let us have a drink.'

Tinnstra shouldered past him. 'I must apologise for my friend,' she said to the barman. 'He's a self-confessed idiot.'

'He's more than that,' said Irnus.

'I'm just being polite, trying to spare his fragile ego,' said Tinnstra. 'Even so, I'd be grateful if you'd let us have a jug of wine. Perhaps the *captain* will pay you for some of the damage he caused as well?'

Irnus gave him another glare, but Ralasis knew Tinnstra had won him over. 'Go on, then,' he said. 'Seat yourselves.'

'Thank you, my friend,' said Ralasis. 'And your finest wine – not the gut-rot you normally serve me.'

'Wonders will never cease,' muttered Irnus. 'Fancy women *and* fancy taste?'

Tinnstra headed to the table in the far corner. She took a chair and positioned it so she had her back to the wall before sitting down.

'I don't think any assassins will come looking for you here,' said Ralasis, taking the seat facing her – the only view he was interested in.

'Is that what you thought the last time you were here?'

'Ha. You have a point there.' Ralasis stood up again and moved his chair next to Tinnstra's, with its back to the wall and facing the room. When he sat down, their elbows touched. 'Better safe than sorry, eh?'

'Quite.'

Irnus brought over a jug and two cups. He plonked them on the table and growled at Ralasis. 'And where did you get the alcohol for your bombs, eh? Want me to add those bottles to your bill?'

'I'm not sure. That night was quite the blur. People were trying to kill us, after all,' said Ralasis. 'But yes, bill me if that makes you feel better.'

'It will.' Irnus stomped off, leaving the two of them alone.

Ralasis poured the wine. 'He's normally a charming man. Must've had an argument with the wife.'

'He's married?' Tinnstra laughed, then took a sip of wine. 'Hmm. Definitely not the gut-rot.'

'It's good to hear you laugh.' Ralasis raised his cup in a toast to Tinnstra and then drank. The wine was rich, smooth and full of flavour. Only the Gods knew how much Irnus was going to charge him for it, but Tinnstra was worth it.

'It feels good.' She peered into her cup as she swirled the wine. 'It feels strange.'

'Laughter does appear to be in rather short supply these days.'

Tinnstra looked up, took a sip of wine, then another, before her gaze dropped back to her cup. 'Do you know – this is the first time in over a decade that I haven't been worried about the Egril trying to kill Zorique or myself?'

'A decade?'

'Closer to fifteen years, actually. I was nineteen when all this ... nonsense started. I'm thirty-three now.'

Ralasis knew his jaw had dropped, that he must look a fool. After all, he'd noticed that she'd aged – he wasn't blind – but he'd thought it was magic, not time, that had caused it. 'How … ?'

'We went to a place where time worked differently than it does here. So Zorique could grow up and become who she is today – and maybe I needed to grow up, too. Become who I am.' Tinnstra tried to laugh again but failed. 'We were gone nearly fifteen years. Fifteen years of waking up every day wondering if that was the day the Skulls would come to kill us. Wondering if they'd succeed or if I'd be good enough to stop them.'

'I can't even imagine what that must have been like,' said Ralasis.

'Not good.'

'And did they?'

Tinnstra gave the faintest of nods. 'Yes. But we killed them all.'

'That must've felt good.'

'It did. Felt even better when we came here and killed more of them. I like killing Skulls.'

'Won't be long before you can do it again,' said Ralasis.

'*Souls I will send you.*'

'That's nice – but please, don't go to any trouble on my part.' It was a bad joke, even by Ralasis' standards, but the best he could manage.

'It's from an Egril prayer to Kage – *Blood I will give you, O Great One. Souls I will send you. My body is your weapon. My life, your gift.*'

'Cheerful.'

'Quite. They think it's their holy duty to kill any non-believers and send us off to their one-eyed demon God in the Great Darkness. The more they kill, the more they'll be rewarded in the afterlife. And if they die in the process? That's the biggest honour of all. It's the opposite of what we're taught – that all life is precious, that to kill for no reason whatsoever is evil.'

'I know which version I prefer,' said Ralasis. He drank some wine but found no satisfaction in his cup this time.

'Believe me – so do I. But to the Egril, Sekanowari isn't the end of everything, it's the start of something far better. In their minds, they're putting the world right, either in this life or the

96

next. That's why they'll never stop trying to destroy us.' Tinnstra paused for a heartbeat. 'That's why I mean to enjoy this brief respite.' She drained her cup and poured herself another before offering to top up Ralasis' own. 'Tell me about yourself.'

He allowed her to fill his cup. 'What would you like to know?'

Tinnstra shrugged. 'I don't know. Anything. How did you get to be commander of Meigore's fleet? That's quite the promotion from a captain.'

'Well, normally, one obtains such a high title either by right of birth or through bribery and corruption,' said Ralasis. 'However, it became apparent during recent events that neither of these approaches would give us very good military leaders. Tian Galrin has decided, in his infinite wisdom, to try a different way.'

'You.' Tinnstra's smirked. Somehow it suited her more than her smile.

'Yes, me. Apparently, he was impressed by the way I uncovered Tian Kosa's treachery and rallied our forces during the Battle of Layso. He wanted an inspirational hero to lead us to victory instead of some rich, inbred fool.'

'He's a wise man.'

'Or we're all fools. Either way, here I am – Lord Commander of Meigore, with one hundred and twenty ships and forty thousand men at my command.' The title still didn't sit well with him, no matter how many times he said it out loud. Now it was his turn to down his wine. 'Off to save the world.'

'My hero.' Tinnstra leaned in, her shoulder pressing against Ralasis. 'Now tell me one more thing.'

'Anything.'

'Why don't you want to sleep with me?'

13

Yas

The Ascalian Mountains

'How long's it been?' Yas glanced over to the cave entrance for
the six hundredth time. Four guards loitered around the hole in
the rock face, but there was no sign of the others, the ones she'd
sent out.

'The patrols will be back soon,' replied Hasan. 'They know
what they're doing.' They were sitting around a small fire, waiting for a pot of water to boil.

Yas had a cushion underneath her, a small concession to comfort that was missing from almost every other aspect of their lives.
'Maybe. I'll just be happier when they're home.'

'You worry too much.' The Shulka leaned over and kissed the
side of her head.

'I know.' It was something he'd told her many times since
they'd abandoned Kiyosun to live in the mountain caves, but she
couldn't help herself. It was what she did now she had the whole
city to think about.

Yas rubbed her cheek, then noticed a grimace flicker across
Hasan's face and dropped her hand. He'd not been happy when
she had the two tears tattooed beneath her eye, but the Weeping
Men had insisted when they took her for their leader. Two tears
for two kills – Raab and his Skull paymaster. She didn't mention to anyone the three hundred she'd poisoned in the Council
House a few days beforehand. Not that she needed any marks to

98

remind herself of those. Those deaths were a heavy weight on her shoulders as it was.

She looked around. Little Ro, as always, was nearby, being looked after by Daxam and his wife, Timy. Her beautiful boy was playing with a few other children, laughing away. Some were orphans from the war, while others had parents in the caves. They all knew the safest place for the young ones was near Yas. And it wasn't just because Daxam and Timy watched over them.

The two Weeping Men who loitered another few yards away ensured that no one made the mistake of threatening Ro again. Dean and Sorin stood alert like always, Skull scimitars hanging off their belts, with orders to kill anyone who tried to take Ro or any other child without her permission. Her son's life had been threatened twice – it wouldn't happen a third time.

Not that she should have any enemies in the caves. Not now.

It had been nearly three months since she, Ro and the other survivors from Kiyosun fled into the mountains. Nearly eight hundred of them. Eight hundred out of a city of thousands. Not many when you thought about it. Not many at all – but all that was left.

Even so, the Skulls had tried to come after them. It was what they did. Once they'd laid waste to Kiyosun, they sent troops into the mountains, hunting for survivors. The Hanran sent corpses back. That wasn't enough of a deterrent, though. Still the bastards hunted her people. And that's why she worried. The Skulls never gave up.

Yas glanced towards the entrance again. 'The patrols should be back by now.'

Hasan gave her a look that said she was worrying again, but he didn't tell her she was wrong. They'd got together a few weeks after they moved into the caves. Neither of them had planned it but she was glad that it had happened. Hasan was a good man with a good heart, her bit of happiness in a world gone crazy. He even put up with her fussing.

Hasan called to one of his troops standing nearby. 'Nika, go and check outside. See if there's any sign of the patrol.'

'Will do, Boss.' Nika set off at a run up the slope.

They both watched her go. 'Do you remember when you had that much energy?' said Hasan.

'Not since I had Little Ro,' replied Yas.

'How's he doing?'

Yas shrugged. 'Not bad considering his father and grandmother were murdered, he was kidnapped, his mother's leading an organisation of cut-throats and his home is a cave.' She allowed herself a smile, though it had no humour in it. 'Oh yeah, and we're waiting to be invaded again.'

'At least this time the invaders are on our side.'

'Do you think this Zorique will be as powerful as Wenna said?'

'The Meigorians wouldn't be coming if they didn't believe they had a chance,' said Hasan. 'That means something. It makes me hopeful, at the very least.'

'We've not had much of that for a long time.'

'Not since the Skulls turned up.'

'Sometimes I think it'll be the hope that kills us.' Yas waved her hand at the cave. 'It's certainly not done us much good so far.'

'We're still alive, Yas,' said Hasan. 'We still have each other.'

Yas raised an eyebrow. 'You got the short straw there.'

'Not at all. We're doing good here. Yes, we're living in a cave, but we're alive and things will get better.'

'I'd just settle for the patrol coming back at this point.'

Three Hanran – Asker, Sadir and Tavis – had left early that morning to check on the Skulls, then put an arrow through an animal or two; anything that could be added to the vegetable stews that made up most meals in the caves. They were good people. Smart. Like all of Hasan's troops, they knew how to look after themselves.

Ange and Garo made up the other patrol. They weren't much more than kids themselves – members of Dren's old crew – but they had war smarts. They were in Kiyosun, looking for weapons or anything they could sell on for food or money. Yas had been using the Weeping Men's network to get supplies, but those bastards didn't work for free. The tears on her cheek meant nothing when it came to business. The Weeping Men worked solely for cash.

She looked up to the small holes puncturing the cavern's roof. The sky outside was bloody and bruised. Not long before nightfall. Well past the time the patrol should've been back. Yas tried to shake the thought from her head. 'Has there been any word from Wenna?'

Hasan nodded. 'We've been getting messages regularly. Everything's as good as it can be. The Skulls are cracking down on them but the Hanran in Aisair are getting organised for when the time comes.'

'So, we all just wait for the queen to make her grand appearance, eh?' Yas scratched her tears again. She'd had them three months and she could still feel the needle. Three months since she'd become a killer. She wasn't sure what bothered her more, the tattoos or the murders.

'They'll be here soon.'

'We can't go on like this – sleeping in caves, living off shrubs and roots, scrabbling in the dirt for coins.' Yas leaned closer, kept her voice low but did nothing to hide the anger she felt.

'I know, Yas, I know. We just need to be patient a bit longer.'

Yas bit back what she was going to say next. There was no point getting angry with Hasan. The man was doing his best, like everyone else. He'd not asked to be put in charge of the Hanran in Kiyosun. The responsibility had been dumped on him, like it had on her. By the Gods, how she wished she could go back to how things were before the war.

'Should we send some people out to check on—'

Thunder cut across her words. Odd, that. She looked at the sky again. No clouds.

'Where's that storm coming from?'

Another roar of thunder, closer this time. Yas saw more heads looking up.

'That's no storm,' whispered Hasan, as if he was too scared to say the words out loud.

More thunder, loud and brutal. Dust and dirt rained down from the cave roof.

They all knew what it was then. The people of Kiyosun knew only too well.

'Bombs!' shouted Yas, already moving. 'Take cover!'

She scooped Ro up without breaking stride and just had to hope the others would get the rest of the children to safety. She heard shouts and screams as all her people scrambled away from their homes and the stream – the danger areas if the roof collapsed.

Another explosion boomed overhead, so close this time that she felt the ground shake. Small bits of stone rained down from the roof.

With the cave wall at her back, Yas looked up. They'd talked about what would happen if the Skulls bombed the mountains. They'd thought the roof of the cave was thick enough to withstand an assault – now they were going to find out. She searched the little patch of sky she could see for any sign of the Daijaku carrying the bombs, but they must've been too high up, too far away. That was something, at least.

Ro started to cry as more bombs pounded the mountainside.

'It's okay,' whispered Yas. 'It's just noise. We're safe here.' As Ro snuggled closer, she caught Hasan's eye. 'Do they know where we are?'

Hasan shook his head. 'No. The bombings are too random. I think they're just trying their luck.'

Yas looked up again. It was all too easy to imagine a bomb falling through one of the holes in the cave's roof. The Daijaku only had to get lucky once for the damage to be horrendous.

'Why now?'

They both looked at each other, sharing the same fears, no doubt. 'It's just a coincidence,' said Hasan.

'I don't like this.'

'Me neither,' said Hasan. 'I'm going to check outside.'

Yas nodded. 'Be careful.' She watched him sprint off to the tunnels that led outside, with some Hanran in tow, and tried not to think about what might happen to him.

She couldn't lose another man she loved.

She sat huddled against the cold stone, Ro wrapped up in her arms, the other children pressed around her, for at least an hour. Every time they thought the bombs were moving away, the next one landed right overhead, rattling the rock and filling the caves with thunder.

By the Gods, she hated waiting there, scared witless, unable to do anything – unable to protect her child. When was it all going to stop? When were they going to get their lives back?

Surviving was enough.

And where was Hasan? The others? The patrol? She wanted them all back, all safe.

She checked the sky again, but night had fallen. The Daijaku could be right on top of them and the Jians wouldn't know until it was too late.

A new fear gripped Yas. She looked around the cave and saw fires still burning, lanterns lit, torches flickering.

'Dean! Sorin!' called Yas. The Weeping Men were with her in an instant. 'The Daijaku will see the light from the fires and they'll know where we are. Get whoever can help and put out all the lights.'

Gods bless them, the Weeping Men didn't hesitate. They had half the men moving a few moments later. They ran down to the camp and were soon stamping out fires and snuffing lanterns, but to Yas they seemed to be moving in slow motion. Every second lasted a minute, every minute an hour. And all the while, the bombs continued to fall.

Slowly, too slowly, darkness fell across the cave. Even with Yas's ears ringing from the bombing, she could hear her own heart pounding away, the ragged breaths of the people around her, the sniffles, the cries. Even the men returning to their families after putting out the fires seemed to make enough noise for three times their number.

Still no Hasan. Still no patrol.

So, Yas sat in the dark, holding her child, with that awful fear in her gut that everything had gone wrong again. And still the bombs fell.

14

Ange

Kiyosun

Ange wanted to kill Garo. That much she knew. Especially if he said just one more word.

'This is a waste of time,' said Garo for the thousandth time, and it took everything Ange had to ignore him. It was bad enough they were picking their way through the ruins of Kiyosun without having to listen to his moaning. Three months had passed since the Egril had bombed her home to almost nothing and it still stabbed her in the heart to see what those bastards had done. Three months since they'd been forced to flee to the mountains. Three months since Dren ... Ange took a breath. Three fucking months. It felt like yesterday. It felt like a lifetime ago.

Sometimes it felt like she'd died with him. Sometimes she wished she'd died with him.

Especially now she was stuck with bloody Garo. The Gods must really hate her.

He kicked a small rock out of his way. 'I mean, haven't we got more important things to do?'

Ange spun on him then, fists clenched, and Garo took a step back when he saw the look on her face. 'This is important.'

Even then, the idiot still didn't catch on. 'I thought the Meigorians were coming. I thought we were supposed to be getting things ready for them.'

'Fuck's sake, Garo. Just because they gave you a chest plate and a sword, it doesn't mean you're a soldier.'

They were both dressed in a mishmash of armour they'd picked up along the way, most of which had come from dead Skulls. They'd painted the white plates a mix of rust and ochre to blend in with the mountains – and to make sure no one actually mistook them for Skulls. Garo had an Egril scimitar hanging from his hip whereas Ange had a shorter Shulka blade that Hasan himself had given her.

'First of all,' she said, 'Hasan has other people getting ready for the Meigorians – his Shulka and some of Yas's Weeping Men. People who know what they're doing. That's why they're guarding the gate up at the top of the bloody mountain and we're not. Second, you know bloody well why *we're* here and it's not because you're just one big, moaning waste of space. We have to look for abandoned weapons. That way, we can make sure everyone's got something to fight with when our friends turn up. And – maybe – find something we can sell for food.' Ange spat the taste of ash out of her mouth. 'I think that's kind of important. Don't you?'

Garo had the decency to glance away, at least. For a moment, he looked every bit the dumb sixteen year old he was. Even his fluff of a beard couldn't hide that. 'I hadn't forgotten. It's just—' He kicked another rock. 'It's just ... there's nothing here. Just rubble and burned-out homes. I don't like being here.'

'Grow up, eh?' Ange set off without waiting for Garo, angry that she all but agreed with him. She didn't like it there, either. Kiyosun had far too many memories for her. Too many reminders of what she'd lost. Too many ghosts following them around. But orders were orders. 'We've got a job to do.'

'How long do we have to be here?' Garo's voice echoed through the ruins.

Ange turned on him again. 'Keep your fucking voice down,' she hissed. 'Bad enough I have to listen to your moaning without it getting me killed as well.'

He had the cheek to laugh. 'Who's going to kill us? You said yourself there are no Skulls left.'

'Godsdamn it, are you really so fucking stupid? Just because they left doesn't mean they won't come back – or that they're not back already.' She jabbed a finger against his chest plate. 'That's why we've come out all dressed up and with steel on our hips. We ain't got rid of the Skulls yet. There's still a war on. Better safe than dead and all that, eh?'

'I'm sorry.' His voice dropped with his shoulders.

Ange took a deep breath. It wasn't Garo's fault he was stupid. It wasn't his fault he wasn't Dren. 'Look, we stay here until we find enough blades to fill our sacks or a few coins or anything else the Weeping Men might think is worth something. It's not hard work, it just needs to be done. So be happy. Unless you want to go and tell Hasan that you think you're too good for what he's asked you to do – or better yet, you can tell Yas.'

Garo took a step back at that and had a quick look around, as if mentioning Yas's name was enough to make her suddenly appear. 'No. No, I don't want to do that.'

'That's probably the first sensible thing I've heard you say today.'

They cut left down Houseman Street, aiming for the far end, where it met Brewer's Lane. The houses on that side were still more or less standing, if you didn't mind the odd missing wall or floor.

Ange knew there'd been a lot of fighting around there. Maybe they'd get lucky and find some usable blades, but even she had to admit they were after short pickings. Crews had been through Kiyosun plenty of times already.

'I gotta tell you, Yas scares the shit out of me,' muttered Garo. Still Ange said nothing. Yas wasn't a topic any sensible person wanted to talk about. If Garo had any brains, he'd realise that. 'Do you think it's true?'

Gods, Ange really hoped he wasn't taking the conversation where she thought he was. 'Whether what's true?'

'You reckon Yas killed all those people they say she killed?'

And there it was. The idiot. Ange shook her head. The lad had a death wish talking about Yas like that. About *that* subject. 'You've seen the tears on her cheek. The Weeping Men don't give those out for being nice to strangers.'

'She's only got two tears. I'm talking about the others. At the Council House.'

Ange moved a rotten piece of timber that was blocking the street. 'What does it matter if it's true? We've all killed people. You have. I have. The Gods know Dren certainly did. That's the world we live in.'

'They say she poisoned her friends on top of all the other Skulls, that she just watched as they died. Three hundred people. Three hundred. That's fucking cold, that is.'

'First off, that's just a rumour that no one – as you well know – should be talking about. Second, if those rumours *are* true, she did it to kill the Skulls so she could rescue Jax and – more importantly – Dren. So that makes her a bloody hero in my book.'

'Yeah, but—'

Ange stuck a hand over his big mouth and hauled him into a doorway. Something had caught her attention.

Something in the air.

She watched the sky, heart racing, praying to the fucking useless Gods above and below that she'd been mistaken, that it was just a bird or—

They both shrank further into the ruins as fast as they bloody could as more of the things filled the sky.

There were only a few at first. If Ange and Garo didn't know better, the shapes could've been mistaken for seagulls. But they did know better. They'd learned the hard way; seen friends die, others snatched, run from the demons themselves. They were no birds.

They were Daijaku.

More and more flew out over the ocean. Ange lost count after thirty. And that was just the start of the bastards. In the end, there had to be hundreds of them. Thousands, maybe. A swarm large enough to almost blot out the sun.

'Not looking for us,' she said, still wanting to crap herself all the same.

'What did you say?' said Garo.

'I said the Daijaku aren't looking for us.'

'How d'you know?'

Ange gritted her teeth. 'They're flying out to sea, not going inland.'

'Thank the Four Gods for that.'

'Yeah, but they're not doing it for the fun of it, are they? They're here for a reason.'

'What reason?'

Ange chewed on her lip. Only one thing made sense. She looked out to sea herself, trying to spot what the Daijaku were searching for. But there was nothing to see – yet.

'Do you think they know?' asked Ange.

'Know about what?'

'The fucking Meigorians, you fucking idiot.' Gods, the urge to hit him was almost too much.

'How could the Skulls know about them? I thought we were keeping it secret.'

'How do I bloody know?' she hissed through clenched teeth.

'I just—'

'Come on, we need to have a better look at what the Skulls are doing.' Ange set off, moving with care. Fire had laid waste to most of the ground floor of the house and it didn't look like it would take too much to bring the rest of it down on top of them. She had to pull a rotten piece of timber out of the way just so she could reach the stairs.

'I think we should head back, tell the others,' said Garo, still following.

'Not till we know what's going on,' replied Ange from the top of the stairs. She entered a bedroom that was missing a wall, giving her a perfect view over the city and out to sea. The ocean glistened in the spring sunshine, looking as beautiful as it ever did. Except the view was ruined by Daijaku flying in formation over the water. Not that there was anything for them to attack. 'I've never seen so many in one place. Not even that night when they bombed the city.'

'Do you think they're here for a reason, then?' said Garo, still not putting two and two together.

Ange didn't take her eyes off the Daijaku. 'They're not here for a fun day out, are they?'

She followed some Daijaku as they flew back to shore, landing over at Omason Beach. It stretched for five miles, from Kiyosun at one end to the Hosing Cliffs at the other. When she was a child, Ange's parents used to bring her there, to swim in the sea on hot days and laugh around open fires with other families well into the night. Happy days long gone. It had been a beautiful place back then.

Now? Now there was movement down there. A shit-load of movement. The Daijaku weren't the only ones who'd turned up. 'I wish I had an eyeglass.'

Garo looked over her shoulder. 'What's going on?'

'I don't know. We need to get closer. Have a proper look.'

'Cl ... Closer?' Garo almost choked on the word. 'No fucking way.'

Ange gave him the eye again. 'I thought you wanted to be doing something important?'

That shut him up.

It took them most of the afternoon to get close enough to see what was happening on Omason Beach. The Daijaku might well be flying in sweeping arcs over the ocean but that didn't mean Ange and Garo could wander around without a care in the world. They crept and they crawled and damn well hid when they had to. Under bushes, sticking to shadows, hugging rocks – they used every trick they knew. Ange lost track of the times she nearly pissed herself with fear when a Daijaku flew too close. Slow going but they made it to the cliffs overlooking the beach somehow still alive.

Now, Ange wished they'd stayed in Kiyosun – or, better still, that they were back up in the caves with everyone else. But no, she was lying on the top of a cliff overlooking Omason Beach, bloody Garo shaking with fear next to her, covered head to foot by an old sand-coloured cloak and not much else. When the Shulka had trained her, the idea of hiding under a bit of cloth sounded like suicide to her until they'd shown her how well it blended with the ground from above. She just hoped today wasn't the day she was proved right after all.

The beach was covered with Skulls as far as the eye could see. And they definitely weren't there for a picnic. They were fortifying positions; digging trenches, installing stakes and spikes all along the shoreline. And they had enough timber to build a city of their own by the looks of it.

'There are so many of them,' whispered Garo in the understatement of the year.

'Whole fucking army by the looks of it,' replied Ange.

'We're dead.'

Ange glared at Garo to keep his bloody mouth shut. Not for the first time, she wished it was Dren next to her. He had the knack of making everyone feel safer just by being there, and if shit went down, there was no one better at dealing with it. Then again, even Dren wouldn't have anything good to say about what was happening below. Of course, being dead and all, he'd not be saying much about anything.

'Come on. Let's get back. We better tell the boss what's happening.'

'Thank the Gods.'

They crawled away, taking their time, brushing the dirt with some leaves to erase any trail they might leave. It was a slow process but, as Dren used to say, careful never got anyone killed. Then he had to go and prove his point by getting sloppy and getting himself dead.

What a stupid idiot.

It made her angry just thinking about Dren. Angry and a hell of a lot more sad. He might have taken out a whole bunch of Skulls when he killed himself, but it was a waste of a life to go out like that. She understood why he'd done it, why he'd gone on that suicide run and blown himself up; dying from orb poisoning was a nasty way to go, but if he'd stayed with her instead, Ange could've had a few more days with him, at least. Instead, she'd barely got a goodbye.

Stupid, selfish idiot. Why did she miss him so much?

When she and Garo were far enough away from the cliff edge to be out of sight from below, they rose to their feet and scampered back towards the caves. It was a tough climb and involved some precarious balancing on paths that barely looked wide enough, just to make things even more difficult.

She paused halfway up the mountainside and licked her dry

lips. There was a good view over the Golden Channel from where she was, the water turning red with the setting sun. A good view of the Daijaku patrolling the waters, too.

In the distance was Meigore. Too far away to see properly. No sign of any ships coming to save the day yet either. She'd seen the Shulka who'd turned up months back with the news about the invasion. She didn't quite believe it at the time, but now, having seen all those Skulls, she reckoned she'd been convinced. Now, the bastards couldn't turn up quick enough for her liking.

They climbed on, keeping their eyes open, watching the skies, still being careful. There was no point dying a mile from home.

That's why they spotted the Daijaku coming towards them. Lots of them. Ange grabbed Garo, dragged him down between some boulders and held her breath.

They were going to die. She knew it. They'd see her and Garo somehow. They'd ...

The Daijaku flew straight past, straight towards the Ascalian Mountains.

'Shit.' She scrambled off after them. She needed to see ... Gods, she hoped she was wrong.

'Ange!' Garo was easy to ignore but the explosion stopped her dead in their tracks. It wasn't somewhere close, but that made the loudness of it even more terrifying.

'What did they bomb now?' said Garo, catching up.

Another explosion boomed. Then another.

Only one thing worth blowing up on Ascalian – the bloody gate that was the key to all their plans. She had to look. Had to be sure. 'We better check it out.'

'Fuck no,' said Garo, grabbing her arm. 'Let's just go back. Let Hasan send someone else.'

She jerked her arm free. 'Shut up.'

They didn't have to go far before they saw the smoke drifting up from near the top of Ascalian. From the temple.

Ange slumped down on a rock, the air gone from her lungs and her hope with it. Everything was fucked.

But if that wasn't bad enough, things got worse pretty damn quick. The Daijaku weren't finished.

The demons still had plenty more orbs to drop.

They swooped this way and that, carpeting the mountain range with their bombs. On and on they went, an endless swarm intent on destroying everything.

All Ange and Garo could do was hunker down and hope a bomb didn't fall straight on them. The very air shook with the force of the explosions. Dirt, rock and rubble fell like rain. Smoke stung their eyes and choked their lungs. It was like the night they'd destroyed Kiyosun but, somehow, a thousand times worse than that hell.

Ange tucked herself into a ball, hands pressed over her ears, elbows tight against her face. She might've screamed. She might've cried. She had no idea in that maelstrom of destruction.

It was a long time after it stopped before she had the courage to open her eyes, amazed that she was still alive. Garo was already sitting up, eyes wide and bright against his blackened skin. 'You hurt?' she called, not that she could hear over the ringing in her ears. 'You hurt?'

The idiot didn't move, didn't look at her, so Ange had to crawl over and give his arm a tug. 'Garo. You hurt?'

He looked then, eyes slowly focusing on her, fucking tears welling in their corners. For once, Ange didn't think bad of him. Instead, she hugged him, grateful that they'd both made it, and ignored his sobs.

When she thought she was up to it, Ange let go of him and got to her feet. The ground felt like it was still moving, but there was nothing she could do about that. 'We need to head back. See if everyone's okay.'

'What?' shouted Garo.

'Fuck. Keep your voice down.' Ange could see the fool was going to shout again so she put a finger to her lips and shushed him. Even if he couldn't hear her, he was smart enough to work out that bit of sign language. She then pointed towards the caves. 'Home.'

Garo nodded.

They were halfway there when they came across Tavis and a couple of his mates, looking as shaken up as Ange.

'Were you out in that?' asked the Shulka.

'Yeah,' said Ange. Not much else needed saying. 'You been back yet?'

'Going now,' said Tavis. 'I hope—'

'Don't,' said Ange, cutting him off. She didn't need anyone putting into words what she truly feared.

Tavis nodded. He understood. They all did.

No one spoke on the way back, all too caught up in their own thoughts about how bad it was. They were only weeks away from this Zorique turning up with their army and it had all gone to shit.

Hasan was with the guards at the entrance to the tunnels. 'Thank the Gods,' he called out. 'We were about to send search parties out for you.'

'We were on our way back from Arlen's Farm when the bombing started,' said Tavis. 'Got caught on the side of the mountain until the demons went home.'

'They've not gone home,' said Ange. 'The whole Skull army's setting up camp at Omason Beach.'

'We'd better get you all inside,' said Hasan. 'Sounds like you have a story that needs telling.'

It was quiet inside the cave. Not surprising after what they'd all gone through. There were only about half the normal number of lit torches, adding to the gloom, but fires were springing up near people's homes as they began to go back to their usual routines.

'Yas was worried the Daijaku would see the firelight from above,' said Hasan, 'so she had everything put out.'

'A good call,' said Ange.

'Come on, let's go see her and you can tell us everything.' Hasan led them to the corner of the cave he shared with Yas. Someone had already got a fire going and a pot dangled over it.

'Took your time, didn't you?' said Yas when she saw them approach. 'I was worried sick.'

'Things were bad out there,' said Tavis. 'Real bad.'

'Well, they weren't a barrel of laughs in here, either,' said Yas. 'Anyway, sit down, warm up. Timy's got some tea brewing.'

Once they were all settled around the fire, Ange realised how exhausted she was. She certainly had to admit she felt a lot happier now she was back inside the cave. Back in the shadows with rock all around them. Safe now she was home.

Home. Odd to think of a cave in that way, but it was what it was.

'So, what's what?' asked Yas.

'That attack isn't going to be a one-off,' said Ange. 'The whole Skull army's turned up at Omason Beach. Thousands of Skulls – with more Daijaku than I've ever seen in one place. And they're not leaving anytime soon.'

Hasan exchanged looks with Yas. 'Why's that?'

'They're digging trenches, and they're covering the beach with spikes and only the Gods know what else,' said Garo.

Ange nodded. 'Yeah, and they've got timber and stone with them. They're building all sorts down there. They're expecting visitors. A lot of them.'

'The Meigorians,' said Yas.

Ange shrugged. 'There's no one else.'

Yas shook her head. 'So much for keeping it bloody secret. You think someone's talked?'

Hasan looked around the cave. 'No one here.'

'You sure?' asked Yas.

'As sure as I can be.' Hasan had another look around. 'So not very sure at all.'

'What about Wenna? They could've caught her,' said Tavis.

'Last we heard she was safe,' said Hasan. 'We've been getting messages from both her and Kos over the last couple of months. If the Skulls had got one of them, the other would say.'

'Then why are the Skulls here?' asked Yas. 'I don't like it.'

'The Skulls aren't stupid,' said Hasan. 'We learned that the hard way. The beaches around here are the best place to get a large number of people ashore quickly. Maybe the Skulls have worked that out for themselves. Maybe this is just them guessing lucky – or maybe they're building barricades up and down the whole coast?'

'They'll be well dug in by the time the Meigorians arrive,' said Ange. 'It'll make landing bloody difficult.'

'Then it's up to us to make sure they don't get too settled,' said Hasan. 'What about the temple?'

Ange shook her head. 'It's rubble.'

'Shit,' said Yas. 'Shit. Shit. Shit.'

'How many people did we have up there guarding it?' asked Hasan.

'A dozen,' said Tavis.

Hasan glanced over at Ange, but she shook her head.

'That's the whole plan out the bloody window,' said Yas.

'What are we going to do now? Send word to the Meigorians?' asked Tavis.

'We do that and they might decide not to come,' said Yas. 'I say we keep this bit of news to ourselves.'

'We need to warn them that the whole Skull army is waiting for them,' said Hasan.

'I think it's better for us if they find that out for themselves,' said Yas.

Ange stared at Yas for a moment. Garo had been right. She was one cold bitch. She closed her eyes and tried not to think about how fucked they were.

Part II

Homecoming

15

Tinnstra

The Golden Channel

Tinnstra stood on the prow of the Meigorian transport ship, wondering how everything had fallen apart so quickly.

Overhead, Zorique flew amongst the Daijaku, burning bright, smiting them from the sky as quickly as she could. But there were still hundreds of them – thousands of them – attacking the Meigorian armada, and only the one of her.

After three months of planning and building a fleet and recruiting and outfitting an army, they'd left Layso with one hundred and twenty ships, carrying forty thousand men and women, full of hope and belief, but now? All along their line, ships burned while others had already sunk. Only the Gods knew how many they'd already lost and how many more they'd lose before they reached Jia's shore.

If we reach shore. Tinnstra wasn't feeling too confident about that right then.

Lightning crackled from behind Tinnstra as Aasgod lent his might to the fight. She was glad now he'd returned from the past. His blast tore through a clutch of Daijaku, detonating their bombs high above the fleet where they could do no harm. He moved on, fuelled by precious Chikara water, sending up bolt after bolt of magic, killing more and more of the demons, but it was like pissing on a fire. The allies might've planned well, but had Raaku outthought them? If someone told Tinnstra that the

Emperor had sent every Daijaku he possessed against the armada, she'd have believed it right then.

Archers shot wave after wave of arrows into the sky along with the mage's lightning. But still the winged monsters came, sweeping through the ships with their Niganntan spears, dropping bombs, leaving corpses and shattered ships in their wake.

Drums beat in a frenzy, driving the fleet's oarsmen on – as if the threat of death wasn't enough. They were all eager to reach the Jian shore. Better to die fighting on the sand than to drown in the sea. Tinnstra had put herself through too much for that to be her end. She glanced over at Ralasis, his face set with grim determination. Gods, so much rested on all their shoulders.

This was Sekanowari, after all. The Last War. And if her mad plan was to work, she had to live long enough to see it through.

Zorique twisted and turned high above the fleet, throwing fireballs at the winged demons, battering more away with her shield. She was Godlike up there, shining bright amidst the smoke. The Daijaku flew at her, like moths to a flame. They screamed in hate and screamed in death. They threw their bombs and charged with their spears. All it would take was for one to get lucky, for Zorique's attention to wander or her strength to wane, and then where would they be? So much hope was riding on her daughter's abilities.

Tinnstra tightened her grip on her spear, eager for the beach. Everyone around her was fighting and dying and she needed to do more than just watch.

The drums beat on. The oars bit and clawed at the waves, adding their might to the wind filling the sails. At least that was with them. The fleet was east of Kiyosun, heading for the beaches of Omason where a five-mile-long stretch of sand awaited the Meigorian ships. Every boat had been adapted to Ralasis' flat-bottomed design so the troops could disembark onto solid ground 'easily'. Tinnstra scoffed. Well, there was nothing easy about their approach. She knew the Egril would have a say in how they reached land. She knew every boat that reached the Jian shore would pay a heavy blood price, and by the Four Gods she was right. But would it be too much?

'Prepare yourselves,' screamed Ralasis over the chaos. 'When we hit the beach, move quickly. Anything gets in your way, kill it.'

Tinnstra wasn't going to argue with that advice.

Men and women rushed to form lines on either side of Tinnstra, down the length of the ship. White cranes on their black tabards in honour of their murdered king. Helmets strapped on tight. Shields on arms. Spears at the ready. She could hear their breathing, fast and ragged, feet shuffling on the wooden deck. Two men with axes waited at the ship's prow, ready to hack away the ropes that held the front ramp in place. They would set to work the moment the boat hit the shingle, creating a platform for everyone to run down.

Someone vomited but no one cursed whoever it was, nor mocked them. Any one of them might have done the same. They all felt the fear.

All except Tinnstra. She'd given that up long ago. Now there was only a storm where once there'd been ice. Now there was only fury.

She watched the beach draw closer, watched the Skulls line up, ready to meet the allies. So many to fight. So many to kill. She smiled. That was something she could do well. That was why she was there. She just had to get ashore first.

A spike of pain stabbed at her brain, making her catch her breath. Magic. There was magic waiting for them among the Egril – and that could only mean one thing: Chosen.

Arrows flew overhead. The drums drove the oars on. Lightning crackled across the sky. Explosions rocked the ship. Daijaku screamed and howled. Tinnstra ignored it all.

The Skulls had dug in well, filled the first thirty yards of beach with spikes, behind which row after row of Skulls waited to greet them. And Chosen, too. Always Chosen.

Tinnstra's hands went to the pouch on her belt and found a vial of Chikara water without even thinking about it. She only had five on her but the rest were in her bag in the hold. That didn't seem the cleverest place to store it now the bombs were falling, but if the ship was destroyed it was more than likely she'd be blown up with it.

Tinnstra hadn't drunk any in months, saving it for the invasion, but now there was no need to ration herself. Now, she needed all the strength she could muster. She uncorked the vial and downed the contents, welcoming the rush as the water raced through her already powerful body.

Gods, it was almost too much. Her breath caught in her throat as her heart punched against her chest. Tinnstra forced herself to breathe, to allow the Chikara water to do its job. She didn't need to fight it or hold anything back.

Her power exploded to life and it was as if she could suddenly see the world as it truly was. Light swirled all around her as Zorique and Aasgod threw their magic at the Daijaku. She could even see red light pulsing through the demons as they swooped amongst the ships.

Tinnstra turned her attention on the beach, looking for the Chosen. If she could spot their magical auras, she could determine how many of the bastards were waiting for them – and where. They had to be her first targets when she made it ashore.

A bomb exploded off their starboard bow, showering them all with water as the ship rocked from side to side, to remind Tinnstra she might not get that far.

'Try and kill the Daijaku before they have another chance to sink us, please,' shouted Ralasis. 'And let's pick up the pace. I want to be on that beach today.'

The drums quickened their beat and Aasgod fired more lightning in reply. It crackled and spat through the demons, burning them from the skies. Arrows flew from the ships. Everyone did all they could, but it wasn't enough.

Zorique shot through the Daijaku ranks once more, her sword flashing bright and furious, drawing the demons to her and away from the ships. If the allied forces still had hope, it was because of her. Then fire flew up from the rear of the Egril lines. Four distinct blasts. Chosen magic. All aimed at Zorique. Every single one hit their target.

They knocked Zorique cartwheeling across the sky and Tinnstra's heart missed a beat. Had they ... ? An explosion filled the sky with smoke. She couldn't see anything. Fire rained down on Tinnstra, on the boat. A Meigorian collapsed with an arrow in his chest. Another took one in his eye.

'Get ready,' shouted Ralasis. 'We're nearly there.'

Tinnstra forced her attention back to what she had to do, marking the positions of the Chosen in her mind as she decided who she'd kill first.

Ten yards to go.

Now arrows flew towards them from the Skulls in a wave so great, it all but blocked out the sun. Tinnstra dropped behind her shield a second before a dozen struck its surface. Men and women less quick screamed around her. More bodies fell to the deck.

And yet more arrows fell towards them.

'Get ready,' shouted Ralasis once more.

Arrows littered the deck of the ship, beating a tattoo as they rained down. More screams filled the air and not just from Tinnstra's ship. By the Gods, she wasn't sure how much more they could all take.

Then the ship shuddered as it finally hit the shingle.

The men with axes swung powerfully. Two thunks later, the ramp fell away and Tinnstra could see the beach. 'Let's go,' she screamed. A slash of her spear broke the arrows off her shield and she was up and running.

'Move! Move! Move!' shouted someone behind her. It might have been Ralasis but Tinnstra wasn't turning around to look. She jumped into the water. It was deeper than she expected, filling her boots a heartbeat later, cold and biting, but she ignored it as she waded forwards, trying to keep her shield up, desperate to reach the beach.

Other ships, many on fire, made it to the shingle as well, spilling their troops out into the sea and sand. Smoke billowed angrily as explosions pounded them from one end of Omason Beach to the other.

An arrow hit Tinnstra's breastplate as she stumbled ashore. More hit her shield. She shouted and screamed, noise to drown out the chaos, and charged forwards as Skulls ran down the slope to meet the allies. One got her spear in his chest, knocking the bastard off his feet, but there were plenty after him, all more than happy to try and kill her.

Tinnstra drew her sword. Time to send Kage more Egril souls.

16

Ange

The Ascalian Mountains

'I'm not fucking touching those,' said Ange.

'Fuck's sake,' said Garo, holding out the orbs in his gloved hands. 'Take them.'

'*You* take them,' Ange spat back. Orbs petrified her – they'd killed Dren, they weren't going to kill her. 'I've got enough weapons.'

'I don't bloody want them. Go on – take them.'

'No.'

They stared at each other for a few heartbeats more before Garo gave up and put the orbs back in the sack at his feet. 'If I end up dead—'

'I'll have done the world a favour.' By the Gods, she hated him sometimes. He knew how Dren had died – why he'd died – and he still made a comment like that? Fuck him.

All around them, anyone fit and strong enough was strapping on armour and blades. The Meigorian fleet had been spotted and the Hanran were going down to do what they could to make sure their allies made it ashore. Chances were it would be a lot of people's funerals.

It had been a rough few weeks since the Skulls turned up at Omason Beach. The Daijaku had spent most nights bombing the shit out of the mountainside and the Skulls had come hunting during the day. Any plans they'd made to hurt the bastards on the beach had gone straight down the shitter. All their effort went into keeping the Skulls out of their home, rather than scaring them away from Omason.

Things had got so bad that Yas had sent some of the weak and the infirm out and away from the caves, happier to get them somewhere safer. She used the Weeping Men's smuggling network to do it, too. Someone had suggested Yas go with the children as well, but she'd refused without hesitation.

'My place is here, with you all,' she said, and Ange had to admit she'd been impressed by the woman's resolve. Yas was no Shulka, but she had the balls of one for sure.

And now there was nothing left to do but fight.

Ange checked her own armour. Most of it had been stolen off dead Skulls, but she didn't care where it had come from as long as it stopped her getting killed. Even so, she'd painted *Skull Killer* across her chest plate just in case some idiot mistook her for an actual Egril. That thought made her glance over at Garo. Killing her by mistake would be something he'd do all right.

'You okay?' asked Tavis. He was dressed up in all his Shulka gear. A black plume running over his helmet like a bird's crest apparently told people his clan, back when that kind of shit was important. There were red, blue and green plumes amongst the other Shulka, but Ange hadn't bothered learning what they all meant. She only cared that they knew how to use their spears and swords, and she'd not met a Shulka yet who wasn't a bloody good killer.

'I'm fine. I just don't want to touch those bloody orbs.'

'I don't blame you.' He smiled, white teeth showing through his grey beard. 'Unnatural things. I'm always convinced I'll blow my own hand off when I use them. At least I know where I am with a sword.'

'I can't even say that much.'

'Ah, you'll be fine. Everyone knows you can look after yourself. Besides, it's not going to be about skill down there. There's too many Skulls for that. It'll be about who wants to live more – you or the person you're fighting. And they can't match your heart.'

Ange allowed herself a smile. 'I bet you're telling everyone that bullshit.'

Tavis raised an eyebrow. 'Only the good ones.'

'Don't worry about me. I won't let you down.'

'I know you won't.'

From somewhere in the distance came the cracking of explosions. Everyone stopped to listen, all looking up as their imaginations told them what was happening. They all knew how many Daijaku were ready to meet the Meigorian fleet, how many soldiers waited on the beach. It was bad odds all around.

In the end, it was Hasan who broke the silence by clapping his hands to get their attention. Yas stood on his left. 'All right, everyone. No surprise the battle's started. We all knew the Skulls wouldn't let our friends turn up without a say in the matter. That's why we're here, all dressed up. Now it's our turn to get involved.'

Hasan got nods and murmurs back.

'Our job is simple: go straight down the mountain, hit the Skulls where they're not expecting it and do as much damage as we can so that the Meigorians have a chance to land. We have bombs, arrows and spears, so let's use those first before anyone thinks about getting clever with their sword.'

'Yes, Chief,' said Tavis, slapping his sword against his shield.

Other joined in, but Hasan held up a hand for silence. 'This is the day we've been waiting for. This is the hour. This is the moment. Today, we take back Jia. We take back our homes. We take back our lives.'

This time the applause was thunderous as swords pounded shields and spears stomped the ground. 'We are the dead,' someone cried. 'We are the dead.' Ange had always hated that stupid Shulka prayer, but even she found herself shouting it. It rang off the walls and shook her bones.

Hasan let it go on and on before holding up his hand once more. The shouting and the banging stopped, but Ange's blood still roared in her ears. 'May the Four Gods look after us all. Now, let's go and kill the bastards. For Kiyosun. For Jia. For all our friends and loved ones who aren't here to fight anymore! For us!'

Tavis led the Hanran out, Ange with them, down the narrow

passage from the caves to the mountain trail. She saw a few nervous faces around her as explosions rang out with alarming frequency somewhere over the water but they kept moving somehow. Suddenly her makeshift armour and second-hand sword didn't seem like much for a proper war. She'd been taught by Dren to stab people in the back, not go toe-to-toe with them like a real soldier.

Fuck, she wished he was beside her now. He'd have made her feel better. Braver. Instead, she had Garo. Ange glanced over at him, all bug-eyed and panting like he was about to piss himself. At least he wasn't running his mouth off like he normally was. Still, he was a shit replacement.

She glanced down at the bag of orbs on his hip. They were still too close to her for her liking. Could she get sick from them? She moved a couple of steps to her left just in case, then almost walked straight into the back of the person in front of her.

'Oi, get mov—' Ange shut her mouth. The end of the passage was up ahead, and no one looked keen to go out onto the mountainside. It was understandable the way the very air shook from the power of the explosions. 'Keep going,' she shouted, even though she wasn't keen to do so herself.

'Maybe it's the Daijaku,' Garo shouted back.

For once, Ange didn't argue with him. So many bombs were falling now that the explosions were blending into a single constant roar. 'I'm going to look,' she said, needing to do something before her own nerve went.

'Stay in line,' hissed Garo, but she was already off, squeezing her way down the side of the Hanran.

The sound of war grew louder as she neared the end of the passage. She could make out Tavis's helmet ahead. Even the ground felt like it was shaking with the fury of it all, but that had to be her imagination. Nothing could shake a mountain.

Then she reached Tavis and she had a perfect view of what had stopped the Hanran cold.

'By the fucking Gods,' she said.

The world was on fire. Or rather, the Meigorian fleet was. It stretched from east to west. There had to be more than a hundred ships, but she doubted there was a single one not burning. Daijaku swarmed above the fleet like a cloud of death, dropping bombs and slashing with their Niganntan spears. But there was something – someone? – amongst them, shining like the sun, setting the demons on fire. What was it? *Who* was it?

Tavis looked over his shoulder at her. 'Quite the sight, eh?'

'I ... I ...' Ange didn't know what to say – she only knew she was bloody petrified. 'How ... how do we fight in that?'

'Same way we normally do – with plenty of heart and sharp bloody weapons.' Tavis turned to the Shulka next to him, a woman wearing a bronze helmet with a blue plume. 'Enough gawping. Time to move. Get down the bloody mountain quick as you can. That fleet is heading to shore. It still needs our help and I sure didn't get dressed up to stand here playing spectator.'

The Shulka did as she was ordered, and people began moving with her. Each and every person stopped, like Ange had, when they saw the madness over the ocean, but somehow they pushed on.

'I didn't think you'd wait for me,' said Garo when he reached her. He actually looked relieved.

'Of course I waited,' replied Ange. Not intentionally, but he didn't need to know that. 'Someone's got to look out for you.' She fell in step beside him but maintained her distance. He still had those bombs. Although even worrying about those felt stupid now. Chances were they would all be dead in a few short hours.

'Who's that?' Garo was staring skywards.

Ange followed his gaze. The shining light fighting the Daijaku had drawn closer. Close enough to see it was woman in armour – but no one human could do what she was doing. 'She must be a God.'

'I hope so.' Garo sounded lost, yet there was something else in his voice. She looked at him again, saw his eyes weren't full of fear now. Even he'd found some bloody hope.

'Come on,' said Ange. 'Let's kill some Skulls.'

It was the last thing she wanted to do but, by the Gods, it was what Dren would've done. And maybe, just maybe, they actually had a chance to win.

17

The Invasion

Omason Beach

There wasn't much left of Tinnstra's shield, just a few stubborn bits of wood stuck to the strap on her arm. Enough to ram into the face of a Skull, shattering his mask and most of his jaw. Enough to make sure he wouldn't get up again.

She flung the remaining splinters of the shield to the ground and drew her axe. She stabbed another Skull in the gut at the same time, then blocked a descending scimitar with the axe's shaft. A twist removed the weapon from the Egril's hand, then, as he stared at his empty hands, Tinnstra buried the axe between his eyes.

Lightning crackled from behind her, taking out another half-dozen foes. It was Aasgod. The mage had trained hard while they waited for the Meigorian fleet to be ready. He was still nothing like the older man she'd first met back in Aisair, but at least he wasn't the weak intellectual she'd met in the past. He might even be of some use after all.

Zorique was caught up in a maelstrom in the skies. The Egril seemed to have an endless supply of Daijaku, and in any brief respite she found, the Chosen bombarded her with their baton blasts, smashing her this way and that. Fear unlike anything Tinnstra had ever known gripped her as she watched her daughter fight, because it looked like she was going to get killed any second.

But Tinnstra couldn't do anything to help Zorique. It was bad enough down on the ground. The Skulls were swarming over the allied forces and it was taking everything Tinnstra had not to be swept away.

Tinnstra hacked and chopped, sliced and slashed, cut and thrust at anything in Skull armour. Riding the rush from the vial she'd drunk and full of rage and hatred, she killed and killed and killed. No armour could withstand her Chikara-water-enhanced strength. No shield could stay her blows. She was death incarnate, and she sent soul after soul back to bloody Kage.

She twisted as a scimitar came perilously close to her face and paid the bastard back by taking off his knee. A spear skidded across her breastplate so Tinnstra rammed her elbow down, snapping the shaft in two. She stabbed the Skull in the neck, driving her sword all the way through to the hilt. The soldier fell, threatening to take her sword with him, but she freed it with a yank and drove her axe into the balls of the next Egril to get in her way. Blood splattered her face, but she had no idea whose it was and didn't care. All that mattered was it wasn't hers. She pushed on, aiming for the Chosen on the escarpment, killing anyone in her path.

The allies drove a wedge into the enemy ranks as they gained another yard. Two more. With each life claimed, with each yard stolen, Tinnstra could tell they were winning.

Then something caught her eye. A Daijaku broke from the swarm above, a glowing orb in its hand, and headed straight for her.

She dropped the sword and switched the axe to her right hand – her throwing arm. They locked eyes with each other, and the Daijaku's wings flattened against its sides as it shot down, that damned orb burning ever brighter.

Tinnstra threw the axe.

Everything slowed as her axe flew at the Daijaku and the Daijaku flew at her.

The axe struck home, straight between the demon's eyes. Knocked off course, it spun to the right, away from Tinnstra but into a pack of Meigorian soldiers.

And the orb exploded.

The blast hit Tinnstra and everyone around her, Skull and

Meigorian alike, washing her with fire and sending her flying. She smashed into the ground, and for a petrifying moment she found herself in silent darkness. There was no war, no people, no ground, no air.

Nothing.

Fear surged through her. Then air hit her lungs and the world came flooding back into focus. She lay face down in the sand, covered in blood and gore. It was a miracle she was still alive. There was a crater, some ten feet deep, where her troops had been, littered with corpses.

The blast had shocked the allied forces and she could see their momentum faltering. Then Ralasis stepped out of their ranks, screaming blue bloody murder, and charged towards the Skulls. There was a slight hesitation, then his troops followed, all bellowing their war cries.

Tinnstra pulled herself upright, snatched up a sword and, her head still ringing, staggered after him.

Ralasis didn't know what he was doing. Somehow, he was leading a charge towards the Egril forces. Not his preferred option, but he'd had no choice. A Daijaku bomb had taken out only the Gods knew how many, just as he thought the allies were starting to turn the fight in their favour. Suddenly his troops looked like they'd break any second. Battles were lost or won in such moments, and in moments like that, troops needed leaders. It was Ralasis' bastard luck that there weren't any others nearby. So he'd screamed his best curses and charged, praying it wasn't going to get him killed. A stupid, mad thing to do, but Ralasis was anything but clever.

The Skulls were thirty yards away and closing on him, screaming curses of their own, getting their own swords good and ready to gut him. A sensible man would have retreated. A clever man would have run away and lived to fight another day. But no, not Ralasis.

He swung as the first Skull reached him, his momentum carrying him past and into the second man without the faintest idea if he'd scored a hit. They collided with a smack of armour against armour and both men went down. Somehow, Ralasis landed on top, so he smashed his sword hilt into the Skull mask, screaming and spitting again and again before he was knocked sideways, and this time he was on the bottom and about to get fucked.

He wrapped an arm around the bastard's neck, trying to pull the Skull off him. There was no room to use his sword, so he dropped it and snatched up the knife from his belt, jerking his head out of the way of the Egril's scimitar, and stabbed up. He hit armour, felt the blade skid, stabbed again, felt the blade slide again, then it was in and warm blood spilled over his hand as he thrust, pushing the blade up as hard as he could. A fist or a boot caught him across the face, cracking his nose, making him spit blood, but the Skull on him fell away and he was on his knees, quick as possible, and blocking a sword thrust with his knife. Ralasis grabbed the Skull's wrist, pulled him down to one side and buried the knife in the man's neck.

Ralasis got his hand around his sword's hilt, pushed himself up to his feet somehow, chest heaving, and tried to shout something, anything, but he had no air spare for words. He doubted anyone would've heard him anyway. On every side individual battles raged between his troops and the Skulls and no one had time to pay him any heed.

Good. He glanced around and stabbed the first Skull he saw in the back. Sliced another's hamstrings, then stamped on the man's face when he went down. Fuck fighting fair. War was about winning any Godsdamned way they could.

Aasgod was nearby, shooting energy blasts out of his fingertips, but he should've been shooting it out of his arse because a Skull was about to gut him from behind. Ralasis screamed as he threw himself on the Egril, dragging him down onto the blood-soaked sand as he rammed his sword through the man's side. Before Ralasis could get free, another body fell on him, then another, then another. The weight multiplied until he couldn't see, couldn't breathe, and he realised he wasn't going to die from a sword thrust but from being squashed like an insect.

What the *fuck* was he doing fighting in a war?

★

Ange crouched amongst the rocks, trying to steady her nerves. There were twenty Hanran with her, including Tavis and Garo, some one hundred and fifty yards behind the Skull lines. She couldn't see how the battle was going, but it sounded worse than ever.

The God was still up and flying, but the Daijaku were after her like flies on shit and four Chosen weren't making it any easier for her, either. By the Gods, she hated those black-masked bastards.

Tavis must've thought the same because he pointed to her and Garo, then pointed to one of the Chosen, a woman. She was halfway down Omason Beach. Ange nodded, feeling sick, not wanting to go, but she had her orders. Garo was white-faced, but he gave a nod, too. After that, there was nothing else to do but get going.

They moved carefully through the rocks, watching where they stepped, making sure they did nothing to catch the eye of anyone who might look their way by chance. Most likely no one would, as the Skulls were caught up in the battle, but all it would take was a bit of bad luck and Ange was no stranger to that. Of course, trying to be sneaky when you're dressed up in a load of ill-fitting stolen armour didn't help. At least Garo had the good sense to keep his mouth shut for once.

It took a few minutes to position themselves a stone's throw away from the Chosen. Far too many minutes for Ange's liking. Her heart was hammering away, sweat dripping off her face, like this was her first time on a mission. Fuck knows what Dren would've said if he could've seen her. Probably would have told her to pull her shit together, but that was easier said than done.

When they were more than close enough for her liking, she signalled Garo to stop. He was sweating more than she was and, by the Gods, his hands were shaking so much he could barely open the sack. He withdrew an orb and promptly dropped it.

Ange jumped back. 'For fuck's sake,' she hissed. 'What are you doing?'

'You do it,' asked Garo, not even attempting to pick the orb up.

It looked so small lying there. Hard to believe it contained so much death. Hard, but not impossible. She took another step back, aware that she was the one shaking now. 'No.'

'Shit.' Garo gave her a sullen look, then pulled a glove off. His knife shook in his hand so much that Ange thought it was more likely to cut his thumb off than nick it, but nick it he did, enough to release a drop of blood and squeeze it onto the orb. The moment the blood hit it, the orb reacted. The liquid or whatever was inside it began to swirl and glow.

But Garo still didn't pick it up.

'Go on – throw it,' said Ange, not hiding her panic as the liquid grew brighter and swirled faster.

'I can't do it,' said Garo. By the Gods, there were tears in his bloody eyes.

'Garo!'

'I can't.'

'Shit.' How much time did they have? Ange grabbed the orb and ran out into the open. The bomb burned in her hand as she drew back her arm.

The Chosen turned, shouted, raised her baton, but Ange had already thrown the orb, only too keen to get rid of the fucking thing before it blew her up. She hit the ground, swallowing a load of sand and dust, just about covering her ears before it went off.

Tinnstra ducked under a Skull's scimitar, came up within his swing and rammed her sword in through the man's armpit. Felt the blood pour over her hand before she pushed the corpse away. *Another soul for Kage. I'll be his favourite before this day is done.*

'Tinnstra!' Aasgod ran towards her. He was still throwing lightning around but it spluttered and sparked where once it had roared. 'Give me a vial.'

Why doesn't the idiot have his own? The last thing Tinnstra wanted to do was share her supply. Still, she reached into the pouch on her hip and pulled a vial of her precious Chikara water out as Aasgod reached her. 'Here.' Tinnstra flipped the vial to the mage. 'You owe me.'

Aasgod caught it, uncorked the vial and drank its contents

almost in one motion. A Skull lunged at him, but Tinnstra rammed her sword into the man's gut, shattering his armour and her blade with the force of the blow. He went down and she stomped on his face to make sure he never got up again. She replaced her broken sword with the dead man's and looked around the battlefield at the mountains of corpses. The fighting raged on even so. There were many more lives still to be lost.

'Are we winning?'

'I don't know. I honestly don't know.' Aasgod wiped his brow and gulped air. 'This is my first war.'

More baton blasts crackled across the sky, chasing Zorique, reminding Tinnstra of what she had to do. 'We need to get to the Chosen – before they hurt Zorique.'

Aasgod sucked in more air. 'Agreed.'

They set off, Tinnstra in the lead, heading for the rear of the Egril lines, towards the escarpment that led to the newly built walls. She just hoped there weren't more legions of Skulls waiting for them on the other side. They'd need the Gods' help if there were.

They charged up the beach, smiting their foes with sharp steel and magic lightning. Tinnstra concentrated on her hatred for the Skulls. For each soul she sent back to Kage, she remembered the lives he'd stolen from her; her father, her mother, her brothers Beris, Jonas and Somon. Greener, Monon, Anama, Maiza – the list went on and on. She remembered the innocent dangling from nooses, the bodies left to rot in their homes, the poor who just disappeared.

This was the day they would be avenged. It was the moment to free all of Jia from Egril rule. The day would be theirs – she'd damn well make sure of it.

Hands hauled Ralasis from the press of bodies. A boot clipped him above the eye, then caught him in the mouth on the way out, but he didn't care as he blinked away the daylight and breathed air once more.

'You all right, Commander?'

Ralasis couldn't see who it was. Just a shadow against the sun, but he owed the man a drink. Owed him his life.

'Help me up.' The words came out slurred through swollen lips and dry mouth. His hands were covered in blood and sand as he was hauled to his feet. The world swirled around him, deafening him with the roar of battle. He couldn't tell which way was which, who was winning, who was living, who was dying. Fuck, he had no weapon. 'I need a s—'

Blood splattered his face. His saviour was gone. Dead. Ralasis had no idea what or who had killed him. He didn't even know which corpse at his feet had saved him.

A Skull charged at him, screaming his lungs out, scimitar up and ready to cleave Ralasis' head from his shoulders. Well, Ralasis wasn't having that. He grabbed a sword from the ground, came up with it and blocked the scimitar. His arm shook with the force of the Skull's blow, but his legs didn't give way and he punched the Egril in the mouth. A feeble jab, as tired as he was, but it bought him time to slash with his new sword, hoping for a lucky strike. The Skull wasn't having that, either, and did some blocking of his own. They grabbed each other's wrists, trying to force the other off their feet, trying to kill the other, trying to stay alive, dancing in the sand and blood. Their heads touched, both shouting gibberish, and Ralasis knew it could go either way. Life. Death. And Ralasis' only thought was that he didn't want to die.

He kicked the man in the balls as hard as he could. Unconventional but, by the Gods, it worked. The tension went out of the man's grip as the Egril's legs buckled. It was all Ralasis needed to stick his sword in the man's eye.

The Skull dropped and Ralasis heaved in air, grateful to still be standing. Then the next Skull came at him.

Stone, sand and rock showered down on Ange. By the Gods, she'd been too close to the explosion for her liking, could still feel its heat – its evil – on her skin, hear the echo of its violence in her ears. Would it make her sick like Dren? Was hers to be a slow death, too?

She opened her eyes, saw destruction where the Chosen had been – at least she'd done that right – but in her place were a shit-load of Skulls coming for some revenge.

'Get up!' Garo had a hand under her arm, lifting her, his sword in the other, trying to prove he wasn't useless. 'We have to get back to the others.'

But they didn't need to go anywhere, because Tavis was on his way with all the Kiyosun Hanran, all screaming blue murder, eager for some revenge of their own.

Ange had her sword out as they passed and flinched a second later as the two armies smashed into each other. Then there was nothing else to do but get stuck in herself. At least there was no magic to kill her now. Only sharp blades.

A quick death, if it happened. She could handle that. Not that she wanted to.

She fought like Dren taught her. Fast and furious. Quick and deadly. Stabbing and screaming. It was madness. Hard to focus on anything but what was in front of her. No time to think. No time to worry. Kill or be killed. A spear skidded off her chest plate. She slashed at a Skull, cut nothing but air. Someone knocked her and she went with it, turning, using the momentum to thrust into a Skull. Maybe it was the one she'd missed. Maybe it wasn't. Didn't matter. On to the next. Mouth dry. Sweat in her eyes. Burning in her arm. Everyone screaming. The living. The dying. The Hanran. The Skulls.

Then the woman – the God – flew overhead. Low enough to touch. Burning bright like the sun. Burning Skulls in her wake.

Ange froze as she watched the God disappear down the far end of Omason Beach, then turn around and come back. She had a spear – or at least that's what Ange thought it was – and it was on fire, too, cutting a swath through anyone in its path. A Chosen fired a baton blast at her, but it hit a bubble of air that surrounded the God and that was that. All the Chosen had done was get the God's attention. She flew straight at the blasts and Ange would have laughed if she wasn't so bloody petrified.

Then she was gone, and the battle certainly wasn't, and Ange couldn't worry about Gods anymore. She had to keep her head on her neck. A scimitar came at her, a screaming Skull behind it.

★

There were still Chosen left. Tinnstra knew that much. The pain in her head roared from their power with such force she dreaded how many waited for her.

She pushed on even so, up the escarpment, ignoring the pain, earning every inch with her enemies' blood. For all their numbers, all their magic, the Egril were the ones retreating.

Above, Zorique was more than a match for the Daijaku – and for any other monster they threw at her. Only a few remained to bother her and already Zorique was turning her attention to the Skulls on the beach. She'd taken out at least one Chosen, if not two, but the strongest ones remained.

Thankfully, Aasgod was with Tinnstra still, clearing a path with his magic, leaving charred corpses at their feet. For a brief moment, Tinnstra remembered Anama's warnings about bringing someone from the past to fight in the future. But damn the consequences. Aasgod's might made any risk worthwhile.

Ralasis was to her right, a mad grin on his face, leading the Meigorians. By the Gods, the man knew how to fight, and his troops loved him. He was a man much like Tinnstra's father. A man to win wars.

More Skulls came at Tinnstra as she reached the top of the escarpment, but even as she cut them down, she realised that they weren't attacking her but retreating from something else. She smiled when she saw the Shulka helms and armour. The Hanran had come to help.

More Meigorian troops came up behind her, joining the fray, and Tinnstra knew the day was theirs. The beach was all but won.

Then a burst of magic punched a hole through that thought. The Chosen. They still needed killing before victory was declared.

'Aasgod, follow me!' Tinnstra cut her way east, fixed on her enemy, the pain in her head growing. The Chosen were together, or as good as. Perfect. It would make her job easier.

Another pulse of magic and more bodies fell. Tinnstra fixed her feet and lowered her head against it as it roared past. When she looked up, she saw them, surrounded by dead bodies. The Chosen, batons in hand. Only two of them, both men, but emanating incredible power. It hurt Tinnstra even to look at them, but she let her hate fuel her fury and charged.

Aasgod shot lightning as she ran. It crackled past her, but one of the Chosen waved a hand and a shield formed in front of them. The lightning skittered over its surface, but neither man was touched.

Another wave, the shield fell and both men raised their batons. They fired.

'Get down!' screamed Tinnstra. Time slowed as she threw herself to the ground. The baton blast arced towards her, angry and red. Tinnstra ducked her head but she was too late, too slow. Pain seared across her face.

Ange spun around, looking for her next opponent, finding none. She blinked, throat raw, and wiped sweat and blood and only the Gods knew what from her face. Garo was still standing but his left arm hung limp at his side, a bloody gash along its length. Tavis was nearby, ramming his sword into the face of a Skull already on the ground. Others, too, thank the Gods. Alive and wondering what to do next.

'Vanless! Vanless!' shouted a Meigorian soldier, his eyes bugging out of his face. Ange had no idea what it meant, but she grinned back. People all around her were hugging and shouting, amazed they were alive – amazed they'd won.

Then explosions boomed from the far end of the beach and the cheering stopped.

'We've not won yet,' roared Tavis. 'Come on.'

Ange watched him lead another charge, hating the fact it wasn't over. Taking a deep breath, she raised her sword and set off after them.

Ten yards on, the charge slowed, then stopped. Everyone stopped. Some started retreating. And, by the Gods, Ange didn't blame them. She would've done the same if she could've got her legs to work. If she wasn't too scared to move.

A dark-skinned Jian stood over the body of a woman as he threw magic against two Chosen and they fired back with their batons. Flame and lightning crashed together, shaking the ground, burning the air. Ange had to shield her eyes with her hand and, even a good five hundred yards away, she could feel the heat, the violence.

Then the girl – the God – flew past, no more than a streak of light.

This time, Ange got her legs moving. This was no fight for her. Not for any human.

18

Zorique

Omason Beach

There were limits to Zorique's power after all, and she knew she was perilously close to reaching them. She could barely feel the fire that had burned inside her since the Battle of Layso and she had to concentrate to stay in the air. And yet still more Daijaku rushed towards her.

How many had she killed that afternoon? Hundreds? Thousands? The Egril seemed to have an endless supply of the creatures to fill the skies.

'*Kasri.*' Zorique said the word for fire and a second later more demons burst into flames. But even that magic came slower to her than before. It took effort to make it work. Zorique wasn't used to that feeling. She didn't like it.

She looked around, searching for the next threat. For a glorious moment, there was nothing but blue sky in every direction, and she had time to catch her breath. The battle on the beach looked like it was going well, too. The Meigorians had the main stretch of sand in their control and even the higher ground appeared to be theirs. Zorique had helped as much as she could, burning swathes of Skulls, but there were still Chosen to deal with.

Chosen that scared her.

The first time they hit her had felt like she'd been hammered by a mountain. It had been like nothing she'd experienced before. Certainly not at Layso. Killing Chosen then had almost been easy. They didn't have the power to hurt her then. But now?

Now they could.

She'd been at full strength when she took that first blast, and it had sucked so much energy from her. So much that she'd been grateful the Daijaku had attacked her again and she didn't have to continue to fight the Chosen.

Luckily for her, an explosion had killed one of the Egril mages and she'd found the strength to kill another. Even that had been touch and go. The woman's blasts had leached at her, burning around Zorique's shield, doing their best to extinguish her flames. Only by thinking of Tinnstra had Zorique found the courage not to run. Her mother wouldn't have been scared. Her mother wouldn't have given up. So Zorique had howled and flown straight at the Chosen, flooding what magic she had left into her spear. And, by the Gods, it had felt good when she'd driven it through the woman's chest.

Now there were two left and, judging by the havoc they were causing, they were the most powerful of all.

Four more Daijaku swooped towards Zorique, Niganntan spears in their hands.

'*Shirudan.*' Zorique thrust her hand forwards as she said it, shoving her shield at the demons. Their spears splintered a second before their skulls.

She turned back towards the beach, towards the Chosen. She had to deal with them now, before she became too weak, too exhausted.

A pulse of magic told her where they were. Bodies fell like wheat in the harvest, revealing two men in black, batons in hand. Zorique flew towards them, gripping her spear, charging it.

On the beach below, a group was racing towards the Chosen with Tinnstra and Aasgod at its head.

A Chosen raised his baton. Fired. The blast hit Tinnstra and she went down.

'No!' screamed Zorique. She couldn't lose Tinnstra, not now.

Aasgod stood over Tinnstra's body and threw lightning at the Chosen. One of them raised a shield and not even a spark hit them. Then the other raised his baton again.

'*Shirudan.*' Zorique formed the shield in front of her, curving it until it was like a giant ball. '*Oso.*' Push. The word contained all her will, her speed, her fury as she sent the shield towards her enemies. '*Kasri.*' Flames erupted across its surface as if the sun itself had fallen from the heavens.

The Chosen looked up. The shield-maker raised his hand.

Zorique's magic smashed into them. The sound of the impact was louder than any bomb, as if the world itself had been cracked in two. Sand and dirt and dust flew into the air, and Zorique had to use even more of her power to clear her path through it. The smoke twisted and twirled as she shoved it aside, eager to see the Chosen's corpses.

Except the Chosen weren't dead. The two men stood on a square of undamaged land, with not a mark on them. They both raised their batons at Zorique as she hurtled towards them. She saw energy crackle along their shafts and swerved to her left. Felt the air spark and throb as the blast missed her by inches.

She hit the ground hard, rolling with the impact and getting to her feet just as another blast lashed towards her. '*Shirudan.*'

The Chosen's energy blasts smashed against her wall, and again it was different from anything she'd experienced at Layso. The Egril magic ate away at her shield, clawing at her strength. Dear Gods, what were they doing to her?

Then lightning filled the air. Aasgod had rejoined the fight.

Immediately, she felt relief as the Chosen's attack stopped. The shield-maker had to rebuild his defences as Aasgod threw everything he had at them.

'*Kasri.*' The flames leaped from Zorique and raced towards the Chosen. They enveloped the Chosen's shield, mingling with the lightning, trying to find a way past the Egril's defence.

She took a step forwards, focusing her magic through her spear. Sweat dripped off her brow as she took another step, then another. She could see fear and doubt on the Chosen's faces now, and that gave her strength. They'd have to drop their shields to fight back. And the moment they did that, she and Aasgod would have them.

They had to. They couldn't fall at the first hurdle.

The Chosen's shield rippled as fire and lightning battered it from every angle. The man wavered under the pressure as the other Egril crouched behind him.

Zorique watched their faces, tried to see their eyes behind their masks, and knew they weren't beaten yet.

She took another step forwards. Her power burned inside her. Not the way she was used to. Not a song to be relished. This was raw. Painful.

She really didn't like it.

But she couldn't – wouldn't – give in. She took another step forwards, gritting her teeth, ignoring the exhaustion pressing down on her, the fear that her power could fail her.

Zorique focused like Anama had taught her. '*Oso*,' she hissed. A command to push, as much to herself as to her magic. The Chosen's shield rippled and buckled for a heartbeat before re-forming, but it was enough to give Zorique hope.

The Egril were only twenty yards away. The second man was still hiding behind the shield-maker, watching Zorique as she approached. He ignored Aasgod, ignored the lightning. The Chosen just kept his eyes on Zorique. But she could tell he wasn't afraid. Perhaps he saw dying for his God as a reward of some sort. Perhaps …

But what did it matter, as long as he died?

Zorique advanced again, feeling the strain. She spared a glance towards Aasgod. The mage was faring no better, his lightning no longer full of fury.

It was a battle of attrition now between the Jians and the Egril. Whose will was greater? Who wanted to win the most?

Zorique pushed on. If she had to carve the Chosen's shield apart with her sword then so be it. Fifteen feet separated her from the Egril now. Soon they would feel her blade.

Then the second Chosen stood up, placed a hand on the shield-maker's shoulder, whispered something in his ear. The man nodded. The Chosen started to glow.

And Zorique knew that this was the moment they'd been waiting for – had planned for all along. She knew she'd made a terrible mistake. 'Aasgod! Get back.'

The Egril's shield fell before her.

'*Shiru*—'

The Chosen exploded.

Zorique screamed from the brutality of the Egril magic as she confined it within her own shield, holding it back from her friends, her allies. It roared like Kage himself, full of anger, eager to kill, pummelling her mind with its desire to be free.

She was on her knees, one hand clawing at the sand as she held the magic, unable to breathe, unable to think. Her whole being was consumed by the effort of keeping her shield strong as the Egril magic buzzed like a dragon trapped in a jar, searching for its way out.

Aasgod was beside her, shouting something. Words lost in the maelstrom.

Zorique shook, every muscle in her body threatening to shatter from the strain of holding on to the Chosen's fire.

'Throw it!' screamed Aasgod. 'Throw it.'

'*Oso!*' Zorique thrust both hands in the air as she sent the ball of fire skywards, holding it tight. One mile. Two miles. Three. Four. Then she let go.

The explosion shook the world. Its light blotted out everything. Its heat washed over them all, burning skin.

Zorique lay coughing and spluttering, covered in sand, dirt and blood. But alive. By the Gods, she was alive. She opened her eyes, saw Aasgod on his knees, a mad look on his face as if he couldn't believe he had survived. He wasn't the only one, either. Her soldiers were also getting to their feet. She'd saved them. She'd saved them all.

Then she remembered Tinnstra. The thought snuffed out victory's joy. Zorique scrambled to where her mother had fallen, clambering over the dead, pushing the living aside. 'Tinnstra!'

Zorique could see her mother a few yards away. Not moving. *Not dead. Please, not that.* Tinnstra was face down, so Zorique hauled on her shoulder to turn her over – and fell back at the sight of Tinnstra's face. The left side looked like it had borne the brunt of the Chosen's baton blast, leaving a scorched mess. Taking an eye.

Zorique shook the fear and the shock from her head and felt

for a pulse in her mother's neck. At first, there was nothing, so she pressed harder, desperate to feel anything.

'Is she alive?' Aasgod staggered over, an arm hanging limp at his side, blood from his nose staining his beard.

'I don't know.' Zorique might've been crying. She had no idea. She moved her hand to Tinnstra's wrist, pressed two fingers down on the vein, praying to feel something that said her mother was still alive.

19
Vallia

Kagestan

Vallia stepped through the gate into Kagestan and wondered how she was going to tell her Emperor that she was no longer Vallia the Victorious. She had tasted defeat at long last, and it was not something she wished to repeat. The thought burned her, gnawing at her guts. She walked quickly through the castle, running her mind over the battle and pondering what she might have done differently but couldn't come up with a satisfactory answer. She had planned it perfectly. She had a vastly superior force on good ground. They should've destroyed the heathens and yet all her troops were now in the Great Darkness.

Astin awaited her near the stairs to the caverns, wringing his hands as he watched her approach. Even a fool could tell she was the bearer of ill news.

No words were exchanged. She followed him back down the stairs, into the darkness and the heat.

The chancellor led Vallia deeper than she'd ever been before. Raaku was in a small cave, alone. Not even his bodyguards were present. He was waist-deep in the holy waters again, working on a single orb, one almost as big as he was.

He looked up as Astin and Vallia fell to their knees and bowed.

'It is good to see you, Commander.' Raaku's voice cut through Vallia, intensifying her shame. 'Tell me what happened.'

'I failed you, Your Majesty,' she replied, her head pressed to the wet stone. She heard him wade closer, felt his shadow fall over her.

'Rise.'

Vallia straightened her back and found herself looking the Emperor in the eye.

'Tell me.'

'We met the heathen army in Kiyosun as you directed, with thirty thousand infantry, ten thousand Daijaku and a well-fortified position,' said Vallia. 'It should've been enough to destroy both their fleet and their army. Instead, all our forces are with Kage in the Great Darkness.'

'What happened?'

'The False Gods' champions, Your Majesty. They were too powerful for us.'

Raaku cupped his hand around the back of Vallia's head. It fitted easily into his palm, still warm and wet from the holy waters. She closed her eyes, expecting Raaku to crush her skull like she had seen him do to so many others.

'You witnessed the whole battle,' he said instead.

'I did, Your Majesty, from a nearby cliff.'

'Tell me what you learned about the False Gods' champions.'

He removed his hand and, for a moment, Vallia missed its warmth. 'The mage, Aasgod, has a limited power supply. He threw lightning at us from the moment the Daijaku attacked the fleet and yet, in the middle of the battle on the beach, it spluttered out for a time.'

'He regained his magic, though?'

'Yes.'

'Did you see how?'

'No, I didn't.'

'And the others?'

'The Shulka is quite possibly the best warrior I have ever witnessed on a battlefield. I lost count of the troops she personally sent to the Great Darkness. If I had a legion of fighters like her, I could conquer the world for you.' Vallia paused for a moment. 'I also saw the Shulka take a Chosen's baton blast full in the face. She fell on the field.'

'But you do not think she is dead.'

'No, Your Majesty. I underestimated them once. I will not do so again.'

'What about the other two?'

'There was only one other that I saw. The one we believe to be Zorique. She is … different from the others. Unique.'

'What powers does she have?'

'Only what we heard she can do from the attack in Layso. She can fly and command fire. She has some sort of shield that can protect her from almost any assault and I saw her send some troops flying with a wave of her hand.'

'Formidable.' There was a note of respect in the Emperor's voice.

'We did hurt her, though,' said Vallia. 'The changes you made to the Chosen's batons affected her. I could see her slowing down, and her fire lost some of its ferocity.'

'What about the fourth champion?'

'There wasn't one. Not that I saw.'

Raaku glanced back at the orb before returning his attention to Vallia. 'What about the rest of their army?'

'Most of their ships are destroyed and their casualties are heavy. They paid a high price for their victory.'

'They had no victory, Commander, and you did not fail me. I told you this would be just the first skirmish. You have done all I wished of you, and my father is grateful for the blood and souls you have sent him.'

'Yes, Your Majesty.' The words were bitter on her tongue.

'Our soldiers gave their lives to Kage, as they had sworn to do. Tonight, they dine by his side in the Great Darkness and will enjoy everlasting glory. The bones and blood of the faithful have formed the foundations of our Empire since the beginning.'

'Yes, Your Majesty,' said Vallia, unable to meet her master's eyes.

He tilted her head up. His gaze burned through her. 'Do you believe in me, Commander?'

'Yes, Your Majesty. With all my heart.'

'Then believe me when I say that Jia will be drenched in both Egril and heathen blood before the final battle is fought. You and

I will stand together in Aisair and we will destroy everything the False Gods hold dear.' Raaku let go of her head and turned back to the orb. 'Our victory on that day will be unlike any other.'

Vallia bowed for a final time, her strength restored. It had been hubris to think Sekanowari could be won so easily. She would not make the same mistake again.

Back in Aisair, Vallia headed straight to the chamber she'd designated as a war room and to the map on the table. At least with all the gates destroyed, there was only one road the heathens could take and plenty of opportunities for her to destroy them.

'You can leave me now,' she said to the aide who'd followed her. 'Send up some food and wine as quick as you can.'

'At once, Commander.'

'One last thing. The city closest to Kiyosun ...' She glanced at the map. 'Anjon.'

'Yes, Commander,' said the aide.

'Send the spikes there tonight. Tell the men to get to work immediately.'

'Yes, Commander.'

She looked down at the map once more. 'Blood I will give you, O Great One. Souls I will send you.'

20

Larius

Aisair

Larius bolted upright when his bedroom door opened. There had been no knock. No request for permission to enter. Instead, the Egril commander, Vallia, walked in as if these were her own private quarters and not the private chambers of the King of Jia. As if he meant nothing.

To make matters worse, the bitch was right.

His consort startled awake as the door banged shut. The stupid woman, Grace, gave a squeak of fright and dragged the bed sheet up to cover her breasts. Truth be told, Larius wanted to do the same, but that wouldn't have been kingly. At least he was wearing his nightshirt and didn't have to face the dreadful Egril general naked. Instead, he had to pretend he wasn't bothered by Vallia's insults, and that he was, in fact, superior to her.

'Who do you think you are? Walking in unannounced like this?' He tilted his head back so he could look down his nose at her. 'Where are your manners?'

Of course, it was obvious neither he nor Vallia were convinced by his act. Vallia was tall, thin as a dagger, with her grey hair cropped so short it was as if she couldn't allow even a single strand to be out of place. So very unlike Larius's shoulder-length locks – which, no doubt, looked as big a mess as his life. Her uniform was immaculate: a simple black dress uniform, not unlike a Chosen's, except she wore a red brooch on the left breast marked only with the black eye of Kage.

However, it was her mask that Larius found the most unsettling. It was unlike any other he'd come across, all black except for red lines that ran around the eyes and down the centre of the nose. Some tribal pattern, no doubt, that told the history of her family for the last thousand years or some nonsense like that. He could've asked for details, he supposed, but Larius didn't care to find out. He had no interest in history. It was his future he was more worried about.

'I need to speak to you in private,' said Vallia in Jian, her accent flawless. Even with the mask, Larius could see in her eyes that being in his presence disgusted her. Typical of the woman to not even pretend to apologise for decorum's sake. Not even a 'good morning' or a 'by-your-leave'. There was a piece of paper in her hand, but Larius couldn't make out what was written on it. He was too busy looking at the ancient scimitar hanging from her hip. He'd never actually seen her draw it, but her hand was constantly on its hilt as if she was just waiting for any excuse to free its blade.

He forced himself to look Vallia in the eye with his most defiant stare for as long as he dared. Of course, it wasn't long before he had to look away, turning to Grace. 'Leave us.' Thank the Gods, his voice didn't crack.

The girl didn't need telling twice. She all but ran from the room, trailing the sheet behind her. After he watched her leave, Larius realised that he rather wished she'd stayed. Not that she offered him any protection, but Larius had never wanted to face his last moments with no one by his side, and he had a feeling that this might be the day death called.

'Well?' he managed to say.

'There has been an invasion in the south of the country,' replied Vallia.

'An invasion?' The word didn't make sense. Not now. The Egril had invaded. They'd won. Who else was left? Who would dare?

'Yesterday, a force made up of Meigorians and a small group of exiles from the faithless lands crossed the Golden Channel and engaged us near Kiyosun.'

'What?' Larius's mind raced. It sounded impossible, but why would Vallia bother to lie about such a thing? He was relieved, scared, confused. He needed a drink. Some wine. There was a flask on a table on the other side of the room, but he couldn't get to it. Couldn't show weakness in front of Vallia. Instead, he straightened his back and tried to act like a king. 'What happened?'

'We met it with a considerable force. Casualties were heavy on both sides but, unfortunately, the invaders were victorious in the initial battle.'

'So, they are still here? In Jia?'

'We presume they are moving north at present.' Vallia made it sound as if her information was of no importance but, by the Gods, it was. It damn well was. It changed everything.

'Are they coming here? To Aisair?' This time, Larius couldn't help himself. He was on his feet and looking out through the window before he knew what he was doing. He didn't know what he expected to see. His castle already under siege? But no, there were only near-empty streets under grey skies, still too early for people to risk leaving their homes after curfew. The only colour was those damned red flags of the Egril dangling off the buildings. As if his city was smeared with blood. The invaders weren't in his city yet, but then his gaze drifted to the distance, past the city walls, to the construction the Skulls had started some time before. 'You've known they were coming for weeks, haven't you? Months even. That's why you're here. That's why you're building more walls and digging trenches.'

Vallia glanced out through the window. 'Of course. The city needs to be defended if our enemies manage to get this far.'

'*Your* enemies, you mean.'

Vallia's smile chilled him to the bone. 'Oh no, they are *our* enemies, Your Majesty. Make no mistake.'

Larius smoothed out his nightshirt, as if that would make everything better. Like him, it had seen better days, but he didn't want it to look ruffled in case it made *him* look ruffled. Kings – even puppet kings – didn't panic. 'What do you intend to do to stop them?'

'Their destruction is a foregone conclusion. Preparations are well underway to destroy the invaders long before they reach the capital, but there's no need to trouble yourself with the details,' replied Vallia. 'However, there is a matter that does affect you.'

'And what, pray tell, is that?'

'The invasion is led by someone claiming to be Zorique, your niece.'

Larius stared at the Egril commander, open-mouthed. 'She's ... she's dead. I was told she was dead.' The girl certainly haunted his dreams enough. Her, her brother, mother and good old Cariin were always happy to come and visit him in the depths of the night. To remind him of his betrayal, of their murder. To scream and curse at him.

'That was a lie. She survived and escaped to Meigore.'

Dear Gods, Larius wanted to be sick. 'But ... but even if she did survive ... she's four years old. No one would follow her. How could she lead anything?'

'The woman claiming to be Zorique is a child no longer.' Vallia pursed her lips. 'She also has magical abilities. We've heard rumours that some believe she is the daughter of one of your False Gods.'

'Like Raaku?'

'His Imperial Majesty? No, our beloved Emperor is the one true son of Kage, the one true God. This ... Zorique simply has some tricks that impress the faithless.'

Larius had to sit down before his legs went from under him. 'But you have powers – your Chosen have powers – to stop her, stop this ... impostor.' That word sounded better than any other Larius could've used to describe Zorique – like *niece* or *queen*.

'Of course, and we will.' Vallia made it sound inevitable but, somehow, Larius got the impression it was far from it.

'So why are you telling me this now?'

'We are concerned that your subjects may flock to the invaders' banner. The Hanran have been busy spreading word of this *charlatan* and asking for aid. We need to curb their enthusiasm.' Vallia placed the paper she'd been holding on the desk next to Larius. 'This is a proclamation declaring anyone who helps the invaders a traitor and subject to the death penalty. You will sign it.'

Larius stared at the words written on the paper as if they were poison. 'You don't need my permission to kill anyone.' They'd certainly killed enough without his approval.

The woman smiled. 'It's nice to have it on occasions like this.'

By the Gods, Larius hated the Egril, but he especially hated Vallia. Did she think he didn't understand what they were doing? 'You just want everyone to hate me more, don't you? Are you scared I'll try to broker a deal with the invaders? With this Zorique impostor?'

'Just sign the paper,' replied Vallia. Not a denial, then.

'What if I don't? What will you do? You need me.'

'Please, we both know that's not true.' Vallia managed to contain her laughter. She pointed at the paper again, like a teacher to a naughty child.

Again, Larius went through the motions of resisting. He didn't really know why he did it, because the result was always the same – acquiescence. But he felt it was expected, the sort of thing a king should do before a conqueror. But was he even king if Zorique was back? And with that thought, any spine he may have pretended to possess crumbled to dust.

He took the quill on his desk, dipped it in ink and signed his soul away for the thousandth time. One would have thought it would become easy after so much practice, but it never had. He felt the pain as if it were his first betrayal.

Vallia whipped the paper away without waiting for the ink to dry. 'Thank you. Enjoy your day.'

He watched the general leave before burying his head in his hands. What had he done to deserve this hell? It wasn't as if the Egril ever gave him any choice in anything. Even the betrayal. Even the deaths.

Well, there was a choice – do it or die. Was he to blame for not choosing the latter? Anyone would have done the same thing in his shoes. To say otherwise would have been to lie, and while Larius was many things, he wasn't a liar. He was a man of his word. The trouble was, his word was worthless. The gold in his crown had more value than the head beneath it.

No, he was a victim, much like his brother, much like his brother's wife and their silly children. Perhaps more so. Their pain had been swift. His was endless, a horror to wake up to and somehow endure.

The far door opened and Grace peeked out. 'Has she gone?'

'Of course she's bloody gone,' snapped Larius.

Despite his assurances, the girl still tiptoed into the room as if expecting Vallia to suddenly rematerialise. Oh, why couldn't they have given him a woman with some brains to go with her face? If he'd been a real king, he could've had a proper queen. Instead he had ... whatever Grace was.

She rubbed his shoulders. 'Are you all right?' Her voice sounded so full of sympathy. Larius knew better. What she meant was, *Am I all right?* The woman might be dumb, but she was more than aware that her fate was tied to his. When the end came for Larius, it would come for his strumpet, too.

'Just go and get me some food. I'm hungry.'

'Talk to me,' she said instead. 'I can help.'

Larius shot to his feet. 'Talk to *you*? *You* can help?'

'Larius. Please don't get angry. I ...' Now it was someone else's turn to offer mock defiance, and he didn't like it one bit.

'*Please don't get angry?*' he roared and, by the Gods, it felt good. '*Please?* There's no pleasing in this world. You should know that by now. I certainly do.' He glared at her with all the hate he felt for himself.

'Why are you being like this?' Grace's lip quivered and tears appeared in the corners of those big, wide eyes of hers. 'I love you.'

He hit her before he knew what he was doing. A good right with the back of his hand across her cheek, sending her flying. He shook his hand, feeling the sting, regretting the violence instantly and the pain it caused him. It was beneath a king to beat someone personally. He only hoped he'd not damaged his hand. As if he needed his day to get any worse.

'I'll fetch your breakfast,' mumbled Grace as she crawled away from him. Hopefully she'd learned her place, like he'd learned his. Everyone is under someone's boot heel. Everyone has a master.

But what to do now? Larius had no idea. Everything depended on whether the Egril defeated these invaders, these liberators. But Vallia was right. There was no if. The Egril would emerge victorious. No one had ever beaten them. That wouldn't change.

However, there was something about this Zorique that Vallia feared. Was she his niece or the daughter of a God? Both options seemed impossible. But everything in life seemed impossible.

Memories flooded him of the little girl who loved to sit on her uncle's lap and hear him tell tall tales of princesses long ago, the girl who giggled when he produced a coin from her ear and clapped her hands so ferociously when he sang her songs. He hated thinking of those happy days, when he was a better man, a prince who should never have been king. When he was loved and loved himself.

He walked back over to the window and opened it. It was a long drop down. A fast end to his punishment. An escape from his prison.

But there was no dignity in that route. Only shame.

A king had his pride to think about. What little of it he had left.

A pretence of pride, perhaps.

Larius rang a bell for his servants to bring his clothes.

21

Tinnstra

Omason Beach

Tinnstra heard voices. People talking. So she wasn't dead, then. The left side of her face felt strange. She reached up, touched the bandage covering her eye, and winced at the pain. Her face *burned*. She wanted to scream but ground her teeth together instead. She could deal with pain. She knew pain.

Tinnstra opened her other eye, saw canvas above her head. She was in a tent. She tried to move her head, but the fire flared across her whole body so fiercely that Tinnstra closed her eye again and lay back. Controlling her breathing, she relaxed as best she could, moved past the burning, focused on the voices around her. Listened to the conversations. Most were far away, an incoherent buzz intermingled with the moans and cries of others in pain. There was a man and a woman nearby, though, close enough to hear.

'They say she's the Queen of Jia,' said the woman, her voice full of energy, young.

'We haven't got a queen. Larius is king,' croaked the man. He didn't sound much better than Tinnstra felt.

'They say she's Cariin's daughter.'

'But she's dead ... and even if she weren't, I thought she was a baby. Not a ...'

'God?'

The man tried to laugh but ended up coughing in pain. 'She's not a God.' There was a pause. 'Is she?'

'Well, she's not human,' said the woman. 'I know that much. Not the way she flies around and throws fire and stuff. I'm just glad she's on our side.'

'Makes a change.'

'Yeah, well. She scares the shit out of me, so if she wants to be called queen, then I'll call her queen.'

Tinnstra tried to say something, but her tongue felt too big for her mouth and she knew the effort was beyond her. Besides, the fire on her face had reached her brain and, by the Gods, it hurt. There was no moving past this. It consumed her, burning the edges of her thoughts, turning the world black.

The fire was gone when Tinnstra woke next. She reached up, touched her face, felt the bandage once more, felt a rush of her old friend, fear. *How bad is the injury beneath it? Dear Gods, I don't want to be half-blind.*

No, whatever it was, she'd heal. The Chikara water would do its work. That's why she'd drunk it over the last fourteen or so years after all. That's why she'd sacrificed so much to become ... *what? What have I become?*

She reached out with her mind. Zorique was nearby. Aasgod, too. But no other magic users. No Chosen. No demons. Thank the Gods. Tinnstra took a deep breath and sat up. Her ribs protested, but the pain was minor, all things considered. In truth, she was lucky to be alive. She'd turned as the Chosen fired his baton and she'd only caught a fraction of the blast. Even so, without the healing powers the Chikara water had given her, she would've been dead.

Shit. So much for an easy victory. So much for my great plans.

She wasn't the only injured person in the tent. It stretched a good hundred feet in length and was rammed full of cots containing men and women injured during the fighting. Tinnstra ran her eye over them, assessing their wounds. Some had what looked like minor injuries, easily cured with some rest. Perhaps they'd not get back to their best, but well enough to fight some more. Others, covered in bloody bandages, would be on their way to see Xin sooner than later.

Again, Tinnstra's hand went to her covered face. *Lucky, stupid girl.*

There were no Skulls, though. No guards. This wasn't a prison. Still, she didn't have any weapons and she didn't have her pouch. And what of her bag? A shiver of fear went through. Her bag with her supply of Chikara water had been in the hold of her ship, along with her book and the map. *What if they're all at the bottom of the ocean?*

Outside, soldiers moved about their duties, the sun already high. Tinnstra must've slept through the night. She could smell food cooking somewhere and her stomach grumbled in response. Hunger was a good sign. She'd find Zorique and Aasgod, get some Chikara water from the mage and fix herself before the army moved on. Why Aasgod hadn't given her some while she slept was a question she'd ask the fool of a man the next time she saw him.

She gulped down a cup of water someone had left beside her cot and climbed to her feet, holding on to a tent pole for support. It felt like a lifetime since she'd last stood upright.

Passing soldiers gave her furtive glances as she stepped out of the tent, but she ignored them and headed for Zorique and Aasgod.

The Ascalian Mountains loomed overhead, bringing back memories from long ago, of being hunted by the Egril. Strange to think it was less than a year ago for everyone around her, yet over a decade and a half had passed for Zorique and herself. A long time to be away from home. A long time to wait for vengeance.

The camp was large, built in what looked like the remains of the Egril base, and filled not just with Meigorian soldiers but Jians in Shulka armour. There were others, too, Hanran wearing cobbled-together armour, part-Skull, part-Shulka, even some Meigorian. But no matter who they were, all wore tired expressions, and plenty carried injuries. *Dear Gods, what a price we paid to win this beach.*

The central command tent was easy enough to find, even without Zorique's magic lighting Tinnstra's way. A crowd had gathered around it, full of eager people desperate to see Zorique. At least they weren't singing prayers and other such nonsense, but

Tinnstra recognised the same maniacal gleam in their eyes. *Good. They'll fight all the harder if they believe in Zorique.*

Zorique was there, Aasgod next to her, a bruise on his face but otherwise unmarked. With them was a man who had the air of a Shulka, someone strangely familiar, and a woman with two tears tattooed on her cheek – a Weeping Man. She looked up as Tinnstra entered and shock ran across her face.

'Do I look that bad?' Tinnstra growled. She'd never liked gangsters.

'Tinnstra!' Zorique ran over and wrapped her arms around her mother. For a moment, Tinnstra forgot about everything and just enjoyed the embrace.

'It's good to see you, my love,' she whispered, kissing the top of Zorique's head.

The girl stepped back, smiling. 'It's good to see you, too. I thought I'd lost you.'

Tinnstra tried a smile back. 'I'm not that easy to get rid of.'

'Stop charging straight at a Chosen's blasts,' said Aasgod, coming to join them.

Tinnstra leaned in and whispered in his ear. 'I'll do what I have to – now give me some Chikara water.'

'You've had more than enough. I fed you three vials while you slept,' said the mage.

'Stop bloody arguing with me and give me some,' she said through clenched teeth, need fuelling her fury. She stepped back, let him see what she'd do to him if he dared say no. Aasgod looked for a moment like he would, but then he sighed and removed a small vial of green liquid from a pouch.

'You don't need it,' said Zorique.

'Really? Maybe if I hadn't lost an eye, you might be right.'

Aasgod shook his head. 'This isn't the way.'

'It is mine,' she snarled. *Losing an eye isn't going to stop me. Nor do I need their pity.* She took the water from Aasgod and felt all the better for having it in her hand. She just needed a moment to drink it.

'Are you going to say hello?' asked a man from behind her. 'I'll be hurt if you don't.'

Tinnstra had to turn to face him, even though she didn't want him to see her like that. 'Ralasis. You're alive.' She kept her voice painfully cold.

The Meigorian sea captain made a sweeping bow. 'A miracle if ever there was one.' When he straightened, she saw the cuts and bruises that even his easy smile couldn't hide. 'Good to see you up at long last, Tinnstra.'

She glanced over at the man and woman who'd been talking to Zorique earlier – the Shulka and the gangster. Now she looked closer, they both seemed familiar, the man especially. 'Is that ... Hasan?'

'Aye,' he replied. 'How are you, Tinnstra?'

'Alive.'

The Shulka looked uneasy. 'Dear Gods, they told me you'd changed, but I never imagined ... You were a barely a woman when I last saw you ... and now you're a giant!' Hasan shook his head.

'I'm no giant.' But she was a good head taller than the Shulka, and just as broad – far different from the scared girl he'd known. It felt so good to see him, like reuniting with family, in a way. 'We've all been through a lot since then,' she said instead, her only explanation. 'Who's your friend?'

Hasan stepped aside so the woman with the gangster tears could join them. 'We've met before, too. I'm Yas.'

'The maid?'

Yas gave a tight-lipped smile. 'I was.'

'When did you get the tears?' asked Tinnstra.

Yas grimaced. 'Sometime when I was trying to stay alive.'

'That happens,' said Tinnstra. 'What about the old man, Jax? Where's he?'

Hasan shook his head. 'He died when the Egril bombed Kiyosun a few months back.'

'A sad loss for us all. We could use warriors like him. And Dren?' She looked around, expecting to find the kid lurking somewhere. If ever there was anyone she owed for her life, it was him.

'He died taking out a Skull command post,' said Yas.

Of course he did. That bit of news really hurt. He'd burned bright, got Tinnstra going when all felt lost. Another one to avenge.

'Probably saved the rest of Kiyosun in the process,' said Yas. 'It was a good death.'

'There's no such thing as a good death,' said Tinnstra.

'True,' replied Yas. 'But dying's all anyone seems to do these days. You gave it a proper go yourself by the looks of things.'

Tinnstra touched the bandage over her eye. 'How long was I unconscious for?'

'Three days,' said Zorique.

'Three days?' Tinnstra couldn't believe it. The rage within her grew at the news.

Aasgod nodded. 'You were all but dead. It's a miracle you're on your feet at all.'

Ralasis put a hand on her shoulder. 'We lost fifteen thousand of our troops taking the beach. With thousands more injured.'

'Dear Gods,' said Tinnstra. 'That many?' It didn't seem possible. Couldn't be. She felt fear stir in her gut, but she forced it down and smothered it with her anger.

'The land was hard won,' said Ralasis.

'I know. I was there,' snapped Tinnstra. 'That still doesn't explain why you haven't already gone through the gates and attacked Aisair.'

'We ... lost the gates two weeks ago,' said the Shulka.

Of course we did. Tinnstra took a deep breath. 'Two weeks ago?'

'Daijaku flew straight to it and dropped only the Gods know how many bombs on it,' said Hasan. 'We've had word that they hit the other gates in our control at the same time. All of them were destroyed.'

'All of them?' repeated Tinnstra. Gods, she needed to drink the Chikara water, needed its magic. This was all too much. All her plans ruined. 'Why didn't you bloody well let us know before we left Meigore?'

Hasan glanced at Yas. 'I sent ships on two separate occasions to warn you and I watched both get bombed out of the water by the Daijaku. I didn't send any more after that.'

'So how did the Skulls know what we were doing? Who bloody talked?' Tinnstra knew she was raising her voice but she couldn't help herself.

Again, Hasan exchanged looks with Yas. 'No one that we know of.'

'Why do you keep looking at her? What aren't you telling me?' said Tinnstra.

'Oh, fuck off. Who do you think you are?' said Yas, stepping forward. 'I thought the girl over there was supposed to be the bloody queen.'

Hasan held up a hand. 'No one's keeping secrets. The Skulls have a new commander in Aisair, a woman called Vallia. Maybe she just worked out what we were planning.'

'I don't know what's worse – a traitor or a clever Skull.' Tinnstra took another breath, tried to calm herself. *When will our luck change?* 'Have we heard from Wenna?'

'She's been in Aisair for three months,' said Hasan. 'She's been sending us information when she can. It's pretty bad there.'

Tinnstra almost didn't want to ask. 'How bad?'

'As bad as it can get. The Skulls have built a barricade around the city and dug trenches in front of that,' said Hasan.

'Nothing we can't push through.'

'Except the Skulls are bringing in more reinforcements every day, plus Chosen on top of that. It makes what we faced at the beach seem like a walk in the park.'

'Does she have numbers?'

'Last count was around twenty thousand Skulls and a couple of hundred Chosen.'

'Two *hundred* Chosen?' Tinnstra almost couldn't believe it. *But why am I surprised? It's the Egril way.*

'That's what she said,' said Hasan. 'It could be more by now.'

'We still outnumber them,' said Ralasis, ever the optimistic fool.

'Didn't you hear what Hasan said?' Yas snapped. 'There are two hundred Chosen in the city – that's too many. They'll kill everyone.'

'What about the other cities?' asked Tinnstra.

'We sent messages all across Jia the moment we heard you were coming,' said Hasan. 'Told them that Zorique was on her way and they had to get ready to fight. No more than that, though. We didn't let anyone know plans or dates or locations.'

'How many do you think will answer the call?' asked Aasgod.

'Thousands, I would hope,' said the Shulka. 'Perhaps even tens of thousands.'

That was something. 'Then we do this the hard way. We move quickly. Straight up the Northern Road to Aisair,' said Tinnstra. 'If we set a good pace, we can be there before the next moon.'

Hasan shook his head. 'That's three weeks away.'

'Time enough to gather our forces from across Jia,' said Tinnstra. 'Tell them to meet us at the Kotege. From there we go to Aisair for the final battle.'

'This Vallia will be waiting for us,' said Hasan.

'This is Sekanowari,' said Tinnstra. 'Once you lost the gates, it was never going to be easy.'

Ralasis shook his head. 'It's not what we hoped for, is it?'

'Nothing ever is. How many troops are fit to fight?'

'Of those that sailed with us?' replied Ralasis. He rubbed his head. 'Nearly everyone is carrying a wound of some kind, but we have just over twenty thousand that can still fight.'

'What about the Shulka and Hanran here?' asked Tinnstra.

'I have about one hundred and fifty Shulka and another hundred Hanran that will come with us,' said Hasan.

'And the rest of Kiyosun?'

'There's not many of us left,' said Yas. 'And we've got children and old 'uns to take care of. We're staying here.'

Tinnstra raised an eyebrow. 'What about the Weeping Men? Will they help?'

'I can't speak for them, whatever my position here may be. They find food for us, but we pay with gold or coin, same as everyone else. They won't fight – not unless you've got some wagons full of money tucked away somewhere.'

'Thought as much,' said Tinnstra. 'Still, we'll need food and supplies. We could use your help with that, if possible.'

Yas nodded. 'Once we've got ourselves sorted here. Anything we have to spare after that, we'll send your way.'

'Thank you.' Tinnstra pressed the bandage over her ruined eye. By the Gods, she was tired.

'Do you need to rest?' asked Ralasis.

'No,' she snapped. 'We've wasted too much time already. I'll rest when this is all over.'

'I meant no insult.' Ralasis held up his hands, tried that easy smile of his. It didn't have the effect it used to.

'How soon can we move out?' said Tinnstra.

'In the morning. We'll have to leave some people behind. The ones who are too injured to move.' It hurt Ralasis to say that. Tinnstra could hear the pain in his voice.

'We'll look after them,' said Yas. 'I promise you that.'

Ralasis bowed. 'Thank you.'

Tinnstra turned to Hasan. 'There's a city a couple of days' march from here, isn't there?'

'Yes. Anjon,' replied the Shulka.

'Can you send some people there straight away? Tell the local Hanran to make things difficult for the Skulls until we get there,' said Tinnstra.

'No problem,' said Hasan.

'Good. Now, if you'll excuse us, I'd like to speak to the queen alone.' Tinnstra stepped back and crossed her arms. The meeting was over. Not that the others looked keen to be dismissed.

Ralasis was the first to react. 'Time to eat, everyone,' he said loudly. He put his arm around Hasan's shoulders. 'Let me show you the magic of Meigorian spices.'

Aasgod was about to follow the others out the tent, but a shake of Tinnstra's head stopped him in his tracks. 'You stay.'

Aasgod didn't look too happy at being ordered around, but Tinnstra didn't care about his feelings. 'Why are you and the army still here?' she said when they were alone. 'We had a plan of action. You've wasted three days, waiting here.'

'We had too many injured and dead from taking the beach,' replied Zorique. 'Including you. Everyone thought it best to allow people to recover first.'

'Since when did everyone's opinions matter? You're the queen.

You make the decisions. You should've moved on. I would've caught up.'

'It was my decision,' said Zorique. 'I thought you were worth waiting for!'

'Well, it was the wrong decision. Beating the Skulls is all that matters. We can't give them any more time than we already have to prepare for us.' Tinnstra knew she was losing her temper, but she couldn't help herself. 'You heard Hasan – they have two hundred Chosen waiting for us in Aisair, and you can bet everything we have that there'll be even more by the time we get there.'

'Didn't you hear how many people died taking this beach?' said Zorique, finding some fire of her own. 'People lost friends – family, even. I couldn't ask them to march off into the sunset without a moment to mourn.'

'Yes, you can! We are the dead, remember? Stop thinking about your army as living people. Every single one of us – including me – is already dead. Any mourning should've been done in Meigore. We are the dead who fight.' Tinnstra looked from Zorique to Aasgod, then back again. 'Accept that.'

'I don't want everyone to die.'

'We were all dead the moment we boarded those boats. So, you need to harden up and lead and you –' Tinnstra jabbed a finger at Aasgod '– start advising her to do the right thing.'

'I thought I had,' replied the mage.

'Waiting won't win this war. Giving the Skulls time to dig in, to reinforce themselves, won't win this war,' snarled Tinnstra. 'We have to push on. Let everyone in Jia know we're here to save them. Inspire them to join, to fight beside us, beside you. Then our army of twenty thousand becomes an army of millions.'

Zorique's head dropped, looking every bit her age. 'They won't follow an eighteen-year-old girl.'

The sight calmed Tinnstra. She wasn't angry at Zorique, anyway. She was angry at herself – for getting hurt, slowing them all down, making them wait. 'I heard people talking about how they think you're a God. If they believe that, they're not going to question whether you deserve to lead them. They won't care who your father may or may not have been – or how old you are.'

'That's easy to say.'

'Do you remember a man named Greener? He helped us escape to Meigore.'

Zorique looked up. 'He was the giant who carried me for days.'

'That he was. And he gave you some advice once. Good advice.'

'I remember. "Act like a queen to be a queen."'

Tinnstra nodded. 'Don't ask for permission. Don't ask for consensus. Don't even ask for advice if you don't want to. Just lead. If they won't follow the queen that you are, then be a God. Be the star they *will* follow. Give them hope and they will tear down anything in front of them.'

'I can't do it without you.' Zorique's voice was barely a whisper.

'You can, and you will,' said Tinnstra. 'I nearly died on that beach. I may well die on the next battlefield. When I fall – and I will fall – shed a tear, but no more than that. Definitely don't stop to mourn or wonder what to do. Just keep fighting until every Skull in Jia is dead or running for their life. Honour me by freeing our country.'

'Tinn, I ... I'm scared. Back at the beach ... The Chosen hurt me. I felt my power drain away when their blasts struck my shields. It wasn't like before.'

Tinnstra took her in her arms. 'My beautiful girl, I wish it wasn't so, but things will only get harder from now on. Raaku isn't a fool. He'll throw everything he has at you. Every damn monster in the world and every trick he can think of.'

'What if I'm not strong enough to beat him? What if I can't do it, can't free Jia?'

'Believe in yourself, girl. Believe in yourself like I believe in you. Remember there's more power in you than what you've used so far. More than any of us can imagine. The smart Aasgod told me that.' Tinnstra glanced over at the mage, gave him a nod to let him know she believed in him, too.

'Okay,' said Zorique.

'Even now, there are people outside this tent, just as they were outside the embassy in Layso, who think you are sent by the Gods to rid us of the Egril. Use that. Play on that. Be their inspiration. Be their hope.'

'I will.'

'Good. Now, did anyone find my things? I need my pack. The map and the book are inside it.'

'Our ship's still on the beach,' said Aasgod. 'Ralasis had his men gathering what supplies were left, but I don't know about your bag.'

Tinnstra nodded. 'I'll go and check. I need to find more weapons anyway. I'll see you both later.'

'Tinn,' said Zorique before she could leave. 'I'm sorry. I promise I'll do better.'

'I know you will. We all will.'

'This is why we trained.' The girl said it with a smile.

'I'll see you later,' said Tinnstra, bowing. She left the tent, needing to be away from there, only too aware it was the wrong thing to do. She pushed past the devoted worshippers, ignoring their looks and their whispers, hating them for being in her way, for being weak, but not as much as she hated herself.

As she walked, she pulled the stopper out of the vial of Chikara water and drank it without breaking stride. Once it was empty, she tossed the vial aside, wincing at the taste, desperate for its power.

Desperate for anything that would help her win.

22

Jax

Lastwin

Jax crouched in the shadows of an oak tree, with Moiri beside him, and watched the house. It was a small cottage on the outskirts of a village called Lastwin, two or three days north of Chita. Smoke drifted up from the chimney at the building's centre, disappearing into the night. Light glowed behind shuttered windows at the far end of the house.

'Just the lantern in the front room,' whispered Jax.

'Probably only one or two people,' said Moiri. 'Maybe some children.'

'Worth the risk?'

'We need news. We've spent so long hiding from the Skulls that we have no idea what's going on. We don't even know if the Meigorians have invaded yet.'

'Then it's worth the risk.'

They returned to the others, hiding in a copse nearby. There were eleven of them in the scouting party, having left the rest a mile or so back. Hard to move quietly with a small army. The months on the road had only swelled their numbers. There were nearly two hundred of them now.

Almost an army.

Jax had to admit it felt good to have soldiers around him once more, to have a purpose. No one looked down on him. No one felt sorry for him. No one thought he was mad.

He was the general again. *His* Hanran acted on *his* commands.

Jax was also glad that he couldn't remember what happened in Kagestan. It was easier that way to pretend it had never happened, that he'd never been that helpless, that broken – especially now Monsuta no longer taunted him, either. He could leave that part of the past behind.

'Looks safe,' said Moiri to the others. 'Building's well taken care of, too, so chances are no one's starving inside. They might even have some food to spare.'

'Who's going to talk to them?' said Petrik. He was a Shulka, from Clan Rizon, like Moiri. Older than both Jax and Moiri, he'd never risen in the ranks, he was just happy to follow, happy to fight. The battles had taken a toll on him, though, as there was hardly a part of him that wasn't battered or scarred.

'Not you,' said Moiri. 'Not unless we want to frighten them to death.'

Petrik rubbed at his cauliflower ear. 'My mother always said I was the best-looking of her children.'

'Not saying much,' said Dev. 'I've seen the rest of your family.'

That got a snicker from everyone else, but Moiri shushed them pretty quick. 'All right. Let's stay professional. I'll do the asking. Jax can come with me. Two old folks like us should make them feel safe enough. The rest of you keep your eyes open and your blades close to hand. We're deep in Skull territory here. First sign of trouble, come in hard and heavy. Okay?'

Even Sarah and Remie drew their swords. They'd joined in as the Shulka trained on the way south and at least knew which way around to hold their weapons now. They might not be as skilled as the others, but they had good hearts and that made up for a lot.

'Leave your sword here,' said Moiri. 'But keep a knife or two, out of sight.'

Jax nodded. How many times had he been told as a cadet that it was better to have a weapon and not need it than need it and not have it?

They didn't talk as they approached the cottage, both of them too busy listening for anything out of place, looking for anything that betrayed a trap.

But it was just a cottage and they reached the front door

without any trouble. A man and a woman were talking inside. Jians.

Moiri took a deep breath and knocked.

The voices stopped. Jax could imagine their panic. Nothing good knocked on a door in the middle of the night.

'We're just some travellers after a bit of help,' he said, roughing up his accent so it wasn't obvious he was a Shulka. Better to appear a commoner than a Shulka.

A shutter over one of the windows opened a crack, spilling some light outside before a body blocked it once more.

Jax stepped away from the door so whoever it was could get a good look. 'It's just me and my wife.'

'What do you want?' asked a man, sounding nervous. 'You're breaking curfew.'

'Hoping you might have some food to spare,' said Moiri. 'We've not eaten for a few days.'

The man at the window hesitated for a moment, then closed the shutter and bolted it. A tense, murmured conversation followed before footsteps approached the door. Another bolt was dragged back and then the door opened. 'Come inside. Quickly.'

Jax and Moiri did as they were asked. The man shut the door again the moment they were inside. He was young, maybe a little younger than Kaine would've been, with short hair and broad shoulders that came only from hard work.

A woman stood by the fire, a sleeping baby in her arms, looking none too happy to have guests. A rocking chair moved back and forth behind her. To her right was a small table with benches on either side. Past that was a curtained-off area, probably where they slept. The cottage was simple but well made and cared for; a nice home that could've done without Jax's intrusion.

'Sorry to disturb your evening,' said Jax, getting a nod back.

'You're breaking curfew,' the man said again. 'You shouldn't be out of your homes.'

'Unfortunately, we've not got homes to go to,' said Moiri. 'We're heading south. Jax is from there.'

'Long road, that,' said the man. 'Still, you should've waited till morning. If the Skulls followed you, we'll all end up swinging.'

'We were careful,' said Jax. 'No one saw us coming here.'

'I'll put the baby down and then warm up some stew,' said the woman. 'There's not much left, but it's better than nothing.'

Jax watched her disappear behind the curtain, listened to her make cooing noises and remembered his own wife, Iss, doing the same with Kaine. The memory made him smile and hurt at the same time.

As the woman reappeared and headed over to a shelf with bowls and cups, the man held out his hand. 'I'm Beaden.'

'I'm Moiri.' She shook the man's hand. 'Thank you for taking us in.'

'I told him not to,' said the woman.

'That's Kiln,' said Beaden. 'She doesn't mean it.'

'I do.' Kiln hooked a small pot over the fire. 'Coming here puts us and our baby at risk.'

Moiri held up her hands. 'I know and I'm sorry, but we're desperate. We've been hunting most days, but there's lots of Skulls about these parts and we've been doing our best to avoid them.'

'We used to only see them once in a blue moon,' said Beaden, 'but something's got the bastards worked up. They've been around checking on us most days.' He gestured towards the benches. 'Please sit.'

'We don't want to impose,' said Jax.

'It's fine. Enjoy the fire,' said Beaden. 'The nights are still cold.'

Jax glanced over at Kiln.

'Do you know why there are so many Skulls about?' asked Moiri. 'Has something happened?'

Beaden glanced at his wife. 'I don't go asking questions if I can help it. That leads to—'

They all heard the whistle.

'What was that?' said Beaden, going white.

'I don't know,' lied Jax. He knew. Moiri knew. It was a warning from one of their team. He went to the window and peeked through a gap in the shutters. Skulls were heading their way. At least a dozen on foot and another four or five on a cage wagon. No, there were two wagons. Both already contained prisoners.

Jax had been in one of those wagons himself once. He had no intention of being in one again.

'What is it?' asked Kiln.

'The Egril,' replied Jax, dropping his accent. 'They're coming.'

'Did they follow you here?' said Beaden.

Moiri ignored him. 'How many?'

'Maybe twenty. They've got prisoners, too,' said Jax.

Kiln covered her mouth with her hand. 'They're going to kill us.'

'Don't panic,' said Moiri. 'Go and wait in the back with your baby.'

'Wha— What do you mean?' said Kiln.

'Go in the back,' repeated Moiri. 'We'll deal with the Skulls.'

'By yourself?' said Kiln. 'You're mad.'

'We're not alone,' said Jax.

'I should help you,' said Beaden. 'This is my house.'

'Better you stay out of the way,' said Moiri. 'Look after your family.'

'I ... You need my help ...' Beaden looked to his wife, who shook her head. He dropped his. 'May the Four Gods protect you.'

She led him into the back room.

'Stay here and wait for them to knock on the door or go outside and meet them?' asked Moiri.

'Outside,' said Jax. 'Less risk of these folk getting hurt.'

She nodded. 'Agreed.'

'Will the others be ready to help?'

'They'll be ready.'

Jax took a deep breath. 'Let's do this.'

Moiri opened the front door and they both stepped outside. Gods, she was brave. Confident. A true Shulka.

It was then that Jax realised he wasn't afraid of the enemy anymore. In fact, he was excited. Relishing the prospect of killing some Egril. The last time he'd felt like that was the night of the invasion, back at Gundan. Back when he'd thought himself invincible.

He liked the feeling.

'Stop!' shouted a Skull in bad Jian. 'Do not move. Run, we kill you.' The wagons rolled to a halt fifteen yards away. A lot of scared faces watched from behind the bars of the cages. Men and women of all ages. Children, too. All packed in tight.

'What do you want?' shouted Jax, controlling his anger.

Two Skulls came forwards, spears in hand. 'Get on knees.'

'We haven't done anything.' Jax and Moiri took a couple of steps towards them.

'Get on knees,' screamed the Skull. He lowered the spear and jabbed it at Jax, his partner tight on his heels. No intention to kill, though. They wanted prisoners.

Jax got down on his left knee, let the knife fall into his hand out of sight. Moiri stepped to one side, giving him room. The Skulls always went for the men first. They still hadn't learned that Jian women were just as deadly. Fools. One even stepped in front of Moiri, keeping his eyes on Jax.

'Please,' said Jax. 'Leave us alone. We've done nothing.'

'Don't speak,' said the Skull, lowering his spear. 'Put hand up.' The soldier let go of the spear with one hand and reached for a rope on his belt. Jax knew what was supposed to happen next. He'd been captured before. Tied up before. But he'd been weak then.

He wasn't now.

The moment the Skull was close enough, he pushed up with his right leg and drove his knife straight up into the man's chin, giving it a twist for good measure. Moiri moved a heartbeat later, yanking back the helmet of the Skull near her, exposing his neck before slicing from left to right.

Arrows flew from the sides of the road and more Skulls fell.

Jax drew the scimitar from the man he'd killed, Moiri picked up a spear and they ran towards the remaining Skulls. Another wave of arrows reached the enemy before they did, thinning their ranks further, and then Jax and Moiri were in amongst them. The others ran to join them, screaming war cries, swinging swords.

Jax was stronger than he'd ever been. Even left-handed, he struck with power and precision, attacking the Skulls' weak spots, drawing blood, taking lives. There was no stopping him. No weakness. No mercy.

Moiri and her Shulka were just as efficient, well used to fighting as a team. They struck in pairs, attacking Skulls from opposite sides. Relentless. Shulka. Jax's heart swelled at the sight of them.

The Skulls had no chance. In moments, they were all dead.

By the Gods, it felt good to stand over their fallen bodies, to be victorious again. Jax wasn't even out of breath. He threw his borrowed blade onto the pile of corpses, then looked over at Moiri to share a grin.

'Well done,' she said. 'Well done.'

He nodded, enjoying the moment. It was like the old days, when he'd killed Egril for fun. Then, for a heartbeat, he thought Monsuta would say something to him – tease him, goad him, haunt him – but there was only silence. Even that monster was gone from his head.

'Open up the cages,' said Moiri, clapping her hands. 'Get those people out. Fin, Dev, get people watching the road in case any more Skulls decide to join us, then get a crew clearing the dead away. Dump them in the barn or something out of sight. Stick their wagons in there, too.'

'Yes, Chief,' replied Fin and off they both went.

Beaden and Kiln came out of their house as Moiri's team opened up the wagons. There had to be at least fifty people crammed in the two cages.

'They're our neighbours,' said Beaden, rushing over to a couple as they were helped out of a cage. 'Dahir! Asli! What happened?'

The man had been beaten badly in the face. 'They dragged us from our homes. Shoved us in here.'

The woman clung to the man. 'We were at home, asleep, when they kicked our door in.'

'Why?' asked Beaden. 'Did they give a reason?'

'What do we do now?' interrupted Kiln, her voice shrill. 'More Skulls will come and then they'll kill us.'

Her panic set off the rest of them; crying, shouting, begging for help, demanding answers.

'Everyone!' called out Moiri. 'Peace, everyone. Peace.'

Heads turned her way.

'You're safe for now, but Kiln is right – the Skulls will come back. They will try to take you again.'

'What should we do?' cried out a woman.

'Go back to your homes. Get supplies that will help you live. Leave anything that isn't essential for your survival. Then return here as soon as you can. Bring anyone you know who wasn't captured with you.'

'And then what?' said Kiln. 'People can't stay here.'

'No, they can't,' said Moiri. 'Is there anywhere you can all hide? Build a camp? Perhaps with fresh water nearby?'

'There's a gorge a couple of miles away,' said Dahir. 'It's hard to get to, but not impossible.'

'Then that's where we'll go,' said Moiri. 'If any of you need help bringing your belongings from your homes, my Shulka can help.'

'What about going south? Finding Zorique?' whispered Jax in Moiri's ear.

'We'll leave after we know everyone's safe.'

'But we can't afford to waste time. We need to join the others.'

'Helping these people isn't a waste of time,' said Moiri. 'Don't worry. The war's not going to be over in a few days.'

'Okay,' said Jax, feeling almost breathless. 'A few days.'

Jax watched the villagers set off towards their homes. Deep down he knew Moiri was right, but he still didn't want to wait. More than anything, he knew he had to get to Zorique and join her army. He was a Shulka again and his sword could help change the tide of the war.

He had to reach the queen.

23

Yas

Omason Beach

'You stay alive,' said Yas. 'You hear me? No matter what – come back.'

Hasan nodded. 'I have no intention of dying, I promise you that.'

She glanced over at the army, all lined up and ready to march off along that bloody road. Hasan was taking two hundred and fifty of *her* people with him. People she'd come to know over the months living in the caves, listening to their tales around fires, being amongst their families. More than just their names, she knew all the little things that made each and every one of them who they were. 'I wish you were staying with us. I need you here.'

'You're not still angry at me for trying to warn the Meigorians about the beach?' His eyes flickered over to her tears and, for an instant, she could feel them burning on her cheek. She had no pride in earning the ink, only shame.

'I didn't like you going behind my back. We'd agreed not to say anything.'

'I never agreed, Yas. Warning them was the right thing to do.'

'Fat lot of good it did.' Yas shook her head. 'How many people died on those boats, eh? How many—' She stopped herself. They'd argued enough about it the night before. There was no point going over it again now. Not when he was about to walk out on her. 'I'm not the hero you are, am I? I just want to keep everyone alive.'

'Listen, if it wasn't for you, this little society we built up in the mountains wouldn't have worked. There's people preparing to march who are only alive because of you. And if I were a betting man, I'd say there will be a hell of a lot more before this is over.'

Yas shook her head. 'How did this all end up on my shoulders, eh?'

'Because when the shit came down, you didn't run.'

'Well, maybe I bloody well should have.'

'Can you get word out to the Weeping Men? See if they'll help?'

'I'll see what I can do.' Yas paused. 'The leader is a man named Kenan. I've not met him, but from what I've heard, he don't do favours. He'll want paying.'

'Men like him always do,' said Hasan. 'See if he'll take credit. We'll pay double when this is over.'

'Another reason you'd better stay alive, you big, dumb fool, if I'm going to run up debts with the Weeping Men.'

'I'd never abandon you to that fate.'

'You better not.' Yas pulled him close and kissed him hard. 'I've got used to you by my side.'

Hasan chuckled. 'You just like being warm at night.'

'Yeah? If that was the case, I'd just get another blanket. Blankets don't snore.'

'I don't snore.'

Yas gave him a look that let him know what she thought of that.

'You're a good woman, Yas. Better than I deserve,' said Hasan.

'That's the truth at last.' She sniffed and hoped she'd not start crying some real tears.

'Look after yourself, Yas.' Hasan rubbed her cheek with his thumb, then kissed her with a tenderness that caught her by surprise. 'I'll see you when it's over.'

'I'll hold you to that,' she replied, feeling the tightness in her chest.

Hasan hoisted a bag over his shoulder, then picked up his shield and spear. He looked like he was about to say something else, but all she got was another smile and then he was off down the slope to join the army below.

Another one gone. Gods, she hoped he didn't die like all the rest of the men she … loved. 'You bloody idiot, Yas,' she muttered to herself.

Yas pulled her cloak tighter. It was cold for a spring morning, especially for Kiyosun, but maybe it was just her mood. Maybe it was just her heart.

Back in the old days, she would've loved a chilly day, wandering to the market arm-in-arm with her husband, Rossi, trying to imagine what it was going to be like when they had a child. A magical time, looking back now. Little diamonds of life to be treasured. Moments she'd never have again.

She should return to the cave. Little Ro was there with the other children. Daxam was looking after them all with Timy so she knew her son was fine, but still, she didn't like being away for too long.

She'd just watch for a while longer, see Hasan and the others off. It was the right thing to do, after all. Watch and try not to think about how many would never come back.

Dust filled the air as the army marched off, thousands of feet stomping down that bloody road, following that glowing girl who claimed to be their queen.

Yas had to admit she was no fan of magic. It didn't matter that this time it was on the Jian side. Nothing she'd ever seen would convince her it belonged in the world. Even that girl, shining bright like some star, was an abomination. She was certainly no queen Yas wanted to follow.

And as for Tinnstra? She petrified Yas. If there was anything the war had given her, it was the ability to spot a killer, and Tinnstra was one of those all right. Nothing more dangerous than someone with a cold heart and cold steel. She was leaving, too, thank the Gods.

Then again, maybe Tinnstra and Hasan were the clever ones. Leaving. After all, what was there to stay for?

Kiyosun was a blasted ruin. Yas wasn't even sure there was

any point in rebuilding it. Without any rooftop towers, they'd be gasping for drinking water in a week.

Maybe the rest of them should leave, too. With one last look at the departing soldiers, Yas began the hike back up to the cave. Maybe a fresh start wouldn't be a bad thing.

Eyes followed her as she entered the cave. She could feel them, feel the expectation, the worry, the fear. Many had watched the battle from the mountain and celebrated the victory. They'd said goodbye to their friends and family who were now marching off to fight alongside the Meigorians. But she knew they were all wondering what was going to happen next. They had to be. Yas certainly was.

No one dared approach her, though, as she walked to her corner of the cave. It wasn't just because of the three Weeping Men following close behind her, either. They knew her well enough now to give her time to see her son first. Once that was done, they would ask for permission to speak to her through others before coming over. They treated her with respect, and Yas appreciated that.

She spotted her boy a second before he saw her, his little head popping up and a big grin spreading across his face. By the Gods, it made her heart sing to see that. After everything he'd been through, he still smiled. He still loved her.

'Mama!' Little Ro ran over to her as best he could, looking like he might tumble to the ground at any point. The boy was nearly two and could hardly be called little anymore, but he was still her baby.

Yas scooped him up in her arms and kissed his cheeks. 'I missed you.'

'Miss you,' repeated Ro.

'Were you a good boy for Uncle Daxam?'

'Good boy,' said Ro. 'We played games.'

Yas glanced over at Daxam, who stood a respectful distance away. Timy, his wife, was playing with the other children. Daxam nodded back. All was well. She could tell he had questions, same as everyone else, but he also kept his silence, patient enough to wait until Yas was ready.

Nearly eight hundred of them had made a home in the mountains. Eight hundred out of a city of thousands. Not many when you thought about it. Not many at all. But they'd filled the space and settled down well enough. Yas hadn't wanted to be in charge – she certainly hadn't asked to be – but after everything that had happened, the refugees hadn't given her a choice. It was what it was. All Yas could do was try and make the best of it for everyone.

Was moving everyone now the right idea? They were safe here with solid rock all around them. It was perfect, apart from the fact they couldn't grow any food or raise livestock. They only managed because of the Hanran. Without their help now, staying in the caves might kill them all.

What to do? By the Gods, Hasan had only been gone an hour and she already missed him something bad. At least he was someone she could ask for advice, someone to talk through her ideas with. Who did she have now?

She looked around at her men; killers, smugglers, thieves. But not a mind amongst them.

'Daxam?'

The man couldn't hurry over quick enough. 'Yes, ma'am?'

Yas still grimaced at the moniker. She'd tried to persuade everyone not to call her that, but it was the one order they'd all ignored. 'Can you ask the council to gather tonight after evening meal? I'd like to talk to them about some things. And find Bros for me. I'd like to speak to him now.'

'Will do, ma'am.' And off he ran, just like that. Rossi would have laughed his head off to see her now, making grown men jump at her words. He used to joke she was barely as loud as a mouse.

Times had changed them all. Rossi was dead and Yas had done what she had to in order to stay alive. There was no way she was going to let Little Ro grow up an orphan.

Bros sauntered over a few minutes later. He'd been pretty tight with Raab, the previous leader of the Weeping Men, and he'd been the last to give his fealty to Yas. He had six tears inked on his cheek, but word was he was being modest about his kills. He was a small man but built for trouble, all jutting jaw and large forehead. If she was being honest, Yas didn't like having him around – which made him the perfect candidate to send on an errand.

'You wanted to see me.' Even the man's voice sounded like he wanted to start a fight. His lips barely moved.

'Hasan's gone with the army. They're heading to Aisair to take on the Egril.'

'So?'

'He'd like the Weeping Men to help.'

'I take it you said no.'

'I said I'd ask.'

'We don't do battles.'

'But we like getting paid.'

'Yeah. That we do.'

'I want you to go and see Kenan over in Felix. Tell him about what's going on, about Zorique. Tell him she'll pay for any men he can send to fight.'

'Did you get the money up front?' Gods, the man looked so bloody happy with himself. Talking to Yas like he was her boss and not the other way around. 'I'm not hiking all the way over to the coast for someone who's got no money to pay.'

'Hasan said he'd pay double if Kenan will take payment after we've won.'

The man laughed. It was truly an unpleasant sound. 'No fucking way he'll do that.'

Yas took a deep breath. 'Well, go and ask him bloody nicely, then. Use that charm of yours.'

Bros said nothing, just stared at her, doing his best to intimidate her. Yas stared back. She might not have liked the man, but she damn well wasn't scared of him. She'd dealt with far worse than that little bulldog.

'It'll be a waste of time,' said Bros eventually.

'I'm sure you can work some magic,' said Yas. 'I look forward to hearing some good news when you get back.'

The man nodded, then walked off, probably muttering to himself about what a bitch she was, not that Yas cared. Being nice had only ever got her beaten up and her son near killed. Nice no longer had any place in her world. Anyway, what did it matter if it was a waste of time? By the time Bros got over to Felix over on the east coast and made his way back with nothing but a flea in his ear, Yas would've been spared his company for a good few weeks. That was a win as far as she was concerned.

She spent the next hour or so playing with her boy, singing songs together, clapping hands. He had a giggle that evaporated all the darkness in her heart, and for a short while she could pretend all was normal.

Timy brought food over for them both; bowls of stew with fresh bread, a luxury these days. Ro was still a messy eater, so Yas took her time making sure he got most of the food in his mouth and not all over himself and the ground. Surrounded by hungry people, it wasn't good to waste food, no matter how unintentionally.

The council turned up not long after Yas had finished her last mouthful of bread. Daxam had probably kept them waiting for a signal from Timy before they came over.

There were five of them now where there had been six; another reminder that Hasan was gone. She hoped she wasn't going to miss the steel his words carried.

Yas stood and waved an arm towards her fire. Large stones had been set up in a circle around it to form makeshift seats. Not the most comfortable in the world, but better than the floor. 'Good to see you all.' To her side, Timy scooped up Little Ro and took him over to the other children.

'Evening, Yas,' said Sala as she sat down to Yas's right. She always liked that spot. Made her feel important as she pursed her lips and clasped her hands in her lap. Her grey hair was wound up as tight as she was. Never anything let loose. Harmless enough and well liked by the people she represented.

The same couldn't be said for Sykes from the northern quarter. Despite being a small man, or perhaps because of it, he'd been a bully back in Kiyosun and wasn't much better now. Everything with Sykes was an argument, and many a time Yas had thought about sending a Weeping Man to have a word with him. But Hasan had always talked her out of it. Looking at him now, all scowls and sneering, she was starting to think her way would've been better after all.

Venon, the lad from Cresswell, couldn't have been more different. He was about twenty years younger than Sykes for a start and there wasn't anything he wouldn't do to help. His family had come from the farms, so he knew that part of the world well. He blushed as he took his place, dropping his eyes as he sat down. 'Hello, Miss Yas.'

'Good to see you, Venon,' she replied, and the lad blushed some more.

Mayes, a single mother like Yas, sat next to Venon. She had two kids to look after and didn't take any nonsense from them – or anyone else. She had eyes that saw through any bullshit and she didn't mind telling you when she had. Yas liked her a lot.

Last up was Anan. An old fisherman, Kiyosun born, bred and bled. He'd lost a wife, four sons and only the Gods knew how many grandchildren. Enough to break anyone, but Anan was solid and bore his wounds as well as any. He wasn't one for talking, but when he did, he made a lot of sense. Anan was well respected by everyone and Yas had wanted him to be in charge. His big, white beard was testament to the years behind him, but Anan had just shook his head and pointed at Yas. And that was that. He gave her a nod now as he took his place on the stone to her left.

It wasn't quite like the grand meeting room she used to clean in the Council House, but their little stone circle suited them fine.

'Thanks for coming over,' said Yas. 'You know I hate dragging you away from your family and friends, but I thought it best we not wait before we spoke. I know you and your people all want to know what's going on.'

'That would be bloody nice,' said Sykes. 'It's been four days with naught but rumour and nonsense to go by, and now you're back without any of the Hanran.'

Yas tried to smile but failed miserably. 'I'm sorry for the delay. As you can imagine, there was a lot going on.'

Sykes crossed his arms. 'Hmph.'

'As for the Hanran,' continued Yas, 'they've left with the allied army to help liberate Jia.'

'And left us high and dry,' said Sykes. 'Who's going to protect us now?'

'With any luck, we won't need protecting. The Skulls are gone and won't be coming back.' Yas paused, watching the faces around her. 'So we can start planning to leave here.'

'What? Go back to Kiyosun?' asked Mayes.

'That's one possibility,' said Yas.

'The place is a ruin,' said Sykes. 'Nothing to go back to.'

'But we could rebuild,' said Sala. 'Maybe even give ourselves some room this time – now there's not so many of us.'

'Or we could go somewhere else.' Yas left the suggestion hanging.

'You got somewhere in mind?' asked Mayes.

'Now we've lost our hunters, we need somewhere we can look after ourselves more easily,' said Yas.

'Plenty of fish in that there sea,' said Anan. 'Always done us good up to now.'

'Granted, but there are no towers anymore to catch the rainwater and my old well won't provide enough for all of us,' said Sala. 'We wouldn't last a week.'

'Better we stay here,' said Sykes. 'Train some new hunters.'

Mayes held up a hand. 'Let Yas get a word in, eh? Can't you see she has an idea already?'

Yas managed not to smile. 'Obviously, my first thought was to go back to Kiyosun. It is and always will be our home. But the Skulls left nothing standing and – as Sala says – without the towers, water will be a serious problem. So, I was thinking … what about Arlen's Farm?'

Venon sat up. 'It's got a good river running through it. Apple orchards. Fertile soil.'

'What do we know about bloody farming?' said Sykes with a

wave of his hand. 'As I said, we stay here and send some of the young 'uns out to hunt.'

'Try listening to others for once,' said Mayes. 'Don't you want blue sky above your head again?'

'I want to stay alive more,' he snapped back.

'The facts are we need food and water,' said Yas. 'We have water if we stay here. We can have food if we go back to Kiyosun – once we build some boats and make some nets. If we go to Arlen's Farm, we can have both. From what I've heard there's good fishing in the river, fruit in the trees and hunting to be had in the woods nearby. Maybe some of Arlen's crops will sprout soon enough – or we can plant our own. All in all, it sounds like the best of our options.'

'What about protection?' asked Sala. 'Now the Hanran and Shulka are gone.'

'There's plenty of abandoned weapons down on the beach,' said Yas, 'and enough of us left who can learn how to use them. The Gods know I picked it up easy enough when I had to.'

That killed the debate. Even Anan had to shift in his seat. No one looked at her, but Yas could feel the ink on her cheek as if the tattoos were only freshly done. There was no denying the power in those marks, no matter how hard won they were.

'When should we make the move?' said Mayes eventually.

'We could send a small group down to the farm tomorrow. They could start getting things ready while everyone else packs up their belongings. Perhaps a dozen from each of your communities?'

'It'll be a pleasure, Yas,' said Venon. 'I know just who to ask – and I'll go with them, too.'

'You just want the best spot for yourself,' said Sykes, getting to his feet. 'I'll go with my lot, too. Keep you fair.'

Anan stood up, taking his time to straighten until he towered over the other man. 'We'll all go because it's the right thing to do.'

'Wonderful,' said Yas, rising as well. She gave them a smile then. 'I think you've all made the right decision. This will be a fresh start for everyone.'

Mayes gave her an arched eyebrow back.

Venon jumped up. 'We'll be off at first light, then?'

'That we will,' said Sala. 'Thank you, Yas, for your … guidance.'

'Sleep well, everyone.' Yas kept her smile as they all left and watched them wander back to their neighbourhoods. Sykes was still grumbling, but he had a knack for that. The man could probably find a pot of gold and see the bad side.

Yas was about to turn away and ask Timy to bring Little Ro back when something caught her eye – a woman lurking in the half-shadows. Someone she hadn't seen in a while.

Rena. The sister of Arga, who Yas had poisoned at the Council House. The woman who'd paid the Weeping Men to kill Yas in return. The woman the Weeping Men had offered to kill for Yas. The woman had kept a low profile over the months since Yas had spared her life, and it felt odd to see her again now.

Rena made her way past some fires, went up to Sykes, slipped an arm around his. She looked over then and met Yas's gaze before turning away and walking off with Sykes. Long enough for Yas to know Rena still bore hard feelings towards her. Not surprising, really, but disappointing all the same.

Yas wasn't sure how she felt about Sykes and Rena being together, either. Hopefully it meant nothing, but life had taught Yas the hard way that it likely meant something bad.

Her hand went to the knife hidden in her jacket. A touch of cold steel was always a good way to ward off ill omens.

24

Jax

Lastwin

Jax was up early, eager to be away. He'd not slept much. Every time he closed his eyes, he'd dreamed of being underground, of drowning, all red everywhere, like blood. Each time he'd woken with a start, eyes wide, gasping for air, heart going like a stampeding bull. After the third time, he'd been too scared to go back to sleep.

Now, as the rising sun slowly lightened the sky and the memories of the dream began to fade, he had his kit all packed, ready to go. It was stuff he'd scavenged from the ruins of Gundan, spare clothes, a bedroll, a blanket and a few knives – even his boots had come from a dead body – but it was more than he'd owned in a long time, and like any good soldier, he knew to take care of it all.

Despite urging the villagers to hurry, it had taken most of the previous day for them to pack and then make their way down to the gorge. Some stubborn fools, who'd not been caged by the Skulls, had refused to leave their homes and the Hanran had wasted even more time forcing them out of their houses. They'd moaned and cursed all the way to the gorge, but at least they were alive. The Skulls wouldn't have treated them so kindly.

Jax had been impressed when they finally reached the gorge later that afternoon; fresh water, high cliff walls on three sides, plenty of trees for timber and well hidden. No one would find the place unless they knew exactly where it was. The villagers had settled quick enough and they'd slaughtered one of Beaden's pigs to cook. In many ways, it had been an enjoyable night, despite everything.

The others had gone to sleep after that and Jax had tried. The Gods knew he'd tried, but his mind was elsewhere. Obsessing over the queen, as usual.

He knew Zorique was out there somewhere. She might already be in Jia for all he knew, and he had to find her. It was hard to think of anything else. He felt the call to be by Zorique's side as if it was a message from the Gods themselves. To help her, to stand by her, was why he'd been saved. It was the reason why he'd escaped. This was his redemption, a chance to be a hero again.

The thought was enough to make him want to pick up his bag and set off that very moment, but he had to be patient. Better the others came with him. Better to bring an army with him for Zorique. Especially Moiri. He needed her. There might be people down south who knew how bad he'd been before he got captured, how messed up his mind had become. Moiri could vouch for Jax, tell everyone he'd recovered now. Back to his old self. Better, in fact, if the previous night's fight had been anything to go by. For a one-armed old man, he'd given a pretty good account of himself.

He glanced at the route out of the gorge, all but hidden amongst the tall pine trees, felt the pull again. Day had broken. It was time they were off. Off to Zorique.

Jax needed to do something. Distract himself somehow. Best to be busy. The time would pass quicker that way.

He started gathering some fallen branches, stacking them up in the centre of the camp, ready for a fire. He'd light it himself, but the one hand made it almost impossible to strike a flint. Someone else would be up soon, though, so he'd get it ready for them. It was the right thing to do. A good thing.

Moiri stirred as he passed but didn't wake up, still wrapped in her blanket against the morning chill. Dagen had done well in marrying her. It was no wonder they'd had good Shulka children. She reminded Jax of his own wife, Iss, in many ways. Too many, perhaps. She was a strong woman. A beautiful woman. A good woman to settle down with if things were different.

But they weren't.

There was a war to win for Zorique. His queen.

Movement caught his eye. Beaden and Kiln were up, their baby in Kiln's arms. He watched the two villagers wander down to the gorge's pool and scoop up water to wash their faces. By the Gods, how their life had changed. Jax felt sorry for them, but it could've been worse. If not for Jax, Moiri and the others, all the villagers would be in a Skull prison now – or in Egril.

Images flashed through his mind. Red and horrible, full of monsters, pain, tears. Nothing clear.

'You doing all right, Jax?' It was Remie, his blanket draped over his shoulders, hair tousled.

'I'm fine,' replied Jax.

Remie stretched his back. 'Some spot this, eh?'

Jax nodded. 'It's beautiful.'

'A nice change from Raaku's palace.'

The very mention of the Egril Emperor's name made Jax flinch, like touching a raw wound. 'Yeah, much better.'

'Me and Sarah were talking last night. We were thinking we wouldn't mind staying here – if the locals would let us. Neither of us has a home to go back to.'

'Not a bad idea,' said Jax. He looked over at the path through the pines. He knew where he wanted to be.

'We could all live well here.'

'Not me.'

'Why not? You've been through enough. We all have. We could hide away here until the war's over.'

'I can't do that,' said Jax through gritted teeth. He couldn't even contemplate it. 'I have to find Zorique, help her win this war.'

'But Jax—'

'No,' Jax snapped. A bit too loudly, truth be told, but he wasn't going to hide away again. Not ever.

'It was just a thought,' said Remie, looking hurt.

Jax had to take a deep breath, calm himself. 'I'm sorry. You're right. You and Sarah should stay here – if that's what you want. I ... I just can't. The Gods were looking after me when we escaped, and I have to believe there's a reason I've been given a second chance. I must take it.'

'You've been given a second chance to live – not a second chance to die.'

'It's not that simple. Did you know I was the one trusted to stop the Egril from invading Jia?'

Remie shook his head.

'That ruin back at Gundan was my command,' continued Jax. 'Good soldiers are dead because I failed them. I failed the whole country.' Jax realised he was shaking. He clenched and unclenched his hand, trying to get back control. 'I must repay the debt I owe this country.'

'Then Sarah and me will come with you,' said Remie. 'Because we owe you a debt, too.'

'No. No, you don't.'

'You might think it was the Gods that helped you escape Kagestan, but I know it was you who got us out of there. If you believe in life debts, then we have one of our own.'

Jax shook his head. 'Remie, please. There's no debt. I don't even remember escaping.'

Remie took a step back. 'You don't?'

'No. No, I don't. I don't remember anything about Kagestan – the prison, the escape, you, Sarah – nothing. Believe me, there is no debt.'

'That's just your mind trying to protect you. You don't need to remember that shit. Not now we're here. Back in Jia. Free.'

Jax placed his hand on Remie's shoulder. 'Then repay the debt by staying here. Make a home with Sarah. There's only death down the road I'm on.' He left Remie and headed over to wake Moiri. It was time they were going.

An hour later, they were on their way. Sarah hadn't wanted to stay without Jax, either, so both she and Remie were with them. He'd tried talking them out of it one more time but they had refused, going on about that blasted debt. They were fools, but Jax was glad they'd stayed if he was honest.

The Hanran had also picked up a few more recruits, villagers who wanted to help rather than hide. Dahir and Asli, keen despite their injuries, and a kid named Rin. Only the Gods knew if they'd be any use in a fight, but it felt good to grow in number for once instead of leaving the dead behind.

A few of the villagers had begged the Hanran to stay, but the only way to ensure all of Jia remained safe was to go and fight.

They moved slowly, avoiding the main roads, sticking to the woods and forests, hiding at the first sign of trouble. The Skulls were everywhere, setting up checkpoints on the main roads and stopping and searching everyone who travelled on them.

'Something's got them all riled up,' said Moiri as they edged away from yet another squad of the bastards. 'I've never seen so many out and about at the same time.'

'They're slowing us down,' snarled Jax. 'We should be miles away from here by now.'

'Would you rather be captured again?' asked Moiri.

'No … I just … We need to get south.'

'And to do that, we need to stay free, eh?'

'I know.'

'Should we snatch one?' asked Fin. 'Find out what's going on?'

Moiri mulled it over for a second or two. 'Not yet. It's not worth the risk. Let's keep going west. We head for the coast, towards Chita. That way we circumvent Aisair and avoid the main Skull army before we cut South again.'

'We've already gone too far west as it is,' said Jax. 'We should head straight for the Southern Road. We could move quickly.'

'I don't want another fight with the Skulls yet,' said Moiri. 'For all we know there could be a battalion of them over the next hill.'

'There won't be,' said Jax. 'These are lone patrols. We should kill them and move on, head south.'

'I said no, Jax.' Moiri fixed her eyes on him so he knew not to argue any more. It wasn't good to argue in front of the troops. Jax knew that. Except he knew he had to—

Go to your queen.

He spun on hearing the words. Remie was behind him. 'What did you say?' asked Jax.

'I didn't say anything,' replied Remie, confused.

Jax peered over his shoulder, glancing down the line, at those closest to him, to Sarah, Dev, Jen, Jakota, Cal. None of them were even facing his way. None of them looked like they had spoken.

'What's wrong?' whispered Remie.

'Nothing,' said Jax. 'Just my mind playing tricks on me.'

'Are we good to go now?' asked Moiri.

'Yes,' said Jax, feeling sick, feeling scared.

They headed deeper into the forest. Everyone was alert but Jax was on edge, searching his mind more than his surroundings. Had he heard a voice? *His* voice? Dear Gods, no. Jax must've imagined it. Monsuta was gone. He couldn't be back, not now Jax was close to being a true Shulka again. Not now he had a mission once more. A calling.

The path they followed descended into a valley thick with silver birch. At first, light danced off leaves and tickled the boughs as they passed. On another day, it would be a place of beauty, a journey to be enjoyed. But not that day.

Not with ghosts in every shadow.

Not with a monster on Jax's mind.

Down the path wound, taking them further from the light step by slow step. The only sound was the crunch of their feet through the undergrowth.

Jax tried to concentrate on their surroundings, looking for danger, but his mind was full of memories, taking him back to the Council House, to the prison beneath, to that room, to Monsuta.

Darus Monsuta was one of the Emperor's Chosen, a cruel man with the gift of healing. He'd stopped Jax from dying after Jax had taken the poison Kaine provided and then regrown Jax's missing arm, only to chop it off over and over again. No horror was too much for Monsuta to inflict on Jax. There was nothing he wouldn't do.

He'd broken Jax in that room, mentally and physically, but that wasn't enough for him. No. After Jax had killed Monsuta, the monster took root in his mind, haunting him, tormenting him, tricking him into doing awful things.

But Monsuta was gone. Jax had left him in Raaku's castle, back in Kagestan.

Jax was free.

Wasn't he?

25
Ange

Anjon

Ange could still feel a tingle in her hand from where she'd held the bomb – or she thought she could. Why had she picked it up? Why had she thrown it? It was a stupid thing to do. And yet, if she hadn't, she'd have been dead, most likely. Blown to smithereens. But maybe better that than a slow, painful death. She could still remember how bad Dren got, and she didn't want that. No way.

She glared at Garo's back and hoped he could feel how pissed off she was with him. It was all his fault if she was dying. Why hadn't he thrown the fucking bomb like he said he would? Because he was a chicken shit, that's why.

And yet, here she was, stuck with him on another bloody mission. Ange had obviously pissed someone off to get lumbered with him all the time.

Walking to Anjon had been the last thing she'd wanted to do straight after the battle, but Hasan had asked. 'Tell the Hanran in Anjon that we're coming. Get them ready to fight so we can hit the Skulls from every direction the moment the rest of us arrive,' he'd said. 'There's no one else I trust more.'

How could she say no to that? Of course, he'd then told Garo to go with her, so maybe it wasn't quite the compliment she'd thought it was.

Yas had sent one of her Weeping Men with them, too, a thug called Beni. Apparently, he knew a way into the city that didn't involve wandering through the main gate. He'd stayed about ten yards ahead of them, keeping himself to himself the whole bloody way.

They'd moved quickly down the mountain road that first night, keeping an eye out for Skulls but seeing none. A good job, too, because they'd left their armour with the others, and most of their weapons as well. There was no chance they'd sneak in anywhere the Skulls still controlled if they were dressed up as soldiers.

They'd caught a few hours sleep around dawn, tucked in some bushes. Not that it had done them much good. Ange had woken up feeling even worse than ever. Every part of her body ached from the battle and her eyes stung something rotten. They'd eaten a breakfast of stale bread and sour water in silence, then Beni had them off again.

They'd passed some spots during the day where there'd been fighting at some point, past some craters in the road and a few mounds that could only have been graves, which got a lump going in Ange's throat. Only the Gods knew why. There was probably nowhere in Jia that didn't have such things by now. Not after nine months under Egril boots.

Hopefully not for much longer, though. Not now they had the God girl helping them.

'Hey, Garo.' She kept her voice low, but he heard good enough. Even the Weeping Man glanced back over his shoulder at her.

Garo was all frozen, hand on the hilt of his knife. 'What? What have you seen?'

'Keep walking.' Ange slapped his arm as she passed. 'I haven't seen anything.'

He let out a big sigh of fucking relief. 'So, what then?'

'What d'you think of her?'

'Oh.' Garo started moving again and fell in beside Ange. He didn't need to ask who 'her' was. 'She's pretty damn scary, that's for sure. I mean ... you saw how she wiped those Chosen out, and when she's flying around ...' There was no hiding the awe in his voice. 'But then when you see her walking about, looking normal and everything ...' Garo shrugged. 'She's just a kid.'

'She's looks like she's our age. Maybe a bit older..'

'Oh,' said Garo, sounding surprised. 'Well, I don't feel young. Not after what we've been through. Sometimes I feel older than my old man was ... before.'

'Yeah, well, you're not. We're not.' Ange didn't want to talk about anyone's parents, particularly hers. She didn't need any more memories to get maudlin over. As far as she was concerned, the war had made them all orphans. 'And who's to say what Zorique's gone through? She might feel a hundred years old herself.'

'With power like hers, I bet she's not had to worry about the shit we've dealt with,' said Garo.

Ange shook her head. 'Everyone has shit to deal with. It's the first fucking rule in life.'

'You two,' hissed Beni. 'Shut your holes.'

Ange and Garo didn't say anything after that. Night came and they carried on walking, eyes twitching this way and that, looking for danger. They stopped for more breadcrumbs and a splash of water but none of them wanted to sleep, despite the fact they were all exhausted.

On they went, pushing tired legs and cursing as the road climbed upwards, until both of them needed all the air they could get to reach the top of the rise. Beni waited for them as the road flattened out again. Ange, for one, was bloody glad he'd stopped. She plonked herself down on a rock and stretched out her burning legs.

'That's Anjon down there,' whispered the Weeping Man as Ange took a slug of water from her gourd.

Ange looked past the Weeping Man, amazed she'd not noticed the city by herself, especially as the place was a damn sight bigger than anywhere she had seen up to that point, with big, high walls and even bigger buildings behind them. They made the Council House look like an old ruin. 'How the fuck do they make houses like that?'

'Some of them come from the old days – the magic days,' said Beni. 'Others just took a lot of sweat and money to make. But don't you worry, the place has its slums just like everywhere else.

They called where I grew up the Rats' Den. It's a maze of streets, packed up tight on top of each other.'

'Huh,' said Ange. 'How many live in the city, then?'

Beni shrugged. 'I dunno. Seemed like the whole world when I was a kid. Maybe five, six thousand.'

'Bloody hell. I don't think I've ever seen that many people,' whispered Ange. She took another pull from her gourd. It tasted rank even by Kiyosun standards, but not as bad as some she'd drunk.

'A crowd's a crowd. Nothing special about it.'

Garo crawled over. 'Give us some of your water.'

'Where's yours?' asked Ange.

'I finished it ages back,' replied Garo.

'Why should you have mine?'

'Aw, come on, Ange.'

Ange slapped it into his arms, hard enough that Garo would realise she wasn't happy.

But Garo gave no sign it bothered him. He just started gulping it down, looking as if he was spilling more than he was swallowing.

'Take it easy, Garo,' she said. 'You can have some of it – not all.'

'Sorry.' Garo passed the gourd back. A quick rattle of it told Ange he'd left her nothing but a dribble.

'You selfish fucking—'

'You two lovebirds need to stop squawking,' the Weeping Man interrupted. 'We've a job to do.' He set off without waiting for a reply.

Rest time over, Ange stood up with a sigh. 'Best get it done,' she muttered, more to herself than Garo.

'What if the Skulls are waiting for us?' said Garo, holding on to her arm.

'What if they are? We sneak past them.'

'What if we get caught?'

'By the Gods, Garo. If your nerve's gone, why the fuck did you come all the way here with me? Why didn't you say no when Hasan asked you and saved yourself a bloody long walk?'

'There was no way I was saying no to Hasan.'

Ange took a deep breath. Punching the idiot wouldn't help her. 'Look, we're not going to get caught because we're crafty. That's why Hasan picked us.'

This time it was Garo with a look that suggested she was the mad one.

Ange gave him a smile to make him feel better. 'Don't worry, anyway. I won't let them capture you.'

'No?' His face lit up as if all his problems were solved.

'I'll kill you myself before I let any Skull have that pleasure.' By the Gods, she felt good watching his shoulders slump again. What sort of fucked-up world kept wastes of space like Garo alive, while people like Dren got dusted? It wasn't right.

She set off after Beni, not looking back to see if Garo followed. Not caring, either.

The sky was blood-red by the time they got near enough to the city to realise something was really wrong.

It was the birds that did it. At first, they thought they were Daijaku. Hundreds of them. But, when they moved closer, they could see it was gulls that were filling the sky and squawking away.

'I've only heard them get that excited when the fishing boats come in,' said Garo.

'Feeding time,' said Beni.

'They're all over the city,' said Ange. 'Not at the docks.'

'This doesn't look good,' said Garo.

'Follow me,' said Beni. 'Keep your heads down and try and stay out of sight.' He led them off the road and up the slope, darting between rocks and boulders, following a path that only he knew.

Ange followed, trying to not break her ankle in the dark, all the while watching for Skulls and keeping an eye on the birds. For some reason, she would've been happier if they'd been Daijaku. At least she'd know what was up. Instead, she just had a sense of dread building within her.

'Ground's pretty churned up below,' said Beni, crouched down behind a boulder. 'A lot of horses came this way not long ago. Headed for the Northern Road.'

'You reckon it was the Skulls?' asked Ange.

'Either that or half the city's done a runner.'

Garo chewed his lips. 'I've got a really bad feeling about this.'

Ange and Beni ignored him. They carried on towards Anjon.

A small copse of trees grew along the mountainside facing the city, as dried out and gnarled as the ones around Kiyosun.

'This way,' said Beni.

They moved in a crouch, avoiding snagging branches as best they could, as the city grew larger to the south. They didn't bother to keep quiet – the seagulls were making more than enough noise to drown out the approach of an army – and Ange couldn't help but think they should've come with one instead of just the three of them.

Five hundred yards from the main gates, Ange could see gulls perched all along the city walls and nearby rooftops, while others circled up above before swooping down out of sight. 'No Skulls,' said Ange.

'No,' said Beni.

'That's good, isn't it?' said Garo.

'There should be Skulls on the walls or down by the main gate,' said Beni. 'But there's no one.'

Garo peered towards the city. 'Maybe we can't see them?'

Ange sighed. 'If they were here, the gulls wouldn't be sitting around, shitting on the walls.'

'Someone's written something on the gates in red paint,' said Beni.

Now it was Ange's turn to crank her neck towards the city. 'I can't make out what it says.'

Beni rubbed his face as he stared at the city, his brow all furrowed. 'I think we give up trying to sneak in.'

'Thank the Gods for that,' said Garo. 'Let's rejoin the others.'

Beni started moving again, down the slope and towards the city.

'You're going the wrong way,' Garo called out after him.

Ange slapped him around the back of the head. 'Idiot.'

She followed Beni out of the copse and straight up to the main gates. They were about fifteen feet high and had once been painted black. The sun and the sea and the wind had stripped that back to a mottled grey, but it only made the words stand out more.

Gulls watched them approach, but no guards appeared, no challenge was shouted.

Ange stopped next to Beni about five feet from the gates, Garo on her heels. 'What's it say?'

'Dunno. It's not Jian as far as I can tell – but I've never been that good with words.' The Weeping Man walked up to the gate and touched the paint, then smelled his finger. 'Fuck.'

'What?' asked Ange, not wanting to know.

He glanced over his shoulder. 'It's blood.'

'Shit.' She couldn't even guess how much blood the Skulls would have needed to cover the gates with whatever that message was. It was no friendly greeting, that was for sure.

Beni pushed the gate and it started to move. Ange held her breath as it opened, dreading how bad things were going to be.

26

Tinnstra

Tinnstra marched from Kiyosun with twenty thousand soldiers, give or take. Everyone was on foot because the Daijaku had sunk the Meigorian ships bringing all their horses, and most carried less than half the rations they should've had, again courtesy of the Skulls. It was a disaster of a start, losing half their army in their first battle. The only good thing was that they were all armed to the teeth.

They'd left under the cloak of darkness and marched long and hard through the day. Now dusk approached and soon they'd have to make camp for the night. They'd need their rest, for on the morrow they would all have to fight again.

Zorique and Aasgod led the column, with Tinnstra and Hasan following behind them and Ralasis in the next rank. Zorique had protested at first, wanting her mother beside her, but Tinnstra had insisted. Zorique was the queen and Aasgod the royal advisor, and both had to be seen to lead. Tinnstra was merely a bodyguard.

A bodyguard with one eye.

The Chikara water had helped, clearing up her burned skin in hours, but her eye? There was nothing left to save. Aasgod had given her a mirror so she could see the mess the Chosen had made of it. The sight had turned her stomach. For now, she kept a bandage over her ruined socket, angry at herself for letting it happen in the first place, and worried over how long it would take her to adapt. Right now, she had no sense of depth. Even walking was a challenge.

She hated how it made her feel. It took all her concentration just to put one foot in front of the other. She was supposed to be the best, but now? How was she going to carry out her plan? *Dear Gods, you have a sick sense of humour.*

Still, she was alive, and she would adapt. She always had.

Her bag hung over her shoulder, with her book on Sekanowari, her map and her precious Chikara water. At least they'd survived the landing. From now on, she'd not let them leave her side again. Same as her weapons. She'd replaced her sword with a traditional Shulka blade, and she'd found a short axe that was even better made than the one she'd lost. Added to those were three knives, her brass knuckles and the pouch full of poisoned throwing stars. Quite the weight to carry, but that was what the world demanded. If she didn't have miles to walk each day, she would've added more to the arsenal.

'Tinnstra.'

The voice came from her blind side and Tinnstra had to turn her whole head to see Hasan. There was a lightness about the man that was so very different from the darkness swirling inside Tinnstra. 'Hasan.'

She glimpsed the flash of a smile through Hasan's beard. 'I've got to say it's good to be part of an army again. I've missed it. I've been living in a cave since you left.' He paused, chewing on what he had to say next. 'Hiding.' He almost spat the word out. 'Hiding while the Skulls destroyed my country.'

'You only did what you had to do. There's no shame in that,' said Tinnstra as she stared ahead along the Northern Road.

'Doing what's right, what's necessary, doesn't have to sit well. I'll eat a rat if it means staying alive, but it doesn't mean I'll enjoy it.'

'True.' The Gods knew she'd done far worse to herself.

Hasan filled his chest with air. 'Soft grass to sleep on under a warm, dry sky will be a luxury by the time this is over. A lot of us will be left cold in the dirt on the way. But at least we're doing something, at long last. We have a chance. Thanks to you.'

'I'm not the one who's going to make a difference. That's Zorique. She'll win us this war.'

'If that's so, it's only because you kept her alive. You raised her. You trained her.'

Tinnstra smiled. 'If you follow that logic, then everything's down to you. You got me to leave the cave in Rascan's Bay. Maybe I'd still be there now, crying my eyes out, too scared to move, if not for you.'

'Hard to believe that was you. It seems impossible now,' said Hasan.

'Oh, it was me all right.' The memory still burned.

'You were only what? Nineteen? Twenty? It's been three ... four months since then and look at you now. More than a grown woman, you're bigger than me, armed to the teeth, looking like you're ready to take on the whole Skull army by yourself. It's some change.'

'A necessary one,' replied Tinnstra. 'I've found it's best to be prepared.'

'Can I ask you something?'

'Sure,' replied Tinnstra, feeling far from it.

Hasan took another deep breath. 'What really happened to you? To Zorique? How'd you get so old?'

For a moment, Tinnstra didn't know what to say. When Ralasis had asked her in Layso, she'd brushed him off. It was the easiest way. It was hard enough for her to understand, and she'd lived through it. 'As you said, you do what's necessary.'

Hasan nodded, respecting her lack of an answer. Soldiers always understood.

That only made her feel worse. Hasan needed to know more – deserved to know more. She really did owe him for what he'd said to her that night in the cave, when she'd given up. 'I'm sorry. It's just hard talking about it.'

'That's okay,' said the Shulka.

'No ... it's just ... Aasgod – the other Aasgod – had built a gate in Meigore that was linked to his home in Aisair. We used that to escape from a Chosen. But the gate didn't just transport us from one place to another, it took us from one time to another – a thousand years in the past.'

Hasan stopped dead in his tracks. 'By the Gods.'

Tinnstra gave a small shake of her head. 'No. By that annoying mage.'

'He's that powerful?'

'Not the one I brought back with me. But he will be one day – if he stays alive. As much as it pains me to say so, I hope he reaches his full potential quickly. We're going to need all the help we can get. Until then, he's just as likely to irritate someone to death.'

'I used to be terrified of that man,' said Hasan.

'Most people were. I certainly was.'

'Not Jax. He hated mages and he hated Aasgod most of all. He'd rather have a legion of Shulka than depend on Aasgod. He told him that to his face, too. On more than one occasion.'

'The Egril showed us you need both.'

'Aye. That they did.'

'I'm sorry Jax didn't make it,' said Tinnstra after a moment. The general was someone else she owed a debt to.

'It was probably for the best,' replied Hasan. 'He was never the same after you escaped. Whatever they did to him, it damaged his mind. He even cut his arm off again after the Chosen had grown it back. Killed a couple of our lads, too, who I'd left to keep an eye on him.' Hasan wiped something from the corner of his eye. 'I loved that man.'

'I hope he's found peace with Xin.'

'Do you believe in all that still? The Gods, I mean?'

'I don't know. I've spent most of my life praying to them without it making one damn bit of difference – and yet this is Sekanowari.'

'The Last War. You really think so? I wasn't sure if that was just something you were using to get everyone geed up.'

'It is Sekanowari – and we can't afford to lose. So maybe I'll keep on praying and hope those bastards above and below finally take notice.'

'Huh. Good advice.'

'And of course, I find it helps to make sure you've got steel close to hand.' Tinnstra smiled and patted her sword.

'Spoken like a true Shulka.'

'Thank you. It means a lot for you to say that. Especially after what you saw ... before.'

'I've seen worse than that in my time. Being scared is nothing to be ashamed of. Being scared is part of being human. Only Raaku's monsters feel no fear.'

Tinnstra said nothing. She knew not all monsters were of Raaku's making.

When they camped that night, Tinnstra's head was full of unseen dangers. There was no hiding an army that size, spread along the road. She made sure there were plenty of sentries watching for any sign of Daijaku in the skies. Occasionally, Zorique took to the air, flying up the mountainside, looking for Skulls or other, far nastier, surprises. Even over the stomp of feet on the dry gravel, Tinnstra enjoyed the buzz of chatter that sprang up every time Zorique shot skywards. She glanced back and saw mouths drop and eyes bulge. The awe was contagious, spreading through the ranks.

Let them think she is a God. That's better than a queen. Let her be their light against Raaku's darkness.

'Anjon's over the next rise,' said Hasan as the sun started to set on the second day's march.

'I hope your people have the local Hanran ready for us,' said Tinnstra. 'We need more troops. We need food. We need equipment. After the disaster on the beach, we need to swing things back in our favour – or we've lost before we've even begun.' She grinned. 'And I want to kill a Godsdamn lot of Skulls in the process.'

'Ange and Garo may be young, but they're two of my best,' said Hasan. 'They're just street kids, but I rate them as much as any Shulka.'

'My father would've been outraged if he'd heard you say that. He believed in the purity of families. Of good stock.'

'No offence to your father – he was a great man – but we were wrong about a lot of things back then. Shulka families might've been better, but that was only because we could afford to feed and educate our children and train them to be better. A fisherman doesn't have that luxury. As soon as their children are big and strong enough, their parents have them out working. Knowing thousand-year-old poetry isn't much use when you're worrying about where the next meal's coming from.' Hasan took a slug of water from the skin on his belt. 'This ... shit we've gone through has made me think that back then we didn't really do right by anyone we were supposed to protect. How many people did we execute because they failed to show us enough respect? How many people starved because we taxed every penny they earned? How many people died because we weren't as good as we thought we were?'

'You make us sound as bad as the Skulls,' said Tinnstra.

'Maybe we were back then, in our own way. Certainly, when the time came, we didn't fulfil our duty to keep everyone safe.'

'Tinnstra,' said Zorique, cutting through their conversation. 'Look.'

Someone was running towards them. A tiny figure in the distance, moving quickly.

Only trouble moved that fast.

'Stop the column,' said Tinnstra. 'Stop it now.' Hasan gave the order as Tinnstra searched the skies. No monsters were coming for them – yet. She glanced at the Shulka. 'Make sure everyone's ready to fight.'

'I will,' he replied with a nod.

As the figure drew closer, Tinnstra recognised the runner. 'It's your girl. The one you sent to Anjon.'

Hasan started forwards. 'Ange?'

The girl skidded to a halt, all red-faced and panting. 'Hasan,' she managed to say, before glancing at Zorique. She might've bowed. It was hard to tell. 'Your Majesty.'

'What is it, Ange?' asked Hasan, passing her some water.

'The city, Chief. It's ... it's ...' said Ange.

'How bad?' asked Tinnstra.

'As bad as can be.'

'And the Skulls?' asked Hasan.

Zorique took off before the girl could answer, with a burst of light that had them all covering their eyes. They watched in silence as she burned through the darkness towards Anjon. Only when she disappeared behind the city walls did anyone move.

'The Skulls?' repeated Hasan.

'Long gone,' said Ange.

'Let's catch up with Zorique and see for ourselves,' said Tinnstra.

Hasan ordered the column on as Tinnstra's heart filled with dread.

You knew this was no easy road. Time to find out how hard it's going to be.

27

Zorique

Anjon

Zorique didn't hold anything back as she sped to the city. Let her light shine. Let her enemies see her. Let them know her might. She didn't care if they were waiting for her with all their weapons drawn, she would smite them where they stood.

But the dark city told her no Skulls were waiting for her. She flew lower, saw two people outside the city gates, watching her approach. The other Hanran sent by Hasan.

Zorique passed over the city wall and skimmed along the rooftops, her light reaching the streets below, revealing the citizens all lined up in single file outside their homes. Not moving, not looking her way. So still. All through the city. Outside the grand mansions. Filling the narrow alleys around the docks. Young. Old. Men. Women.

Tears filled her eyes and she screamed into the night. Screamed at the horror. Full of anger. She let the wind take her pain away, promised that she would be strong for the people of Anjon, strong for her warriors following below.

When she couldn't put it off any longer, she landed by the main gates.

The dead watched her land, spikes jutting from mouths, agony frozen in their eyes. The bodies were lined up on either side of the street like some macabre welcoming committee. It looked like every man, woman and child had been impaled. The Skulls had shown no mercy.

There must've been at least two hundred people along either side of the entry road alone. Most had already been pecked at by the gulls and were starting to stink. The birds had gone for the easy takings first; eyes and cheeks and lips. Even now, the foul creatures perched on walls and awnings, watching Zorique and squawking at the disturbance to their feast.

Then she spotted the paper stuck at the base of the first spike, a notice of some sort. She walked over and tore it free.

By order of King Larius, any citizen who aids and abets the invaders of Jia will be declared a traitor and subject to the death penalty.

Larius was her uncle, her blood. Tinnstra said he was the one who betrayed her father, that he was responsible for her family's deaths. But how could he order his own people to be executed in such a horrible way? What sort of monster was he?

She crumpled the paper in her hand, feeling overwhelmed by it all. Fighting Skulls was one thing, but to fight Jians, to fight her only family?

She jumped as a creak cut through the silence. A Weeping Man stuck his head through a gap between the gates. He stared at Zorique, mouth open.

'I can't believe this,' said Zorique. 'What human being could do such a terrible thing?'

'It's bad,' said the man. He walked over to Zorique, followed by a younger man all but hiding behind him, like a frightened child. Zorique let her aura fade just in case he was more scared of her than of the Skulls' atrocities.

'It's horrible,' said Zorique.

'Do you think they were alive when they ... they ...' The young lad couldn't finish the sentence.

'Of course,' said the Weeping Man, his voice cracking.

'Dear Gods,' said Zorique. She didn't know what else to say. 'Did anyone escape?'

'Not that we've seen,' said the Weeping Man.

'What's your name?' she asked.

'Beni, your ... Your Majesty.'

'And yours?' she asked the young lad.

'G ... Garo.' His cheeks flared red and he couldn't meet her eyes.

'I'm Zorique.' She smiled. 'I'm sorry to meet you both under such circumstances.'

'Er ... likewise,' said Beni.

'The Skulls wrote something on the gates outside,' said Garo. 'A message of some sort.'

'Show me,' said Zorique. She followed the men, grateful to be away from the dead of Anjon for a moment.

'Here it is.' Garo pointed to a red scrawl across the main gates. At first, Zorique thought it was paint. But no, of course it wasn't. 'Do you know what it says?'

'It's the Egril prayer to Kage,' said Zorique. '*Blood I will give you, O Great One. Souls I will send you. My body is your weapon. My life, your gift.*'

'Well, they fucking lived up to that,' said Beni. 'Er ... excuse my language.'

'If ever there was a time to swear, this is it,' said Zorique.

'It's just ... I knew people here. I had family here,' said the Weeping Man.

'We'll avenge them all,' said Zorique. 'I promise.'

She waited with the two men until the others arrived. Beni and Garo stayed outside with the army while Zorique took Tinnstra, Aasgod, Ralasis and Hasan in to see the horrors.

Their reaction was no different from hers.

'How could they do such a thing?' said Ralasis.

'Easily – if you think your God will reward you for it,' replied Tinnstra. 'It doesn't get any better than massacring a whole city to earn your eternal rewards in the Great Darkness.'

'Read this,' said Zorique, handing her the notice she'd found.

Tinnstra ran her eyes over it. 'That bastard. He ordered this?'

'Who?' asked Hasan.

'King Larius,' snarled Tinnstra. She passed the notice over. 'I swear I'll kill him before this war is over.'

'Is the rest of the city like this?' asked Ralasis.

Zorique nodded. 'From what I've seen, yes.'

Aasgod couldn't take his eyes off the dead. 'We'll search for survivors and then build pyres for the dead. These poor souls need to be released to Xin's kingdom – we owe them that freedom, at least.'

'It's a waste of time,' said Tinnstra, her voice brutally cold. 'We need to move on.'

'What about the dead?' said Aasgod, aghast. 'We can't leave them like this.'

'Why not? They're past caring,' sneered Tinnstra. 'We can't afford to waste any more time.'

'Waste time?' said the mage. 'How can caring for the dead be a waste of time?'

Tinnstra closed the gap between her and the mage in an instant, her face suddenly an inch from his. 'Anything we do that isn't fighting the enemy is a waste of time. *Not* fighting is what allowed *this* to happen. *You* waiting in Kiyosun for days allowed *this* to happen.'

'By the Gods, you're as bad as they are,' said Aasgod, stepping back.

'Godsdamn right I am. We all should be if we're going to win.'

There was an ugliness to Tinnstra's face that scared Zorique, a need for violence that didn't care what it was taken out on – or whom. 'Enough,' she shouted. 'This is neither the time nor the place.'

Tinnstra stepped back, but she still looked ready to attack Aasgod, given half a chance. 'Yes, My Queen.'

'We'll do as Aasgod said: search for survivors, then send these poor souls to Xin's kingdom.' She looked her mother in the eye. 'We need to be better than our enemies.'

'As you command,' replied Tinnstra, her lip curled in distaste. She turned and stormed off without another word, leaving Zorique feeling so very much alone.

28

Tinnstra

Anjon

Pyres of the dead burned across Anjon, filling the sky with smoke and blotting out the sun. It was a dark start to the day – and a complete waste of time as far as Tinnstra was concerned. The army should have been moving north, not sitting around watching as dead people were being burned. She could already see the effect of the Skulls' atrocities on the army, particularly the Meigorians, who only had limited experience of what an Egril was capable of. *My plans are going so horribly wrong.*

Her hand drifted to the bag at her hip, with its book on Sekanowari. She needed its secrets now more than ever – some clue that would guide her to victory over Raaku – but she'd yet to decipher if that secret was within. Only her gut told her it was worth hanging on to, that she'd eventually see the answers she was looking for.

Her hand slipped inside the bag, not for the book but for the pouch with the Chikara water. She was tempted to drink another vial. She'd not get back her sight, but at least it would make her feel better. Stronger.

But they only had a limited amount from the past and there was no way of getting more. She had to ration the Chikara water for when she really needed it. It was madness to waste it for no reason whatsoever. And Aasgod wouldn't be happy if she had to ask for some of his supply. He'd made that clear enough back as Omason Beach.

She pulled out a vial all the same, feeling better for holding it. It was so small, so fragile. It was hard to believe it was so full of power.

And to think Aasgod suggested she didn't need it – when he, of all people, knew what it could do. Perhaps the mage wanted to take her supply to add to his own. Tinnstra wouldn't put it past him. After all, he was useless without it.

Tinnstra didn't blame him for his greed, if that was the case. If they were to win Sekanowari, they all needed as much power as they could get.

I need it more than anyone else.

She opened the vial and drank, shivering at the taste, feeling its bite as it rushed through her body. Feeling its strength. Feeling all her weakness flee.

The world came alive around her, so vivid and clear, even with her one eye. Suddenly she was aware of everything. She could hear soldiers working in the city, the others waiting outside. She could smell their sweat in the air, taste their fear, their hope. Thousands of voices buzzed around her: orders, complaints, questions, answers, gossip, prayers, greetings and grumblings.

By the Gods. It was almost too much. Tinnstra gritted her teeth, clenched her fists, tried to hold her body together. Her soul.

She shouldn't have taken it. She'd drunk too much. Not enough.

No, it was just the rush. She knew that. She craved it, after all. Needed that magic to fix her, make her stronger. She didn't fear it. Tinnstra feared nothing. Not now. Not ever again. No, she could control it. She had to.

Magic flared in her mind. So bright. Agony. Pain. Zorique.

She shielded her eye as Zorique landed beside her. Her daughter's skin blazed from within, warm and humming with energy. Colours swirled around Zorique like Tinnstra had never seen before – flickers of light that danced across her armour and sparked in her eyes before drifting into the sky. Tinnstra blinked, knew it was the Chikara water working through her, making her see things, but it was all so real, so pure, so beautiful, so painful.

Tinnstra knew she should say something, but words failed her, mesmerised as she was.

'You're staring,' said Zorique, with a smile that lit up the world.

It took all of Tinnstra's willpower to answer. 'I am?'

'You are.'

'How are you feeling?'

Zorique glanced back at the city. 'I'll be better when we've left here.'

If you'd listened to me, we'd already be gone.

'You did the right thing staying,' Tinnstra said instead, the words like ash on her tongue.

'I'm glad you feel that way,' said Zorique, suddenly looking a hundred years younger. 'Because I need to ask you to do something.'

'Anything.'

'I need you to stop arguing with Aasgod, especially when we're with the others. It's not doing anyone any good.'

It took Tinnstra a moment to register what Zorique had asked. Anger rose within her. 'Is he going to stop being an idiot?'

'He's not an idiot.'

'Really?'

'Mother – he's a good man, doing his best. Like all of us.'

Tinnstra had to close her eye. The Chikara water was making it hard to concentrate. Zorique's magic was making it too painful to think. *Why must we have this conversation now?*

'Fine. As you wish.' Better to agree than argue.

'Are you feeling all right?' asked Zorique.

'I'm fine,' replied Tinnstra, but she knew that wasn't enough of an answer. 'I'm still getting used to having one eye. It hurts.'

'I'm sorry.'

'What are you sorry for? It wasn't your fault.'

'I should've stopped the Chosen before he had a chance to hurt you.'

'You had enough to worry about.'

'I know, but—'

'There's no buts,' said Tinnstra. 'It's my job to protect you, not the other way around. It's always been that way and it isn't going to change now – no matter how powerful you are.'

'I know, but ... I don't want to lose you.'

'Nor I you.'

Zorique slipped her hand into Tinnstra's, just like she used to do as a child. A precious moment between mother and daughter. Then light crackled around their hands as Zorique's magic reacted to Tinnstra's touch. The light travelled up Tinnstra's arm almost with a hunger, following the water in her veins, burning as it moved, forcing Tinnstra to let go, breaking the connection.

Zorique gave her a look. Hurt, baffled.

'This isn't the time,' said Tinnstra, a little too harshly.

'Fine.'

Tinnstra hated hearing so much pain in such a small word, hated herself even more. She'd turned herself into a weapon, but she couldn't control who she hurt as a result. 'I'm sorry,' she said. 'I'm on edge. My eye. This war. Everything.'

'You don't have to carry the weight of the world on your shoulders,' said Zorique. 'You don't have to carry me. Not this time.'

Tinnstra glanced at her daughter, all raging magic in a tempest of colour. 'It's you who carries the world.'

A sad smile flickered over Zorique's lips. 'That's why I need you. And Aasgod and everyone else. I don't think any of us can win this on our own. We can't fight amongst ourselves.'

It hurt hearing Aasgod's name in the same breath as hers. 'None of us is as strong as all of us,' said Tinnstra. 'That was one of my father's favourite expressions.'

'Do you miss your father?'

'Some days he doesn't even cross my mind. Then there are times when I feel his loss like a hole in my heart.' Tinnstra had to take a breath. Her memories swirled around her mind, riding the Chikara water, making some so vivid it was as if they were all happening right then. She had to concentrate on her words. 'My relationship with my father was ... complicated.'

'In what way?'

'I never felt as if I was who he wanted me to be. I was just good at pretending – at being brave, at being a good Shulka, a good daughter, at being someone he could be proud of.'

'He'd be proud of you now.'

'Would he?' Tinnstra wasn't so sure. She couldn't help but think Grim Dagen would be making a much better job of things than she was. Grim Dagen wouldn't need Chikara water to be strong.

'He would. I am.'

If only you knew me. Truly knew me. 'You don't have to be.'

'But you're my family. The only family I have. I don't even remember what my father was like, let alone his favourite expressions.'

'He was a good man, too,' replied Tinnstra. 'His heart was with his people.'

'They called him Cariin the Gentle, didn't they?'

'Aye, they did. He liked his music and the arts, and they're strange things for a Shulka to understand. He wanted to build a peace that would last a thousand years.'

'Maybe one day I can do that,' said Zorique.

'He would've liked that. It would be a fitting legacy.'

Zorique smiled. 'We just need to kill all the Skulls first.'

'That we do,' said Tinnstra. *Every last one of them.*

Another spike of pain shot through Tinnstra's mind, one she knew only too well. She turned to see Aasgod approaching.

'Your Majesty.' The mage bowed. 'Tinnstra.' A nod for her.

'Is all well?' asked Zorique.

'Yes, Your Majesty,' replied Aasgod. 'Hasan has informed me that the last of the pyres will be lit in the next hour, and he hopes we can be away this afternoon.'

'Thank you, Aasgod,' said Zorique. 'What would I do without you?'

Tinnstra stopped herself from answering that question.

Zorique headed back into the city, and when Tinnstra went to follow, Aasgod stopped her.

'Yes?' she asked.

The mage assessed her through narrowed eyes. 'Have you taken more Chikara water?'

'No,' she spat, the lie obvious.

'You need to be careful,' said Aasgod. 'We can't afford for you to become ever more dependent on the water.'

'I'm not dependent on it. I've not drunk any since yesterday.'

'And you've still got all your vials?'

'Are you calling me a liar?' Tinnstra stepped towards the mage, fists clenched, forgetting Zorique's request, happy to let her anger grow.

'No, I'm not.' Aasgod stood his ground, but she could see it was taking all his willpower to do so.

'Good.'

'We need to be at our best for Zorique, that's all.'

Tinnstra shook her head. 'Don't you think I, of all people, know that?'

Aasgod swallowed his reply and shook his head instead. 'I'll let you get on.'

Tinnstra watched him scuttle after Zorique. He might not have been turning into the feared mage she knew, but he was quickly mastering how to hang around royalty.

By the Gods, she wanted to smash something. Hurt someone. The last thing she was willing to do was wait around for hours more.

She found Hasan easily enough, watching bodies being thrown onto a pyre. A pile of steel spikes lay nearby, stained with dried blood. *How long did it take the Skulls to murder a whole city? There really is no limit to their depravity.*

The Shulka leader saluted her as she approached. 'Grim work.'

'I was thinking about the Skulls,' said Tinnstra. 'The ones who did this.'

'The bastards.'

'When do you think they left Anjon?'

'Maybe a day before we got here. No more than that.'

'Any thoughts on where they've gone?'

Hasan spat on the ground. 'Best case? They're retreating north. Worst case? They're hiding somewhere, waiting to ambush us.'

'Knowing the Skulls, I'd go with the worst-case scenario.'

'Yeah, me, too. I have some crews watching the roads so we

don't get caught unawares if they decide to come back.' Hasan waved towards the bodies.

'There're better places to attack us than here,' said Tinnstra. 'There's no advantage in street fighting.'

'Not for them, anyway.'

Tinnstra watched the smoke drift up into the sky. 'That smoke will be visible from miles away. They'll know when we're on the move again.'

'You got a plan?'

'Give me a small crew. We'll scout ahead. See what's what.'

'Looking for trouble?'

'Better safe than sorry.'

'You find any, you'll come back for the rest of us before you wade in. Okay?'

'Of course,' she lied. 'Wouldn't dream of doing anything different.'

'How many bodies do you want to take on this stroll?'

Tinnstra shrugged. 'I don't know. Ten? Seems a good number.'

Hasan rubbed his beard. 'Leave it with me. Come back in half an hour.'

'Just make sure they're a vicious crew, eh?'

'Oh, I think we've got a few here that'll suit you.' Hasan gave her a look then, part bemused, part impressed. 'What happened to the scared girl I found in that cave?'

Tinnstra gave him a look back. 'Nothing good.'

Part III

Bad Choices

29

Yas

Arlen's Farm

Yas was happy for once as she walked through the new village at Arlen's Farm, holding Little Ro's hand. Two Weeping Men, Dean and Sorin, followed on behind, more out of habit than necessity, making sure no harm came to her, either by accident or by design. She felt as safe as she ever had, but that didn't mean she was going to grow careless.

The refugees from Kiyosun had left the caves the day after the council meeting and moved en masse down to the farm. Temporary shelters had gone up almost instantly and now, two days later, real homes were starting to take shape. It was amazing to see the speed at which they were being built – but then again, everyone had had good practice at it these past few months. Hopefully – and Gods willing – this would be the last time.

She nodded and said hello to people as she passed, noting that they all bowed deeper and longer in return. It was to be expected. They were all very grateful to be out of the caves. No doubt that gratitude was enhanced by the Weeping Men behind her, but still, it was nice to see.

The sounds of hammers, saws and axes at work filled the air while children giggled and laughed, happy to have blue skies to play under and soft grass to run on.

The water was clean, and the hunters had found enough game in the nearby forest to keep everyone relatively well fed for now.

Even Sykes had yet to find the need to complain about anything. All in all, things were about as good as they got.

Of course, in the distance, towards the beach, smoke marred the perfect blue. Another body being burned. Another death.

She'd left the hospital tents where they were, down by the sea, instead of moving them with the refugees. She told everyone it was for practical reasons – the farm was too far away to transport the grievously injured – but the truth was the farm was for new beginnings, not painful reminders of what they'd all endured. Everyone had seen far too much death to want to see any more.

The fact of the matter was ... it was better for all concerned that the Meigorians stayed where they were, until they recovered or died. And, judging by the near continuous smoke, more were on their way to Xin than not.

Yes, best they stay away and not come to the farm. Cold-hearted, perhaps, but practical – an approach Yas found worked for most of the problems her community faced. She was grateful to the foreign soldiers for what they had done, but that didn't mean she could spare precious time for needless ceremonies to see off their dead. It wasn't as if she had a priest to officiate and she certainly wasn't going to stand in for one.

Once the injured were better, they could join her new community if they wished to stay in Jia. For Yas wanted Arlen's Farm to be a place of hope for what tomorrow could bring, and that meant a world where all were welcome, irrespective of family, country or religion. In fact, she'd had quite enough of Gods. Too many had died in their name and she hadn't seen any sign they gave a damn about their sacrifice.

And, as the Gods were no good, she wanted to make sure her community could look after itself, especially now that Hasan had gone with all the Shulka and anyone worth a damn with a sword or a spear. That's why the first thing she'd done was set up watch posts covering every approach to the farm, and she'd made sure everyone knew to retreat to the caves at the first sign of trouble.

But trouble came in all forms, as Yas well knew. The sad fact was that often the worst of it didn't come dressed in Skull armour.

As if to prove that point, Mayes was standing at the corner of what was going to be her house, watching Yas walk towards her, clearly with something on her mind.

'Everything okay?' asked Yas, even though she didn't really want to know.

'Wouldn't mind a word,' replied Mayes. 'In private, if possible.'

'I don't think Little Ro's going to repeat anything you have to say,' said Yas. 'He's good at minding his own business.'

Mayes glanced over Yas's shoulder. 'I was referring to your ... friends.'

'Sure,' said Yas with a smile and turned to Dean and Sorin. 'Wait here. Keep your eyes open.'

Still holding Little Ro's hand, Yas walked with Mayes. 'So ... what's got you worried?'

'Thought you'd want to know that Sykes is up to no good again.'

Yas nearly laughed. 'When isn't he? That man could start a fight in an empty room. He's nothing to worry about, I promise you that.'

'He's not as dumb as he looks. He's been getting a fair few people stirred up.'

'What about?'

'You, of course.'

'Nothing new, then.'

'I don't know.' Mayes looked around. 'He has a few people helping him out this time. People with more than enough bad things to say about you.'

Yas sighed. 'Like what?'

'That you were a collaborator, selling out your neighbours.'

'That's a new one on me, at least,' said Yas. 'Total nonsense, of course.'

Mayes nodded. 'Of course. Then there's the one about you poisoning the Jians who worked at the Council House.'

'Now, I forget – were they collaborators working for the Skulls or freedom fighters about to kill the Skulls?' Yas couldn't help the sarcasm in her voice. She was sick to the eye teeth of all this nonsense.

'They were people who have friends and family still alive and building homes here.'

227

Yas stopped walking and cracked her neck from side to side. 'Look, I like you, Mayes. I really do. I appreciate your straight talk and I'm grateful for the heads-up about this. But do me a favour, eh?'

'Sure, Yas.' The woman shifted her feet.

'I'm going to tell you the truth of things and you can, with my blessing, tell everybody else, because I'm not repeating myself again. First, I was not a collaborator. In fact, I was in the Hanran when a lot of these good people were hiding under their beds. Second, I only worked at the Council House because I was in the Hanran. I – no one else – was the lucky sod spying on the Skulls. For that pleasure, I got beaten up and near damn well killed. Now, because of that beating and near-killing, I wasn't at the Council House when everyone else died. But that don't mean I was the one who murdered them.' Yas leaned in closer to Mayes and made her voice go cold. 'And third, the most important fact of the lot. The last time those rumours went around, someone looking for vengeance paid the Weeping Men to kill me. They failed, and that was the day I earned my tears. That was also the day I swore I'd kill anyone dumb enough to spoil my good name. Now, I suggest you tell anyone who needs telling of that oath because, as the Gods were my witness then, I intend to keep it now.'

Mayes stepped back, dropping her eyes. 'Of course I'll put the word out, Yas. Be my pleasure.'

'I know you will.' Yas squeezed Mayes' shoulder. 'I'm counting on you.'

'Don't worry.' The woman was shaking, which Yas felt bad about. But it needed doing.

Yas gave her a smile to make up for it. 'Good chatting with you, Mayes. Look after yourself, eh?' She glanced down at Little Ro. 'Come on, love, let's go home. Get you something to eat?'

'I am hungry,' said Little Ro, bless his heart.

Yas led him back the way they'd come, back towards her men. She stopped by Sorin. 'Can you do me a favour later?'

'My pleasure, Miss Yas,' replied the Weeping Man.

'Go and see Sykes when he's alone. Have a word. Make it clear it's not good to tell lies about people.'

Sorin nodded. 'No problem.'

And Yas had no doubt that was true. Sorin had eight tears on his cheek. The man knew how to get things done.

30

Tinnstra

Anjon

Tinnstra had asked for a vicious crew and by the looks of them, at least, Hasan hadn't disappointed her. They were assembled by the city gates, right next to the bloody message left by the Egril. Six men, four women, Shulka all. They wore light armour – good for moving fast and keeping out of sight – but they'd not cut back on their weapons. They looked ready to fight the Skull army all by themselves.

'The Skulls left here two days ago, far as we can tell,' she said as they ran a last-minute check of their gear. 'That's two days to dig in somewhere and prepare a nasty surprise for when our little army leaves here in a few hours. Our job is to make sure that doesn't happen.'

Tinnstra got nods back. Not a talkative group. That was good, too.

'Any of you know the land well?' she asked.

'Aye,' said one, an older man named Tavis. 'I've been hunting the trails around here since I was a lad. There's a few places I can think of that would be good for an ambush. Where's Hasan planning to camp tonight?'

Tinnstra pulled out the hastily drawn map she'd been given and pointed to a spot about ten miles north of Anjon, where a small river cut across the road to the sea. 'Here, all being well.'

Tavis nodded. 'A good spot. Great visibility for miles in every direction. Easy to defend.'

'Where do you think the Skulls are going to be waiting?' asked Tinnstra.

Tavis followed the road with his finger. 'The road turns inland here and away from the mountains. It cuts through a valley, narrow, high rock walls on both sides. Only one way in, one way out. If I wanted to kill a lot of people, it'd be here. You wouldn't even need many soldiers.'

'How far is that from here?'

'Our army will reach it late tomorrow morning.'

Tinnstra nodded. 'Sounds perfect.'

'It is,' said Tavis.

'Okay. You lead, but find us a path where we won't be spotted – just in case the Skulls have left people hidden in the mountains waiting for us. I'd rather we took them by surprise instead of the other way around.'

'And when we do?' asked a woman, Nika. Tall and wiry, her hair shorn to the scalp.

'Depends where we find them and how many,' said Tinnstra. 'If it's their army, our orders are to come back and tell our comrades what to expect.' She paused. It was time to find out if they really were her kind of people. 'Of course, depending on how many of them there are, that might not be necessary. Might be there won't be time to run for help.'

'We can look after ourselves,' said a man called Sadir, from Clan Mizu. Two short swords were strapped across his back.

'It'd be good to find some justice out there, General,' said Nika.

'I'd be happy with some good old-fashioned revenge,' said another.

Tinnstra grinned. They certainly were her people. 'Don't worry. I won't object if you want to send some souls back to Kage if the opportunity arises. Far as I'm concerned, any scouts we find are fair game. Sound good?'

'Very much so,' said Sadir.

'Good,' said Tinnstra. 'Let's move out.'

Tavis took them north into the mountains, down half-forgotten paths, through hidden gullies and across sun-baked clearings, before cutting to the east along trails that would have made a goat think twice and then drifting back to check the road from various vantage points. Only the Gods knew what game Tavis used to hunt in this wild land, but Tinnstra was glad she had him with her. Coarse grass grew in patches along narrow streams, while gnarled trees stood watch as they clambered on. A cool breeze followed them from the ocean, taking the edge off the sun's rays, but it was still hard going, especially for Tinnstra with her one eye. She had to think twice about every footfall, every handhold, slowly getting the distances right, adjusting to her handicap.

Walking's one thing, fighting another. She shook the thought away. She would be ready.

It was easy to keep track of where Anjon was, though. A glance over her shoulder was enough to spot the drifting smoke, and each time Tinnstra checked, she became more convinced the Skulls would be watching, too – but from where?

She reached out with her mind, trying to sense any magic users. A Chosen would flare up long before they were within visual distance, but there was nothing. How she longed for that spike of pain in her head or the sight of some white armour hidden amongst the rocks.

But they found no sign of the enemy, except when they checked the main road, which was all churned up by the Skulls' passing.

'How many do you think came this way?' she asked Tavis.

'Hard to say. Maybe two, three thousand. Maybe five or six. Anjon was a big town. Bigger than Kiyosun. Stands to reason they'd have a bigger garrison to look after it.'

They stopped mid-afternoon to drink and rest, hidden in a small depression. They sat with their backs to the rock, enjoying the cool shadows.

'The army should be leaving Anjon soon,' said Tinnstra. Her hand rested on her bag and she was painfully aware of the Chikara water within. *Not the time or the place for that. Later. Perhaps.*

'And no sign of any Skulls,' said Dale, a Shulka with a broken nose. He dug at the dirt around his feet with a hunting knife.

'Yet,' said Nika.

'Oh, they're out there. Somewhere,' said Tinnstra. She turned to Tavis. 'Where's Hasan's proposed campsite from here?'

'About a mile or so away,' said the scout.

'And if I told you to watch it without being seen, where would you go?'

Tavis took a few moments to think about it. 'There's a two- or three-foot slope down to the riverbed. A few men could hide there well enough, amongst the tall grass.'

'Can you see the smoke from Anjon from there?'

'I'm not sure,' said Tavis. 'I'd stay in the hills for that. Watch the road from one of the spurs, then move out the moment I saw the army.'

'Take us there first,' said Tinnstra. 'Then the river.' *And by the Gods, I hope I get to kill something.*

They found the Skulls in the hills, near the end of the mountain range. Four of them sheltering under an awning, their eyes fixed on the Northern Road. They didn't hear Tinnstra, Nika, Tavis and Dale come up behind them. In fact, three of them were dead before they even knew they were in trouble. The fourth had Tinnstra's knife tight against his throat.

'Hello,' she whispered in Egril. 'Fancy finding you here.' She pulled him back from the edge of the spur, down into the shadows of the rock face. 'You got any other friends nearby?'

'N ... no.'

Tinnstra enjoyed hearing the fear in the man's voice. 'You're not lying to me, are you?'

'There are more scouts, but not close. We have a mirror ... to signal each other.' The man pointed with his boot, back to where he'd been standing. Sure enough, there was a small hand-sized piece of silver glass.

'How far away are the next scouts?'

'Three miles. By the river.'

Tinnstra glanced at Tavis and translated what the Skull had said. He gave her a nod back.

'And how many in your main group, the one waiting in the valley?' she asked.

'Just under five thousand,' said the Egril.

'Any Chosen? Any monsters?'

A pause. 'No.'

Tinnstra ripped the man's helmet from his head and threw it over the edge. His mask followed. She spun him around then and straddled him, so he could see her, so she could see him. The soldier was young, like she'd been once. Blue eyes shining bright, unsure whether to look at her or at her knife, full of fear, like she used to feel. She cut away the armour from his arms and then pressed her knife point into the flesh under his eye. She wanted his attention on her. 'You're a pretty boy, aren't you?'

'Please, my face ... only Kage may see it.'

'Think of me as him,' said Tinnstra. 'I even have only one eye.'

'That's ... blasphemy.'

'Maybe.' Tinnstra shrugged. 'What's your name?'

'Bastion.'

'Well, Bastion, as I look on your face and you look on mine, now's the time to tell me the truth. Any Chosen? Any monsters?'

'No.'

Tinnstra stabbed him in the biceps, twisted for good measure and left the knife embedded there. She smothered the man's scream with her other hand. 'Any Chosen? Any monsters?' she asked again.

'No,' he said when she removed her hand.

She covered his mouth an instant before she dragged her knife down, slicing the man's arm all the way to the elbow, pulling the blade free when she hit bone. The man passed out, blood pouring all over the stone.

'General? Is he ...' asked Dale.

'Dead? No, not yet.' She slapped the Skull's face, switched back to Egril. 'Wakey-wakey.'

The Skull's eyes fluttered open, slowly focusing on Tinnstra, then popping wide.

Tinnstra smiled. 'Any Chosen? Any monsters?'

The man nodded. 'One Chosen. A dozen Daijaku.'

'What's the Chosen's power?'

'Fire. She can control fire.'

Of course. I should've expected that. They're trying to take one of Zorique's weapons away from her.

'Say hello to Kage for me. Tell him Tinnstra sent you.'

'Wai—'

Tinnstra rammed the knife into his temple, shutting him up. The Egril barely twitched. She stood, not caring. 'Collect the helmets. It's time we left a few messages of our own.'

'What about the bodies?' asked Nika.

'Leave them. The animals and the birds all have to eat.' Tinnstra set off to rejoin the others, happy again. 'Hurry up,' she called over her shoulder. 'We've plenty more work to do.'

31

Zorique

Anjon

Zorique is coming.

Three words written on a wall, not with blood like the Egril had used but in blue paint instead. Not recently done, either. The Hanran had spread the word as Tinnstra had wanted, and someone in Anjon had believed help was on its way.

She ran her fingers through her hair. Was that why the city died? Or was it because the Egril lost the battle for Kiyosun? Either way, Zorique couldn't help but feel responsible.

The streets were empty now, the stakes removed and the last of the bodies placed on the pyres, but she could still feel their presence. If she closed her eyes, she could still see the people's faces. Gods, how she wished to be far away. Far away from the ghosts.

'It was never going to be easy,' said Aasgod from behind her.

She didn't turn but continued to stare at the words, written in hope by someone now dead. 'I didn't think it was going to be this difficult. So many people have died already and we haven't achieved *anything*.'

Aasgod moved beside her. 'We are here. We won our first battle. We are still alive to fight on.'

'That doesn't feel like much to be proud of.'

'The alternative is much worse.'

'I know. I just didn't think it would be … that it would hurt so much.' She looked at him then, eyes wet. 'It's as if I can feel every death.'

Aasgod put his hands on her shoulders. 'That's good. Life is precious. We must never forget that or take it for granted. The men and women outside may be willing to sacrifice everything for you, but that is a gift we should not accept unless there is no other option.'

'I don't think Tinnstra feels the same way.'

'But you are not her. Tinnstra has her own battles to fight. Concentrate on what lies ahead of you.'

'I don't want anyone else to die.'

'But they will. On both sides. You can't stop that from happening.'

'I should be able to! Isn't that why you created me? To stop all this?'

Aasgod stepped back as if slapped. 'That wasn't me. I mean … It was, but …'

Zorique rubbed her face. 'I know. I know. I'm sorry.'

'You certainly don't have to apologise, either,' said Aasgod. 'Yes, you have great powers, but despite what some of your soldiers may be saying, you are not a God. You are as human as the rest of us. And I'm glad of that.'

'Someone once said to me that to be a queen, all I had to do was pretend to be one. Everyone thought it was good advice. Now I'm not so sure. It feels like I've been pretending all my life. I feel like a fraud. An impostor.'

'There's nothing wrong with doubt or fear. We should question what we do. We should worry that things may go wrong. That's how we prepare. That's how we push ourselves to be better than we are.' Aasgod smiled. 'And believe me, you're no fake. Be proud of who you are.'

'I thought I could win this war with a flick of my fingers.' She shook her head. Such stupid thoughts. Childish.

'You are only human. You can only do your best.'

'What if it's not good enough?'

'It will be. *You* will be.'

'Thank you,' said Zorique. 'I'm glad you're here.'

'So am I, Your Majesty. So am I.' Aasgod looked around the

empty streets. 'Shall we join Hasan and the others? The army is ready to leave.'

Zorique sighed. 'A minute ago, I couldn't wait to leave, but now? I don't want to go. More death waits for us.'

'Death calls across Jia, no matter what we do.'

Zorique took a deep breath, filling her lungs, straightened her back and placed her helm on her head. She let her magic flow around her as she picked up her shield and spear, enjoying the glow it created, knowing the effect it would have on the others, giving her something to hide behind. It was time to play the part once more.

Time to be a queen. Pretend to be a God?

She wished she was better at it, that it felt more natural, but she still felt like the girl with three mothers, used to being told what to do and how to act – except now Anama and Maiza were dead and Tinnstra was ... only the Gods knew where.

Oh, how she wished they were all by her side, like they were meant to be, like she needed them to be. Aasgod was wonderful, full of calm reassurance, but he wasn't *them*.

She walked out through the city gates to her waiting army. Those nearest her dropped to one knee, heads bowed, and she shone brighter because of it. It wasn't intentional and a part of her thought it was more from embarrassment than pleasure. Another part of her didn't want it. If she could, she'd rather have been just Zorique, a girl without title or powers. Just ordinary like everyone else. Silly dreams, best left in the past with a farmer's son.

'Please rise,' she said.

Hasan was the first to stand, yet he bowed once more. 'Your Majesty, we're ready to move.' He indicated for her to walk on, past the lines of soldiers.

'Thank you, Hasan,' she replied. The Shulka stayed one or two steps behind her, and Aasgod was two steps behind Hasan. Silently, she cursed them both – she'd rather they were both beside her, sheltering her from the eyes that watched from the ranks. She could only imagine what the soldiers thought, what their whispers said. Nothing good, certainly. Disappointment, perhaps. Doubt. Regret. An army needed strength in leadership. Confidence. Not a girl playing make-believe as a queen, dressed up like a soldier.

All she could do was fix her eyes on the road ahead, keep her back straight and march like Maiza had taught her. The old Shulka would have disapproved of her light tricks, but Anama would've smiled. She had been an illusionist after all.

Zorique took her place in the centre of the army and then, with a series of shouted orders, Hasan had the warriors moving.

'Well done, Your Majesty,' whispered Aasgod.

'All I did was walk,' she replied.

Hasan had told her that the army could comfortably walk three miles an hour all day and still be fresh enough to fight at the end of it. They could also double that speed for a few hours if they had to, but for now he kept the pace slow and steady.

It was hard going all the same. The sun beat down and the marching feet stirred up dirt and dust. It got in Zorique's eyes and irritated her throat, but water was rationed so she did her best to ignore it. And even amongst all that, she could feel the eyes on her, could hear the whispers. Zorique knew it was only natural and her actions invited it, but she hated it all the same. She didn't want to be worshipped.

After an hour or so, though, she'd had enough. Her eyes were constantly drawn to the blue sky above. She told herself she was watching for the Egril, that the enemy were out there some-where, and she needed to make sure her army was safe. But if she was being honest with herself, that was a lie.

The sky promised freedom.

She turned to Aasgod. 'I'm going to fly for a while. Make sure there are no surprises waiting for anyone.'

'As you wish, Your Majesty,' replied the mage.

'*Tobo*.' She took off at speed, far faster than was necessary, but she was eager to be elsewhere. Wind whipped past her face, cold and sharp, clearing her mind and blowing away the smell of Anjon's pyres.

She went straight up – a thousand feet, two thousand, three thousand, four. Too far to be able to see what was happening below, too far for her to be truly seen. She was just a spark above.

Zorique looked north, past the mountains, over the rolling hills, to where the grass grew and forests stretched across the horizon. How long would it take her to reach Aisair? A day? The urge to find out, to test herself, was immense. She could fly there and battle the Skulls by herself like she'd done in Layso. Tinnstra had told her no when she'd suggested it before, but now, more than ever, it felt like a good thing to do. The right thing to do. No need for any more lives to be lost.

Then she glanced down at the trail of soldiers on the Northern Road. What would they think if she took off? Would they think she was running away? That she was deserting them after everything they had been through? And what if the enemy attacked them while she was gone with Chosen and Daijaku and only the Gods knew what else? Their deaths would be on her shoulders then, and she couldn't bear that.

Most of them were Meigorian anyway, ordered to fight in a foreign land by their tian, to fulfil an imagined debt because she freed their country. Truth was they owed her nothing. The Skulls had only invaded Meigore because of her. The debt was hers.

And then there was the memory of what the Chosen had done to her at the beach. The pain they'd caused. In Meigore, their blasts had bounced off her shields like rain on stone. But now? They burned her in a million different ways. What if she flew to Aisair and more Chosen like that waited for her? What if her powers were not enough?

No, she wasn't going to fly to Aisair.

Zorique stayed airborne for another half-hour, enjoying the solitude, relishing the silence, but in the end, her duty called and she returned to the ground. She approached slowly, knowing the eyes were on her again, making sure she appeared confident and comfortable, acting like a queen. Back straight, head up. She could almost hear Maiza's voice correcting her posture.

'Your Majesty,' said Aasgod, bowing as she landed beside him.

Ralasis was with him and the Meigorian gave her a rather less reverential bow in greeting. 'Your Majesty,' he said with a smile.

'Hello, Commander,' she replied. 'Is all well?'

'That depends on what you consider "well", My Queen,' said Ralasis. 'There's no sign of the enemy, so that's something. We're making good progress and will soon be clear of the mountains, with hopefully softer ground and some cold water ahead.'

'But?'

'I'm a sailor, not a soldier. My legs are meant to stand upon a ship. Marching is not a natural thing for me – or for anyone, I would presume. As such, my feet are pure agony,' said Ralasis. 'Luckily, I'm not one to complain.'

'No?' said Aasgod.

'My father always told me it was best to suffer in silence,' said Ralasis.

'A wise man,' said Aasgod. 'I think I'd like him a lot.'

'Of that I have no doubt.' Ralasis arched an eyebrow. 'You both enjoy giving unwanted advice.'

Zorique laughed, then immediately stopped herself.

'Something I said, Your Majesty?' said Ralasis.

'It doesn't feel right to laugh,' she said quietly. 'Not now.'

'Far from it,' said Ralasis. 'War is the best time to laugh. It reminds us that we are alive.'

'Did your father tell you that?' asked Aasgod.

They all laughed then, and Zorique had to admit that it felt good.

The buzz of chatter from the ranks ahead stopped further conversation. 'Something seems to have everyone talking,' said Aasgod.

Ralasis craned his neck to try and see over the soldiers' heads. 'What's going on?'

'I have no idea,' replied Zorique.

The column slowed. The chatter at the front turned into a cheer that rolled through the ranks.

Hasan appeared at a trot. 'Your Majesty. Aasgod.'

'What's happening?' asked the mage.

'Someone's left a present for us. Tinnstra, I presume.'

'A present?' asked Zorique, confused.

'Best I show you, Your Majesty,' said Hasan. 'It's about half a mile ahead of us.'

'You're not suggesting the queen should run, are you?' said Aasgod.

Zorique held up a hand. 'There's no need – besides, Ralasis' feet wouldn't like that.'

'I can wait here, if you'd like,' said the Meigorian.

'*Shirudan*.' Zorique formed the shield in a bubble around the four of them. '*Tobo*.' The group rose slowly above the soldiers. Hasan had to stop Ralasis from falling, whereas Aasgod remained stiff and upright like it was something he'd done a thousand times before. When they were high enough not to hit anyone, Zorique flew them straight over the column.

She was showing off to an extent. She knew that, knew it would bring the conversation back to her, bring all their eyes back to her, but maybe that was a good thing.

They saw the 'present' soon enough, lined up on some rocks, all neat and tidy if not for the blood. Four Skull helmets. Four dead enemies.

Zorique lowered the group to the ground beside them.

'Definitely Tinnstra's work,' said Aasgod.

'The girl has style,' said Ralasis.

Zorique glanced around the mountainside, expecting to see her mother looking down on them, feeling all pleased with herself, but there was no sign of her. Knowing Tinnstra, she was most likely still hunting.

'I presume they were scouts, watching for us,' said Hasan.

Aasgod nodded. 'So the enemy haven't fled completely after all.'

'The Egril never give up,' said Zorique softly, echoing Tinnstra's words to her from when she was a child.

'Does this affect our plans?' asked Ralasis.

Hasan shook his head. 'No. It was to be expected – that's why Tinnstra set off earlier. We'll proceed to tonight's campsite, set up sentries, have everyone take shifts on duty.' He looked north. 'The road we're on? Nowhere's going to be completely safe until the Skulls are gone for good.'

'I'd rather march at the front of the army from now on,' said

Zorique, following his gaze. 'When trouble finds us, I'd prefer to be the one to deal with it first.'

'As you wish,' replied the Shulka.

Their next sign of the enemy was waiting for them at their intended campsite. Four more bloody helmets lined the side of the road, and this time Tinnstra and her little team were there as well. All with big grins, enjoying the cheers they got from the troops. It still shocked Zorique to see her mother's bandaged eye, and she felt another stab of guilt that she'd not been quick enough to stop the Chosen.

Her mother seemed to have adjusted to the loss and gave Zorique a theatrical bow when she saw her. 'Welcome, Your Majesty, to your home for the night.'

'Mother,' replied Zorique. She took her time drinking some water. 'You've been busy.'

'My crew did good work. Found out what the Egril have planned for us.'

Zorique glanced back towards the others. Ralasis and Hasan were in discussion with some of their troops while Aasgod was watching Zorique's conversation. 'Let's get the others and hear it all.'

'Sure,' replied Tinnstra, but sounding far from it.

Zorique said nothing. At some point her mother had to learn to work with the others – to trust them. She couldn't win the war on her own. Of course, the irony wasn't lost on her that she'd thought of attempting that very thing only a few hours before.

Tinnstra brought one of her men, a Shulka named Tavis, with her and they moved to the riverbank while a camp was built around them. Ralasis immediately took his boots off and waded into the river, sighing loudly in delight at the effect the cold water had on his feet.

When he realised everyone was watching, the Meigorian simply shrugged. 'Sometimes it's the simple pleasures in life.'

Even Tinnstra smiled.

'What have you found out?' asked Aasgod.

Tinnstra nodded at Tavis, who unfurled a map on the grass.

'Five thousand Skulls plan to ambush us tomorrow. We're going to ambush them instead.'

32

Tinnstra

The Northern Road

Tinnstra looked down at the camp from her perch on a rock. She'd been there for at least an hour, watching the shadows chase the sun out of the valley. She'd not told anyone where she was going, as she didn't want to explain her almost desperate need to be alone. She knew she'd strayed too far from the others, but the army was safe for now. Tomorrow another test would come, and by the Gods, she couldn't wait.

Just thinking about it made her smile. At last, something had gone right. Tavis knew a path that would bring a small group right up behind the enemy, which Tinnstra would lead herself. They planned to set off an hour before dawn to get into position. Aasgod would be with them, to add his magic to her steel. Their job was to kill the Chosen and then signal Zorique to come in and lay waste to the majority of the Egril. Tinnstra and the others would mop up the rest.

It was time the Egril got a taste of their own medicine.

Soon enough a chill found the air and the scent of that night's carefully rationed meals filled her nose. So much of their supplies had been lost aboard sunken ships during the invasion. Even with their reduced numbers, there wasn't enough left for everyone to have full rations. Sooner rather than later they'd have to find food from local sources. A hard ask from people already suffering to give up what they had, but it was what it was.

Tinnstra rubbed her bandaged eye. So much had been lost. So much to win back. But they would do it. They had to.

The night grew colder, making Tinnstra regret not bringing her cloak. Still, she'd done enough moping. *It's been a good day. Tomorrow will be better.* Best to get some food and some rest while she could. She stood and stretched and smiled once more. The Skulls were probably settling down as well, thinking they would hurt the Jians once more on the morrow. By the Gods, Tinnstra couldn't wait to prove them wrong.

A pulse in her mind froze the smile on her face and stole the confidence from her heart in a single breath.

It was faint, barely noticeable, but it was there. A needle of pain. A trace of magic. A warning.

Her head shot up. She scanned the sky, searching with her mind for the cause. It was coming from the north, from the far hills.

Another spike, sharper, closer. Enough to recognise it, now. Oh, Gods. She knew it. Dreaded it.

A Tonin.

And if there was a Tonin, that meant the whole Egril army could be there in seconds. *Shit. Shit. Shit.*

Tinnstra started running down the mountainside, trusting her instincts to find sure footing. Why had she left camp? Why had she gone so far up the mountain? Why had she believed that bastard of a Skull? He'd lied to her. Fucking lied to her!

'Tonin! Tonin!' she screamed, but the wind dragged her voice away. 'Tonin! Tonin!' She tried to pick up the pace, but the damn dark and her one bloody eye made it all but impossible.

How long did she have before they attacked? She could feel the damn creature getting closer. Close enough that she could tell there were others with it. A Chosen. No, two Chosen. Shit.

'Tonin! There's a Tonin!' On she ran. Jumping over boulders. Throwing herself down drops. She could see the camp, the sentries. One stepped forwards to challenge her, but she didn't slow down. She couldn't afford to.

'Sound the alarm!' she cried. 'The Skulls are coming!' She didn't stop, didn't look back. She just ran past them, shouting as she flew by tents and startled soldiers, heading for the command tent, half-falling over a rope she hadn't spotted. Bouncing off some hapless soldier who got in her way and spinning around another. 'Tonin! Tonin!'

A horn sounded behind her, thank the Gods. The sentry had done as she had ordered. They might have a chance, if everyone was quick. Quicker than the bastards coming for them.

Soldiers scrambled out of tents and up from fires, grabbing weapons, donning armour, all looking around for the enemy, the attack.

'Tonin to the north! To the north!' she shouted as Zorique and Aasgod ran out of the command tent, both dressed for war.

'Tonin?' said Zorique.

'To the north, on the—'

The screech drowned out everything. That sky-shattering howl they all knew so well. Tinnstra didn't need her magic to spot where the Tonin was – it shone bright in the darkness, its power rushing through the trees, ripping the air apart. Fire and light swirled as the damned creature opened a gate. A mile outside the camp, maybe.

Zorique shot into the air, shield flaring around her, and headed towards it. No hesitation, fire of her own dancing across her spear. Lighting up the night, crashing through the trees as if they weren't there. She'd stop the danger before the Skulls could get too many of their troops across the gap.

'Follow me!' screamed Tinnstra. She raced off after her, sword in one hand, short axe in the other, ready to kill any Skulls that came her way.

Then two angry red streaks burned through the forest. Two Chosen blasts. Straight at Zorique. They struck her shield, stopping her dead. Two more blasts followed a heartbeat later. Both hit home, flaring bright against her shields, sparks shooting everywhere, and this time their force sent Zorique tumbling. Trees shattered around her as she hurtled towards the earth. She hit the ground hard in a burst of fire.

The sight was enough to stop Tinnstra in her tracks. She'd not seen the Egril do that before. Gods, was Zorique ...

Her daughter hauled herself to her feet, the forest burning around her. She staggered, straightened and just got her shields up in time as more blasts smashed into her. Tinnstra could see Zorique's shield cracking under the pressure, her magic dimming with each attack. But may the Gods bless her daughter, the girl didn't give up. Once more she pushed forwards, inch by painful inch, thrusting her shield out ahead of her, blocking the Chosen's blasts. Somehow, she stood up to them. But that was all she could do. There was no fighting back.

The Tonin was free to work its magic. Free to bring more monsters.

Even over the chaos of Zorique's battle with the Chosen, even over the burning forest, Tinnstra heard them. Heard the flap of their leathery wings. She looked up, peering through the smoke and burning trees. Saw the shadows. Saw the Daijaku, red orbs glowing in their hands.

Zorique saw them, too. She thrust her hand up and fire burst across the front line of the demons, then it was gone, snuffed out. Zorique looked confused, and her shield shuddered under the Chosen's attack. *One of them controls fire. The Skull hadn't lied about that.*

'Daijaku,' screamed Tinnstra, still staring at Zorique, suddenly so scared at what the enemy might do to her daughter. 'Daijaku. Shoot them down.'

Arrows zipped up, but it was pointless. The creatures were too high, too fast. The trees too dense. All Tinnstra could do was watch. Watch as the first bombs fell.

The ground shook as explosions ripped her army apart. A blast from only the Gods knew where sent her flying. She felt splinters pierce her skin, felt shards of tree fly past her face. Tinnstra hit the ground hard, all air knocked from her lungs. She lay there, trying to breathe, amazed she was even alive and all her limbs intact. And considering the howls around her, she was one of the lucky ones.

Get up. Get up. Get up.

Tinnstra grasped her sword, her axe already lost, and forced herself to her feet, ears ringing, ignoring the swaying ground.

'Keep moving!' she roared, dragging anyone she could along with her. 'Head for the Tonin. Keep moving. We have to kill it. It's our only chance.'

Tinnstra stumbled on, through the smoke and ash, climbing over the dead and dying, across craters, mouth dry, full of rage, feeling helpless. Others came with her, trusting her or perhaps just because they had no idea what else to do. It didn't matter. To charge was their only option. To run was to die.

Lightning arced up from the rear – so Aasgod was still alive, at least – and sent a Daijaku spinning from the air in a ball of fire. More lightning followed but Tinnstra couldn't see if it struck home.

A Daijaku flew straight towards her, a Niganntan spear already swinging. She threw herself to one side, slashing out with her sword, felt the thunk of her blade biting. Then it was wrenched from her hand as Tinnstra tumbled across the bloody grass.

By the time she was upright again, her troops were on the felled Daijaku, hacking and stabbing at it. It felt damn good to see the creature die – for all of a second before another bomb wiped them from the earth.

Tinnstra picked up another sword and staggered on, not knowing what else to do, her mind too numb to think of a better plan. She hauled along anyone she could, leaving those she couldn't help. Leaving too many.

Another wave of Daijaku swept in. Dear Gods, how many were there? The army – her army – couldn't take any more of a pounding. Orbs glowed blood-red in their hands. Maybe a dozen in total. Not many, but more than enough.

Where was Zorique? Tinnstra couldn't see her through the smoke, didn't know if she was even still alive. She thought she heard more of the Chosen's blasts, but there was no way to be sure. Not in that chaos.

She looked up, some sixth sense warning her, saw red orbs falling. One by one the bombs fell, down through the dark, down towards her. Dear Gods, it was over.

Light flared above her head. For a moment, Tinnstra thought it was Aasgod's lightning, but no, it was something else. It cut through trees and smoke and fire, so bright. It was a shield. Zorique's shield.

The bombs exploded fifteen feet from the ground. Fire rippled over the shield's surface, the roar of the explosions suddenly muted like far-off thunder, and Tinnstra knew they were safe for a few moments, at least. The Chosen's blasts hammered away at it, sending cracks scattering across its surface, but they fused shut a second later.

A surreal calm fell over them all, safe in their bubble, watching death dance around it. Some Daijaku flew straight into the shield, as if hoping their very fury could tear it asunder, but all they did was splatter themselves in vain. The survivors cheered with each death – but not Tinnstra.

Zorique was easy to spot, standing alone, burning bright, a star shining amidst the darkness, her power protecting them all. Her legs were braced and her whole body shook from the pressure, as if she was holding a mountain up above their heads. Tinnstra wanted to run to her, to help, but there was nothing she could do.

The survivors stood frozen, smoke swirling around them, looking bewildered, unsure of what to do. Tinnstra felt much the same, but she knew she couldn't waste that moment of calm. Who knew when the bubble would burst and the attack resume? There was only one way to stop this.

'Stop gawking,' she roared. 'Arm yourselves. Get shields. It's not over. The enemy is still out there. They still want to kill us. Come on.' Tinnstra clapped her hands as she moved amongst the soldiers. 'Where are the orderlies? We have wounded that need our help.'

Slowly her words sank in. People shook off their fear and shock and responded to her orders.

'Come on! You're soldiers! Are you going to let the queen fight alone?'

Some looked at her as if she were mad but Tinnstra didn't care. Soldiers needed orders, they needed action and she would give them that. It didn't matter how right or wrong her decisions were, anything was better than dying on their knees.

Tinnstra moved on, heading towards the Tonin. She had it focused in her mind, a spike of pain that told her exactly where the bastard creature was. Killing it was still the best way to stop the attack. 'Archers! Where are the archers?' By the Gods, it was impossible to organise anything in this insanity. She needed to find a signalman, a horn, anything to carve order out of the chaos.

The Daijaku still buzzed around above the shield, still dropped bombs, looking for weak spots, finding none – yet. Tinnstra still couldn't tell how many were out there. The explosions that rippled across the shield made it impossible to see what was going on.

She spotted Aasgod, lightning crackling around his hands, a gash of red across his forehead. 'Aasgod!'

The mage looked up and there was no hiding his relief at seeing Tinnstra. 'Thank the Gods, you're alive.'

'Find some captains, some signalmen. Get whoever's still standing to form battle lines, and have some bloody archers ready to shoot the demons the moment the shield falls.'

'I will,' said Aasgod.

Tinnstra turned to leave but then stopped. The spike in her head was gone. Just like that.

'The Tonin's disappeared,' she said. 'Shit.' She ran towards Zorique, still burning like a star in the centre of what was once their camp, channelling her magic through her spear to form the shield above their heads. 'Zorique! The Tonin's gone. The Chosen, too. There's only the Daijaku left.'

The girl looked over, eyes on fire. 'How many?' A simple question, but Tinnstra could hear the exhaustion in her words.

'Does it matter?'

'No.' Zorique reset her feet and dropped her arms. The shield fell and the outside world rushed back in. The screeching of the Daijaku, louder than before, filled the air. Seeing their prey, they rushed down.

'*Kasri!*' screamed Zorique and thrust her spear towards them.

Fireballs blossomed across the night as, one by one, the Daijaku burst into flames. This time there were no Chosen to protect the demons. Soldiers cheered as the creatures tumbled from the sky. Tinnstra had to admit it was a beautiful sight.

As the last ones fell, Zorique relaxed and her aura, so bright a heartbeat before, blinked out. The sudden darkness was all but blinding. Almost enough for Tinnstra to miss the strength go from Zorique's legs as she, too, fell to the ground.

Tinnstra rushed over and cradled Zorique's head in her lap.

The girl's eyes fluttered and she smiled. 'We stopped them.'

'*You* stopped them,' corrected Tinnstra. 'You saved us all.'

Zorique's smile faded. 'Not all. Not enough.' Then her eyes closed.

'Is she going to be all right?' asked Aasgod.

'She'll be fine,' hissed Tinnstra through gritted teeth. *She'd better be. Dear Gods, she'd better be.*

Tinnstra looked around at the ruin that had been their camp. Saw the dead and dying. Would they even have an army after this?

33

Vallia

'A massacre,' said Vallia as she looked up from the map at the two Chosen before her.

'Yes,' said the woman, Torvi.

'How many of the heathens did we kill?'

Torvi took a deep breath and straightened her back. 'It's hard to estimate. The first wave of Daijaku bombs was devastating.'

'Devastating?' snarled the other Chosen, a man named Bryak. He glared at Torvi. 'We were supposed to destroy them. If we hadn't run like you ordered us to, we could've succeeded.'

'We'd be with Kage now if we'd tried,' said Torvi. 'Our orders were to return here with an update on the attack once it had been carried out.'

'We ran – like cowards.' Bryak spat. 'I would gladly give my life to achieve what my Emperor asks of me. There is no greater honour.'

'Don't worry, you'll have your chance – when the time is right,' said Vallia. She rubbed her thumb up and down her sword hilt.

'We have over fifty Chosen here in Aisair now,' said Bryak. 'That's more than enough to deal with one heathen girl. Send us all and we'll end this farce of a war today.'

'Underestimating the heathen queen got the Monsutas killed. It got Lord Bacas, his elite Chosen and over five thousand soldiers killed. I lost my first ever battle because I didn't take her seriously enough. I won't make that mistake again.'

'So you would rather have us stand by and watch while our armies get killed and we achieve nothing?' shouted Bryak. 'You shame us all.'

'Curb your tongue, Chosen.' She leaned in closer still, her mouth to his ear. 'Disrespect me again and I'll feed your balls to the Daijaku.'

'Do your worst. I have no time for cowards.'

Her sword flew from its sheath in a perfect arc. She barely felt the blade bite it was so sharp. Bryak's head fell from his shoulders and, a heartbeat later, a torrent of blood spurted from his neck.

Vallia flicked the blood from her blade and sheathed the weapon as the Chosen's corpse crumpled to the ground.

She returned to the map. She'd stared at the thing so often she could probably draw it blindfolded. Red blocks showed her own forces and blue blocks marked the heathen army's. She moved them forwards to where the attack had taken place. It would be interesting to see how quickly they moved on. An Egril commander would leave the dead where they lay – after all, when the souls were in the Great Darkness, the shells left behind in this world were of no consequence. The Jians, on the other hand, were weak when it came to their dead, needing ceremony – as if that made a difference in the afterlife.

Torvi joined her at the table. 'How long will it take for the heathens to march here?'

'Three weeks, four at the most,' said Vallia.

'Commander ... we hurt the heathens, but their queen ... once we'd lost the element of surprise—'

'Her powers are incredible. So, too, are the powers of the others with her.'

'Can we defeat them?'

'We can – but it will not be easy. It might well take all we have.'

'Have you informed the Emperor?'

'Of course. He is no fool. He doesn't need people telling him falsehoods to feed his ego. Only through honesty and knowledge can we decide the right course of action. There is no strength in lies.'

'And?'

'He was the one who reminded me that it was the war we must win, not the individual battles.'

'So what do we do?'

'We carry on as planned,' said Vallia. 'Each attack we launch will be more ferocious than the last. For every life we lose, we will send ten of theirs to the Great Darkness. They will march during the day, then they will have to fight through the night. They will have no rest, no respite and no aid. The dead will welcome them at every town until they dread seeing another city's walls. If they reach here, their numbers will have dwindled, their hearts will be strained and their stomachs will be empty. And then they will die before the greatest Egril army ever assembled.'

'A good plan,' said Torvi.

'The only plan,' said Vallia. 'The Emperor's plan.'

Torvi looked down at the map again. 'This is different, isn't it? From all the other wars we've fought?'

Vallia glanced over at the aide, patiently waiting in the corner of the room. 'More wine, please.'

'Yes, Commander.' The aide filled Vallia's cup and then filled another for Torvi.

'Thank you. You can leave us now,' said Vallia.

The aide bowed and left the room.

'Praise be to Kage,' said Vallia, raising her cup.

'Praise be to Kage,' replied Torvi.

They both drank. The wine was a Dorwanese red, rich and full-bodied. Vallia rolled the liquid around her mouth, enjoying the dark, fruity flavour and the smoky aftertaste.

'I was with His Imperial Majesty at the beginning,' she said eventually. 'I was there when he returned from his pilgrimage across the steppes and spoke of his vision for an Egril Empire that encompassed the continent. We thought he was just a man then – this was before his magic had developed – but we all believed in what he said. He had this way of talking that made any doubts disappear. There were some, the Bryaks of the tribe, who voiced their fears, who wanted life to stay as it was. But Kage spoke through Raaku in a way that could not be ignored.'

'You were truly blessed to witness that,' said Torvi.

'It didn't feel like it at the time. We simply fought for our chieftain, for our God, with clubs made from bone and spears tipped with sharpened stone. We fought with tactics that Raaku seemed to conjure from the air, like no Egril had ever fought before. We started wearing masks made from the skulls of our fallen enemies and relished the fear it created. And we defeated each and every tribe we encountered. It was glorious.

'And then we met the Yifling.'

'The final battle in the War of Unification,' said Torvi.

Vallia took another sip of wine. 'It was.'

'My father told me about it. He fought there, too.'

'Then I hope he told you the truth, because it was not like the tales make out today. Raaku didn't ride a chariot with flaming wheels, smiting all enemies from his path.'

'My father never said that,' said Torvi. 'He told me he fought for five bloody days, and each night he was amazed to still be alive. He said the dead covered every inch of the battlefield for miles in all directions.'

'Then your father spoke true. For it was a battle unlike any other,' said Vallia. 'We were some fifty thousand strong by the time we faced them at the River Otra, but the Yifling had been busy while Raaku conquered the rest of the north. They had gathered all of the southern tribes together, so their army matched ours in number – and they had proper steel.'

Vallia refilled her cup. Talking about the Battle of Otra always made her want to drink. Sometimes the memories alone were enough to make her seek oblivion in whatever bottle was nearest. 'It was the first time His Imperial Majesty gave me a command of my own – his reserve forces, ten thousand of his finest warriors. Some were insulted at first because they wanted to be in the front lines, fighting alongside Raaku himself. Others thought he was protecting us from danger because many were from Raaku's own tribe.

'We watched as the two armies clashed, and I had to hold my warriors back from rushing to join in. And the Yifling appeared behind us, on horses twice the size of any we were used to. We barely got inside our shield wall in time.'

'My father said their horses would run over the shields,' said Torvi, 'crushing the men beneath them.'

Vallia nodded. 'The battle – the war – was nearly lost on that first day. By the time Raaku called our retreat, half our number were with Kage, and we ran from the field with the cheers of the Yifling ringing in our ears.

'A normal king would've given up, but Raaku is the son of Kage. He doesn't give up.'

'What did he do?' asked Torvi.

'He sent my command back to the battlefield that night,' said Vallia. 'We armed ourselves with swords from the Yifling dead and then crawled for miles through corpses until we were as close as we could get to the enemy's camp. Then we lay amongst the fallen, covered in their blood and guts, listening to the Yifling celebrate their prowess over us, and we waited. By the time the morning came, we were half-frozen but still we didn't move. One of my men even had his eye pecked out by a crow, but he had to endure it – otherwise any movement would've betrayed our plans. Then the Yifling came out to face Raaku once more. They marched right by us, laughing and joking about how Raaku would be with Kage that night – and still we didn't move.

'The battle resumed. Raaku told us to wait for one hour before we rose. But rise we did, blood-red and ready, our stolen swords in our hands. We charged into the Yifling from the rear, howling behind our skull masks. And still it wasn't enough.'

Vallia swirled the wine in her cup. 'Like your father said, we fought for five days and each day was worse than the last. I remember being so tired I could barely raise my sword, but Raaku? He was everywhere, rallying us when all seemed lost, pushing the enemy back when they had broken through. It was then that I first saw the divine in him, as did so many others.

'The Yifling saw it, too, and that was why we won. They could not fight against the son of Kage. They could not defeat him. Once the Yifling accepted that, they surrendered and swore their undying fealty to Raaku.' Vallia sipped her wine, dark and bitter on her tongue. 'The Emperor gave me this sword in honour of the victory we won that day.' She pulled the sheathed blade from its fastening and placed it on the table. The scabbard was scratched and scuffed, the hilt worn smooth from her endless rubbing.

'He gave you a priceless gift,' said Torvi.

'Whenever I touch it, I feel his presence and I remember that day. We won despite everything the enemy threw at us. This battle will be no different.'

'Why do you say that?' asked Torvi.

'Because I know that, if all seems lost, then Raaku will be here by our side, and no mere mortal can defeat the son of Kage, no matter what powers the False Gods have gifted them,' said Vallia. 'This is Sekanowari and Raaku will be victorious.'

34
Yas

Arlen's Farm

Shouting woke Yas.

She had her hand on her knife before she'd opened her eyes, then she took in Little Ro still fast asleep, bundled up next to her, safe. She rolled out of her cot, listening to the commotion outside as she pulled on her boots and picked up her coat. The yelling had stopped, but someone – a woman – was crying. Yas relaxed. Whatever had happened, it wasn't the Skulls attacking. Panic over.

Dean gave Yas a nod of greeting as she emerged from her tent. She had to admit she liked having a guard outside her door. It certainly helped her sleep better at night now that Hasan was gone. By the Gods, as glad as she was to be away from that damn cave, she missed the old Shulka. He would've enjoyed Arlen's Farm and what they were building. Being outside felt like living again, like progress. She just prayed he was keeping safe while she built something special for him to come home to.

The town was starting to take shape. There were rows of tents and lean-tos, but the odd building frame had already gone up. A month or two and there'd be proper homes as far as the eye could see. Yas made a note to herself to check with Daxam and find out when he and his crew intended to start building her own home. The tent was better than a cave, but she was excited by the prospect of having walls around her once again.

Timy was already up and cooking something over a small fire.

She flinched when she saw Yas, then straightened up again and found a smile. 'Morning, Yas.'

'Morning.' Yas tilted her head towards Rena, who was the source of the crying. 'Any idea what that fuss is about?'

'You know me, Yas. Keep myself to myself.' Timy tapped the pot with her spoon. 'Breakfast won't be long.'

'Thank you,' said Yas. 'Would you mind watching Little Ro while I see what's going on?'

'My pleasure,' said Timy. 'He's such a lovely boy.'

'Well, I think so.' Rena was easy to spot – she was making enough noise, after all. A small knot of people stood around her, offering comfort, but not managing to shut up her wailing.

Rena was quite possibly the last person Yas wanted to speak to, but it would be odd if Yas, as town leader, didn't go and see what was wrong.

'Do you want me to come with you?' asked Dean.

'I'll be fine,' said Yas. 'You stay here.'

'Er ...' Dean chewed on his lips, clearly uncomfortable.

'What is it?'

He grimaced. 'You might want to put the knife away before you go over. Don't want to give everyone the wrong idea.' He nodded down towards her hand.

Yas hadn't even noticed she was holding one. She slipped it inside her coat, into a special sheath Timy had sown there. 'Thank you. That would've been awkward.'

'Aye,' said Dean, with a smile. 'That it would.'

With a shake of her head, Yas wandered over. Sala and Venon were with Rena, and a couple of others Yas didn't know so well. Rena was sobbing away on a woman's shoulder – Tricia or something like that.

She was the one who spotted Yas approaching and gave Rena a tap on the shoulder and a few whispered words. The woman looked up, her red, wet eyes suddenly full of anger and hate.

Yas kept her own face neutral. 'What's happened?'

'You damn well know what's happened,' spat Rena.

'I'm sorry but I don't,' said Yas. 'I've just woken up.'

'It's Sykes,' said Sala.

'Sykes?' Yas looked around as if she expected to see him nearby.

'He's dead,' Rena howled.

'Down by the river,' said Venon. 'Must've slipped or something and hit his head on some rocks.'

'Dear Gods.' Yas covered her mouth with her hand. Sorin must've had that chat with Sykes and Sykes probably hadn't wanted to listen. But killing him? That wasn't what she'd wanted. Not at all.

'He didn't slip,' said Rena. 'Why would he slip?'

'Accidents happen,' said Sala. 'It was dark, too.'

Rena wasn't having it, though. She jabbed a finger at Yas. 'She did it.'

Yas held up both hands, hoped she didn't look guilty. 'I was asleep, Rena. I know you think I've done some bad things – and I have – but not what you think I've done. I got these tears for looking after my son. No more than that.'

'You're a liar!' screamed Rena. 'You murdered my sister and now you've murdered Sykes.'

The others looked petrified. 'I think you need to have a lie down,' said Tricia. 'You've had a shock.'

'She didn't mean it, Yas,' said Venon.

'Don't worry,' said Yas. 'I understand. We all say stupid things when we get upset.'

'I *do* mean it,' Rena roared, spit flying everywhere, so red-faced she looked like her heart might burst. 'She's a killer.'

'Tricia, take Rena to her tent before she says something that can't be forgiven,' said Yas. Everyone noticed the coldness in her voice.

'I will,' said the woman. Even Rena must've realised she'd overstepped the mark, because she let herself be led away with no more fuss.

'Please take no notice of her,' said Sala. 'She's just upset.'

'She and Sykes had become close,' said Venon. 'She didn't mean anything that she said.'

'It's already forgotten,' said Yas. 'Get a couple of the lads and have them take Sykes's body over to the beach. No doubt the

Meigorians will still be burning their dead today. They can add Sykes to one of their pyres.'

Venon glanced at Sala before turning back to Yas, his cheeks colouring. 'We were thinking we could have a ceremony here. People will want to pay their respects.'

'Oh, no,' said Yas. 'Anyone who wants to can go to the beach and do it there. Arlen's Farm is about the future. We're building hope here. A funeral would lower the mood, distract everyone from their tasks. Don't you think?'

Hesitation rippled across all their faces, but Yas was patient enough to wait for them to work things out for themselves. She looked back over at Dean by her tent and gave him a nod.

That helped make everyone's minds up. 'Oh, we do,' said Sala. 'You're right, of course. We'll see to it. Don't worry.'

'Thank you,' replied Yas. She liked Sala. The woman had a sensible head. 'This is a tragedy, but we need to move on quickly.'

'Leave it with us,' said Venon, his cheeks still red. 'And I'll have a word with Rena later. Let her know she's got things all wrong.'

'Thank you,' said Yas and sighed. 'What a start to the day, eh? I better get back, see to Little Ro. The pair of you take care, eh?'

Yas walked away, wondering if things might've just got a good sight worse. One thing was for sure, Rena would need dealing with sooner rather than later. The woman had done her best to get Yas killed once before and could very well try again. Of course, Rena had needed the Weeping Men's help that time, but they weren't an option now. Yas doubted Rena had it in her to do the dirty work herself. She'd be looking for another Sykes before long.

Sorin was back and talking to Dean when Yas returned to her tent. More importantly, Ro was up, sitting in Timy's lap and eating his breakfast. He broke into the biggest smile when he saw Yas. 'Mama!'

Yas bent down and kissed his head. 'Hello, gorgeous. Are you being a good boy for Auntie Timy?'

'Yes, Mama.' His eyes shone with love and, for that short moment, nothing else mattered.

Yas would make this world safe for him. That was why she'd done everything she'd done so far, and she'd do whatever it took in the future to achieve that ambition. 'I'll be back in a minute, my love.'

'Morning, Miss Yas,' said Sorin as she joined the two Weeping Men.

'Sounds like you had an eventful night,' replied Yas.

Sorin shook his head. 'I tried reasoning with him, Miss Yas. I promise you, I did. But that man ... Well, some people don't ever want to listen.'

'Even so, I'm not sure you had to kill him,' said Yas.

'I didn't. The mad fool stomped off, cursing you and me both. Next thing I know he's slipped. By the time I got to him, he was dead.'

'Seriously? It was an accident?'

'As the Gods are my witness,' said Sorin.

'Well, keep your ears open for anyone else that fancies causing trouble,' said Yas. 'Pay Rena particular attention.'

'You want us to go see her now?' asked Sorin.

'No,' said Yas, quickly. 'Things need to calm down, if possible.'

Sorin nodded. 'You're the boss.'

'Can't believe Sykes slipped and fell,' said Yas. 'Maybe someone up there is looking after me.'

'I don't think too many people are going to miss him,' said Sorin. 'Good riddance if you ask me.'

'You've a point there,' said Yas. 'By the way, either of you heard from Bros yet?'

Sorin shook his head. 'Nah. Knowing that one, once he hooks up with Kenan, he'll just get drunk for a few days and cause a bit of trouble. Kenan tends to bring out the worst in people.'

Yas did not like the sound of that. 'I don't think Bros needs much encouragement to be a right little shit.'

'Some people are just born that way, Chief,' said Dean.

She sighed. 'Go get yourselves some breakfast. I'm off to play with my son.'

'Right you are, Miss Yas. Will you be fine without us?'

Yas looked over the tents that made up her town. People were starting to move about, readying for the day ahead. They'd be building and hunting and digging and clearing and a hundred other things. All good things. 'I think we're going to be just fine.'

35

Tinnstra

The Northern Road

Tinnstra stood, surrounded by the dead. She'd not slept. How could she after what had happened? And now her eye – her one remaining eye – burned so much she wanted to stab it out herself. A mad thought, especially since every other part of her was in agony already. She'd come back to Jia feeling invincible and it had taken just over a week for the Egril to relieve her of that hubris. Just like they'd done for the Shulka before her.

What was worse, Tinnstra didn't know what to do. Her plan – her great plan – was a disaster. Move fast, take the enemy by surprise? What a joke. They'd been waiting for her every step of the way, and now thousands upon thousands of her soldiers were dead.

Did they still have enough to fight? To win? Or would another attack wipe them out altogether?

She glanced over to the tent where Zorique was resting. The girl was awake, but weak. They'd all thought Zorique would be more than enough to counter any of Raaku's demons, but whatever magic the Chosen had hit her with had taken a toll. Yet another sign that the Egril were more than one step ahead of Tinnstra.

Always ahead.

She pulled her precious book out of her satchel, the book she'd stolen from some Jian lord centuries before. It had been old even then, its pages stiff and cracked, ink faded, and Tinnstra's constant thumbing through it hadn't helped. If she wasn't careful, the blasted thing would fall apart before she found the answers she needed – if it even had them to begin with. She was starting to doubt that more and more.

The Egril priest's handwriting was thin, as if he'd written with a needle instead of a quill. Perhaps he had? There was certainly nothing decorative in the book, none of those ornate illustrations the Jians adored. Kristoff's book was nothing more than a journal of his visions of the future. He'd written it as a warning to the Egril because he believed Kage would lose Sekanowari.

The priest's words swam before her tired eye, making sense but not making sense. The Four against the One. Death comes for all that live. The Great Darkness waiting. The Light fading. Hope lost. She still wasn't sure if she was reading it right. Seeing paths forward that weren't there.

Tinnstra slammed the book shut. Maybe she was just too stupid to understand what Kristoff was trying to say. If only she had someone else she could talk to about it – but there was no one. She was on her own.

Tinnstra returned the book to her satchel and then her hand strayed to the pouch with the Chikara water. She found a vial, opened it and swallowed its contents quickly, almost without thinking, barely tasting it, and held her breath as she waited for the rush to hit. *Yes, here it comes.* The tingle that made the hairs on the back of her neck stand up, the cold sweep that preceded the roar. Her blood caught fire, destroying any tiredness, fuelling her muscles, clearing her mind. Burning up her doubt. Bringing strength where there had been weakness.

Again, her senses flared alive. She could hear the whispers, the fears, the complaints, the cries of everyone around her. She could taste the death in the air, smell the stink of bodies beginning to turn. She could see the flies eager to feed.

Light flared from Zorique's tent, growing stronger by the second, making Tinnstra's head hurt. She was recovering, her magic returning, and that was a good thing. They'd been wrong, though, to put so much hope on her daughter's shoulders. Tinnstra had to do more. Be more. Help more.

Dear Gods, they would win somehow. *She* would win. She was a killer. *The* killer. Being good wasn't enough. It was never enough. Raaku knew that – that's why he created monsters. Well, she could play that game. She would be the monster.

The Chikara water crashed through her veins. She had to trust in it, let it do its work, and when it was time, she'd be ready. She could be a God, too.

Hasan approached, weaving his way through the corpses. 'Tinnstra.'

She stood, knowing what news he brought. She let the Chikara water harden her soul. 'Yes.'

Hasan looked away for a moment, uncomfortable. 'I have the tally.'

'And?' The Chikara water crushed her weakness, turning her voice to stone, her heart to rock.

'Just over three thousand dead, another twelve hundred too injured to fight, and almost the same again carrying wounds but fit enough.'

Tinnstra did the sums. 'Our army is down to sixteen thousand?'

'Yes.'

'Dear Gods.' Eight days ago there had been forty thousand of them.

'Ralasis' men have taken it pretty hard. Most of the dead are Meigorian,' said Hasan. 'Dealing with everyone is going to hold us up a good while and take a dent out of what rations we have left in the process.'

'Nothing's going to hold us up again,' said Tinnstra. 'Haven't you learned from your mistakes yet? I have.'

'What?'

'Send the wounded back to Kiyosun. The rest need to be ready to move on as soon as possible.'

'The queen—'

'Will be ready soon as well.' Tinnstra checked Zorique's tent. Her daughter's aura was brightening, her colour returning. 'We go today – this afternoon.'

'We can't do that. We need to care for the wounded and the dead.'

'We leave them.'

'But—'

'The people of Anjon died because you hung around after we landed in Jia, "caring for the wounded and the dead". Wasting more time on the corpses in Anjon there gave the Skulls time to prepare last night's attack. So no, staying here isn't an option.'

'The troops won't like it.'

'They're soldiers. They follow orders. See that they do.'

Hasan shook his head. 'You really have changed, haven't you?'

'Perhaps it's time you did, too,' said Tinnstra, leaving the Shulka standing there. She'd been more curt with Hasan than she'd intended. It was the Chikara water that made her like that. She knew it. Holding a conversation in the midst of a rush was like trying to light a wick in a hurricane. But she'd spoken true, too. The Egril had shown them this war had no place for weakness. No time for complacency. It was kill or die. Mourning could wait till after the last Skull was dead. The sooner the likes of Hasan understood that, the better.

I am the hurricane. I am the force the Egril can't stop. I will find a way to win.

The pain in her head grew as she approached Zorique's tent, but it was nothing more than a reminder of what needed to be done. Pain was good. Pain was right. It signalled change. It made her strong. It made her a monster.

The crowd was there as ever, gathered around the tent. They knelt in circles with heads bowed, praying, while others gazed on the tent with unblinking eyes. Tinnstra noticed a few had painted a white star on their armour as well. That was new.

Zorique was upright and strapping on her armour when Tinnstra entered the tent. A whirlwind of colour surrounded her and Tinnstra had to blink furiously to clear her vision.

Aasgod was sitting on a stool, looking a hundred years older than he had the day before. A bandage covered the cut across his head, but it only highlighted how out of place he was. His aura was a pale reflection of Zorique's. A spark next to a star. It was hard to remember why she'd been frightened of the mage when she was younger, because the man before her was far from exceptional. Of course, she'd been scared of everything then. Even waking up to a new day had filled her with dread.

'How are you feeling?' asked Tinnstra, not that she needed to ask. She could see the magic.

'Better,' replied Zorique. 'Thank you.'

'I told her she needs to rest more,' said Aasgod.

'I don't have that luxury,' said Zorique, before Tinnstra could.

'She's right,' said Tinnstra. 'I've told everyone to be ready to move out this afternoon.'

'Where to?' asked Aasgod, rising to his feet.

'Towards Aisair.' A rush of Chikara water ran through Tinnstra and she had to clench her fists to keep calm.

'You can't mean for us to go on? We haven't got enough troops.' The mage looked from Tinnstra to Zorique and back again. 'None of us are in a fit state to win this war.'

'I'm sending the wounded back to Kiyosun,' said Tinnstra, despising his weakness. 'You can go with them if you want.'

Aasgod glared at her. 'Just because I think we should be cautious doesn't mean I want to abandon you.'

'We should be so lucky,' said Tinnstra.

'What is your problem? Have you addled your brains with that bloody water—'

Tinnstra punched him in the mouth before he could say another word. The mage went down, tumbling over the stool and spilling a jug of water. She stepped after him, eager to hurt him some more, when a wall of light cut her off from the others.

Zorique rushed over to Aasgod and helped him sit upright. Blood ran from a split lip. They both glared at her through Zorique's magic.

'Tinnstra – calm down,' said Zorique. 'You're both right. We need more soldiers to fight the Egril, yet our numbers make us an easy target, especially if we stay here.'

Tinnstra tried to swallow her anger. 'What ... do you propose we do?'

'We have asked the people of Jia to help us and they will. Reinforcements will be waiting for us at the Kotege. We must continue. You will scout as before. We need to find the Skulls before they find us. Strike first.' Zorique's face was grim but determined. She'd never looked more like a queen. 'We shall be ready for them.'

'I'll be by your side,' said Aasgod. 'You can count on me.'

'Thank you,' said Zorique. 'I'll visit the wounded before we go. Everyone needs to know their sacrifice means something.'

The sight of the damn mage worming his way around Zorique was too much for Tinnstra. She left the tent, her thoughts a storm. The devoted crowd all stirred, hoping it would be Zorique, but they were quickly disappointed when Tinnstra appeared. Tinnstra paid them no heed.

This was always going to be a hard road to walk. It has been from the very moment Beris appeared in my bedroom. Nothing has changed.

Except me.

She couldn't hold back now.

She wouldn't hold back.

Her blood sang. She didn't need anyone else.

Death comes for all that live.

Even the one, true God.

36
Jax

Chita

They could smell the salt on the air for over an hour, but Jax was still unprepared for the sight that welcomed them as they came over the rise – the Drasus Sea, all turquoise and gleaming under the pure blue sky.

Moiri and Jax knelt in long grass caressed by the wind. The rest of the Hanran were spread out on the slope behind them. Everyone kept low, with grass, branches and leaves tied to their bodies to help them blend in with their surroundings. Even so, most watched the skies. There wasn't a cloud in sight – perfect weather for Daijaku to come swooping down.

'That's Chita,' said Moiri, pointing to a smudge in the distance, nestled in the hook of the bay.

'I know it,' said Jax. 'I was stationed there once, fighting pirates … With your husband.'

'He hated the sea,' she replied.

Jax smiled. 'He hated pirates more.'

'That he did.' Moiri's eyes drifted to his. 'I'm glad we found you, Jax. It was a good omen.'

'I'm glad you did, too. I'd be dead if you hadn't turned up.'

'True.' She smiled and Jax felt a lightness he'd long forgotten.

'What's the plan?'

'Same as before. We head south, follow the coast past Inaka, then cut across to the Southern Road. We'll meet up with the Meigorians soon enough.'

Jax looked down the beach towards Chita once more. 'Worth sending some people to speak to the local Hanran? Might be able to pick up some bodies for the cause.'

Moiri nodded. 'Good call.'

'I know the name of the man who runs things here – Danni. Think I remember where to find him, too.'

'Okay – go. Take a couple of people with you. Just to be safe?'

'Jen and Cal?'

'Sure.' She put a hand on his arm before he could move. 'Be careful.'

Jax nodded, then slithered back down the slope to the first Hanran and passed the names down the line. A couple of minutes later, two heads bobbed up out of the grass. Keeping low, they moved quickly towards Jax. He pointed to Moiri, sitting just below the ridge, and the Shulka headed towards her.

'Jen, Cal, I've got a job for you both,' said Moiri.

'You name it,' said Jen.

They removed their camouflage and left most of their weapons and armour with the others before heading down the slope to Chita.

'Thanks for asking us along, General,' said Jen. 'Means a lot.'

Jax nodded. 'Pleasure.' In truth, Jax was glad he had the others with him. The thought of being in a city again made him nervous. After however long living in the wilds with Moiri and the others, it was hard to imagine walking down streets amongst people going about their business, trying to maintain a semblance of normal life under occupation. In truth, he was as nervous as could be. Some Shulka he was.

The best.

The words drifted past in the wind, accompanied by an echo of laughter. No more than a whisper, but enough to have Jax drop to his knees and pull his knife out.

Jen and Cal reacted a heartbeat later, falling into defensive postures, eyes roaming everywhere looking for danger, seeing none. 'What is it?' asked Cal. 'What have you seen?'

Jax scanned the slopes of long grass, not able to admit what

– who – he was looking for. 'I ... I thought I heard something.'

'Daijaku?' asked Jen.

'I ... maybe ... It's nothing,' said Jax, rising to his feet. He slipped the knife back inside his coat. It was just his imagination. 'I'm getting old.'

The others stood up, too. 'We'll have to be careful in town,' said Cal. 'Weapons are still illegal for non-Egril.'

'Better to have them and not need them,' said Jen. She looked at Jax, eyes bright. 'You taught me that.' By the Gods, she was so young, so keen. Not even the war had dimmed her energy.

'A long time ago.'

'Gundan wasn't that long ...' Jen caught herself, stopped. No one needed that reminder.

'Where else did you serve?' asked Jax. 'You said you took your vows three years ago?'

'The usual places,' said Cal. 'We were with you in Aisair in the Royal Palace, two stints up at ... and the rest of the time in Kiyosun.'

'We both grew up in Kiyosun, General,' said Jen.

'Did I know any of your parents?' asked Jax.

'My father never had a rank,' said Cal. 'He said he was happy taking orders.'

'Nothing wrong with that,' said Jax. 'What was his name?'

'Sojon. He died five summers ago. Over in Gambril.'

'Gambril?'

Cal gave a sad sort of laugh. 'He didn't die in action, if that's what you're asking. He got sick, something wrong with his lungs. The clan sent him to Gambril to see a doctor there. He died a while later.'

'I'm sorry.'

'Not the way he wanted to go – but who gets that wish?'

'True,' said Jax. 'Especially these days.' Memories of Kaine flashed through his mind, in that prison cell, passing the poison to Jax, taking it himself, dying in the dark and filth. A wasted death.

He focused on the city of Chita instead. Better to concentrate on what they had to do. It was once a great sea-trading port, built in the hook of a deep-water bay, but that was before the Skulls came. Now there were only a couple of wrecks in the harbour and no boats out fishing in the ocean.

Buildings were tightly packed around the docks then spiralled out from there. From what he remembered, the port governor's mansion was in the northern quarter. He'd been invited to a gala dinner there once, after they'd defeated some Egril pirates who'd been harassing the coast. Jax had hated it. There was nothing worse than making small talk with people full of their own self-importance. The governor in particular had been a pompous man, and Jax wouldn't have put it past him to have done a deal with the Egril like Aisling had back in Kiyosun.

'What shall we say if they stop us from entering the city?' asked Jen.

'They're normally more worried about people leaving than coming in,' said Cal.

'If they do,' said Jax, 'then we say our family farm burned down and we're coming to stay with my brother, Danni.'

'And hope they don't search us for weapons,' added Jen.

Jax nodded. 'That, too.'

There was a small trail of people and carts heading into the city and it was easy for Jax and the others to slip in amongst them. Ten or so Skulls stood guard by the main gates, but they were only interested in the wagons and what they contained. He could hear questions being asked about weapons and contraband, but really the Skulls seemed intent on stealing whatever food they could. Maybe things weren't going so well for the Skulls after all.

The thought made him smile.

When it was their turn to enter, a Skull looked them up and down and waved them through when he realised they had nothing of value on them. And, as easy as that, they were in Chita.

They reached the first crossroads and Jax had to stop. Tightly packed streets, full of looming buildings that reduced the sky to slivers of blue. It was like Kiyosun before the invasion. Almost normal.

But not quite.

The city was deathly quiet.

'No one's talking,' whispered Cal.

'What's going on?' asked Jen.

'Nothing good,' said Jax. The Jians that were out and about all moved with purpose. There was no idle chatter. No one dallied. Jax could almost taste the threat of violence in the air. 'Let's get to the docks. Find Danni.'

Like everyone else, they moved as quickly as they could without drawing attention to themselves.

The Skulls were everywhere. They weren't stopping anyone on the streets or at checkpoints, but they were just *there*, as if they were expecting trouble.

It was Cal who spotted the writing on the wall. 'Look,' he said, voice no more than a breath. The words covered the wall in white paint. Big and bold.

Jax felt his heart race.

Zorique is coming.

They saw it again a few streets on. This time someone had thrown more paint over the wall to cover the words, but they were still legible.

The closer they got to the docks, the more the graffiti appeared. The message brought more Skulls, too, who loitered on street corners, watching everyone who walked past.

When they were in sight of the ocean, they saw four Skulls beating a man for no good reason. Cal made a move to help, but Jax pulled him back. 'It's not our problem.'

Cal glanced back at the man, now curled up on the ground with his hands covering his head while the Skulls worked on him with spear shafts, then nodded. 'Where do we find Danni?'

'He lives on one of these streets, from what I remember, but I've no idea which one. We need to find someone we can ask,' replied Jax.

'Not the best time to be asking questions,' said Jen.

'Not the best time to be doing anything.' Jax led them down narrow streets, digging out memories from long ago, back when he'd walked with pride and held his head up high.

The Half-Moon Inn was what he was looking for, and he finally found it down the third street they checked. The windows were shuttered and all seemed quiet inside. Jax tried the door all the same, but that, too, was locked. He pointed to an alley alongside the inn and the three Shulka slipped off the main street.

'What are we looking for?' asked Jen.

'I was hoping to find a friendly face here,' said Jax. 'The owner and I were acquaintances, back when I was stationed here. Probably the Skulls took her like every other decent person.'

'What do we do now?' asked Cal.

'Stick to the alleys. See who else we can find.' Movement from above caught Jax's eye, and he looked up to catch a glimpse of a head disappearing inside. 'Or who'll find us.'

The alley twisted and turned, sometimes barely wide enough for Jax to squeeze down, other times opening up almost wide enough to fit two abreast. There were no Skulls and Jax took that as a good sign. Hopefully they'd learned the hard way to stay out of the narrow passages.

Jax and the Hanran were definitely being watched, though – not that Jax could spot from where. He just had that itch that said eyes were on them.

'Keep your weapons handy,' he whispered as they took another left turn.

And sure enough, someone stepped out of a doorway ten yards in front of them. 'You look rather lost, friends,' said the man, tall and lean with a narrow-brimmed hat shading his eyes. He tucked a thumb into his belt, revealing a sword under his long coat. In his other hand was a long steel rod that looked perfect for breaking heads.

'Not lost,' said Jax. 'Just looking for someone.'

'Who's that?' said a woman, somewhere behind Jax. Jax glanced over his shoulder. She was petite with long, black hair falling down her back and half-covering her eyes. She was fixing some metal claws onto her hands.

'A friend of mine,' said Jax. 'His name's Danni.'

'Danni doesn't have any friends,' said the man. Two more men and a woman appeared behind him, with swords and a spiked club.

'Then why does he have you as a welcoming committee?' asked Jax.

'We're more like the unwelcoming committee,' said the woman with the claws.

Jen reached for her knife, but Jax put his hand on her arm and shook his head.

'Easy,' said the man with the iron rod. 'Let's find out who these fine folks are before we do anything hasty.'

'My name is Jax. I was a general once. Of Clan Huska.'

The man laughed. 'Nice try. Jax is dead. Try again.'

'I lost an arm and nearly died at Gundan,' said Jax. 'Since then I've poisoned myself, been tortured, had my skin burned up by a Chosen's blasts and got taken to Kagestan itself, but I'm still very much alive. Last I heard, I was in charge of all the Hanran in Jia – so I suggest you take me to see Danni right now or we might as well start with the killing.' Jax bared his teeth in a tight grin and, Gods help him, right then he would have been happy if it came to a fight.

The man watched him, weighing his options, so Jax waited, acting like he didn't have a care in the world while his blood pumped through his body, preparing itself for action. He'd loved that feeling when he was younger. When he knew he'd win every fight.

Then the man nodded and removed his thumb from his belt, letting his coat fall over his sword. 'Let's go and talk somewhere private.' The man stepped back into the doorway and banged twice on the door. It opened a heartbeat later. 'Come on. Let's hear what you have to say.'

Jax and the others followed the man inside, along a dark corridor and up some creaking stairs to the third floor. Two guards waiting there nodded greetings to the man before giving hard stares to Jax, Cal and Jen. They had no effect on Jax. After everything he'd been through? A mean eye did nothing.

One guard opened the door to a set of rooms and the man led Jax and the others inside. Windows offered a grand view of the harbour, and the sudden light made Jax squint. The woman with the claws was the last in and shut the door.

'Take a seat,' said the man, pulling a chair over for himself. He swung it around so he could lean over the back of it. It was an old soldier's trick; easy to get up from, plus it left some wood between the sitter and a possible blade in the guts. The rest of his crew took up spots on either side of Jax, Cal and Jen, trying to make them feel crowded, trying to scare them into revealing that they weren't who they said they were.

Jax found it easy to ignore them. He sat down and stretched his legs out. It had been too long since he'd had a half-comfortable chair to settle down on. 'Nice view,' he said, tilting his chin towards the window.

'If you're Jax like you say you are, you should be in Kiyosun, not here up north,' said the man.

'Chita's not the north,' said Jax. 'Gundan's the north. Egril is the north. This is just a seaside town.'

'Still – what the fuck are you doing in my town?'

'Just a courtesy. Say hello. Find out what the Skulls are up to.' Jax rolled his neck. 'Pretty quiet on the streets. The whole city looks scared stiff.'

The man laughed. 'You did see the Skull army out there while you were wandering around?'

'Aye, there's a lot of them.'

'And more and more by the bloody day.'

Jax leaned forwards. 'Is it because of the signs? About Zorique?'

The man's face froze. 'Is that what you're after? Information about the queen?'

'Yes, we are. We're heading south, over two hundred of us, to join up with the Meigorians. Thought some of the Hanran here might want to come with us. But at this rate, I'm going to die of old age before you're happy that I am who I say I am.'

The man glanced over at the woman with the claws and got a nod back. 'You might have a point there.' He held out his hand to shake. 'I'm Danni.'

Jax waved his stump of an arm at him. 'I'm still Jax. These two with me are Jen and Cal. They were Shulka, now they're Hanran.'

'You met Nicola outside,' said Danni.

The woman glared at them through her mess of hair, but she was taking her claws off so Jax took that as a good sign.

'What brings you and your crew here?' asked Danni.

'As I said, we're just passing through and looking for

information,' said Jax. 'Hopefully some news about the queen.'

'Zorique is coming, eh?' said Danni with more than a hint of irony.

The tone touched a nerve in Jax. 'She is.'

Danni laughed. 'That's as may be. We've spread the word like we were asked. Told the stories we got told to tell – how she can fly like an eagle and shoot lightning bolts out of her arse and how she's going to crush the Skulls like ants beneath her feet – but it sounds like horseshit to me.'

Jax glanced over at Cal and Jen, who shrugged. 'We've not heard those stories,' said Jax.

'Have you not?' said Danni. 'Well, you're in for a treat, then. I hope you're sitting comfortably.'

And Danni told them of a girl who was a God and the army that travelled with her, how she was going to free Jia and rid the world of the Skulls.

Behind him the sky turned from blue to blood-red. Someone brought some food and some wine but Jax wasn't hungry except for more information about Zorique.

'Do you know when the invasion is going to happen?' he asked.

'It could've happened already,' said Danni. 'It's not just the graffiti that's got the Skulls all riled up. They've nearly doubled the men they had stationed here in the last week, and they've been even quicker than usual to arrest anyone they suspect of being Hanran.'

'Just being Jian is enough to get you picked up,' said Nicola.

'They've always been like that,' said Cal.

'This is different,' said Danni. 'Mass arrests. Mass executions. Next time they send the wagons out, we're going to put a stop to them. We've spent the last week passing around weapons, preparing everyone to take to the streets. There might be a lot of bloody Skulls, but I've got a whole city ready to kill them all.'

'Were you given any orders from Zorique? Is there a plan?' asked Jax.

'Only to have our people ready for when the time comes,' said Danni. 'Wait for the signal.'

'Did they tell you what the signal was?'

'Apart from a flying girl shooting lightning out of her arse?' Danni chuckled and poured himself a mug of wine. 'I didn't think to ask.'

Jax's gaze drifted towards the harbour, half-hoping to see Zorique fly past. 'She is coming.'

'Maybe she is,' said Danni, 'but she'd better bloody hurry. The Skulls are up to something and we may not be able to wait much longer.'

'If you have to fight, then fight,' said Jax. 'That's what happened in Kiyosun.'

'Yeah? How did that work out for you?'

'The city burned. Hundreds, if not thousands, died. But if we hadn't, Zorique would not be alive today.'

'She'd better be worth it,' said Danni.

Cal leaned forwards. 'We should be getting back to the others.'

Jax nodded and stood up. 'Thanks for the company and the information, Danni. May the Gods look after you and everyone in this city.'

Danni got to his feet but didn't offer to shake Jax's hand this time. 'You, too. Maybe when this is over, we'll meet again and you can buy me a drink.'

'That'll be good.'

They were halfway down the stairs when a woman came running in the opposite direction. 'Danni! Danni!'

The big man pushed in front of Jax. 'What is it, Sal?'

'It's the Skulls!' the woman gasped, trying to catch her breath. 'They're rounding up people in the northern quarter. Dragging them out of their homes.'

'How many are they taking?' asked Jax.

'Everyone,' replied the woman.

'Look's like it's time to fight,' said Jax. He turned to Cal and Jen. 'Go get the others fast as you can.'

'What about you?' said Jen.

'I'm going to lend my one hand to Danni here. See what we can do.'

37

Ange

Lanaka

'I don't see why we have to do this,' said Garo for the thousandth time. 'Why couldn't we stay with the army?'

'Alo's balls, Garo,' hissed Ange. 'Can't you talk about something else?' It'd only been a few days since they'd left Hasan and the others, but it was a miracle that she hadn't stabbed the idiot yet.

'But why us? Anyone could've gone.'

'Anyone?'

'Yeah.' Garo glared at her, daring her to say otherwise. Well, more fool him.

'What? Like the Meigorians?'

'Well ... no, not them. I wasn't talking about them. Most of them don't even speak the language.'

'What about Tinnstra or Aasgod or Hasan?'

Garo started to colour. 'Obviously not them.'

'What about Zorique?'

'You're being stupid.'

Ange's laugh wasn't kind. 'Right. *I'm* the one being stupid.'

'I meant other Hanran.'

'They weren't going to send any Shulka because, unlike you and maybe me, they know what they're doing when it comes to fighting. That's why you and me have been sent out to try and recruit other people who know how to fight – because, if you haven't noticed, we've been getting beaten to a pulp every time we fight the bloody Skulls, and if we don't do this, we're going to lose the whole bloody war. So, here we are, heading north, you moaning worse than a Kiyosun fishwife and me wondering who I've pissed off to keep getting stuck with you.'

'It's just I felt safer with the army,' said Garo. 'Anything could happen to us out here.'

'Oh, shut up.' She shifted the small pack on her back, trying to get it more comfortable. She was hungry, but eating would have to wait till nightfall. Hasan had made sure they were given some supplies to take with them, but it wasn't much. The old Shulka had joked about the pair of them 'living off the land', but Ange was a city girl. What did she know about finding food to eat or catching game? Especially when all she could see in front of her were miles and miles of open grassland.

'But the way Zorique destroyed all the Skulls at the beach,' said Garo, still going on. 'The way she made the Daijaku burst into fire ...' For a moment, there was a lightness to his face and his eyes went wide with wonder.

Ange slapped him on the arm. 'You'll be telling me you love her next.'

'She's a gift from the Gods.'

'Yeah, yeah.' Ange stalked off, not wanting to talk about it anymore. She could understand Garo getting all weak at the knees about Zorique, but Ange could still feel the fury of the beach and remembered how insignificant she felt. She could still hear the explosions ringing in her ears, see all the dead and the dying. Just thinking about it made her want to be sick, to scream, to cry.

Truth was, she was glad to be away from the army. She'd felt so helpless. She'd expected to die. Maybe a part of her had wanted to. It was a way out of the war. A way to be with Dren again.

If there was a fucking afterlife. She wished she could believe in Xin's kingdom the way her parents had. It'd be good to see them and Dren and her nanna again, sitting around and eating endless feasts. One big happy reunion.

It sounded too good to be true – and that's why she didn't believe it existed.

Hard to believe in anything anymore. Certainly not anything good.

Not even Zorique and her magic powers impressed Ange. Scared her, certainly – but lots of things did that. But if all their hopes rested on that girl's shoulders? Jia was fucked.

That's why Ange had been more than happy to leave them all behind when Hasan asked. In fact, she was tempted to keep on walking and forget all about revolutions and the Hanran. All she had to do was find somewhere she could disappear and try and forget all about it.

It was a shame that Garo was with her. She couldn't very well desert with him tagging along. She didn't want any disapproving looks from him or, even worse, have him feeling sorry for her and thinking she couldn't hack it. Of course, there was always the possibility that he'd want to run with her, and that thought really made her feel sick. Imagine being stuck somewhere with bloody Garo?

'I must've really pissed someone off,' said Ange.

'What you say?' called Garo from behind her.

'Nothing.'

'How are we supposed to get recruits, then? Just walk into a town and start asking people to join us?'

'Yeah, that'll work,' said Ange. 'Maybe we can say a few words before the Skulls hang us, too, if a good crowd shows up to watch us swing.'

'What's your great idea, then?'

Ange spun on her heels and glared at Garo. 'I don't fucking know. I'll just be happy to find everyone alive – or have you forgotten Anjon?'

Garo went white. 'No.'

'Thought not. So no, we're not going to just walk into a town. We're going to be bloody sneaky, and if the Skulls haven't impaled everyone, we're going to be even more sneaky when putting the word about – because there aren't any magical Goddesses keeping us safe this time. There's just me and you. Got it?'

'Yeah. Got it.'

'Now can you please stop bloody talking?' Ange pointed to the north. 'We've a long way to go and I am sick to death of your voice.'

Garo started to say something back but stopped himself. Maybe he wasn't completely dumb after all.

They set off once more, still heading north but a bit west now. Ange wished she knew where she was going or, at the very least, had a map. All Hasan had said was, 'Head up the coast and see what you find.' Apparently, there were plenty of fishing villages and some ports in that direction.

It was warm, too, but nothing she wasn't used to. She'd spent her life in Kiyosun, after all. It'd have to be scorching to slow her down. Still, the open fields were a bit more disconcerting, with nothing but grass as far as she could see. There wasn't even a tree anywhere. In some parts of Kiyosun, she could touch one side of the street with one hand and the opposite side with the other. That's why Dren liked running the roofs. He said he felt free up there. Nothing holding him back or fencing him in. A wolf on the loose.

Fuck. Why was she thinking about him again? How'd she get from empty fields to Dren?

By the Gods, she missed him. Sometimes, she could go nearly the whole day without thinking about him, then something stupid would bring it all back. Other days, he was in her mind from the start. Turning up in her dreams, lingering until she wanted to scream. She'd even hear his voice sometimes, or think she'd seen him. Stupid, really, but what could she do?

Ange had been in love with Dren for as long as she could remember, even back when the world was normal. Not that he knew, of course. Too busy being a wolf. Trying to be the big man. Going after the girls who wouldn't even give him the time of day. Like that Sasha, who worked at Old Man Hasster's place. That one would've flirted with a bucket of water if it had a gold coin at the bottom. Twisted Dren around her little finger with a flutter of her eyelashes and a glimpse of cleavage.

He'd gone mad when the Skulls made Sasha disappear. Probably why he blew up Old Man Hasster's place in the end – not that anyone would've called him on it. Dren really wouldn't have liked that. That would've got him right riled up and no one wanted Dren angry at them.

Still, she loved him, for all his faults. She knew what he was really like, knew how big his heart was, how hurt he was by what the Skulls had done.

Maybe that was why it took so long for him to see her, really see her, for them to get together. Stupid idiot left it too long. Too late. There had to be a war on before he kissed her. He had to be bloody dying before he made a move.

So much wasted time.

'You crying?' asked Garo.

'What?'

'You're crying.'

'No.' But she was. Bloody hell, how'd that happen? Ange blinked her eyes and rubbed her nose with the back of her hand. Crying in front of bloody Garo, of all things?

'It's okay,' he said. 'I understand.'

'You do what?' Last thing Ange needed was Garo's bloody sympathy.

'I cry, too. Sometimes. When no one can see me.' His voice was quiet. Different. Not full of his usual posturing – or whining. Whatever it was, it stopped Ange getting her back up. She couldn't start a fight with Garo if he was being like that.

'What about?' she sniffed.

'Nothing. Everything. I miss my mother, my father, even my bloody sister.'

'I didn't know you had a sister.'

'Her name was Arwen. She was only young. Right pain, she was. Would never do what my parents wanted her to do, always causing a racket. Drove me mad at the time, but I miss the noise now.'

'There was only me in my family,' said Ange. 'I wasn't their first kid, though. There was one before me, but they'd not lived long. A sickness or something. I don't really know what happened. No one would talk about it, but I could see my mother getting sad every now and then.'

'Like we do now,' said Garo.

Ange flared up at that, on instinct. In no way whatsoever did she want to be like Garo, but she forced it down, smiled instead. 'Yeah. Like us.'

'Do you ever ... think about if we can win or not?'

The question threw Ange. She'd not thought about it. Not dared to. 'We're going to win.' By the Gods, she hoped they were. 'You think that, too, don't you?'

Garo shrugged, looking younger by the second. He even rubbed at that silly beard of his as if he were suddenly embarrassed by it. 'I don't know. I hope we do. I mean, now we have Zorique, I think we can. Maybe.'

'Why are you fighting, then? What's the point if you don't think we can win?'

'What else can I do? I mean, I hate the Skulls and I don't want them here,' he said, looking over his shoulder as if he was expecting to see a bunch of Egril eavesdropping on him. 'I've got to fight – same as you. I mean, if we don't do it, who will?'

'True.'

'And I owe it to Dren, too.'

'You do what?' Hearing Dren's name was like a slap across the face. One she wasn't expecting.

'I owe Dren. He took me in. Looked after me. Taught me how to look after myself. I made a promise to him that I'd give everything to get rid of the Skulls.'

'He never said.'

'He didn't know. He was dead when I made the vow, but all the same, I reckon it still counts.'

Ange reached over and squeezed his shoulder. 'Yeah, I think it counts.'

38

Tinnstra

Tinnstra didn't wait for the rest of the army to get moving. She took her ten and headed out. 'Find where the Tonin was,' she ordered Tavis. 'Find out where it went.'

The man didn't need telling twice. They all knew the direction the Daijaku had flown from. Tavis led them away from the carnage and up into the hills beyond, heading north. There was no pretence this time about what their mission was, and woe betide any Skull they found. Tinnstra had left any mercy she'd once had back at the river with the dead.

The others shared her bloodlust. She could see it on their faces. The attack had only intensified their need for revenge. *Well, Gods be damned, I'll give it to them.*

Tinnstra wasn't mad enough to try and take on five thousand Skulls with her ten, but she as sure as hell meant to kill as many of them as she could. They would know they were in trouble. Their free ride was over.

The Great Darkness called for them all.

Once more, Tavis led them along goat trails and rabbit runs, along paths that no army could take. They moved fast and silent, eating up the miles, moving ever higher. Anger drove them on. Hate fuelled their muscles.

They reached a small valley by late morning. Trees lined the slopes on either side of the basin floor below and Tinnstra could feel the absence of a breeze. Not even a bird stirred. It was a beautiful, secluded spot and it stunk of magic.

'This is the place.' She looked back and had a perfect view of their camp, smoke still drifting into the sky. The campfires of the previous night would have been an easy target to aim for.

Tavis waved them down as he scampered between rocks, looking for signs of the enemy. Tinnstra watched him, heart racing, axe gripped tightly in her hand, waiting – hoping – she'd have someone to kill. She thought about taking some more Chikara water, but she knew there were no Chosen nearby and she didn't need its power to deal with ordinary humans. *Better save it for the monsters.*

Still, her hand lingered near her bag and her thoughts stayed on those small vials. She had twenty-five phials left. Enough to have one a day, but that didn't seem enough. Not for now. Not for this war. Not for what she needed to be. Her fingers worked the bag's catch—

'Tinnstra.' She looked up. Tavis crouched a few yards away. 'You need to see this.'

'Skulls?'

The man shook his head. 'They're long gone.'

The words rippled through her, filling her with disappointment, but they were oil to Tinnstra's fire. She stood suddenly and screamed her rage and frustration to the sky. She needed to murder someone, and she would not be denied.

It was the others moving away from her that gave her pause. She looked at each of them, one by one, and saw the fear in their eyes – fear of *her*. And through her fury, she knew that wasn't right. They were her ten. She was their leader, not their enemy.

Tinnstra took a deep breath, thought of apologising, but just as quickly dismissed the idea. *Let them be scared, for I am death.* 'Show me,' she said to Tavis.

He led her into the valley, pointing out signs and impressions as they passed. 'They were here. Maybe twenty, give or take.'

Tinnstra nodded. Twenty wasn't many. Nothing they – she – couldn't handle.

'This is where the Tonin was,' said Tavis. He didn't have to point out the spot. There was no mistaking the scorch marks on the valley floor. It was a violent, unnatural act when a Tonin opened a gate, burning the very air – and everything around it.

Again, Tinnstra looked back and could see the Daijaku flying straight through the gate and down towards the Jians' camp. 'We made it so easy for them.'

'We didn't know they'd do this,' said Nika. 'We were told—'

'Lies,' cut in Tinnstra. 'We were told lies by that bloody Skull. And we should've anticipated this. We should know the Egril by now.' Her voice was cold, constrained. She looked around the valley, not seeing the slopes or the beauty of the land anymore. Her mind was far away. 'They could be anywhere now ... If they all left through the gate.'

'What do you mean, "if"?' asked Dale.

Tinnstra turned to Tavis. 'Search the ground now. I want to know exactly what happened here.'

'I presumed they had ...' Tavis swallowed whatever else he'd been about to say and immediately set to work, checking the ground, darting from spot to spot, moving further out, away from the burned and trampled ground.

Tinnstra watched, patient. She knew what he'd find. Knew what the Skulls planned to do.

The tracker suddenly stopped, halfway down the valley. 'They didn't leave through the gate. They headed north.'

'Of course they did,' said Tinnstra as the others headed over to join him. Tinnstra looked at the ground but couldn't see anything. 'Are you sure?'

'Yes,' said Tavis. He moved on a few yards. 'They had three horses waiting here.'

'For the Chosen and the Tonin,' said Tinnstra.

'The rest left on foot with them,' said Tavis.

'Do you think they'll send more Daijaku after us tonight?' asked Nika.

Tinnstra shrugged. 'Or some other monsters. It worked once. They've no reason to think it won't work again.'

'Dear Gods,' said Sadir, 'how can we survive another attack like that?'

'Because this time, we'll catch them and kill them first,' said Tinnstra.

'They have a good start on us,' said Tavis, 'but the tracks are easy enough to follow. If we move fast—'

'If you need to eat something, now's the time,' said Tinnstra. 'Drink some water. If you need to piss or shit, do that, too. Whatever you have to do, do it now. We're not stopping after this until we have Skull blood on our blades. Got it?'

'Yes, General,' said the ten.

'You have five minutes.' Tinnstra left them and headed up the slope and into the trees, her hand already in her pouch. Just touching a vial sent a thrill racing through her.

She wanted the power it held.

They were going up against two Chosen and a Tonin. She knew that. Plus more than a dozen Skulls. She'd need the water's magic if she was going to kill them all, but should she drink it now or later? The enemy had a six-hour lead on them, plus horses. Chances were they'd not catch up with the Egril at all, and then what?

So, no, she'd not drink the Chikara water now. She'd save it for later. Save the pleasure.

Tinnstra drank some ordinary water but didn't eat. Her fury left no appetite for food. Only one thing was going to sate her hunger.

She returned to the others. 'Let's go. We've wasted enough time.'

Tavis led them once more, setting a fast pace. The old Shulka was like a hound now he had a path to follow, chasing it without hesitation, further into the wild country.

Where are you? Where are you? Where are you? The words ran through Tinnstra's mind like some sort of magical mantra that would reel in the Skulls.

It was early afternoon when Tavis put his hand up, signalling them to stop. Everyone sank down into cover, hiding in long grass or bush or bracken. The guide turned to look back at Tinnstra and showed her his clenched fist. *Enemy are near.* She nodded, then passed the message down the line.

Tavis signalled again. *I'm going to look.*

Tinnstra nodded. She watched the Shulka disappear into the undergrowth and then opened up her senses to see if she could spot the Chosen's magic or the Tonin, but there was nothing.

Then she smelled the smoke. Someone had a little fire going, cooking something judging by the scent. Was that what Tavis had spotted? Maybe it wasn't the Egril. Maybe it was a hunter having a meal. *Don't get excited. Be patient.*

Her eye roamed everywhere, looking for that telltale sign of white armour that marked her enemy, but all she saw was green. She couldn't even spot the smoke from the fire she could smell.

Then Tavis reappeared, hand signs flashing. *Four men on the other side of the hill.*

Tinnstra was up and running a heartbeat later, not even pausing to pass the information to the others. Her sword and axe were in her hands and her enemies waited for her. She passed Tavis, who tried to fall in step beside her and failed.

Tinnstra knew she was being foolish, that she should wait for the others, be cautious, but her blood was up and she wanted revenge.

She sprinted over the top of the hill and saw them straight away. Four Skulls, like Tavis had said, sitting around a fire, an animal of some sort on a spit. They looked up and she saw their eyes pop wide with shock. They scrambled for weapons and one fell into the fire with a yelp. The other three were quicker, snatching up scimitars as Tinnstra closed the gap between them.

Time slowed as Tinnstra attacked, her enemies' actions obvious to her before they'd even thought of them. Fifteen years of Chikara water had made her stronger, faster. Fifteen years of training with Maiza, of fighting in the pits, had made her deadlier. Fifteen years of hate had made her more ruthless than her enemies.

She slashed her sword across the first Skull's stomach, cutting through armour and skin alike, opening him up with a howl, leaving his entrails for the crows as she moved on to the next. The man raised his sword so Tinnstra's axe took the arm. She turned as the limb fell and rammed her sword through the Skull's heart. He dropped as she pulled the blade free.

The third man took her axe in his face and that just left the fool still trying to climb out of the fire. Tinnstra kicked him in the face, flipping him over onto his back. As he hit the ground, she was on him, sword in his heart, and another soul went to the Great Darkness.

Tinnstra stood and flicked the blood from her weapons. Four dead and she wasn't even breathing hard.

She looked back to the top of the hill and saw Tavis walking towards her, mouth open. She grinned but didn't get a smile back. He stopped ten yards from her. 'I've never seen anyone move that fast.'

'Every Shulka knows speed and aggression win fights.'

Tavis shook his head. 'No one can move that fast.'

'I can,' said Tinnstra, not liking the way he was looking at her. The way people looked at Zorique.

The others appeared over the hill, slowing from their run when they, too, saw the dead.

'She killed them all,' said Tavis, 'in the space of a heartbeat.'

'I caught them by surprise,' said Tinnstra. 'Now, let's move on, there're still others out there. We need to find the Chosen and the Tonin.' She glared at Tavis. 'Focus on what you need to do.'

The Shulka hesitated, then bowed. 'As you wish.' He set off once more, checking the ground, looking for the trail, while the others watched and waited.

'She's not human,' one of them whispered from behind Tinnstra's back.

She didn't look to see who'd spoken, but she was grateful no one agreed with the man. Still, the words lingered in her mind as they waited. She felt a flutter of her old friend, fear, resurface for a moment and she welcomed it. There was still a small part of the old her inside. She wasn't lost yet.

Tavis returned. 'The tracks head off in two directions. The horses went that way.' He pointed to the north-east. 'The rest left on foot in the other direction. Maybe a dozen people.'

'Take me to where they separated,' said Tinnstra.

She followed Tavis down the slope for another two hundred yards until the path split as he'd described. 'It's here. You can see the hoofprints but nothing else with them. Just the three horses.'

'That'll be the Tonin and the Chosen,' said Nika, repeating what Tinnstra had said earlier.

Now, Tinnstra wasn't so sure. 'Why split up?'

'Maybe they wanted to move quickly,' said Dale. 'Get somewhere before dark?'

She stared down the path, trying to imagine who was on those horses. 'Or they want us to think that.' Tinnstra turned to look at the other route. 'Tavis, can you tell if it's just Skulls that went that way?'

The Shulka shook his head. 'The ground's too churned up for that.'

Tinnstra closed her eye and opened up her mind, hoping to find some trace of lingering magic like she had at the valley. She expanded her senses as best she could, like Aasgod had taught her so long ago in Aisair, but sensed nothing. 'How far are we from tonight's campsite?'

'If we go hard, we can be there before nightfall,' said Tavis.

'We can't afford to follow the wrong tracks. Better we rejoin the main army at the campsite,' said Tinnstra.

'But you said they'd attack us again tonight if we couldn't stop them,' said Nika. 'We can't give up.'

'No one's giving up,' said Tinnstra. 'I'm just not going to do what they expect me to do. We need to start changing the way we play this game if we're going to win.'

'Have you got a plan?' asked Sadir.

'The Tonin has to come to us so, we'll hide in small groups around the campsite,' said Tinnstra. 'Once it turns up, we'll kill it and everyone with it.'

39

Raaku

Kagestan

Raaku was submerged up to his waist in the holy water, working on the large orb, when Astin entered the small cavern.

The chancellor stopped by the water's edge, knelt and bowed. 'Your Majesty.'

'Summon all the Chosen from Chongore and Dornway. I want them here within two days. I will adjust their powers again now we know more about the Four Gods' champions. Then send them to Jia before the week is out.'

Astin looked up, shocked at the request. 'Your Majesty, we would need to have the Tonin working day and night across the Empire to achieve that schedule.'

'And?'

Astin bowed his head. 'It will be done.'

'Increase the transportation of soldiers as well. Make sure Commander Vallia has whatever she needs.'

'I will action it immediately, Your Majesty.'

'What progress with the runes retrieved from Meigore?'

'Illius is ... close,' said Astin. 'He has sworn he will have them working within days.'

'Let him know he will have to explain any failure to Kage himself.'

'I will, Your Majesty.'

'Leave me now.'

Astin rose, keeping his head bowed, and backed out of the cavern, leaving Raaku alone once more.

For a moment, Raaku was tempted to visit Laafien and make the Jian drink the holy waters again, but he had visited too often these past few weeks. Laafien would see it as weakness, of doubt in his victory.

But Raaku had no doubt. No uncertainty. He just had to find the way to victory, and Laafien was no longer the guide he'd once been. The man fought against the visions, tried to deny the truth within his riddles.

Sekanowari would be won, whether through feats of arms or by unleashing the contents of the orb beside him. The means mattered not, only the result.

He turned to face the orb, his greatest creation, and watched the swirling liquid within. If he had to kill the world to win, he would.

40

Szal

Chita

'Wake up.' Szal's wife Kat sounded scared, shaking him in case her words weren't enough.

He opened his eyes, a rush of blood countering the tiredness that had driven him to his bed what felt like minutes before. 'What's happening?'

'Danni's in the front room. There's fighting in the north of the city.' As soon as Kat spoke, Szal could hear the shouting and the clash of steel from outside. It sounded like war.

'Alo's balls,' he grunted. He rolled from his bed and stuck his head out of the window. He wasn't the only one, either. Half his neighbours were doing the same. Not that they could see much. Chita was all narrow lanes, turning this way and that, with all roads leading down to the docks. Szal lived a few streets from the seafront, but the few coins he used to earn hadn't been enough to get him a view of anything but his neighbour's balcony opposite.

The street below was rammed with people, though the fighting was happening somewhere else in the city.

He ducked his head back inside and picked up his shirt from where he'd thrown it earlier. 'Did Danni say if this is it?' He didn't have to say what *it* was. The invasion. It had been six or seven weeks since they'd received word it was on the way. Six or seven hard weeks of getting ready, waiting, hoping.

'He just told me to wake you up,' replied Kat. 'He has someone with him, too.' She'd put on a heavy padded jacket while he'd been looking out of the window, so he knew what she thought. No one puts on fighting gear if they think they're going dancing.

'Fuck. This is it, isn't it?' Szal had his trousers on now, his belly full of nerves. Gods knew, they'd talked about fighting the Skulls long enough, planned for it, too. Especially after they got word about Zorique and what she could do. He'd even painted a few walls himself, enjoying how fucked off it made the Skulls. But now? He felt like shitting himself.

Danni was by the window of the front room, looking out through a gap in the curtains. He was tall and lean and hard as fucking stone. He didn't take no nonsense from anyone if he could help it. Kowtowing to the Skulls all this time had been torture for the man. A long butcher's knife hung off his belt and a long metal rod leaned against the wall. But if Danni was tough, the old man next to him looked like he could take on the Skulls by himself – and he only had one bloody arm.

'You ready, son?' asked Danni.

'This is it?' asked Szal.

'It isn't what we planned,' said Danni. 'Things have kicked off in the northern quarter. Skulls have been trying to round everyone up and no one wanted to go. There's no more waiting for help from elsewhere. It's down to us. Go get your tools.'

'Shit.' Szal moved the table and hooked a finger into a small hole he'd made in a floorboard. Hidden beneath it were his weapons: a club he'd made with nails jutting from it in every direction, his dad's old hunting knife, a knuckle-duster and two kitchen knives attached to sticks. He passed those to Kat and took the rest for himself, hands shaking. Then he caught a glimpse of the old man watching him, taking in his nerves. Szal didn't like that. 'Who's your friend, Danni?'

Danni pointed a thumb at the old man. 'This is Jax, the head of the Hanran. He's come to help.'

'Fucking great,' said Szal. 'How many fighters have you brought?' Suddenly Szal was feeling better about things. Always good to have an army of their own.

'It's just me for now,' said Jax, 'but some more are on their way.'

Szal straightened, his good mood gone. 'How many?'

'Two hundred or so.'

Szal turned to look at Danni. 'Two hundred against all those fucking Skulls?'

'What's it matter how many he's bringing?' said Danni. 'We've got the whole city fighting for us.'

'Shit.' Szal glanced over at Kat. 'You should stay here.'

'No bloody way,' she said. 'I'm not leaving your side.'

'You sure?'

'You'll get yourself killed without me watching you and I'm not having that,' said Kat, and Szal couldn't have loved her more. She was a bloody fighter, that woman. His warrior.

'Come on, then.'

They followed Danni and Jax down the stairs and into the street. Just being outside at night felt like an act of rebellion in itself. Curfew was on, but no one cared. The Skulls would have to hang the whole city at this rate.

Others spilled onto the street, too; Mad Nevik, Stev, Ti, Arina, Andre, Pet'r, Farrell, too – the whole crew. Someone must've been knocking on doors while Danni was rousing Szal. Half of them were still getting dressed, but everyone was tooled up. Knives, clubs, sticks, axes, spikes – anything that could be used in a ruck. A lucky few even had swords.

Nicola was there, her black hair flowing behind her like a wild thing, a set of metal claws on each hand. She fell into step beside Szal and Kat. 'You ready?'

'I am,' said Szal. 'Time for some payback.'

'Bloody lovely,' she cooed.

'Come on,' screamed Danni, rattling his iron rod at the sky. 'For Jia!'

Jax waved a big knife in the air. 'For Jia!'

'For Jia!' screamed Szal, feeling his blood race.

'Jia! Jia!' The chant went up around them, drawing more to the street, to their army.

They wound their way through the city, moving north, excitement building. The chant filled their ears and charged their blood. More people joined them until they were a heaving mass of bodies and Szal wondered how the hell he could've ever worried about anything. Kat was next to him. His friends were all around. His neighbours, his city, everyone was out to take back what was theirs.

The chant died when they saw their first Skulls. Maybe a dozen of them, laying into a load of Jians with their bloody swords. They must've sensed something because they stopped their attack and turned almost as one. Probably crapped themselves as one, too.

'Get them,' screamed Danni. Then they were all running, howling, screaming.

Szal threw himself at one of the bastards and they went down together. Szal landed on top. There was no room to swing his club but that wasn't going to stop him. He used the blasted thing like a pestle in a mortar. Bam, bam, bam. Kept going until he was covered in blood and brains and he was pounding nothing but stone.

'Szal!' Kat grabbed his arm, pulled him back. She was all wild-eyed, covered in blood, her knives as red as she was. 'He's dead.'

'Yeah, right,' said Szal, looking down at the Skull beneath him. He was a fucking mess. The bastard barely looked human. And Szal had done that to him. He'd never killed no one before. 'Shit.' His stomach lurched and he staggered to one side and spewed his guts up. 'Fuck.'

'Come on, lad,' called Danni. He had a big chunk of cheek hanging loose, blood all down his neck and over his shirt, but it wasn't going to slow him down. 'There's more waiting.'

'For Jia!' roared Szal, flecks of vomit flying.

'For Jia!'

On they marched. For their country. Their homes. Their lives. Straight into more Skulls.

It was chaos. Danni waded in, swinging his iron rod. Jax was next to him, slashing a Skull sword to and fro like some kind of fucking expert. Nicola pounced onto a Skull's back and plunged her claws into the scum's eyes, screaming rage. Mad Nevik had his hammers smacking left and right, cracking heads. Arina and Kat ganged up on a Skull, forcing him back against a wall before their blades found the Egril's heart.

Farrell wasn't so lucky. He'd stolen a scimitar somewhere along the way, but he was no expert like Jax. In fact, he had fuck all ideas on how to use it. He went down a heartbeat later, not even scratching anyone else in the process.

The Skull who killed him came at Szal next, but Szal was no mug – he knew how to use his club. This time, he had plenty of room to swing. Szal put all his weight into it, from right to left, down to up. His arms shook as he made contact, the spikes biting into the Skull's chin as the wooden club shattered bone. The Egril dropped instantly and Szal followed up with an overhead strike down, pulping the Skull's helmet and head.

He'd barely straightened when another Skull came straight for him, levelling a spear at his gut. He battered the weapon away with his club but the Egril was quicker, whipping the spear back. Szal danced away. The Skull advanced. Then Danni was there, whacking his metal rod into the man's legs. Down the Skull went, simple as that.

Szal wasn't one to ignore an opportunity and his club did its work once more. He nodded at Danni. 'Thanks.'

The big man grunted and left him to it.

The street was one massive brawl as far as Szal could see. It looked like everyone in Chita was involved, swarming wherever there was a white-armoured Skull to kill. They moved along Cassin Street, through the Main Square, down Babbras Road, then north again.

A wave of bodies swept everyone along and Szal was caught up deep in the middle of it, shouting, screaming, raging. Everyone was packed so tight, it was shoulder to shoulder in there. Szal's face was inches from the person in front and he could feel breath on his neck from the person behind. He lost sight of Kat at some point, but he knew she'd be all right. Nothing could stop this mob.

They moved on, excitement growing, numbers growing, fury growing. They'd put up with the Skulls for nearly a year and enough was enough. They cheered the sight of Skulls hanging from lamp posts. They cheered at another enemy torn apart or stamped underfoot. They cheered each other and the fact they were all still alive. They cheered at taking back their city.

They surged out into King's Avenue and Szal suddenly had room around him once again. He looked about, hoping to find Kat or Nicola or Danni or anyone he knew, but he had no luck, so he kept moving with the crowd, down the avenue to the port governor's mansion.

The Skulls had grabbed it as theirs within minutes of turning up in Chita and turned it into their little home from home, a fortress by the sea. Now it was time they grabbed it back.

'For Jia!' screamed Szal. He could see Skulls watching from the walls and hiding behind the iron bars of the gates. A lot of them, for sure, but nothing close to the mob he was with. They'd swarm the mansion like they'd swarmed everywhere else.

Then the world screamed. Bright, white light shone from the mansion's windows.

Everyone stopped. Some fell to their knees, clutching their ears. Others took a few steps back, their courage faltering. They all knew what that howl meant. That sound, that light, heralded their army's arrival in the city. The Skulls were opening a gate.

'They're getting reinforcements,' someone shouted.

'Or running!' added another.

'They're running!'

'Come on! Let's get them!'

'For Jia! For Jia!'

The mob continued to advance. Szal was right there with them. He waved his club over his head, bits of flesh caught on its barbs. 'For Jia!'

They reached the gates, home-made weapons stabbing through the railings. As the enemy retreated, bodies threw themselves against the iron bars, rocking them back and forth. The hinges groaned, then moved, then gave.

Another cheer went up as Szal and the mob surged into the mansion's grounds. If only Kat was by his side, to share this moment with him.

Then the monsters appeared.

The blue-skinned giants burst through the doors of the mansion, taking half the walls down with them. At least twelve feet tall, horns curling out of their foreheads, bulging with muscle, carrying clubs that looked like fucking trees.

'Kojin,' whispered Szal, remembering stories from his childhood, wishing he could go back there right then. Be safe with his mother and father. Far from where he was now.

The mob halted as quick as it could, but it wasn't quicker than the monsters. They waded into the Jian ranks, clubs sweeping back and forth. Killing people like bugs.

A shadow fell over him. Szal screamed. Thank the Four Gods Kat wasn't with him. He wouldn't want her to—

41
Jax

Chita

The arrival of the Kojin was unexpected. Things had been going well until that point, with the local Hanran in spitting distance of the port governor's mansion and whatever Skulls were left in full rout. Then that Godsdamned Tonin did its work and now the Jians were the ones retreating.

'Build barriers!' shouted Jax. 'Block off the roads.' But no one could hear him over those monsters smashing buildings and squashing people and the shriek of the Tonin's magic. If it went on unhindered, every advantage the Jians had gained would be lost. The Skulls could flood the city with reinforcements.

Then he saw Danni, face cut open, blood-red from the neck down, trying to stop his people running. He had a few of his Hanran with him, jabbing spears at the Kojin, trying to hold them back.

Everything hinged on this moment. Victory or failure. Life or death. If the Jians broke now, the Egril would win. It was as simple as that and Jax couldn't let that happen.

He barged his way over to Danni, grabbed the man by his jacket. 'We need to build barricades and block the streets off,' he shouted.

'What?' said Danni. 'Barricades? Against them? They'll just smash them to bits.'

'Not if we set fire to them, too. We can stop the Kojin from doing more damage and give ourselves a chance to regroup.'

'The whole city could go up in flames if we do that.'

'We take the risk. We're dead if we don't.' Jax stared into Danni's eyes, daring him to say no.

'Fuck. You're crazy, but we'll do it. Nevik, Stev! Ti, Pet'r! Get your arses over here.' Danni's words had more effect than Jax's. The four men rushed over and Danni told them what needed doing. 'Build the barricades further down the road. We'll hold them off as long as we can, but leave room for us to get through. Okay?'

'On it, Boss,' said one.

'Then set fire to the fucking thing the moment we're clear,' added Danni.

'Fire? You can't be serious?'

Danni jabbed his bloodstained iron rod in the man's chest. 'Just do what I tell you to do. Leave the thinking to those better at it.' He got nods back. 'Good. Now go and do it while I try not to get my brains pulped by the big scary fuckers. And send someone around the back to close off the street from the other end. Let's keep them trapped here.' With that said, the big man was as good as his word, not wasting any time to rejoin the fray around the Kojin.

Jax wasn't much use with a spear, so he hung back behind the front ranks, shouting encouragement and watching the others ready the barricades. Everything from tables and chairs to carts and beams from fallen buildings were hauled into the street behind the retreating Hanran.

The Kojins' shrieks rattled off the buildings as Danni and the others poked at them with their spears and fishing hooks. Each time a club smashed down, they danced back, keeping injuries to a minimum.

'We're ready,' shouted one of Jax's men from the barricade, waving a torch.

'Time to go, Danni,' called out Jax.

'All right, boys and girls, you heard the man,' said Danni. 'Fall back NOW!'

They turned and ran as one, Jax with them. The Kojin hollered in delight, thinking the fight won. They chased, clubs swinging.

Two men weren't quick enough. A club sent them flying across the street and they crashed through a shop window, the breaking glass silencing their screams.

Jax and the others burst through the gap left for them and then it was quickly filled with more debris. The torches went in a second later, just as the Kojin arrived. Flames shot up, creating a wall of fire. It stopped the monsters in their tracks. Their howls turned to pain and frustration as it was now their turn to retreat. The creatures smashed their clubs into the sides of buildings and pounded the ground beneath their feet, but there was no way around the fire for them.

A whoosh and a blaze of light signalled that the other end of the street was closed off as well.

'Keep the fire going,' shouted Danni. 'Get more wood.'

'What about archers?' asked Jax, panting from the run.

Danni laughed. 'We're sailors and fishermen, not bloody Shulka.'

'Hopefully we'll have some of those soon,' said Jax. 'In the meantime, get people on the roofs with spears or rocks – or better still oil jars, with burning rags stuffed in the mouths – anything they can throw on the Kojin.'

'You're determined to burn my city down, aren't you?' Danni shook his head then clapped his hands at the nearby Hanran. 'You heard the man – spears! Rocks! Jars of oil! Jump to it! Let's see the monsters burn!'

And burn they did. The watching Jians cheered as the creatures went up in flames, they cheered as the Kojin howled in agony, they cheered as they crashed into buildings and each other trying to escape the flames and they cheered as they fell to the ground and lay still.

'Celebrate later,' shouted Jax. 'We've a city to win. Danni, take us back to the port governor's mansion. As long as the Tonin's alive, no one's safe.'

Danni pressed his torn cheek against his face as if that would heal the wound. 'Give me a minute.'

'We haven't got—'

A Hanran ran over with a knife, its blade glowing red-hot.

Danni took it and thrust the blade against the cut skin. He screamed as his cheek burned. Smoke drifted off his bright-red flesh when he took the blade away. He groaned through clenched teeth and squeezed his eyes shut as he gathered himself. When he opened his eyes again, there was a madness in them. 'Let's go.'

Ash and embers floated around them as they ran. Smoke stung Jax's eyes. Fighting and dying filled his ears and, somewhere, behind it all, there was the Tonin's screech. That gate was still open.

Danni led them back into the boulevard, the screech growing louder, closer. Dead lay everywhere. A mess of blood and bodies; a fair few Skulls but a damn sight more Jians squashed by the Kojin. It was a nightmare.

That ungodly howl was easy to locate now. A grand building lay at the end of the avenue, with a fury of fighting before it. Skulls and Jians battled back and forth, with more Skulls coming out of the building to join in. So many more.

'Jax!'

He turned at the sound of his name and thanked the Gods. There was Moiri and the others, sprinting over from the opposite side of the boulevard. Two hundred Shulka, armed and ready to wreak havoc. Jax grinned. Perfect timing.

There was only one order to give. The last thing to do. 'Charge!'

He didn't wait to see if anyone obeyed, he just set off running as fast as he could, sword in hand, towards the melee.

Then he was in amongst it, with no time to worry, no time to think, his sword doing its bloody work. Hacking left, slashing right. Everywhere he looked there was a Skull to kill.

But a heartbeat later, he felt a shift in the wall of bodies as the Skulls stepped back, giving room, and Jax knew the others were with him, adding their spears and swords to his. And he roared with joy. This was what he was born to do.

More enemy fell as Jax and the others advanced, Jians united in heart and action.

'Kill them all,' he shouted over the madness. Only the Gods knew if anyone heard him.

Danni was with them, his cheek still red-hot, mad-eyed, swinging his rod, cleaving Skulls. Then Nicola, the dark-haired woman, slashing with knife-tipped hands while another madman went to work on an Egril with a blacksmith's hammer.

It was glorious, and they were winning.

The Egril sensed it, too, and their ranks shattered, all discipline gone, giving up the fight and running to save their lives. Straight back to the mansion. Straight back to the Tonin.

'After them!' screamed Jax. 'Don't let them get away. Kill them all. Show no mercy.'

No one needed telling twice to kill a running foe. The Hanran sliced hamstrings, stabbed through backs and plunged swords into necks. No one cared how they did it as long as every Skull died.

There was no hiding in the mansion, either. The monsters had conveniently smashed the doors out of the front of the building so the Hanran poured in unhindered, screaming at the top of their lungs, taking more lives. But still that Tonin's magic rattled.

Jax stopped in the main entrance hall and stepped out of the way of the mob. He was panting, eyes rattling with that Godsdamned scream. Let the others have the fun and the glory. 'Find the Tonin!' he called as the others ran past. 'Find the bloody Tonin.'

He looked around, trying to locate that howl, but it was all too loud, Skulls everywhere. Fighting. Dying. It was chaos.

Then silence fell. So sudden it stopped everyone mid-swing, mid-thrust. Even the wounded and dying seemed to stop screaming. Heads looked around in wonder, momentarily confused. But everyone knew what had happened – the gate was down, the Tonin most likely dead.

'Keep fighting!' roared Jax as if he were shouting into a hurricane. And, just like that, the spell was broken and the war resumed.

He watched, a mad grin on his face, proud as the Hanran did their bloody work, picking off the last of the stragglers, the battle won.

Danni staggered over, skin stained scarlet with his own and enemy blood, leaning on his iron rod, but by the Gods, he looked happy. 'We've done it! Chita's free.'

'Aye,' replied Jax. 'And Jia next.'

Danni wrapped an arm around Jax's head and pulled it close to kiss. 'May the Gods bless you and all yours, you mad bastard. You saved us all.'

Jax pulled himself free. '*We* did this, my friend. We did this.' He scanned the room. Only the allies remained alive from what he could see. Then he spotted Moiri.

She rushed over and they fell into each other's arms. 'Thank the Gods you're alive,' she said.

'Thank the Gods you arrived when you did,' replied Jax.

They looked at each other then, deep into each other's eyes, and something passed between them, unspoken but all the more powerful for it.

Hours later, Jax lay in a bed for the first time in he didn't know how long, in a room in the port governor's mansion. There was still fighting going on in the city, but Chita was back in Jian hands. Moiri lay next to him, curled up against his chest, his arm around her shoulders. She had fallen asleep soon after their lovemaking had finished. Jax had tried to sleep as well, but every time he closed his eyes, he saw the red cave, the blood, the monsters – and he heard Darus's Godsdamned laughter.

Some things even a battle couldn't shake loose. Better he stay awake. Better keep that monster away.

42

Tinnstra

The Northern Road

Tinnstra and the others arrived at the campsite ahead of the main army. It was once a small farm on the River Silik, nestled between small hills that offered protection from the elements. The farm's owner wasn't going to object to an army taking over their land, either, as they were long gone, or more likely long dead. That was the Skull way, after all. Perhaps their body lay buried beneath the tall grass that filled the fields instead of crops. Maybe they'd not even been afforded that simple kindness.

When she saw the others arrive, Tinnstra didn't greet them with smiles this time. She was under no illusion that her job was done. *The Skulls never give up. It's not their way.*

'Find anyone?' asked Hasan.

Tinnstra shook her head. There was no need to mention the four she'd killed. 'They'll come tonight.'

'Great,' replied Hasan. 'I'll double the guards, move them further out.'

'A good idea.' *It won't be enough.*

Ralasis raised an eyebrow in greeting. 'Fancy a romantic dinner by the river while I soothe my feet? My treat?'

Despite her mood, the Meigorian made her smile. 'Tempting, but not tonight.'

He pointed to the river. 'You know where I'll be if you change your mind.'

'I'll think about it.' *If only this was a world for such things.* Those last days in Meigore felt so long ago now. Precious moments gone too soon.

Aasgod and Zorique came next. She ignored the mage and went to her daughter instead. The queen looked tired. 'How are you feeling?'

Zorique tried to smile. 'Been better.'

'Try and rest, if you can,' said Tinnstra. 'Tonight will be … dangerous.'

'Will they attack?'

'They'll try.'

Zorique's head dropped. 'I … I'm not sure I can take another attack like last night.'

'I'm hoping you won't have to.'

'You always said hope was for fools.'

'We'll stop them before they can hurt anyone.'

'You don't know that.'

'I do. They caught me off guard last night. I won't make the same mistake again.'

'You know how I told you the Chosen's baton blasts hurt me at the beach?' said Zorique. She sounded hesitant, as if she was scared of what Tinnstra would say.

'Yes.'

'It was worse last night. Worse than at the beach.'

'In what way?'

'It felt like I was being bitten by a thousand sharp teeth that were eating away at my magic. It took everything I had to keep my shield up.'

'Maybe they're doing something different, changing something, after what happened in Layso – and at the beach. Trying to find a way to stop you.'

Zorique's head dropped. 'To kill me.'

'They've been trying to do that since you were four years old,' Tinnstra replied. 'They've not succeeded. They won't now.'

'What if they do?'

'Believe in yourself. You will only grow stronger. You will defeat them.'

'I hope so.'

'I know so. That's why we've trained all these years. So we can do this.'

That got a smile from the girl. 'That's why we train.'

'Go and rest while you can.'

'What about you?'

'I'll rest once I've checked the perimeter and made sure everyone knows what to watch for.'

'We need you, Tinn. Don't do anything foolish.'

'I'll be back soon.' Tinnstra left her bag with Zorique's attendants as they started to set up the queen's tent and wandered around the campsite. Tinnstra didn't like leaving her supply of Chikara water but she needed to travel light. There would be fighting soon and she needed to be ready. She had five vials in the pouch on her hip anyway. More than enough to get her through the night.

Tinnstra ignored the south and focused her attention north and towards the rolling hills and long grass. Perfect for an enemy to approach unseen.

That's where she would go once it was dark.

A small cluster of hills in particular drew her attention. She had no idea why except a feeling that, if she were the Egril, that's where she would choose to attack from. She could imagine the Daijaku swooping down from there, eager to repeat the previous night's destruction. Were they there now, watching her?

She stretched out her senses, seeking the spike of pain that would confirm her enemies were near. But they weren't. Not yet. But the bastards were coming. They always did. In that regard at least, the Skulls were predictable.

Tinnstra found a spot on the edge of the farm and perched on a piece of fencing that somehow remained standing. From there she watched as the soldiers raised their tents and cooked food around small, scattered fires. There was little chatter and certainly no laughter. The air stank of fear, something Tinnstra had once been such an expert on, which made her angrier still. She hated the fact that everyone looked so beaten after just a week. And she hated the fact they'd been beaten so easily. That *she'd* been beaten so easily.

She rubbed the bandage over her lost eye. None of them was quite what they once were.

Not even Zorique.

The remains of the day hung in the sky, but it would soon be dark. Tinnstra played with a vial of Chikara water in one hand, rolling it between her fingers. She wanted to drink it right then, get rid of the tiredness that dragged at her body and made her eye burn, but she had another long night ahead of her and couldn't peak too soon.

By the Gods, she needed to kill someone. And tonight she'd get her chance. She knew the Skulls would be back. They must know they had the Jians on the ropes. A few more attacks like the previous night and it would all be over.

But to do that, they needed to get a Tonin close enough. *That* was Tinnstra's opportunity. She just had to take out the creature before it could work its magic. And work some magic of her own.

Nika, Tavis, Dale and the rest of her ten approached. Tinnstra slipped off the fence and dropped to the ground. 'How did you get on?'

'No one out there now,' said Tavis, 'and hasn't been for a long time.'

'Maybe we'll get lucky tonight and they won't attack,' said Dale.

Tinnstra ignored the naivety. 'Half of you rest now. The rest join the sentries and patrols. Change over in four hours' time.'

'What about you, Chief?' asked Nika.

'I'm going to stay solo. I'll call you if I need you.'

'Take care,' said Tavis, with a look that said he didn't believe she would.

Tinnstra ignored it. 'Get some sleep.'

Alone once more, she watched the last streaks of colour sink behind a hill. Shadows soon covered the farm, quickly followed by the darkness. She watched and waited as the night settled and the moon rose high above them all. All the while, she played with the vial of Chikara water, rolling it back and forth between her fingers, happy to know it was there, ignoring the temptation to drink it. She was stronger than her urges.

Then it was time to go. Still clutching the vial, she set off north, avoiding the road, cutting through the long grass.

The allies had patrols a good mile outside of camp, all armed with horns and with orders to blow them at the merest hint of trouble. Some of Ralasis' best, she'd been told, but Tinnstra slipped past them all unseen. Even her own didn't know she passed them by. Better to be a shadow to all. Better to be alone.

The darkness seeped around her, shielding her. Once it would've scared her to be out on her own at night; now she welcomed it. Still, she kept her pace slow and steady, her ears open and her eye always moving.

Her eye. Maybe she was getting used to that.

She searched with her mind, too, waiting for that first prick of pain, that first sign of nearby magic, but all she felt was Zorique and Aasgod's presence behind her. Even as she drew further away, their position remained anchored in her mind.

Tinnstra headed towards the cluster of hills she'd spotted earlier, then veered to the west as she drew near, looking for a spot to hide. In the end, she almost tripped over a small hollow in the darkness and she thanked the Gods because it was exactly what she needed.

She slipped down and out of sight and started to wait once more.

And wait.

It was the last thing she wanted to do. Time dragged on, the cold reached her bones and tiredness dragged at her mind. How long had it been since she last slept? Two days? Three?

At least she had a solution to that problem.

Without looking, she pulled the stopper out of her vial and raised it to her lips, eager for the water's bitter taste.

Except the vial was empty.

Tinnstra stared at it disbelievingly. Had it spilled while she was running? No, she would've felt that. Her hand would've been wet.

Had she drunk it earlier? While they were chasing the Egril across the country? She'd have remembered that, surely. She'd thought about it, but she knew she'd decided not to, to save it for later.

Dear Gods, the only truth was that the vial had always been empty.

Tinnstra threw it aside and then reached into the pouch on her hip for another. She picked one, unwrapped it from its protective cloth, saw that it was empty, too.

Her temper flared. Had Aasgod swapped her vials for empty ones? Was this some sick trick of his? Another way of controlling her?

She wouldn't have put it past the hateful mage.

Tinnstra rooted around for another. It was full. She checked the last two. They, too, were full, thank the Gods. So what happened to the others? It made no sense.

Unless I drank them.

No, I'd remember that. Wouldn't I?

Tinnstra didn't want to think about what that meant. It was a problem for another day. She uncorked the vial and this time she drank, shuddering at the taste. Immediately, the world brightened. She heard a soldier in a patrol grumble about being in Jia when he should have been back home in Meigore. She sensed a rabbit darting through the field. Instead of the faint echo of Zorique and Aasgod's power that she had felt before, now their magic thrummed in her mind as if they were standing right next to her.

She dropped the empty vial at her feet, breathing deeply of the night air, thinking about nothing except the hum of the Chikara water racing through her veins. By the Gods, she felt more alive than ever, connected to the world on a level that was—

There they are. The Egril were near. A Tonin, two Chosen plus ... four others. Skulls. On the other side of the hill, maybe two miles away, moving slowly, doing their best to keep quiet. But to her ears? Every footfall sounded as if they were beside her. Every clink of their armour rang like a bell.

She smiled. *Kage calls, you bastards. The Great Darkness waits for you.*

She ran, silent as the grass, swift as the wind, sure as death. The distance disappeared beneath her feet. She had them.

One of the Chosen separated from the rest and headed towards the top of the hill. The others remained on the far side, out of sight. The Tonin was nervous ... no, scared. It didn't like being outside. It wasn't used to it. Tinnstra could smell its rotting skin, hear its ragged breath.

She cut around the hill, a shadow in the grass. She slipped free her axe, her hunger growing. For justice, for revenge, for blood.

Kage was going to have his souls this night.

She saw them from half a mile away, as bright as day. The Tonin's magic throbbed with its heartbeat, while the Chosen's hummed an angry red. The Skulls wore black armour to blend with the night, but they needn't have bothered. Their life forces had songs that were loud as any orchestra. Their spirits shone like a fire she couldn't wait to snuff out.

Tinnstra didn't slow down. Why should she? They couldn't see her, they didn't hear her. On she came, full of fury, full of hate, closing the distance to six hundred yards, five hundred, four hundred.

The Chikara water surged through Tinnstra and she grinned with the sheer, mad pleasure of it. Finally, it was her turn. Her time.

She threw the axe when she was forty feet away and chased in after it, drawing her sword as it spun through the air. Three turns and its blade bit deep into the Chosen's temple. Then Tinnstra was on them.

The Skulls had barely registered the Chosen was dead when she took one of their heads. A quick turn to the next and she drove the blade into his face. She left her weapon buried in their head and seized the third Skull's helmet by the chin. A yank and his neck was broken. One Skull left, his hand moving too slowly for his scimitar. Her knife was a hundred times faster.

The Tonin backed away, but there was no running from death. She leaped on it, driving it to the ground, one hand over its mouth, ignoring its stench. She stared into its eyes and, by the Gods, she loved seeing the fear there. She loved smashing her fist into its face even more, breaking bone, destroying teeth. Over and over, hammering away, shattering the Tonin's skull. Even when she knew it was dead, she continued pounding because why the hell not? How many of her friends, her countrymen, had died because of this creature or others like it?

She stopped only when she sensed the last Chosen, a woman, returning, unaware all her comrades were with Kage in the Great Darkness.

Tinnstra rose, covered in blood and brains, and retrieved her axe. She raced up the hill, keeping low, moving like a snake in the grass, as the Chosen wandered down towards her. The urge to kill still roared inside Tinnstra with an intensity a thousand deaths would never satisfy.

The Chosen was tall, dark hair blowing in the breeze. She held her baton in her right hand. No doubt she was picturing Daijaku swooping down upon the Jians' camp with their cursed bombs again. Thinking about the mayhem they would cause. *Bitch. I've got a surprise for you.*

With no need to be quiet, Tinnstra screamed her rage as she jumped out of the grass, axe swinging.

The Chosen raised the baton. Energy sparked bright at its tip. All too slow, too late.

Tinnstra took the Chosen's right arm first, baton tumbling into the night. She spun and hacked off the woman's left leg below the knee a heartbeat later. The Egril went down, spurting blood, her screams drowning out Tinnstra's laughter.

Tinnstra kicked her in the head to shut her up.

She got to work quickly, tying off the amputations, not wanting the woman to bleed out just yet. Not when she had so many questions to ask. No one was going to take her for a fool again. This time she'd make sure she got the truth.

Once that was done, Tinnstra straddled the woman. She pulled a knife from her belt and tapped the Chosen's face with it. 'Wake up.'

No response, so Tinnstra stuck the knife through the woman's cheek until the blade's tip touched her teeth. The Chosen's eyes shot open, her body bucking in a futile effort to free itself of Tinnstra's weight. She tried to scream, but Tinnstra's other hand quickly smothered that. Tinnstra leaned in close. 'Shhhh.'

The Chosen's eyes twitched as she took in Tinnstra and the

bloodied knife and saw her death before her. She went silent and still, sucking in air through her nose as best she could.

Satisfied, Tinnstra removed her hand. 'Hello,' she said in Egril. 'My name's Tinnstra. I'd like to have a little chat with you.'

Zorique was asleep when Tinnstra got back to the camp, but Aasgod was still awake, watching over her from a chair. He started as Tinnstra entered the queen's tent, then his eyes bulged at the state of her. At the blood that covered her hands and clothes.

'Where have you been? What happened?' he spluttered.

Tinnstra dropped the two Chosen's masks on a table. 'We don't have to worry about an attack tonight.' Her head pulsed with the pain from being so close to Zorique and Aasgod, making her wince. She had to concentrate, shut down her feelings, ignore the fire in her mind.

'You fought two Chosen?' hissed Aasgod, trying to keep his voice low.

'I killed two Chosen,' she corrected, 'as well as a Tonin and some Skulls.'

'Where?'

'In the hills to the north. They were preparing to attack us again.'

'And you fought them alone?'

'Yes.' Tinnstra spat the word out, her blood still up, the pain in her head destroying all patience. She didn't like the way he was looking at her, either – as if she'd done something wrong. 'You'd rather I'd let them be? Let them attack us?'

'I'd rather you'd taken someone with you,' said Aasgod, getting to his feet, his voice rising with him. 'Someone who could've helped you, or at least warned the rest of us if you got yourself killed.'

'You're just a coward,' Tinnstra spat back.

Zorique sat up. 'What's going on?'

'Aasgod's upset that I went out and killed some Egril before they could attack us,' said Tinnstra.

'You did?'

Tinnstra glared at Aasgod. 'I did.'

'Why didn't you tell me you were going to do that?' said Zorique. 'I could've gone with you. Or Aasgod. You might've been killed.'

'What? You're taking *his* side?' Tinnstra couldn't believe it. Not her own daughter.

'I'm not taking anyone's side,' replied Zorique, swinging her legs out of the bed. 'But what you did was dangerous.'

'We're fighting a war. Everything about this is dangerous.' Tinnstra's voice grew louder as her frustration escalated. 'You should all be thanking me – unless you like losing every battle.'

Aasgod held up both hands. 'Calm down, Tinnstra.'

Tinnstra jabbed a finger at the mage. 'Don't you tell me to calm down. I was the one out there, saving everyone's lives – not you.'

'Because you didn't give any of us the opportunity to help,' said Aasgod.

'And why would I want you with me? I should've left you in the past, for all the good you do.'

'Enough!' Zorique shouted. She stood, glowing, looking every bit as if she was ready to fight if need be. 'Tinnstra, Aasgod is right. Next time, take some soldiers with you. By the Gods, take me.'

'As you wish, My Queen.' Tinnstra inhaled sharply through her nose, trying to calm the fire in her blood. She wasn't going to argue with Zorique. That wasn't why she was there. 'I questioned one of the Chosen before they died.'

'And?' said Zorique, her eyes flicking to the bloody masks on her table.

'You were right. Raaku's done something to them all so they can hurt you.' She walked over to the table and filled a cup with water. 'He summoned them all back to their capital – to Kagestan – after our victory in Layso. There are caverns under his castle where he makes his monsters. Caverns filled with pools of water.'

Aasgod arched an eyebrow. 'Chikara water?'

'The Chosen didn't call it that, but Raaku submerged them one by one and charged them with his magic, changing them. Some got extra powers, but he altered how their batons worked

318

as well. Still lethal to us ordinary folk of course, but now their magic affects Zorique, too.'

'Damn.'

'It changes nothing,' said Zorique. 'We knew they could hurt me.'

The mage sat down, his anger gone. 'Chikara-water springs. This explains Raaku's power – how he's done what he's done.'

'It's not all bad news. This proves Raaku is no God – or even the son of a God. He's just a human like you or me – and humans die,' said Tinnstra. 'They can be killed.'

Aasgod shook his head. 'Who by? No one would be able to get close enough to do it. Not even if we took the whole army into Egril. We don't even know where Kagestan is in Egril.'

Tinnstra said nothing. The fool didn't have the imagination to see things the way she did. She had a plan now. She'd turn the Egril's own weapons against them – as long as Wenna had found out where the Tonin were being kept in Aisair like she'd asked. *Then I'll go and say hello to Raaku.*

43

Wenna

Aisair

'Where is he?' asked Wenna, peering through a gap in the curtains.

'He's not late yet,' said Royati from the other side of the room, but she sounded far from relaxed. They were in a set of rooms on Salin Street, a quiet cul-de-sac in the east of Aisair. It was their seventh hiding place since arriving in Aisair, and they'd already been in these rooms for two days. It'd be time to move again soon. Maybe even later that day. But for now, they waited for Kos.

They took turns watching the street, no matter if it was day or night. They couldn't afford having the Skulls catch them unawares. Wenna had been camped at the window for nearly two hours now, while Royati sat at the small table. Sami was asleep in the room next door, having taken the previous shift. Out of them all, he seemed to be holding up the best. Maybe he didn't realise how dangerous things were, or perhaps he didn't care, but give him a bed and the boy could sleep for days if they let him.

Wenna peered out into the street once more. Curfew had ended about an hour before, but she hadn't seen anyone walking by. People were staying in their homes more and more as the tension built in the city. Word had reached them that the invasion had been a success, that Zorique and her army were marching north, but the Skulls had plastered notices everywhere promising death to any that offered them aid or shelter. Hangings had followed quickly after – not that the Jians were guilty of anything. There was no army to shelter yet. The Skulls were just making a point. They wanted everyone good and scared.

Some had been from Kos's crew, picked up here and there, more often by chance than by design. Others, though – most of them – were just civilians who were in the wrong place at the wrong time. Their deaths clawed at Wenna's heart, but there was nothing she or the Hanran could do to save them.

Instead, they worked tirelessly to smuggle as many people as they could out of the city. Doing it via the south of the city was impossible, what with the barricades and the trenches, but the north was still relatively open for now. Ironically, the hangings had made the evacuations easier – not many people argued to stay any longer, especially when they realised things were going to get a whole lot worse in the days ahead.

Nerves weren't helped, either, by the continual screech coming from the king's castle. Kos's informant in the palace had told them that the Skulls had brought in more Tonin and had them working non-stop transferring more and more troops and monsters into the city. Wenna could've worked that out for herself, though. The wail of open gates was never-ending and a constant reminder that whatever information Wenna gathered on the Egril forces was next to useless the moment she got it.

The Tonin, as ever, were the key to everything. If it were down to Wenna, she'd have launched an attack on the castle somehow, tried to kill those evil creatures, but she had her orders from Tinnstra herself.

She wanted to know where they were, how she could get to them, but she'd made it clear that under no circumstances were the Tonin in the city to be harmed. Only the Gods and Tinnstra knew why, but Wenna wasn't one to argue. Not with Tinnstra.

Wenna wanted to speak to the insider herself but getting to them had been impossible – until now. The insider had sent word that they could leave the castle for one hour just after curfew ended. Kos was going to bring them to Salin Street to meet Wenna and Royati.

So where was he? First light, he'd said, and that was long gone now. Had the Skulls caught him? Were they coming for Wenna and Royati next?

She glanced over at her friend. 'Go wake Sami up and get our stuff ready – just in case.'

Royati nodded and got up without any argument. After all, no one ever died for being overcareful.

Wenna smiled when she heard Sami complaining. The boy could cope with anything – except being woken up.

Then movement caught her eye at the far end of the street. Kos ... with someone. Whoever it was had a hood over their head and a long cloak, but she guessed it was a woman by the way they moved. They walked quickly, like everyone did these days. Not wasting any time, but not so fast it drew too much attention.

Wenna watched them and the street behind them, making sure they weren't being followed. If anything, this was the most dangerous time. The Egril could be lying in wait, hoping to catch everyone together. But the street remained clear except for Kos and the woman.

As they reached the steps to the house, Wenna opened the door. They slipped inside and she shut it quickly after them. 'Any trouble?'

Kos shook his head. 'No more than usual.'

Royati reappeared. 'Hello. You made it, then.' Sami followed close behind, then peeled off to sit in the corner of the room.

'Aye,' said Kos. 'You two okay?'

'Never better,' said Royati. She took Wenna's place by the window. Someone always watched the street. 'Who's your friend?'

'This is Grace,' said Kos. 'She's my daughter.'

'She's too pretty to be related to you,' said Wenna, and it was true. The woman had taken her hood down and she was utterly beautiful. Maybe even the most beautiful woman Wenna had ever seen. Shame someone had smacked her in the mouth recently. The fading bruise on her left cheek could only have been caused by the back of someone's hand. 'I'm Wenna. Have a seat.' She indicated the chair where Royati had been sitting.

'Thank you,' said Grace. Kos sat next to her and Wenna took the chair opposite. Now she could see the resemblance between the two, especially around the eyes. She brought a brightness to her father that made him seem younger. She, on the other hand, looked not even twenty.

'Grace ... lives in the castle at the moment,' said Kos.

The girl glanced at her father, then turned to Wenna. 'I'm the king's consort.'

Kos squirmed and Wenna could hardly blame him. 'Right. Is that who gave you the bruise?'

'The king's not a very nice person.'

'We needed someone close so we could relay as much information out of the place as possible,' said Kos.

'The Egril are too careful around strangers to let things slip, but Larius's ego doesn't allow him to think that someone is with him for any other reason than lust or love,' said Grace. 'I have to sit and listen while he complains about how unfair his life is. He tells me everything.'

'Have you met this general of theirs? Vallia?' asked Wenna.

'A few times. They normally send me away when she speaks to Larius, but he rants about her for hours afterwards. Apparently, she doesn't treat him with respect.' Grace laughed, but it was a cold and bitter sound. 'Everyone's complaining about the number of troops she's bringing in – especially Larius. We're running out of room to accommodate everyone, and food stocks are getting low. But it's the noise that's the worst – from the Tonin.'

'How many are there?' asked Wenna.

'Larius said there are three of them now, opening gates around the clock. Apparently, they can only work their magic for so long before they need to rest.'

'Do you know where they keep them?' asked Wenna.

'Down in the basement, past the cells. They're always under lock and key and only Chosen or Vallia are allowed in to see them,' said Grace. 'I've never been down there myself, but some of the kitchen staff have taken food to the guards.'

'Not to the Tonin?'

'No one knows what they eat.'

'Has Larius said much about the invasion?'

'Only that Vallia will stop it. He's petrified, though. He thinks he'll be put in prison if the Egril army is overthrown.'

'If he's lucky,' murmured Kos.

'Don't worry,' said Grace. 'He won't live a minute longer than he has to. I promise you that.'

'Why does he think Vallia will win?' asked Wenna.

'She has over eight hundred Chosen here alone,' said Grace. 'Plus fifteen thousand Skulls. And Larius says there are other monsters, too dangerous to keep here, that Vallia will bring over when the Jians arrive.'

'Do you know where Vallia sleeps?' asked Wenna.

'I asked Grace to map out where everything and everyone is inside the castle,' said Kos.

Wenna perked up at that. 'And have you?'

Grace reached into her cloak and produced a folded piece of paper. 'Here.'

Wenna all but snatched it from the girl's hand and unfolded it on the table. 'Well done.' Grace had drawn and marked every level of the castle, from top to bottom. It had everything, from the Skull barracks to the Daijaku nests, from Larius's quarters to the cells in the basement. 'This is priceless.'

'I'd best be getting Grace back,' said Kos. 'Before ... that man misses her.'

'Thank you, Grace,' said Wenna. 'But you don't have to go back now. Your father can take you to safety.'

'People will get suspicious if I don't return,' said Grace.

'Who cares? You've given us the information we need,' said Wenna. 'Two weeks from now and they'll all be worrying about the army on their doorstep.'

'I told her the same thing,' said Kos.

'And I said I'm going back,' said Grace. 'What if something happens that you need to know about? Something that might affect the outcome of this war? What then?'

Wenna and Kos said nothing. She had a point.

'I'll leave when Zorique arrives,' said Grace.

Wenna nodded. 'All right.'

Kos stood up. 'Come on, then. Let's take you back.'

'May the Four Gods watch over you,' said Wenna as Grace got to her feet.

She pulled her hood over her head again. 'And over you.'

'Not an easy job that girl's got,' said Royati once Kos and Grace had left. 'Not for Kos, either.'

'There are no easy jobs left,' said Wenna. 'Look at us.'

'So what do we do now?' asked Royati.

Wenna held up the map of the castle. 'We leave the city and find Tinnstra.'

Sami sat up. 'When?'

'No time like the present,' said Wenna. 'You've packed our bags already, haven't you?'

44

Vallia

Aisair

The Daijaku squawked and flapped their wings, eager to be off, eager to drop death on the Jians again. A hundred of the creatures were waiting in the grounds of the royal palace for the Tonin to open the gate.

The Daijaku weren't the only ones growing restless. Vallia watched from the window of the war room with Chosen Torvi next to her, waiting for word that the latest attack was underway.

'They should've gone by now,' said Torvi, as if reading her thoughts. 'The Tonin should've opened the gate.'

'I know,' replied Vallia. Already, the sky was starting to lighten over Aisair.

There was a knock at the door.

'Come in,' said Vallia.

An aide entered and bowed. 'I apologise for disturbing you.'

Vallia waved the man closer. 'What news?'

'There was an uprising in Chita, on the north-west coast.'

Vallia didn't need to look at the map. She knew where it was. 'And?'

'We had the uprising under control, but the Hanran were re-inforced by an outside force who turned the battle in their favour. The city is now in Jian hands.'

'The Tonin?'

'It was brought back here before the city fell.'

'Do you know how large the Hanran force was that came to Chita's aid?'

'Reports from the survivors put the Hanran force at a few thousand.'

Vallia nodded. This wasn't the news she wanted to hear. 'Send the Daijaku back to their aviary. Give them plenty to eat – five or six prisoners from the dungeons should keep them happy. And get the Tonin to open a gate to Kagestan once it's back in its cell downstairs.'

'I'll see to it now, Commander,' replied the aide.

'I'd gladly lead the reinforcements to take back Chita,' said Torvi, once the man was gone.

Vallia glanced over at the Chosen. 'No, I'd rather you were here. There are others that can deal with the Hanran in the north.'

Torvi nodded. 'As you wish.'

Vallia watched the sun rise over the city. 'Hope is contagious. It will spread from heart to heart until we destroy its source.'

'The girl, Zorique.'

'Yes.' Vallia moved back to the map. The blue blocks were making good progress, despite all she'd done to slow them down. She'd not expected that night's assault to be stopped before it had begun. She'd promised Kage more heathen souls and she'd failed him. 'I think I'll need to get more creative in dealing with our enemies.' Vallia cracked her neck from side to side, aware of how tired she was and of how much there was still left to do. 'Anything interesting in the reports from our spies?'

'Nothing new. Every day, the queen marches in the heart of the army with the mage next to her while the Shulka scout ahead, looking for any sign of ambush.'

'For all her power, they keep their queen well protected.'

'She's never alone – except when she flies off by herself.'

Vallia looked up from the map. 'By herself?'

'She leaves the army and flies off on her own. Sometimes she's gone for minutes, other times it's hours.'

'Interesting. Do the reports say what's more common?'

'No.'

'Still – it opens up all sorts of possibilities. Any sign of the fourth champion?'

'Not that we've seen.'

'Why keep that champion secret? They're not hiding the others.'

'Perhaps there are only three after all – just the queen, the mage and the Shulka?'

'Four Gods. Four champions.'

'Then the fourth one hasn't met up with the others yet.' Torvi ran her hand through her hair. 'Perhaps if we can find whoever it is before they do—'

Vallia shook her head. 'They could be anyone, anywhere. No, we focus on the other three. They are foolish enough. Their strength is together but the Shulka and the queen seem not to realise that. Perhaps this gives us an opportunity we can take advantage of.' Already her mind was racing with the possibilities. 'Now, if you'll excuse me, I must go to the capital and speak to the Emperor.'

Torvi saluted. 'Praise be to Kage.'

Vallia nodded. 'Indeed.'

Astin was waiting for her. 'He asked me to bring you straight to him.'

There was no need to ask who *he* was. 'Lead on.'

For once, Astin didn't take her down into the caverns. Instead, he took her to Raaku's throne room. It was rarely used. Raaku, after all, was not one for needless pomp and ceremony. Even so, the chamber stretched half the length of his castle, with a ceiling some thirty feet high. The face of Kage had been carved out of the eastern wall and the morning sun streaked into the room through a single window in the place of Kage's right eye.

Raaku was sitting on the throne below his father's face. His bodyguards stood two on either side. The men were nearly as large as the Emperor himself and wore the red armour and demon masks of the First Legion. Their scimitars were twice the size of a normal soldier's. Vallia had seen the guards cut a man in half with a single stroke on more than one occasion.

Other members of the First lined either side of the chamber, along with at least a dozen Chosen, but the person that piqued Vallia's curiosity was the man in grey robes kneeling in front of the Emperor. There was a parchment laid out before him on the floor.

When Astin and Vallia reached the throne, both knelt and bowed, keeping their foreheads pressed against the stone.

'Rise, my friends,' said Raaku. 'It is good to see you.'

Vallia straightened and looked upon the face of her master. It was hard to remember a time when she had thought him merely human, back before the War of Unification. Now he radiated his divinity and she found her breath catching in her throat at the sight of him.

'My father thanks you for the souls you have sent him, Commander Vallia. Over half the heathen army are now slaves in the Great Darkness,' said the Emperor.

Vallia bowed once more. 'With many more to follow, Your Majesty.'

'Of course, Commander. Especially now that you will have some help.' Raaku indicated the grey-robed man. A mask, carved like a hawk's beak, covered the upper half of his face. 'This is Illius.'

The man gave a curt bow. 'Commander.'

'The king's palace in Meigore had wards inscribed into the walls,' said Raaku. 'These wards were not only effective against the Chosen's powers, but they also removed the heathen queen's magic when she crossed over them.'

That was news to Vallia, but she said nothing. Her place was to listen to her master.

'Lord Bacas's spy found documentation in the palace's records detailing the wards,' said Raaku. 'Those documents were passed to Illius. He has discovered how they work.'

'You can remove the queen's powers?' Vallia asked the scholar, unable to control her excitement.

The man smiled. 'Yes.'

Vallia's mind raced. Without her powers, Zorique was just a girl who could die all too easily. She bowed to Raaku once more. 'Thank you, Your Majesty, for this gift.'

'Commander,' said Raaku. 'Prepare your army. Prepare the city. When the time comes, I will join you for Sekanowari.'

Vallia bowed, deep and long. 'As you command, My Emperor.'

45
Yas

Arlen's Farm

The horn sounded from the north. It was one of the sentries Yas had set up a good distance from Arlen's Farm, watching for anything or anyone coming their way.

Everyone stopped what they were doing when they heard it. There was that lull before realisation dawned on them all that danger could be approaching. Yas was no different. She'd been playing with Little Ro and the other kids, rolling stones on a patch of dirt. She froze, stone in hand, mid-throw, mouth open.

Then everyone moved, may the Gods bless them. Just like they'd practised. The men and some of the women took up weapons and ran to positions along the barricades they'd built. They were nothing more than bits of tree and bushes tied together, but it was something. Enough to block a spear or stop some arrows. They'd dug trenches in front of them to make things that much harder. The holes were filled with spikes, all covered in shit. It wasn't a good smell, but it made people think twice about touching them, and if they got stuck by one, the wound would go rotten sure as night followed day.

The children were taken to one of the fields and hidden in pits. The wooden traps were covered with grass, so once they were lowered, they were all but invisible. Some of the women went in, too. Their jobs were to look after the kids and keep them quiet. It only took one to start bawling to give everyone away.

The hiding pits had been Yas's idea. Even so, the last thing she wanted to do was leave Little Ro in one of them. But she couldn't keep him with her, either, so she passed him over to Timy and watched the two of them climb into one of the bigger burrows. 'Keep him safe,' said Yas. Timy looked petrified but nodded all the same.

Dean and Sorin were waiting for her, armed with cutlasses. Dean even had one for her. She took it without a word and headed to the main barricade, the Weeping Men following behind.

She saw Anan, standing head and shoulders above the rest of them at the barricade, with a long fisherman's spear in his hand.

'We know what's coming yet?' she asked.

'I've sent one of the lads to have a look,' replied the old man. 'He's quick, so we'll find out soon enough.'

Yas stared off into the distance, towards the mountains. 'We should've worked out a better system. Different horn blasts or something. One for a friend, two for Skulls or something.'

'Aye,' said Anan. 'Well, we aren't quite Hanran yet, are we? Next time we will.'

'If there's a next time,' replied Yas, under her breath.

Anan heard her all the same. 'It's going to be all right.'

Yas kept her opinion to herself that time. Instead she watched the road, waiting for who knew what horror, trying not to think how good things were looking after just under a week at the farm. Almost like normal life should be.

'Lad's coming back,' said Anan, with a tilt of his beard towards the road.

Yas squinted, seeing nothing at first, then spotting the tiny figure sprinting for all he was worth. 'By the Gods, your eyes are good. What do you think?' She tightened her grip on the cutlass. 'Trouble?'

Anan shrugged. 'Or not.'

Yas didn't know why she said anything. Life had taught her what the answer always was. Nothing good.

The boy continued to run towards them. Whatever it was had put some speed under him and given him stamina, too.

Yas stared, trying to work out if the kid was scared or not, was running from a threat or …

'Help!' the lad shouted. 'They need help!'

Yas glanced at Anan. 'Help?'

'They need help,' the boy yelled again.

The people of Arlen's Farm rose from behind their barricades, but Yas shouted them down again. 'We still don't know what's going on. It could be a bloody trap.'

'Doesn't look like a trap to me,' said Anan.

Yas glared at the old fool. 'That's the whole point of a trap, isn't it?'

Anan waved his spear at the lad. 'Over here, Jessup.'

Jessup stopped on the other side of the spike-filled trench, panting and heaving. 'They ... they ...'

'Catch your breath, son.' Anan slapped the man next to him on the shoulder. 'Take him some water, eh?'

Jessup managed to get some wind before the man reached him. 'There's injured soldiers on the way. Thousands of them. They need help.'

'Thousands?' repeated Yas.

The lad nodded. 'Looks like it to me. Most are in a bad way.'

Yas looked at Anan, not daring to say what she feared. Gods, was Hasan amongst them? She closed her eyes. She needed to toughen up. This wasn't a time to be weak.

'We always knew people would get hurt,' said the old man. 'Best we do as Jessup asks and offer our help.'

'Half of us should stay here to defend the village – just in case,' said Yas. 'And let the children out for now.'

'What about you?'

'Let's see the wounded.'

Yas, Anan and two hundred of her people followed Jessup back to the Northern Road. They brought some carts with them, scavenged from the ruins of Kiyosun, loaded with water skins and bandages. They had no doctors, but a few of the villagers knew enough basics to be of use. Or at least Yas hoped they did.

She'd also brought Dean and Sorin along – just in case.

Her mind was a mad mix of fear and dread. How many more

people would they have to watch die? Dear Gods, let them all be Meigorians.

It took an hour to reach the wounded. An hour of walking through the mountain paths, each step taking Yas away from her perfect little village and back to the realities of the world. Back to the war.

At one point, she could see Kiyosun, a blackened ruin in the distance. Once that had been all she knew. Now she'd rather it was wiped from existence. It was nothing more than a painful reminder of what she'd lost. Better to concentrate on the future, on what could be.

And when they saw the injured? Her heart sank even more. They filled the Northern Road, stretching back as far as she could see. Not thousands like Jessup had said but more than enough. And may the Gods help her, but Yas's first thought was that she didn't want any of them near her village. Not if they were foreigners.

She walked down the line as her people went to work, passing out water skins, treating injuries or simply saying a few kind words when that was all they could do.

Yas smiled and nodded, playing her part, but she was checking faces more than anything else. Seeing who was hers and who was theirs. Who was Jian, who was Meigorian. And, of course, looking for Hasan, praying that he wasn't there, that he was alive and uninjured, not dead. Not like the rest of the men she'd loved.

There was every type of injury, from broken bones to missing limbs, from burned skin to sliced flesh. The stink of rot filled the air and it didn't take a doctor to know there were a good number who wouldn't see out the end of the week, and some not even the day. Death lingered over so many of them.

Too many.

It took everything Yas had not to cry or turn away. She forced herself to look at their pained faces, feeling pity one moment and then relief the next as she still didn't find the Hanran leader.

'He's still alive,' she told herself. 'Please let him still be alive.'

'Yas!' Anan waved her over. There was a woman with him that she recognised – Simone. She'd been married to a Meigorian, knew the language and had volunteered to go with the army to help translate. Now, she looked like she wished she'd stayed behind. One of her arms was bandaged and in a bloodstained sling, and her face was covered with cuts and small burns.

Standing with them was a Meigorian officer, judging by what was left of his jacket. His dark hair was unkempt and his eyes had a tired glaze to them. He leaned on a makeshift crutch to help a heavily bandaged leg.

Yas hurried over. 'I'd say it was good to see you, Simone, but it looks like you've been through hell.'

'Yas,' replied the woman with a nod.

Yas glanced back down the line of soldiers. 'Dear Gods. What happened?'

'The Daijaku attacked us up in the farmlands, past the mountains, four or five days back,' said Simone. 'Zorique stopped them in the end, but not before ... before ...'

'It's okay. You don't have to go into the details. I can imagine,' said Yas. 'Hasan ... is he ...'

'He was fine, last I saw him,' said Simone. 'He's taken what's left of the army on to Aisair.'

Relief washed over her. 'I'm glad you've made it back to us, Simone. You can tell me everything later when you've had some rest.'

'Thank you.'

'Who's your friend?'

'This is Captain Portis. He's in charge of the injured,' said Simone.

Yas gave the man a nod that could've, perhaps, been considered an attempt at a bow. 'Pleased to meet you, Captain. I'm Yas.'

Portis looked at Yas with what appeared to be a rather disapproving expression, then said something to Simone in Meigorian. She replied in a whisper, sounding almost embarrassed. The conversation went on, while Yas and Anan stood waiting. In the end, Yas had enough. 'Something wrong?'

Simone shook her head. 'The captain is just a bit ... thrown by your ... you know ...' Simone touched her own face just under the left eye, where Yas's tattoos were. 'In Meigore, it has bad ... connotations.'

'It does here as well,' replied Yas, a little too sharply.

'I told him that it's different with you,' said Simone. 'That you look after everyone. That you're not ... a ... one of them.' Her eyes went to Dean and Sorin.

'Oh, but *I* am,' said Yas. 'Make no mistake about that. These tears didn't get put on my face because I thought they looked nice. I *earned* them. Earned them the same way my two friends back there earned theirs.'

Simone stared at her, wide-eyed, scared, speechless.

'You not going to translate that?' asked Yas.

'Easy now,' said Anan quietly. 'No one means no harm. We're all on the same side.'

Yas smiled, but there was no warmth in it, and she let the Meigorian see that. 'Of course we are.'

'We're glad you're here,' said Simone. 'Honestly, we are. Some of the men ... well, they need your help if we're going to get them to the cave.'

'We're not up in the cave, lass,' said Anan. 'We're over at Arlen's Farm.'

That brought some life back to her eyes. 'You are?'

The big fisherman nodded. 'We're building proper homes again.'

Simone started saying something to Portis, but Yas held up a finger. 'Hold on. Before you start promising things, none of these soldiers are going to the farm.'

'They're not?' said Anan.

'No,' said Yas. 'The Meigorian hospital is at Omason Beach. They can go there. Plenty of good shelter – better than what we have at the farm, in fact – for everyone while they ... recover.'

'But they need help ... people to look after them,' said Simone. 'Zorique promised ...'

Again, Yas smiled. 'Zorique shouldn't be promising anything she needs other people to do. She's not queen yet. There isn't room at the farm for ... how many of you are there?'

'About twelve hundred started the trip,' said Simone. 'Some haven't survived the journey south.'

336

'The population of the farm is only eight hundred or so. The Meigorians would overrun the place.'

'But after what they've done ... sacrificed—'

'We appreciate everyone's sacrifices, Simone – you know that. We just want what's best – and the beach is best. We'll send people to help look after them, of course. We'll even provide what food we can – down at the beach.'

Simone translated to Portis, who again gave her that look that made Yas not want to do a bloody thing to help him, but he nodded all the same. 'Captain Portis agrees to go to Omason Beach.'

'That's good,' said Yas. 'It's much closer to here, anyway. The injured can get settled quicker.'

Simone gave a half-bow of her own. 'Yes, Yas. As you say.'

Yas turned to Anan. 'Take whoever you need and help our heroes to the beach. I'll come along later with some food and supplies for them all.'

Anan cleared his throat and rolled his shoulders, but whatever was on his mind, he decided against saying it. 'Will do,' he said. He put his arm around Simone's shoulders. 'Come on, lass. Best be on our way.'

Portis remained behind for a moment. He tapped his cheek under the left eye, just like Simone had done, then pointed at Yas, before spitting on the ground.

'Nice to meet you, too.' Yas gave him a real smile this time, showing plenty of teeth. 'Get well soon.'

Yas watched Portis limp off after Simone and Anan, then turned back to Dean and Sorin. 'Let's go home.'

'The man going to be a problem?' asked Sorin.

'I hope not,' said Yas. 'But if he is, we'll sort it.'

She was done with being messed about by anyone.

46

Wenna

Aisair

Wenna, Royati and Sami had tried to leave Aisair by the main gate the afternoon after they'd met Grace. They still had their passes, after all, so it shouldn't have been a problem. Should've been easy. Except when they arrived, it looked like the whole Skull army was there waiting for them.

They'd watched for a while as some others tried their luck with the guards, arguing about their rights and waving papers, saying they had permission to leave. The Skulls didn't care. The gates were locked and no one was getting in or out.

Wenna and the others went back the next day but nothing had changed. The gates were shut tight.

'It was to be expected,' said Wenna, watching the chaos. 'Zorique will be here soon enough.'

Royati spat on the ground. 'They could've waited a couple more days before they closed everything off.'

'What do we do now?' asked Sami. He stood between them, holding on to a hand each. Sometimes, he looked just like the child he was. Not a Hanran. Not just a good disguise. Just a kid.

'We're still leaving,' said Wenna. 'Make no mistake about that.'

It turned out that was easier said than done. They'd tried other gates but it was the same situation everywhere. No one was leaving the city.

The gates weren't the only place where there were a lot of Skulls either. They were all over the city. Checking papers.

Harassing innocent Jians. Arresting alleged troublemakers and Hanran. Causing distress. It seemed everywhere she looked Skulls were carting Jians off in caged wagons to only the Gods knew where.

Wenna and the others avoided the checkpoints when they could and handed over their papers when they couldn't, keeping their heads bowed and looking scared – for once, that didn't take much pretending.

They spent another night at the safe house on Salin Street, expecting the Skulls to kick the door in at any moment. Daijaku circled above the city, squawking away, making sleep next to impossible.

'Do they know something we don't?' asked Royati as she watched the demons from the window.

'Maybe they're just spreading their wings,' said Wenna. 'As long as they're not looking for us, I don't care what they do.' That was easy to say, much harder to believe. The Daijaku had them cowering with every shriek.

Shortly after dawn, a knock on the door jolted them all awake. It'd been Sami's turn to be on watch but the kid had obviously fallen asleep as well. So much for not being caught unawares. Wenna picked up a knife, wishing it was a sword.

'Who is it?' asked Royati, her blade out as well.

'Kos,' came the old man's voice from behind the door.

Royati glanced over at Wenna. 'Check the street,' she whispered.

Wenna pulled the curtain back a crack. 'Street's empty.' They both knew that didn't mean anything. Wenna moved so she'd been hidden when the door opened. 'Let him in.'

With her knife behind her back, Royati did as she was told.

Wenna watched Royati's reaction, ready to pounce if she had to, but Royati let out half a laugh and stepped back. 'Get in quick,' she said.

Kos walked in on his own and Royati swung the door shut. He gave a jump when he saw Wenna with a knife in her hand. 'Fuck. What you are doing – creeping up on me?'

Wenna shook her head and smiled. She tucked her knife away

339

in its sheath and slapped the old man on the arm. 'Sorry. Thought you might be trouble.'

Kos rubbed his face. 'Yeah, well, there's enough of that going on out there without me bringing you any more.'

Royati sat down on a chair. 'You know what's going on?'

'Nah,' replied Kos. 'I've not seen Grace either. Whatever it is, it's got the Skulls all worked up. I've lost track of the number of people they've arrested. I came here expecting to find that you've been picked up as well.'

'We need to get out of here before we are,' said Wenna.

'Well, that's the other reason I'm here. I've got an exit for you all sorted,' said Kos. 'A woman named Jo is waiting for you round at her house.'

It took Wenna and the others the rest of the morning to make their way to Jo's house, choosing a long, circuitous route that avoided as many checkpoints as possible. The building backed onto Crescent Avenue, a road that ran parallel to the city wall. The Hanran had dug a tunnel that ran two hundred feet, under the wall and to the fields beyond. It had taken the Hanran six months to dig it, burrowing away like moles, pushing the dirt back down the tunnel for others to collect and disperse around the city. It had taken them so long to make, it had only been in use for a week or so, smuggling a few families out every night.

Kos had said only a few people knew about it and the Skulls certainly didn't.

But he was wrong.

A caged wagon was parked outside Jo's. A Skull sat in the driver's seat, but he was alone as far as Wenna could tell. However, the front door to the house was open. That was never a good sign.

'Do we go back?' asked Royati.

'No,' said Wenna. 'There's only the one wagon. Must be a small squad. Maybe three or four Skulls.'

'So?'

'We take them. We're getting out of the city today and this is still the best way.'

'You sure?'

'I am.' Wenna turned to Sami. 'Go and distract the driver.' She pulled her knife from its sheath at the small of her back.

Sami nodded. He headed straight over to the wagon, calling out to the driver. 'Have you seen my ma?'

'Go way,' said the Skull.

'I lost my ma,' cried Sami. 'I can't find her. Will you help me?'

The Skull raised his whip. 'Go way now.'

'Please,' continued Sami. 'I want to find my ma.'

'Go way.' The Skull cracked the whip down. Sami got his arm up in time to protect his face, but the whip left a bloody streak on his forearm.

By then, Wenna had reached the rear of the wagon and came up behind the driver as he pulled back his arm to strike Sami again. There was a sweet little gap between the plates of armour covering the Skull's waist, back and belt, too good to turn down, so Wenna shoved her knife in as hard as she could, pulling the Skull back towards her once it was good and buried. He gave a yelp as he fell, but Wenna made sure he hit the ground hard. She pulled her knife out of his back and rammed it under his chin and up into his brain just to make sure he was dead.

She was up a moment later, the Skull's sword in her hand. She ran over to Sami and checked his arm. It was a nasty cut and the boy had plenty of tears to go with it. She sliced off the bottom of his shirt and tied the cloth around the wound. It wasn't much but it was all she had time to do. 'Stay here, you brave boy,' she told Sami with a fake smile. 'Things go bad, scarper and find Kos.'

The boy nodded, biting back the pain. Then Wenna and Royati entered the house, knives in hand. A Skull stood with his back to them at the end of corridor, watching whatever was going on in the kitchen. It certainly didn't sound pleasant, judging by all the shouting in Egril. No wonder they hadn't heard their friend dying outside.

Wenna didn't waste any time. She slashed with the scimitar across the man's hamstrings – one of the few places not protected by armour. He crumbled and Wenna stomped on his face as she ran into the kitchen. There were two more Skulls inside, with

Jo and her family tied up on the floor between them. Both their heads snapped up as their friend went down.

Wenna went right and crashed into one of them with all her momentum, trusting Royati to take the other. The bastard couldn't even draw his sword before they crunched into the wall. A shelf got knocked and shit fell on Wenna's head, but she was too busy screaming in the Skull's face and forcing the edge of her sword under the man's chin to notice. He fought back, tried to knee her in the crotch, but it was a dumb move and, off balance, down he went. Wenna was on top, but he had hold of both her wrists, stopping the sword from slicing his throat open. He shouted some shit at her in Egril. She screamed right back. Up came his knee again, but it didn't have any punch to it. Wenna tried raising herself up so she could get some weight behind the sword, force it down, but he was too fucking strong, and sitting up allowed him to straighten his arms. Now *she* was the off-balance idiot. The Skull threw her aside and Wenna rolled into a table, knocking it over so it crashed down on top of her. She pushed it away, but the Skull threw himself on her, grabbing her neck, squeezing the life from her. She'd lost the sword somewhere, so she punched him the face, cracking her knuckles against his helmet, doing no damage to him in the process.

She went from trying to kill him to trying to save her own life. She tried bucking the Skull off, but he was too strong, with his heavy armour digging into her everywhere and his stinking breath panting in her face. She couldn't even scream now, let alone fight. She clawed at his arms, but they were locked and she didn't have the strength.

Wenna was going to die.

She managed to glance at Royati, but she was having enough problems with her own Skull, each trying to bring their sword to bear, wrestling for their lives.

Wenna tried to breathe, tried to fight, tried to live. Her vision started to darken. The roar inside her mind quietened. Her legs stopped kicking.

Shit. Tinnstra ...

The Skull cried out and spat blood all over Wenna's face. His back arched and he let go of her throat. It took a moment or two for air to find her lungs as the Egril fell off her, trying to reach something behind him. He flailed wildly, crashed into a wall, eyes wide, screaming, blood running from his mouth and all over that white armour. When he stopped moving, she saw the knife in his back and Sami standing behind him.

'Thanks,' she croaked but, by the Gods, it hurt to talk.

The kid rushed over, helped her sit up as she sucked in air.

But there was no time to recover – Royati needed her. It took Wenna two attempts to pick up a fallen scimitar and she half-crawled, half-fell towards her friend. She stabbed out with the sword, more an irritant than a threat, but it was enough to get the Skull's attention. He turned, loosening his grip on Royati, and the Shulka didn't waste any time. She shoved the blade into the Skull's face, straight into his screaming mouth. He backed away, trying to escape, and fell over Wenna on the floor. She kicked at him, scrambling free, while Royati stabbed him a few more times for good measure.

'Free Jo,' wheezed Wenna, throat raw. Sami pulled the knife out of the back of the Skull he'd killed and ran over to the woman and her kids.

'Are you hurt?' asked Royati.

Wenna tried a smile. 'Yeah, but I'm alive.' She got to her knees, coughing and spluttering, fully aware of how lucky they'd been. 'You?'

'Alive.'

Wenna got to her feet as Sami freed the last of the children and they scrambled into their mother's arms.

'Thank the Gods you arrived when you did,' said Jo. 'I thought we were done for.'

'Did they know about the tunnel?' asked Wenna.

'They just asked where the Hanran were,' said Jo. 'They said they'd kill my kids in front of me if I didn't tell them.'

'You have two choices,' said Wenna. 'Go and hide somewhere else in the city or leave with us now, because you can't stay here. More Skulls will be coming. They might even be on their way now.'

'But this is our home,' said Jo.

'You can come back to it after the Skulls are gone.'

Jo gave her a look that said she didn't believe that for one instant. 'We'll get our stuff.'

'Show me the tunnel first,' said Wenna.

The trapdoor was located in the floor where the kitchen table used to be, which was now lying smashed in one corner, replaced by the Skulls' bodies. Wenna, Royati and Sami dragged the corpses into the hallway, leaving a trail of blood behind.

The trapdoor was still all but invisible – except for a small hole, barely big enough for Wenna to hook her finger into. With a tug, the trapdoor came up, revealing a narrow shaft beneath dropping ten feet to a tunnel.

'You and Sami get the Skull from outside,' said Wenna to Royati once Jo had gone to pack her belongings. 'Hide him in the house.'

'What about the wagon?' asked Royati.

'Nothing we can do about it now, but it won't draw as much attention as a dead Skull lying in the street.'

Royati tapped Sami on the arm. 'Let's be quick.'

Jo returned with her three kids, all clutching little bags. She grabbed whatever food she had left in the kitchen and stuck it into a bag of her own. 'Not much for a whole life lived here.'

'It could be worse,' said Wenna, pointing her chin towards the dead Skulls.

'Are we off?' said Royati as she walked back into the kitchen.

'All right, everyone. Pay attention,' said Wenna. 'Royati will go first – she'll make sure the Skulls aren't waiting for us on the other side of the wall. Then the kids go, then Jo, Sami, and me last. When it's your turn to leave the tunnel, wait for Royati's signal that it's safe to go. Don't go if she doesn't say it's safe.'

Everyone nodded, even the kids, trying to look brave.

'Good,' continued Wenna. She crouched down so she was eye level with Jo's kids. 'It'll be dark in there and you might bang your head or scrape your knee, but I want you to keep going until you can't go any further. It'll be over before you know it.

Your mother will be right behind you and Royati will make sure nothing bad is waiting for you.'

'Thank you,' mouthed Jo over her children's heads.

The shaft was a tight fit for Royati and she had to hold her sword tight against her body as she went down. Then Wenna counted to fifty before she let the first child follow, then counted again before the second followed. The last child was Jo's youngest and she was crying by the time she stepped on the ladder.

'I'm scared,' she said. 'I don't want to go down there.'

'It's just dark,' said Jo. 'You'll be fine. I promise you.'

'Why don't you both go down together?' said Wenna. 'Then you know your mother is with you all the way.' That suggestion seemed to placate the child enough for her to climb down and Jo followed.

'Thanks for not staying outside like I told you to,' said Wenna to Sami, when it was the boy's turn. 'You saved my life.'

The kid grinned. 'Pleasure. You'd do the same.'

'I would. Now get going.'

The boy dropped down, leaving Wenna alone in the kitchen. She took a scabbard off one of the dead Skulls and slipped a scimitar into it. There was no point strapping it on until she was on the other side of the wall, but she was damn glad to have it.

Holding on to the sword and her own small pack, Wenna descended into the tunnel. It took some manoeuvring at the bottom to turn herself around and get on her hands and knees, but she managed it somehow, keeping any new cuts and bruises to a minimum. Then, pushing her sword and pack in front of her, she crawled into the darkness. She could hear Sami shuffling along in front of her, but she couldn't even see her hand in front of her face.

The darkness pressed down on her, making it hard to breathe as she shuffled along, stretched out in the tunnel, pulling herself forwards with her fingers and pushing with her toes. Dirt fell from above, all the more frightening in the dark. It didn't take much to imagine the whole thing collapsing on top of her and that would be it. Dead and buried in one. Gods, she didn't want to die down there.

She tried to move quicker but it was impossible. There was no room to hurry, only enough to panic. Wenna concentrated on taking deep, measured breaths. It was going to be fine. She'd be away from Aisair soon. She had the map. Everything Tinnstra needed.

Then she saw light ahead, sneaking around the shape of Sami's body, and she knew she was near the end of the tunnel.

Then Jo screamed. Her kids screamed. Royati shouted, 'No!'

Wenna flinched as she heard swords clash, then Royati cried out in pain, and a heartbeat later, Jo and her family fell silent.

Wenna lay frozen in the tunnel, not willing to believe what she'd heard. It had to be Skulls. They must've killed Royati, Jo and her kids. Sami must've thought the same because he started to shuffle back towards her without being told.

Someone above shouted in Egril. Someone else laughed.

Wenna heard the crackle of a Chosen's baton charging up.

'Sami!' she screamed.

The boy looked back at her, eyes wide and bright in the tunnel, full of fear. 'Wenna?'

Light. Heat. Darkness.

Wenna opened her eyes. Somehow, she was alive. Every part of her hurt. Her cheeks and hands stung from burns. Dirt covered her face, pressed against her body and filled most of the space around her and she couldn't hear a thing – but she was alive.

She could see a few specks of soft light ahead of her, offering hope of a way out. Some primordial instinct kicked in and she started to push dirt past her, burrowing her way forwards, not caring what waited above. She just knew she had to get out of that tunnel. Get out of the dirt.

It was slow going and agony with her burned hands, but she kept moving, just like she'd told Jo's children to do. Blood ran between her fingers as she spat mud from her mouth.

Then her hand touched something. Not dirt. Hard, curved, jagged, cold. It was part of Sami's skull. No more than a shard. But her fingers found more flesh and bone and scraps of clothes around it. The boy had taken the full brunt of the blast, saving

Wenna one last time. Dear Gods, she hoped he was at peace. He deserved it.

Bile rushed into her throat, but she swallowed it back down as she pushed what was left of Sami past her. On she crawled, forcing herself through what was left of the tunnel until her face felt fresh air and she was looking up at the evening sky. She didn't move as she listened for soldiers, keeping her breathing shallow. Above, stars sparkled with a beauty that jarred against the suffering on the world below. Wenna didn't know what hurt more – her body or her soul. She'd thought being back in Jia would make things better but, somehow, it was worse. In Meigore, she had expected to die. Here, she wanted to live. She wanted her friends to live. She wanted this Godsdamned war over and done with.

Finally, when she was as sure as she could be that she was alone, Wenna dragged herself into the last part of the tunnel. She reached up, hooked her fingers over the top and pulled herself up. She tried using her feet to help push, but she couldn't get a grip on anything. The heat from the Chosen's blast had turned the walls of the tunnel leading up to the surface into glass. She dropped down, defeated, arms aching, fingers bleeding even more.

She tried again, jumping this time to give herself some momentum, but again her feet slipped and slid against the walls, and for all her effort, Wenna ended up on her arse at the bottom of the shaft as before.

Tears came, but Wenna brushed them angrily away and stood up. There was a way out – there was always a way out. She pulled her boots and socks off and then threw them out of the tunnel. It was time she used the narrowness of the chute to her advantage.

Wenna placed her back against one side of the shaft and then manoeuvred her legs up so she could push herself tight into the space. Wedged like that, she shuffled upwards, hurting all the way, feeling stupid she'd not climbed like this in the first place. It took an age but, by the Gods, was she happy when she all but fell onto the scorched earth outside.

Then she remembered what had happened on the blackened grass and her good humour disappeared with the breeze. Her friends' bodies were gone, but they'd left plenty of their blood behind.

'I will avenge you.' Wenna prayed that it wasn't an empty promise, even though she had no idea how she'd keep it.

She was a hundred feet from the city walls, with the same distance between her and the cover of the nearby woods. Luckily, the Skulls hadn't got around to clearing the area yet, concentrating all their efforts to the south. Time for one last push with her knackered body.

Wenna got to her feet, snatched up her boots and half-ran, half-stumbled to the woods. She ducked under a branch and skirted around some bushes, welcoming a different kind of darkness. She felt safe now. Protected.

She carried on, deeper into the trees, until the ache in her lungs made her stop. She slunk down behind an ancient oak, gasping for air, amazed she was still alive. The tears came then, the tears she'd promised not to cry, the tears she couldn't stop. Her body shook with the pain of it all. Gods, how much more of it could she take? How many more people would she have to watch die?

47

Zorique

The Northern Road

Zorique woke up angry. She'd not slept much as it was; the thought of all their losses – *her* losses – had swirled around her head all night, no matter how tightly she'd shut her eyes.

Twelve days ago, she'd had an army. An army she thought she was going to lead to victory and cleanse Jia of the Egril stain. Truth be told, she thought she was going to be able win Sekanowari by herself – like she had in Layso. Now she wasn't so sure. Now she felt vulnerable. She needed her army. She needed Aasgod and she needed Tinnstra more than ever.

But it was Tinnstra who had her mind racing. She was furious at her mother. It was bad enough she'd lost at an eye at Omason Beach leading a mad charge, but her antics since had been almost suicidal. Tinnstra really didn't seem to care whether she lived or died. What was worse, she didn't seem to care about Zorique, either.

Zorique slapped on her armour, strapped on her sword, trying not to think about what a mess everything was. By the Gods, how she wished she'd never left the past, and stayed in Aisair with Wex. Married him. That would've been enough for her. More than enough. Better than now.

'Your Majesty?' called Aasgod from outside the tent. 'Are you awake?'

Zorique wanted to scream. She'd just woken up and already people were making demands on her. She couldn't have even a moment to herself. To think. 'Yes.' She forced the word out through gritted teeth. Pretending to be calm. Pretending to be a queen. 'Enter.'

Aasgod pulled the flaps to one side and ducked in. He smiled. 'Did you sleep well?'

'No, I did not,' she snapped back.

'I'm sorry,' replied the mage. 'It was a stupid question. More habit than anything. I doubt anyone did.' He ran a hand over his head. 'I certainly didn't. I was still expecting another attack.'

The man's honesty took some of the anger out of Zorique. 'Don't apologise. I was rude. I'm tired and ... frustrated.'

'Understandable.'

Zorique looked up. 'I'm glad you're here. I'd be lost without you.'

'I'm glad I'm here, too – most of the time. I must admit there have been occasions when I've wished otherwise ... that I was safely back in my library in Aisair.'

'I was just thinking the same,' said Zorique. 'I was thinking about Wex ... the man I met. He asked me to marry him once.' It was strange saying the words out loud. She'd never mentioned it to anyone before. Not even Tinnstra. 'I said no.'

'He seemed like a good man.' Aasgod squeezed her shoulder. A simple gesture, but it was what she needed. 'It's important you remember that love – treasure it in the dark days ahead. It might just make all the difference.'

'Aasgod ...' Zorique stopped, unsure whether to say what worried her.

'Yes, Your Majesty?'

She turned away from him and picked up her helmet. 'It's nothing. Don't worry.'

'If something is bothering you, Zorique ...'

She closed her eyes. 'It's just ... talking about it feels like a betrayal ... Especially talking to you.'

'Ah,' said the mage. 'Tinnstra.'

She looked up as the tears began to form. 'Yes.'

'You can trust me. What we talk about stays between us.'

'It's not just what she did that worries me. It's her. She's ... changed so much.'

'Haven't we all?'

'Have you spoken to Tinnstra lately?' asked Zorique, her voice low.

'No. Not for a few days. She's been keeping to herself and, as you know, we've never been the best of friends.'

'I'm worried about her. Stupid, really – she, of all people, doesn't need anyone to worry over her – but I do.'

Aasgod paused, choosing his words with care. 'She ... wants to win this war.'

'At what cost, though? Do you know what the soldiers call her?'

'I do. Some say she's Xin's daughter while others say she's Xin herself. They think she's Death.'

Zorique wiped the corner of her eye. 'She's my mother.'

'She'll always be that.'

'Then how come I don't recognise her anymore?'

'Tinnstra will come back to you – when this is all over. Deep down, she's a good person. You know that.'

'Once. Before she started drinking the Chikara water. Before it changed her.'

Aasgod paused, as if he was trying to work out what he should say. 'It's true, she is drinking too much of the water. Every time I see her, it looks like she's had some more. But it's not just what it's doing to her that I'm worried about. We only brought so much from the past, and Tinnstra must be running low by now. I'm worried she'll start drinking my own supply soon.'

'We can't let that happen. You'll be powerless without it.'

'Well, talking to her doesn't work. I'm amazed she's not stabbed me already.'

'What do we do?'

'I don't know.'

'I'm scared,' said Zorique. 'Scared she'll—'

'Scared she'll do what?' Tinnstra's voice made them jump.

They both turned, red-faced, Zorique feeling guilty. Her mother was standing in the tent's entrance. 'Tinnstra! I didn't know you were there.'

'Obviously.' Tinnstra had swapped the bandage over her face for a black eyepatch. 'Is there anything you'd like to say to my face that you were happy to say behind my back?'

Aasgod stepped forwards, putting himself between the two women. 'Tinnstra, it wasn't like that.'

'Shut up or I'll cut your tongue out,' snapped Tinnstra. She turned on Zorique. 'After everything *I've* done for *you* – given up for *you* – this is how you repay *me*? You tell *him* that you're scared of *me*? Dear Gods, I'm the closest thing you have to a mother.'

'You *are* my mother,' said Zorique. 'You're misunderstanding what I was trying to say.'

'Of course,' said Tinnstra. Her smile was cruel, cutting. 'I should've realised the mistake was mine. Please forgive me.'

'Tinnstra, you are overreacting,' said Aasgod.

Suddenly, there was a knife pointed at Aasgod's face. 'What did I tell you about speaking?'

'*Shirudan.*' The shield snapped between Tinnstra and Aasgod, preventing her from attacking the mage, but it didn't stop Tinnstra's scowl towards Zorique from striking Zorique's heart.

Her mother slipped the knife back into its sheath. 'If I may be excused, I will return to trying to protect your life.' Her bow was curt, formal, cold, then she turned on her heel and left the tent.

The only sound was the crackle of the shield as both Zorique and Aasgod stared after her.

'I'm sorry,' said Zorique as she dispersed the shield. 'I thought she was going to ... I'm sorry.'

Aasgod let out a deep breath. 'I did, too.'

'I should go after her ... explain.'

Aasgod held out a hand. 'Leave it for now. I think she's just taken some Chikara water. No matter what you say, she won't hear it, and things might escalate.'

'She wouldn't hurt me,' said Zorique. 'She couldn't.'

'She might try.'

'It's the water doing this to her, isn't it? Making her angry? Dangerous?'

'It's the water. It's the war. It's probably everything.' Aasgod scratched his head. 'Tinnstra's spent the last fifteen years trying to make herself into something she isn't, burying herself beneath rage and magic. But the real her – the woman who raised you and loves you – she's still there. Of that, I'm sure.'

Zorique stared out through the tent opening, her heart broken. 'I hope you're right.'

This time, Aasgod's smile came easily. 'Do you know what the soldiers call you?'

'Do I want to?' Zorique doubted it was anything good.

'Hope. They call you Hope.'

'That's something, I suppose.'

'That's everything.'

48

Ralasis

The Northern Road

Another morning.

Ralasis groaned. He was starting to hate them. More than he ever had.

Ralasis had never been one of those annoying 'morning' people who jumped up out of bed at the crack of dawn. Most likely, he'd be staggering home at that point, as drunk as a man could get. He'd then fall into bed, hopefully with some company, and sleep through the rest of the day until it was time to do it all again, washing away his headache with more of the same poison that had made him feel so wretched in the first place.

In fact, he looked back at those hung-over moments in Layso with renewed perspective. Given half a chance to experience them once more, he'd not complain. He'd not think the world was ending because he'd drunk three or four bottles of bad wine or a flask or nine of Irnus's home-made spirits. No, he'd think he was the luckiest man alive.

After all, a bath would have been on hand to soothe his aches. Clean clothes would have been waiting. A good breakfast. Fresh water. A cup of tea. A smile, perhaps, from a beautiful woman.

Even at sea, he had food and wine, a ship beneath his feet, a crew he adored and new horizons to chase.

But now? All he had was misery. Why had he agreed to this? Why? Why? Why?

Of course, he knew the reason. Knew only too well why he'd

said yes. Knew who he'd wanted to impress. Who he'd wanted to be with. Gods, he was a fool – just like his father had said.

And no wonder she wasn't interested in him. Dirt was ingrained into his skin so deeply that he doubted he'd ever be clean again, and his clothes – what was left of them – stunk to the heavens. Even his hair itched in a way that made him think lice had taken up residence there.

But the worst part was his feet. Bruised, blistered and bleeding. Every night, if he was able, he washed them in whatever river or stream he could find, letting the cold water soothe them and keep any infection away. But, by the Gods, it was little relief. It was a miracle he slept a wink with the burning pain that radiated upwards all night long.

He'd even asked Zorique if she could perform some magic on them, but apparently there were limits to her powers.

They said an army fights on its feet and his were just a reminder of why he'd become a sailor. Not much walking aboard a ship, and a good thing, too.

He winced as he pulled back his blanket and stared at the ruined lumps of meat at the ends of his legs. By Nasri's breasts, he was tempted to take his sword to them and put himself out of his misery. Of course, amputating his own legs wouldn't be very attractive to *her*, let alone any ladies he might meet in the future if he survived this war. So, instead, he sat up, winced as his feet touched the razor-like grass and wondered how he'd get through another day of marching across the Godsdamned country.

Oh, to be back in Meigore.

He found a pair of socks that were almost dry and pulled them over his agony. Then on went his boots and Ralasis could've screamed the camp down. It was a miracle, in fact, that he didn't.

He brushed dirt off his trousers, not that it made much difference. They were stained with far worse things than mud after all. He'd wash them if he had a chance but, to do that, he'd have to take them off, and there was no way he was going to risk that. Not when he expected a Skull attack at any moment. The last thing he needed was to try and fight those bastards in his underwear.

He pulled his jacket on over his shirt and buttoned it up, convincing himself he almost looked smart, then scratched his beard and knew he didn't. A hot shave was another luxury he missed.

Finally, he buckled on his sword and knew he couldn't put off facing the world any longer. Still, he hesitated before leaving his tent, knowing what he had to face, the guilt he'd feel.

Dear Gods, no wonder his father thought him a fool.

When he stepped outside, he saw Guil, Siren, Jamie, Iris and a few of the others from his old crew sat around a miserable fire, with faces that looked a hundred times even more miserable.

'Morning,' Ralasis said, with a beaming smile full of forced cheer. 'Are you looking forward to another delightful day?'

'Morning, Commander,' said Guil. 'Doubt it's going to be delightful. Far from it.' His first mate glanced at the others, got nods back. Never a good sign. Ralasis had spent his whole life aboard ships and knew the look of mutineers before the thought of treachery had even crossed their minds.

'Come now, Guil, we're all alive and we're not missing any limbs. No one attacked us during the night – unless I slept through it.' Ralasis smiled. 'I know I'm a deep sleeper but even I'd have woken if a battle had been raging.'

'I don't know about that, Commander,' said Siren. He'd got that name because of his way with the women of any and every port. 'You've snored through a fair few storms before.' He laughed at his own joke, but Guil nudged him silent.

It was serious, then.

'Something on your mind, Guil?' asked Ralasis. Better to get the poison out in the open than let it fester.

The first mate cracked his neck and tried a smile. A thin, pathetic thing, it was. 'I was hoping you'd perhaps reconsider things. Set a course south and west.'

'What? Back to Meigore?'

Guil gave an innocent shrug of his shoulders. 'That's not a bad idea, Commander. The men would be happy to follow you.'

'Would they indeed?'

'Yes, Commander.'

'And this is the view of . . . of all our brave soldiers here?'

The man looked sheepish then, as if reluctant to let Ralasis know he'd been conspiring behind his captain's back.

'Come now, Guil. Don't get shy on me,' said Ralasis. 'You started this conversation.'

'Yes. Most of them.'

'You *have* been busy.' Ralasis pretended to think about it, gazing at the sky, finger on chin. 'Stay or go. Stay or go. Stay or go. A hard choice, my friend. What's best?'

They watched him, all looking nervous and unsure. Ralasis dragged it out, as if he really was thinking about it.

'Godsdamn it!' he shouted, making them all jump. 'You've persuaded me. Give the signal, Guil, my friend. Gather the men. Let's be off.'

'Back to Meigore?' Guil's eyes brightened.

'Of course. What better way to honour our brave dead, whose blood stains every inch of land from here to Kiyosun, than by running back home and deserting our allies when they need us the most. What a way to ensure our names will live for eternity, eh? They'll be singing songs about us when we get back. Might not be nice songs. But our names will be known. Every time we go somewhere, they'll say, "There they are, the clever ones who ran away." We'll be called cowards and turncoats and stuff like that, but what does that matter? We'll be alive!' He hooked an arm around Guil's neck, pulled him in tight so the man was all but off balance. 'Thank you for suggesting it. What would I do without you?'

'Doesn't sound so good when you say it like that, Commander.' Guil tried to pull himself free, but Ralasis had him.

'No? You don't think so? Surely you all talked about that when you were conspiring behind my back?' He looked from face to face, but no one would meet his eye. 'Perhaps you thought about actually stabbing me in the back for real if I didn't agree? Leave me here in the dirt with the rest of our friends and countrymen.'

'We'd never do that, Commander,' said Jamie. 'We do what you tell us to do.'

'Shall we stick with the original plan, then? You know the one – where we go on and help to save the people who saved us?

Where we act like men of honour, not cowards?' Ralasis leaned in close to Guil, close enough for their noses to all but touch. 'Or do you want to discuss it with the others, like fisherwomen from Skorn?'

Guil tried to pull his head away, but again Ralasis held him tight. 'No, Commander,' he said eventually.

They stared into each other's eyes for a moment, just so Guil realised how much shit he was in, then Ralasis let him go and stepped back. 'Well, I'm glad that's settled. Now, let's make ready to move out, eh?'

The men got to their feet, but none looked too happy about the prospect. Ralasis couldn't blame them. 'Listen, don't think I don't know this is a shit job we've got. We're all hungry, tired. I'm filthy. Siren's ugly.' That got a chuckle. 'The Skulls want to kill us and – between us girls here – I'm not keen to die just yet. Unfortunately, this is the job we've got, and a lot of people are depending on us to do it.'

Jamie kicked some dirt onto the fire. 'But we don't know them, Commander.'

'But I know you, Jamie. And I know Siren, as much as I wish I didn't. And, Gods help me, I know Guil, the treacherous little bastard. And I promise I'll do everything I can to keep you safe and alive and get you back to Meigore so that you can finally lose your innocence to some poor lass.'

They all laughed at that, because the odds of Jamie actually finding someone desperate enough to sleep with him were pretty slim, and Ralasis knew he had them back. 'But the thing is, I'm depending on you to keep me alive as well so I can go home and drink myself to death. So, don't do it for the people you don't know. Do it for me and Guil and Siren and every Meigorian here. Together, we're stronger. Together, we can get through this. Together, we can win.'

Ralasis could see their backs straighten.

'You can count on us,' said Siren.

'I've always known that. You just need to remember it.'

'We will, Commander,' said Guil.

'Now, get on and pack up,' said Ralasis.

'Commander,' said Jamie. 'Did you mean it when you said I'd find a girl when this is all over?'

Ralasis winced. 'I might've lied about that one. But we can hope, eh?'

His men roared and Siren slapped Jamie on the back. The others began to move off, but Ralasis caught Guil by the elbow before he could leave.

'Yes, Commander?'

Once more, he leaned in, bringing his mouth to his first mate's ear. 'If I ever even think you're stirring shit up again, I'll have you hanged. Got it?'

'Yes, Commander.'

'Good. Because I hate making speeches before breakfast. See that it doesn't happen again.'

'Yes, Commander.'

Ralasis let go of his elbow. 'Now fuck off.'

Guil didn't move. 'Do you want me to find you some food, Commander?'

That brought the smile back to Ralasis' face. 'Of course I do.'

'I'll see to it immediately, Commander.'

Ralasis watched him scuttle off. What a start to the day – and he had no doubt it was only going to get worse from there.

Guil was back quick enough with a small bowl of the slop they were passing off as food. Ralasis took it gratefully enough, because he knew there'd be nothing better. Then, eating as he walked, he headed over to the queen's tent.

He'd not gone ten feet before he saw Tinnstra storming towards him. She had a murderous look on her face. 'You're not looking for me, are you?'

She did a double take as her mind switched to the present. 'No. Not you. I need to be alone.'

'Ah, I can appreciate that sentiment. Solitude is hard to find when you have an army for company.'

'Quite.'

Ralasis tilted his head to one side and gave Tinnstra his smile that won over every heart except hers. 'Would you like some company while you're being alone?'

'That makes no sense,' replied Tinnstra. 'No, I don't.' But she didn't walk away.

'I'm a good listener.'

'I'm a bad talker.'

'We seem perfect together.' Again, he gave her his smile and got nothing back. He was starting to think he'd imagined ever sleeping with her. But again, she didn't leave, so perhaps things were improving.

'I'm just angry. Zorique and Aasgod ...' Tinnstra waved a hand back towards the centre of the camp, then shook her head. 'It's probably me.'

'Why do you say that?'

'I scared them last night. I ... went out on my own. The Skulls were about to attack again. I killed a Tonin and two Chosen.'

'That was brave of you.'

'*They* think it was stupid of me.'

'Well, I'm grateful. I got to sleep and rest my feet because of you.'

Tinnstra glanced down at his boots. 'They did look sore the other night.'

Ralasis laughed. 'I think the Skulls have the right idea – get a Tonin to open a gate and just step across to where you want to be. None of this marching nonsense.'

'We'll reach Aisair soon enough. You can rest your feet then.'

'Ah! But then it'll be fighting day after day. You'll have to listen to me complaining about my aching shoulder, or perhaps I'll end up with some horrific scar that will ruin my good lo—' He stopped himself from finishing the sentence, but he'd already said too much.

'Like I did?' The edge to Tinnstra's voice cut as sharp as any blade.

'I'm sorry. I say stupid things without thinking. I do it all the time.'

'No offence taken. You speak the truth.'

'You're still beautiful—'

'Dear Gods, man. Quit while you can.' With that, she stormed off.

'Tinnstra,' he called after her. 'I didn't mean to …' But she was out of earshot already. 'And you're supposed to have a way with the ladies.'

The trouble was, Ralasis had been telling the truth. Yes, Tinnstra was scary, downright dangerous and her injury had made a mess of her eye, but there was so much more to her that he found compelling and, yes, beautiful. He'd noticed it the moment they met on the *Okinas Kiba*; a defiance against all the world could throw at her. Even when she'd returned from her mysterious journey, the years had been both harsh and kind. He could see how she bore the weight of her responsibilities, and yet that same defiance he'd liked when she was younger had only grown with her, strengthening her. She walked like a warrior out of myth, with eyes that could see into a man's soul. She was no damsel to be rescued; she was going to save the world by herself.

Tinnstra was the reason he'd volunteered to lead the Meigorian forces in Jia. She was the reason he was probably going to die in some foreign field, far from the sea, and he'd just managed to make her hate him. Brilliant.

No doubt some Egril would chop his head off later and make his day perfect.

49
Ange

Lanaka

Ange stared at the dead, tears running down her cheeks. She didn't try to stop them. Didn't know how, truth be told.

Even though she'd known what to expect as they approached the town, she'd hoped to be wrong. Even when she'd seen the birds circling overhead, just like at Anjon, she'd still clung to that hope.

Such a fool she was. There was no pretending the stink in the air was anything normal. No way to explain the way the damned birds squawked uninterrupted as anything good.

There was no message written in blood on the city gates to greet them though. Instead, they'd simply been left open as if it didn't matter. After all, the citizens inside weren't going anywhere.

No, they waited inside.

Impaled, just like Anjon.

Had she really travelled halfway across the country just to see more atrocities? She put a hand across her mouth to stop the bile from rising and closed her eyes. She could handle this. It was bad but she was strong. She—

'Let's go,' said Garo. 'I don't want to hang around here.'

By the Gods, Ange agreed with him. She wanted to say yes, but she knew that wasn't right. She opened her eyes. 'We need to look for survivors,' she whispered.

'No, we don't,' replied Garo, all but shouting.

Ange blinked away her tears. 'Queen Zorique ordered us to do that in Anjon, so we do it here.'

'We didn't find any survivors in Anjon!'

'We still look,' she snapped.

It was only a small town, big enough to warrant a wall around its edges, but small enough for Ange not to recognise its name – not that she was any sort of expert. She knew the main cities like everyone did – Inaka, Gambril, Myoshia, Selto, Chita, Aisair – but she'd never heard of Lanaka. She doubted anybody had unless they lived there or nearabouts.

They'd passed plenty of other, smaller towns and villages on their way east, spreading the word about Zorique like Hasan had asked, looking for fighters and finding farmers. People had been kind to the both of them, whether it was giving them a hot meal or a roof to sleep under, but no one seemed keen to stick their necks out and join the Hanran.

A kind old bloke gave them a lift in a hay cart for a couple of days and a husband and wife let them travel down the river on their barge, allowing them to cover twice as much distance in half the time. They hid from Skulls when they had to, then poached game for their meals. On occasions, the war seemed very far away. Certainly, if someone had told her she could spend ten or twelve days in Garo's company and not killed him by the end of it, she wouldn't have believed it. In fact, if Ange was being honest with herself, she'd really enjoyed Garo's company, talking shit with him in the sunshine. It'd been like having a holiday from the real world for some of the time.

But the real world was back now, with all its horrors, and Ange felt fucking guilty for being so bloody happy only a few hours before. How could she have been laughing and joking when these poor sods were getting murdered?

Looking up at the faces of the dead, all twisted in agony and warped with pain, she had no doubt that small town had meant the world to the people who did live there, just as Kiyosun had to her and Dren. And she knew they'd done nothing to deserve their fate – no matter what the flyers said.

There were enough of them about, though. Littering the place, they were.

'What they say?' asked Garo, holding one up.

'You've got eyes, haven't you,' she snapped, more out of habit than any reason.

'I can't read none.'

Ange shook her head and then straightened out the paper. She squinted, not the best at letters herself. 'By order of King Larius, any citizen who aids and a ... abets the invaders of Jia will be declared a traitor and subject to the death penalty.'

'What's "aids and abets" mean?'

'Helps – I think.'

'Why don't it just say that, then?'

'Maybe that's how royals talk,' said Ange.

'I don't get it, though. How did anyone here help us?' said Garo.

'They didn't. This –' she screwed up the paper and threw it into the gutter '– is just a crock of shit.'

'So why did they do it, Ange?'

'Because they're evil bastards. They want to scare us all. Stop us fighting back.'

'Makes me want to fight more,' muttered Garo. 'Makes me want to kill every Skull there is.'

'Yeah. I know what you mean.'

Still, walking past the dead like that might have got her rage up, but it also reminded her how bloody small and insignificant she was. What could she or Garo do to stop the Skulls? They'd murdered hundreds, if not thousands, of people in Lanaka just because they could. Just like they had in Anjon, and in other towns and cities as well. Of that she had no doubt.

To make it worse, every house they entered told its own sad story; a broken door, a half-eaten meal, a discarded toy, a dropped knife. Lives had been lived in those rooms and then those lives were taken.

Each empty home stabbed at Ange's heart. She wanted to cry more. She wanted to scream. If Garo hadn't been with her, she would've. But instead, she pushed the pain down, bottled it up as best she could. She had to survive this somehow.

'This is pointless,' said Garo for the thousandth time as they entered another home.

'We've got a job to do,' replied Ange for the thousandth time. She shouldered past him, opened a cupboard door and then slammed it shut, not even bothering to look inside. She hated the fact that he was right. Hated the fact the Skulls had killed everyone. If Dren was with her, he'd be ready to tear the world apart to get revenge. She wanted to be like Dren. Trouble was, she was worried she was more like Garo. And she hated that even more. Dren would've hated her feeling helpless. He would've told her to sort herself out, to be a wolf, not a sheep.

She stomped up the stairs.

Of course, Garo followed. 'Why don't we head back to the army? Everywhere we go will be like this.'

She spun on her heels. 'What about everyone waiting for us in bloody Aisair, eh? You going to give up on them, are you? What if they all die because we listened to you?'

'No one listens to me,' moaned Garo.

Ange jabbed a finger at him, wishing it was her knife instead. 'With. Good. Fucking. Reason.' She continued up the stairs, driving her boot down with each step, rattling the boards, needing to vent her anger on something.

'Do you think you should be making so much noise?' whispered Garo.

'You worried we're going to wake the dead?' she shouted back. 'Fat ch— Fuck.' She stopped in her tracks, eyes wide and mouth open.

A boy had stepped out into the corridor from the last room down, clutching a filthy blanket to his chest like it was some sort of shield. His wet eyes shone under a mess of hair. He could only be nine or ten years old.

'What is it? What've you found?' shouted Garo from behind her, coming up the stairs like a bloody elephant now.

'Shush.' She waved him back, keeping her eyes on the boy and popping her best smile on her face – hard work after all she'd seen that day, but needs must and all that.

The boy just kept on staring at her. At least he didn't run away.

'Hello,' said Ange.

The boy didn't move, didn't speak.

'What the fuck's going on, Ange?' Garo shouted again. Again, she waved him quiet. How she kept smiling was a miracle.

'Do you live here?' she asked the boy. 'Is this your home?' She took a step forwards, but that spooked the kid. He tensed up as if he was about to bolt. Ange didn't want that. She stopped and held up her hands. 'It's okay. We're friends. Look, no masks.' She tried a bigger grin, showed some teeth.

The kid scarpered. Back through the door he'd come from. Fast. So much for her smile.

'Shit.' Ange went after him. She clunked down the corridor in her armour, sword banging against the wall. She reached the end room, bundled into it. It was a bedroom. A cot in the corner. Straw mattress. Nothing else. Definitely no kid. Shit.

Ange went to the window and stuck her head out. Below, the dead hung from the spikes, but there was no sign of the boy. He couldn't have jumped, anyway. Too much of a drop for anyone, if they wanted to walk away from it.

'What's happening?' said Garo, finally catching up.

'It's a kid. A boy,' said Ange. 'He ran in here but ...'

'Where is he now, then?'

'I saw him run in ...' Ange grabbed the corner of the cot and hauled it away from the wall, revealing a hole big enough for a ten-year-old boy to wriggle through. 'Quick, run next door. Try and cut him off.'

'What?'

'Just. Fucking. Do. It.' Thank the Gods the fool listened to her because Ange was pretty close to ramming her sword up Garo's arse. As his footsteps disappeared off down the corridor, Ange hauled her chest plate over her head, dropped it to the floor and unbuckled her sword belt.

She crouched down and stuck her head through the hole. It was dark, musty, and it took Ange a second or two to work out that she was looking at the base of another cot. She wiggled an arm through and pushed the bed to one side, revealing another room almost identical to the one she was in.

The kid's blanket lay on the floor, but there was no sign of the boy. 'Fuck.'

It took a damn sight more effort squeezing the rest of her through the hole but, scratched and scraped, she made it and set off after the child. Luckily for her, he'd left a well-worn trail along a dusty floor.

'Hey, kid, we're trying to help you,' she called. 'We're Hanran.' Down the corridor she went, following the boy's footsteps, checking the rooms despite the trail leading straight on, because Dren had taught her not to be careless or take anything for granted. For all she knew, the kid could be trying to lure her into a trap. That was the sort of trick Dren would have pulled, after all. Suddenly she didn't like not having her sword and armour. Dumping it might've been a really dumb move.

Garo pounded up the stairs, appearing too late as ever at the other end of the corridor. 'Where is he?'

'Not here,' she replied, not bothering to hide her anger. The trail led straight to the stairs. Garo should've found the boy, unless ... Ange stopped, looked in the room to her right. There was a bigger bed in this one, some rugs, furs, a fireplace. No kid, but she stepped in all the same.

She checked underneath the bed. Nothing. Garo gawped at her from the doorway but at least he kept his damn mouth shut for once. She looked around the room again. There was nowhere to hide except ... She walked over to the fireplace. With its chimney.

'Are you in there, kid?' She kept her voice soft as she could, trying to copy the way her mother had spoken to her long ago, when kind words healed all.

Something moved behind the stone. A scrape. Nothing more.

'We're here to help,' said Ange. 'You must be hungry? Thirsty? We've got food and water.'

Another scrape and a foot dangled from the chimney for a second before being pulled up again.

'Is this where you hid from the Skulls?' said Ange. 'That was clever of you. Brave. I'm sorry we got here too late to stop them from ... doing what they did. But we're here now. You don't have to be on your own anymore.'

Silence.

'Come down,' she said. 'It can't be nice up there.'

The foot reappeared, then the other, followed by a grunt and then legs.

'Hello,' said Ange as the boy's face emerged from the chimney. She tried the smile again and maybe did a better job at it because the kid didn't run this time, thank the Four Gods.

'Hello,' he said back, his voice cracking like he'd not used it in a while.

'I'm Ange. That big lump behind me is Garo. What's your name?'

'Linx.' It came out more of a sob than anything, and Ange felt her heart break a little bit more.

'You hungry?' she asked and pulled out a scrap of bread she'd been saving for herself.

He snatched it from her hand and started nibbling on it double quick.

'Eat slowly,' said Ange. 'You're safe now. No one's going to hurt you.'

He stopped mid-bite. 'The Skulls will.'

'The Skulls are gone,' said Ange. 'We're the only ones here now.'

The boy didn't look too convinced. He started eating again. Quicker this time, as if he knew something Ange didn't, that they weren't safe no matter what she said.

'Why don't we take you to see our general? He can say hello and it'll make you feel better.'

Linx glanced at the window. 'I'm not going outside.'

Ange understood. It was his friends and neighbours all lined up out there. Maybe his mother and father, too. She tried her smile again. 'How long have you been on your own, Linx?'

'Two days.'

Ange glanced at Garo. Two days was nothing. The Skulls might not even be that far away. She wished she had her armour back on and her sword to hand. She wished she had the whole bloody army with her.

'It was clever of you to hide in the chimney,' said Garo.

'My mother told me to,' said Linx.

'Your mother was clever,' said Ange.

Tears welled up in Linx's eyes. 'She's outside.'

Garo bent down and offered the boy his water skin. 'Here. Have a sip of that. It'll make you feel better.'

Linx took it and had a tentative sip.

'Well done,' said Garo. He sat down on the floor and leaned back against the wall. 'That's better.' He looked up at Linx, then patted the space next to him. 'Do you want to keep me company?'

The boy did as Garo asked, and Garo put his arm around him.

Ange watched, just a little bit open-mouthed. Maybe the big lump wasn't so bloody useless after all. 'I ... Just going to get my sword and stuff.'

Garo nodded, almost looking happy with the boy snuggled up next to him. 'We'll be here.'

'Right.' Ange walked the first few steps backwards, still confused at the change in Garo and unable to take her eyes off him. It was the second time he'd surprised her and she wasn't sure how she felt about it. Maybe she was a little less likely to stab him. In fact, she was almost glad he was with her.

When she got down to ground level, Ange took a tentative peek out into the street. She wasn't sure why, but the boy had got her spooked and she half-expected to see a fucking army of Skulls waiting for her. But there were only the dead and the birds and the flies. Bad enough but better than a sword and a Skull. After all, Ange had no intention of ending up with a spike sticking out of her mouth.

She sprinted along to the house next door, keeping her eyes down and off the dead. She rushed up the stairs and straight to her armour. By the Gods, she felt better with it back on and her sword on her hip. Still, she had the jitters good and proper, so she didn't dawdle. Who'd have thought she'd ever be keen to be with Garo, but she bloody well was.

Garo and Linx were where she'd left them. The boy had fallen asleep and Garo signalled for Ange to be quiet. 'What do we do now?' he asked, and for the first time ever, Ange knew he wasn't thinking about himself.

She lowered herself down next to him. She knew what she should say – Gods knew she'd said it all before – but now? 'I don't know.'

'We can't leave him.'

'No one's saying we should.'

Garo looked relieved at that. 'He doesn't stand a chance without us.'

'I know.'

'So, what do we do?'

Ange shrugged. 'I don't know.'

Garo held up a small piece of dried meat. 'You hungry? It's all I've got but it's yours if you want it.'

Ange stared at the food. It was no more than a morsel – one or two bites at the most – but, by the Gods, did she want it. Her stomach growled just to make clear how hungry she was. 'What about you?'

'Don't worry. I'm not hungry.' Garo was lying. She knew that, and he knew she knew, too, but she was more than happy to pretend if she got to eat.

'Thanks.' The meat didn't taste of much and was hard to chew, but Ange was grateful all the same. She leaned back against the wall, against Garo's arm. 'We should get out of the city as soon as we can.'

'Not tonight,' said Garo. 'Let the boy sleep. We can go at first light.'

Ange wasn't about to argue. She was warm, dry, and Garo's arm was surprisingly comfortable. 'Sure.'

Ange woke with a start. She didn't know where she was for a few brief, mad seconds or who she was lying on. Then she saw Garo and remembered the town and its horrors, the boy they'd found and Garo being all protective. She sat up slowly so as not to wake him, feeling awkward that she'd slept with her head on his chest.

She got to her feet and went into one of the bedrooms. The sky was starting to brighten outside the window. Another day of only the Gods knew what. They had to leave the city, but maybe the kid knew where to find some food first. Everyone had only been dead two days, so there had to be something somewhere they could still eat.

Then where? Take the kid back to the army? Hasan wouldn't be impressed they'd not done what he'd asked, even if it was to save someone. Maybe they could dump the kid somewhere, find someone to look after him? But Ange knew she'd not be able to do that, not when he could still end up on a spike.

She rubbed her tired eyes. There was only one real choice. They'd keep Linx with her and Garo and still try to carry out Hasan's mission. The Skulls couldn't have staked out the whole country. Not yet.

Dear Gods, she hoped not, anyway.

Suddenly she felt trapped being inside. She needed air. She needed space.

Ange took the stairs up, not down, and headed to the roof. It's what Dren would have done.

The roofs in Lanaka weren't flat like in Kiyosun. Here they were sloped and covered with tiles, but there was a ledge wide enough for Ange to climb out on, if she was careful. She hesitated for a moment, but she could hear Dren mocking her for being scared and she wasn't having that. So out she went, watching her step, moving slowly, one hand on the tiled roof.

Good job there was no wind, but even so she could feel the ground calling her, wanting her to fall. She stopped five yards along the ledge, far enough to satisfy her ego, close enough to get back inside easily enough.

Ange closed her eyes and breathed in. The air had a tinge of the dead about it, but it wasn't so bad up that high. She could pretend everything was all right. The sun was coming up and Ange could still hear the waves breaking if she tried hard enough.

No, not the sea.

She opened her eyes, scared now, as she listened. Suddenly she felt very alone on the roof, very exposed. Trapped.

Slowly, she crouched down, hoping that some early-morning shadow would hide her as the sound grew louder. She was a fool for thinking it was the waves. She should've recognised the noise that marching feet made.

The Skulls were back.

50

Tinnstra

The Northern Road

By all the Gods, Tinnstra needed to kill some Skulls. It was either that or she'd kill Aasgod, or Ralasis, or any poor fool who happened to rub her the wrong way next. She knew she was being irrational, that she was tired and maybe, just maybe, she'd had too much Chikara water, but that did nothing to quell the fury inside her. Only violence could sate that. Only death.

So yes, her useless Gods could drop some Skulls in her path and she'd happily send them all off to Kage in the Great Darkness.

Her gut told her the enemy were out there, likely preparing for another night attack, but so far she and her ten had found nothing.

The main army was marching up the Northern Road, making slow, painful progress. The road itself wound through a series of rock-strewn valleys that were perfect for an ambush. So where were they?

Tavis called Tinnstra and the others to a stop near midday, when they were high up on a western slope. They huddled together, hidden amongst the tall grass and boulders, and looked down on the road while water skins were passed around. The distant stomp of marching feet told them that the army wasn't far away.

Tinnstra alone still stood, scanning the undulating slopes for anything that looked out of place, straining her ears for any odd noise, but all was quiet. The only flicker of magic she could feel came from Zorique and Aasgod back with the main army. There were certainly no Tonin or Chosen nearby.

She should be happy. There'd been a few skirmishes here and there but no big battles had been fought, no heavy losses suffered. In fact, the Skulls hadn't launched any real attacks on them for nearly two weeks now. But no, Tinnstra wasn't happy. She was damn miserable and on edge. She knew that if the Skulls had left them alone, it meant they were up to something and that had her worried.

Damn bastard Skulls.

'You doing okay, Chief?' asked Tavis as he joined her.

'I'm fine,' replied Tinnstra, sounding far from it.

The Shulka held out an unwrapped cloth, offering her bread and dried meat. 'You want some?'

'I'm not hungry.' She was never hungry these days, not for food anyway. The Chikara water killed any appetite she had.

'You need to eat, Chief.' Tavis's voice was calm, quiet and full of nothing but care, and still it stoked Tinnstra's ire.

'You need to mind your own business.'

'I didn't mean any offence, Tinnstra. Just ... I'm worried about you.'

'Worried about *me*?' Gods, the nerve of the man. 'Who do you think you are? Why don't you concentrate on finding the fucking Skulls, eh? Like you're supposed to?'

Even the Shulka knew when to back off. 'We're all doing our best. We can't find what's not there.'

'They're somewhere, I promise you that. You just have to—' She swallowed her ire. Took a breath. Reminded herself that it wasn't Tavis's fault she was pissed off. '*We* just need to find them.'

'Maybe you killing the Tonin has cut off their ability to bring troops to fight us. Maybe we'll get a break for a while.'

The man had a point. 'Maybe, but I doubt it. It's not the Skull way.'

'Aye, they're bastards when it comes to killing.'

'We're not too bad ourselves – we just need something to kill.'

Tavis nodded. 'We'd best be off then, eh?' He turned back

374

towards the others, but Tinnstra took hold of his arm, stopping him from leaving.

'I'm sorry … for snapping at you.'

'That's all right. I've been known to stick my nose in where it's not wanted.'

'It's not your fault. I just … It's the Skulls. I know they're waiting for us and I don't want any more surprises. We've lost too many people already.'

'I know. There's no need to apologise.'

'All the same, I am sorry.' She let go of his arm and watched him head back to the others. They were good people, her ten. Trying to do their best. It wasn't their fault the world was a fucked-up place – almost as fucked-up as she was.

Her hand drifted to her pouch. Chikara water was always the answer. Tired? Drink some. In danger? Drink some. Midday? Drink some. She'd be needing it to breathe next.

It didn't help that she'd run out of the bloody stuff. The thirty vials she'd brought with her were long gone, guzzled on the Northern Road while she fretted about an attack that hadn't materialised. So much for it lasting the whole campaign – but what did she expect? She was downing two or three or four vials a day.

What was worse was the fact she now had to get more from bloody Aasgod, that sanctimonious shit. She'd told him that her bag had got knocked, that her vials had been smashed but he knew she'd been lying. He'd known but had been too scared to say anything.

But he was loving the power he now had over her, handing a vial here and there out to her like she was some sort of child. Each vial came with a lecture, too.

Gods, she wished she'd never ever started drinking the stuff. She wished she'd stopped when she knew it was changing her. She wished, she wished, she wished. *Stupid thoughts. Childish thoughts. There was no other option then. There's no other option now. It won't kill me before this war does. I just need to stay strong enough to …*

No, she didn't even want to think about that now. Her plan was secret. Best keep it that way.

Tavis led the others over. 'You ready, Chief?'

Tinnstra nodded. 'Let's go up. Make sure nothing's hiding on the other side.'

'You got it.'

They moved off, silent as all good killers are, with eyes open and steel close to hand as they climbed up the slope, traversing the dips and bumps of the valley side and clambering around or climbing over the rocks and boulders. And, all the while, the same thought plagued Tinnstra: *Where are the Skulls?*

She didn't believe they were safe. She didn't believe the Egril wouldn't attack again.

Tinnstra felt Zorique's magic flare and looked back in time to see a flash of bright light from within the heart of the marching column, then her daughter shot up into the air. Tinnstra watched Zorique soar into the clouds, all but disappearing from sight. She envied her daughter right at that moment – having that freedom to leave the mess of the world behind.

Tinnstra didn't have that luxury. She was neck-deep in the shit of it all.

And whose fault's that?

Tinnstra and her ten kept climbing as the army continued to advance along the Northern Road. She tried not to think about how few their numbers were now. Over half their troops gone and they'd only fought one major battle.

And whose fault's that as well?

Some leader she was. Some hero.

One thing was for certain, she wasn't her father. Without the Chikara water, she was nothing.

Zorique flew past, following the path of the road, dropping ever lower until she was all but skimming across the ground, until she was but a bright spark in the distance.

Tinnstra smiled. Zorique was the only speck of light in Tinnstra's world. That morning's argument had been stupid. Tinnstra had been hurt by her daughter's words and lashed out. She should've been braver, though. Talked about what scared Zorique, admitted that she was scared herself, scared of herself, scared of getting everyone – especially Zorique – killed, scared of just fucking it all up for everyone.

Forgive me for what I've done, my love. I've done it all for you.

'Tinnstra!' Tavis's voice pulled her from her thoughts.

She looked up. He was near the crest of the slope, crouched, waving her down, too.

Tinnstra sank into the tall grass and slipped her axe into her hand as she searched around for whatever Tavis had seen. The sky was clear of Daijaku and there was no trace of Chosen nearby. What had Tavis spooked?

'Come here,' he hissed, waving her to join him.

She moved quickly, passing Sadir, passing Nika, passing Dale. 'What is it?'

He pointed back along the valley. 'See those rocks down there? They look blue from up here.'

'Blue rocks?' She almost laughed. He was worried about blue rocks?

'They don't look natural.'

She followed his directions, saw the cluster of boulders. They were massive even from that distance, with a faint blue wash. They'd not have noticed them from the road. Grass and moss covered their sides – almost too well. Almost as if they'd been placed there deliberately. The smile fell from her face. And what was that across the surface of the rocks? 'Has someone written something on them? Drawn something?'

'Yes,' said Tavis, 'but I don't recognise the patterns. Maybe they're runes or wards.' Both answers meant magic. Magic where it shouldn't be. Tinnstra reached out with her senses, scared that she'd missed something, but there was nothing to find.

Just an awful feeling in her gut that something bad was about to happen.

'I don't like this,' said Tinnstra. She looked back down the road, towards the advancing column, and the pain in her gut got worse. 'There's more over there. On both sides of the road.'

'How did we miss them?'

'We weren't looking at the rocks. We were looking for Skulls.'

'I think we should head back down,' said Tavis. 'Have a closer look.'

'I think you're right.' She started to move, the others following.

Time slowed as it always did when bad things were about to happen and yet the army still marched towards her, the blue boulders on either side of the column now. 'Tavis, take those.' She waved towards the first rocks she'd seen. He peeled off, half their team with him.

Tinnstra and the others ran towards the army.

She wasn't fast enough. The boulders began to move.

51

Zorique

The Northern Road

Zorique shouldn't have flown off and left the army, but she needed to be alone. She needed time to think. Everything was going wrong and she didn't know how to fix any of it – especially whatever was going on between her and Tinnstra. Gods, they were in the middle of a war and she was more worried about why she was fighting with her mother. She felt selfish and petty for even thinking about it, let alone flying off and leaving everyone. But the army would survive without her for a few hours. Her disappearance wouldn't cause any harm except annoy Tinnstra – not that her mother would notice.

Once, she'd never been able to escape her mother's eye. Frustrating as it was, Zorique had known it was because Tinnstra loved her. But now?

All she cared about was the Chikara water. They'd barely spoken for weeks. She was always off hunting day and night, looking for the Egril. Avoiding her daughter.

Zorique flew faster, letting the cold wind strip the thoughts from her mind, getting lost in the sheer joy of her magic. Feeling stronger the higher she went.

She could cope. She'd find a way to deal with everything, with Tinnstra. She'd talk to her mother later.

Scorched fields pulled her from her thoughts. Black and brown amongst a sea of green. There was a scattering of houses, too, what was once a village.

Zorique was tempted to fly on and pretend she'd not seen anything. She knew nothing good waited for her there. Only bloody work left by the Skulls.

Sure enough, Zorique saw the bodies next. Rows of them across one of the charred fields. Impaled like scarecrows. She tried not to count, to spare herself some pain, but it was impossible. There had to be over a hundred dead, at least.

Over a hundred men, women and children, all impaled on spikes. Probably the whole village. The Skulls, after all, never left survivors if they could help it.

Zorique circled the village in case the Skulls were still nearby, but she couldn't see any sign of the white-armoured monsters. Just blackened land and smashed-up homes. No doubt the Skulls had poisoned the water supply as well.

Godsdamn them all. Why had they done this? What possible harm could these villagers have done to the Egril? It was all so unnecessary.

'*Shirudan.*' The shield activated around her as she lowered herself to the ground. Better to be careful in case there were Skulls she'd not spotted. In case their Chosen waited for her. She still remembered the pain from their baton blasts and suddenly wasn't so sure she wanted to meet the enemy on her own.

But no, there were no enemy to be found.

She walked towards the field. Her shield crackled around her, but it offered no protection from what she had to do next. She could've turned back, of course, left the dead to nature, but Zorique wouldn't have been able to live with herself if she did that.

She smelled the dead first. The Godsawful stink that comes from rotting bodies, which stuck in her nose and clung to her clothes, an odour that never seemed to leave her these days. She wished her shield could protect her from it, but no magic was that strong.

There was that buzzing, too, from the flies feeding on the bodies, and when she saw the villagers, she could tell the birds had also been along to have a peck at an eye here and a cheek there.

She stopped and closed her eyes for a moment, building her

strength, building walls around her feelings. She was only eighteen after all, and the world shouldn't hold such horrors for her. But she was Zorique, Queen of Jia, and there was no hiding from any of it.

The villagers were planted on spikes, row after row, like some sort of demonic crop. Each one frozen in agony, their lives ended because someone somewhere believed in a different God.

She stopped by a child; a boy of no more than seven summers, his eyes wide open in terror. What were Gods to him? Did he care who ruled the heavens or who he was told to worship in this world? And yet his life had been taken.

It wasn't fair.

It wasn't right.

Zorique let her shield drop so she could touch the boy's face, offering him a gentle caress that had been missing in his final moments. Her finger traced the white streaks tears had made down his dirty cheeks, then she brushed his eyes shut and whispered a prayer just for him.

When she had gathered her strength, Zorique walked on. Past row after row of faces, knowing they would stay with her for the rest of her life.

When she had looked on the last, she headed to the edge of the field and turned back to the dead. 'Forgive me for not coming here in time to save you. I promise you will never be forgotten for as long as I breathe. I will avenge you all. I will set Jia free so no others will endure your fate. Now go, leave this horrid world and join Xin in her kingdom.' Zorique pointed her spear at the impaled.

'*Kasri.*'

Fire bloomed like red flowers from one end of the field to the other, engulfing each and every person who had ever called that village home. *Let their spirits find Xin now. Let them find rest.*

Zorique watched the village burn, for everyone should have someone bear witness to their final moments in this world. Even when smoke stung her eyes and obscured the fires, she stayed, tears running down her face, listening to the crackle and pop of the flames.

Maybe that was why she almost missed the creak of wood behind her. She turned as the shattered houses shook from within. Walls collapsed and roofs fell as monstrous shapes emerged from their ruins. A dozen at least, over twice her height and just as wide, blue-skinned monsters with curling horns growing from their foreheads and giant tusks jutting out of their lips. Some carried spiked clubs and spears in their hands while others brandished man-sized swords. They roared at Zorique, and she felt the ground shake as they charged towards her.

Kojin.

Zorique had fought them – slaughtered them – in Layso. These would die just the same.

'*Kasri.*' She summoned the fire into her hand, letting it build for a heartbeat, for two, three, then she threw it with all her might at the leading giant. The fireball struck it square on the chest and ... there was a flash of light, the flames disappeared and the monster charged on.

Disbelieving her own eyes, Zorique threw another fireball without thinking. Again, light flared around the creature and her fire turned into smoke. Then the beast was on her, dipping its head, charging with its horns.

'*Shirudan!*' The shield crackled to life as the Kojin slammed into her, lifting Zorique off her feet and sending her flying through the air. She had wits enough to realise she'd been a half-second from death, but that was all as she slammed into the ground. She rolled, her spear lost, trying to catch her breath, but the Kojin resumed its attack. Others joined in, giant clubs smashing down on her shield.

Zorique fell back onto one knee by instinct and put up a hand to protect herself as the first club crashed into her shield. More light flared around the impact and Zorique gasped as if hit, pain filling her chest, worse than even a Chosen's blast. A second club hammered her shield, knocking her sideways, rattling her bones.

She tumbled head over heels, suddenly so scared.

It wasn't like Layso at all. The Kojin could hurt her now, but her magic couldn't hurt them.

'*Tobo!*' Zorique took to the air but a hand shot out and batted her to the ground once more. The Kojin pounded her shield mercilessly, driving her into the earth, giving her no time to think, no time to breathe, no time to do anything. She could feel her shield weakening. Cracking.

Dear Gods, she was going to die.

52

Ange

Lanaka

Ange inched her way back along the ledge, scarcely breathing, eyes darting to the skies in case there were Daijaku in the air, cursing herself with every step. Why had they stayed the night? They should've left straight away, left this cursed city far behind them.

But she had to remain calm. They weren't fucked just yet. They still had a chance. If they were quick.

Ange hooked her foot under the windowsill and crawled back inside, feeling all the better for having walls around her once more.

Garo and the kid were awake when she came down the stairs. Garo greeted her with a smile, but it disappeared the moment he got a good look at her face. 'What's wrong?'

'Skulls.'

Linx whimpered at the news and Garo pulled him in tight. 'How many?'

Ange shook her head. 'Does it matter?' She went to a window and peeked out. The street below only had the dead in it. No Egril. 'I was on the roof. I heard them. Marching. Lots of them.'

Garo came up beside her. 'What are we going to do?'

'We go now.' Ange looked past him, to the boy. 'How do we get out of the city, Linx?'

'The main gates ...' said the boy, pointing out through the window.

Ange went over to him and bent down, smiling her fake smile. 'We can't go that way. Is there another way out? A back gate?'

'I ... I don't know.' Linx's lip wobbled. 'I ... I've never left the city before. My mother ... My mother ...' Tears sprang into his eyes.

Garo was there in an instant. 'It's all right, Linx. Don't worry. You've got us. We can work it out. Can't we, Ange?'

'Yeah, of course we can.' The words didn't sit well on her tongue, but there was nothing else she could say.

They scrabbled their stuff together as quick as they could. Garo shoved an extra blanket in his backpack for Linx. Neither of them mentioned the lack of food or water. What was the point? They both knew it was bad.

When they got downstairs, Garo picked Linx up. 'I'm going to carry you, okay?'

The boy nodded.

'Now, I want you to keep your eyes closed as long as you can. Keep them closed until I tell you to open them. Do you think you can do that?'

Another nod.

'Good lad.'

Ange was at the door, pulled it open a crack, listened. Someone somewhere was screaming, and she heard a man shout in Egril. A pig language, Dren called it, and with good reason. The Skulls must have prisoners with them.

Heart racing, she chanced a peek outside. Still no sign of them. Just the dead. Dear Gods, she didn't want to become one of them. 'Let's go,' she hissed to Garo. Then they were out, exposed, running down the street, Garo holding Linx tight against his chest. Their feet sounded so fucking loud, echoing all around them.

Ange didn't know where she was leading them, just that they were going in the opposite direction from the city gates. The dead stared at them as they passed, down one street, a turn left, a turn right, down another.

It didn't help that every street looked the same; bloodstained cobblestones and impaled bodies. It was like trying to escape a nightmare.

'Ange,' puffed Garo. 'We've got to stop.'

Stopping was the last thing she wanted to do, but stop she did. 'Why?'

Garo lowered the boy to the ground. 'He's too heavy for me to run far with.'

'Fuck.'

'Don't leave me,' said Linx, his eyes still closed.

'We're not going to do that,' said Ange.

'Linx, I need you to be brave,' said Garo, 'and open your eyes.'

Slowly, the boy did as Garo asked. He'd seen the dead before, but still he balked at them for a moment before, somehow, pulling himself together.

'You both ready?' asked Ange, desperate for them to say yes and, thank the Gods, she got nods back.

They moved slower this time. Every now and then a scream cut through the silence, only to stop suddenly. Ange didn't want to think what that could mean, but what she wanted never meant much. Each shriek made her flinch. Each howl made her eyes water.

Garo kept his arm around Linx, covering him with his body, and for once, he didn't complain or ask any stupid questions. And, as much as she hated to admit it, Ange was glad he was with her.

She took a left down a long, wide street. They got halfway before she realised the road was curving back on itself and they were going in the wrong direction. 'Shit.' She stopped, trying to spot a turning or a crossroads up ahead, then looked back the way they had come.

'What's up?' said Garo.

'Nothing,' she replied. 'Just took a wrong turn. We need to go back.'

'Right,' said Garo, and Ange was just so damned happy he hadn't argued. She didn't have the strength for that.

Turning around, they retraced their steps, passed where they had made the turn and carried straight on, looking for a crossroads to turn left. But the bloody road started to curve right again. Committed, they carried on for a few minutes longer while Ange grew more agitated, hoping they'd get lucky, knowing they wouldn't.

'Do you recognise where we are?' she asked Linx.

'N ... no,' replied the boy, not even glancing up.

'Are you sure?' she tried again. 'Have a look at the buildings. Maybe you came here with your mother one time?'

'Easy, Ange,' said Garo. 'He said no, okay?'

'It's just ... we're going back on ourselves again.'

'Do we turn around, try another route?'

'But how far back should we go? Where did we go wrong?'

Garo looked around as if he'd suddenly see the path they needed to take, fool that he was.

Ange whacked his arm. 'Come on, let's keep going. There has to be a turning somewhere.'

Garo didn't move. 'What about the houses?'

'What about them?'

Garo shrugged. 'Go in the front door, out the back. We'll either be in the next street or there'll be another house to go through before we find it. Either way, we'll be heading in the right direction.'

Ange stared at him open-mouthed. 'When did you get clever?'

'It's obvious, isn't it?'

'Apparently not,' said Ange. 'Come on.'

The first door they tried was locked but the second opened easily enough. Someone had died inside the hallway, judging by the blood smeared over the floorboards, but Ange ignored the stains and led the others through the house.

The kitchen table was overturned. A broken chair. Another lying on its side. Some bowls shattered over the floor. The Skulls had come at dinner time, apparently.

Ange spotted the pot hanging over the cold hearth and chanced a look. There was a stew of some sort inside, the top all brown and congealed, but she was hungry enough not to care. She grabbed a spoon and dug in, shovelling the goop into her mouth. It had been sitting there for two days at least but she'd eaten worse.

She stuck the spoon in again and waved Linx over. 'Here. Eat.'

The boy didn't need asking twice and rushed to join her,

followed by Garo. They took it in turns, eating quickly, spilling as much as they ate.

Ange stopped them when they were halfway down the pot. 'Enough. We have to go.'

Again, there were no arguments. Ange found the back door. It opened into a small garden, which seemed a bloody odd thing to have in a city, but there it was; a patch of grass and a tree and another house backed onto it. There was nothing like that in Kiyosun – they didn't have the space or the water to waste. Ange felt a tinge of jealousy at the luxury as they crossed from one house to the next, but then she remembered whoever owned it was now dead and that was nothing to envy.

The door to the other house was locked, so Garo put his shoulder to it and got it open with a crack. They all froze at the loud noise, listening in case anyone heard it, and that was when Ange realised how quiet the city was now. No more screams. No more murders.

No more Skulls?

Would they have gone once they'd killed whatever prisoners they had?

A stupid thought. She stepped into the next house. It was much the same as all the others. A nice home, full of ghosts.

The front door had been smashed in and Ange could see the street through the open portal it left behind, see more dead lined up, planted like trees. A peek outside told her there were no Skulls to worry about. Ange just had to work out whether to turn left or right. She concentrated on the map in her head, trying to picture their path. They couldn't afford for her to get it wrong this time.

'What's up?' asked Garo. She looked back, saw he was tucking a small loaf of bread into his pack. He smiled. 'It was just sitting there, back in the kitchen.'

'Well done.' Ange returned her attention to the street. Which way? Which way? Had to be left. Had to be. She bloody hoped so.

Off they went, back out in the open, the only moving things in a city of the dead, noses full of corpse stink, hearts full of dread.

Doubt ate away at Ange, making her question every decision. Maybe they should've stayed in one of the houses. Laid low there until the Skulls moved on. They wouldn't search the buildings again, would they? Not after they'd killed everyone?

But what if they did? What if they turned up mob-handed with a load of spare spikes to ram through the three of them?

There were no right choices, just bad options that she had to make the best of.

They went along more streets, turning when they could, heading in what she hoped was the right direction. The city wall had to be close now. She prayed that it was and that they'd find a gate easily enough. The Gods knew they needed some luck.

She wished for a moment that they'd not gone on Hasan's mission, that they'd stayed with the army, but she stopped herself. She was turning into Garo with thoughts like that.

Ange glanced back, feeling guilty. Garo was right behind her, looking nervous, but still he had his arm around Linx, whispering encouragement to the kid. He played big brother well.

As they moved through the city, the number of dead lessened until they finally found themselves walking down empty streets. For some reason, though, it made Ange feel even more exposed. She was convinced a Skull was going to appear and had to fight the urge to hide in a doorway every few seconds.

Then they turned a corner and there it was – the city wall. 'Thank the Gods,' said Ange. 'Thank the fucking Gods.'

It wasn't as high as the wall around Kiyosun, but it was high enough. Maybe fifteen feet. Whoever had built it knew what they were doing. Shame it hadn't done any good against the Skulls.

'We're not going over the top of that,' said Garo. 'That's for sure.'

'There'll be a gate somewhere,' said Ange, looking left, then right along the wall, not seeing anything. She looked down at Linx. 'Don't suppose you have any ideas?'

The kid shook his head.

That left Garo. 'You?'

He did what she'd done, looked left, then right, then shrugged. 'Fuck.' She checked the sky, trying to work out her north from her south, but she'd always been crap at that. At least there weren't any Daijaku swooping around. Not yet, anyway. 'This way.'

She went left, hoping and praying, and knowing what Dren would've said about that. Maybe there weren't any Gods, but luck was a thing, wasn't it? She deserved some of that. They all did.

But the further they walked, the less lucky she felt. It was all wall and no bloody gate. Garo and the kid were getting nervous, too, and Ange didn't blame them.

She drew her sword. No bloody idea why except it made her feel better having it in her hand. And, of course, Garo copied her. So there they were, inching their way along the wall, blades out, hearts in mouths, expecting things to go wrong any minute because they sure as hell weren't going right.

'What's that?' said Garo, from over her shoulder.

'What's what?' she asked, not seeing anything.

'That.' He pointed along the wall with his sword.

Ange peered ahead, didn't see much, just more bloody wall, and then she spotted it, too – a column sticking out. She stepped left to get a better look and started grinning. There was an archway and an oak door. Just what they were looking for. 'We bloody found it.'

Garo picked up Linx and they sprinted to the gate. Ange was nearly laughing, she was that happy.

On another day, a heavy bar would've been placed across the door, locking it shut, but now it was leaning against the wall doing nothing. Good job, too, because it looked heavy enough to have been a problem for both her and Garo to move.

Whether it was down to the Gods or just a nice slice of luck, Ange wasn't going to complain. With one last check of the streets around them, she pushed the gate open.

And found two Skulls standing guard on the other side.

They were as surprised as she was, but Ange had her sword ready. She screamed, hurling herself at one of them, jabbing forwards with her Shulka blade, not really aiming at any body part in particular. Ange felt the impact in her arm first as the sword stopped against something solid, then she was on top of the Skull, screaming and spitting fury, battering away at his mask with her other hand.

Something hit her in the side and she went flying off and rolling in the dirt. By the time she was on her feet again, Garo was wrestling with the other Skull, holding on to both his wrists as best he could, with Linx crying a few yards behind.

The Skull Ange had jumped on lay dead with her sword in his chest. So that was something, at least. She pulled her knife out of its sheath, bloody grateful she had it, and lunged at Garo's Skull. She was screaming again, a stupid thing to do, but she couldn't help herself as she jumped on the bastard's back and stabbed for all she was worth. The Egril struggled, trying to shake her off, but as big and strong as he was, it didn't mean shit after she'd stuck her knife in his neck a dozen times.

The Skull's legs went from under him and he collapsed with Ange still clinging to his back, stabbing away.

Garo grabbed her hand and stopped the knife going in one last time. 'He's dead.'

Ange stood up, covered in blood. 'Shit. Run!'

She shouldn't have screamed, of course. More Skulls raced towards them.

53

Tinnstra

The Northern Road

Kojin.

The boulders were Kojin. They emerged from the ground where they'd been half-buried, shaking off lumps of dirt and grass. Their roars filled the air a second before they fell on the army column. They didn't have any weapons, but that was no mercy.

Dozens were dead before anyone could react. The giants' big fists pulverised anyone close to them. Tinnstra saw men ripped asunder, blood and guts flying everywhere, while others were pulped into the ground. Some tried to form a shield wall, but a Kojin swatted it aside like a pack of cards before falling on the men behind it.

Tinnstra sprinted towards the battle, but her weapons felt small in her hands, inadequate. Men and women screamed in agony and despair as the slaughter continued.

Already there were a dozen Kojin causing mayhem amongst the troops, but more were coming down the valley slopes to join the attack. If they couldn't stop these monsters somehow, the whole war would be over.

Tinnstra spared a glance over her shoulder, hoping that she'd see Zorique blazing back from wherever she'd gone, ready to save the day at the last minute. But the skies were clear. There was no sign of her daughter.

'Pull back!' she screamed. 'Get out of their way!' No one

could've heard her over the carnage, but she kept hollering the orders as she ran. The ground was littered with the dead, with more joining them by the second.

Lightning bolts flashed out, a sign that Aasgod had joined the fray, but when they hit the Kojin, light flared along the runes painted on the demons' skin and the magic fizzled without even slowing the monsters down.

A Kojin had its back to Tinnstra as it ripped the head off a soldier and then used the corpse to batter another five into the road. Screaming with all her fury, she leaped into the air, axe already swinging.

She landed square on the Kojin's back as the axe came down on the spot where neck met shoulder. It went deep, but not deep enough. The beast howled in pain, twisting its back to dislodge her, but she used the axe to stay in place and dodged a flailing fist. Pulling herself up, she drew her sword with her free hand and, using every ounce of strength she'd gained from the Chikara water, she swung the blade towards the side of the Kojin's head. This time the sword sliced into its skull. The demon went rigid beneath Tinnstra's feet, then toppled forwards like a felled tree. Pulling her weapons free, she jumped clear, already looking for her next kill.

Another Kojin lunged at her with its massive hands. Every instinct told her to run, but she ignored them all and charged at the demon instead, ducking under its sweeping arms, stabbing her sword deep into the Kojin's groin. The Kojin howled as she slipped, blood-drenched, between its legs and took her axe first to one set of hamstrings, then the other. The Kojin crashed to the ground and Tinnstra strode along its back until she could bury her axe in its brain.

Nothing is invincible. Anything can be killed. She spat on the dead creature and turned to find more prey.

It was mayhem, a slaughter. Aasgod was throwing his lightning around even though it did nothing but make him feel better about himself, but she spotted Ralasis and Hasan organising the troops to fight back more efficiently.

They had the soldiers forming spear rings around the Kojin.

One side retreated as the demon attacked while the rear side moved in, stabbing with spears. As the creature turned to deal with the assault, the other side would strike. Ralasis had his archers lined up on the slopes and peppering the creatures with arrows. It was slow work, but Tinnstra could already see some of the Kojin slowing down, weakened by a multitude of wounds. They had the better of the creatures.

Thank the Gods for men, at last, who knew what they were doing.

Then Tinnstra heard a scream from behind her and spun. She'd forgotten about Tavis and the others! He ran towards her, clutching a bloody arm, with Dale and Nika hot on his heels, chased by four Kojin. There was no sign of the other two she'd sent with Tavis.

'Ralasis!' she howled. 'I need help!'

The Meigorian's head snapped towards her, then to the road and the charging monsters. Gods bless him, he didn't hesitate. He sent a dozen archers her way. Even joined them.

'Line them up in two ranks and get ready,' she called as she watched Tavis and the others sprinting towards them. The Kojin weren't that far behind, the ground shaking with every monstrous footfall. The Jians weren't going to make it.

Tinnstra charged towards them.

'Tinnstra! Come back!' shouted Ralasis. 'You'll get yourself killed!'

Not if I can help it.

She passed Tavis clutching his bloody arm, passed Nika, but she wasn't fast enough for Dale. A Kojin reached out, snatched him off his feet and tore him apart.

Tinnstra screamed and threw her axe at the demon. It smacked home, right between the Kojin's eyes, but this time it did not fall. Instead, it backhanded Tinnstra off the road.

She lay there, head spinning, spitting blood, scared for a moment that every bone in her body was broken, and only too aware she'd lost her both her sword and her axe now. And the Kojin was coming for her again.

A volley of arrows from Ralasis' archers did little to slow its fury as it charged towards Tinnstra, head down, horns ready to finish her off.

Move, you fool, move.

Ignoring the pain, Tinnstra snatched some throwing stars from the pouch on her side and threw them at the creature. They struck its chest, but still the demon came, despite the poison on the tips of the stars.

Tinnstra dived to one side a heartbeat before the Kojin's head smashed into the ground. It reared up, her axe still stuck in its forehead, roaring and howling, and then grabbed her arm, yanking her upwards. Tinnstra had to go with it, lest her arm be ripped from its socket, and she was lifted into the air, straight towards its gaping jaws.

Straight towards her axe.

She swung herself around, reaching out with her free hand to snatch her axe loose, before kicking the Kojin in the face. It howled as she sent a tusk flying, but it didn't let go.

Good.

She swung back, her reach just long enough now with her axe in hand. The blade slashed straight across its face, straight across its eyes.

It let go of her, and the sound of the Kojin's cries made her forget her own pain. Tinnstra dropped to the ground, her left arm numb, but she still had her axe and her fury. She attacked the creature like it was a tree. She chopped at its knee, hacked its hamstrings, took a chunk out of its side as it toppled.

The Kojin crashed to the ground, its legs gone, and Tinnstra ran along its back and buried the axe in its skull. She spun around, saw Ralasis' archers had felled another two of the beasts while soldiers harried the last with spears. It swatted at the soldiers, but they kept out of its way as others jabbed deep. Already, the Kojin was bleeding from a dozen wounds. It, too, would fall.

She checked down the line, saw the other Kojin lying dead along the path and hundreds of her soldiers lying with them. The dead were everywhere.

Dear Gods, how many have we lost this time? Wiping blood from her mouth, she walked over and picked up her sword, checking for damage before sheathing it once more. *Every time the Egril attack, we pay too high a price.*

And there was still far to go before she could enact her plan. Now, more than ever, she was convinced that if it worked, she could end this war and save so many lives.

If it worked ...

'Tinnstra!' Aasgod ran towards her.

She was surprised he wasn't still throwing his lightning around, even though the Kojin were dead. 'What?'

'Have you seen Zorique?'

The question stabbed Tinnstra in the gut. 'No.' Zorique had flown ahead of the column how long ago?

'She should have returned by now,' said Aasgod. 'The sound of battle alone should've brought her back.' His eyes were wild, darting, searching the skies.

Tinnstra reached out with her senses. Zorique's magic had grown since they'd been back in Jia, and Tinnstra was more sensitive to it than to anyone else's, but there was no sign whatsoever of that bright spark. There was nothing.

'She's not close by at all.'

'What if something's happened to her?'

'Don't say that,' snapped Tinnstra. She didn't even want to think it. She glanced around, saw Tavis with his bloody arm, Nika not looking much better as she comforted Sadir. Only the Gods knew what had happened to the rest of her ten. At least three were dead, if not more. They weren't going to be able to help her. 'I'll find her.'

'I'll come with you,' said the mage.

'You won't. You'll only slow me down.'

'I—'

Tinnstra didn't care what Aasgod had to say. She set off at a run. Zorique was out there somewhere and she'd find her – or die trying.

54

Jax

Lanaka

Jax rode with Moiri by his side, leading the Hanran south. Since the victory in Chita, their ranks had swollen to more than five hundred soldiers. Even Danni had joined them with his crew. Over fifty horses had been reclaimed from the dead Skulls and, by the Gods, it felt good to be riding once more, leading an army of well-armed Jians.

He wasn't taking anything for granted, though. He spent two hours every morning drilling the new recruits before they set off, and Jax intended to do the same every morning going forward. His soldiers might not be Shulka, but he was going to train them as best he could. And he knew more battles would harden them further. More victories would give them strength. Would give them hope.

They had a taste of it now, and he would ensure that continued.

He glanced over at Moiri, who smiled back. The night in Chita had changed everything between them in the best possible way. The Shulka had always encouraged each other to find love within their own ranks. They knew such bonds made their warriors fight harder, and any offspring from such unions secured the future. Now, with this woman by his side and the fine Jians following them? Dear Gods, the Egril didn't stand a chance.

'You look like your old self,' said Moiri.

'I was just thinking the same thing,' said Jax. 'It's been a long time coming.'

'I'm glad,' said Moiri. 'You've made such a difference in a short time already – just when we needed it the most. I thank the Gods.'

'You don't need to do that. You're the one who kept it going all this time. I'm just here to help you.'

'Gracious of you to say that.' Moiri tilted her head in appreciation. 'Even if it's not true.'

He smiled. 'We make a good team.'

'That we do.

'Any word from the scouts?'

'Not yet, but we'll have it soon enough. They know what they're doing.'

'Good. We don't want to ride into the Skull army by accident.'

'Relax. We won't.'

Worry. Worry. Worry. You do it so well, sang Monsuta.

Jax didn't react to the voice. He didn't look for where it came from. It didn't make him scared or uncomfortable. Not anymore. He knew what it was.

It wasn't Monsuta and it wasn't Monsuta's ghost. It was nothing more than a lingering nightmare. An echo. His own memories tricking him. Reminding him not to get too confident. It might all go wrong again if he wasn't careful, and Jax couldn't allow that.

The truth was, his nightmares bothered him more than the voices in his head. Every night he'd had the same dream, of the red cave and the red waters and that monster of a man. It felt so real, so utterly terrifying. Every time, Jax would wake, drenched in sweat, doing his best not to scream.

It was another hangover from everything he'd been through. He knew that. He'd seen it before in Shulka who'd come back from the border wars. He knew it was his trauma haunting him, but he still wished it gone. He should be stronger than that. Better.

But you're weak. I proved it in that room. With my little knives.

Jax flinched at the thought.

'Something wrong?' asked Moiri. 'You look like you've seen a ghost.'

'Seen one? No. I carry enough with me as it is,' replied Jax. 'And I can never seem to let them go.'

'I know that feeling.'

Jax wanted to tell her that she didn't really know – no one could – that his ghosts were different, more vicious than any other, but he kept quiet. Any explanation would involve talking about what happened in Kiyosun ... in that room. It would shatter her faith in him, and he didn't want that. He was the general again. The leader. Not the failure. The betrayer.

His eyes drifted back to Moiri. With her, he could exorcise all his ghosts, bad memories and failures. Once the Egril were defeated, they could build a life together, perhaps even rebuild the Shulka. Jia would need them to ensure the enemy did not simply return. With Moiri, he could do that. It would be an honour. A second chance. Redemption.

Of course, they had to win this war first.

He focused on the road ahead instead. It looked peaceful enough as they followed the dirt track though low rolling hills under a clear, blue sky, and yet ... some sense told him there would be fighting soon. He could almost smell the violence in the air. Hear the dead calling.

Or was that his imagination as well?

He kicked his horse forwards, wanting to get to the top of the next hill.

'Jax?' said Moiri, moving with him.

The horse sensed something, too, picking up speed without any more urging from Jax.

Before he could reach the hilltop, a horn sounded. It was his scouts. An alarm. He kicked his horse into a gallop before pulling it to a stop at the peak.

There was a walled city in the distance, maybe two or three miles away. His scouts were about a mile from there, racing towards something – no, someone. Someone being chased by Skulls.

The Skulls were on foot, but their white armour stood out against the green surroundings. More were spilling from the city, drawn by the scouts' horn. No way to tell how many there were, but Jax couldn't leave his people to die.

He heard Moiri ordering their horse to charge and that was all the permission he needed to set off at a gallop. By the Gods, he hoped the scouts would be alive by the time they reached them.

The ground shook with the thunder of fifty sets of hooves charging towards their enemy. Jax gripped his reins with his one good hand and bent low over his horse's neck, grinning like a madman as the wind whipped his face. He watched the scouts reach the smaller group of Skulls, saw swords flash up and slash down.

They were good men and women who knew what they were doing, so he had no fear for them in that skirmish. Horses always win over infantry unless the numbers are overwhelming. That's why it was the larger group of Skulls coming from the city that offered the greater threat. That's who Jax was charging.

The scouts had won their fight and were riding back towards Jax and the others, but slower, weighed down with whoever the Skulls had been chasing. He hoped their lives were worth the cost of what came next.

The fifty galloped past the scouts in a swirl of dirt and dust, on towards the Skulls. There had to be a hundred of them, maybe two hundred, drawing swords, pointing spears, getting ready to meet the charge.

'Line up. Line up. Line up,' urged Jax through gritted teeth. He didn't want them bunched together.

The Jians drew swords of their own. Jax swapped his reins to his teeth and did the same. The weight of the blade felt so natural in his left hand now, as if it had always been there. He guided the horse beneath him with his thighs, as comfortable as if he'd been riding every day for years.

And yes – the Skulls spread out before them. A line of white, waiting for death to arrive.

The fifty crashed through the Skull ranks, killing with sword and hoof, slaughtering all before them. The thunder of hooves, the clash of steel, the screams of men all mixed together. On the first pass through the enemy lines, Jax's horse trampled one Skull, while Jax hacked down another, splitting his head open in a shower of red. He wheeled the horse around and charged through the Skull line again and again. Tireless. Remorseless.

It was a massacre.

It was glorious.

It was everything Jax had loved about being a Shulka.

Invincible and victorious.

When there was no one left to kill, Jax almost felt disappointed, but then he saw the sheer joy on his soldiers' faces, Shulka and Hanran alike, and their euphoria seeped into him. Moiri rushed over, her face and armour splattered with Egril blood, and they fell into each other's arms and kissed with a hunger that only battle creates.

Of course, it couldn't last.

'Generals! Generals!' Fin and Dev rushed over, ashen-faced. 'You have to see this.'

'What is it?' asked Jax, pulling away from Moiri.

'We went into the city,' said Dev, before her voice broke.

'Best you see for yourself,' said Finn.

There was no euphoria once they saw the dead, staked throughout the city.

'Find the scouts,' said Jax. 'Bring whoever they rescued to me. And see if any Skulls survived. I want to talk to them as well.'

'I don't believe this,' said Moiri while they waited.

Jax put his arm around her and pulled her close. 'We'll make them pay.' He kissed her head. 'By the Gods, I swear they will pay.'

She looked up with tears in her eyes. 'I'll hold you to that.'

The scouts appeared, accompanying a young man, a woman and a child. The man was doing his best to stop the boy seeing the corpses. 'This is no place for a child,' said Jax. 'Take the boy back outside.'

Two Hanran tried to take the child, but both the man and woman took up fighting stances before they could lay a hand on him.

'Take the kid and I'll rip your bloody eyes out,' snarled the girl.

Jax stared at her. She looked familiar. He knew her from somewhere, and her accent ... 'Are you from Kiyosun?'

401

She looked over and her eyes went wide. 'Jax? Fuck! Jax! We thought you were dead!'

'Have we met?' asked Jax.

'Yeah, in Kiyosun,' said the woman. 'I was with Dren at the house on Compton Street.'

Jax flinched at hearing the address. That was where he'd cut his own arm off, where he killed the two lads looking after him. He shook the memories from his mind. Best forgotten. 'You know Dren?'

The woman turned to the man. 'Take the kid outside, like they say. I'll do the talking here.'

'You sure?' asked the lad.

The woman glanced at Jax. 'Yeah, I am.' She waited for her friend to leave, then walked over to Jax. 'My name's Ange. It's good to see you. Real good.'

'Likewise,' said Jax. 'What are you doing this far north?'

'I'm with the Hanran. I came up with Hasan through—'

'Hasan?' interrupted Jax. 'Where is he?'

'We left him back down south,' said Ange. 'Zorique sent us—'

'You're with the queen?'

Moiri laid a hand on Jax's arm. 'Let Ange tell her story.'

Jax nodded, his heart racing. This was all too much to take in.

'We're all with the queen now. Zorique landed with a Meigorian army at Kiyosun,' said Ange. 'They met more Skulls than I've ever seen, and thousands of Daijaku, and she beat the fucking lot of them.'

'But she's a child,' said Jax. 'How could she?'

'Not anymore, she's not,' said Ange. 'She's my age. Maybe a bit older.'

'Zorique is four years old,' said Jax. 'I saw her myself less than a year ago.'

'Was she flying back then?' said Ange.

'No.'

Ange shrugged. 'Then I'd say she's done a fair bit of growing up since you last saw her.'

'That's not possible,' said Jax.

'She flies, shines like a star and shoots fire from her hands.

Wiped out most of the Skull army by herself.' Ange shrugged. 'Seems to me, growing up quick is the least of her skills.'

'I ... I don't know what to say,' said Jax, trying to picture his queen fully grown, flying. Not that it changed anything. He felt the urge to rush to her side even more strongly than before. If she was putting her life in danger for her subjects, he had to join her. He could keep her safe.

'Wait till you see her,' said Ange. 'You'll really be lost for words then. A lot of people, including that dumb idiot with me, think she's a God.'

Jax glanced over at Moiri, who shook her head. 'Don't look at me. I've given up trying to make sense of everything.'

'Where are they now?' asked Jax.

'I'm not sure,' said Ange. 'They were heading north with the main army and they sent a few of us ahead to recruit more soldiers. We're to meet up with them at the Kotege in about a week.'

A warm rush came over Jax. Finally, he knew where Zorique was heading. He was going to meet her and fight for her. He was going to win this war for her. 'We ride to the Kotege, then.'

Moiri nodded. 'After we deal with the dead here.'

'Of course,' said Jax.

Moiri turned to Ange. 'Was my daughter with Zorique?'

'Your daughter?'

Moiri nodded. 'Her name is Tinnstra.'

Ange's eyes went wide. 'Yes, yes, she is. She lost an eye during the invasion, but that hasn't slowed her down.'

Moiri's hand went to her mouth. 'Thank the Gods.'

'And Dren?' asked Jax. 'You said you were with him back in Kiyosun.'

'Dren's ... dead.'

'Oh.' Not another one. Jax should have been used to hearing such news, but he felt a stab of sorrow all the same. 'I'm sorry.'

'Aren't we all?' She glared back at him, clearly upset, too, despite her efforts to hide it.

Jax stood there, unsure what to say, regretting his choice of speaking to her now. He'd have been better off with his memories of what had been, rather than the knowledge of what was now. In the end, he said, 'He was a good kid. I liked him.' Stupid words that wouldn't change a thing.

Except the girl brightened, her darkness lifting, if only by a little. 'He liked you, too. He said you made him want to be better.'

Jax smiled, her words chasing back the darkness inside him. 'I don't think he could've got much worse. Dren was a ... wild thing.'

'He was pretty sick by the end, though,' said Ange. 'Could barely stand. The Skulls' bombs poisoned him.'

'I'm sorry.'

'Yeah, well.' Ange looked around at the corpses. 'It's a shit world.'

'That it is.'

Fin, Dev and the other scouts returned a second time, dragging a Skull between them. His hands were tied and his helmet had been removed, but they'd left the Skull mask in place. Jax was glad of that. It would make what he had to do that much easier.

'Ange, why don't you and your friends go and get something to eat? Fin and Dev will show you where,' said Jax. 'While you're doing that, I'll have a chat with our friend here.'

Ange nodded. 'Okay. We'll do that. Promise me one thing, though?'

'What's that?'

'Don't go easy on this piece of shit.' She spat in the Egril's face. 'Not after what he's done here.'

'Don't worry,' said Jax, producing a knife, his favourite. 'I won't.' He nodded at the scouts holding the Skull. 'Take him inside one of the houses. Might as well have a bit of privacy while we chat.'

'Let go,' said the Skull in bad Jian. 'Let go.'

'The Great Darkness waits for you,' replied Jax in Egril. He waved the knife at the man. 'But not just yet.'

He followed the scouts into one of the houses. It was a modest little place, but it had what he needed. 'Tie him to the tabletop.'

The scouts got to work. The table wasn't big, so the Skull's

404

legs and arms dangled over the sides, but that made it all the easier to tie his limbs to the table legs, arching his back quite uncomfortably. The man was still begging and whimpering, making beautiful sounds, but he knew he wasn't going anywhere.

It was just part of the game. The wonderful game.

'You can leave,' said Jax to the scouts, once the Skull was secured.

'Are you sure?' asked one.

'Absolutely,' replied Jax, trying not to smile. He had a knife and a prisoner – what more could he want? He knew how this worked. He leaned over the Skull, let him see the knife once more. 'Are you feeling brave?'

55
Zorique

The Northern Road

Zorique's shield was the only thing keeping her alive and even that was about to fail. It fizzled and cracked, spluttering with every blow from fist and club. She didn't understand how the Kojin had such power, not when she'd killed them so easily before. She didn't understand how she could be losing so badly. Not now.

A giant's boot lifted her off the ground and sent her flying across the scorched earth of the village. A club knocked her back the way she'd come. A sword hacked down and shattered against her shield, taking a chunk of her magic with it.

Gods, the Kojin didn't stop, didn't slow down. They could sense they had her, and only her death was going to satisfy them. Their roars rang out as they pounded her shield again and again.

Zorique curled up in a ball, her arms covering her head, her eyes closed. It was all over.

Nothing's over. Zorique could remember the snarl in Tinnstra's voice as she'd said it.

Never give up. Never surrender. Maiza had told her that time and again.

There is more power in you than you can ever imagine. Anama's promise.

What would her mothers think if they saw her now? After all they'd done? All they'd sacrificed?

'No.' She barely heard herself under all the roaring and the hammering, but it was enough.

Zorique reached deep inside herself and found the small ball of light that was her magic. She set it free.

There was no flash of light. Zorique blazed like the sun.

The Kojin fell back, covering their eyes, their skin smoking, and howled.

At last, Zorique could get to her feet, could suck air into her lungs and she could fight back.

She saw her sword lying twenty feet away and reached out with her hand. The sword twitched once, twice, then flew straight into her grasp.

Some of the Kojin were already on their knees. Others staggered. All were blind. Zorique walked amongst them, butchering one and all. She worked without anger, without cruelty, just with calm efficiency.

As she dispatched them, Zorique couldn't help but wonder how these creatures had been created. Tinnstra had told her of Raaku's lake of Chikara water and how he'd used it to give the Chosen their powers. Was that how he'd made these dreadful monsters? Had they once been human?

And then there were the runes painted over their blue skin. She couldn't remember seeing those on the Kojin she'd fought in Layso and, if she touched any, they shimmered with light as if reacting to her magic. She stepped back from one and tried to set it on fire.

The runes glowed in response and her flames were snuffed out, leaving not a mark.

Tinnstra had been right. The Egril were learning, adapting. Zorique would have to do the same if the Jians were going to win.

She sheathed her sword and reached out a hand. Her spear flew to it.

Anama's words came to her again: *There is more power in you than you can ever imagine.* If that were true, Zorique had to discover what else she could do. She couldn't rely on her old tricks. Nor could the others.

With one last look at the monsters, Zorique took to the air. She'd been gone from her army for too long.

She'd nearly been gone for good. She'd made so many mistakes, become overconfident, careless. Wasn't that how the Egril had beaten the Shulka in the first place? Tinnstra had told her about that enough times and yet there she was, repeating the same mistakes.

Zorique watched the ground as she flew, worried what other surprises might be hidden, while her mind ran over and over the fight with the Kojin. That's why she saw the lone figure sprinting down the Northern Road. Even from half a mile up, she recognised Tinnstra.

Zorique twisted in mid-air, changing direction, and shot down, down towards her mother, happy to see her, yet scared she was going to be told off once more. Then, when she was close enough, she saw the blood that covered Tinnstra.

'Tinn!' she called as she skidded to a halt a few yards from her mother.

'Zorique!' Tinnstra's face was full of joy as she swept her daughter into her arms. 'Thank the Gods, you're safe.'

Nothing else needed to be said. For that moment, everything was all right. They held each other, their hearts beating together, breathing in the other's scent, savouring their warmth, their touch. Zorique closed her eyes and all the years fell away until she felt like a child again, safe under Tinnstra's wing.

When they eventually stepped apart, Zorique saw that Tinnstra had been crying. It shouldn't have, but it made Zorique happy to see the tears. It meant she cared, that Tinnstra still loved her.

As if sensing her thoughts, Tinnstra wiped a tear away with the back of her hand and smeared blood across her cheek. 'I thought you might be in trouble.'

'I was,' said Zorique. She glanced back the way she'd come. 'I found a village. The Skulls had spiked everyone. When I went to investigate, Kojin attacked me.'

'They attacked us as well,' said Tinnstra.

'By the Gods, is everyone okay?'

'No. They killed hundreds before we could stop them.'

'I need to get back, see if there's something I can do—'

Tinnstra put a hand on Zorique's arm. 'They can wait for you a bit longer. Tell me what happened.'

So Zorique told her of the fight with the monsters and the runes that negated her powers.

'Our Kojin had markings, too. Aasgod's magic was useless against them,' said Tinnstra when she was finished. 'Are you sure the ones in Layso were unmarked?'

'As much as I can be.'

'The Egril are learning. They're adapting.'

'Too well. They nearly killed me.'

'Thank the Gods they didn't.' And Tinnstra hugged her daughter once more.

'Tinn?' Zorique's voice quivered.

'Yes, my love?'

'Are we okay? What I said earlier ... I didn't mean it the way it sounded ... I—'

'Oh, my dear, beautiful girl. Of course we're good. There's nothing you could say or do that would make me love you less. You are my everything and you always will be.'

'You seem so angry with me all the time.'

'It's not you I'm angry at – it's the world. Life shouldn't be like this – our lives shouldn't be like this. This war ... I—' Tinnstra took a deep breath, as if she'd said enough. 'We'd better get back to the others. They'll be worried.' The warmth was gone from her voice. Whatever moment they'd just shared was over.

Zorique formed a shield around them and raised it into the air. As they flew back towards their army, Zorique glanced at Tinnstra. She stood to one side, staring straight ahead, all her barriers back in place. A million miles filled the space between them.

56

Raaku

Kagestan

Raaku stood on the edge of the Red Lake and closed his eyes. The morning prayer was over. Over a hundred Jian prisoners had been sacrificed to his father and their blood scented the air and stained the waters. On the other side of the lake, the faithful still chanted his name over and over again. 'Raaku! Raaku! Raaku!'

For that moment, he felt the weight of destiny lifted from his shoulders as his father's presence filled his heart. The end was close, his duty all but fulfilled.

'Raaku! Raaku! Raaku!'

He remembered the boy he'd once been, driven by vain ambition before Kage had opened his eyes and shown him the way. He wished he could show his younger self what he would achieve, the glory he would create.

'Raaku! Raaku! Raaku!'

The journey to Sekanowari had taken more than a century to complete, but it was here, now, and soon his father, through his son, would be victorious.

He opened his eyes. There was much to be done. With a nod to his priests, he walked back inside the castle. His guardians fell into step behind him as he headed down into the caverns.

Fewer eggs grew in the waters, a sign of his distraction. The levels were still acceptable, though, and once the war was won, he would replenish the stocks quickly enough. After all, there were still other lands to conquer in his father's name. Meigore would be next, and then further west, across lands unknown.

He walked on, past the Veksters, ignoring their bows, heading towards the prisoner's cell. Raaku hadn't planned on visiting Laafien, but now he was drawn there, his father's will guiding him.

When Raaku entered the cell, the prisoner was sitting cross-legged on the floor, facing him, a strange smile on his face. 'You were expecting me?' asked the Emperor.

'I do see the future.'

Raaku sat down on the stool. 'That's why you still live.'

'When will you go to Aisair?'

'Don't play games with me. We've known each other far too long for that. You know when.'

The man nodded. 'I do.'

'It's been a long time since you were last this ... calm. You remind me of when we first met. The man you used to be.'

'The man I have always been.'

'Not since I locked you away from the world.'

'Ah, yes, to be a guide that never travels,' said Laafien. 'To witness the future but never live it.'

'One day, my father will reward you in the Great Darkness for the service you have done him. One day in the next life, we can talk like we once did around the campfires on the steppes.'

'When I thought you were my friend?'

'Yes.'

'I used to enjoy talking to you back then. You were always so eager to learn.'

'You had much to teach.'

'Do you miss those days?'

Raaku remained silent. It was another person's life.

Laafien smiled. 'I can't imagine you have too many conversations now – especially with anyone your equal.'

'I have no equal.'

'For now. The Four Gods' champions will meet you soon enough.'

'There are only three of them and they grow weaker by the day.'

'No, there are four. But you'll find that out for yourself in the days to come.'

Raaku stood. 'You're right. I do miss our conversations. There was an innocence to that time before I first saw the world for what it would be.'

Laafien smiled. 'Remember what I told you. You must stop death if you are to win Sekanowari.'

'If that is what I must do, it will be done,' said Raaku.

He left the cell, the prisoner's laughter following on his heels.

He walked to the small cavern next. The orb sat in the centre of the water. It had grown substantially since he'd last seen it, despite the fact there was nothing living inside it.

It contained only death.

Raaku waded into the holy water and put his arms around the shell. 'Blood I will give you, O Great One. Souls I will send you. My body is your weapon. My life, your gift.'

Part IV

Lost and Found

57

Tinnstra

The Northern Road

The Chikara water burned through Tinnstra's veins. It no longer gave her a rush, a thrill. It just kept her going. Awake. Alert. Dangerous.

She slipped the empty vial back into her pouch and shifted her position. A shadow amongst shadows. She and the six survivors of her team were a mile outside camp, hidden amongst rocks, watching, waiting, desperate for the Egril to show up. It had been seven nights since the last attack. Now, there wasn't much left of this one. Not long at all if the enemy were planning to attack.

Where were they?

The Jians were close to Aisair now, with only the Olyisius Mountains and three days' march between the allies and their goal. Close enough that the Egril wouldn't even need a Tonin to launch an attack, and yet there was still no sign of the bastards.

Close enough that Tinnstra was also thinking about what she had to do next. Her plan. Her mad plan. Hopefully Wenna had the information Tinnstra needed. Then she'd have no excuse not to go through with it.

Tinnstra stretched out with her senses, searching for the spike of pain that warned her of the enemy's proximity. The irony wasn't lost on her that she was now praying for the Egril to turn up, whereas she used to pray they'd stay away.

Different people, different times.

Each night, Tinnstra and what was left of her crew had gone

out to hunt. Each morning, they'd come back empty-handed. Now it looked like they faced yet another night with nothing to show for their efforts.

What was worse was that Tinnstra knew her team were suffering. They stole a few hours' sleep before the day's march and then a few more after they'd made camp, but it wasn't nearly enough to counter the demands she made of them. Even now, she knew at least three of her soldiers were asleep in their positions.

Then again, am I any different? Tinnstra couldn't remember the last time she'd had decent sleep herself; an hour here or there didn't count, and she was relying on the Chikara water more than ever. It was as necessary as the air she breathed – almost more so.

Aasgod had taken to hiding the Chikara water from her because there was so little left, but she always found it. It was as if it called to her, and she couldn't resist the summons. What worried her most was the fact that she only had two vials left in her pouch and there were only ten vials left in Aasgod's box. Twelve vials for both her and Aasgod to see out the war. *It's not enough – but it has to be. Especially for what I have to do.*

She told herself that she wouldn't need the water anymore after the war was over. She could live that normal life she'd dreamed about so long ago. Perhaps she could hide away in a small cottage somewhere. Be nobody, with nothing to do. No one to kill. Anonymous.

Concentrate. You have a job to do.

Tinnstra shook the thoughts from her head. By the Gods, she was tired. Her hand drifted to her pouch once more. Another vial would do the job. A bump to keep her awake. But how many had she drunk that day, that night? Never enough.

There was movement off to her right. Tavis crawled into the space beside her. 'Anything?' he whispered.

She shook her head.

'Maybe they'll attack while we're on the move?'

Tinnstra stared into the night. *Why can't the Egril ever do what I expect them to?*

'Shall we call it? Head back? We could all use some sleep.'

It was the last thing Tinnstra wanted to do – admit defeat once more and return empty-handed. Nor did she want to see Aasgod's smug face at yet another failure. He still opposed the plan, even in its present form. Only the Gods knew why. Tinnstra would've thought he'd be happy to be rid of her, but apparently not.

She sighed. 'Call it.'

Tavis raised himself up on his knees and let out a low whistle. Five bodies rose from where they'd been hiding. They moved quickly on Tinnstra's position, and Tavis tapped each one as they passed and pointed them back to camp.

'You coming?' he asked once everyone had gone.

Tinnstra shook her head. 'I'm going to stay here for a little longer.'

'Are you sure? We've a long march today. Hasan wants to be at the Kotege tonight.'

'I'm sure.' She almost flinched at hearing the words 'the Kotege'. She had so many memories tied to that place. It was the last place she wanted to go to – even though it had been her idea – but somehow it was fitting. She'd run from there twice before. Now, she was marching back.

She glanced up at the dark shadow of Olyisius Mountain against the sky. She'd left good people up there. People who'd given their lives for Zorique and Tinnstra, who believed the Egril could be defeated. She owed it to them to honour that debt.

The army was ready to move out when Tinnstra walked back into camp. It had grown over the last week or so as more and more Jians flocked to join them, pushing their number back up to somewhere around seventeen thousand. It truly felt like an army of allies now, with soldiers from the four countries of Jia, Meigore, Dornway and Chongore gathered together. The four of them against the one, true enemy.

She could sense Zorique and Aasgod. Their magic blazed with myriad colours, burning in her mind. *Another reason to avoid them. Avoid the looks, the questions, the judgements. Dear Gods, avoid my daughter.*

What am I doing? Why do I feel like I'm in the wrong?

Her team waited to one side of the main ranks. Their uniforms were still stained black and their faces covered with charcoal and mud from the night's mission. Now, in daylight, they looked so very different from the other soldiers – and their attitude didn't help, either. None of them was ready to depart like the rest of Zorique's army. Sadir was stretched out on the ground, asleep by the looks of it, and Nika was cooking a rabbit over a small fire, drawing envious looks from the other soldiers. Their dark-ringed eyes watched every flicker of flame as the meat roasted. Despite everyone's best efforts, most of their army was going hungry.

Tavis sat near the fire, sharpening his knives. He gave Tinnstra the most casual of salutes as she walked over. 'Good to see you, Chief. We were starting to worry you might not come back.'

'And leave all the fun to you? Never.' Tinnstra stretched her back and cracked her neck from side to side. 'You've worked out a route for us to the Kotege?'

'Of course.'

'Ambush points?'

Tavis shrugged. 'Every step of the way. The forest provides a hundred places to hide and then the mountain slopes offer exposed ground for us to cross. None of it's good.'

Tinnstra didn't argue. She knew what the ground was like, both from her time at the Kotege and from her escape south with Zorique. She remembered being chased through the woods by the Skulls. 'We need to get out ahead of our soldiers. See if we can spot any surprises.' She glanced down at Nika and Sadir. 'Tell them we go in ten minutes.'

'Do you want anything to eat?'

'I'm fine.'

Tavis nodded. 'We're all running pretty close to the wind, Boss, but no one more than you. You need to look after yourself.'

'Don't worry about me,' replied Tinnstra. She had no need of sleep or food, not after the Chikara water she'd drunk. She had more than enough energy coursing through her veins to get her through the day. Later, perhaps, she could sleep for a few hours, before another night of waiting for Skulls.

Tavis nodded at something over her shoulder. 'Your friend's come to see you.'

Tinnstra turned and saw Ralasis walking over. They'd not spoken much since he'd … what? Spoken the truth?

'Good morning, Commander,' she said. 'How are your feet this morning?'

'They don't hurt anymore,' replied Ralasis. 'Not since I lost all feeling in them, anyway.'

'Maybe you're getting used to all the marching.'

The Meigorian laughed. 'I don't know about that. Give me the sea any day.'

Tinnstra had no idea what to say next, and an awkward silence grew between them. Ralasis didn't leave, though. 'Have a good day, Commander,' she said in the end.

'You know you can still call me Ralasis, don't you?'

'I do.' Gods, he had that look in his eye that made her feel like he was imagining her naked or something. Her cheeks reddened.

'That's good, because I have a favour to ask.' He actually winced as he spoke.

'A favour?'

'I was … wondering if I could join you today,' said Ralasis hesitantly.

'Why?'

'Why not? I thought you could do with the help – or, rather, that *I* could do with the help. We're going to be fighting again soon. I really need to be at my best, and who better to learn from than the best this army has to offer?' For once, Ralasis' words weren't full of posturing or false modesty or needless flirting, and for some mad reason, she actually found him even more attractive.

'I'm not sure that's a good idea,' said Tinnstra. 'We'll be moving fast, looking for the enemy – and we've got our own way of working. I don't want to disrupt that.'

'I'm not a soldier, Tinnstra. I'm not used to any of this. I need to know how you do it – before it's too late. A battlefield's no place to learn.' The man actually looked quite vulnerable in his honesty.

'A fair point,' replied Tinnstra with a smile. 'We're leaving in ten minutes. Try not to get yourself killed, eh?'

★

The army had started their march when Tinnstra, Ralasis and her crew left. Because they had to get ahead of the main column, she made them all run, setting a cruel pace. Her team were used to it, despite the packs on their backs and the weapons in their hands and on their hips. Ralasis, though?

Let's see how he copes. The Egril will show no mercy and nor will I.

So they ran, and Ralasis, for all his complaining of sore feet and sea legs, kept up. If he was in any pain, he kept it to himself, and he certainly didn't ask to rest or slow down. Tinnstra maintained the pace along the Northern Road, waiting to see when he'd break. After an hour, Ralasis' face was red and he was drenched in sweat, but still he ran and, when she checked on the others, she saw her six were faring no better. In the end, it was Tavis who called out for her to stop. 'We're not like you, Boss. We're only human,' he puffed.

Ralasis slumped to the ground and started gulping down water, but Nika pushed the water skin from his mouth. 'Drink too much and you'll be sick. Swish some water around your mouth before you swallow.'

Ralasis nodded. 'Th ... thank ... thank you.'

'Enough wasting time,' said Tinnstra. 'Let's go.'

The others groaned – but not Ralasis. He climbed to his feet and put his water skin away. He even gave her nod to say he was ready.

'You want me to lead for a bit?' asked Tavis. 'Get off the main road?'

'Find me some Skulls,' said Tinnstra.

Tavis took them off into the forest and up the slopes. They moved slower this time, but it was no less hard on their legs and lungs. Tinnstra kept looking back, checking on Ralasis, but again he didn't falter. She could see the determination in his eyes, and she knew he would give everything he had.

Some of the trails Tavis took them down started to feel familiar to Tinnstra. Memories returned of exercising on the mountain when she was a student at the Kotege, learning escape and evasion techniques and how to hunt human prey. Back then, she'd been scared of catching anyone, petrified of what would happen next, not wanting to fight or risk getting hurt. She'd been a pathetic little girl. Thank the Gods, she'd made herself grow up.

All day they hunted, clambering over the slopes of Olyisius, finding nothing except old tracks. Tinnstra grew frustrated once more, her anger rising. For the most part, the others kept silent, concentrating on the job, saving conversation only for when they stopped to eat or rest. Just because they hadn't found the enemy, it didn't mean they weren't out there.

And Ralasis? He continued to surprise Tinnstra. He found it hard going – there was no hiding that – but he made not one complaint and he maintained the pace set by the others, following their lead on what to do and how to behave. It many ways, it felt like he'd been part of the team since the beginning.

Every now and then, he'd catch her watching him and give her that easy smile of his, as if he was enjoying himself. And every time she saw that smile, it took the edge off her fury and calmed her soul. *Perhaps the man has a rare gift after all.*

It was late afternoon when they saw the waterfall, a twenty-foot-high column of water tumbling into a pool below. The sight stopped Tinnstra like a punch in the face. Suddenly, her mind took her back how many years? To that night, standing at the top, holding Zorique's hand, surrounded by Skulls. She'd jumped then, believing Aasgod's lies, trusting that some non-existent magic in a sword would keep her safe. It was a miracle she and Zorique survived the fall and didn't die of hypothermia.

No, not a miracle. Sheer, bloody dumb luck.

The others noticed she wasn't moving and immediately dropped into cover, searching for whatever danger they thought she'd seen.

'The Kotege is up there,' she said, pointing to the waterfall. 'I recognise it from my time as a student.' Her words took some of the tension out of the others, who used the respite to ease water skins from packs or nibble at whatever food they had to hand.

Tinnstra followed the river with her eye, her mind still in the past, trying to spot where she and Zorique had come out of the water after they'd jumped, but she didn't recognise any-where. And why should she? They'd stumbled about in the dark, half-drowned and half-frozen, and collapsed amongst some bushes and a fallen tree, staying awake just long enough to get a fire going that saved their lives.

Of course, it was the arrival of Monon and Greener that ensured Tinnstra and Zorique lived. Two great men, long dead now – to her, at least. It had only been a few months for everyone else. She glanced up at Olyisius. Monon's body was still up there, along with the others that had stood their ground against the Egril.

I will avenge you all. I promise.

'Let's push on,' she said at last, knowing more ghosts waited for her at the Kotege. Would the bodies of her friends still be there? Would Aasgod's?

So what if they are? They're just bones. No more, no less. Hard thoughts that did nothing to quell the emotions roiling inside her.

They were halfway up the slope when Tavis waved them down, and it wasn't long-forgotten memories that drew his eye. His hand signalled Tinnstra and the others: three people, up ahead and to the right, armed, not Skulls.

Tinnstra signalled Nika to go with Tavis and circle around them, then signalled the others to do the same to their other side – all except Ralasis. He was going with her, straight up the main path towards them. They might not be Skulls, but she wasn't taking any chances.

Once the others had moved off, Tinnstra stood up, followed by Ralasis. He gave her a look that asked if she was sure about this, and she just grinned in return. There was no magic nearby, and even if the others weren't there to help, she had no worries that three normal people could hurt her.

They walked forty yards before a man's voice ordered them to stop. It came from some foliage off to the right, but she could see the voice's owner.

'Who are you? What are you doing here?' asked the man once they had obeyed him.

'I could ask you the same,' replied Tinnstra. She started walking again before anyone could reply.

'Don't move! One more step and we'll shoot!' shouted the man.

Tinnstra held up both hands. 'Friends, there's no need for threats.'

'We're not your friends. Who are you?'

'Neither of us is a Skull by the sound of it. That makes us friends.' Tinnstra took another step forwards, but an arrow thudded into the ground before her. She looked down at it then up at the undergrowth. 'That wasn't very nice.'

'I warned you.' The man's voice grew shrill.

'Be careful. He sounds scared,' whispered Ralasis. 'He might shoot you by mistake.'

Tinnstra chuckled. 'Don't worry. I'll use your body as a shield.'

'It would be an honour,' muttered Ralasis.

Somewhere, a sparrow sang a short song.

'Do it,' said Tinnstra.

There was sudden movement through the foliage. The man cried out, then another. A fist struck flesh. Something heavy hit the ground. Then silence.

'Shall we?' said Tinnstra, setting off once more.

She found Tavis and the others twenty yards ahead. They stood guard over two men and a woman kneeling on the ground, who stared at Tinnstra with sullen faces. One of the men had taken a blow to the face and his eye was already swelling. By morning, he'd not be able to see out of it. *I know how that feels. He's lucky his eye will get better.*

'Hello. My name's Tinnstra.' She smiled. 'I see you've met my friends already.'

'Bitch,' spat the man with the swollen eye.

Tavis whacked him around the back of his head. 'Be nice.'

Tinnstra bent down. 'Look, I know you're not Skulls. Nor are we. You're carrying weapons, which means you don't care that the Egril made that a capital offence, and as you can see, my friends and I don't care, either. So, I think that makes you Hanran. If you are, we really are on the same side.'

'So why did you jump us?' snarled the woman.

Tinnstra pointed at Ralasis. 'He was worried you'd shoot us by accident, and I didn't want to take any chances.' She looked around the woods. 'We're heading up to the Kotege in a minute to make sure things are safe for our army. Are we going to find any more friends waiting for us up there?'

The three exchanged quick looks. 'You have an army?' asked Swollen Eye, looking happy all of a sudden. 'Zorique's army?'

'That's the one,' said Tinnstra.

'Thank the Gods,' said the woman. 'That's why we're here. To join you.'

'There's nearly two thousand of us at the Kotege already,' said Swollen Eye. 'My group came with Ange and Garo, but there's people from all over.'

Tinnstra glanced at Tavis, who nodded. 'Two of Hasan's kids.'

'Hasan from Clan Huska?' asked the other man.

'The very same,' said Tavis. 'That's my clan.'

'Our leader is General Jax from Clan Huska,' said Swollen Eye.

'Jax?' repeated Tinnstra.

'Jax is dead.' Tavis drew his knife. 'Why are you lying to us?'

'He's alive,' said the woman. 'Burned skin, one arm?'

Tavis nodded. 'That's him.'

'He's alive.'

'Once, I'd have said that was impossible,' said Tinnstra, 'but not anymore.'

'Best bloody news I've heard all day,' said Tavis.

'Does this mean we're all friends now?' asked Tinnstra.

The three nodded.

'Good,' said Tinnstra. 'Then let's go and say hello to Jax.'

The Hanran led Tinnstra and the others up to the Kotege.

It was just as Tinnstra remembered it, yet nothing like it at all. Back when her father had brought her to the school, it had been an imposing building – towering above her and echoing with shouts from the practice fields as wooden swords clashed and marching feet stomped. Now, she saw it for what it was, a mock castle where children played Shulka, hiding behind its semi-high walls and pretend watchtowers. No wonder it was overrun so quickly when the Egril attacked. A part of her wondered why the Skulls had even bothered storming it.

But it was full of Hanran, and that was a good thing. Men

and women watched them approach from positions on the walls and from the main gate. Others worked on repairing the damage done during both the Skulls' initial attack and, later, when she, Zorique and Aasgod had been attacked by the Chosen. Tinnstra could tell some were Shulka, while others were ordinary Jians drawn to their cause. No matter their origins, it made her heart glad to see them. They would all be needed to win back Jia.

Swollen Eye led them through the gate and into the courtyard. The ruin of the main building stood waiting for Tinnstra, scorched and broken, a round hole in its heart. She felt sick at the sight of it; a mix of guilt, remorse, anger and hate. How long had it been since she'd last set foot here? Fifteen years? A long time, yet not nearly long enough. Memories threatened to overwhelm her. Names, faces. Deaths. Carnage.

They'd cleared the dead away, but Tinnstra could still see their ghosts everywhere; Jono decapitated by a Daijaku, Lina blown apart by a bomb, Darn cut down by a Skull. How many people had she watched die that night? Her friends and peers, all so young, their futures taken.

Then her eye drifted to the main building. She could see the hole where Aasgod had fought the Chosen; could see him standing there, on the edge, looking invincible, throwing lightning. She could see the Chosen, just a shadow, just smoke, striking him down with her axe. She could see him falling, taking all her hope with him.

She could hear that crunch as he hit the ground. She remembered the anguish she'd felt, the despair, the fear. Worse even than when her own brother, Beris, had died. His body was gone now, thank the Gods, yet she couldn't help but think how different her life would have been if he'd lived.

She'd been so young when it all happened. So useless.

No. I am not that person. She dug deep, found her rage instead, let that flare up and consume the weakness. *I am the fury that will set things right. I am death.*

'Tinnstra!'

She spun around at hearing her name and saw Wenna running towards her. Thank the Gods, she was alive. Then she saw the burns on her friend's face and realised Wenna's road to the Kotege had been just as hard as hers. 'It's good to see you.'

Wenna's hand went to her face. 'Not as good as it was.'

'All the best people have scars these days,' said Tinnstra, pointing to her own. 'What happened?'

'A Chosen. When I was leaving Aisair.' Wenna tried to make it sound like it was nothing, but Tinnstra knew the opposite was true.

'I'm sorry.'

'It is what it is.'

'How did you get on?'

'Good. The city's a mess and the new Egril commander, Vallia, is busy turning the place into a fortress, but I managed to find out everything you asked me to. The Hanran have someone inside the castle – Larius's consort, of all people – and she's mapped out the castle interior.'

'Well done. Well done indeed. Let's find somewhere we can—' Tinnstra winced as she felt a spike of pain shoot through her head. It was different from any she'd experienced before, almost as if she was sensing magic that was both far away and close by. But, as suddenly as it had come, it disappeared. Almost like it had never been.

'You okay?' asked Wenna.

'I'm fine. It's ...' The words caught in Tinnstra's mouth. A man and a woman approached. Though Tinnstra had only met Jax once before, she recognised him instantly. But it was the woman with him that made her doubt what she was seeing. A woman she thought was long dead.

Tinnstra's hand covered her mouth. It was impossible. Her chest grew tight as tears filled her eyes.

'Mother?'

The word came out almost as a sob.

It stopped the woman in her tracks. She stared back, confused, then her eyes widened. Her hand went to her mouth. 'Tinnstra?'

58

Tinnstra

The Kotege

Tinnstra couldn't move. She didn't know what to do. Her mother was dead. She had been for so long. For fifteen years of Tinnstra's life.

But only a year had passed here. Not even that. No time at all. Still, she couldn't move.

'What is it?' said Ralasis, looking from Tinnstra to her mother and back. 'Do you know each other?'

'She's my mother,' said Tinnstra.

'Your *mother*?'

'Yes.' Tinnstra felt herself cracking inside. All her walls, all her barriers. Everything she'd built. Her strength. Her hardness. All undone by the sight of the woman who made her.

'Tinnstra?' Her mother said her name louder now, but she wasn't paralysed like her daughter. She took a few faltering steps forwards, then found her feet and rushed over, taking her daughter in her arms, burying her head in Tinnstra's neck.

Still, Tinnstra couldn't move, didn't know what to do, what to say, what to think, what to feel. Then her mother started crying, big, chest-heaving sobs, and Tinnstra's arms finally, almost of their own volition, wrapped themselves around Moiri, and she could feel the life in this woman she'd thought dead. Feel her heart beating. Feel her breath on her neck, her tears on her skin.

'Mother.'

Tinnstra held on tight, not wanting to let go, scared in part that if she did, her mother would disappear. Scared, too, at what she'd become since her mother had last seen her – scared that would drive her mother away. She wasn't Moiri's little girl anymore. Tinnstra was a monster of her own making, a creature of hate and anger and violence. What would her mother say?

'I thought I'd never see you again,' said Moiri. 'Dear Gods, this is a miracle.'

She stepped back then to get a good look at her daughter. Tinnstra flinched as her mother touched her face, but there was no fear or revulsion in Moiri's expression – only love. She smiled. 'You've got older.'

'Mother ...' whispered Tinnstra. She wanted to apologise. She wanted forgiveness. She wanted ... Gods, she didn't know. 'It's hard to explain—'

'Hush,' her mother whispered. 'I've found you again. That's all that matters. Not how we got here. Not what we've done. Nothing matters other than we're together again.'

Tinnstra hugged her mother tight. It was her turn to cry. She wept because this was the last thing she wanted. Another reason to stay. Another reason to abandon her plan. Was this the Gods' work? Some attempt by them to stay her hand?

It was impossible, and yet ...

'Moiri?' It was the one-armed general, Jax.

Tinnstra looked up, wiping the tears from her eyes, trying to find the stone that she'd built around her heart once more.

Jax hovered nearby, uncomfortable, awkward. The burns he'd suffered in Kiyosun the night Tinnstra and Zorique escaped had healed somewhat, but he still looked a mess. *Just like everyone else. We all have scars.*

'Jax,' said Tinnstra. 'It's good to see you alive. Hasan said you'd died back in Kiyosun.'

The man looked as if he'd been struck. 'I ... I was captured.' He took a breath. 'Have we ...?

Her mother slipped her arm through his. 'This is my daughter, Jax. This is Tinnstra.'

There was a familiarity between her mother and Jax that Tinnstra found unsettling. 'You helped Zorique and I escape Kiyosun.'

'You've changed,' said Jax.

'Haven't we all?'

His head went down. 'Yes.'

'We rescued Jax from some Egril hunters at Gundan. He'd escaped from Raaku's castle itself in Kagestan,' said her mother.

'He did what?' Tinnstra couldn't believe what she'd heard. Someone had been to the Egril capital. 'How?'

'I was captured in Kiyosun and they transferred me by Tonin,' said Jax, unable to look at her, his voice breaking.

'What was Kagestan like? Did you see Raaku? Did—'

Her mother held up a hand. 'Tinnstra. Give the man a moment to catch his breath—'

A commotion broke out across the courtyard. People shouted as they pointed in the air. Tinnstra didn't need to look to see its cause. She'd already felt the spike in her brain that told her Zorique was on her way.

She watched the reactions of her mother and Jax instead. They'd not seen the queen before, and no stories ever prepared anyone for seeing Zorique for the first time. Their eyes widened as their mouths dropped, and all other thoughts no doubt vanished from their minds.

Tinnstra only turned when she knew Zorique was close, and even she had to smile when she saw her daughter, shining bright. Whatever arguments they'd had didn't matter. At that moment, she felt nothing but love, pride and hope.

Tinnstra would do her part to win Sekanowari, but it would be Zorique who'd create a new world for the survivors.

'Is that ...' said her mother.

'Yes,' replied Tinnstra. 'Queen Zorique of Jia.'

'She's certainly no child,' said her mother.

'No. No, she's not.'

'I hear she has you to thank for that.' There was something about the way her mother was looking at Tinnstra. Her gaze was full of love, pride and hope, too.

Tinnstra smiled, the monster within her forgotten. 'I'm her mother.'

And she'd do anything to keep her safe.

Moiri smiled. 'And a good one, too.'

The praise made Tinnstra uncomfortable. 'I just tried to do my best – do the right thing.'

'That's all any parent can do. The Gods know your father and I got it wrong often enough.'

'I'm proud of her, Mother. After everything she's been through, she still wants to do the right thing.'

'She's like you.'

'She's ...' Suddenly words were hard to find. There were too many emotions running through Tinnstra. It was unsettling. She felt like her old self – her mother's daughter, scared and unsure of everything. 'I'm nothing like her. Zorique is the best that the world can offer, while I'm—'

'You're her mother. Whatever Zorique is, she learned it from you.'

'I tried to be like you and Father. Sometimes, though ...' Tinnstra looked at her mother. It had been so long since she'd last seen her, and yet Moiri had barely aged a day. She still looked perfectly composed, like nothing could ever bother her. Perfect as she always was, while Tinnstra ... She rubbed her face. She felt lost. Empty. Broken. 'I don't know what the right thing is anymore.'

'Of course you do.'

'I don't. I thought I did, but ...' Tinnstra took a breath. So many bad choices from terrible options. 'I just want Zorique to be safe. That's all I've ever wanted.'

'That's all any parent wants.'

'Is it?' said Tinnstra. She glanced at Jax, but his attention was on Zorique. It was as if she and her mother had ceased to exist. 'Can we go and talk somewhere? I still can't believe you're alive.'

'Of course.' Her mother's smile was as warm as she remembered. Somehow it made Tinnstra feel like everything would be all right with the world. They walked over to the main building of the Kotege – or what was left of it. Past where Aasgod had died.

They stepped through a hole in the wall, into darkness. Tinnstra saw an overturned bench lying half-buried in rubble. She pulled it free, set it upright and hesitated. 'Is this ...'

'Sit down,' said her mother. She lifted the strap of a water skin over her head and offered it to Tinnstra. 'You must be thirsty.'

Tinnstra took it as her mother sat down and stretched out her legs. The water was cool and fresh, but it wasn't what Tinnstra wanted to drink. Already, she could feel the call of the Chikara water, her need for its energy. 'How did you survive Gundan?'

Moiri shook her head. 'Same way anyone did – sheer luck. A bomb went off, bringing down a wall that separated the group I was with from the main battle, then some Daijaku forced us back further. When it was clear we were overrun, we got the hell out of there, saving as many Shulka as we could.'

'Did you see Father die?'

'No. No, I didn't. Nor any of the boys.'

'Beris survived.'

'He did?'

'He came and found me in Aisair. He was in the Hanran and he needed my help. A Chosen killed him a few hours later.'

'Dear Gods, my poor boy.' Moiri covered her mouth with her hand as she took a deep breath. 'What about you? How did you survive? You were here when the invasion started.'

'Only just.'

'What do you mean?'

'The night of the invasion ... Harka had expelled me for cowardice just before the Egril attacked.'

'Cowardice?' Moiri gave a little shake of her head, as if she couldn't believe her ears. There was a part of Tinnstra that enjoyed seeing her unnerved. It made her more human, somehow. Less perfect.

'During my trials, when we were in the arena – I ran instead of fighting. The prisoners came out to attack us and I ... I just couldn't do it. I thought I was going to die, so I dropped my weapons and ran. I did it in front of everyone. I ran and the whole Kotege watched me, jeered at me, laughed at me.

'When we came back here afterwards, I was going to kill myself. The shame was too much.'

'Oh, Tinnstra.' Her mother slipped her arm around Tinnstra's shoulders.

'I sat on my bed, with a knife in my hand, and I couldn't think of a single reason not to do it and a million reasons why everyone would be better off if I did. But I couldn't go through with it.' Tinnstra let out a laugh. 'I wasn't brave enough.'

'I'm glad you didn't,' said her mother. 'Your father and I would've understood if you'd told us. We could've helped you, worked something out.'

'How? The Egril attacked a few minutes later. Father was too busy dying to help me.'

Moiri winced at Tinnstra's words, but there was no stopping them now.

'Do you know what? When Harka asked me to leave, I was happy. Maybe for the first time in my life. Happy it was over. Happy I could stop pretending I was like you and Father and Beris and Jonas and Somon. I was happy that I could be me, at long last.' Tinnstra looked out of the window at the darkening sky. 'Happy for all of ten minutes, until the first bomb fell.'

'I'm so sorry, Tinnstra. I really am.'

'Do you know what's even worse?' Tinnstra looked at her mother. 'After the invasion, after I thought you were all dead, a part of me was glad.'

'Glad?'

'I was glad that I didn't have to tell any of you what happened, that you'd died not knowing how much I had failed you. Glad that I'd been spared that shame.'

'Oh, Tinnstra. We'd have understood.'

'Would you? Would Father?'

'Of course. I promise you. We loved you. I love you.'

'It didn't feel that way when I was growing up. Father seemed determined to put us in danger. Wanting us to be perfect little Shulka.' She didn't mean to sound bitter, but she couldn't help herself.

'Believe me, we only wanted the best for you.'

'Your "best" wasn't what *I* wanted.' The words came out sharper than she'd intended, full of long-buried memories and resentment, of always being pushed in a direction she'd been unsuited for, of always feeling that she wasn't good enough. What parent wanted their child to feel that?

Her mother said nothing for a moment, then sighed. 'Deep down, we both probably knew that. You weren't like the boys. It was all so easy for them. They were little versions of your father. I used to joke that Beris was waving a sword around in my womb, Jonas would run into a fight without a second's thought about whether he could win or not, and Somon wanted to be like the heroes from the old myths.' Moiri's smile was full of sadness. 'Then you came along. You struggled with everything and we could see you hated it all, but you never gave up. You worked harder and practised longer and you became better than all of the boys. You never realised how ferocious you were. That's probably why you were our favourite.'

'Favourite? It never felt like that to me. Quite the opposite. I was scared that you'd like me even less if I ever let you down.'

'You could never have let us down.'

'I let everyone down.'

'I can't believe that.' For a moment, her mother's famous composure wavered.

'I never planned for any of this to happen. I was hiding when Beris found me. I only met Aasgod and Zorique because I had nowhere else to go. I only became her guardian because Aasgod died. I even ended up in the past because of Aasgod's plans.'

'The past?'

'Zorique was four when I met her. The mage needed time for her to grow older, come into her powers – so he sent us a thousand years back in the past.'

'How long were you there for?'

'Fifteen years. Fifteen years of training, of worrying, of waiting for the Skulls to find us.' She looked at her mother. 'This war has only been going on for a year for you. I've been fighting it for half my life and I never wanted a minute of it.'

Her mother slipped her arms around her and pulled her close. 'My beautiful baby girl. I'm sorry. I really am. But sometimes the world choses the heroes it needs when it needs them and all we can do is try and answer the call as best we can. And thank the Gods, you have risen to the challenge better than anyone could've hoped.'

Tinnstra had forgotten how wonderful it felt to be held by Moiri; the way her mother smelled, the weight of her arms around her, the rise and fall of her chest, the beat of her heart. It was a gift Tinnstra didn't deserve, a treasure from the past, long lost. She hadn't realised how much she needed it. 'I love you, Mother.'

'And I love you. I always will, no matter what happens or what you do or where you go. Remember that.'

'I will.'

'And another thing.' Moiri leaned back so she could look Tinnstra in the eye. 'You could never disappoint either your father or me. You will always be the best of us. I know you've been through a lot, but look what you've achieved. Only you could've done all that.' Moiri kissed Tinnstra on the forehead. 'And look at you now. Everyone's counting on you.'

'What if I let them down?' asked Tinnstra. 'What if I fail when it counts the most?'

Moiri smiled. 'You won't let anyone down – no matter what happens. I know you'll do your best and you'll keep fighting until your last breath.'

'I'll try,' said Tinnstra.

Moiri glanced out of the window. 'We should go and find the others. Get something to eat.'

'You go. I still have a few things to do. I'll find you later.'

Moiri stood and smiled. 'Okay.'

'Mother,' said Tinnstra, getting to her feet. 'I …' Again, words failed her. Nothing felt even remotely adequate to express how she felt. 'I've missed you.'

Her mother simply smiled and kissed her once more, her lips soft against Tinnstra's hard skin. 'And I, you.'

Tinnstra watched her mother leave, feeling like that short conversation had all but destroyed the woman she'd worked so hard to become. Ten minutes with Moiri and she felt like a child again.

A part of her wanted that: to be innocent, to be told what to do, taken care of, protected, all the weight from her shoulders gone.

But that was a stupid dream. If anything, the pressure on Tinnstra had only increased. She had her mother to worry about now, too.

Tinnstra took out her book from her bag. The book she'd carried across time and halfway across Jia. She flicked through the pages, seeing the words but not reading any. What was the point? It didn't mean anything. There were no clues, no map to follow. Just a load of gibberish that she'd been hanging on to because it made her feel better. There were no champions coming to save them, only Zorique – and Tinnstra couldn't bear the thought of losing her, either.

By all the Gods, she wished she had killed herself that night in the Kotege, spared herself all the misery that had followed. If only she'd known then that it would have been the easiest route, the least painful way forward. She'd have used that knife.

But it was what it was and the road she was on only had one future. One destiny.

It was time to fight like an Egril.

The Jians had built a wall to keep the Egril out, so Raaku had his Tonin open gates across the country. In Layso, the Meigorians locked up every foreigner, so he sent just one man, disguised as one of their own, to kill the king. It was a simple plan.

One man – or one woman to kill a king.

She smiled. 'God or man, Death calls for you.'

59
Jax

The Kotege

Jax watched the woman descend from the sky, shining gold, and knew it was Zorique. His queen. To say she was beautiful was an injustice. To say he was awestruck was an understatement.

She was perfection.

A God in the world.

His heart swelled with love and adoration. He would die for her – of that he had no doubt. Every trial and tribulation he had endured, every loss he had suffered had been worth it for Jax to experience this moment.

He was vaguely aware of the silence that fell across the Kotege as she landed on the parade ground.

He knew every eye was on her. Every hope pinned to her.

She wore a God's version of Shulka armour. Her helm's plume was pure white, because how could she belong to any one clan? Her spear sparkled with flames. Her shield glistened with power.

She walked with poise and grace over to some of Jax's soldiers and spoke a few words to them. Jax watched as the Hanran's eyes lit up and smiles spread across their faces. Others drew near, attracted by her light and wonder, but Jax stayed where he was.

He wasn't afraid to approach Zorique, he was just happy to be near her for now, watching her. There was more of her mother, Florina, than of her father in Zorique's features. Thinking of King Cariin made Jax smile more. He wondered what Cariin the Gentle would've thought of his daughter dressed for war. He'd never seen the king so much as raise his voice, let alone carry a weapon. The king had been a good man, but ill-suited for these times.

Then again, how many people were? Even the greatest Shulka had failed that test. Even he had. But he'd learned his lessons. He'd grown stronger than ever before. And now, with Zorique as his queen, he would rectify all that had gone wrong. He could see a free Jia, rising to ever greater heights, a nation above all, ruled by a God.

More soldiers flooded into the grounds of the Kotege – Zorique's army. Most wore Meigorian armour and colours, but there was Shulka armour amongst them, plus others dressed in whatever they could scavenge, like Ange and Garo. True Hanran. The best of Jia.

Then he saw another face. One he knew like a brother's. Hasan.

Tears came to Jax's eyes. It was almost too much to take in. He'd heard from Ange that Hasan was leading the army, but to see him? It was yet another relationship to reclaim, a failure to redeem.

He watched as Hasan issued orders and took status reports. He waited while his friend organised defences and allocated tasks. He waited until Hasan looked his way and their eyes met, and then Jax smiled and gave him a nod. There was a moment of shock as recognition dawned on Hasan that Jax was alive.

Hasan ran to his friend and the two men embraced. Jax pulled him close, tears flowing, full of joy. 'Hasan. My friend.'

'Jax! You're alive!' Hasan leaned his head back so he could look at Jax properly, before hugging him once more. 'By the Gods, you're alive.'

'It's so good to see you,' said Jax. 'I thought I never would again.'

'How did you get here? How did you survive the bombing of Kiyosun?'

'I was captured, taken to Kagestan. I escaped, came south.'

'You've been to Kagestan?' said Hasan, stepping back. 'You've actually been there?'

'Yes,' said Jax. 'I was a prisoner at Raaku's castle.'

'By the Gods, I'm so sorry. To go through that—'

Jax shook his head. 'It's I who must apologise. Before I was captured ... I ... I wasn't well. My mind wasn't right. I did some terrible things.'

'It's okay. It's okay. All best forgotten. That was then. This is now. You're back. That's all that matters. You're here when we need you the most. You're a gift from the Gods, as far as I'm concerned. Our best general, just in time for the final battle.'

'Thank you, my friend. It's good to be with you, too.'

A woman approached. The woman from before. Moiri's daughter. 'Tinnstra.'

'General,' she replied, inclining her head. 'I'm sorry to interrupt, but I was wondering if I could have a word with you.'

'Don't mind me,' said Hasan. 'I've plenty to do. We'll chat later, eh?' He gave Jax's arm one more squeeze and then left.

'What can I help you with?' asked Jax.

'Do you mind if I ask you some questions about Raaku's castle?'

'Can I ask why?'

'Just curious. I like to know as much as possible about our enemy.' There was something in her voice. She was trying to make it sound like a trivial question, but it was obvious that she had an ulterior motive. That thought worried him, but he had no idea why.

'I'll tell you what I can.'

Tinnstra pointed to a low wall. 'Shall we sit here?'

Tinnstra moved with a fluidity Jax had only ever seen in the very finest of warriors, gained through a total dedication to the martial arts. He wondered who had trained her. It had been a true master, whoever it was.

'How did you end up at Raaku's castle?'

'I was captured in Kiyosun and they used a Tonin to transfer us to the Emperor's castle,' replied Jax. 'They had hundreds of Jian prisoners in the castle cells.'

'Why did they take you there?'

'They execute prisoners every morning ... every morning at sunrise ... Blood for Kage,' said Jax. 'Sometimes Raaku himself would oversee the executions. They draw crowds from all over the city to watch. Some Egril would even commit suicide themselves at the same time as the executions.'

'Blood for Kage,' said Tinnstra. 'Where did the Tonin connect you to? What part of the castle?'

'We entered a courtyard, then were taken straight to the cells.'

'Did you see any other parts of the castle?'

'I ... I ...' Flashes of the red cave and the red water passed through Jax's mind. 'I don't think so. No.'

Tinnstra stared harder at Jax. 'Are you sure?'

'The truth is, I don't remember much from my time there as a prisoner. I've blanked most of it out.'

'What about Raaku? You said he oversaw the morning executions? What's he like?'

'He's ... big. Bigger than any man I've ever seen. His voice is cold like death.' More images rushed through Jax's mind. Raaku looking at him. Touching him. Hurting him. But that had only been in his dreams. Not real.

'What about guards?'

'There were soldiers with him at all times. Like Skulls, except their armour was red and they wore demon masks.'

'How did you escape?'

'One day, it was my turn to be sacrificed. They took a group of us up to the lake, but we weren't tied up. I ... I managed to kill a Skull and a group of us swam to freedom, then trekked south to Jia. The Egril chased us all the way to Gundan. They caught us, too – it was just luck that Moiri arrived in time to save us.'

'What was the city like? Kagestan?'

Jax closed his eyes, tried to remember. He could recall his view from the cell window but nothing else. 'It's a big place. Buildings all grey, as if they're made of stone. The only colour came from Raaku's flags. They were everywhere.'

'And the people?'

'Everyone wore masks but, other than that, same as anywhere else.'

'One last question,' said Tinnstra. 'You're a soldier. Their Emperor, Raaku ... do you think he can be killed?'

'Kill Raaku?' Jax had to steady himself. He was horrified by the question. 'He is the son of a God. Perhaps Zorique could—'

Tinnstra's face was grim. 'I'm talking about someone shoving a good blade into his heart.'

Jax was on his feet in an instant, his anger rising. 'No. No. Impossible. He is the son of Kage.'

'Okay.' Tinnstra held up both hands. 'It was just a question.'

Jax seethed. 'I have to go.'

'Sure,' said Tinnstra, standing. 'Thank you for your time. I appreciate it. It was good talking to you. I'm glad you made it here. Everyone's happy to have you with us.'

'Thank you,' said Jax. He left then, not running despite how much he wanted to. He had to get away from Tinnstra, away from her questions.

You need to kill her, said Monsuta, *for daring to ask that question.*

Jax stopped, took a breath. He had to be calm. He was just unsettled, seeing everyone again, being part of an army once more. Too much remembering the past for his own good. He had to concentrate on now, not then. Never then.

The bad thoughts still lingered when they gathered later in what had once been the Kotege's mess hall. The windows were all shattered, but the walls still stood and the ceiling looked intact. Year-old dust swirled around as tables were righted and benches dragged over.

As he waited with Moiri by his side, Jax considered the others standing closest to him. According to Hasan, they were Zorique's inner circle, the ones she trusted most.

There was a Meigorian captain called Ralasis, a handsome man despite the war's best efforts, who had an easy smile. He stood near Tinnstra, who was deep in conversation with another woman, a Shulka by the looks of her, not paying attention to anyone else – except, occasionally, to look at Jax. Each time she did so, her eye narrowed, as if she could read Jax's mind. Hoping to rape his memories again, no doubt. Why couldn't she leave his shame alone?

At the opposite end of the table was a man, bald with dark skin, who reminded Jax of someone he once knew. Unlike Tinnstra, he didn't look like a fighter, but there was still something dangerous about him.

And between them was Zorique, shining brightly, even more beautiful up close. She stood still as she waited, her eyes closed. She'd placed her helm on the table so there was nothing obscuring the serenity in her face or her beauty.

Jax stood frozen to the spot. The sight of her, so close ... he could see the magic in her. Feel it.

He'd done it. He'd found her like he knew he had to. Like he'd promised.

Down in the red caves.

His heart began to race, his breathing quickened. A terror unlike any he'd ever known seized him. His arm began to tingle as the room spun. Raaku's face loomed in his mind. Memories of his words pounded through his soul. Memories of drowning in the red water. Of burning again and again. Of endless suffering.

He remembered the orders he'd been given. The promises he'd made.

But it wasn't him. It wasn't.

He was a good man. A brave man. A Shulka.

He ... he ...

Dear Gods, what had he done? What had he done?

Bile rose in his throat. He had to get away. Far away – before it was too late. Before ...

Zorique's magic touched his heart.

No.

Yes.

The Great Darkness woke within him.

It woke his true self.

And it was glorious.

Darus smiled. He would kill them all.

60

Ralasis

The Kotege

Ralasis was quite surprised by how happy he felt being inside a building again. Perhaps exhausting himself running halfway across the country chasing after Tinnstra had added to his relief. Sitting on a chair was truly wondrous. It took what little self-control he had not to grin like an idiot, and even he knew that wouldn't go down well in his present company.

Smiling wouldn't do with this dour lot.

Not even being reunited with her mother had managed to cheer Tinnstra up. In fact, she looked far more interested in the Shulka with the burned face sitting next to her.

Her mother sat opposite her daughter. They were like reflections of each other; the same-shaped face, the same nose, the same eyes ... well, eye in Tinnstra's case. The main difference between them, apart from age, of course, was that Moiri had a calmness to her that was quite the opposite of her daughter. Maybe Tinnstra inherited her rage from her father. Something he and she had in common, perhaps. Ralasis was, after all, an expert in angry fathers.

Ralasis had no idea who the one-armed old man with Tinnstra's mother was. He looked like he'd been through all the wars already, with his scarred skin and mad eyes. He was staring at Zorique like ... well, Ralasis had no idea what it reminded him of – except someone not right in the head. No doubt he'd fit in perfectly with everyone else in the room.

'Your Majesty,' said Hasan, once everyone was seated, 'it gives me great pleasure to introduce to you two very important people. First of all, General Jax of Clan Huska.' He indicated the one-armed man, who bowed his head in acknowledgement. 'He was the leader of the Hanran just after the invasion. I ... We all thought him dead, but the Gods are with us today, for he has returned – just when we need him the most.'

'I have heard great things about you, General,' said Zorique. 'You saved my life when I was a child, and for that alone I'll be eternally grateful.'

'The honour is mine,' said Jax, his voice quivering as if he had to force the words out. 'My sword – my life – are yours.'

Zorique didn't seem to notice the old man's struggle and beamed at his words. 'I'll gladly take your sword, General, but I'd rather you keep your life. It's a precious thing.'

'Even so, Your Majesty, it is yours to have.' Jax bowed once more.

'And with him,' said Hasan, 'is Moiri of Clan Rizon and the mother of our very own Tinnstra.'

Moiri bowed. 'Your Majesty.'

'You're Tinnstra's mother! By the Gods. We thought you were dead,' said Zorique, jumping to her feet. She rushed around the table and took Moiri in her arms, hugging her. Zorique turned to Tinnstra, who was looking uncomfortable with the meeting. 'You didn't tell me your mother was here. This is amazing.' She laughed, a sound straight from the heavens. 'I can't wait to hear tales of what you were like growing up.'

'We'd all like to hear those,' murmured Ralasis, enjoying himself all the more.

'Definitely,' said Moiri.

'I think we have more important things to discuss,' snapped Tinnstra, ever the spoilsport.

Zorique nodded, a flush colouring her cheeks. 'Yes, of course. Wenna has rejoined us, too.' With a wink at Moiri, the queen returned to her seat at the table.

'For those of you who don't know, Wenna has spent nearly four months in Aisair,' said Tinnstra. 'I gave her two tasks: to

443

evacuate as much of the city's population as possible, and to discover what our enemies have waiting for us.'

'And is it as bad as we thought?' asked Ralasis.

'Worse,' said Wenna.

'I'm not sure I want to know, then.' For once, he'd have liked some good news.

Of course, nothing Wenna had to say was good. She spoke of trenches and barricades and Skull armies and hundreds of Chosen – the very things Ralasis didn't want to hear about. As he listened, all he could think of was how many more of his countrymen would die before this war was over.

'Jax,' said Hasan, snapping Ralasis' attention back to the room. 'What do you think?'

'About what?' The man looked shocked to be asked a question, as if his mind had been a million miles away.

'About the best way to take the city?' said his friend.

Jax gave a little twitch of his head and pursed his lips before answering. 'We must presume that the Egril have already targeted the open ground in front of the city so that the moment we step foot on to it, we'll be under bombardment – whether it's arrows, Chosen blasts or the Daijaku and their bombs,' replied Jax. 'Then we reach the trenches.'

'Which are too wide to jump,' said Hasan.

'We can bring tree trunks of our own,' said Jax. 'Drop them across the trenches like little bridges. Run straight over.'

'I'll get them cut at first light,' said Moiri.

Ralasis was pleasantly surprised for once. For all the man's strange quirks, he seemed to know what he was talking about. 'What about the barricades and the city walls?'

'It'd be best if they weren't there,' said Jax. 'Do we have any Egril bombs? If we do, we could just blow holes through them and rush straight into the city.'

'We have enough for the barricades,' said Hasan, 'but not enough for the city walls.'

'Aasgod and I can take care of the walls,' said Zorique with a confidence that reminded Ralasis of himself.

'Aasgod?' said Jax. 'He's dead.'

'I'm afraid I'm not,' said the dark-skinned man at the far end of the table.

'Not yet, anyway,' added Tinnstra. By the Gods, her tongue could be as vicious as her blades.

Jax stared at the man open-mouthed, as if seeing a ghost. 'But you're too young. Aasgod was older than me.'

'I am the man you knew,' said Aasgod. 'Or … I will be, one day.'

'How is that—' Jax looked around the room at everyone else. No one shared his bewilderment.

Tinnstra just leaned back in her chair and shook her head. 'Magic.'

At least Zorique smiled. 'A tale for another day. But rest assured, we will take care of the barricades and the city walls.'

'Thank you, Your Majesty,' said Hasan. 'We need to get across the open ground as quickly as possible – that's where our losses will be heaviest. Once we're in the city, it'll be easier for us.'

'We'll need to head straight to the castle,' said Aasgod. 'Deal with this commander of theirs, this Vallia, and their Tonin. Once they're eliminated, the Egril can't be reinforced and we'll have a chance.'

'Still, six hundred Chosen?' said Ralasis. He didn't like that one bit. 'I know we have Tinnstra, but that's a lot, even for her.' The Meigorian was trying to be light-hearted, but he got a scowl from Tinnstra all the same. The woman seemed impervious to his charms these days.

'They'll be focused on me,' said Zorique. 'I'll have to keep them busy.'

'Your Majesty,' said Aasgod, 'you will have me by your side.'

'Thank you,' replied Zorique.

Ralasis couldn't help but notice that Tinnstra didn't say anything to that remark. That was strange for her. Normally, she'd be the first one declaring that she'd stand beside her daughter, especially after Aasgod said he would.

'It would help if we had more information about the interior of the castle,' said Hasan, 'so we know exactly where we're going.'

Wenna went to speak, but Tinnstra put her hand on hers.

'Wenna tried to get a map, but she wasn't successful.'

'I'm sorry,' said Wenna, looking at Tinnstra. Something funny was going on between them. 'We tried but it was too dangerous.'

'I know the castle well enough,' said Jax. 'I was stationed there on quite a few occasions.'

Zorique smiled. 'Then we are even more blessed that you have returned to us.'

'When shall we leave for Aisair?' asked Aasgod.

Zorique turned to Hasan. 'When will the army be ready?'

'I'd like a few days here, if we can spare them. We've a lot of new recruits that need assigning and maybe even training,' said the Shulka. 'Especially now we have Jax and Moiri to help.'

'We will stay here for three days, then,' said Zorique. 'On the fourth, we march to Aisair. For Sekanowari.'

Ralasis glanced over at Tinnstra. He knew she hated delays of any sort and yet she remained silent again. That was unlike her as well. There had to be a reason why. What was she planning? Nothing good, that was for sure.

61

Wenna

The moment the meeting finished, Tinnstra stood up and walked out of the mess hall without speaking to anyone. Not to Zorique, not to her mother and not to Wenna. But Wenna had to speak to Tinnstra. She needed answers.

Why had she said there was no map, when Wenna had risked so much to bring one to her? She hated lying – to the queen no less.

Wenna shot to her feet and went after Tinnstra, but by the time she reached the corridor, Tinnstra was out of sight. 'Shit.' She broke into a run, weaving past confused soldiers, all wondering what her urgency was.

Where was Tinnstra, though?

Wenna ran past the wreckage of what used to be the main doors onto the parade ground and stopped. There were thousands of people in every direction. Soldiers and Hanran sat around small fires or under tents and awnings, chatting about this and that. Others walked from here to there, doing only the Gods knew what. There were faces she recognised, more that she didn't, but there was no sign of Tinnstra – and finding her in this crowd was going to be impossible.

'Something wrong?' asked Ralasis, coming up behind her.

'No. I . . . needed to speak to Tinnstra,' said Wenna, still scanning the people around her.

'She left in even more of a hurry than you did.'

'Well, I have to find her.'

'Do you want some help?'

Wenna shook her head. 'Probably best I go by myself.'

'Her team are over by the north wall,' said Ralasis. 'She might be with them. They go out on patrol most nights.'

'I'll do that. Thanks.'

'Good luck. Find me if you need help.'

Wenna set off for the north wall, checking everyone she passed, not wanting to risk walking straight past Tinnstra because she wasn't paying attention. Maybe she was overreacting. Maybe she'd misread Tinnstra's intentions. Maybe. Maybe. Maybe.

The war had turned her head around. Being in Aisair had made it worse. Waiting to get caught. Wondering if she'd be betrayed. Even now, amongst her own people, she didn't feel at ease.

Mostly, she just felt guilty. It had been her plan to leave via Jo's tunnel. Her plan that had got everyone killed. Gods, how old had Jo's kids been? And what about Sami? Why did he have to take that blast for her? She'd have swapped places with him in a heartbeat – except then Tinnstra wouldn't have her map. The map she didn't want anyone else to know about.

It was all a mess. Give her a—

Wenna stopped. There was a boy standing in front of a fire, talking to a man and a woman sitting on the other side. Same height as Darl, her brother, would've been. Same scruff of hair. Gods, was he alive?

'Darl!' Wenna rushed over. The kid turned at her shout. The man rose to his feet, the woman following. Then she got close enough to see his face and all that hope vanished. She stopped, feeling stupid now, crushed. Of course it wasn't Darl.

'You okay?' asked the man, who turned out to be younger than she'd first thought. More of a lad than a man. Wenna recognised him from the cave at Kiyosun.

'I'm sorry. I thought ... the boy ... reminded me of someone,' said Wenna.

'I'm Linx,' said the boy.

'I'm Wenna. Pleased to meet you, Linx.' She held out a hand and the boy shook it. Gods, his hand was so small. He was so young. So like Darl.

'Pleased to meet you,' he repeated.

'I know you,' said the woman. 'You're the one who turned up early. Told us about Zorique and everything else.'

'Yeah, that was me.'

'I'm Ange,' said the woman. 'This big waste of space is Garo. We found Linx in a town a few days' walk from here. Thought it best he come with us.'

'The Skulls killed all my family,' said Linx. So matter-of-fact.

'I'm sorry,' said Wenna. 'They're bad people.'

'Ain't that the truth,' said Ange. 'Anyway, can we help you with something?'

'Don't worry. I was just looking for a friend,' said Wenna. 'Take care of yourselves.'

'Bye,' said Linx.

Wenna had to force herself on, but she kept glancing back. Gods, the kid reminded her of Darl in so many ways. She'd have to find him later. Do something for him. The Kotege right then was no place for a kid. She'd have to get Ange and Garo to take him far away, somewhere safe. Somewhere he had a chance to stay alive. Something she should've done for Sami. War was no place for kids.

When she reached the north wall, she knew she'd found Tinnstra's crew without needing to ask. Even during the short time she'd been back with the main army, Wenna had heard enough stories about them. Frightening stories. Looking at them now, Wenna could believe every word of them. They had more in common with a pack of feral dogs than soldiers; lean, mean, with wild eyes shining bright against their camouflaged skin. All killers. And Ralasis had been right. They were checking each other's gear before they headed into the night.

And, in the heart of them, was their pack leader, the most dangerous of the lot, Tinnstra. She was talking to a man, but she saw Wenna approaching and made her excuses.

'Wenna,' she said. 'What brings you over here?'

'We need to talk.'

'About?'

'The lies we just told to the queen and everyone else.'

'Lies?'

'I gave you a map of the castle. I have all the information they wanted, but you said I hadn't been able to get it.'

'Ah, that.'

'Yes, that.'

Tinnstra reached into a pocket and produced the scrap of paper so many people had died for. 'Give it to Hasan before the army leaves for Aisair. Tell him I asked you to keep it to yourself. Tell him I told you to lie. He'll understand.'

Wenna stared at the map but didn't take it. 'Will he? Because I sure don't.'

Tinnstra sidestepped the question. 'Hasan needs it more than I do. I lived in the castle when I was younger. I know my way around well enough.'

'Then why—'

'Because I need to know where everyone's located in the castle. I won't have time to stick my head around doors to find out.'

'What do you mean? What aren't you telling me?'

Tinnstra laughed. 'Best you don't know.'

'You're not coming with us, are you?' said Wenna. 'That's why you need me to give Hasan the map, tell him you told me to lie – because you're not going to be around.'

'Keep your voice down,' hissed Tinnstra, leaning in. Not much scared Wenna, but she was scared then. Tinnstra grabbed her by the arm and dragged her away from the others. 'I need you to trust me on this.'

'Trust you? I risked my life because I trusted you. People died because I trusted you.'

That took some of the fire out of Tinnstra. 'I know, and I'm grateful. It will be worth it. I promise you.'

'So now you need to trust *me*. Remember I was with you in Layso. I helped get you out of that camp. I came here ahead of everyone else to help you.'

'I do trust you, Wenna,' said Tinnstra. 'That's why I asked you to do all this for me. It's just … some things you're better off not knowing.'

'I won't let you endanger the rest of us.'

'I would never do that.'

'Then tell me.' There was a long, painful pause during which Wenna could almost see Tinnstra weighing up her options in her mind. 'You can trust me.'

Tinnstra shook her head. 'You'll think me mad ... maybe I am.'

'Just tell me.'

Tinnstra glanced around, as if to make sure no one else could hear what she was about to say, then she took a deep breath. 'We can't win this war like this.'

'What do you mean?'

'Every time we fight the Egril, we lose more soldiers. Every time, they get closer to hurting Zorique or, even worse, killing her. We have to do something different. *I* have to do something different.'

'Like what?'

'I'm going to kill Raaku.'

'What?'

'I'm going to kill Raaku. It's the only way to end this war for good. Chasing the Egril out of Jia will never be enough. Not while he lives.'

Wenna struggled to take in what Tinnstra had said. 'But how?'

'I'm going to hunt down a Chosen and take their uniform, put it on and walk straight into Aisair, straight into the royal castle, and order the Tonin there to open a gate to Kagestan. Then I'm going to find Raaku and ram my knife through his temple.' Tinnstra made it all sound so easy, so doable. It was madness.

'But Raaku ... he ... he's too powerful ... He's—'

'Just a man. As human as you and me. That means he can be killed.'

'But it's suicide. Even if you can reach Raaku ... get close to him ... Gods, even if you kill him—'

'Maybe, maybe not. I have another map – a map of Egril. If Jax and his friends could escape without any help, I reckon I can escape with a map in my hand.' Tinnstra's voice was so calm. It made Wenna want to scream. 'Anyway, it doesn't matter if I can escape or not. If I kill Raaku, this war is over. Thousands will be spared. What does my life matter compared to that?'

'And you're going on your own?'

'That's the plan.'

'Tinnstra – I … I don't know what to say. It's madness. It's—'

'It's the only way.'

'By the Gods, no. There has to be another way.'

'There isn't – and believe me, I've looked hard enough. We've all tried hard enough. Whatever we do, the Egril just keep on coming, hitting us harder and harder each time.'

'Tinnstra …' Wenna was lost for words. The trouble was she agreed with her as much as she disagreed with her. 'Does Zorique know?'

Tinnstra looked away. 'No.'

'No? She's your daughter, your queen—'

'You don't have to tell me that! I've given my life to her! If I can kill that Egril bastard, Zorique will be safe and that's all I want. That's all any mother wants. If I have to die so my daughter can live, it's a price I'm more than willing to pay.'

'Tinnstra, I—'

'I love her more than anything. I just haven't got the strength to say goodbye.'

'When do you intend to go?'

'As soon as I can.'

'Gods.'

Tinnstra held out the map of the royal castle again. 'Take this. Give it to Hasan. Tell him what I've done after I've gone. Tell him you tried to talk me out of it but I'm a stubborn fool who wouldn't listen.'

This time, Wenna took the paper. 'Please don't do this.'

Tinnstra's smile was the saddest thing Wenna had ever seen. 'When war calls, you either run or you fight. I tried running and it didn't work out. So, this time I'll fight until the last.'

'You don't have to do it alone,' said Wenna.

'As you said, there's a good chance I won't make it back. I'm not going to ask anyone else to go on that journey with me.'

'I'll go with you.'

'Then who'd tell everyone what a fool I've been?'

'Someone else. Anyone else.'

'I appreciate the offer, I really do, but no. It's better this way.' Tinnstra glanced back at her crew, saw they were all watching her. 'I've got to go. Hunt some Skulls. Maybe find a Chosen. I'll see you around, Wenna, and thanks for everything.'

'May the Four Gods look after you.'

Tinnstra laughed. 'They've done a shit job so far. How about I do my best to look after myself?'

Wenna nodded. 'You do that.'

'I'm sorry.' With that, Tinnstra ran to join her team. She didn't even glance back before they hustled out through the gate into the darkness. She certainly didn't look as if she was even thinking about her conversation with Wenna.

Wenna, though, could think of nothing else as she stared into the shadows. The truth was, there was no stopping Tinnstra. No saving her.

Gods. Wenna wished she'd just let things be. Tinnstra was right – she would have been better off not knowing.

She headed back into the camp.

62

Ange

The Kotege

Ange, Garo and Linx sat around their fire, eating their dinner from bowls. The kid was shovelling his down like his life depended on how quick he could get it in his belly. Ange didn't blame him for that. Who knew when they'd next get something half-decent to eat, let alone something hot?

She stretched her toes out towards the fire, enjoying the warmth, enjoying not having to bloody do anything for a few minutes.

Even Garo was enjoying himself for once. He certainly wasn't moaning. In fact, he'd been a different person since they found Linx. Certainly, he was less annoying. She'd not wanted to punch him or stab him for quite a while. If she was being really honest with herself, she was glad he was around. She certainly wouldn't mind ...

He looked up, caught her looking and smiled. Ange smiled back before she knew what she was doing and felt her bloody cheeks colour a second later when she realised what she was thinking. She lifted her bowl to hide her embarrassment. 'Good, this.'

'Lovely,' replied Garo, not taking his eyes off her. 'Shame there's not more of it.'

'Lucky to get it.' Gods, she was even feeling tongue-tied.

Thankfully, the Shulka who'd spoken to them earlier turned up before Ange could make a fool of herself. 'Can I have a word with you two?'

'Of course you can,' said Ange, grateful for the company. Anything to stop her thinking about Garo in *that* way. 'You find who you were looking for?'

'Yeah, I did,' said Wenna.

'You don't sound too happy about it.'

'I'm not.'

'Anything we can do to help?' asked Ange. Whatever it might be, she hoped it wasn't serious enough to drag her away from the fire and Garo.

Wenna shook her head. 'I'm afraid not. Someone I know is planning on doing something stupid that'll probably get them killed.'

Ange laughed. 'Aren't we all?'

'Yeah. We are.' Wenna sighed. 'It's not right.'

'It's not right?' Ange looked at her, all confused. 'What *is* right about any of this? It's one mad, bloody world of not-right.'

The Shulka crouched down. 'You should leave. The three of you. Leave now.'

'What?' Ange pulled her head back as if she'd been slapped.

'You're right. Most of us here are going to die. Maybe tonight. Maybe next week or next month. But that doesn't mean you three have to.'

The woman was clearly mad. 'We're not going anywhere,' said Ange. 'We knew what we were in for when we signed up for this long ago.'

'Did you?' said Wenna. 'What about the kid? Did he? Or is he here because bad luck got him here?'

'I told you – we saved him from the Skulls.' Ange jumped to her feet. She wanted Wenna gone now, as quick as she could bloody go.

The Shulka stood, too. 'Then you're responsible for him. Save him now. This is no place for kid.'

The boy looked up, eyes wide and afraid. 'I'm not leaving. You can't make me leave.'

Garo put a hand on his arm. 'It's okay, Linx. No one's making you go anywhere.'

'In the next few days, we're heading north to Aisair,' said

Wenna, 'and maybe not many of us will have the chance to go back home again. You two have a great kid here. Take him far away from what's coming. Find a life where you all get to grow up. There's nothing special about dying young.'

'We're not running away,' said Ange, full of fire.

'I'm not asking you to,' said Wenna. 'I just don't want you to die. That's all.'

'Good for you,' said Ange. 'But we're staying. Now fuck off.'

Wenna didn't move. She turned to Garo. 'How do you feel?'

'Me?' replied Garo, pointing to himself.

'Yes, you,' replied Wenna. 'You keen to fight like your friend here or have you got a bit more common sense?' Garo looked towards Ange but Wenna stepped in between them. 'I'm asking you. Not her.'

'We all want to do our bit,' said Garo. 'To … to free Jia.'

'Look around you,' said Wenna. 'There's an army here. Whether we win or lose isn't going to depend on whether you're here or not. But this kid you're looking after? His life depends on what you decide to do next.'

'Bollocks,' said Ange. She pushed Wenna back and put herself in front of Garo. 'I told you to fuck off.'

'Ange,' said Garo from behind her. 'Maybe she's got a point.'

Ange couldn't believe it. Typical bloody Garo, not taking her side. She spun around. 'What do you mean by that?'

'I mean we could go. Go home. Take Linx with us.' And just like that, the old Garo was back. Whiny, pathetic Garo.

'That's called desertion. It's what cowards do.'

'Maybe it's called living.'

'You wouldn't be deserting,' said Wenna from behind her. 'I could make it an order if you want. I can give you permission.'

Ange held up a hand to shut her up, didn't even look her way. 'I told you to fuck off.'

'Ange, please,' said Garo. He got to his feet, Linx with him, holding his hand.

'Look, if you want to go and take the kid with you, then go,' snapped Ange. Fury ripped through her. 'I'll be glad, if I'm being honest. I'm sick to my back teeth of your moaning anyway.'

'But Ange,' said Garo, 'we want you to come, too. We could go back to Kiyosun. Yas would have a spot for us. We could start over.'

Ange waved an arm at him. 'Ah, clear off, you waste of space. You'll be doing me a favour if you pissed off. You've not got the balls for this.'

'I don't want to leave you.'

'Listen to your boyfriend,' said Wenna.

That was it. Ange spun on her heels, a knife in her hand. 'You say one more word and this goes in your fucking eye.'

'I'm just trying to help you,' said the Shulka.

'Well, you're not,' snarled Ange. 'Now, do I have to stab you or will you leave us the fuck alone?'

'All right,' said Wenna, holding up both hands. 'I'll be off.'

Ange watched her disappear into the camp once more and wondered if she'd ever hated anyone as much as she did then. Who the fuck did that bitch think she was?

'Ange,' said Garo. 'Can we just talk about this?'

'Take the kid and go,' said Ange, not turning around. 'You heard the woman. You've got her permission. You don't need mine.'

'But—'

'I wanna go,' said Linx. 'Please.'

'All right,' Garo said, sighing. 'We'll go in the morning.'

'You're doing the right thing,' said Ange, hating the words, hating him.

'Doesn't feel like it,' said Garo.

'It will.' Ange stormed off then, not looking back, not saying goodbye. Just like Dren had done to her, her heart breaking just like before.

63

Ralasis

The Kotege

It was either early or late, Ralasis wasn't sure which. The sun was trying to come up, so it was early, but he'd not been to sleep, so it was also late and he was tired. He'd been waiting for Tinnstra to come back, like a fool. Something was up with her but he didn't know what.

So, Ralasis had wandered the camp, making excuses to himself and others about why he was still awake, while he was really just looking for Tinnstra.

He also knew what would happen when she did get back. Not what he wanted, that was for sure. She'd tell him to go away, to mind his own business, to leave her alone. He knew that and yet he was still hanging around, hoping she wouldn't send him away when he found her, hoping that he could find out what was wrong.

'All right, Commander?' Guil popped up from the other side of the tent. 'Thought you'd be asleep by now?'

'How could I go to bed when I have you lot to worry about, eh?' The old Ralasis would've flashed a smile right then but he was too tired for such nonsense.

'Since you're up, can I have a word, if you got a few minutes?' asked his first mate.

'You're not going to suggest another mutiny, are you? Because if you are, I'm really not in the mood for it right now.'

Guil held up both hands. 'Nothing like that.'

'Thank the Gods. I'd hate to have to hang you.'

'Yeah, well, that's partly the reason I wanted to chat,' said Guil. 'I didn't want to leave things on a sour note between us. I didn't want you thinking badly of us.'

'I'd never do that,' said Ralasis. 'Things are grim. I get that.'

'Well, they'd be a lot worse if you weren't here and that's the truth. So, I just wanted to say thanks, really. From me and the lads. We're glad you're with us.'

'Thanks?' Ralasis squinted at the man. 'You're having a laugh?'

'I'm being serious. We've had some shit commanders in the past – you know that as well as me – and, well, you're not shit and me and the lads wanted you to know that.'

'Oh, Guil, you have such a way with words. I think "you're not shit" has to be the greatest compliment I've ever been given,' said Ralasis. The smile came easily then. So did the laugh. 'Of course, I think even you could be "not shit" compared to Tian Bethos – remember him?'

'How could I forget? He's the only commander of the fleet who ever got seasick a mile out of port,' said Guil, chuckling. 'I think it was the first time he'd ever been on a boat.'

'I thought he was going to sink the boat with all those medals on his chest. There had to be at least thirty of them.'

'And what about Tian Salander?'

Ralasis held up a finger. 'Now, he was a distant cousin to the king, may the Gods bless his soul. I'll not hear a bad word about him – it wasn't his fault he was born with a silver spoon shoved up his—'

There was Tinnstra with her team coming through the gate.

Guil followed his gaze. 'Oh, you're not after her, are you? She'll eat your balls for breakfast.'

'Enough,' snapped Ralasis. 'You go too far.'

The man's head dropped. 'Sorry, Commander.'

'You're dismissed,' said Ralasis, but he was already walking away – towards her.

Tinnstra was talking to her scout, Tavis, when she spotted him approaching. She said something to Tavis, who then looked his way, too, before turning on his heels and leaving her alone.

Ralasis took that as a good sign – unless she just didn't want anyone to see her tear Ralasis apart.

'Commander,' she said with a nod of greeting.

'General,' replied Ralasis.

'Late night or early morning?' There was a ghost of a smile on her lips and he remembered saying something similar to her back in Meigore at the embassy.

'I've not been to bed yet, if that's what you're asking,' said Ralasis, playing along.

Tinnstra looked at him then, as if seeing him for the first time, or maybe seeing him as he'd been back then, before all the shit of war. 'What if I was asking you to bed?'

'Sorry?' Ralasis must've misheard. 'Did you say—'

'I've a room in the Kotege.'

'You have?'

'Come on.' Tinnstra took his hand and led him quickly towards the half-ruined building.

Ralasis couldn't believe it. This wasn't what he'd expected. Not even what he'd hoped. He'd wanted to talk, to find out what was bothering her. Now, she wasn't giving him a chance to say anything. Gods, she didn't even look at him as she dragged him along. A few people saw them pass but she ignored them all. And Ralasis? Well, he didn't know what to say to them, either. Someone even cheered.

Through the shattered doors, up the stairs to the first floor, down the corridor to a room.

It was small; a bed, a desk, a chair and Tinnstra's kit. She dragged him in and started kissing him straight away, then slammed the door shut behind him with a boot.

'Tinn—'

Her tongue silenced him as her hands pulled at his jacket, fumbled with his belt. Her weapons hit the floor in a clatter, his sword and belt a second later. Ralasis had to help her undress him, scared that she was going to shred his last uniform and make him go jacketless for the rest of the war.

'What's the rush?'

'There's a war on.'

Ralasis couldn't argue with that. Clothes and boots and weapons all ended up in a heap on the floor. Everything out of the way but the words he wanted to say.

The bed was barely big enough for the pair of them but Tinnstra pulled him down with a fury that didn't have any need for kind words or gentle touches. She landed kisses like punches, her eye everywhere but on his. A part of Ralasis even wondered if she cared who she was in bed with. She certainly didn't care that she was hurting him.

'Stop. Just stop.' He pushed her off him.

She paused for a moment, gave him a look of confusion. 'What?'

'I don't want to do this. Not like this.'

She sat back, her scars bright-white against her dark skin. 'What do you mean?'

'This isn't right,' said Ralasis.

'I thought you wanted to fuck me. So, we're fucking.' She went to kiss him again but Ralasis put his arm between them, pushed her back.

'Not like this,' he repeated, trying to keep his voice calm.

'What's the matter with you? I thought this was all you wanted – ever since you first saw me. You certainly didn't object back in Meigore, did you? You were more than happy to fuck me then. Several times.'

'Tinnstra, please. Why are you doing this?'

'I thought it was bloody obvious. I want sex. I want to feel something.' She gritted her teeth. 'Something more than this fucking war. I thought that's what you wanted, too – the way you're always looking at me with those puppy-dog eyes.'

'What's wrong? What's happened?'

'Nothing's fucking wrong.'

'Tinnstra, please. Tell me.'

'Fuck.' She slid off him and pulled the blanket over herself as she leaned back against the wall. 'Fuck.'

The room suddenly felt very cold and very small. Ralasis grabbed his jacket and covered his lap. 'Has something happened?'

Tinnstra rubbed her face and then held her head in her hands. 'No.'

Ralasis shifted so he was sitting next to Tinnstra, their shoulders touching. 'You can talk to me.'

'Why? Why should I?'

'Because I care about you.' There were other words he could have used then, to justify his actions, but even he knew some truths were better left unsaid.

'Why haven't you given up on me yet?' she asked. 'Why haven't you told me to fuck off like I deserve?'

'Because I'm an idiot?'

'Be serious.'

'I've never been too good at that,' said Ralasis. 'Easier for me to hide behind a joke than face the truth. Same way I know you use your rage to hide who you are.'

Tinnstra leaned back. 'I'm sorry. I've not been fair to you. I've treated you like shit.'

Ralasis arched an eyebrow. 'Really? I hadn't noticed.'

Tinnstra shot him a hard look with her one eye, then it softened straight away. 'Yes, I have.'

'The world's not been fair to any of us.'

'I know. It's just ... everything I had planned, everything I'd hoped for has gone so wrong. And the more I've tried to force things back the way I wanted, the worse they've got.' She paused for a moment and took a breath. 'And you ... you reminded me of when things were good, back in Meigore, and that made it worse, somehow.'

Ralasis shifted his arm and put it around Tinnstra's shoulders. She didn't resist as he pulled her closer. 'Things will work out. We will win.'

'Not if we carry on doing what we're doing,' said Tinnstra. 'Just letting the Egril pound us into the ground. We've only got a third of our army left and most of our new recruits have never even held a sword properly. It was wrong to try and fight them this way. I was wrong.'

Ralasis kissed the top of her head. 'We all made those choices, Tinnstra. It wasn't just you.'

'Stop trying to be nice to me.'

Ralasis chuckled. 'I can't be cruel like you. I've always worn my heart on my sleeve.'

'Maybe it's time you stopped.'

'Then how would you know where to stab?'

Tinnstra laughed. 'I think I could work it out.'

'Well, don't do it today. Let us pretend we're the only two people in the world and that we actually like each other for a change.'

Tinnstra turned to face him, her mouth only an inch from his. 'I've always liked you – that's the problem.'

'I've always liked you, too.' Ralasis moved closer, his lips drawn to hers. They kissed again but not like before, when it had been full of anger and fear. This time it was soft and gentle, full of love and care.

It was only the howls and the screams that ruined the moment.

64

Zorique

The Kotege

Zorique had stood watch for most of the night – some sixth sense warning her that the Egril would attack again. But, with dawn near, she decided enough was enough. She'd been assigned a room on the first floor of the Kotege. It would've been a student's room at one time, similar perhaps to the one Tinnstra had lived in, small in size with a cot, a desk and a window overlooking the parade ground. But it also had a door, four walls and a ceiling – luxuries she'd not known in a long while. It felt so good just to close that door and be alone. Truly alone.

She was exhausted in more ways than she'd thought possible. Even taking off her armour was too much for her. Instead, she lay on the cot and closed her eyes.

Sleep would be good. Even for five minutes or, Gods willing, ten minutes.

But, as tired as her body was, her mind refused to rest.

There'd been no attack that night, but there would be soon. She knew that. The Skulls wouldn't let her march her army up to the gates of Aisair uncontested. Then the real battles would start. There would be more deaths.

Her mind drifted to a place long ago and a boy she'd loved. A different time. A different life. None of it felt real now, more a dream than a memory. Back when the sun shone and stomachs were full, when a kiss by the river was all that mattered. Simple things. Beautiful things.

Long lost.

Dear Wex. She should've said yes, stayed, had a life instead of this.

Zorique would've been happy. Content.

If only she'd never gone through that gate. She could've destroyed it. Closed it permanently from this world. In time, she'd have forgotten what she'd run from.

But what would Maiza have said to that? Or Anama? Or, Gods help her, Tinnstra? Of course, what did a few harsh words matter? They would all be well and alive if she'd blown the damn gate up. Living in Aisair in their beautiful house. Happy.

Or as happy as Tinnstra and Anama could ever have been under the same roof.

Gods, what Zorique would give to see her mothers argue once more, to hear their raised voices, the sharp back and forth. She'd hated their rows back then. Now she recognised the love for her in their words.

She told herself they were stupid thoughts to have. She should be sleeping. She had to sleep. Not fill her head with silly dreams of things that could never be. She wasn't a child anymore.

She had to sleep.

Zorique willed her mind to be calm and concentrated on her breathing, counting to five with every intake of air and counting to five as she exhaled. In and out, she counted, feeling the tiredness seep into her brain. In and out, she breathed. In and out.

The howls came from so far away. Zorique knew the sound well. From when she was last at the Kotege, from the palace in Layso.

She knew the monsters that made them. She'd run from Kyoryu. She'd fought Kyoryu.

The howls got closer. Louder. Then came the screams.

Zorique's eyes shot open. It was no dream.

She half-fell from her bed, snatching up her sword and spear. She didn't waste time running down corridors and staircases. Zorique flew out through the room's window, showering glass and rubble in her wake.

The sky was blood-red but Zorique burned brighter, banishing

465

the last of the night's shadows. The howls were even more monstrous now she was in the open, the screams more piercing. They came from the front gate. Zorique flew there as fast as she could, leaving a trail of fire behind her.

There were three of the beasts; each one almost twice the size of a man, their fangs glistening in her light, their claws rending all asunder. The Kyoryu looked up as she drew near. One reared up onto its hind legs, roaring a challenge.

Fear struck her. What if her magic was as ineffective on them as it had been on the Kojin?

'Kasri.' The word came out in a whisper, lacking any conviction, but it struck with power.

The demon erupted in flames, burning Zorique's fear with it. She plucked up another with her shield, thrust it a hundred feet in the air and then slammed it back down in the blink of an eye. It left no more than a smear on the landscape.

The last was quicker to move, leaving a disembowelled Meigorian soldier and sprinting straight towards her. Zorique could've burned or squashed it like the others, but she was angry. Angry that these creatures had come to kill her soldiers. Angry that the enemy had thought they could do her harm. Angry that they had thought her weak.

She landed in the path of the Kyoryu and waited as it rushed towards her. When it was fifteen feet away, she threw her spear with all her might, straight at the Kyoryu's open mouth. It was too good a target to pass up.

The spear flew true, taking the creature through the back of its throat and erupting out the other side, lifting the Kyoryu up and off its feet.

The demon hit the floor, twitching as its life faded, and her soldiers cheered. Her victory was the least they deserved, but as she looked around at the carnage the Kyoryu had caused, she knew she'd been too slow. How many lives could she have saved if she'd not gone to bed?

'Take the injured to the medics,' she ordered. 'Be quick.'

'Your Majesty,' said a soldier, pointing back at the Kotege. Zorique turned and saw Tinnstra sprinting towards them, shouting.

Far behind her was Aasgod, also running, plus Hasan, Ralasis, Moiri and Jax. Other troops ran with them, while others gathered weapons. What had them riled? She'd killed the Kyoryu ...

'*Shirudan.*' The shield formed around her and her soldiers a heartbeat before the energy blasts lashed towards her. They hit the barrier with a boom. Light and fire crackled over its surface, pounding it, pounding her. It was utter agony.

Zorique screamed as thousands of tiny needles pierced her nerves, attacked her very soul. It was worse than before. So much worse. How many Chosen attacked her? How many were coming to kill her?

Zorique went down to one knee and the shield shrank with her, cracking and buckling under the assault. She wanted to collapse. The pain was too much. Too much for her.

Gods, she couldn't even breathe. Couldn't think. Everything she had was holding the shield together and it wasn't enough.

She wasn't enough.

The Chosen appeared out of the forest, energy flaring off their batons. So many of them. Maybe ten – no, twenty of the fiends. The Kyoryu had been no more than bait to draw her out, let her think she'd won, while they were the real danger.

As they drew closer, their baton blasts intensified. Tears ran down Zorique's face and the shield shrank once more. She was forced onto her hands and knees, and the soldiers trapped with her huddled closer. They knew their deaths were imminent as more cracks appeared in the barrier.

'I'm sorry,' whispered Zorique with what felt like her last breath.

Something – someone – shot past, and the force of the assault on Zorique suddenly lessened. Not by much, but just enough. She looked up, saw Tinnstra amongst the enemy, dealing death of her own. No hesitation. No mercy.

Then lightning crackled overhead and she knew Aasgod had also joined the battle. Again, the force of the attack on her faded as the Chosen turned their batons on their other foes.

Zorique sucked in air once more and found her hope. More of her soldiers rushed to help. By the Gods, they were brave. Her strength returned as Jians gave their lives to save hers.

She stood up, expanding her shield, screaming from the pain. 'Get out of the way,' she hissed at the soldiers with her. 'Get away.' Zorique opened enough of her shield to allow them to run free, back towards the Kotege. When she was alone, she took one more breath for one more word.

'*Tobo!*' Zorique shot straight into the air, as fast as she'd ever flown before. The ground beneath her exploded from the Chosen's blasts, but she had left any danger far behind.

For a moment, she found herself in silence as the sun flared over the horizon. Zorique closed her eyes and let the light fall on her skin, enjoying the wind, which soothed her raw nerves.

She looked down. The battle raged as Aasgod's lightning flashed and the Chosen retaliated with energy blasts and magic of their own.

She was scared to go back down. Scared to join the fight. The Chosen had the measure of her now. Better to stay in the clouds and pretend she was the only person in the world. Alone. Safe.

'Dear Gods, if you exist, give me strength,' she whispered to the wind.

The sky didn't answer her, and she felt stupid for asking. There were no Gods. Just humans and Chikara water. The worst combination. Magic only brought death.

Zorique drew her sword and formed a new shield on her arm. It sparkled in the early-morning light.

And down she flew, back into the maelstrom.

They saw her coming, of course. How could they not? She was a falling star. Burning bright.

Batons turned her way and she welcomed them. Better to shoot at her than at her people. Red fire arced up, but she was ready for it, twisting and turning around the blasts as she hurtled down to earth.

She saw Tinnstra take advantage of a Chosen's distraction and bury her axe in his temple, while Aasgod's lightning burned another's baton from his hand.

Others weren't faring so well. A giant of a Chosen slapped a dozen Shulka off their feet, leaving them broken and still. Another threw fireballs into Meigorians and Hanran alike. A third hurled daggers of what looked like ice. A fourth flitted here and there, no more than a shadow, leaving death in her wake. And always there were the baton blasts, flying up at her, lashing out at her soldiers.

Zorique counted fifteen Chosen still standing. More than enough to wipe out her army given half a chance.

'*Kasri.*' Zorique waved her hand and the giant burst into flame. She shot past his burning corpse and landed before the fool with the fireballs. Zorique pointed her sword at the man and his magic turned against him, rushing back into his masked face, engulfing him in flames.

She caught motion out of the corner of her eye and spun, slashing with her sword, hitting smoke. She felt an impact all the same, knew her blade had done its job well. Blood spurted out of thin air and splattered across the ground, followed by two halves of a Chosen's body.

Baton blasts flashed at Zorique, hitting her shield, knocking her back, hurting her – but she was prepared for them.

'*Oso.*' She threw her shield with all her might and sent it spiralling through one Chosen after another.

Then it was Zorique's turn to be sent flying as something smashed into her back. She rolled with the impact, bounced up onto her feet as a wall of ice flew towards her.

'*Shirudan.*' Ice was no match for her shield. As it shattered and sizzled, Zorique strode forwards behind the shield's protection. The Chosen realised her folly, tried to draw her baton instead, but Zorique's sword flashed out, fire dancing across its blade as another head fell to the ground.

Zorique glanced around, saw Tinnstra doing her bloody work, saw Aasgod lashing out. Hasan and Jax led a charge of Shulka against a Chosen, and their spears dealt death.

'Abomination!' screamed a Chosen, her voice louder than the battle. 'Face me!' She held a Skull's scimitar in her right hand, a baton in her left.

Zorique rolled her neck and adjusted her grip on her sword. 'Here I am.'

The Chosen charged. With each step she took, a replica of her appeared, multiplying again and again to either side of her.

Zorique smiled. She'd fought illusionists before. Flames licked along her sword's blade once more and she closed her eyes, remembering all Anama and Maiza had taught her. She struck almost before she reopened them, putting all her fury into her weapon. She ignored the replicas and their raised weapons and concentrated on the original Chosen. Their blades met, Zorique's weapon shattered the Chosen's and then she punched the woman with her free hand, driving her fist through the woman's skull.

By the Gods, it felt good. She spat on the corpse. 'That's why we train, bitch.'

Zorique moved on, hunting the Chosen, putting them down one by one. Their blasts bounced off her shield as their power weakened and weakened with their dwindling numbers.

Tinnstra was like Xin herself. There was no finesse to the way she fought, no holding back or fear for her own well-being. Tinnstra rushed in, no matter who she fought, a storm of war, severing arms and hacking through necks.

So different from Aasgod. The mage fought with surgical care and precision, striking from a distance, emotionless. Effective.

Zorique's soldiers fell back under Hasan and Jax's orders, aware that their jobs were done and there was no need to risk anyone else's lives in the last moments of the battle.

Eventually, only one Chosen remained. The man faced the three of them with a shaking baton, energy flickering along its tip. 'Blood I will give you, O Great One,' he said. 'Souls I will—'

The throwing star struck him between the eyes.

'Shut up,' said Tinnstra.

The Chosen stood there for a moment, looking at them as if trying to work out whether he was dead or not. Then his legs buckled and he joined his brethren in the dirt.

'Well fought,' said Tinnstra, walking over to her side. 'Are you hurt?'

Zorique shook her head. 'No. Luckily.'

'You got your shield up in time.'

'Only because you ran to warn me. I thought the Kyoryu were the only threat.'

'Always look for the trap.'

'I will.'

'You'd better – because one day I won't be around to warn you.'

'What do you mean?' asked Zorique. There was something about Tinnstra that worried her. It wasn't her rage this time. It was something else. A sadness. 'Are you okay?'

'I am. And I'm sorry about the way I've been. It was uncalled for.'

Zorique smiled. 'I'm sorry, too.'

'You never have anything to be sorry about.' Tinnstra leaned in and kissed Zorique on the cheek. 'I love you.'

'I love you, too,' replied Zorique, more worried than ever. She was going to say something, but Aasgod walked over towards them.

'Go and get some rest now,' Tinnstra said, spotting him, too. 'I'll see that these bodies are cleared away.'

'Tinnstra, I—'

An alarm rang out.

'Egril at the eastern wall,' someone shouted.

'Go,' said Tinnstra. 'Your people need you. We can talk later.'

Zorique nodded and took to the air, grateful that she still had her mother looking after her. They could fix whatever had come between them later. Once the war was won.

65

Tinnstra

The Kotege

Tinnstra held the knife in her shaking hand. It was a small blade, made of the best Rizon steel and razor-sharp. Perfect for what she needed to do. Perfect for her mad plan.

She sat in her room in the Kotege while the battle raged outside. She felt guilty for not being out there, for not doing her bit, but the longer the fight went on, the more convinced she became that she was doing the right thing.

She had to stop this war.

She'd not seen her mother all day. Moiri had been busy fighting alongside Zorique, Hasan and Jax, and Tinnstra had been grateful for that. She didn't want to tell more lies or, even worse, lose the courage to do what she had to do.

She'd not even spoken to Ralasis after their little moment. That had been an act of weakness on her part – something else she couldn't afford. Why had she tried to sleep with him again?

Because that might've been the last time I'll have a chance to feel something other than hate, a chance to feel loved.

Because there was no turning back. No other way. This was it.

Our only hope.

She looked down at the uniform she wore. The stolen uniform of a Chosen, the Emperor's elite, the enemy. How monstrous they'd once seemed, how petrified they had made her feel. Now she was more than their equal. If they were fear, she was death.

How many have I killed?

Too many to count.

Not enough to make a difference. Yet.

She'd taken the uniform from a woman with a caved-in face – Zorique's work. It was a perfect fit, as if it had been made for her. A gift.

There'd been some blood on the collar, but not enough to matter. No one would notice it against the black wool. Her hand drifted to the skulls at her throat. Such small things to hold such power.

The mask lay on the bed next to Tinnstra's weapons. She'd hated the feel of it when she'd put it on. It was only a simple piece of material, but it made her feel claustrophobic.

Lost.

It wasn't natural for one's face to be covered like that. Bad enough she had lost the sight in her left eye, now her remaining good eye was further hindered by the mask. It had clawed at her peripheral vision, just enough to irritate. Worst of all, it made her feel like one of *them*. She'd taken it off immediately.

Still, it would do its job when the time came.

A fool's hope, but it's all I have. All I'll ever have.

No. She had more than a stolen uniform and mask.

Tinnstra had her strength and her speed and her powers and she had her weapons.

They lay spread over the bed. She couldn't bring them all with her – Chosen didn't carry weapons as a rule – but she could bring enough.

Tinnstra had swapped her sword for a scimitar taken off one of the Chosen who'd attacked the night before. Unlike the typical Skull swords, it was a beautifully crafted weapon and sharp enough to cut Kage himself.

She'd have to leave her axe, but not her knives. She strapped one to the inside of her left arm, slipped another inside her boot, and now she placed the knife she'd been holding into a sheath fixed to her belt at the small of her back. Her pouch with her throwing stars was on her right side, small enough that it was barely noticeable.

The same couldn't be said about her bag. Any way she looked

at it, it was obviously out of place. Trouble was, she needed it more than anything else. There were always more swords or knives to pick up, but the things in her bag were irreplaceable: her map and her supply of Chikara water.

She only had two vials left of the green liquid. There'd not been an opportunity to restock since that morning's attack. Already, she could feel the jitters that came from going too long without. A few more hours and she'd be sweating and her stomach would be cramping. Then the shakes would start. And the headaches – worse than any magic could cause. The water was supposed to make her stronger. Now she needed it just to breathe.

Dear Gods, what have I done to myself?

Tinnstra stood up. She knew where to find more water, after all. In the mayhem outside, no one would notice her sneaking into Aasgod's tent.

Tinnstra strapped on her weapons belt and started packing her bag. In went her last two vials of Chikara water. She was about to put the map tube in when she stopped. The map was too large to be able to use in a hurry. Gods, they'd needed a table and paperweights earlier to look at it.

She opened the tube and removed the map, unrolling it across her bed. The smell of centuries wafted up from the paper, but this wasn't the time to worry about history. 'Sorry, Ralasis,' she whispered as she sliced off the section that showed the Egril Empire. It was easy to imagine the Meigorian's horror at her ruining such a priceless artefact. Of course, he had plenty of other reasons to be upset with her. A ruined map might just be the easiest to forgive.

The smaller portion folded easily, until it was no bigger than the palm of her hand. If she had to dump her bag at any point, she could hide the map on her person without a problem. For now, though, into the bag it went.

The Chosen's mask was the last thing to go in.

She snatched up her cloak, pulled it around her shoulders and flicked up the hood, making sure it was drawn tight against her neck, hiding the skulls. She left the rest of her old clothes folded on the bed with the ruined map. For a moment, Tinnstra thought to leave a note, something to explain what she'd done, but what did it matter? She didn't need anyone's forgiveness or to justify her actions. She'd either win Sekanowari or it would all be over for everyone.

With her bag over her shoulder, Tinnstra opened the door, then stopped. She looked back at the room, identical to the one she used to live in when she was a student. She'd been petrified after her father had dropped her off, standing in the doorway, looking at her new home. It was her first real time away from her family – apart from Beris, that is. He was a few months away from taking his vows and still at the Kotege. His shadow had been everywhere at the school. Everyone had been in love with mighty Beris.

It had felt so daunting back then: the people, the place, the training and the teaching. Running back to her room every night and hiding behind a locked door to cry herself to sleep.

There'll be no doors to hide behind where I'm going. No friendly faces to help me out. But it's been like that my whole life. Everything was training for what I have to do now.

With that, she left the room, not bothering to close the door. Now, she just needed to find Aasgod – or rather his things. She didn't want to see the mage, just steal from him.

Tinnstra opened up her senses. As ever, Zorique shone like a star. She was over on the eastern wall where the fighting was heaviest. Aasgod was near her, as always. That was a good thing, she told herself, when she felt a pang of jealousy. He'd look after her while Tinnstra was gone. Maybe help keep her alive – if he didn't get himself killed first. But knowing where he was didn't help Tinnstra. She stretched out her senses further, hoping to find his scent – a magical trail leading back to where he'd stored the Chikara water.

She picked out the enemy, too; Chosen and Daijaku and only the Gods knew what else – all drawn towards Zorique and her light. All desperate to snuff it out. Tinnstra had to fight the urge to run to her daughter's side. Her plan was still the best way to end the war. To win.

Tinnstra reached the ground floor. The enemy had yet to properly breach the Kotege, but they were trying their best.

Zorique shone above the grounds as she blasted Daijaku from the sky and danced between Chosen blasts.

So where was the Chikara water? Tinnstra could almost hear it calling her.

Most of the army had camped out in the parade grounds, creating a tented village. Now it was a place for the dead and wounded. Tinnstra made her way through it, trusting her instinct, seeking the mage's tent.

A Daijaku came screeching past and hurled a bomb at the Kotege's main building before a thrown spear took it through the chest. The explosion punched yet another hole in the already ruined building, showering half the campsite with debris.

Tinnstra kept going, ignoring the injured, ignoring her guilt.

In the end, Aasgod's tent was easy to find. If he'd put it up any closer to Zorique's, he would've been in it. There were plenty of people around, but no one paid Tinnstra any attention – they were too busy worrying about not dying.

She ducked inside and immediately spotted the small chest where the mage kept the Chikara water, despite his attempts to hide it under his cot. When she pulled it out, she saw the bastard had even fixed a padlock to the blasted thing.

She was sure he was doing it to annoy her. After all, it took her all of a second to break the thing open. The Chikara water, or what was left of it, lay inside. Ten vials.

Fear struck Tinnstra in a way she'd not experienced in years. The water was everything to both Aasgod and her. He needed it to fuel his magic. She needed it to ... live. Without it, they would both be useless.

But what was left wasn't enough, not nearly enough.

Calm down. Think. I don't need that much. Just enough.

Two days to Aisair. A day to get into the castle and find a gate to Kagestan. Two days, maybe three to find and kill Raaku. That was how many vials?

Six vials.

And then, of course, she'd have to escape. Gods, there was no way of knowing how many she'd need for that. She could take everything Aasgod had and it still wouldn't be enough.

Then again, Wenna had been right. It was a suicide mission. She'd be lucky to get close enough to kill Raaku. Even if she succeeded, they'd not let her escape.

So what did it matter? Tinnstra needed enough Chikara water to get the job done. No more.

She took five vials to go with the two she already had. Seven was enough. Aasgod would have to make do with what was left.

She shut the chest, then opened it again. Took one more. What difference would that make? A lot to her. It would get her through the night. Aasgod only needed the water when the army reached Aisiar. Four vials would be enough for him. More than enough. She uncorked it, drank it and placed the empty vial back with the others, like she used to do in Aisair, all those centuries ago with Anama.

Another mage who drove her mad. Another one who gave her life for Zorique.

She stood as the rush hit her, a wave more than a storm, as her senses heightened and the world sharpened. She could almost feel the battle around her, the blows being struck, the lives taken, the magic blasting through it all.

Zorique blazing in colour. Flares of green around Aasgod. Half a dozen red flares marking the Chosen. And then ... what? She didn't recognise it. Someone with magic, but it was hidden or only starting to develop ... It was power, though. Dear Gods. Tinnstra could tell it was dark, evil, Egril ... and it was inside the Kotege.

66

Yas

Arlen's Farm

Yas stared at the field as though it would make the bastard crops grow quicker. Anan and Venon were beside her, while Dean and Sorin waited nearby. 'How much longer before we've got food to eat?'

Venon rubbed his chin and sighed. 'We only planted the seeds three weeks ago. It's going to be a long time yet before we've got anything worth eating.'

'Shit,' said Yas.

'Next year will be better. We'll have more seeds to plant,' said Venon.

'Next year doesn't fill bellies this year,' said Yas. She glanced up at Anan. 'What about the hunters?'

'Not great,' said the big man. 'It's slim pickings out there. We've been taking from the land for too long without returning the favour, and not giving the wildlife time to replenish their herds. At the moment we're catching enough, but we're going further out and coming back with less each time.'

'And the boats?'

'Ah,' said Venon, glancing over at Anan.

'What is it?' asked Yas. She had a feeling she didn't want to know.

'We've got a few problems with the Meigorians,' said Anan, all the same.

Yas turned to face him. 'Seriously?'

Anan nodded. 'They've not been too friendly to our people when we've gone down to fish. They seem to think the sea belongs to them – or that part of it, at least.'

'I hope you put them straight on the matter.'

'We've had words. I even thought we'd come to some sort of agreement, then one of our boats managed to unbeach itself and drift away in the night. The Meigorians denied any involvement, of course, but we know it was them.'

'How?'

'Well, it wasn't the seagulls that cut the anchor ropes.'

'I don't believe it,' said Yas. 'After everything we've done for them.'

Anan didn't say anything, but his silence said enough.

'What?' said Yas. 'You don't think we have?'

Anan glanced over at Dean and Sorin, then sniffed. 'We've not been too friendly ourselves.'

'What do you mean? We gave them somewhere to live, treated their injuries and sent food to them,' said Yas.

'And watched them burn their dead day after day,' said Anan. 'Made them walk half a day for drinking water.'

'There wasn't room for them in the village,' snapped Yas. 'And even if there was, they'd have brought diseases and only the Gods know what else with them.'

'I'm not saying your decisions were wrong. I'm just saying they're feeling aggrieved. And now they're being bloody difficult about us fishing.'

'I'll go and speak to them,' said Yas. 'Try and sort things out. We need to be fishing.'

Yas saw Anan's eyes flick once more to Dean and Sorin. 'You sure that's a good idea?'

'Why do you keep looking at those two? What do you think I'm going to do?' said Yas.

'Not suggesting anything, Yas,' said Anan.

'I'll be off,' said Venon, retreating a few steps. 'You don't need me here.'

'What?' said Yas. 'Are you scared of me, too?'

'No, Yas. Not at all.' Venon held up both hands. 'I'm just a

479

farmer. I know nothing about fishing, is all. Thought I could be more useful elsewhere.'

'Go on, fuck off, then.' By the Gods, she'd had enough of them both. 'And you go with him, Anan.' She watched them leave, shaking her head at the ungrateful fools. They'd all be starving up in that bloody cave if it wasn't for her. The way they were acting, it was as if she had her lads killing people left, right and centre.

'We've not heard anything from Bros yet?' she asked Sorin.

'No. Not a peep,' replied the Weeping Man.

'He's going to come back empty-handed, isn't he?' said Yas.

'Kenan tends to want cash before he'll do anything, and Bros had nothing but your promises to offer.'

'Shit.' Yas pinched her nose, feeling a headache coming on. Why couldn't things be simple for once? Why couldn't they be normal? 'You two carrying?'

'Yeah,' said Sorin. 'You need us to do something?'

'We're going to have a chat with the Meigorians to sort out a few things,' said Yas. 'I want you to be ready in case there's trouble.' Yas had a knife in her own coat lining, but she'd rather not give that little fact away to anyone.

Dean nodded. 'Are we the ones causing the trouble?'

Yas arched an eyebrow. 'I'm hoping no one will be.'

They walked down to Omason Beach. In a normal world, it would've been a nice stroll. Clear skies and that lovely spring heat that made a person feel good about life, complemented by a soft breeze from the south-west. The path was well worn and easy going, taking all of about forty minutes. Almost enjoyable, in fact, if Yas didn't resent the hell out of having to make the trip in the first place – especially when she could've been back at the village, playing with Little Ro or working on her house.

She just hoped Simone would be there to translate, otherwise it was all going to be a waste of time. Of course, if the Meigorians were pissed off with her, it wouldn't matter what Simone said. With any luck, that prick of a captain, Portis, would be reasonable – unlike the last time they'd met just over two weeks back. Still, Yas couldn't see how she could've done things differently. It wasn't as if any of her lot were having a rosy time of things.

Of course, the smoke drifting up into the sky from the beach suggested the Meigorians were having a harder time of it. They were still burning the dead most days, and that couldn't be easy on them.

Maybe she should've made the effort to come down and check on them more than she had, and she felt a bit of guilt about that, but it wasn't as if she hadn't been busy with everything else. Yas was lucky to get a minute to herself these days.

The hospital tent was the first thing she saw. The sides had been opened to allow the breeze through, and there were still a fair few people lying on cots. It had been nearly a month since the invasion. Yas couldn't help but think that if they weren't back on their feet by now, they were never going to make it. No wonder there was no end to the funeral pyres. Poor sods.

To the right of the hospital were the old Skull barracks, now living quarters for the Meigorians. Further down the beach, what was left of the invasion fleet was anchored in the bay, about forty ships in all. Other wrecks jutted out of the water and the shoreline was still littered with debris. There were a few fishing boats on the beach as well, which looked like they'd been assembled from scraps of other ships but were obviously seaworthy enough. No sign of any Jian craft, though. Yas hoped that they were missing because they were being put to good use and not because more accidents had befallen them. Finally, at the far end of the beach, there were the pyres for the dead. One was already burning, while two more lay waiting for whoever died next.

Yas felt another pang of guilt. This was no easy place to live at all.

It took another five minutes before they found Simone. She looked worn out and brittle, and none too excited to see her guests.

'Hi, Simone,' said Yas. 'It's good to see you.'

'Yas,' she replied.

'I was hoping to have a chat with Captain Portis,' said Yas.

'That won't be possible,' said Simone.

'It'll only take five minutes of his time,' said Yas, not liking the pushback. Simone was Jian, after all – she was supposed to be on Yas's side. 'Just want a friendly word. That's all.'

Simone gave a little shake of her head. 'He died a week ago.'

'What? Died? How?'

'His wound got infected. The rot set in.'

'Shit.' Yas didn't know what else to say. She wasn't expecting that.

Simone gave Yas a hard look then. 'It happens a lot here. We don't have enough water to drink most of the time, let alone enough to clean everyone's injuries. Then there's the flies hopping from one body to the next, spreading the germs around. Still, every death means one fewer to worry about, eh?'

'What do you mean by that?'

'Nothing,' said Simone, but again she gave Yas the evil eye.

'Everyone's doing the best they can,' said Yas. 'It's not easy anywhere.'

'Sure.'

'Look, I didn't come here to start an argument with you or anyone else. In fact, I came here to see what we can do to help. We all have to get along. We all need to help each other out.' Yas looked over the beach once more. There were a lot of Meigorians up and walking. Enough to cause real trouble if they wanted to. 'Who's in charge now Portis is dead?'

Simone took a deep breath and straightened her back. 'I am, apparently.'

'You?'

'Don't look too shocked. There aren't any officers left and the others need someone to look after them. They chose me.'

Yas pinched the bridge of her nose again. She could really feel the headache building now. 'Okay. So what can we do to help you, Simone?'

'What can't you help us with? We need more fresh water than we can carry. We need more ways to store the water we have. We need more clean cloth for bandages. We need more food—'

'But you're fishing, aren't you?' said Yas. 'That should be helping with food.'

'We are. It helps,' said Simone.

'I hear a few of the Meigorians have been ... stopping our people from fishing, too.'

'Things can get a bit emotional when you're hungry and your friends are dying around you.'

'I can help you, Simone,' said Yas. 'I can send people down every day with more water. I can get some of the villagers to build water storage for you here. Cloth for bandages might be a problem, but I'll see what I can rustle up. As for food ...' Yas shrugged. 'We need to help each other there. No more hassle from your friends here when we come to fish, and in return, we'll send you whatever we have spare. I won't lie to you, though – we've not got much of anything. Hopefully, when the crops come in, that'll change.'

'Sure. I'll see to things on my side – if you can sort your side out,' said Simone.

'We're on the same side – remember?'

Simone nodded. 'I'll be seeing you, Yas.'

Yas seethed all the way back to the village. Simone had really rubbed her the wrong way. The woman was a bloody Jian. She should've been siding with her own people, making sure they were looked after first. There shouldn't have been any of this 'my side, your side' nonsense.

It wasn't going to be a popular request to get people to lug water down to the beach. It might be a pleasant enough stroll, but not for someone carrying a bucket of water or two. And it wasn't as if people were sitting around with nothing to do. Everyone was busy trying to get the village up and running. Maybe she could work out a rota or something.

'Yas.' It was Dean. He had his neck stretched up as if that would help him see beyond the horizon.

'Dear Gods, what now?' Yas wasn't sure if she could handle any more grief.

'We've got visitors.'

'We can't have. We would've heard the horns.' Yas tried to see whatever it was that Dean had spotted, but he was about a foot taller than her.

'He's right,' said Sorin. 'I can see a lot of horses. A lot of people, too.'

'Maybe it's Hasan,' said Yas, her heart lifting. 'Maybe him and the others have returned.'

'Maybe there's been another battle,' said Dean.

'Or the war's over,' said Sorin.

Yas knew they weren't going to be that lucky. Instead, she walked on to the village with a sick feeling in her gut and glad she had a knife tucked away in her coat. She told herself that no horns meant the visitors were known, that they were friends, but she didn't believe that, either.

And she was right not to.

It looked like most people were gathered in the centre of the village, but no one was saying much. In fact, it was uncomfortably quiet. Their backs were to her, so no one saw her approach. Yas had to push her way past the first few rows before the rest stepped aside and let her through. But she wished they hadn't, because their visitors weren't friends. Not at all.

She knew one of them – Bros – but that didn't make her feel any better, especially not the way he was grinning. With good reason, too – Bros had brought the Weeping Men back with him. There had to be at least a hundred of them, maybe a good sight more. All with tears on their cheeks as far as Yas could see, heavily armed and looking about as dangerous as a bunch of gangsters could.

Somehow the ink on Yas's own cheek didn't make her feel any better about their visit. Four villagers – her sentries – were on their knees and tied up with ropes. Well, that explained why there'd been no warning.

'Ah, is this her?' An older man smiled as he asked the question of Bros. 'The one you've been telling me about?' Both sides of his heavily lined face were almost dark grey with tattoos faded by time. So many tears that Yas couldn't count them.

'Shit,' said Sorin from behind her. 'It's Kenan.'

67

Ralasis

The Kotege

Ralasis slumped against a wall and gulped a mouthful of water. The fighting had gone on all day, with no sign of respite yet. Every part of him ached and it was taking his last remaining strength just to lift his sword, let alone use it. He'd been pulling his lads off the front line when he could and replacing them with fresh bodies, but that luxury was gone now.

Now it was fight or die.

Zorique shot past overhead. Somehow the girl was still going, unstoppable despite everything the enemy had thrown at her. Without her, the allies would've been overrun long ago. If something happened to her ... Ralasis didn't want to think about that. The closer he got to dying, the more he knew he wanted to live.

It was a bit late to work that out, though. He should've had the brains to do that before he volunteered to lead the invasion.

'Get out of my way.'

He looked up and saw Tinnstra racing towards him.

'Get out of my way!' she cried, pushing bodies aside.

'What's wrong?' said Ralasis, climbing to his feet, but Tinnstra ignored him and ran past.

'Shit,' he muttered, hauling his tired body after her. It had to be bad to get her worked up like that.

Tinnstra was going twice as fast as he could manage, drawing her sword without pausing. Up ahead, Aasgod was throwing lightning into the Skull ranks. Tinnstra's mother and the one-armed Shulka were also nearby, marshalling the defences.

Then Tinnstra skidded to a halt and began circling as if she was trying to spot some danger – but there was none to be seen. None that Ralasis could see, anyway.

'What is it?' he asked when he reached her. 'What's wrong?'

'It's gone, Godsdamn it,' hissed Tinnstra. 'Shit.'

'What's gone?' said Ralasis, turning with her, seeing nothing but their soldiers. 'What did you see?'

'Magic. Egril magic,' said Tinnstra, still turning, still scanning the grounds. 'It's in here – with us.'

'Where?' asked Ralasis. He held his sword in his shaking hand, but only the Gods knew what he could do against magic that had Tinnstra scared.

'I sensed Egril magic in our ranks. It was faint – but it was here. I've lost it now ...' Tinnstra glanced over at Aasgod. 'Or it's being hidden by more powerful magic.'

'Maybe it was a Chosen and Zorique killed them?' said Ralasis.

'No,' said Tinnstra. 'It's different, subtler. Maybe ... Maybe I was mistaken.'

'You've never been wrong before.'

'I've been wrong plenty of times.'

'Not about things like this,' said Ralasis.

'Fuck.' Tinnstra rammed her sword back in its sheath but her head kept moving. She was still looking.

'What shall we do?' said Ralasis.

'We do nothing,' said Tinnstra. 'Go back to wherever you were. I'm sure you're needed there.'

'What are you—'

'None of your business.' She looked at him then, her eye wild. Gods, he was glad she'd sheathed her sword, because she looked ready to kill him.

He held up both hands. 'I meant nothing by it.'

'You never do.' Whatever she was going to say next, she bit back and swallowed.

She ran off before he could say anything else, heading north along the wall.

He watched her go, uneasy about the encounter. Not that she would've killed him – he was used to feeling that she might – but she looked crazier than normal, as if she knew she was going to go do something insane.

He had to stop her or help or ... do *something*.

Someone grabbed him. It was Guil, a bloody gash across his cheek. 'Where you going, Commander?'

Ralasis stared after Tinnstra, but she was out of sight already. 'Something's wrong.'

'She looked like she wanted to kill you.'

Ralasis stepped back, smiled and patted Guil on the shoulder. 'If that happens, you can tell my corpse that my father was right about me. Now, keep an eye on everyone, eh? Don't let anyone get killed if you can help it.' He ran off then, following Tinnstra's path.

Guil was right, though. It was the last thing he should be doing. Not with a battle going on around him, his troops fighting and dying. They needed him. Not some crazy woman who'd made it clear she didn't want him.

But if that was true of him, it was even more true for Tinnstra. If she wasn't in the thick of things, there'd be a damn good reason. A terrifying reason.

Then he spotted her, by a hole in the northern wall where some Jians were going toe-to-toe with a load of Skulls. Tinnstra drew her sword again and waded in, a blur of steel, cutting a path through the enemy.

Literally cutting a path. Once she was clear of the fighting, she kept going into the woods, out of sight.

Ralasis should've stopped then, turned back, done anything except draw his sword and go after her. But that's what he did. A Skull swung a scimitar and nearly took his head off, but he managed to get his own blade up, then half-tripped, half-ducked out of the way of the next blow.

Ralasis grabbed someone's helmet off the ground as he righted himself and clubbed the bastard Skull with it, knocking them back, buying him enough time to ram his sword into the man's throat.

Someone or something hurtled into him, sent him sprawling over a load of corpses. It was a miracle he kept hold of his sword as he spat someone else's blood out of his mouth. A Skull's legs stepped in front of him, so he slashed the man's hamstrings while he was still down on his hands and knees and cut the Skull's throat as he crawled over the body. More blood and guts covered him for his troubles, but he saw an opening in the fighting and scrambled for it.

If anyone noticed him, they'd think he was running away, but he couldn't get it out of his head that Tinnstra needed him, that whatever she was doing was more important than the battle at the Kotege.

He got back on his feet and ran into the woods, not knowing where he was going. Ralasis probably had more chance of running straight into a battalion of Skulls than he had of finding Tinnstra. But he kept trying, stubborn fool that he was.

A fallen log lay in his path. He hurdled it without thinking, only realising as he cleared it that the ground dropped away beyond it. Down he went, six feet, maybe. Not far, but far enough.

'Shit!' He landed hard, tried rolling with the impact, but it was more of a fall than a tumble. As he went head over heels, Ralasis nearly stabbed himself with his sword more than once. He took out a bush and ate a mouthful of dirt before he could stop himself, amazed that he'd not run himself through. His sword was next to useless, though. He'd snapped it in half somewhere in the fall. Still, a broken sword was better than no sword.

There was no time to waste. He clambered to his feet, cursing the mess he'd made of himself, sheathed his half-sword and hobbled off after Tinnstra.

She was long gone, but Ralasis had no intention of giving up. Not now. He started to run as best he could in the dark, through woods he didn't know.

Ralasis headed north, instinct and stubbornness driving him on. It was madness – of that he had no doubt. At some point, he'd have to turn around. Head back, defeated, and pretend he'd never gone on this fool's quest. It would probably be for the best if he did that anyway. What was he going to do if he caught up with her? As Guil said, Ralasis would be lucky not to get killed for his trouble.

After about five miles, Ralasis stopped to catch his breath. Gods, he wished he'd brought some water with him to drink – nearly as much as he wished he'd stayed back at the Kotege. Finding Skulls had to be better than this. He bent over, his hands on his knees, as he sucked in air. Sweat dripped from his brow onto the ground and his heart hammered away. At least he was still alive. That was something.

He mopped his brow with his sleeve and straightened up. With his wind back, he decided he'd give it another mile or two and then call it a night. The others must be wondering where he was. Of course, Ralasis was wondering that as well.

He looked around. It was getting dark, but what little he could see offered few clues as to where he was going. He wasn't even sure he was heading north anymore. For all he knew, he'd gone in a circle and was about to stumble straight back into the Kotege.

Then he heard ... what? Footsteps, lots of them, crunching on dirt, breaking twigs. Chinks of armour moving. The odd curse. Whispers. All sounds of trouble heading straight for him.

Ralasis ducked down, trying to see what was coming, trying to pretend he wasn't scared – but he was. There was no doubt about that.

It had to be more Skulls.

A few minutes later, he saw a glimpse of white armour. It was a Skull, all right. Once he'd seen the first, the others were easier to spot. There were enough of them, after all.

An army of them.

He had to return to the Kotege, get out of their way. He—

A hand covered his mouth, pulled him back. A knife appeared in front of his eyes.

'Make a sound and I'll kill you.'

68

Yas

Arlen's Farm

Yas wanted to run. She wanted to snatch up Little Ro and get as far away from Arlen's Farm as possible. She also wanted to ram a knife into the gut of that smug bastard, Bros. How could he bring the Weeping Men here? He'd ruined everything.

But running wasn't an option, and nor was killing Bros – not yet, anyway.

'Welcome to the farm,' she said instead. 'I've heard a lot about you, Kenan.'

'And I've heard a lot about you.' His eyes gleamed against the grey of his skin. 'Not always the most complimentary things, eh, Bros?'

'No. She can be a right bitch,' said Bros, looking very pleased with himself.

Kenan laughed. 'Yeah, well, what leader makes everyone happy? We have to make the hard choices, don't we? Think of the greater good over the individual!'

Yas glanced around, searching the faces of her people, looking for support, looking for those who would be ready to fight – didn't see much that made her feel good about her odds. No one had weapons with them and too many had kids clinging to their legs. Timy wasn't there with Little Ro, though. That was something. Hopefully she had the brains to stay out of this mess until Yas got things sorted.

But how *was* she going to sort it? Five minutes before she

490

would have trusted Dean and Sorin with her life. Now she was nervous with them at her back. They were Weeping Men, first and foremost. Maybe they were as unhappy with her as Bros was.

'What brings you down south?' she asked. 'It's a long way from Felix.'

Kenan sucked at his teeth and then grinned. 'Well, the weather for one. It's so lovely and warm in this part of the world!' Everything the man did was a performance, but whether it was for his men's benefit or her people's, Yas wasn't sure. She found his joviality bloody scary, that was for sure.

'A long way to travel for some sunshine.'

'Yeah, well, there's a war on, too. Lots of fighting and killing and all that nonsense. It's not good for business. So when you sent Bros up to warn us about it, I had an idea. I thought, "Kenan, why stick around in Felix and risk being blown up when you could get away and wait it out until it's all over?" I gotta tell you, it didn't take me too long to make up my mind. Not at all.'

'You're here for a holiday, then,' said Yas.

'That's right,' said Kenan. 'But who knows? We might love it here and want to stay for ever. Depends how welcome you make us feel.'

'We're a friendly bunch down here,' said Yas.

'Are you, though? Are you really?' Kenan wagged a finger at her. 'I'm not so sure. The tales I've heard. The things you've done. I've got a feeling you might be the sort of person who'd put poison in my ale, or perhaps you'd like to stick a knife in my gut like you did to my cousin, Raab?'

He was right on both accounts, but Yas didn't want him to know that. 'Not at all,' she said instead. 'I'm all out of poison. To be honest, we've not got much of anything. We're still waiting for crops to grow, and the hunting's not been great, either. Chances are we'll all be starving before the war's over.'

Kenan glanced over Yas's people and sniffed. 'They all look like they're used to a bit of hardship. I'm sure they won't mind going without for us.'

'I'd rather no one went without,' said Yas.

'Beggars can't be choosers. Sometimes you've got to be happy with the simple fact that your heart's still beating. Now, we've had a long journey and me and the boys are peckish and more than a little bit tired. So, why don't you rustle up some food for us, and while we're eating you can sort out some beds. How's that sound?'

'Absolutely wonderful,' replied Yas. 'I told you, we know how to look after our guests here.'

'And don't get any funny ideas, eh? I wouldn't want to add more tears to my collection if there's no need,' said Kenan with a nasty chuckle.

'Don't worry. There's been too much death already for us to go looking for more.' She glanced around, saw Mayes. 'Go and sort some food out for our guests and get Venon to put some tables together for them.'

'Some ale be nice, too,' called Kenan over her shoulder.

Yas looked back at the man. 'It would, but we ain't got none. Life's full of disappointments, eh?'

'Ooh. Was Bros right about you after all? It'd be a shame if he was.' He wagged a finger at her again. If he tried it a third time, she'd be tempted to see if she could cut the bastard thing off.

'Come on, everyone,' she called out, clapping her hands. 'Show's over. We've more than enough to do without wasting the rest of the day gawking. I'm sure you'll all have a chance to meet our guests soon.'

A few worried looks were exchanged before people began to disperse, but they got moving soon enough. Even better, Kenan didn't try and stop anyone. He didn't take any hostages to ensure the farm's good behaviour, either. Hopefully that meant he was feeling confident about his little coup.

Kenan was just another in a long list of people who'd under-estimated Yas. The question was how much harm could Kenan and his men do before she got the chance to show him the error of his ways?

She found Daxam next. 'Where's Timy with my son?'

'She took him for a walk in the woods when the Weeping Men turned up, but she didn't take any food or water with her – she'll have to come back soon. And you know how your little boy is about you. He won't want to be away for long.'

492

'Yeah. I know.' Yas sighed. 'When Timy comes back, make sure she stays with Ro at your place, don't bring him to me. I'll come and see him when I can. When it's safe.'

'We'll look after him, Miss Yas.' The big man couldn't hide the fear in his voice, though.

'I know you will.' Yas squeezed his arm. 'Just be careful, and if you need to slip away to the caves with him to keep him safe, don't hesitate. Better that than those bastards getting their hands on him.'

As Yas turned to leave, she saw Mayes running over. 'They're asking for you, Yas.'

'Dear Gods,' she muttered. 'Already?'

Walking back with Mayes wasn't the same as having Dean and Sorin at her shoulder, but she wasn't going to let anyone else know that.

Long tables had been set up in the centre of the village and most of the Weeping Men were gathered around them, making the most of the food that had been put out. The sight of that alone made Yas feel sick – it was enough to keep her people fed for a good few days and Kenan's thugs were just shovelling it into their mouths. They had wine, too, and weren't being shy about drinking it.

'There she is,' Kenan called from his spot in the middle of the chaos. 'Come sit with me.' He pushed the man next to him out of his seat to make a place for Yas.

'Very kind of you,' said Yas, sitting down.

'Least I could do. You're one of us, after all.' He tapped his cheek with a knife. 'Of course, we don't normally recommend earning your tears by killing our own.'

'Raab had it coming.'

'You don't have to convince me. Raab was my cousin and I know what a cunt he was. Still, traditions and all. You didn't make yourself popular with the other leaders. Raab, if he was nothing else, was a good earner. You? Not so much.' He picked at something stuck in his yellow teeth.

Yas laughed. 'What's there to earn in a wasteland? We spent three months living in a cave. Not much need for a black market when no one's got any bloody money. Still, we sent what we could.'

'It wasn't a lot.'

'It was all we had.'

'We don't just accept coin.'

Yas stared at him, anger boiling away. 'You are not suggesting—'

'I am.'

'These are *my* people,' said Yas though gritted teeth. 'I'm not selling any of them.'

Kenan sucked his teeth again. 'We're not buying, Yas, my dear. We're taking. Now, you need to decide if you're one of us.' His knife touched her cheek. 'Or not. We can have a very different conversation if you're not.'

'If it's just slaves you want, why didn't you stay where you were? There'll be enough lost souls back there for you to round up once the fighting starts.'

'You're right, but the trouble about being in a war zone is there's a chance you could get killed yourself. Call me pessimistic, but I'd rather that not happen to me. Much better to come down here and take some easy pickings, eh?'

Yas stared at the man, wondering if it was possible to hate anyone more. 'I can see the logic.'

'I knew you were a smart one, Yas. Now, are you really a Weeping Man, or do I have to go about things the nasty way?'

Sometimes the hard choices were no choice at all. 'How many people do you want?'

69

Tinnstra

The Kotege

'Make a sound and I'll kill you,' hissed Tinnstra. Bad enough the bloody fool had come after her, huffing and puffing, making enough noise to wake the dead. Now she'd been forced to save Ralasis from blundering into another load of Skulls.

At least he recognised her voice and stopped resisting. That was something.

She retreated into the darkness, taking Ralasis with her. She kept her hand clamped over his mouth. She didn't trust the idiot to stay quiet as she manoeuvred them both out of the path of the enemy.

There had to be at least another thousand Skulls heading towards the Kotege, alongside a dozen Chosen. Dear Gods, she hoped that Zorique and the others had the strength to deal with them.

Tinnstra felt her rage grow, but she had to remind herself that she wouldn't make much difference if she was still with the others. But if her plan worked? It would change everything.

Until then, Zorique and the others were on their own.

She slipped from shadow to shadow, dragging Ralasis with her, until she was well out of the Skulls' way and she knew they wouldn't be discovered. Even then, she didn't take any chances, forcing Ralasis down into cover, until they were both well hidden and all they could do was watch.

He kept trying to turn his head to look at her, but she tightened her grip, holding him still. His breath raced in and out of his nose, hot on her skin, and Tinnstra could feel his heart pounding away against hers. *Gods, what was he doing? Following me like that? He's lucky I didn't kill him.*

She waited until after the last Skull was long past, waited until she was sure there were no more following, before she let Ralasis go.

He pushed off her, eyes wild, looking at her, then in the direction of the Kotege and the Skulls, then back to her again. 'What are you *doing*? Why didn't you stop them? Warn the others?' The words spewed out of him, full of indignation and disbelief.

'Why don't you shout a bit louder?' she hissed. 'You'll bring the Skulls down on us.'

'That would be better than where they're going!'

'If you're in that much of a hurry to die, let me know and I'll kill you myself.'

'This isn't about me! We've got to go back and help the others. Gods.' Ralasis stared after the Skulls open-mouthed, shaking his head.

'Then go after them. I don't know what you're doing here in the first place.'

'I came after you.'

'I worked that much out for myself,' said Tinnstra. 'After I made it damn clear you weren't welcome.'

'Scared I was going to stop you deserting?'

'Deserting? Is that what you think I'm doing?' She waved a hand at him. 'Go away. Go back.' She marched off, heading north, anger raging. How dare he? How bloody dare he?

Tinnstra could hear Ralasis spluttering to himself, but then the fool was running after her. Shit.

'Tinnstra! Talk to me! What's going on? There's a reason you let those Skulls go by. There's a reason why you're doing what you're doing ... whatever this is. Tell me.'

She turned on him, teeth bared, using all her willpower not to punch his face in. '*Of course* there's a reason – now leave me alone.'

Ralasis stood his ground, with a snarl of his own. 'What is it? I deserve to know!'

'Why? Because you have feelings for me?'

He flinched at the venom in her words, but he didn't back down. 'No – because my friends are dying for you far from their homes. That's why.'

His words gave her pause. 'I'm trying to save lives. I'm trying to stop the war.'

'How? By running around in the dark on your own?'

'I'm going to Aisair.'

'Aisair?'

'I need to get there before the army does.'

Ralasis stared at her as if she was speaking another language, one he didn't understand.

It was pointless. What was she doing talking to him? 'Just go, eh? I haven't got time for this.'

He still didn't move. 'Tinnstra – talk to me. Maybe I can help.'

'Help? Help? You? What help are you going to be? Are you going to smile the Egril to death?' She started to walk off, but he grabbed her sleeve.

'I've saved your life before.'

She looked down at his hand until he let go. When she spoke, there was ice in her voice. '*You* won't be any help where I'm going.'

'Where? Aisair?'

'No. Kagestan.'

'What?'

Tinnstra took a deep breath. 'I'm going to Kagestan. I'm going to kill Raaku.'

Ralasis took a step back. His legs looked like they were about to buckle under him. 'How?'

'They have Tonin in the castle. I'm going to make one of them open a gate to Kagestan. Then I'm going to walk into Raaku's castle, find him and kill him.'

'And the Egril are just going to let you?'

Tinnstra unslung her bag and removed her cloak 'Yes.' She stood before him in her Chosen uniform. 'That's exactly what they'll do.'

Ralasis looked her up and down, seeing her Egril trousers, her

Egril boots, her Egril sword for the first time. 'You look like one of them.'

'It fits rather too well,' said Tinnstra. 'So yes, I'm going to walk through the front gate, straight into that castle, and no one will stop me.'

'And you haven't told anyone you're planning to do this?'

'No. They'd try to stop me.'

'With good reason!'

'Look – we can kill every last Skull, Chosen, Daijaku and Tonin in Jia, and we'll still have won nothing. Raaku will only send more of his monsters to try and kill us, because that's what he does. He never gives up. That's one lesson I've learned the hard way.'

'Then we strengthen the border so they can't attack us again.'

'It won't be enough.'

'And so you plan to kill Raaku.'

'It's the only way to win Sekanowari. Cut the head off the monster.'

'You can't do it alone,' said Ralasis. 'Why not take all of us – take the army – after we free Jia?'

'Because more and more people will have to die until there's no one left. But me? I can walk in unnoticed. They'll see an army coming, but what's one more Chosen in a city full of them?'

'There has to be another way. This is suicide.' A thought suddenly struck Ralasis. 'Is this why you wanted to sleep with me at the Kotege? Was that some sort of weird goodbye?'

'Gods, not everything is about you, Ralasis. Besides, I don't intend to die. After I'm done, I'm going to just walk out again and come home.'

'This plan's insane.'

'But it'll work. Now, go back to the others.'

'Let me come with you.'

'You're not dressed for the part.'

'I can get a uniform the same way you did.'

'You're going to kill a Chosen?'

'I was thinking you could do the killing.'

Of course. The man was impossible. 'If you can't even do that, why do you think you can help me?'

'Because if you're really going to escape, I can help. I've seen that map of yours. It would take you weeks to walk across Egril back to Jia, but we could be at the coast within a day. We steal a boat from there and we'll be back in a couple of days.'

'It's too risky taking you,' said Tinnstra, but she couldn't help thinking he had a point. She'd not thought about how to get away – that was a problem for after she killed Raaku. 'You don't even speak the language.'

'Then I'll be the silent one. You can talk for both of us.'

'What about your troops?'

'As you said, if we do this, we can save lives – put an end to the war for good.'

'I didn't say "we".'

'I can help you.'

Tinnstra shook her head as the sounds of explosions echoed across the night from the Kotege.

'We can do this,' said Ralasis.

70
Ange

The Kotege

Ange was curled over on the ground, no more than ten feet away from where she'd been fighting. The battle had stopped a little while ago, with bodies from both sides piled up high around her, but there was no sign of any more Skulls to kill. Somehow, she'd been luckier than most. She'd survived with just a few cuts for her troubles. The only bad one had been on her left arm, but a hot poker had sealed the wound. It fucking hurt like mad now, but the pain told her she was still alive. Getting her armour off had been an ordeal in itself.

She should probably find some water, some food, but she was too tired even to try to move. The bloody ground was more than comfortable for her right there, right then.

Sleep would also be a good idea but instead she kept looking around, expecting to see Garo, but he'd be far away from the Kotege by then – or she hoped he was. She still couldn't believe he'd really gone and left her – even though she'd told him to. He hadn't even tried to talk her into going with him and Linx. He'd just hotfooted it out of there as quick as he could without so much as a goodbye. For an idiot, he'd done the right thing. Unlike her.

She didn't even know why she was missing him. All he did was complain and moan and say stupid things, and yet ... Fuck. It wasn't like he was Dren. Not even close to being half the man Dren was.

But Dren was dead and now Garo was gone and Ange was on her own, lying in blood and dirt. Feeling sorry for herself.

'Ange.'

Ange jerked out of her thoughts and saw the Shulka Wenna standing above her. The woman had her armour on, a sword strapped to her back, another on her hip and a mad look in her eyes. 'You hurt?'

Ange pushed herself upright, groaning, too tired to fight with the woman. She'd done the right thing telling Garo to go. 'Better than some.'

'That's the truth.' Wenna crouched down, unhooked a water skin from her belt and offered it to Ange. 'What about your friend and the kid?'

'They fucked off right after you told them to.'

'I'm sorry, but it seemed the right thing—'

'Ah, don't worry. You were right. They were right. Gods, I wish I'd gone with them now.'

Wenna looked around, taking in the carnage. 'Might've been a good move.'

'Did you find that friend of yours you were looking for?'

'Yes, but I wish I hadn't.'

'Why's that?'

'She's going to do something foolish – or something dangerous. Both. Maybe get herself killed.'

Ange laughed. 'That any different from the rest of us?'

'No, I suppose not.' That got a smile from the Shulka. 'So, this Garo – you like him, then?'

'Yeah. No. I don't know. Garo drove me mad every bloody day. I mean, there were so many times I could've punched him in the face. But now? I kinda wish he was here, driving me mad. Stupid, eh?'

'No. That's perfectly normal. I find myself missing people I haven't seen in years. People I barely gave the time of day to when they were alive.'

'Who's that, then?'

'I had a baby brother, Darl,' said Wenna. 'I was fifteen when he was born, and I thought he was just a pain to have around.

My last year at home before coming here, to the Kotege, was a nightmare with him crying all day and night. Gods, I certainly let my parents know how I felt about it.

'I hardly went home again after I took my vows. And when I did? I think I talked to Darl maybe a dozen times – even though I could tell how much he wanted to talk to me.' Wenna shook her head. 'I don't think he entered my mind once while I was overseas in Meigore – until the invasion.'

'Is he ... dead?'

'Yes. No. I don't know. Probably. I certainly couldn't find him in Aisair when I was there.'

'There's still hope, then,' said Ange.

'It's the hope that kills you.'

'Better that than a Skull.'

'True.'

Neither of them spoke for a moment, but the silence wasn't awkward. Far from it. In fact, it made Ange feel better than she should, all things considered. She leaned back, propping herself up on one elbow. 'Do you think—'

A whistle cut through whatever she was going to say. It was one of the sentries.

'Skulls. They're back,' said Wenna, on her feet in an instant and off at a sprint, heading to the main gate.

'Fuck,' said Ange as another whistle got the whole camp jumping. She snatched up her armour and slung it over her head as the first explosion went off. Ange looked up but couldn't see any Daijaku in the sky. But that didn't mean shit. Those winged horrors were always about.

She ripped her sword out of its scabbard and ran to her place at the wall, to the right of the main gates, her armour flapping at her sides. She should've tied it up, but there wasn't time. Not now. She was in the second row of defenders because she had a sword. Front row all had spears so they could kill Skulls without getting too close.

'Close the gates,' someone screamed. 'Close the gates.'

Fuck knew what good that would do – the gates were

half-smashed to pieces after the day's fighting. The walls weren't much better. They were more hole than stone.

Some of the lads had built a barricade across the hole in front of where Ange was standing, but it didn't look like much now trouble was approaching. She had a good view of the woods, though, some fifty feet away. No sign of any Skulls – yet.

Beni was to her right and a bag of nerves. 'You see anything? You see anything? You see anything?' For a Weeping Man, he wasn't the bravest.

'No,' she snarled, wishing she could see the bastards, wishing again that she'd tied her armour up or taken a piss or eaten something or that she'd fucked off with Garo when she had the chance.

More explosions erupted further along the wall and somewhere people were fighting. Ange could hear the sword song and the battle cries and the screams.

Zorique flew past, a streak of gold, and energy blasts shot up from the darkness in response. The queen shouted something and sent a wave of fire down into the forest. Where there'd been darkness and shadows was now orange and yellow and gold as the trees went up with a whoosh. More screams, then. Lots of them coming from the other side of the wall.

That made Ange smile, got her thinking that she might not have to fight at all that night, that the queen would take care of all the Egril. But that was stupid thinking, because that's when she saw the Skulls coming out of the woods, screaming and waving their bloody swords about.

'Egril!' she screamed pointlessly. 'Egril!' Shit-loads of them. Some even seemed to be burning, trailing smoke, but it weren't slowing them down none.

'Come on, you bastards!' screamed Beni, thumping his chest with the fist in which he held his sword. He was lucky not to cut his own nose off in the process.

Ange tried to spit, but her mouth had no saliva to spare. It was her bladder that was fit to burst. Fuck, she'd probably wet herself and get killed in the process. She didn't know how that was possible, though, not when she couldn't even remember the last time she'd had a drink.

The Skulls hit the barricade in a rush, trying to power their way through by sheer weight of numbers. The front row lashed out with their spears. Stabbing here and there, some getting lucky, some not.

Killing Skulls didn't do them any favours, though. The dead Egril gave the ones behind them something to push against, as well as protection from the Jian spear points. Sure enough, the bloody barricade began to move the wrong way, back towards Ange and her mates.

It seemed to take an age – probably only seconds – before there was a creak and a groan and the stupid thing collapsed in a heap of wood and dead Skulls. Then the rest of the bastards rushed through the gap. And the fighting was on.

The front row jabbed out with their spears again, but suddenly having a six-foot reach wasn't much use with the Skulls in your face. Two of them went down, just like that.

Beni rushed in to fill a gap, shouting, swearing, swinging his sword. Like a madman, he was. Ange would've gone to help him, but he looked like he might kill her just as easily as a Skull.

Then he took a scimitar through the heart and Beni wasn't a problem she had to worry about anymore. No, the problem was the bastard Skull that had killed him. He still had to get his sword out of Beni's guts, though, so Ange took the chance and went for him. Now she was the one shouting and swearing. Enough for the Skull to look up and offer his stupid masked face for a target.

Ange hacked down with all her might. No skill, no technique, just sheer bloody fear and anger and a will to live. It worked, too, catching the fucker in the sweet spot beneath his eye. The skull mask cracked as the blade bit deep and the Egril went down.

Then it was Ange who was falling, hitting the ground, sword flying from her hand, tripping over Beni's dead, bloody body. She scrambled, trying to get clear of the mayhem, desperate for a weapon as she watched more Skulls come pouring through the gap. More Jians rushed to meet them and someone's boot nearly stomped on Ange's head, but there was no room to stand. She'd just got her fingers around a sword hilt when a body fell over her, sending her sprawling again.

The man smacked her in the head with his elbow as he tried to fend off a Skull with his sword. For all the good it did him. The Skull chopped down with his scimitar, like an axe on a log, and hot blood spurted everywhere. The Jian screamed, wriggling from the pain, arms thrashing, until the Skull hacked down for the second time and shut him up for good.

The Egril's eyes locked on Ange, lying there all helpless. She could've sworn the man grinned at such an easy target, but she saw his sword go up again well enough. Knew what was about to happen.

The Gods help her, she shut her eyes, not wanting to see what came next. But there was a thump and a cry and no sword came down. When Ange looked, Wenna was there, a sword in each hand and a dead Skull at her feet, another about to join him. The Shulka was a whirlwind of precision, single-handedly forcing the Skulls back, giving the defenders a moment to gather themselves, giving them hope. Somehow, she was everywhere at once, with eyes in the back of her head, blocking an attack from one Skull while striking down another.

Ange got back to her feet, soaked in blood that thankfully wasn't hers, and picked up a scimitar. A Skull came at her, but she managed to duck under his wild swing and slashed at him with her sword. The Egril was fast, though, and blocked her, sending shock waves through her arm as their blades clattered together.

She kicked out, aiming for the Skull's balls, but only struck more of his bloody armour, throwing herself off balance in the process. Ange staggered back, scared shitless by the whole bloody thing. What was she doing in a sword fight? She should have gone with Garo.

Dren wouldn't have run, though. Dren knew how to kill. What would Dren do? He'd fight fucking dirty is what he'd do.

Ange grabbed a handful of dirt and threw it in the Skull's face. As both his hands went up to protect himself, Ange lunged and rammed the blade straight into the Skull's chest. The man might as well not have been wearing any armour because it sank all the way in, right up to the hilt. She felt his last breath puff against her cheek, then she pushed him away, grinning for all she was worth. She'd bloody done it.

'Watch out!' Wenna shoved her aside. One sword blocked a Skull's scimitar, aimed at where Ange's head had been, while her second slashed open the Egril's throat in reply.

Ange had to jump out of the way of the falling body, shocked that she'd nearly died again. Then she saw Wenna was laughing in the maelstrom as she hacked and slashed.

'We are the dead!' shouted Wenna, full of a beautiful madness. 'We are the dead!'

Ange, bloodstained from head to foot, ran to join her. If this was to be the night she died, she was going to take as many of the bastards with her as she could. She'd make Dren proud.

71

Zorique

The Kotege

Zorique burned through the sky, shining as bright as she ever had, sending fire down on the Egril and, by the Gods, it was wonderful. She didn't have to pretend to be a queen or a God – she just had to be the warrior she'd been trained to be – and she was good at that.

There were Chosen with the enemy, but she wasn't scared of them anymore. Yes, their batons could hurt her, but they had to hit her first and she was too damn fast for that.

They, on the other hand, made easy targets of themselves each and every time they fired at her. Their red blasts lit a path leading straight to where they were. And Zorique didn't even have to be precise with her retaliation. Not now. She sent wave after wave of flames into the forest around the Kotege until everything burned. There was nowhere for the Skulls and Chosen to hide. She turned them all to ash.

Soaring high, she spun around, waiting for more energy blasts to lash out, looking for more enemies to smite. When none came, Zorique turned her attention to the fighting inside the Kotege grounds.

The Skulls had breached the walls here and there, but Zorique's soldiers were holding their own. The heaviest fighting was concentrated in one particular place where the Skulls were pouring through a hole in the wall where the gates used to be.

The two sides were too entangled for Zorique to use her

flames, but she was just as adept with traditional weapons. Her old teacher, Maiza, had put a sword in her hand from the age of five and made damn sure she knew how to use it.

She landed heavily in their midst, unsettling everyone with her blinding light and the force of her impact. And then she struck, moving fast, showing no mercy.

Zorique thrust her spear through a Skull still flinching from her sudden appearance. She yanked the spear free and used it to sweep another off his feet, opening up his neck with a twist of the spear tip. She shattered another Skull's helmet, driving the butt down through bone and into brain, then spun the shaft to deflect swords aimed at her heart.

Her own people fell back, grateful for the respite, giving her room to fight without fear of harming them. Zorique could've called the fire or used her shield to pulverise the Egril, but that would have ended the fight too soon. She needed it to go on, needed more time not to be the queen.

She left her spear in a Skull's mouth and drew her sword. A dozen Egril remained and Zorique dived into them like a cat amongst the pigeons. A dart of her blade, a slash of her sword. Every move was death. Every strike a hit. Maiza would've been proud. Tinnstra, too, except she'd have told Zorique off for putting herself at risk.

Zorique waded through the Skulls, leaving body after body at her feet. She veered out of the way of an Egril sword and spun to kick the man in the face before thrusting her own sword through the next Skull. She slashed down at an Egril, shattering the man's scimitar as he tried to block her blow, and carved him in two. Zorique spun and took off another man's head.

Three remained. They looked like they wanted to run, but the woods were still burning behind them, cutting off any chance of escape. Even so, Zorique could've been merciful. Once, perhaps, she might've been. But she remembered a town full of spiked people, the dead she'd burned. There was no room left in her heart for mercy.

Zorique was justice. She was retribution. She was Jia.

A cheer went up as the last Skull died and for once Zorique

didn't flinch at her army's adulation. Tinnstra had been right – better they think of her as something more; an invincible soldier, a commanding queen or a divine God. It didn't matter which, as long as it gave them strength and hope.

She walked through them, allowing hands to touch her armour, nodding back when they fell on their knees, gifting smiles as she passed. Victory was the best tonic for worn-out bodies and scared hearts.

Then she saw Aasgod running towards her and the look on his face instantly soured her mood.

'What is it?' she said.

'Someone just told me that Ralasis and Tinnstra headed into the forest right before the Skulls attacked,' said the mage.

They both turned to look at the burning woods, where Zorique had slaughtered the Skull forces. 'No.' The word almost caught in her throat as fear clawed at her guts. No one could've survived the inferno she'd created. Not even Tinnstra.

What had she done?

Zorique was in the air a second later, shining bright, flying over the flames, searching for her mother, all hubris gone. She used her shields to dampen and squash the fire, wishing she'd not been so cavalier in her actions, so indiscriminate.

The Skulls could do that, but not her. Gods, she couldn't lose her mother. She couldn't have killed her mother.

Zorique flew faster, further, past her flames, past her destruction, trying to ignore the despair in her heart. Tinnstra was fast. She could've outrun the flames. She might've not even been in the area when the Skulls attacked.

Could've. Might've. Zorique was grasping for hope out of thin air. It didn't matter how far she flew or how low she searched, Tinnstra and Ralasis were nowhere to be seen.

Then she saw Aisair in the distance, rising over the horizon as she flew ever nearer. The capital – *her* capital – where the Skulls were waiting for her with their army of monsters. And Zorique knew enough was enough.

She had time before she needed to head back to her army. She'd give her enemy a taste of what was coming for them – and may their miserable God help them if they dared try to stop her.

Torches burned from one end of the city to the other, giving it a glow of its own against the night sky. But, somehow, it looked smaller than the Aisair she remembered.

She'd been five or six when Anama had first taken Tinnstra and her into the Aisair she knew. After living in the villa, the city overwhelmed her with its large buildings and overcrowded streets, which were full of magic wherever she looked. She'd seen one wonder after another, and Tinnstra had carried her home at the end of the day, utterly exhausted.

But, like everything the Skulls touched, it looked different now. They'd cleared the forests that had always bordered the city, creating a no-man's land for miles around. Good killing ground, as Maiza would've said. No doubt they had the approach marked for their archers and sorcerers to give Zorique's army a bloody welcome.

There were the trenches that Wenna had told them about, no doubt filled with spikes and only the Gods knew what else, and more barricades behind those.

Egril flags flew high over city walls lined with white-armoured soldiers. The Skulls scuttled around at the sight of her and someone, somewhere, started ringing the alarm.

Good.

Zorique dropped down to skim mere inches above the ground, heading for the main gate. She could see the barricades clearly now, stretching from east to west, disappearing into the darkness around the city walls. They were at least ten feet high, made of felled trees, their tops sharpened to spikes. More soldiers manned them, and she could see them pointing at her, shouting, waving their swords.

As if that could stop her. Once more, she called the fire.

'*Kasri.*'

Flames erupted with a pop in the centre of the barricades and with them, the screaming started. There were no friends' lives at stake to make Zorique stay her hand. No need for control.

Zorique barely had to encourage the flames to rush left and right, adding more power to them as she flew closer and closer.

Off they raced, greedy and eager, feeding on the wood. She grinned at the havoc they caused, imagining the hard work that had gone into building those defences.

The Egril started to react.

The first arrows flew at her. A futile gesture. As if an arrow could hurt her. A baton blast lashed out next, bright red, arcing down from the city wall, promising pain, but she was already past it before it smashed into the ground.

Shapes rushed towards her from the city. Daijaku. Had they not learned their lesson, either?

Obviously not. The Daijaku swarmed her, screeching with fury, armed with their Niganntan blades.

'*Kasri.*'

The demons burst into fire, popping as flames ruptured their chests before spiralling down to earth, screaming in agony. Others crashed into her shield, breaking bones and plummeting. A wave of her hand sent more tumbling into the darkness, never to be seen again. The demons were nothing to Zorique, like gnats to a horse.

But of course, the Daijaku weren't alone.

Another baton blast cut through the darkness from the city wall. Followed by another and another and another, coming from all along the battlements. Red beams crackled left and right, singeing the air around her, blinding her, scaring her. Zorique dipped and swerved, soared and dropped as she did her best to remain unscathed.

How many Chosen were on the walls? Hundreds?

Explosions filled the sky as the Chosen's blasts smashed into each other, sending shock waves through the air. Time and again, they pounded Zorique's shield, forcing her roll one way, then the other. She screamed with rage as pain shot through her, hating them for making her feel weak.

She raced forwards, letting the blasts hit her shield, relying on her momentum to reach the city, going faster than she'd ever gone before. She'd destroy the very walls the Chosen stood on.

She'd—

Someone was flying next to her.

A Chosen matching her for speed.

The man was no more than ten feet from her right side. Energy flared along his baton. Zorique didn't want to know how a blast from that close would feel.

'*Kasri.*'

The Chosen went up like a torch. He screamed, face melting as he dropped out of the sky.

But he wasn't alone. Another blast hit Zorique's shield, fired from somewhere above her, strong enough to crack her magic. Another came from the left and this time she had no anger to hide her agony. The pain was too much. This had been a mistake.

She tried to fly on – the city walls were so close – but she was now being hammered from above and from her flanks. Two more Chosen were in the sky with her, chasing her, attacking her, not giving her time to think, let alone strike back.

She covered her head with her arms. Tried to breathe, but only managed to scream. She had to turn around. Escape.

She shot up, seeking to put distance between her and her enemy, but the Chosen followed, discharging blasts from their batons in her wake. She threw fire back without aiming, without thinking. She just needed some distance.

She glanced down. Far, far below, she could see the city walls as she passed over them, still flying fast.

Her shield disappeared. Her light blinked out.

And Zorique fell like her enemies had before.

Part V

Monsters One and All

72

Darus

The Kotege

Darus Monsuta was back and in control and it felt glorious.

He'd spent too long lurking in the old Shulka's broken mind, taking what little pleasure he could in tormenting and humiliating the fool. Now he was free. Reborn. Just as the Emperor had promised down in the caves. He didn't care that he had to make do with Jax's feeble, one-armed body. It was sufficient for now. Soon enough, he'd change and become so much more.

Jax was still there, of course, niggling away at the back of his mind as Darus had once done himself – but Darus wasn't weak like the Shulka. Darus would enjoy listening to the old man's howls as he faded from existence.

He'd only placed a sliver of his mind in Jax on a whim, when the old man had been his prisoner. It amplified the torture and added to Darus's thrills. He'd not expected to get killed. But then again, who does? Now he was damn glad that sliver was there when Jax had chopped off his head.

Because he wasn't truly dead. Not while that sliver grew, spreading like a cancer through Jax's tiny mind, and oh, what fun that had been. How he'd loved Jax going mad. How he'd loved pushing the Shulka further and further over the edge.

Of course, there was no denying that it was fortunate Jax had been captured and taken to Kagestan. And even luckier that Raaku had sensed Darus in Jax's mind.

Raaku accelerated what would have been a long, slow process

and made him all the more powerful. Darus didn't have his healing powers anymore, but Raaku had promised him an even better gift.

Even now, as Darus stood half-naked in the dark in a room in the Kotege, he could feel it growing within him, changing him. Soon, he would be revealed in all his glory, powerful enough to smite down even their ridiculous queen with his bare hands.

Outside his window, he could see the Jians running around, being busy little bees, trying to organise their disastrous little war after the previous day and night's fighting. Jax should've been out there with them, but Darus had needed time to familiarise himself with controlling the old Shulka's body at long last.

Besides, Darus had plans to make. He had a rebellion to destroy. A task that was getting easier by the minute.

Tinnstra was missing, presumed dead, the Meigorian commander with her. And, most interestingly of all, Zorique had also failed to return. The Jian army was all but leaderless. All that was left was the cursed mage, Aasgod, and the two Shulka, Hasan and Moiri, Jax's oldest friend and his beloved. He would enjoy sticking his favourite knife in both of them. Stab. Stab. Stab. In and out. Just like that. There was nothing better than feeling a blade sink into wet flesh, hearing that squelch as the blood sucked onto the steel and watching the light fade from their eyes.

It would be even more special because they'd think it was Jax who was sending them to the Great Darkness.

You monster. Monster. You can't do this. I won't let you, wailed Jax from his cage in his mind. *You are not me.*

Darus grinned. There was nothing he couldn't do. Wouldn't do. Blood would flow and many would be the souls he'd send to the one, true God.

Just thinking about it got his blood pumping. Too long he'd been denied.

He picked up one of Jax's knives from a small table and ran it across his chest, shivering at the sensation. He pressed the blade down ever so slightly, felt it bite and watched it leave a red trail in its wake. No more than a scratch, but it made him so happy to see that crimson streak, to feel the pain. When he reached his

516

hip, he stopped, then wet his thumb with the blood, tasted it. So bittersweet. *Heavenly*.

At least Jax had kept his blades sharp, like the good soldier he was. Sharp and ready for Darus. Sharp enough to kill a queen? Perhaps.

It was easy to imagine Darus's knife sliding in between her ribs. He knew just the spot. Knew his knife would work its magic. Knew all her magic couldn't stop him.

The thought played over and over in his mind. He could hear Jax's screams, feel his own lust. His own arousal.

No.

'Yes.'

No.

'Yes.'

NO!

'Shut up, old man,' hissed Darus.

Suddenly, his room felt too small. He'd spent too much time imprisoned in Jax's mind. He had to get out, be free. Walk amongst the Jians and choose who would die first. Spill some heathen blood.

Darus pulled on his shirt, feeling clumsy with one hand. It had been fun at the time, convincing Jax to cut his own arm off, but now, perhaps it had not been the best thing Darus had made the Shulka do. Even putting on his sword belt was an ordeal. A shame that pretty little Moiri wasn't about to do it for him. Of course, the way Darus was feeling, he'd no doubt cut the woman's throat as a thank you, and it wasn't quite the time to do that, either.

No, he'd find someone special to kill, but not anyone that would be noticed. Perhaps someone important to Jax, but not important to the army. Just a little practice to get his hand bloody once more.

Finally dressed, he all but ran from his room, along the corridor, down the stairs, out into the courtyard. Out amongst all those people and not one looked his way. Not one knew Darus Monsuta walked in their midst.

Now, who to kill?

Someone Jax knew, someone who trusted Jax. A friend. Or friends.

He needed Remie. He needed Sarah.

After all, they'd 'escaped' Kagestan together. As Raaku had planned. So Darus could be here now.

He felt Jax's anguish at the realisation that it had all been arranged, at the memories of what had been done to him in the red caves, in that cocoon under Raaku's hand, and it made Darus smile all the more. That need Jax had felt to be by Zorique's side was placed there by the Emperor, and it was her very magic that had set Darus free.

Darus glanced up, hoping to see the Jian queen flying back, but the sky was empty. No matter, he had some friends to kill the time with.

Dear Remie and Sarah.

Jax hadn't seen much of them since Chita, but he'd checked in on them now and then, made sure they were being looked after, so Darus knew where to go.

And sure enough, there they were. By their tent. Together. A perfect couple.

They both saw him at the same time. They both smiled. Sarah even waved.

Remie rushed over, hugged him. 'How are you, my friend?'

'Never been better,' replied Darus. 'But I need to speak to you both. In private. Something urgent.'

'Certainly,' said Sarah. 'This way.' They led him into their tent, invited him to sit with them. Sarah was on his left, Remie on his right. Just the three of them. The tent flap fell down, giving them privacy.

Perfect. They didn't even notice the knife in his hand, the gleam in his eye.

He smashed his elbow into Sarah's face as hard as he could. As she fell back, he thrust his hand forwards, stopping when the knife was an inch from Remie's eye. 'It's time you and I had a little chat.'

By Kage, how he loved seeing the fear spread across his friend's face. 'What are you—'

'Shhh.' Darus smashed the pommel of the knife into Remie's temple and he, too, toppled to one side. As much as Darus loved hearing people scream, he didn't need the noise to bring others running. Better to be quiet for now. Better to take their tongues to start with.

Darus was on his way back to his room when he met Moiri. Calm. Luckily, he'd cleaned himself up somewhat after he visited his friends. Not everyone liked the sight of blood, after all. 'Any sign of Tinnstra or Zorique?' he asked.

'No,' said Moiri. 'No sign of either of them.'

'I'm sure they're fine,' said Darus, putting his arm around her, pulling her close so she wouldn't see the grin on his face.

'Thank the Gods you're here,' said Moiri, resting her head on his chest. 'I don't know what I'd do without you.'

'Oh, I'm glad I'm here, too.' Darus kissed her, bloody thoughts on his mind, Jax's wail in his ear.

'Hasan wants to leave at dawn for Aisair no matter what. The Skulls will only attack us again if we stay here.'

'I'll make sure everyone's ready,' said Darus. 'Go and get some rest.'

Moiri looked up, her eyes full of love. 'Thank you.'

'No problem. I'll come and join you if I can.' Darus kissed her again and realised how hungry he was.

'Wake me if you need me,' said Moiri.

'I will, my love.' Darus smiled as she walked off. He'd need to get a frying pan from somewhere and see if anyone had some salt. He put his hand in his pocket, checking that the tongues were still safely wrapped up. Nothing like some fresh meat for breakfast.

He might even save some for Moiri.

Then again, maybe not. Murder made him hungry.

73

Ralasis

The Northern Road

Tinnstra was going to kill him.

Ralasis knew that as he chased after her. Even though she had acquiesced to his joining her, she made no concession in the pace she set. The day he'd spent travelling with her and her troops had been scant practice for what he endured now. She was relentless, as if the very Gods themselves urged her on.

He, on the other hand, was merely mortal. A day fighting and a night running after her had all but broken him.

Ralasis would've said something – asked her to stop – but he had no air to spare for such a small ask. Nor did Tinnstra turn around to check on him. She just raced ahead, a shadow in her stolen uniform, while he did his best to keep up. Puffing away, trying to ignore the pain in his side and the ache in his legs.

Still, even that was better than thinking about the madness of what they were planning to do.

Yes, Tinnstra was going to kill him.

Morning sun streaked through the canopy of leaves, providing some light to see by, at least, but also a reminder of how much time had passed since they left the Kotege. He prayed to all the Gods that the Skull attack had been unsuccessful and no more of his men had died.

Of course, he should've been with them, not chasing after Tinnstra. Not running off to get killed.

Tinnstra stopped eventually by a stream. She was kneeling by it, scooping water into her mouth, when Ralasis arrived. He was less gainly and all but collapsed head first into the stream. He could feel her disapproval as he rinsed out his dry mouth and spat into the grass, but he was beyond caring. Probably a good ten miles past caring, in fact.

Once he'd satisfied his thirst, Ralasis rolled over onto his back and groaned. Tinnstra was already on her feet, looking north. 'Don't you ever get tired?' he asked.

'No,' said Tinnstra, not even glancing at him. Her fingers beat a rhythm on the side of the bag on her hip.

'Well, I don't have your stamina. I need to rest every now and again.' He pushed himself up onto his elbows. 'I don't suppose you have any food in that bag of yours?'

Her fingers stopped their tapping. 'No.'

Ralasis groaned. 'Great. Looks like neither of us planned for this trip too well.'

'I have everything *I* need.'

'At least give me a few minutes to—'

'Shush.' Tinnstra tensed, like a snake about to strike. She slowly crouched down. 'Skulls,' she whispered.

The word got his blood racing. His tiredness was forgotten as he rose to his knees and unsheathed his sword, ready to fight.

Tinnstra, though, had other ideas. She waved him back down. 'Leave them to me.' She pulled off her eyepatch and then slipped her hand into her bag. It reappeared clutching the Chosen's mask.

Ralasis shivered as she put it on. It was the second time he'd seen her wear it and he still wasn't used to it. If anything, it was worse this time. She really did look like one of them. Cold, dangerous, inhuman. So very different from the woman he'd rescued.

Tinnstra stood up and shouted something in a language Ralasis didn't understand – Egril, presumably. Someone shouted back, ahead of them to the left.

'Stay out of sight,' hissed Tinnstra as she set off towards the voice.

Ralasis watched her, then peered through the trees, trying to spot the Egril. He picked out snatches of white and heard a horse before he saw it, ridden by a Chosen. The man had his baton in his hand, expecting trouble.

Ralasis shuffled forwards, trying to find a better view. He counted four – no, five, six Skulls. Too many for Tinnstra? He edged forwards some more, concerned now that Tinnstra would need his help.

But maybe she didn't intend to fight. She certainly didn't slow down when the number of her opponents became clear. She shouted something in Egril again and the Chosen answered. He lowered his baton but didn't put it away.

Tinnstra carried on talking, spitting words out like punches, until she stopped in front of the Chosen. The six Skulls stood in a circle around them, but there was no threat in their stance. They seemed happy to listen to their superiors talk.

Ralasis couldn't believe his eyes. No one suspected a thing. They thought Tinnstra was a Chosen. The Egril on the horse actually laughed at something she said. Ralasis smiled, the fear in his gut disappearing. Maybe it wasn't such a mad plan after all.

Then Tinnstra turned and pointed in Ralasis' direction, saying something. The Chosen on the horse tensed up, looking his way. The Skulls all turned, raising weapons. Ralasis' smile fell. She'd told them about him. Betrayed him.

He fell back, feet kicking against the dirt, scrambling away as instinct took over. He had to get away. He had to—

Ralasis almost missed Tinnstra's sword flash out, but there was no mistaking the jagged red gash that opened up across the Chosen's neck. The Egril toppled from the horse as her sword slashed out once more and a Skull helmet flew through the air. Blood sprayed everywhere as the blade sliced left and another Skull fell. The horse reared up, frightened by the death around it, as Tinnstra's blade hacked down another soldier.

By the time Ralasis got to his feet, four Skulls were dead. By the time he'd taken three steps towards the fight, it was over. From start to finish, it had taken seconds.

'Undress the Chosen,' Tinnstra said when he reached her. 'See if his uniform fits you.'

'You killed them all.'

'Of course.'

'But there were seven of them ... what if they'd—'

'They didn't.'

Ralasis stared at Tinnstra, incredulous. Obviously, he'd seen her fight but on those occasions, he'd been trying pretty hard not to get killed himself. But to just watch her slaughter seven men in seconds? That was something else. He was actually frightened of her, if he was being honest.

'Take the Chosen's uniform,' said Tinnstra as she cleaned the blood from her sword with some grass. 'See if it fits.'

'What?' Ralasis had to force his eyes off her and look down at the fallen Egril. Tinnstra had all but beheaded him with her sword. 'Is that why you killed him ... them?'

'Of course. As devastating as you think your smile is, I think you'll need more than that if you're serious about coming with me. The man looks your size. If it doesn't fit, you'll have to use a Skull's armour instead.'

'Right. Right.' He bent down and started to unbutton the man's jacket.

'I'll get the horse while you're trying on clothes,' said Tinnstra.

'Right.' Gods, why did he keep saying that? What had happened to his famous silver tongue? Ralasis' hands were already red with blood as he fiddled with the buttons, and they were shaking so badly it took an age to undo each one. He hoped Tinnstra hadn't noticed, but when he looked up, Tinnstra had gone.

He took his own shirt and jacket off and slipped the Chosen's on. It was soaked with blood, but it'd dry soon enough, he supposed. At least it fitted well. Almost as if it were made for him. That was something. He moved quicker, taking off the man's boots and trousers and swapping them with his own.

Fully dressed, Ralasis had to admit the uniform looked good on him – and the boots! Dear Gods, the boots. They were soft and snug and a thousand times more comfortable than the ones he'd worn halfway across Jia. The Egril, for all their world-conquering evil, certainly knew how to dress well.

'It fits, then,' said Tinnstra, returning with the horse.

'Almost too well,' said Ralasis.

'Don't forget the mask.'

Ralasis had indeed forgotten about it. Or perhaps he'd tried to forget about it. The rest of the uniform was just clothes, but the mask? Well, that was something different. Even taking it off the dead Egril had an effect. Instead of seeing the body of his enemy, the naked man looked like anyone else now. Quite ordinary, in fact.

Ralasis put the mask on and turned to Tinnstra. 'What do you think?'

'You should probably shave at some point.'

'I'll take that as a sign of approval.' Ralasis was a fool for thinking he'd get any words of encouragement. He picked up a sword, feeling its weight. The Skulls knew how to make swords too.

'You can't take that,' said Tinnstra.

'Why not?'

'Chosen don't carry swords.'

'You've got one.'

'Exactly – but I'm an exception. But if both of us turn up with swords, people will start to ask questions.'

Ralasis stared at her. 'What am I supposed to do if we have to fight?'

'You could always try smiling at them.'

'You're going to get me killed.'

'Take the baton.'

'It won't work for me.'

'I know. But you'll look the part.'

'You haven't got one.'

'I look dangerous enough.'

And so she did. Ralasis picked up the baton, testing its weight in his hand. A substantial piece of wood. Ralasis might not be able to get its magic to work, but it would still crack a few heads if he swung it hard enough. Not quite as good as a sword, but better than nothing. He slipped it into the hoop on the Chosen's belt. 'I suppose we'd best be off again.'

'You ride the horse. Hopefully that'll save me from your whining.'

Ralasis laughed and shook his head. 'You say the nicest things.'

In another world, he'd at least pretend to be insulted by her, but in this one? He wasn't going to argue. He took the reins and climbed into the saddle.

'The Chosen said there were many patrols between here and Aisair. If and when we come across any, let me do the talking,' said Tinnstra.

'Won't it be suspicious if I say nothing?'

'I think it'll be more suspicious if you try to say something. No, keep quiet and I'll tell them Kage took your tongue.'

'Wonderful. Look, teach me something – a phrase or a word that I can use. Something that might buy us some time if we need it.'

'We'd have to be well and truly in the shit for that to help.'

Ralasis said nothing. There was no need to point out they were always in the shit.

'*Ya durak*,' said Tinnstra, eventually.

'*Ya durak*,' repeated Ralasis.

'*Yaaa du-raak*,' said Tinnstra again. 'Roll the R sound slightly.'

'*Yaa du-raak*,' repeated Ralasis. '*Ya durak. Ya durak.*'

'You've got it.'

Ralasis smiled. 'I have a talent for languages. What does it mean?'

'It means "I'm an idiot". Now let's go.' Tinnstra marched off and Ralasis heeled the horse forwards after her. Again, a voice told him to turn back, to leave her – she obviously didn't want him with her – but he rode after her instead.

He'd never been one for listening to good advice. Especially his own.

74

Vallia

Aisair

Vallia looked through the bars at the heathen queen and had to smile. She'd done it – captured the most powerful of the False Gods' champions. If she'd not seen Zorique in battle, watched her kill thousands of soldiers with her magic, she'd have thought the queen quite ordinary. In fact, lying on the floor of the cell, she looked barely a woman. 'And she'll be powerless when she wakes up?'

'I've etched the wards into the stone all around her,' said Illius. 'As long as she stays in that room, you have nothing to fear – and even if she gets out, it'll take some time for her powers to return.'

'Well done.' Vallia glanced over at her aide. 'Send word to Kagestan that we have their queen captive, and let His Imperial Majesty know that the rest of the heathen army will be here within days.'

'Yes, Commander.'

'What about the wards for the rest of this floor of the castle?' she asked Illius.

He bowed. 'Soon.'

'What about armour for our soldiers?'

'I'm sorry,' said the scribe. 'The runes worked on the Kojin because of their size and their skin was essentially one surface. Armour is proving more ... challenging. The very thing that makes it so effective against normal weapons – all the different overlapping sections – prevents the runes from activating together.'

'Have you tried painting their skin beneath the armour?'

'I could, but to test it? With the armour, we can stick it on a pole in the yard before we throw magic at it. No one gets hurt if the runes don't work. We experimented on the Kojin – they are not human. If we try the runes out on people ... many will die before we get it right.'

'Many will die?' Vallia almost laughed. 'We live in a city of Jians. We'll get you as many people as you need to experiment on. Kage will thank you for any that you send to the Great Darkness until you "get it right".'

'As you wish.'

'What about the Daijaku? The Chosen?'

'Alas, to mark their skin would undo the Emperor's magic. They would be powerless.'

Vallia didn't want that. 'But they can fight in the city? The runes on the walls won't affect them?'

'Of course, you saw, when the heathen queen attacked, that they can fight at full strength. As long as they don't cross over the wall – and through the runes' area of influence, we can rely on their magic.'

'Thank you,' said Vallia. 'You have made all the difference to our war.'

'I just do my duty, Commander.' The man bowed and scurried off.

Vallia turned her attention back to her prisoner.

It had been a close call. If the queen had arrived in Aisair a day or two earlier, Illius wouldn't have finished the runes in the city wall. She could've wreaked havoc. Even with all the Chosen amassed in Aisair, Vallia still believed the heathen queen could've defeated them.

But Illius had finished his work and the girl had dropped like a stone the moment she crossed over the city walls. One Chosen had flown up and snatched her from the sky, and now here she was, a prisoner of the Egril Empire. As it had be foretold.

Victory in Sekanowari was theirs.

'Open the door,' she ordered.

The guards had to pull back three heavy bolts before they could do as she commanded. The girl stirred as the door creaked open. She lifted her head as if the weight of it was almost too much. Bleary eyes fixed on Vallia in the doorway, and fear rippled across her face.

She lifted her hands up, only for heavy chains to stop them rising more than a foot above the ground. Still, the girl snarled, trying her best to look brave, and thrust her hands towards Vallia as best she could. '*Kasri.*'

Nothing happened. The girl stared at her hands with real fear, then she squealed something at Vallia.

'If that was an attempt to do magic, don't bother,' said Vallia.

The girl said something else that Vallia didn't understand. 'Of course, you don't speak Egril.' She sighed. 'Get me a translator,' she called over her shoulder.

The girl carried on squawking and rattling her chains, but Vallia ignored her and walked to the window. The war would be over soon. The Four Gods would be defeated. She could finally rest. Go back to her home and ... do what? Grow crops? Raise cattle? Vallia had been a warrior all her life. She wasn't sure what she'd do without a war to fight.

'Commander?' An aide appeared in the doorway, smart in his grey dress uniform and mask. 'I was told you need a translator?'

'Tell the girl who I am.'

The aide rattled off a load of babble to the heathen queen. She spat more words back.

'She says she doesn't care,' translated the aide, looking embarrassed.

Vallia laughed. 'Tell her that her powers will not work in this room. She is as harmless as the next person.'

The aide translated, and once more the girl spat words back, growing redder in the face, finding some fury to go with her fear.

'She says to unchain her if you would like to see how harmless she is without her powers.'

'I think not,' said Vallia. 'Tell her it is best that she saves her strength for when His Imperial Majesty arrives tomorrow.'

The girl went very still when the aide spoke. She made no brave retorts, no threats.

'I'm glad you are not stupid,' said Vallia. 'You must understand that your little war is over.'

That drew a bit of fire from the girl, but it was for show.

'She said we'll never win,' said the aide.

Vallia waved the comment away. 'All I want to know from you is who the Fourth Champion is, and why are you keeping their powers hidden from us?'

The queen looked confused as the aide translated.

'She doesn't understand your question,' said the aide.

'Did you translate it properly?'

'I did.'

'Then what doesn't she understand?'

The aide spoke once more to Zorique, listened while she replied, then turned back to Vallia. 'She says they don't have four champions. They're not keeping anyone's powers secret.'

Vallia sighed and crouched down so she was eye level with the girl. 'The False Gods each have a champion in your little army. We know of you, the Shulka woman and the mage. Who is the fourth?'

The aide translated as Vallia spoke. When he finished, Zorique spat in Vallia's face. Most of it went on her mask, but still. She stood, wiped it from her face and dried her hand on her trousers. 'Who is the fourth champion?'

'She still says there isn't one.'

'Why lie? I can bring in the torturers and the mind readers, drag the answers from your brain. Tell me the truth and I will spare you that suffering, at least.'

The girl laughed when the translator finished repeating Vallia's words. She straightened her spine and put steel back into her words.

'She says do your worst. All you will achieve is to turn her truth into your lies,' said the aide.

Vallia nodded, straightened up. 'I admire your courage, girl. You still have a warrior's spirit even without your powers. Let's see how you fare when the questions come with pain.'

She left while the aide was still translating and headed back to her war room. Did it matter that she knew nothing about the last champion? Probably not. If their powers were something to be feared, the heathens would've used them by now.

Unless ... the champion was so powerful, the heathens wanted to catch her unawares. Perhaps. Perhaps.

Vallia hated not knowing. Knowledge was everything. And Raaku had asked her to find out. That mattered more than anything. If he thought it important, then it was.

She looked down at the map. The heathens were mere days away – but what did that matter? She had their queen already and Raaku himself would be in Aisair to welcome them. The Shulka and the mage were no real threats. It would be a massacre.

Unless the fourth champion tipped the balance back in the heathens' favour.

The aide entered the war room. 'Is there anything else you require of me?'

'Find me Chosen Torvi,' replied Vallia.

'At once.'

Vallia stared out over the city. She would send more troops against the heathens, see if that could draw the fourth champion into the open, and she would introduce the queen to the interrogators, as she'd promised.

She had to know the truth.

75

Wenna

The Kotege

'Who did this?' asked Wenna, staring at the bodies.

'No idea,' said Datt, one of Hasan's Shulka. 'Someone noticed they weren't taking down their tent as we were packing up. Found them like this. They told me, I brought you here.'

Wenna bent down to get a closer look at the dead man and woman. The inside of the tent was covered with their blood. 'No one heard anything? Saw anything?'

'No,' said Datt. 'But with everything that's been going on, it's not surprising.'

The chins of both bodies were stained red, and Wenna used her knife to open the man's mouth. His tongue was missing. Probably the woman's, too. There were plenty of other wounds on both bodies as well. Whoever killed them had really done a number on them both. 'Do you know their names?'

'Remie and Sarah. They were part of Moiri's crew that came down from the north.'

'Does Moiri know yet?'

'No. I've only told you.'

Wenna pulled her head out of the tent and stood up, breathing deeply to try and clear her nose of the stink of the dead. It didn't help much – the air reeked of smoke and ash and even more death. By the Gods, the day was less than an hour old and it had already turned to shit. 'All right. I'll tell her.'

'What do you want me to do with them?' asked Datt.

Wenna looked around. The army – if you could call it that – was packed up and ready to move off. They had no time for burials or cremations. 'Leave them.'

She left Datt and went to find Moiri, not liking what the deaths of Remie and Sarah meant. With everything else going on, the last thing they needed was a murderer amongst their number.

Moiri was with Jax and Hasan by the Kotege's main entrance – or what was left of it. They all had the long faces that only bad news made. 'What's happened?' she asked.

'Zorique's missing,' said Hasan. 'And Tinnstra and Ralasis are dead. Or we think they are, at least.'

'When?' asked Wenna. '*How?*'

'Last night,' said Jax.

'Tinnstra and Ralasis were in the woods when the Egril attacked. When Zorique set fire to them,' said Hasan.

Wenna didn't need to look to know all that was left for miles to the north of the Kotege was blackened earth and shards of trees. Zorique had burned an army to death in that fire.

'Zorique went off to look for them,' said Moiri, 'and we've not seen her since, either.'

'Can it get any worse?' said Wenna. It was all too much to take in. She didn't even want to think about the ramifications if their three leaders were gone. She shook her head. 'None of that means they're dead.'

'I know,' said Hasan. 'But it doesn't look good.'

Wenna closed her eyes 'No. Tinnstra's not dead. I know she's not. Nor are the others.'

'Wenna, I understand that it's hard to accept, but they'd be here with us if they were still alive. You know that.' Hasan squeezed Wenna's shoulder, but she shrugged it off.

'Not Tinnstra,' said Wenna. 'She was never going to be here.' She shook her head, feeling her anger rise once more. 'She wasn't just scouting in the woods last night – she'd left for good.'

'What do you mean?'

'I had a fight with Tinnstra the other night, after our meeting.' Wenna reached into her pocket and produced the map that Grace had given her. 'She said I didn't have details about the castle interior, but I did – because she'd asked me to get them.' She passed Hasan the map. 'I wanted to know why she'd lied.'

'What did she say?' asked Hasan, looking at the crude drawing.

'That she had a plan. Told me to give that to you when she was gone.'

'Did she say what she was going to do?' asked Moiri. 'Where she was headed?'

'No. She said I'd try to stop her if I knew. But I presume she's on her way to Aisair, to the castle.'

'Why would she do that?' said Jax, through clenched teeth.

'She wanted to know where they're keeping the Tonin.'

'The Tonin,' repeated Hasan.

Wenna nodded.

'Why would she need to know that?' said Jax. 'Killing their Tonin isn't going to make any real difference to us, to the war.'

'I don't think her intention was to kill it.'

'What do you mean?' said Jax, grabbing her jacket. 'What's she planning to do?'

'Easy, Jax,' said Hasan. 'We're all on the same side here.'

'I don't know,' said Wenna, once Jax had released his grip on her. 'But I think she was far from here when the Egril attacked. If Ralasis was with her, then I'd say both of them could still be alive.'

'Bah,' said Jax. 'It means nothing. They're either dead or deserted. Either way, they're of no use to us. We need to stop wasting time and move out. We've got a war to fight.' The man was visibly angry, almost shaking with fury.

Moiri put a hand on his chest as if to calm him. 'She's not deserted. She's—'

'Left camp, left us, without orders to do so,' finished Jax. 'That's desertion. Now she's holding us up from our mission. I'm sorry. I know she's your daughter and the queen's ... guardian, but that's the truth.'

'We can worry about that later,' said Hasan. 'But you're right that we should move on. Let's get to it. They'll find us when they can.'

Moiri and Jax nodded and moved off, but Hasan stopped

Wenna. 'I want you to take over Tinnstra's crew. They're the best we have, and I don't want them losing focus now their boss isn't here.'

'No problem.'

'I want you to scout ahead of the main army as we march – make sure we don't walk into any nasty surprises.'

'You can count on me.'

'I know. Losing Zorique and the others isn't a good start, but we've got to keep going.'

'There's some more bad news.' Wenna glanced over at the disappearing figures of Jax and Moiri. 'I was about to tell them that two of their number had been murdered last night.'

'Murdered? Are you sure?'

'Both of them were stabbed pretty badly.'

'That could've happened during the fighting last night.'

'Whoever did it cut their tongues out as well.'

'Shit.' Hasan sucked on his teeth. 'That's the last thing we need.'

Wenna shrugged. 'Maybe it was a feud that got out of hand? But I don't think so.'

'And they were two of Moiri's crew?'

'I was told their names were Remie and Sarah.'

'I know those names,' said Hasan.

'You do?'

'Yeah ...' Hasan frowned as he searched his memory. 'Remie and Sarah. I'm pretty sure they were the other prisoners who escaped with Jax from Egril.'

'Gods,' said Wenna. 'To escape from there and end up murdered here. It's not right.'

'Jax will be upset when he finds out,' said Hasan.

'He seemed pretty on edge as it was.'

'With good reason. Man's been through more than the rest of us put together.'

'Is he going to be okay when we get to Aisair?'

'He used to be one of our finest military minds. Even if he's operating at half that level, he's still better than any of us.'

'I hope you're right,' said Wenna. 'You going to tell him about his friends, or do you want me to?'

'Leave it with me,' said Hasan. 'You find Tinnstra's team and make sure we've got a clear path to the capital.'

'Will do.'

'And make sure you look after yourself. I don't want to lose anyone today.'

Wenna smiled. 'May the Four Gods watch over you, Hasan.'

'And you.'

Wenna left him then, feeling sad and tired and not looking forward to a long day ahead. It was hard to imagine peace. The invasion had happened less than a year ago and yet she could barely remember what it was like before the Egril turned up. No, that wasn't right. She could remember it all right, but the memories felt more like dreams of times so long ago they could never be rediscovered.

The thought of being back in Jia was all that had kept Wenna going in Meigore when everything went bad there. Now she was back, things weren't any better. In fact, they were a damn sight worse. And to think there was a murderer in their midst, too.

And not just any murderer. Whoever killed those poor people had enjoyed it, dragging it out and making them suffer. Gods, she didn't want to think about the pain, the fear they'd endured, unable to cry out for help, for mercy.

If Wenna ever discovered who'd done it, she'd make them suffer, too.

Tinnstra's crew were packed up and ready to go when Wenna found them. She recognised Tavis from back in Kiyosun and walked over. 'You waiting for your chief?'

'Aye,' replied the old Shulka. 'How are you? Not seen you in a while.'

'I'm surviving.'

'Can't ask for more than that,' said Tavis. 'You have news for us?'

'Tinnstra left last night on mission of her own. We won't see her again until we reach Aisair. You've got me instead.'

Tavis looked over to the others. 'You hear that? The chief's gone already.'

'Without us?' said a woman, running a knife over the stubble on her head.

'You know Tinnstra,' said Wenna. 'She thought it best to do this one alone.' She hated lying, but it seemed easier than the truth, that no one knew where Tinnstra was or if she was alive or dead. 'Hasan sent me instead. He wants us scouting ahead.'

The woman scowled as she put the knife away. 'We're still getting the fun jobs, then?'

'Come on, Nika,' said Tavis. 'You love it.'

Nika's laugh was cold and hard. 'Yeah, I do.' Definitely one of Tinnstra's.

'You going to introduce me to the rest of them, then?' said Wenna.

'Sure,' said Tavis. 'You just met Nika. The ugly one is Sadir, then there's Nial, Rhea and the gloomy-looking one at the back is Priya.'

'Good to meet you all.' Wenna got nods and hard stares back. It was only to be expected. They were a tight crew. 'I'm not going to try and replace Tinnstra, but I'm not here to just make up the numbers, either. We have a long day ahead of us, but it's no different from all the others before it. Our job is to make sure there are no nasty surprises along the way – same as it's always been – except this time we're damn close to the enemy and they're expecting us.'

'We're good at finding trouble,' said Tavis. 'And not bad at causing some ourselves.'

Wenna smiled. 'We are the dead whom evil fears.'

76

Ange

The Northern Road

They'd only been marching for about two hours, but Ange was jittery as could be, eyes everywhere, searching the trees and the bushes and the shadows for signs of the Skulls. It wasn't helping her nerves that they'd not seen any yet. That just added to her stress. Because she knew the enemy were out there waiting, and every step she took was a step closer to finding them.

She was a few thousand soldiers away from the front of the marching column, her throat sore after breathing in the kicked-up dirt and her eyes itching with all the swirling dust. There was a rhythm to it that she still hadn't got the hang of. Wasn't surprising, really. She'd been off with Garo, doing their own thing, while the rest of the army had marched halfway up the country together. No wonder she didn't feel like she fitted in. Not with the proper soldiers.

Wenna had given her a big arse of a shield to carry and, for some reason, it had only made her feel even more out of place. She didn't know how to hold it properly, and she was shifting it from one hand to the other every few seconds. It didn't help that the weight of the thing seemed to grow with every step she took. Ange was half-tempted to lob it into the bushes and be done with it, but she'd held on to it so far.

Thankfully, they'd put Ange with some other Hanran; a few faces she knew from Kiyosun and then a lot more gathered from the rest of Jia. A tall, lanky bloke called Danni from up

537

north seemed to think he was in charge, but he appeared decent enough, so Ange had no complaints. If he wanted to be making the decisions, good luck to him.

At least she wasn't missing Garo – well, not too much, at least. Gods, she hated that she missed him at all. Said something about the state of her world if that big lummox was the best thing in it. Not that she'd ever tell him so.

Fuck.

'You all right, lass?' asked Danni, dropping back to walk beside her. A long, nasty-looking metal rod rested on his shoulder as he marched – not as nasty as the scar that covered half his face, mind you – but she could imagine getting smacked in the head would leave a mark of its own.

'Just jumpy,' she replied.

He sucked in air through his teeth. 'You're not the only one.'

'You, too?'

'I'd have to be mad not to be a little bit nervous, eh? Hascombe Woods is a damn good place for an ambush.' He pointed to the side of the road with his metal rod. 'An army could hide in there if it wanted to and we'd probably not notice it. And, of course, there's whatever's waiting for us at the end of this road. I know that's not going to be anything good.'

'No. No, it's not.'

'So, yeah, I'm jumpy – like you.'

Ange smiled. 'You're just trying to make me feel better.'

'Maybe. Or maybe I'm trying to make myself feel better. Who bloody knows these days? Does it matter?'

'No. Don't suppose it does.'

'You from down south with that accent of yours?'

'Yeah, Kiyosun.'

'I heard you had it bad down there.'

'I heard it was bad everywhere.'

'You're not wrong.' Danni's manner reminded Ange of her father in many ways. They were both masters of understatement.

'You're from Chita?' asked Ange.

'Yeah. Born there, thought I'd die there.'

'Maybe you will.'

Danni gave her a look that told her what he thought about that.

'We can still hope, eh?' said Ange.

'Sometimes I think that's all we got left.'

'Who'd you lose?'

'My wife. My daughter – she wasn't much older than you.'

'I'm sorry.'

'I'm no different from anyone else. I know you've lost people. Recently, too. You've got that look.'

'That obvious?'

'Look around. Plenty of others in the same boat. Who was it?'

'My parents died in the invasion. Then the lad I was ... I was in love with got killed fighting the Skulls a few months back. Stupid, really. Should be over him by now.'

'Nothing stupid about it. Grief is its own thing. Some days it feels so big inside you, you can't move. Other days, it fools you into thinking it's gone and then some little thing comes along, reminds you of who you lost, and you're being crushed again.'

'I hate feeling like that. Like part of me is missing. Thinking about all the time I wasted when I could've been with him.'

'All the important things that took up our time don't seem so important anymore, do they? Times I went out drinking at the end of a day when I could've gone home and been with my family ... I'd do anything to get even one of those nights back.'

'Instead, we're here.'

Danni nodded. 'Yeah, we're here, doing what we have to, to make sure other people get to do all those things we've done – fall in love, have a family, have a life. And maybe they'll appreciate it more once they've come out the other side of this mess.'

'I thought we were here just to kill some Skulls.'

'That, too.' Danni patted his steel club. 'That, too. Nothing wrong with getting a bit of vengeance along with everything else. In fact, it makes it all the better.'

Ange smiled. 'I'm glad I'm marching with you.'

'Likewise. And stay jumpy. I find that's the best way to stay alive.'

The smile fell. 'I will.' Gods, Ange hadn't been paying attention.

Her eyes flashed back to the foliage, searching the shadows, looking for signs of things that didn't belong. Not that she wasn't looking at anything a few thousand soldiers hadn't already looked at as they marched past. Still, stay careful, stay alive. It was good advice.

Danni moved off to check on some of the others. There was a right mixed bag of Hanran with them; some young, some old, some who looked like they knew what they were doing and others who didn't – and maybe some like her who were good at faking it. At least, she hoped she was good at faking it.

She'd felt more confident when Garo was with her. Compared to him, she came across like some military genius. She wondered where he was now. How was he managing without her? Probably really well. Gods, she hoped he was – if only out of spite towards her. At least he was taking Linx back through territory free from Skulls. That was something. She kind of wished she'd gone with him, taken the chance when Wenna had offered it, but she had to be stubborn. Too stubborn for her own good, as her father would've said when they were arguing over something totally unimportant.

The army marched at a good pace, like they were in a hurry to get this war over with. 'One last battle and it'll be over.' 'Win Aisair and it'll be over.' 'Kill the Skulls and it'll be over.' It was all anyone talked about whenever they stopped. All anyone talked about as they marched. She hoped it was so. She prayed it would be so. Trouble was … she didn't think it would be. Unless 'over' meant 'dead'.

It took all her willpower to keep going, to not just step out of formation and disappear into the woods. Find Garo. Tell him she'd changed her mind. Instead, she kept marching down that road, watching the back of the man's head in front of her and the woods off to her side.

Watching for the enemy.

Maybe that's why she hadn't noticed that the queen wasn't with them. But when the army stopped for a short rest and something to eat, the thought struck her all of a sudden. She craned her neck up, looking for that glow Zorique had around her all the time, but there was no sign of it, neither in the air nor anywhere in their ranks. Even when she got to her feet, she couldn't see Zorique, and that woman's glow was hard to miss. Especially in the woods, amongst all those dark shadows.

The fact was the queen wasn't with them, and the more Ange thought about it, she knew she'd not been around all day.

'What's up, lass? You look worried,' said Danni. He was perched on a stone nearby, having made short work of a heel of bread.

'I was looking for the queen,' replied Ange.

The big man grinned. 'Why's that? You want to have a chat with her about something? I didn't know you were friends.'

'I just realised I haven't seen her today, is all,' said Ange. 'Normally she's zipping around. I kind of liked it. Made me feel safe.'

That got Danni looking, too. 'Now you mention it, I've not seen her, either. But that doesn't mean anything. She's probably off doing stuff.'

'Yeah, maybe. But what if she isn't?'

'What do you mean by that?'

'Fuck, I don't know. What if something's happened to her? What if she's ... gone?' Ange couldn't bring herself to say *dead* – even if that's what she was thinking.

'No way,' said Danni. 'I don't even want to contemplate that. We're fucked if she's gone. I've been listening to some of the stories the others been telling, of what's happened to them on the way up here. Word is that Zorique's the only thing that's kept them all alive. Without her, they'd have been dead within the first few days.'

'A few days?' scoffed Ange. 'They wouldn't have made it onto the beach. The Skulls had thousands of Daijaku bombing the shit out of their boats. Zorique was the only thing that stopped them all being sunk.'

'You're not making me feel any better.'

'Sorry. I didn't mean ... fuck it. Ignore me. What do I know about the comings and goings of the queen? I'm just nervous. I should've fucked off back home with Garo when I had the chance.'

'Who's Garo?'

'Just a lad from Kiyosun. I kept getting paired up with him on jobs for Hasan. Drove me mad most of the time.'

'Where's he now?'

'We saved a kid in that town where we met you lot, brought him with us to the Kotege. The other night, though, one of the Shulka told us where we was going was no place to take a boy. Told Garo to go back to Kiyosun with him.' Ange sighed. 'Told me to go with them, too. But no, I had to stay here, didn't I?'

'Maybe that wasn't your best decision,' said Danni, laughing ruefully.

'Right? And I always said Garo was the stupid one. Turns out it was me.'

'You're being hard on yourself, lass. You—'

They both heard the shouts at the same time, heard steel sing.

'Watch the flanks! Watch the flanks!' someone shouted. 'Skulls are in the woods.'

Ange half-tripped over her bloody shield as she drew her sword from its sheath, her heart already racing. 'You see anything?' She sure as hell couldn't. Only a load of trees and bushes. Even so, she hunkered down behind her shield, grateful to have a heavy bit of wood between her and whatever was coming their way.

'Nothing,' said Danni. 'Fucking nothing.' He gripped his steel pole so tight, his knuckles turned white. 'Keep your eyes peeled,' he shouted louder to the crew around them, trying to sound calm, confident, even over the din of the fighting and dying that was going on up ahead.

'Shouldn't we help them?' asked Ange, not wanting the answer to be yes, if she was being honest.

'Not until someone tells us to,' said Danni. 'Bastards could be on us any minute.'

'I don't like this,' said Ange. She was a city girl. She fucking hated the woods, especially when there were Skulls lurking about. 'I thought Wenna was going to stop the Egril from attacking us.'

'Maybe she tried,' said Danni quietly. 'Maybe they found her first.'

Gods, the thought of that hurt something bad. Wenna had

saved her life back at the Kotege. She fought like a demon herself. If someone like that could fall ... well, best she didn't think
about that.

'Should have fucking gone with Garo,' she mumbled to herself.

'Shh ... Here they come,' said Danni.

Ange peaked over her shield. Sure enough, there they were.
White shadows moving between the trees and heading straight
her way.

77
Darus

The Northern Road

Darus was having the time of his life. He'd never been a fighter, much preferring the privacy of his rooms and the subtleties of his knives, but he had to admit there was a certain joy in hacking someone's head off with a sword. He didn't even care that he was killing his fellow countrymen. After all, the Egril soldiers had no idea he was one of them. If he just stood by, there was a good chance they'd kill him, and having died once, he wasn't keen to repeat the experience. There'd be no coming back a second time.

So, Darus hacked and thrust and parried and killed alongside the best of them. Even with one arm, he was a master of death, and Raaku's gift had already changed him enough that he was faster and stronger than any mere human. There was no one of any real threat to Darus. No one of his calibre.

Nevertheless, while sending his countrymen to the Great Darkness wasn't challenging, it was great fun. It was taking all his self-control not to laugh out loud as blood sprayed everywhere and limbs went flying. Even though the death cries were so intoxicating, it would – perhaps – raise the odd suspicion if his fellow rebels realised he was enjoying himself so much.

He'd hate to ruin the surprise before he had the chance to kill them as well.

Oh yes, the Egril infantrymen weren't the only ones Darus intended to murder. Hasan, Aasgod and Moiri wouldn't make it out of the forest, let alone see the capitol.

The queen was gone, after all. Tinnstra, too, and the Meigorian – whatever his name was. And once Darus had stomped Moiri's brains into the dirt, feasted on Hasan's heart and cut Aasgod's head from his shoulders, the army would be leaderless – except for Darus.

And what carnage he'd cause then. Death by the thousands.

'Watch out!' cried Moiri, blocking a scimitar that was aimed at Darus's head with her shield and then hacking the assailant's arm off. Darus stepped up and thrust his sword into the man's eye.

He spun, dropping low, and swept his sword across a soldier's hamstrings. He went down with a lovely cry of agony and Darus stomped on his face until only a bloody mess was left. Good practice for when he did it to Moiri.

She had her back to him now, fending off all attackers, a true mistress of the blade, trusting Jax to protect her rear. Darus was almost tempted to stab her there and then. A quick thrust with his sword and it would be done. No one would notice.

Instead, he caved in an infantryman's helmet with his sword, shattering the steel with the force of his blow. He rammed the broken blade into another man's face, then scooped up a dropped scimitar to continue the fight.

The cursed mage, Aasgod, threw lightning everywhere, killing dozens with each blast. He, too, was a formidable man. Darus remembered what it had been like to be burned by the man's spells, but Aasgod hadn't been impervious to Skara's axe. He would definitely enjoy killing that man. And perhaps now was the time ...

Darus allowed the ebb and flow of the battle to push him from Moiri's side and towards the mage. He parried an Egril sword and danced back as the man came again. The soldier raised his arm too high, inviting a thrust from Darus straight into his exposed armpit, but Darus declined the opportunity and waited to block the man's next attempt. Sure enough, the fool slashed wildly at Darus's stomach with no real skill, but it was enough to allow Darus to retreat further and take another few steps closer to Aasgod.

Frustration flared in the infantryman's eyes as he pursued Darus, hacking away as if Darus was some tree to be chopped down. It was like fighting with a child. The man deserved no glory in the Great Darkness, no place at Kage's right hand. Bored, Darus flicked his sword blade out and opened a gash across the Egril's throat.

Darus had no time to enjoy watching the man die. Instead, he found another opponent to help him reach the mage. Aasgod was only ten feet away now, close enough for Darus to feel the heat in the air from the Jian's lightning bolts, smell the burned skin and hear the howls of the dying.

By Kage's infinite fury, how Darus had missed the beauty of war.

Again, he carried out the pantomime of defending for his life, pretending to be weak, pretending to be tired, pretending to be Jax. He retreated and retreated, getting closer and closer, until he was but a sword's length away. Near enough to ...

Hasan came crashing over with a dozen Shulka and threw himself into the battle around Darus and the others. 'Thought you might need some help,' he shouted, killing the infantryman Darus had been dancing with.

The Shulka made all the difference to the battle, fresh arms and clean blades doing their work on the Egril. More of the Jian army joined them, and soon it became a rout as the last of His Imperial Majesty's infantry fled back into the woods.

Darus spat after them. They were a disgrace to Raaku, to Kage. They should've fought to the end and found glory in the Great Darkness.

'Good riddance,' said Hasan, coming up beside him. 'All that attack managed to do was give us fewer Skulls to worry about.'

Darus sheathed his sword and found a knife that was almost a needle. 'Thank you for your aid, brother.'

'It was nothing. You had it all under control. I saw you fighting like a man possessed. You were unstoppable.' Hasan slapped him on the back and then slipped his arm around Darus. 'Better than you ever were.'

Darus turned so they faced each other. 'Oh, I'm definitely better than I ever was.'

Hasan must've seen something in his old friend's eyes that he didn't like, because he stiffened and tried to pull away. Too late, of course, to stop Darus slipping that little needle into his heart. Hasan lived long enough to see the smile on his friend's face as he died.

Hasan's legs went and Darus caught him. 'Hasan!' he cried, faking panic in his voice. 'Hasan!' He looked around, saw Moiri. 'Help! Get help! It's Hasan!'

Everyone rushed over, taking their beloved leader off Darus, laying him on the ground. Darus already had his little knife hidden away as he stepped back, giving them room.

'He's bleeding out,' a man called.

'Hasan, stay with us,' cried another. 'You're going to be okay. Just hold on.'

The fools were talking to a corpse, but Darus enjoyed watching them work. Not even the best surgeon could fix a knife through the heart. Back when Darus still had his healing powers, he probably would've found that a difficult wound to mend.

Adding to his enjoyment of the moment, what little remained of Jax wailed way inside his mind. By Kage, it was a beautiful sound. 'Someone save him! We have to save him.'

Moiri was by his side a moment later. 'What happened?'

'I don't know,' said Darus. 'He must have been injured in the fight.'

'But he was talking to you, laughing. How—'

'We've all seen Shulka wounded in battle and carry on, the blood-rush keeping them upright. This is no different.'

'It's the last thing we need,' said Moiri, pressing herself against Darus's chest.

'I know,' he whispered. 'I know.' He thought about killing Moiri there and then – after all, everyone else was stressing over Hasan – but he didn't want to push his luck. Anyway, it would be best to save Moiri for last. He wanted her to know who he really was before she died and know exactly what he'd done.

'By the Four Gods, I'm glad we found you up in Gundan. I don't know how we'd cope without you – especially now Tinnstra's ... missing. You're our only hope.'

'You might not say that by the end of this.'

Moiri smiled. 'I will.'

He wasn't going to argue the point. She'd find out the truth soon enough.

78

Tinnstra

Aisair

Tinnstra stood in the shadows of the forest with Ralasis and stared at Aisair. Fifteen years had passed since she'd run from the place. It looked a lot different from what she remembered; more battered and bruised than ever, and only the Gods knew what horrors waited inside. The setting sun washed the walls with red and orange as shadows crept across the city, adding to its air of demise. Egril flags fluttered, lacklustrous, from buildings and towers alike while Skulls patrolled the battlements.

The ground in front of the city had been cleared as Wenna described, but something had happened to the barricades she'd mentioned. Only a blackened skeleton remained, still smoking from the fire that had destroyed it.

'Did Zorique make that mess?' asked Ralasis. His horse was tied up a few yards further back and happily chewing grass.

Tinnstra nodded. 'Who else?'

'That girl is a marvel.'

Tinnstra glanced at the Meigorian. 'On that, we agree.'

'What now? We just walk up to the front gates?'

'That's exactly what we'll do.'

'I can't help but think there has to be a better way,' said Ralasis. 'What if there are passwords or papers we need to show?'

'We are the Emperor's Chosen. Who will bar our way?'

Ralasis pointed to the Skulls on the city walls. 'They might.'

'Then we kill whoever is foolish enough to try to stop us.'

'Is that going to be your answer to every problem?'

'It's worked so far.' Tinnstra's hand drifted to her pouch. To the Chikara water. Seven vials. Enough for what she needed to do? By the Gods, she hoped so.

'I'd rather you didn't kill me.'

'Then don't be a problem.'

'As my father often told me.'

'Sounds like a wise man.'

'He certainly thought so.'

'You didn't?'

'That's a story for my deathbed,' said Ralasis.

'Let's hope I don't get to hear it, then.' Even with the fire burning, Tinnstra could see the heavy glow of magic behind Aisair's walls. The Egril were definitely taking no chances. Her daughter would face a serious challenge when she reached the city.

'When do you want to go?'

'Later, when it's dark and people are tired. It should be easier to enter the castle then.'

Ralasis nodded. 'I'll get some rest, then.' He walked back to his stolen horse and started to search the saddlebags.

'What are you looking for?'

He laughed. 'I'm hoping the late owner of this horse was better prepared than we are.' His arm stopped moving and he reached deeper in. 'Aha!'

Despite everything, Tinnstra found herself smiling as Ralasis produced something wrapped in cloth.

He grinned as he unwrapped a heel of bread. 'Tonight, Tinnstra, we dine as kings.'

'You have it all,' she replied. 'I'm not hungry.'

'You're not keeping treats to yourself, are you?' He tilted his chin towards her own bag.

Tinnstra hadn't even realised her hand was on her satchel. Her smile fell with her hand. 'No.'

He tore the bread in two and offered half to her. 'Then eat. It's a long way to Kagestan.'

'I said I'm fine. You eat. I'm going to take a look around.'

Ralasis shrugged. 'Suit yourself. But it looks like fine bread – just the right side of stale.'

She walked off, shaking her head. Was it a mistake bringing Ralasis along? She wished she knew. A part of her was glad she wasn't alone, but was it the old Tinnstra who felt that way? The scared Tinnstra?

No, I killed her long ago.

Tinnstra turned back, annoyed with herself for being weak, having doubts. 'Get some sleep once you've finished eating. I'll take first watch. We can trade places in a few hours.'

'As you wish.'

Tinnstra settled down next to a tree and tried not to think about when she'd last slept properly. She felt worn thin by it all. A candle at the end of its wick. She just had to keep going for a little bit longer. One last push. One last war.

She didn't even think about taking out a vial of Chikara water, didn't even think about whether or not she should drink it. She just glugged it down in one. There was no rush anymore. No sense of sudden power. There was just relief as the tiredness that clawed at her bones vanished. The fog in her brain faded.

Tinnstra watched the light from all the Egril magic dance across the city. Aisair was awash in shades of red. Wenna had said there were hundreds of Chosen in the capital and, judging by what Tinnstra could see, that was a conservative estimate.

Still, it didn't matter. She would walk in dressed as one of them and then she'd use their own magic to travel to Kagestan. *I'll end this war.*

'Ralasis.'

He woke with a jerk, confused, his hand going for a sword he didn't have. Then his eyes focused on Tinnstra and he calmed down. 'How long was I asleep for?'

'Four or five hours.'

'Why did you let me sleep so long?' Ralasis rubbed his eyes then stretched his neck.

'You looked like you needed it.'

'You should've woken me earlier,' he grunted. 'You haven't slept.'

'I'm not tired.'

Light flickered through the forest around them, dancing amongst the shadows. Light that came from the city. 'What's going on?' asked Ralasis.

'They lit torches all along the road shortly before dark and then moved out across the open ground. They must think an attack is imminent.'

Ralasis stared at the well-lit road. 'They'll see us from the moment we leave the shelter of the forest. We'll be in range of their arrows by the time we reach the trench. Easy targets under the torchlight.'

'Having second thoughts?' asked Tinnstra.

'No.'

'Then put on your mask. Let's go.'

At least Ralasis looked the part once he'd donned his mask. As long as he kept his mouth shut, they could do this.

They set off, stepping from the security of the dark woods onto the main road – the same road she'd fled down with Aasgod and Zorique so long ago. How long ago had that been in this time? Six or seven months? She wondered if her room had been taken over by anyone yet, or if it was how she'd left it when Beris called on her.

Beris. What would he make of all this? His little sister coming back to fight Raaku? His mother alive? If there was an afterlife, she hoped he was laughing at the insanity of it all.

Tinnstra could feel the eyes on them as they made their way along the main road. The city was no more than a shadow behind the torchlight, but she knew the Skulls would all be on alert now. Beyond the shadows, the magic emanating from the city flared bright, making her squint, sending spikes of pain through her brain. *Ignore it. Ignore it. Ignore it. One slip and we're dead.*

A signal must've been given, though, because the city gates opened. Immediately, the magic from the walls dimmed, offering some respite from the glare, and for that Tinnstra was grateful. So much so, she didn't care that Skulls spilled out of the open gate.

'We can still turn back,' whispered Ralasis all the same.

'No.' They were beyond that now. They were committed.

They proceeded over a wooden bridge that spanned a trench littered with sharpened wooden spikes, and then passed through the burned debris of the barricades. Tinnstra kept her eye on the Skulls at the main gate, ignoring the ones watching from above. She hoped Ralasis was doing the same.

By the time they reached the gates, there were more than two dozen Skulls waiting to greet them. One with three blood-red stripes on his left breastplate stepped forwards and held up his hand. 'Greetings, Chosen.'

Ralasis brought his horse to a stop so Tinnstra halted as well. 'Greetings,' she replied in Egril, sounding far from happy at the interruption.

'We were not expecting anyone to return to the city this evening,' said the Skull.

'So?'

'Commander Vallia has given orders that no one is to be allowed entry into Aisair.' There was a quiver to the man's voice that Tinnstra liked the sound of.

'Do we look like no one?' Tinnstra tilted her head towards Ralasis. 'Does *he* look like no one?' The Meigorian leaned forwards in his saddle, watching the Skull. If Tinnstra didn't know better, she would've believed Ralasis understood every word.

'I don't mean to give offence, Chosen.' The man's eyes went from Tinnstra to Ralasis and back again.

'And yet you do,' she snarled.

'I have my orders.'

'And I have mine. Whose do you think are more important?'

'Commander Vallia—'

'Commander Vallia told me to bring her news from the latest battle with the rebels,' said Tinnstra. 'Now, I suggest you step aside and allow us past so I can inform her of our victory.'

'Our victory?'

'Delay me one moment longer and I'll have you begging Kage for his mercy in the Great Darkness.'

The Skull bowed and stepped aside. 'Forgive me, Chosen.'

Tinnstra started walking again and Ralasis heeled his horse forwards. She fixed her eye straight ahead and ignored the Skulls she passed. They were beneath her attention.

They passed through the gates and, as easy as that, were in Aisair. Tinnstra allowed a smile to flicker across her lips.

Then the doors clanged shut behind them and a flare of magic cut through her. She turned to look back and had to stop herself from shielding her eye from the glare.

'What is it?' hissed Ralasis.

'It doesn't make sense.'

'What doesn't?'

'The magic. It's as if it's coming from the city walls.' She'd not seen the like since …

'Why do we care?' said Ralasis. 'Walls can't hurt us.'

'Dear Gods.' Tinnstra felt sick. She knew where she'd seen walls like that, magic like that. In Layso, around the royal palace. They'd hurt Zorique then, taken all her powers away. The three of them had barely survived the fall.

Ralasis tugged her sleeve. 'We need to keep moving.'

Tinnstra stumbled forwards, forcing her legs to work. 'Zorique won't be able to destroy the walls. She won't even be able to fly over them.'

'Why not?'

'The Skulls must've painted them with the same runes that were carved into the royal palace in Layso. When Zorique flew over those, her powers disappeared instantly.'

'And they plan to do the same here?'

'Obviously.'

'Why weren't you affected?'

'The gates were open, disconnecting the runes.'

'And now they're shut?'

'We're inside the barrier and away from its influence. I still have my powers.' Tinnstra looked around the city at the light from the Chosen. 'The Egril still have theirs – unfortunately.'

'What do we do? Shouldn't we warn the others?'

'We stick to the plan. Zorique and Aasgod will have to find their own way to deal with this.' It hurt Tinnstra to say it, but she could see no other path than the one she now walked. Victory relied on her killing Raaku. If she succeeded, they'd win Sekanowari.

It was hours past curfew and the city was quiet as the grave. Even so, Tinnstra hated to see shuttered windows and locked doors everywhere as the Jians hid away till dawn. She remembered what it was like to live in fear of any noise, any sign that the Skulls were coming for her. It was all too easy to imagine what the people inside the buildings were feeling as they heard the sound of Ralasis' horse's hooves on the cobblestones. And if they peeped out and saw two Chosen? They'd be praying to all the Gods that there was no knock at their door.

Magic thrummed through the city. The Egril had Chosen spread out across Aisair, waiting for Zorique to appear, no doubt. Another challenge her daughter would have to overcome. *This is why we trained. It was never going to be easy.*

At least none of the Chosen came for Ralasis and Tinnstra. A group of Skulls saw them approaching and snapped to attention, saluting as they passed. They were waved through checkpoints without question and twice when they actually came across Chosen, a nod of acknowledgment was more than enough to see them through.

No one questioned the uniform. No one stopped them from going wherever they wanted to go. Now they were in the heart of Aisair and the enemy had no idea they were there.

Tinnstra allowed herself the faintest of smiles. *This is going to work.*

They reached the Grand Avenue, the road that led straight to the royal palace. Wide enough for an army to march down. As a child, she'd witnessed the Shulka do just that, at a military parade in honour of King Roxan the Wise. Such spectacle it had seemed then, so pointless now.

Once they reached the palace, the gates were opened without question. A Skull ran over to take the horse from Ralasis to stable, and as easy as that, they walked up the main steps and into the palace.

If the city was dark and deserted, the palace was a hive of

activity. There were Skulls, administrators, Chosen and Egril in a half-dozen shades of uniform scuttling everywhere. What faces Tinnstra could see were taut with concentration. Whispered conversations filled the air but did little to dispel the palpable tension. Zorique had them rattled.

The Egril had been busy redecorating since the invasion. In true Skull fashion, they'd removed the portraits of long-dead kings and queens, the rich carpets, the side tables and vases – all the luxuries the Jians loved so much and the Egril despised.

Instead, they'd filled the space with their flags and statues of Kage and Raaku and little else. Candles burned in chandeliers and candelabras from one end of the great hall to the other, but they did little to lift the gloom that clung to the corners of the building. And yet, despite it all, there was no disguising the magnificence of the palace. It was magic-made, after all, and it had been built by a true artist. Her journey to the past had given her a small taste of what life must've been like with such power, but she'd met no one capable of raising a building such as this out of the ground.

After making sure nobody was near enough to overhear, Tinnstra drew close to Ralasis. 'The Tonin are in the basement, past the cells. We'll take the main stairs down.'

The Meigorian licked some sweat from his top lip and nodded. 'Lead on.'

It helped that she knew where she was going. She'd spent a year in the palace while her father was stationed there. She'd only been seven years old at the time, but the route through the castle corridors came back to her like a half-remembered dream. Happy days – or so they seemed now. At the time, she'd no doubt complained about a lot. Never about anything important. Dear Gods, if she'd known then what she was to endure in the future, she would've smiled a damn sight more while she could.

Now she walked through corridors where Shulka had once stood proud, offering protection to the royal family. Now she passed Skulls polluting the halls.

As they moved through the castle, Tinnstra could sense magic users as well. There were Chosen – real Chosen – spread throughout the palace. At least a dozen, their energies pulsing red. None were near her, though, and she preferred to keep it that way. The Tonin's auras were almost too faint to pick out, buried as they were in the palace depths, but she found them eventually and locked on to their pale white glimmer.

The stairs themselves were incredible, forming the palace's spine, anchoring the different levels and towers to one another, stretching up and up almost as far as her eye could see.

She climbed the stairs until she saw the walkway connecting to the eastern tower.

The eastern tower where the royal family once had their private quarters. Where Zorique had been born. Where her family had been murdered. Where Larius now lived.

Larius the betrayer.

Tinnstra stopped, her eye fixed on the walkway, remembering a promise made long ago.

Ralasis went a few steps further before he realised she was no longer walking beside him.

He came back. 'What's wrong?' he hissed.

'Change of plan,' said Tinnstra, heading for the stairs up.

79

Tinnstra

Aisair

'What do you mean, a change of plan?' hissed Ralasis, but Tinnstra ignored him, a knife already in her hand. It was a small blade. Perfect for what she needed to do.

Her thumb covered the steel as she climbed the stairs, her hand hanging by her side. She didn't want anyone to see it. She didn't want to frighten anyone. Not yet, anyway.

The stone steps were worn with age, curves made by generations of feet. Up she went, the irony not lost on her that she'd once been too scared to cross the street. Now it was she that should be feared. Ralasis followed on behind, at least with the good sense to keep his mouth shut.

As she exited onto the fourth level, she saw the Skulls had built iron gates across the landing. The two Skulls on guard stiffened when they saw her and Ralasis approach, and they covered their left eye in salute. It represented Kage's lost eye. The same eye she'd lost. The irony wasn't lost on her.

She didn't bother returning the salute. 'Open the gate.'

One of the Skulls moved to obey, but the other wasn't quite so quick. 'We ... we were not informed you would be visiting, Chosen.'

Tinnstra fixed her eye on him. 'I come straight from the Emperor.'

The Skull glanced down the stairs. 'Is the commander on her way?'

She stepped closer. Not even an arm's length separated them. Tinnstra leaned forwards, looking down, kept her voice low. 'I require no company to obey His Imperial Majesty's orders.'

The Skull couldn't help himself from leaning in as well. 'Our orders—'

Tinnstra stabbed him in the throat. Her knife might've been small but, by the Gods, it was effective. His brain probably hadn't even registered he was dead when she pulled the blade free and turned to the other guard.

'Wait—' The Skull raised both hands towards Tinnstra. As if that would stop her.

'No.' This time her knife found his eye in honour of Kage. It might buy the fool some grace in the Great Darkness.

In two seconds, both men were dead and Tinnstra hadn't broken a sweat.

'You've killed them,' said Ralasis, eyes bulging, but she waved him silent, waiting, knife ready in case anyone had heard, but they were alone with the dead.

'See if he's got the keys for the gate,' said Tinnstra, pointing to one of the dead Skulls with her knife as she set to searching the other one.

'What are we doing?' asked Ralasis once more. 'This wasn't the plan.'

Tinnstra found the keys and held them up. 'We're going to see a king.'

'The king? No, Tinnstra. Let's turn back. Stick to the—'

The gates opened silently.

'Get the other one.' Tinnstra dragged the Skull she'd searched through the gates and dumped him out of sight from the main stairs. Ralasis followed her example. 'Someone will see them and there's blood all over the floor. What do we do about that?' he asked.

'Hope no one comes this way,' replied Tinnstra. She locked the gates all the same.

They moved on.

The floor was still decorated in the old, Jian ways – a portrait of Queen Esme, who'd reigned during the Loss of Magic, hung on one wall in an ornate gold frame, alongside one of King Hiro, who'd led the Shulka to victory during the Great Northern Wars. There were other great kings and queens, leaders who'd stood strong when Jia had needed them the most.

There was a new portrait, though, which Tinnstra had not seen before. This one stopped her. Stopped her dead.

It was no king she recognised, but it was a man she knew only too well. A traitor and a cur. A man who had committed fratricide and regicide.

Larius, looking smug in ornate armour, as much a pretend warrior as he was a pretend king. The man who'd let the Skulls murder his brother, King Cariin, and his wife and son. The man who'd tried to kill Zorique. All so he could wear a crown of gold within a gilded cage.

Bastard. How dare he be honoured amongst the great of Jia?

She glanced through open doors as they moved down the floor, looking for the enemy, searching for her target. Some were in darkness, while others were still lit by candles. She passed a music room, a library and a painting room, anger rising. Her army was living in mud-covered tents with hardly enough food to keep going, while this ... this bastard lived in such opulence? Maybe the Egril had the right idea. Tinnstra wanted to destroy it all.

A set of double doors waited for her at the end of the corridor. This had to be the room. Resisting the urge to just kick the doors down, Tinnstra took her time as she turned the door handle, wanting no noise to alert those within. When the gap was just big enough, she gave Ralasis a nod, then slipped inside. Ralasis followed and closed the door quickly behind them.

The room was in utter darkness. Silent except for light snoring from the far side of the chamber.

Still Tinnstra waited, letting her eye adapt.

Shapes began to form out of the darkness; a dressing table, a standing mirror, a small lounge chair and a four-poster bed with the curtains drawn. How lovely.

She walked over, holding the knife in her bloody hand, pulled back the curtain and there he was, sound asleep, with a woman next to him. Probably Grace, the spy Wenna had told her about.

Brave woman. Tinnstra couldn't have slept with Larius, no matter how good the cause.

Larius himself looked older than she'd expected, certainly older than they'd painted him. Hardly surprising, though. These were ageing times for everyone. His hair was long and streaked with silver, as was his well-trimmed beard. Still, he didn't have that gaunt look all her friends had, though. No sign that he didn't know where his next meal was coming from.

And definitely no idea he'd eaten his last.

Tinnstra looked around the room for any clue what that might have been, but there were no plates left lying around. Anyway, Larius would've eaten in that grand dining room she'd passed, waited on by servants and flunkies laughing at his jokes.

She wandered around to the other side of the bed, to get a better look at Grace. She was attractive, Tinnstra would give her that. A classic Jian beauty. The sort that turned heads without trying, the sort other men would lust over. A perfect trophy for a trophy of a king.

Tinnstra placed her hand over the woman's mouth. Her eyes shot open, instantly awake, instantly petrified, breath snorting through her nose as she took in Tinnstra's Chosen uniform.

Tinnstra put a finger to her own lips to warn her to be quiet. Hanran or not, Tinnstra wasn't going to let her scream. Having a bloody dagger in the same hand didn't harm things, either. Made the message that much more powerful.

Luckily for her, Grace turned out to be quite the smart one and she nodded back. Tinnstra pointed to Ralasis, who held up a robe for the girl. Always the gentleman.

Another nod and Tinnstra let go of the girl's mouth. Grace slipped from the bed and straight into the robe, then Ralasis helped her to a seat.

Time now for the main act, the reason Tinnstra was there. Time for Larius to die.

Except it wasn't going to be quick. This time she'd make sure her victim knew why he was going to be killed.

Again, the hand over the mouth. 'Wake up, Your Highness.'

His eyes bulged open and he tried to suck in air through her hand, a scared little cat. Then he saw her mask and managed, somehow, to grow calmer yet more frightened at the same time. Then he saw the bloody knife and got terrified real quick. *Good.*

'Don't scream. Don't shout,' said Tinnstra. 'You don't want to know what I'll do if you so much as squeak.'

Larius probably had a good idea of what that could be, though, as he tried to sink into the bed. Such a pathetic man.

Tinnstra removed her hand and Larius scampered back, sitting up against the headboard. 'Chosen,' he said in Egril, his accent terrible, not registering that Tinnstra had spoken Jian to him.

His eyes flitted around the room, taking in Ralasis standing next to Grace.

Tinnstra slapped him to get his attention back on her, then she removed her mask. 'I'm no Chosen,' she said in Jian. 'I am a loyal servant to the crown.'

He took in her ruined eye and the scars on her face before focusing on her blade. 'Jian?'

Tinnstra nodded. 'Shulka.'

Relief flooded his face. 'Are you here to rescue me?' By the Gods, there was even hope in his voice.

Tinnstra shook her head. 'I serve the rightful ruler of Jia – Queen Zorique. Not you. Never you.'

Larius shook his head – or Tinnstra thought he did. It was hard to be sure as the man was quivering so much from fear. 'Zorique ... Are you here to rescue her?'

That took some of the fury out of Tinnstra. 'Rescue her? What do you mean?'

'She's here in the castle,' said Larius, as confused as Tinnstra. 'She was captured last night.' He shifted position, angling his feet towards the edge of the bed, his crafty eyes flicking to the door.

Tinnstra was on him in an instant, before he could pluck up the courage to run. Again, her hand covered his mouth as she shoved him back against the headboard and thrust her knife into his cheek for good measure.

He screamed against her hand, but she smothered the sound, then gave the knife a little twist before removing it. Blood ran down the usurper's cheek, mixing with his tears. Judging by the new smell in the room, he'd wet himself as well.

Tinnstra leaned closer, their noses all but touching, the knife against the corner of his eye. 'I'm here for justice, *King* Larius. I'm here for your brother, his wife, their son and every Jian you betrayed, just so you could stick a circle of gold upon your head.' She removed her hand, but not the knife. 'Now tell me, before things get bad, where is Zorique?'

'She's in the western tower,' said Grace. 'The Egril commander has her in a room next to her quarters.'

'Is she alive?' asked Ralasis.

'I think so,' said Grace.

'Think so' wasn't good enough for Tinnstra. She turned on Larius. 'Is she alive?' she snarled.

'Yes,' said Larius. 'She's alive.'

Thank the Gods for that. 'How did they capture her?'

'She flew over the walls when the wards were activated. Her powers stopped working.' Larius looked from Tinnstra to Ralasis and back again. 'She fell from a mile up in the air. She would've died, but a Chosen caught her and brought her here.'

Of course, Tinnstra had seen the magic in the walls as they'd passed through, but the wards hadn't been activated because the gates were open. 'And she's in a room in the western tower?'

'Yes. On the fifth level.'

Tinnstra reached out with her powers, searching for her daughter. Normally, her magic shone brighter than the sun but there was no trace of her. 'I can't sense her. There's no sign of her magic.'

'The ... the room she's in ... it's warded. She has no magic.'

'Then why haven't they killed her?'

'They're going to,' said Larius. 'They're just waiting.'

'Waiting for what?' asked Ralasis.

'Raaku.'

'The Emperor is coming here?' said Tinnstra.

Larius nodded. 'Tomorrow night.'

'By the Gods, that's when our army will reach Aisair,' said Ralasis. 'Without Zorique, it'll be a massacre.'

Tinnstra stepped back from the bed, all her certainty shattered, her mind reeling over what to do.

Everyone was watching her, waiting for her to say something.

'Tinnstra, we need to go,' said Ralasis. 'We need to go back, warn the others. Come up with a plan to deal with Raaku.'

'Go back? That's the last thing we'll do,' she hissed. 'This changes nothing. Raaku still needs to die. He *will* die.'

'You're not still thinking about going ahead with your plan? After what we've just found out?' Ralasis shook his head in disbelief.

Out of the corner of her eye, Tinnstra saw Larius inching towards the edge of his bed. She threw her knife and it thudded into the headboard, an inch from Larius's already bleeding cheek. 'Don't fucking move again.'

Larius sank back into his bed and pulled his sheets up to his neck, as if they would offer any protection.

'We go tonight,' said Tinnstra. 'Kill Raaku and then come back and free Zorique.'

'And what if we fail? What then? Raaku kills Zorique? Slaughters our army?' said Ralasis. 'The odds for success were never good in the first place. Now there are too many lives at stake to even try it.'

'There were always too many lives at stake!' By all the Gods, Tinnstra wanted to smash something. 'That's why I have to do this.'

'Just think for a minute,' said Ralasis. 'For once, think.'

'I'm not leaving here to go back to the others,' said Tinnstra. 'We either free Zorique or we kill Raaku.'

'I can get word to your army,' said Grace. 'My father – he runs the Hanran here.'

'Your father does *what*?' boomed Larius, bolting upright.

Grace looked at the usurper with sheer hate in her eyes and a smile on her lips. 'My father is the head of the Hanran in Aisair. And I'm their spy.'

'You treacherous little bitch,' sneered Larius.

Tinnstra backhanded him across the face, sending more blood and a tooth flying across the room. 'When I said don't move, that included your mouth. Another peep from you and I'll cut your tongue out. Do you understand?'

Larius starting blubbering, but at least he followed her orders.

Tinnstra turned back to the girl. 'Can your father get out of the city?'

Grace nodded. 'The Skulls haven't found all our secrets yet.'

'And you can leave the castle without any problems? Take a message to him tonight?'

'It's not easy. There's a chute in the kitchens that they dump all the waste down. I might be able to get out that way. But the Skulls are as paranoid as anything at the moment. They're crawling all over the castle.'

'What if I cause a distraction?'

'That would help,' said Grace.

'Do you have a plan?' Ralasis asked Tinnstra.

'Not much of one. If I hadn't killed the Skulls by the gate, I'd suggest we stay here until Raaku arrives and then free Zorique so she could help us kill him.'

'Kill Raaku?' spluttered Larius. 'That's impossib—'

Tinnstra slapped the usurper again. 'Shut. Up.'

'I could go and get the bodies,' said Ralasis.

'No point,' said Tinnstra. 'As you said, there's too much blood on the floor.'

'So what do we do?'

Tinnstra turned to Grace. 'Wait for my signal, then use the chute. When you see your father, tell him to go to the army. They're on the way here from the Kotege. He needs to find Hasan, Moiri or Jax and tell them Raaku's coming here. Tell them Sekanowari starts tomorrow night.'

'I'll leave immediately. What about you?' asked the girl, putting on her clothes.

'We're going to free my daughter and then we'll hide in the city,' said Tinnstra. 'Wait for the Emperor to arrive – and kill him.'

'Zorique will be well guarded,' said Ralasis.

'So?'

'What about him?' said Grace, tilting her head towards Larius. 'He'll betray you the first chance he gets.'

'I won't,' protested the king through bloodied lips.

'Don't worry about him,' said Tinnstra. 'Now go. Quick as you can.'

'What's the signal?' asked Grace.

'When the alarm bells go off, scarper.'

Grace glanced over at Larius. 'Make him suffer.'

Tinnstra grinned back. 'Don't you worry. I'm going to take good care of him.'

Larius gave a yelp and made a run for the door. He only managed two steps before Tinnstra had him by the collar, yanked him off his feet and hurled him across the floor. The usurper crashed into a table, squeaking as it fell on him.

Grace gave a nod and then she was out through the door and off. Ralasis, for his part, said nothing. He knew they were both committed now.

'Would you mind opening the window?' asked Tinnstra.

Ralasis walked across the room and opened a set of double windows. The view over the city was spectacular and the Meigorian paused for a moment to take it in. 'Very different from home. Not a bad place to die.'

'You're not dead yet,' said Tinnstra. She reached into her pouch and drew out a vial. She didn't bother trying to hide it as she drank. They were past that point.

'What's that?' asked Ralasis.

'A magic potion.' She laughed. 'Keeps me strong.'

The world sharpened into focus and Tinnstra felt the eternal weight of life lift from her shoulders and, with it, the belief that she could rip the world apart with her bare hands.

Tinnstra cracked her neck from side to side, locked her fingers together and stretched them out. 'Right, let's be off, then.'

'The king?' asked Ralasis.

'Hadn't forgotten.' She marched over to the whimpering man, hauled him up and off his feet. 'Of course, he's no king of mine.' His toes barely brushed the floor as she carried him over to the window. 'He's the distraction.'

'Please, I'll give you anything,' said Larius. 'I can make you rich. I can give you whatever you desire.'

'How about some justice?' said Tinnstra. 'Maybe some revenge?'

'What? No. Please!' The king was still begging as she threw him out through the window. Still, he managed a solid scream on the way down and hit the ground good and hard at the end of it.

Tinnstra peeked out after him as a bell started to ring. Skulls ran over from every direction, but there was no way Larius was getting up again. Not unless he knew how to stuff his brains back into his head. 'We'd best be off.'

80

Wenna

The Northern Road

'So much for us finding the trouble first,' said Tavis. The old Shulka looked like he was about to weep. Wenna didn't blame him. She felt like having a good cry herself. But it wasn't the time or the place, and besides, she'd made an oath that she meant to keep.

They were back with the army, with Jax and Moiri and Hasan's dead body. 'They must've come up behind us,' said Kira.

'There are only six of us,' said Sadir. 'We can only cover so much ground.'

Wenna didn't want to hear it. 'We should've spotted them. Hasan's death is on ... me.'

'Yes,' said Jax with a sneer. 'It bloody well is. He trusted you to do a job and you failed.'

Moiri put a hand on his shoulder. 'It's not her fault—'

He shrugged the hand away. 'Yes, it is. This is a war we're fighting, and everyone needs to start doing their damn jobs and acting like soldiers. What scout doesn't spot a bloody army lying in wait?'

'We'll do better next time,' said Wenna. 'We'll take some more people with us, cover more ground—'

'You'll do no such thing,' said Jax. 'I wouldn't trust you to find a hole to shit in, let alone keep us safe. No, you'll join the ranks and we'll move on.'

Tavis stepped forwards. 'Hey, who put you in charge? We—'

'*You* put me in charge, you fool,' snapped Jax. 'When your ineptitude got my oldest friend killed. Look at him. *You* did this!'

'Jax,' said Moiri, 'you're being unfair.'

'It's okay,' said Wenna. 'The general's right. We'll fall in.'

'Good,' said Jax.

'I am sorry, General. Hasan was a good man.' Wenna knew her words wouldn't make either of them feel any better. Nothing could.

Jax turned his back on them. 'Get everyone up and moving. We've no more time to waste here.'

'What about the dead?' said Moiri. 'We can't just—'

'We can and we will,' said Jax. 'The longer we wait, the greater the chance others will join them. We'll come back for the bodies if we win.'

Moiri stood there, looking as if she'd been slapped. 'Right.'

'Come on,' said Wenna to her team. 'Let's find a spot.'

'He didn't need to speak to us like that,' muttered Tavis as they wandered through the ranks, past too many injured and too many dead.

'He's just under pressure,' said Wenna. 'Doing the best he can along with the rest of us.'

Tavis glanced back. 'He doesn't sound anything like the man the Shulka talk about. They say nothing got him riled up and he treated everyone as if they mattered.'

'Different days,' said Wenna. 'We're all different people now.'

'Not that much,' muttered Tavis.

'It doesn't matter,' said Wenna. 'We—' She stopped, seeing a familiar face a few yards away. 'Ange?'

The girl looked around, saw Wenna and smiled. 'Hey.'

'Good to see you,' said Wenna and she meant it.

'You, too! You made it through that last scrap all right, then?'

'We did.'

Ange's face fell. 'You heard about Hasan?'

'Yes. We just left him. He—'

'It's fucked up, is what it is,' said Ange. A tall man with a badly scarred face was standing behind her. 'This is Danni, by the way. Good man to have around when violence is needed.'

'Hi, Danni. I'm Wenna.' She held out a hand. Only the Gods knew why. It just felt like the right thing to do. The man shook it, gave her a nod back.

'You looking for someone?' asked Ange.

'We've been told to join the ranks so we're trying to find a spot,' said Wenna.

'Join us, then,' said Ange. 'We could use some more people who know what they're doing.'

Wenna glanced over at the others.

'It's all right by us,' said Tavis.

'It'll be our pleasure,' said Wenna, and Ange grinned back.

'You don't want to carry that shield you gave me, do you? It's bloody heavy.' Ange held it up. It was scarred and its edge had plenty of bites taken out of it.

'Doesn't look like there's much of it left,' said Wenna.

'Saved her life, that did,' said Danni. 'Some Skull got his sword caught in it. Gave me time to cave his head in.' He held up the metal rod in his hand.

'Told you. Good at violence,' said Ange with a wink.

'You're the right man for this little army, then,' said Wenna.

Orders were passed down the line and everyone started to move once more. On to Aisair. Past the dead.

Wenna tried to lose herself in the tramping of feet along the road, in being surrounded by warriors again, but it was impossible. She knew Hasan was lying beside the road, and a sense of dread built within her as each step took her closer to his body. He'd been a good man, an honourable leader and a true patriot. She knew war wasn't fair, that there was a significant chance all of them would be reunited in Xin's kingdom before too long, but that didn't make the hurt any less.

She remembered the woman back at the caves near Kiyosun, the one with the Weeping Man's tears – Yas. She and Hasan had been close. She'd probably not hear about Hasan's death for months, if ever. Maybe she'd just get that slow dawning that he was never coming back as she watched the horizon waiting for him.

There was a murmur in the ranks as they drew closer, as others saw Hasan's body first, which only added to Wenna's discomfort. She understood Jax's decision to move on and not attend to the bodies of the fallen, but no one liked to see a hero of Hasan's standing tossed to the side of the road.

It was stupid, being afraid of seeing one body, especially since she'd already seen it, but Wenna was. It was as if the accusations of her failure grew louder the closer she got. Hasan had been the one who'd entrusted her with keeping the army safe from ambush and he'd paid for that folly with his life.

And there he was, on the side of the road. One body amongst many, without so much as a blanket to cover his face. Eyes still open as if watching his troops march past.

A sob escaped Ange's mouth.

'Poor fucker,' muttered Danni.

'That's not right,' said Tavis.

Sadir broke from the ranks and ran over. He closed Hasan's eyes with a brush of his hand and then covered the body with his own cloak. For some reason, that simple act of kindness made Wenna feel worse. She should've been the one to do that, not Sadir.

The man returned with a face like thunder. 'He deserves better than that.'

'We'll come back for him,' said Nika, but even she didn't sound like she believed it.

We are the dead indeed, thought Wenna.

81

Ralasis

Ralasis had always thought himself a brave man, but he didn't have the nerves for what they were attempting to do. While Tinnstra walked along like she didn't have a care in the world, he expected to be recognised any minute for the impostor he was. And by recognised, he meant horribly murdered.

At least it was chaos everywhere. Throwing the king out of the window had certainly shaken the Skulls up. Someone was still battering the bell to death, making sure everyone knew there was a drama. Down on the ground floor, Skulls ran this way and that and there were Chosen – real Chosen – everywhere. Some already had batons in their hands, ready to blast some unfortunate soul to ash.

An unfortunate soul like Ralasis.

Thank the Gods, they weren't going down there just yet.

Of course, it was highly unlikely that it would be any better where they were going. Somehow, he didn't think the Skulls would leave Zorique unguarded.

Tinnstra didn't look bothered, though, as she led him back downstairs. Only the Gods knew what that green liquid was that she'd drunk, but it had put a fire in her. She looked fit to do a bit of massacring herself. In fact, she looked right at home amongst the Egril. It was hard to see the woman he ... what? Loved?

No, she fitted in too well with the Egril. She scared him almost as much as the enemy did.

She took the walkway off to the western tower without breaking stride and started up the next set of stairs. Two floors later, they reached another gate. Half a dozen guards stood in front of it, with another two on the far side. Too many for Tinnstra's little knife to do its bloody work.

If ever there was a time to turn back, it was then.

But no.

Tinnstra snapped off a few words in Egril, all but shouting to be heard over the ringing bell, and for about the thousandth time, Ralasis wished he understood what she'd said, not least because he was more than half-convinced she'd happily betray him if it meant getting past this set of guards. What would he do then? Run?

Instead, he stood stock-still while Tinnstra acted as if she owned the place. And whatever she said worked, because keys were produced and the gate unlocked. Tinnstra marched through without a second's hesitation and Ralasis followed. He tried not to flinch as the gate was locked behind them.

There was no easy way out now – unless they left through a window like Larius. Not an option Ralasis was keen on.

They turned a corner and were out of sight of the Skulls. That was something, at least. Doors lined the walls on either side, some open, others not. The question was which one was Zorique beh—

'Aargh.' Tinnstra staggered and fell against the wall.

Ralasis rushed to her side and managed to keep her on her feet. 'What's wrong?'

Tinnstra's head rolled around as if she were drunk. 'Runes. They've put runes in the walls.' Her hand went to her blind eye. 'My powers ... they're gone. I'm blind.'

'Blind?' Ralasis didn't understand. 'You still have one eye that works.'

'But everything else is gone.'

'Can you walk?'

'Yes.'

'Then walk, Godsdamn it. We're here for a reason and we're only going to get one chance at this.'

'I know that.' Tinnstra pushed herself upright and shrugged off Ralasis' hand, then took a step, then another. She looked like a drunk staggering around. She wasn't going to fool anyone.

'Damn it,' said Ralasis. 'Stay here. Don't move. Try and get your head together.'

She must've felt bad because Tinnstra didn't argue. 'What are you going to do?'

'Find Zorique, of course.' He left Tinnstra leaning against the wall, looking fit to drop at any second. What was it they said about best-laid plans? They don't mean shit.

He glanced into the open rooms and ignored the closed ones for now. They all looked ordinary to him – not the sort in which one would keep an important prisoner. No, for that they'd need—

Guards.

He'd turned another corner and there they were. Two Skulls, at the end of the corridor. They both looked his way and one said something. Even if he understood a word of Egril, Ralasis couldn't hear over the ringing of the bloody alarm bell. Ralasis waved in response and walked straight towards them, wishing he had Tinnstra's sword or at least one of her knives. Instead, all he had was a Chosen's baton, and a powerless one at that.

He pulled it out of its belt-loop as he closed the distance to the guards and slapped it into his palm as casually as he could, giving the Skulls his winning smile.

Ralasis passed a large room with a map spread over the table and a magnificent view of the city through large, open windows.

One of the Skulls spouted off some more nonsense and held up a hand in the universal sign to stop. Neither had drawn their weapons, though. That was something. The door they stood in front of had three bolts securing it and a small window with iron bars three-quarters of the way up. Perfect for checking on a prisoner.

The Skulls blocked the corridor, shoulder to shoulder. The one that had been doing the talking kept yammering away, sounding more pissed off the closer Ralasis got. Both had their hands on the hilts of their swords now.

He stopped an arm's distance away and smiled again. '*Ya durak.*'

'*Yon durak?*' repeated the Skull.

Ralasis nodded. '*Ya durak.*'

The skull looked at his friend, and that's when Ralasis hit him with the baton. Gave him a good crack with all his strength, right in the middle of his stupid Skull mask, smashing it open and pulping the bastard's nose. As the Egril dropped, clutching his face, Ralasis swung the club back, going for the other Skull.

The guard got his arm up in time to block the blow, maybe breaking some bones in the process, maybe not. He still had it in him to give Ralasis a good right hook.

Ralasis blocked it with his mouth, went sprawling back and fell over Broken Nose, still on his knees behind him. Ralasis kicked Broken Nose in the face again, putting him down for good this time.

Ralasis got to his feet as the second Skull drew his sword. Ralasis couldn't let that happen, so he lunged, swinging the baton at the Skull's sword-hand. He made contact and got a good yelp of pain out of the bastard before he stumbled past and ended up sprawled across the floor, knocking the air out of himself. Heaving for breath, he managed to turn around, managed to keep hold of that bloody baton.

The Skull came after him, one arm hanging by his side in a way that made Ralasis a bit more confident he'd broken it. The Skull's other hand was still working, though, because the fucker's sword was in that one now. Up close, the scimitar looked twice as big and twice as sharp as any Ralasis had faced. Just his bloody luck.

Thank the Gods, his lungs started to work again – just as the Skull raised the sword high, all set to bury it in Ralasis' head. There was no way he could allow that.

Ralasis clubbed the man in the balls.

The sword clattered out of the Skull's hand as his knees buckled. Ralasis gave him another good swipe as he sank down – straight across the jaw this time. The baton broke from the impact as blood and teeth went flying.

Ralasis dropped what was left of the baton as he climbed to his feet, sucking air into his lungs, sweat dripping from his brow. He gave the Skull a good kick before picking up the fallen scimitar.

He didn't waste any time cutting both men's throats. Tinnstra wasn't the only one who knew how to kill – he just didn't enjoy it as much as she did – but better the Egril were dead and not him.

He staggered to the window in the door and looked through. Zorique looked back, battered and bruised. Their eyes met and Ralasis thanked all the Gods. The queen's eyes were scared, though, and Ralasis remembered he still had on his Chosen mask.

He pulled it off. 'It's me.'

That got a smile. 'Ralasis.'

'Wait there,' he said. A stupid thing to say – the girl was locked in and not going anywhere. 'I'll be back.'

He retraced his steps, found Tinnstra not looking much better. 'Ralasis,' she croaked, more sweat-drenched than he was.

'I found her.' A better thing to say. That brought some life back into Tinnstra, got her moving as he half-carried her towards her daughter.

They were almost there when silence fell over them. Someone had, at last, stopped ringing that bloody bell. For whatever reason, though, it made Ralasis more scared. There had been comfort in that cacophony, a sense of cover. Now, he felt exposed.

He propped Tinnstra against the wall as he searched the dead Skulls. The keys were on the second body, of course, but at least they were there.

The locks sounded painfully loud as he turned the keys. Loud enough to bring the whole castle chasing after them, but there was no stopping now. He rushed in. 'It's okay. Everything's going to be okay,' he promised.

'Ralasis,' croaked Zorique, bloody cuts running in lines across her face.

Gods, he wanted to cry just looking at her. How could anyone human do such a thing? His hands shook as he tried key after key in her shackles. 'Hold on. We'll get you out of here.'

'The room stops my powers,' she said.

'I know. The corridor, too.' Relief hit him as a key slipped into the lock and turned. 'That's it. Nearly done.' He was talking more to himself now – he knew that – but the words helped him focus. The second shackle fell away. 'Can you stand?'

'I think so.' Zorique reached up and Ralasis hooked his arm around her waist.

She felt small and fragile as he lifted her. 'Tinnstra's right outside.'

He half-dragged her into the corridor and released her to Tinnstra's embrace.

'My beautiful girl,' said Tinnstra. 'What have they done to you?'

'Tinn, I'm sorry,' Zorique whispered back.

'I'll go and see if there's a way out,' said Ralasis. He left them, knowing there wasn't. He and Tinnstra might be disguised as Chosen, but Zorique wasn't, and even if she was, she'd not fool anyone. Not after what the Skulls had done to her.

He started to walk back to the main gate then stopped. The runes were in the corridor and the cell, but what about the other rooms on that floor? He pushed another door open and saw no runes. And there was the map room near Zorique's cell, which had no bars over its windows ... and no runes that he could remember.

He ran back, hoping and praying that he wasn't the idiot his father had always believed he was. The two women looked up as he hurtled around the corner towards them.

'What's wrong?' said Tinnstra.

'In here.' Ralasis helped them into the map room and settled Zorique on a chair.

'What are we doing in here?' said Tinnstra, on her hands and knees. 'We need to get out.'

'There are no runes in this room,' said Ralasis, pointing to the walls. He went back to the corridor and dragged the Skulls in one by one, then retrieved their weapons as well, before shutting the door. He thought Tinnstra already had some colour back in her face, but maybe it was just his imagination. 'How are you feeling?'

'You came for me,' said Zorique.

'Of course we did,' said Tinnstra, her voice no more than a

whisper. She used the table to haul herself upright. 'We came the moment we knew you were here.'

Ralasis knelt beside the queen. 'How are you feeling?' he asked again. 'Your powers ... there are no runes here.'

Tinnstra looked around the room. 'There are no runes,' she repeated. Her hands went straight to her bag, rummaged inside and produced two vials. 'Help her drink this.' She passed one to Ralasis.

Zorique saw the vials and shook her head. 'No. No. I hate that stuff.'

'Listen to me,' said Tinnstra. 'It might be our only way out of here. It could take days for your powers to come back without it.'

Ralasis didn't understand what was going on, what the green liquid was, but if it could help, then it was worth taking. He uncorked the vial and held it to Zorique's lips. 'Here.'

She hesitated, staring at Tinnstra, who nodded. She drank, wincing at the taste. Tinnstra knocked hers back in one swallow.

'Now what?' said Ralasis.

Tinnstra shook her head. 'Nothing. It's not working.'

He looked to the queen, who just shook her head.

'What's is it supposed to do?'

'Activate our magic,' said Tinnstra.

'And it's not working? But we're away from the runes.' This wasn't what he wanted to hear.

'Maybe we need to be further away,' said Zorique.

'What if you drank more?' asked Ralasis.

Tinnstra's hand went back into her pouch. 'I haven't got much left.'

'There might not be any point in saving it,' said Ralasis when they heard the noise in the corridor.

He tried moving the table but it weighed a ton. 'Help me block the door.' Tinnstra got to her feet and hauled the table with him and, by the Gods, it moved then. Ralasis grinned as they dragged it against the door. 'You are getting better.'

'Not better enough. Not enough to fight.' She produced two more vials. This time Zorique didn't need help to drink hers.

Voices came from outside the door. Ralasis had no idea what they were saying but they were quickly raised in volume until the men were shouting to each other. 'They're going to start ringing that bell again,' said Ralasis.

Tinnstra drew her sword. 'Get ready.' Someone tried opening the door. It didn't move, causing more shouts. Then shoulders slammed against it. 'We'll take as many as we can with us.'

But Ralasis was looking out of the window, an even worse idea forming. 'You said we're too close to the runes in the corridor for your powers to work.'

'Maybe,' said Zorique.

'I hope you're right.' He threw the window open, then made the mistake of looking down. 'Come on.'

The hammering on the door intensified as the table moved an inch, then two.

'I say we fight,' said Tinnstra, as wild-eyed as Ralasis had ever seen her.

'No,' said Zorique. 'Ralasis is right. Our fight isn't today.' She staggered to the window as Ralasis pulled a chair over to help them climb up. He went first and straddled the window ledge, holding on for dear life with one hand, and helped Zorique up.

Except Tinnstra was staring at them as if they were mad. Behind her, the door banged open further and a Skull tried to squeeze through the gap. She lunged over the table and stabbed him in the arm. He jerked back but two more Skulls started to shove their way in. Tinnstra hacked at one of them, but the other got his sword up in time to block her.

'Tinnstra!' shouted Zorique.

Tinnstra looked from the door to Zorique then back again. 'Shit.' She threw the sword at the Skull before turning and running for the window.

She leaped up and her momentum carried Zorique and Ralasis out through the window with her.

Ralasis screamed as they fell.

82

Darus

The Northern Road

Darus sat in the dark. He could feel Raaku's magic working, its glorious strength changing him. Soon, he would reveal himself to the fools around him. Soon, he would murder them all.

Moiri had made him call a stop for the night with Aisair still a half-day's march away. He'd wanted to continue, but visibility in the forest was minimal and the chances of stumbling into Egril forces were only increasing.

So now, while others slept under their hastily erected shelters, he passed the time thinking about all the blood he would spill. How lucky he was to worship a God who encouraged such brutality, an Emperor who demanded it. He almost pitied the Jians for what was to come – almost, but not quite.

The mood amongst the soldiers was delightfully sombre. Their journey to Aisair had been long and full of death and now, with their talismanic leaders gone, few had hopes of victory. His pointed chastising of some of the more capable Shulka had only heightened the melancholy. Even the hero-worshipping of Tinnstra's special soldiers was finished. They were lost in the ranks, heads full of shame, broken by his words.

Movement snapped him from his thoughts. Moiri sensed it, too, and sat up, rubbing sleep from her eyes.

'Jax. Moiri.' The hushed voice came from Jen. She'd been out on sentry duty, but now she and Cal were ushering two people – an old man and a woman – towards him.

'Who's this?' he asked, getting to his feet.

'Hanran from Aisair,' said Cal. 'Said they've got a message for you both from Tinnstra.'

'Tinnstra's alive?' That wasn't what Darus wanted to hear.

The old man nodded. 'Aye, she is. She's with a Meigorian called Ralasis in the royal palace.'

'Thank the Gods,' said Moiri.

'How do you know this?' asked Darus.

'My daughter ... er ... works there. Met Tinnstra and the other one. They sent her to tell me to find you. So here I am.' The old man sounded too damn pleased with himself for Darus's liking.

'What's her message?' asked Moiri.

'She said Raaku himself is coming to Aisair tomorrow night.'

Moiri's hand went to her mouth. 'Dear Gods.'

'His Imperial Majesty is coming here?' said Darus. The moment he said it, he knew he'd slipped. No Jian would call the Emperor that. Better to laugh it off. 'The high and bloody mighty himself?'

'He is,' said the man.

'Cal, go and get Aasgod,' said Moiri. 'Best he hear this, too.'

Cal shot off like an eager puppy. Now they had to wait and already Darus's mind was back on his knives and what he could do with them.

'What are your names?' asked Moiri.

'I'm Kos,' said the man, 'and this is Emras.'

Darus didn't care who they were. They were dead as far as he was concerned. Their souls already with Kage in the Great Darkness. Like everyone else around him.

The mage came bumbling along. It was hard to believe this Aasgod would one day become the man who had all but killed Darus at the Kotege. 'Tinnstra's alive?' said the mage.

'She was a few hours back, at least,' said Kos. 'The Meigorian and her were going to rescue the queen.'

'What? You didn't say anything about the queen,' snapped Darus.

'She's alive, too?' said Aasgod. 'Thank the Gods!'

'The Egril captured her two nights ago,' said Kos. 'They've

done something to the walls that took away her powers. My daughter wasn't sure what.'

'The Kojin we fought had runes painted on their bodies that stopped our magic,' said Aasgod. 'Same as the Meigorian palace in Layso.'

'How could the Egril have found out about those?' asked Moiri.

Aasgod shook his head. 'It doesn't matter how – only that they have.'

'That's not all the news,' said Darus.

'Raaku is coming to Aisair tomorrow night,' said Kos. 'To fight Sekanowari.'

Aasgod had to sit down at that, visibly shaken. 'The Last War.'

'But if Tinnstra and Zorique are alive and free ...' said Moiri. 'It changes everything.'

'Tinnstra said she'd meet me at my house before sunset, if she manages to free the queen,' said Kos.

'*If* they succeeded,' said Darus. He scoffed. 'Who knows if they rescued her or if they're all prisoners now, waiting to be executed by the Emperor?'

'And Raaku arrives tomorrow,' said Aasgod.

'That's right,' replied Kos.

'If we can take Aisair before Raaku gets there,' said Aasgod, 'we'll give him a welcome he'll not expect.'

'Can we do that?' asked Moiri.

'Perhaps,' said the mage, lost in thought. 'How did you get out of the city, Kos?'

'We have some tunnels the Skulls don't know about,' said the old man. 'We've been using them to smuggle people out of the city like you lot asked.'

'Can we use them to smuggle people *into* Aisair?'

'Yes.' Kos pursed his lips. 'If we're careful, a good few.'

'And how many Hanran have you got in the city?'

'There's about five hundred of us scattered across Aisair.'

'What are you thinking, Aasgod?' said Moiri.

Darus stared at them all, not liking one word of this discussion. 'That I take fifty of our best to Aisair now, with Kos. If we move fast, we'll be there before daybreak. Kos can gather the rest of the Hanran in the city while we wait for you and Jax to arrive with the army. When you attack the city walls, we'll attack the palace – either with Tinnstra or without.'

Moiri nodded. 'It'd be nice if you could get the main gates open for when we arrive. Make it easier to enter the city.'

'I can make that happen, sure enough,' said Kos.

'It could work,' said Aasgod.

'It *will* work,' said Moiri.

All Darus knew was that he wasn't going to let it work. 'I'll come with you, Aasgod.'

'Aren't you needed here with the army?'

'There's no one better than Moiri to lead them,' said Darus, giving the stupid woman a smile. 'No offence, but you're not a military man. I can be of greater use to you in the city.'

'How long will it take to get the fifty ready to go with us?' said Aasgod.

'No time at all,' said Darus with a grin. He'd pick the very best – to stay behind.

Thirty minutes later, they were ready to go. Darus just had one last thing to do. A change of plan. He pulled Moiri aside. 'Come with me.' He led her away from the others, into the woods.

'Is something wrong?' asked Moiri once they'd stopped.

'Not at all.' He looked around. They were alone. 'I was going to wait till later. Save the moment for when Tinnstra was with us. But who knows if we'll have that opportunity?'

'Opportunity for what?'

Darus stepped in close and kissed her on the lips. It was a small, hesitant peck at first, but Moiri took the invitation and the second kiss was deeper, longer. Her arms wrapped around him, pulling him close. She pressed her groin against him, feeling his arousal, thinking it was for her, no doubt. Perhaps, in a way, it was, but not in the way she thought.

He adjusted his grip on his narrow little knife and thrust it deep into her.

Moiri's eyes popped open as she broke off their kiss.

'I wanted you to see me kill your daughter before I killed you, however Tinnstra deprived me of that pleasure by running off. Still, I've always been happy to improvise. This isn't perfect but it's something special all the same.' He smiled as she looked at him in shock. He smiled as he gave his knife a little wiggle, making sure it did enough damage. He smiled as he watched the light fade from her eyes. And, with that, he let her drop into the bushes. He barely had to move the body until she was hidden from sight.

Ah, yes, killing Moiri had been quite delightful.

Darus wiped the knife clean with a leaf before slipping it back into his coat pocket, then returned to the others.

'Shall we be off?' he said.

Aasgod looked around. 'Where's Moiri?'

'She's gone to check on the rest of the troops,' said Darus. 'She wished us good fortune.'

'Then let's head out,' said the mage. 'It's time to win this war.'

'Yes, indeed,' said Darus. He was going to do that all right.

83

Zorique

Aisair

For Zorique, losing her powers had been worse than losing a limb. People survived such losses, carried on with their lives, which might not be as they once were but were lives nonetheless. Even Tinnstra had coped with losing an eye, to the extent that Zorique almost forgot she'd been injured. But Zorique without her powers? That was like trying to live without a heart or a brain – impossible.

When Ralasis suggested jumping from the window, Zorique hadn't needed to think twice. Either she would have her magic back, or she would die. Simple as that. Both options were better than staying a prisoner of the Skulls, to be tortured and interrogated, and then have Raaku do only the Gods knew what to her.

Better to die free if her powers failed to return.

She could feel the Chikara water bubbling away inside her, doing its awful work, trying to ignite a spark of magic within her where there was only darkness. Only emptiness.

Only hell.

Then Tinnstra had jumped, taking both Zorique and Ralasis in her arms, and they fell together.

So fast.

Ralasis screamed.

The castle flashed past as the ground rushed up.

Death waited for them.

Yet Zorique cared not, for her light flared back to life. It sparked as Tinnstra launched them out of the window, and now it blazed brightly as they plummeted down.

It was beautiful. It was glorious. It was freedom.

'*Tobo*.' Zorique almost sang the word.

They jerked in the air as their momentum suddenly halted and Zorique almost lost her grip on the others, but somehow she kept hold of Tinnstra and Ralasis as they began to rise once more.

Light flared from her as her strength returned, but she kept low, skimming over the palace walls and into Aisair. Her power was back, but it wasn't enough. It wasn't what it once was.

'Go east,' shouted Tinnstra over the roaring wind and Ralasis' screams.

Zorique did as her mother asked, dropping below the skyline, trying to lose herself in the maze of Aisair's streets, hoping the buildings would hide her. The Egril would be after them and she knew she wasn't strong enough to fight them yet.

Maybe she never would be again . . .

Even now Zorique could feel her light flickering as the darkness threatened to snuff it out. She dropped lower and lower, slowed and then stopped on some dark street. Her light spluttered and disappeared as they stumbled into an alleyway.

Tinnstra hugged her. 'You did it, you beautiful girl. You did it.'

'By the Gods,' said Ralasis. 'Never again.' He crouched down, then vomited over the cobbles.

Tinnstra examined Zorique's face, not hiding her anger at the cuts. 'Are you okay? Are you hurt elsewhere?'

'Nothing that won't heal,' said Zorique. By the Four Gods, she hoped she would.

'Did they—'

'Nothing that matters.' Nothing that Zorique wanted to talk about. Plenty she wanted to forget.

'We need to get off the streets,' said Tinnstra, looking around. 'They'll be following us soon enough.'

'Where shall we go?' asked Zorique.

'I know a place.' Tinnstra reached down and hauled Ralasis to his feet. 'You can rest there.'

'That ... would ... be ... good,' said the Meigorian.

They moved off together, each helping the other, Tinnstra leading them through the ruined streets, using the shadows for cover. Zorique had never seen Aisair after the invasion – or if she had, she'd been too young to remember. She only knew the Aisair of the past, a place of beauty and magic, of love and laughter. This was nothing like that. Red Egril flags hung off buildings still standing, but more were damaged and broken or all but destroyed.

The three of them were no different. The Egril destroyed everything they touched.

Overhead, Daijaku screeched through the sky, making them stop every few yards. Chosen, too, were flying here and there, their cursed batons glowing in the dark, ready to strike.

Just seeing them made Zorique shiver. Even with the Chikara water still burning through her, she wasn't looking forward to fighting those monsters again. She wasn't sure she could fight anyone.

'This way,' whispered Tinnstra, leading them down a narrow terraced street. She stopped halfway along and entered one of the buildings. The inside was dark and dusty, as if no one had walked its halls in an age. Tinnstra took them upstairs to the third floor. She went straight to one of the doors, reached up and found a key hidden on top of the door frame.

She unlocked the door and ushered them inside.

The room was small: an unmade bed, a small stove, a table with two chairs, a teapot and two cups next to it, another chair by the door and a small chest of drawers near the window. It looked like the occupant had just popped out for a moment, except that everywhere was coated with thick dust.

Tinnstra locked the door and propped the chair under the door handle. She found a small candle in a box over the fireplace, put it in a holder and lit it with a match. 'Welcome to my home,' she said, setting it in the centre of the table. She removed her mask and threw it next to the candle.

'Your home?' said Ralasis, drawing the curtains.

'In another life,' said Tinnstra, staring at the empty teacups.

She shook her head, as if to clear the memories away, and turned to Zorique. 'Do you need to lie down?'

'A chair will be fine,' replied Zorique. Tinnstra helped her sit, handling her with a gentleness long forgotten. It was help she very much needed. Whatever rush the Chikara water had given her was wearing off and she needed to get off her feet.

Ralasis took the other chair, stretching out his legs with a groan. 'Thank the Gods.'

With a shake of her head at the man, Tinnstra turned her attention to Zorique's face again. 'Your cuts are healing quickly. You probably won't even be able to tell that you were hurt by this evening.'

'Good.' Zorique didn't want any more reminders of what had happened. She could remember only too well what it felt like as the Egril carved those wicked lines from cheek to cheek, how they'd cut her elsewhere and remained expressionless the entire time. Somehow, that was the worst of it – that they weren't doing it out of anger or hate or lust. They appeared bored, if anything.

'How's that possible?' said Ralasis.

'The Chikara water,' said Tinnstra. Without a mask or an eyepatch, the ruin of her left eye looked all the more vivid. 'It's one of the benefits.'

'I think I could do with some of that, then,' said Ralasis, dabbing at his bloody mouth.

'It wouldn't work on you,' said Zorique. Even though the water had saved her life, she still hated it. 'You'd need to drink it for years before it will do anything. If you're lucky, it might even send you crazy first.'

'I did it for you,' said Tinnstra, her voice a whisper.

'I didn't ask you to,' said Zorique.

'It was the only way to become strong enough to protect you.'

'And Aasgod gave it to my mother so I'd be strong enough to stop the Egril. Do you feel strong enough to protect me now?'

Tinnstra looked away. 'No.'

'Nor do I. In fact, I've never felt so weak in my life.'

'But we're free,' said Ralasis, full of false cheer. 'And your powers are returning. We have another chance.'

'Do we?' said Tinnstra. 'How many parts of the castle are warded with runes that make us powerless? How many more of their Kojin are immune to our magic? What else do they have waiting for us? It doesn't matter what we do, they're always five steps ahead.'

'What are you suggesting? That we give up?' said Ralasis. 'Only a few hours ago, you thought it was a good idea to go to Kagestan to kill Raaku.'

'You were going to do *what*?' said Zorique.

'It doesn't matter,' said Tinnstra, not meeting her eyes.

'It *does* matter!' said Zorique. 'You weren't in the castle to rescue me, were you? You're not dressed as Chosen because of me.'

'No.'

'We were going to Kagestan,' said Ralasis. 'Except Tinnstra decided she needed to kill your uncle first. He was the one who told us you were a prisoner and that Raaku is coming here to-morrow.'

'You went to kill Larius?'

The Meigorian nodded. 'Tinnstra threw him out of a window. He couldn't fly like you.'

Zorique turned to Tinnstra. 'And how were you planning to get to Kagestan?'

Tinnstra stared out of the window through a crack in the curtains. 'I was going to get a Tonin to open a gate for us.'

'It would have been suicide.'

'To kill Raaku, it would have been worth it.'

'Why didn't you tell me what you were planning to do?'

Tinnstra looked at her daughter then. 'Because you would've stopped me – or I wouldn't have been able to leave you.'

'Gods! Do you know why I got captured?'

'No.'

'Because I thought you were dead. I thought I'd killed you fighting the Skulls and I flew to Aisair in a rage, looking for ...' Suddenly, she was lost for words. It was always the same with Tinnstra. 'I got caught because of you.'

'I'm sorry. I didn't think you'd—'

Zorique shot up, knocking over her chair. She jabbed a finger at Tinnstra. 'You never do. You only ever think of yourself!'

'That's not fair, Zorique. I've given my life to you.'

'I never asked you to.'

'You'd be dead if I hadn't.'

'Ladies, please,' said Ralasis, raising his own voice. 'None of this matters. We're here now, together. Our army is on its way to Aisair and, may the Gods help us, Raaku is coming here, too.'

That shut them both up.

'Now,' continued the Meigorian, 'for months I've listened to you talk of Sekanowari. Thousands of my countrymen have died getting us to this point, and more will die before this is over. So ... save your grievances and recriminations for then. When we're either victorious or dead.'

Zorique shook her head and laughed. 'I suppose there's no point asking you to change if we're all going to die tomorrow.'

'We're not going to die,' said Tinnstra, placing her hand on Zorique's shoulder.

'How are we going to win, then?' asked Ralasis.

'I have no idea,' said Tinnstra.

84

Wenna

The army was in chaos. The sun was up and they should've been moving off, but instead, men and women stood around waiting for someone to give them orders. Wenna pushed through the confusion with Tavis and Nika on her heels. Ange was with them, too. It might not have been the best move bringing the kid along, but Ange had asked and, what with everything else going on, Wenna hadn't felt like saying no.

'Where's Jax?' she asked over and over, but no one knew. 'Where's Moiri?'

'I don't like this,' said Tavis.

'You don't like anything,' said Nika.

'For once, he's right,' said Wenna. Armies relied on their leaders and right then, their army didn't appear to have any. She had a bad feeling that was only getting worse the longer they went without finding anyone in charge. She'd not even seen Aasgod. She stopped by a Shulka she recognised. 'Have you seen Jax or Moiri?'

'Jax left last night with Aasgod,' said the Shulka. 'Moiri should be up ahead, though.'

'Jax left?'

The man nodded. 'We got a message from the Hanran in Aisair. Tinnstra's there with Ralasis. Jax took fifty of us to meet up with them.'

'They did? Why didn't anyone tell me?'

591

That question got a shrug back, but Wenna knew the answer already. Jax didn't think much of Wenna, so why should he tell her?

'Thanks,' she told the Shulka and moved on.

'I told you Tinnstra's alive,' said Tavis. 'She wouldn't run out on us or get herself killed.'

'Aye, that's some good news, at least,' said Wenna. 'We just need to find Moiri now.'

'Over there,' said Ange, pointing to a group loitering on the right-hand side of the road. 'I know them. They stopped some Skulls from killing me over Lanaka way. They're part of Jax's crew. The tall woman is Jen and the bloke with her is Cal.'

They were Shulka, too. That was something. 'I am Wenna of Clan Inaren,' she said as she walked over.

'Jen from Clan Huska,' said the tall woman.

Wenna nodded. 'Ange said you helped her out of a scrape in Lanaka.'

Jen smiled when she saw Ange. 'That's right. Had a troop of Skulls chasing after her. Good to see you're still with us.'

'I'm not sure staying was a great idea,' said Ange, 'but I'm here all the same.'

'I hear Jax left in the night,' said Wenna.

'That's right. Aasgod went, too. They found out that Raaku is arriving in Aisair. They've gone with a man named Kos who knows how to get past the Skulls and into the city.'

'I've met Kos.'

'He's going to open the city gates when we arrive. Aasgod wants us to take Aisair before Raaku gets there.'

'We should be on our way already, then.'

Jen bit her lip. 'We were just saying that ourselves.'

'Have any of you seen Moiri?'

'Not since the others left. Jax said she was checking the ranks, but she's not come back all night.'

'She's not been down our way, either,' said Wenna. 'And we've seen no sign of her since we came looking this morning.'

Jen glanced over at Cal. 'That's not good.'

'Do you remember when you last saw her?' asked Wenna.

'As I said, just before the others left. She went off for a private word with Jax and then he came back on his own.'

'A private word?'

'Yeah, they were lovers. I presumed they wanted to say good-bye properly. After all, there's no guarantee they'll ever see each other again. Not the way this bloody war's going.'

'Where did they go for this chat?'

Jenna pointed into the woods behind Wenna. 'Over there somewhere. I can't say for sure.'

Wenna glanced back at her team. 'Tavis, Nika, go have a look.'

'You think—' said Tavis, but Wenna cut him off with a wave of her finger.

'Don't say it. And if you find anything, leave it where it is. I don't want to spook anyone here.'

'Understood.' The scout and Nika disappeared into the forest.

'Jax wouldn't have hurt her,' whispered Jen. 'They were in love.'

'Do you remember Remie and Sarah?' asked Wenna.

'Yeah,' said Cal. 'They were with Jax at Gundan.'

'Someone butchered them both at the Kotege. Sarah alone must have been stabbed at least thirty times – and whoever did it also cut their tongues out.'

Jen's hand went to her mouth. 'Dear Gods.'

'He was with Hasan when he died,' said Cal. 'He was holding him.'

'Bastard,' said Ange. 'That fucking bastard.'

'Easy now,' said Wenna. 'Let's see what Tavis and Nika find first.'

They didn't have to wait long. The two Shulka came back with faces that told their own tale well enough.

'We found Moiri,' said Tavis, keeping his voice low. 'She's been stabbed through the heart.'

'Jax is a dead man,' said Cal.

Jen shook her head, face white with shock. 'What if he kills Aasgod?'

'The mage can look after himself,' said Wenna. 'We have our own problems.'

'It'll kill this army when word gets out,' said Tavis, 'better than any Skull.'

'Then we make sure that doesn't happen,' said Wenna. 'This stays between us. We act as if Moiri is leading us. Any commands we give come from her.'

'What if someone wants to speak to her?' asked Jen.

'Then Moiri is busy somewhere else and we deal with it.' Wenna stared each one of them in the eye, stopping at Ange. 'Not a word to anyone.'

The girl nodded, but she looked shaken by it all. She was just a street kid, not a Shulka.

'Not even Danni,' said Wenna.

'I promise,' said Ange, not looking Wenna in the eye.

'So what do we do?' asked Tavis.

Wenna stretched her neck from side to side. 'How far away is Aisair?'

'A good half-day's march down the Northern Road.'

'And the Skulls will be expecting us to come that way.'

The old Shulka nodded. 'I reckon so. It's the only way.'

'Is it?'

'Unless we traipse through the forest,' said Tavis. 'But that'll slow us right down and we'll end up being spread out over miles.'

'The Skulls will hear us coming,' added Jen. 'Ten thousand troops stomping through woodland? Might as well ring a bell.'

'And why not?' said Wenna. 'They know we're coming. They know when we'll get there. The only thing we can change is the route we take. So let's go through the woods, spread out as we go, and when we get close enough to Aisair, let's make enough noise to wake the Four Gods themselves. We might just put some fear into the Skulls for once.' Wenna smiled. 'And it'll let Kos know when to open the bloody gates.'

'What if Jax stops him from opening them?' asked Nika.

'Then we get in the old-fashioned way – with blood, sweat and tears.'

85

Yas

Arlen's Farm

As the sun rose, Yas stared at her new village and wondered how it had all gone wrong so quickly. Little Ro was up in the mountains with Timy and Daxam and his absence hurt like a knife in the gut. She knew it was for the best. He was safe there, but Gods, she missed him. They'd managed to sneak out a few other families since the Weeping Men had arrived, but not all of them. If there were no children in the village, it would raise suspicions and then they'd all be in the shit. A hard fact for the ones left behind, but she could only do what she could do.

And it never seemed good enough.

Early-morning mist wove through the tents and huts while most people still slept. With food in short supply, no one had the energy for much else. She'd seen Anan leave with a hunting party a short while before and Venon had taken his crew off to the beach to try their hand with their fishing nets. But what they caught was barely enough to keep the Weeping Men fed.

If Kenan and his men stayed much longer, there'd be bodies dying from starvation left, right and centre. Of course, when they did leave, he wanted to take one hundred of her people back with him as slaves. Fuck knows who he was going to sell them to, but Kenan didn't seem bothered by little details like that. 'There's always a market for flesh,' he'd said.

Bastard.

Yas had sent word down to Simone, asking for the Meigorians' help, but she'd refused. Said they were all too bloody injured to be of help. Bitch.

Now it was up to Yas and her crew to make things right.

Someone stirred from a nearby tent, the sudden noise making Yas jump. It was Sorin, sticking his head out to have a look around. He spotted Yas, gave her a nod and ducked back inside his tent, then came to join her, pulling a shirt on. 'Morning.'

'Yeah, morning.'

'You sleep?'

'Nah,' said Yas. 'Not much.'

The man wiped something crusty from his eye, kept his voice low. 'Things are pretty fucked up, eh?'

'You could say that.' Yas looked at the man, who she'd trusted with her life a few days before, and saw a stranger beside her. 'Then again, you've fitted right in with your old crew.'

Sorin at least had the decency to look embarrassed. 'I'm sorry about that. It's just—'

'Just what? Is it just too hard to turn down getting pissed with your mates or too hard to stop them raping your neighbours?'

'Me and Dean ain't done nothing like that, Yas.'

'But you've stood by while it's been done. Had a good laugh while some poor sod's getting ridden against her wishes.'

'We're just trying not to get our throats cut! You don't know how it is. They're always watching us, testing us, waiting to see where our loyalties lie. One wrong move, one wrong word and we're dead.'

'And where are your loyalties, Sorin? Eh?'

'You know where they are.' Sorin's voice was so low now, Yas could barely hear him.

'Do I?'

He looked around, jittery as could be that someone might hear him. 'I'm with you. I like it here. I like what you're trying to do. I was born into a Weeping Man's life, but it don't mean I wanna die in it.'

'We fight back, there's a good chance you'll end up dead anyway.'

'I might not be keen to get my throat cut, but that don't mean I won't do my bit when the time comes. I promise you.'

'How do I know this ain't some trap to get me killed, eh? Kenan put you up to this? Did he tell you to have a cosy morning chat with me to see where my loyalties are?'

'Yas, none of them trusts you. You're dead the moment they decide to leave. Kenan wants payback for you murdering Raab.'

'Fuck.' If Yas was being honest with herself, she already knew that. But to hear it put into words ... 'How much time have we got until they're off?'

Sorin shrugged. 'Dunno. Not long. They're already complaining about the lack of food and booze. Might be a day, might be three.'

'What about Dean? He on our side?'

'Yeah, Dean's with us. Bros ain't.'

'That bastard'll be one of the first to get killed, I promise you that,' said Yas. 'What about the rest of them?'

'It's not worth even trying to guess,' said Sorin. 'They're a tight crew, been together years. You've seen the stuff they've been doing since they got here. I don't think anyone's kept themselves out of it, apart from me and Dean – and that's already been commented on.'

'Well, we'll need help if we're going to take them on. You, me and Dean won't be able to handle a hundred Weeping Men by ourselves.'

'What about the beach?'

'I sent Venon down to have a word, but Simone said no.'

'Maybe you could ask her in person?'

'Kenan's watching me like a hawk. I've not had the chance.'

Sorin looked around again. 'They're all asleep now.'

Yas gave him a hard look. 'You sure you're not trying to set me up?'

'I promise you, I'm on your side. I like living here.'

Yas took a deep breath. It wasn't like she had much choice. They were dead if she didn't get help. 'All right. Cover for me if they come looking. Say I've gone to check on the crops or something.'

'Will do, Chief. Good luck.'

'When have I ever had that?' With a shake of her head, Yas picked up a water skin from her tent, double-checked she had her knife and set off. She moved carefully through the tents and huts, hoping no one would call out her name. Last thing she needed was a ruckus to wake up the Weeping Men.

So much for being the brave leader.

Luckily, she made it onto the path down to the beach without anyone noticing. Unfortunately, that was where her luck ran out.

He was one of Kenan's men; not very tall, bald on top with scraggy sides, and a long knife on his hip. He was coming out of some bushes when he saw Yas, doing up his trousers after having a piss. The little shit had wound up on sentry duty because he puffed out his chest and tried giving Yas the evil eye. 'Where you off to, then?'

Yas smiled like she was just taking a merry little stroll. 'You been out here all night, lover?'

Scraggy wasn't up for a chat, because his hand was on his knife's hilt a heartbeat later. 'Kenan said no one's to go anywhere.'

'I know,' said Yas, looking down but still walking all the same, closing the gap between them. 'But my son's hungry. *I'm* hungry. Thought I could go and look for food before anyone woke up. Didn't think it would be a problem if no one saw me.'

'*I've* seen you.'

'Have you, though?' said Yas. 'Maybe you didn't?' She was almost within touching distance, so she glanced up then, eyes all big and enticing.

Scraggy checked her out from top to toe, like he really had to think about things, as if he could have a woman like Yas any day of the bloody week. And maybe he could, the bloody rapist. Then he looked around and Yas knew she had him. 'I could forget ... maybe.'

'How about you show me what's behind those bushes?' said Yas with a tilt of her head. 'Maybe there's a spot over there that'll help you forget.'

'Come on, then,' said Scraggy. He turned his back on Yas and headed off the way he'd come, hands already busy undoing what he'd just done up.

The moment he reached the bushes, Yas stabbed the dirty bastard in the back. Turned out after killing a few hundred people, another one didn't bother her none. Her knife was sharp and she put a fair bit of muscle behind it, so it stuck him good and deep – a killing blow like Hasan had taught her.

Scraggy squeaked as it went in, then Yas pushed him into the bushes and out of sight. He went down face first, dead as could be. She pulled her knife free and wiped the blade clean on Scraggy's shirt before slipping it back inside her jacket.

Yas dragged the body further into the undergrowth, grateful that Scraggy hadn't been a few inches taller and a few pounds heavier. Hard enough work as it was, and she had to stop and catch her breath a couple of times before she found a hollow perfect for him. She shoved some dirt over him and then covered him with a few branches. Not the best effort, but it would have to do.

She took another minute to compose herself and then set off again, sticking to the woods until she was well out of sight of the village.

Halfway there, she noticed there were little flecks of blood on her hand. She tried to wipe them off on her dress, but only succeeded in smearing the stains some more. Yas uncorked her water skin and splashed some water over her hands. That got rid of most of the blood but she could still see a bit of a pink stain on her skin. She hoped no one else would notice. If they did ... well, she didn't want to think about that.

The Meigorians had been busy since Yas's last visit. They'd built a barricade of their own using some of the Skulls' demolished defences. And, unlike the Weeping Men, they had proper soldiers manning it.

'I'm here to see Simone,' Yas called out as she approached.

'Wait,' said a guard before sending one of his countrymen off towards the main tents.

Simone didn't bother trying to look like she was happy to see Yas. In fact, she had a face to turn milk sour when she showed up. 'Yas. Been a while.'

'Sorry about that,' said Yas. 'Things are difficult up at the farm.'

'I heard.' Simone just stood there, arms crossed, not inviting Yas past the barrier.

'Can we go somewhere and talk?' Yas glanced at the guards. 'They don't understand Jian too well.'

'Still.'

Simone stared at Yas a bit longer before muttering something in Meigorian. The soldiers moved aside and Yas stepped through the gap in the barricade.

'Thank you,' said Yas.

They walked along the path to the beach. The sun was still quite low over the water, but it was already starting to get warm. Back in the day, Yas had loved mornings like this; blue skies full of promise, the sun glittering gold across the water as her husband Rossi got ready to go out on his boat, especially in the days when she'd been pregnant with Little Ro, both of them caught up in the joy of what was going to be, imaging their lives as parents.

'You've been busy,' said Yas, nodding towards the huts and tents that had been put up along the escarpment. Further along, she could see more of the transport ships – those that had brought the Meigorian troops to Jia – were up and floating once more.

'Not much else to do – except watch people die.'

'It can't have been easy for you all.'

'No.'

'It's not been easy for any of us, Simone.'

'Really? Just how many people are you putting on pyres every day, eh?' Simone stopped walking. 'None. You even had the cheek to send your dead down to us to burn.'

'I just did what I thought was right.'

'Do you know what it's like watching your friends die every day, then watching them burn?'

'I imagine it's not very nice.'

'Nice? It's bloody horrible.' Simone shook her head. 'What's worse is the stink from the fires clings to you so no matter what you do, you're constantly reminded. You can scrub your body in the ocean and it's still there. You can go as far away from the pyres as you're able and the stink chases after you. Even the fish we catch smell of death.'

'I am sorry. I really am.'

'Yeah? Well, we could've done with that sympathy earlier, when it mattered – not now, when you need *us*.'

'We do need you.'

'Tough. The Meigorians have done enough dying for you. Your problems aren't theirs anymore.'

'Come on, Simone. You're one of us. You're from Kiyosun. You grew up a few streets away from me, for the Gods' sake. They're your friends, your neighbours, up at the farm.'

'And not one of them came down here to help.'

'That wasn't personal. Everyone's been busy trying to survive.'

'Ain't that the truth – and that's why the answer's no.'

'The Weeping Men want to take a hundred people with them as slaves when they leave and will probably kill the rest of us as a parting gift.' Yas chewed on her lip. 'I can't let that happen.'

'Then don't.'

'But we have no fighters up at the farm – they all left with Hasan.'

'Anyone can use a knife – you should know that better than most.'

Yas glanced down at her hand, at the pink stain on her fingers. 'It's not as easy as that.'

'It is if you want to live, Yas.'

'So, you won't help us? You're just going to let us be raped and murdered and dragged off as slaves?'

Simone looked away for a moment. When she turned back, some of the steel was gone from her eyes. 'I'm sorry, but the answer's still no.'

'Come on – please. We need to do something tonight,' said Yas. 'I don't think we got much more leeway than that. People are going to die if you don't help.'

'No.'

'Thanks very bloody much, Simone.'

'Yeah? You left us on our own.'

'I told you that was a mistake.'

'Well, as you said, I'm just doing what I think is right.'

'You can put that on my bloody grave.' Yas began the long

601

trudge back to the village, feeling sick. She was out of ideas. Out of bloody hope. She'd been worried about Hasan dying and leaving her alone again. Instead, there was a good chance she'd end up eating dirt herself.

Before she got too close to the village, Yas veered off the main path and headed back through the woods, making sure she avoided the spot where she'd hidden the body. She caught glimpses of the huts and shacks as she made her way around to the eastern side. All seemed quiet still, which was good. She'd be able to slip in unnoticed.

But it was Yas who failed to see the shadows detach themselves around her until it was too late. By then, she had a dozen Weeping Men encircling her.

Bros was amongst them, with his evil grin. 'Kenan wants to see you straight away.'

They took her to the village square where Kenan was waiting at one of the tables. The body of the Weeping Man Yas had killed had been laid upon it. Sorin was bound at his feet.

'Look who's back?' Kenan said with a grin. 'You've been busy this morning.'

'I said you went out with the hunters—' A slap stopped Sorin saying any more.

'It's not your turn to speak. It's lovely Yas's.' Kenan fixed his eye on her. 'I hope you're not going to tell me any lies. My friend Haggers is dead, and I'm thinking this is your handiwork, isn't it?'

'It is.'

Kenan looked surprised by her answer. Maybe he wasn't expecting honesty so quick. 'Mind telling me why?'

'When I tried to leave the village, he stopped me. Asked me to see something in the woods. When I followed him, he tried to rape me.'

'What a naughty boy.'

'Yeah, well, he was the one who ended up getting stuck.'

Kenan nodded. 'He ended up more than that, Yas. He ended up dead and that puts us in somewhat of a pickle.'

'Why's that?'

'You killed a Weeping Man – one of my men – and we have rules about such things. Consequences and punishments and so on.'

Yas didn't like the sound of that. 'What about me? You saying I should have let him rape me? I'm a Weeping Man, too.'

'True. But I liked Haggers. And now you and I know each other better, I can safely say I don't like you.' He leaned forwards so his elbows were on his knees, his face a whisker away from the top of Sorin's head. 'And you managed to turn this fine lad away from his brothers. Maybe that's down to your pretty face or that little hot spot between your legs, but neither is a good enough excuse as far as I'm concerned.'

Yas stared at him. 'What are you going to do?'

86

Vallia

Vallia wanted to be sick. She was standing in *her* war room with Torvi, her aides, Illius and a dozen infantrymen, staring at the open window. She had failed when victory had been in her grasp. 'How did the heathens get inside this building? How did they get onto this floor?'

'We don't know,' said Torvi.

'Were they anywhere else?'

The Chosen nodded. 'We found some dead guards near the gate to the royal quarters. Most likely they were the ones who threw the king out of the window to create a diversion.'

'Well, they certainly did that.' Vallia turned on the scribe. 'And how did their magic work? I thought the runes were supposed to strip them of their abilities.'

'We only placed runes in the cell and the corridor outside the cell,' said Illius. 'The prisoner was never meant to be in this room, so we didn't ward it.'

'And what? They dragged her in here and her powers came back just like that?' Vallia snapped her fingers. 'You told me that couldn't happen.'

'It shouldn't have been so easy. When we've tested the runes against Chosen, it's taken days for their abilities to return,' said Illius. 'The heathen queen should've been similarly affected.'

'But instead she managed to fly straight out of the window!'

'Yes.'

'By Kage, I'm surrounded by incompetence.' Vallia sighed. 'Send word to the Emperor that we have failed him.'

'I will go at once to Kagestan,' said one of the aides.

'In the meantime, let us see if we can rectify the situation. I want this city torn apart – brick by brick, if need be. Use everyone. Use Kojin. Use the Daijaku. Use the Chosen.' Vallia glanced at the aide. 'If they have Kyoryu in Kagestan, bring them back with you.'

'Yes, Commander,' said the aide.

'I'll start organising the search parties,' said Torvi.

'Show no mercy,' said Vallia. 'I don't care if we have to kill every man, woman and child in this city to find the heathen queen and her allies.'

'As Kage wills it.'

'Go, then,' said Vallia. 'Find the girl.'

The others saluted and left. Only Illius remained behind.

'Yes?' said Vallia. She took deep breaths, trying to calm herself. Getting angry now wasn't going to change things. She had to accept the situation.

'I was wondering if you would like me to ward your skin?' asked the scribe. 'Before Sekanowari.'

'The troops are more important.'

'A third have already been warded and my assistants will do more throughout the day. But you are the Emperor's right hand. There is no one more important than you in the city. You must be protected from the heathen's magic.'

'You have everything with you to do the work?'

The man patted a small bag on his hip. 'Yes.'

'Come with me.' Vallia led him from the war room, down the corridor and up the stairs. Her chambers were quiet, tidy and rarely visited by her or anyone else.

As she undressed, Illius lit candles taken from his bag and placed them in a circle by the window that overlooked the western half of the city. When only her mask remained, Vallia stepped into the light. 'How long will this take?'

Illius pulled over a small stool and sat down by her left leg. 'We can ward a soldier with rudimentary protection in twenty or thirty minutes, but I would like to spend more time with you. Be more careful.'

'How long?'

'Two hours ... perhaps. But when I finish ... The magic of Raaku himself could not harm you.'

'That is blasphemy. Raaku is the son of Kage.'

'Nevertheless, it will be true.'

Vallia looked down on the man. She should have killed him for even suggesting such a thing. But this was Sekanowari. Nothing would matter if the Egril did not win. 'Do it.'

The ink was cold on her skin as Illius worked, and his breath warm. Each rune was no more than an inch in height and they curled around her body in lines, forming wards Vallia did not understand. She cared not how their magic worked, in the same way she'd never learned how to forge a sword. That they worked was enough for her, and that she knew how to use them.

She watched the sun chase the last of the night across Aisair's rooftops, aware that by the same time the next day, the war would be over one way or the other. She shivered at the thought and Illius's hand stopped its work.

'Do you need to rest?' asked the scribe. 'Are you cold?'

'No, I do not need to rest. And no, I am not cold. I was raised on the steppes of Egril, forged in its winters and chosen by Raaku himself to lead his armies.'

The man began to paint his runes once more across her upper back. 'You are scared?'

'I have fought for the Emperor for fifty years,' said Vallia. 'Together, we conquered first Egril, then the continent. I personally have lost count of the souls I have sent to the Great Darkness to serve the mighty Kage. Every man, woman or child that has raised a sword against me has died. Until I came to Jia, I had never lost a battle. But I had not fought Gods before, nor their champions. Now all I know is defeat.'

'The scriptures say we will win.' Illius's words were soft and kind.

'The scriptures were written long ago.' Her voice was a whisper.

Illius stopped once more. He had reached her neck. 'May I ward your face?'

'It is death to ask that. Only Kage may see my true face.'

'And yet I ask.' The man smiled. He reached up and removed his own mask. Age had marked his face with its touch, leaving lines and wrinkles across his pale, white skin. 'Like you, I have served our Emperor for fifty years. I haven't wielded a sword, only the brush, but I am happy that I have played my part as Kage desired. I also know you are the last person I will ever ward. When I am finished, I wish to go to the Great Darkness and be with my God. I have no desire to witness what must come. It would be an honour if you sent me there.'

Vallia looked at the man's face. She beheld a beauty there, an innocence, a purity that she'd never seen before. 'You are a godly man, Illius. The honour will be mine.'

She reached up and removed her own mask. No one except her mother had ever looked upon her true face, not even Raaku. She shivered, feeling naked for the first time, but she was aware that this was a day to end all days. The brush was gentle on her skin as Illius painted his runes from one side of her face to the other. He had to stand on his stool to finish the last markings on her forehead, squinting as he worked, chewing on his lip.

The candles were nothing but stubs when he stepped down and examined Vallia. 'Magnificent. Gods will tremble before you.'

'Would you like to pray with me?' asked Vallia.

'It would be a pleasure.'

Vallia walked over to the far side of the room, aware of the runes on her skin as if they were clothes she was wearing for the first time. She retrieved her prayer bowl from a side table and placed it in front of the window, along with a small knife. She and Illius knelt before the bowl and bowed.

They could hear the Daijaku already sweeping over the city looking for the heathen queen. Vallia's troops would be out on the streets, breaking down doors and putting Jians to the sword.

It was, after all, the blood hour.

They began to pray, speaking in unison, speaking the ancient words that were the core of their faith, making their promises to Kage, feeling his presence.

'Blood I will give you, O Great One. Souls I will send you. My body is your weapon. My life, your gift.'

Vallia picked up her knife, nicked her thumb and let the blood drip into the bowl. They were but the first drops of her life that she would shed that day.

She stood, then, runes rippling across her flesh, and walked behind Illius.

'I will see you in the Great Darkness,' he said, tilting his chin upwards.

Vallia held Illius's head with one hand and then swept the knife across his throat, opening up the jugular. Blood sprayed across the room, drenching the bowl and covering the floor and wall below the window.

When she let go, the scribe toppled forwards, already with Kage in the Great Darkness.

And so the day began.

87

Darus

Kos got Darus, Aasgod and the others into Aisair easily enough just before dawn. The woman, Emras, left them immediately with errands of her own to run, while Kos led them to an old, disused inn called the Crook'd Billet and ushered them inside. Streaks of early-morning light sneaked through gaps in the boards covering the windows, illuminating swirling dust disturbed by their entry. It was a filthy hole, a perfect place for the heathens to hide like rats. Still, Darus was in Aisair, close to his own people once more – and soon his Emperor would be there as well, and the killing would start in earnest.

He was happy to be out of sight, too. The Emperor's magic was working away inside him, changing him, hurting him. He could manage the pain now, but if it became worse he'd have to hide from the others until he could get it under control.

'There's some basic supplies in the kitchen,' said Kos, 'but I wouldn't go lighting any fires if I were you. People might notice if there's suddenly smoke coming out of the chimney.'

'We'll be careful,' said Aasgod.

'Right,' said Kos. 'I'll be off. Spread the word about tonight. I'll be back the moment there's any sign of the others at the walls.'

'You be careful, too,' said the mage.

'Goes without saying,' said Kos. 'Lock up after me.'

'I'll see you out,' said Darus. 'I want to check the street one more time. Make sure we weren't spotted.'

'No need, General,' said one of the Shulka. 'I'll go.'

'I didn't ask for volunteers,' snapped Darus. 'I said I want to do it myself.'

'Easy, Jax,' said Aasgod. 'The man's just trying to help. You look tired.'

'There's some beds upstairs you can use,' said Kos. 'Get some sleep before the fighting starts.'

'I will,' said Darus, smiling. 'Now, let me see you out.'

'Good luck, Kos,' said Aasgod. 'May the Four Gods watch over you.'

Dawn stained the streets red as Darus followed Kos outside. Curfew would soon be over, but for now they were alone. It was perfect.

'Which way are you heading?' asked Darus.

Kos pointed east. 'About a dozen streets that way.'

'I'll walk with you a bit further. It's been a while since I was in Aisair. It'll be good to get my bearings.'

'Where were you when the Egril invaded?' asked Kos as they crossed the road, sticking to the darker side of the street.

'Gundan.'

'I heard it was bad up there.'

There was a narrow passageway a few yards ahead of them. It looked nice and dark. 'It was bad everywhere,' said Darus. *In the best possible way.* After all, he'd certainly enjoyed himself in Jia.

'Sometimes I think it's a miracle any of us survived,' said Kos.

Darus stopped suddenly by the passageway. 'What was that?' He looked behind him and Kos followed suit.

'What?' said Kos, looking around. 'Oh.'

His sister, Skara, had made a similar sound when Darus stabbed her. Almost as if they were disappointed at being murdered. Still, it was what it was. Using the knife embedded in Kos's back for leverage, he dragged the man into the darkness of the alley. Once out of sight, he looped his arm around Kos, hauled him up and dumped his body in the garbage. Darus didn't really care if anyone found Kos. Word wouldn't get back to Aasgod and the others even if someone did.

Instead, the mage and his little elite force would sit in blissful ignorance, believing all was well and that Kos would open the gates for Wenna and everyone else.

He cleaned his knife on Kos's body and slipped it into his jacket pocket. There was some blood on his hand, but not enough to worry about. He wiped it on his trouser leg and headed back to the inn.

'All clear,' said Darus once he was back inside. 'We're safe.'

'Good,' said Aasgod. 'Now we wait.' He lifted the straps of his bag over his head, placed the canvas sack on a table and sat down, his hand resting protectively over it.

'Something important inside?' asked Darus, pulling a chair over to join the mage.

'Unfortunately so.'

'And what would that be?'

'It contains—' Aasgod stopped, as if realising he was about to make a mistake. 'It doesn't matter. Just some trinkets of personal value. I probably shouldn't have dragged them all over Jia with me, but I couldn't leave them behind. Silly of me, really.'

It was all lies. Any fool could see that, and Darus was no fool. Something else to look into later. 'I understand. In this world where we have nothing, small things take on new meaning.' He glanced at the door. 'Can we trust this Kos? We only have his word that Tinnstra sent him.'

Darus liked the look of worry that flashed across the mage's face. 'He's one of us.'

'Treachery and death are the only certainties in war.'

The mage's hand stiffened on his bag, making Darus all the more curious as to what it contained. Definitely something important. A weapon, perhaps? 'Make sure we have people watching the street at all times.'

He smiled. 'I'll see to it.'

He left the mage sitting there clutching his bag and assigned a few Shulka to watch duty. Not too many, though, and he'd let the ones he selected get tired and bored before he even thought about replacing them.

There'd be plenty of fighting before Sekanowari was over, and

Darus was going to ensure his soldiers were in as poor shape as he could manage.

No one noticed as he slipped into the kitchens. A barrel of water sat next to a sack of bread and dried meat. It took barely any effort to loosen the cork near the barrel's base so that water began to dribble out. He watched it run straight for the sack and smiled as the cloth quickly darkened. Lovely.

A wave of pain ran through Darus. Raaku's magic was still growing stronger. Pain was good, he told himself. Pain was might. And yet ... his whole body shuddered as if he were being stretched from the inside. Even his stump of an arm burned.

Sweat dripped down his brow as he peered through a gap in the door leading to the main room. No one was watching.

He slipped into the room and made his way straight to the stairs. There were three bedrooms on the floor above, so Darus took one for himself. Once inside, he dragged a small table over and pushed it against the door. It wouldn't stop anyone determined to enter the room, but it would put off a casual visitor.

Once that was done, he took off his jacket and shirt and gasped. Lumps protruded from underneath his skin, running up and down his stomach, over his shoulders, his back, as if something bubbled away beneath. Seeing Raaku's magic at work somehow intensified the pain, and Darus gripped the back of a chair to help keep himself standing.

Pain was good. Pain was necessary. But what was he going to become? Raaku had promised him it would be glorious.

When he was ready, he'd strangle the mage and laugh as the life went from the fool's eyes. He'd kill them all and bathe in their blood.

He'd ... By Kage, it was hard to breathe, hard to think.

He wanted to scream.

He picked up Jax's stinking shirt and bit down on the sleeve as he collapsed on the bed, heart racing, body twitching. Changing.

What would he become?

88

Laafien

Laafien was scared.

He had moments left to live – a fact he'd known for hundreds of years – but that wasn't what had him petrified. It was the changes to the future that worried him the most, the new variables he'd not foreseen and didn't understand, all of which combined in the realization that he had no idea what was going to happen next.

Laafien had his first glimpse of the future when he was fourteen. In that vision, he saw his father dying, withered with cancer, a shell of the man Laafien knew. It was so real, so horrifying. He rushed from his room howling and in tears, only to find his father laughing over breakfast with his brother, Aasgod.

'It was just a bad dream,' said his father, stroking his cheek. 'Best forgotten.'

But Laafien knew it was no dream. He could still see the echo of it in his father's face. The vision and the reality, overlapping and merging, as each moment became a memory marching towards tomorrow.

More visions came. He knew when the rains would arrive and when the sun would shine. He watched seeds sprout, blossom into flowers and then wither away in the blink of an eye. He saw houses appear in fields where wheat grew. He walked down the street and met people not yet born, knowing instantly how they would die.

Often, his mind felt strained by what he saw, threatening to

613

break under the weight of knowledge and the relentless pain that accompanied it. Some visions came in flashes, while others would last for hours, leaving him shivering and shaking on the floor.

His father gave him Chikara water for the first time a few months later, and the vision that followed was clearer and brighter than ever, as if he was living the moment rather than glimpsing something out of the corner of his eye. Skull-faced warriors marched through streets adorned with red flags; while corpses danced in the wind as they dangled from gallows.

He learned then not to speak of what he saw. No one deserved to share the horrors of what he knew.

In many ways, the hardest thing for Laafien to bear in those days was the uncertainty of how much time would pass before his visions became a reality. Some occurred within minutes, but they were the minor things. It was three years before the cancer struck his father. Three years of watching and waiting for the first hint of decay. Even then he saw the first coughs come before they left his father's lungs. He met the healers peddling hope when he knew they would fail.

And he began to wonder how he could change what he saw.

There were things that he obviously had no power over, like the sun appearing through clouds, but there were other things that perhaps he could change, other futures that could be found.

The next day, he reached out and stopped a lady from stepping in front of a carriage. A word in the right ear prevented the robbery of a family friend's home.

And from that moment on, Laafien saw the visions within the visions, the possibilities that shadowed the most probable.

That was when he took Chikara water again and saw his father die over and over, no matter the attempted cures, no matter the men and women sought out. No matter what was done, the final future was always the same: his father dead after months of agony, not just for him but for all who had to witness it.

That was when he foresaw the poison in his hands, the mercy he slipped into his father's wine, the suffering he saved him from, the only future he could stand.

Actually doing it – poisoning his father – was easy after that.

After all, in his mind, he'd already done it and he knew it was the right thing to do.

He waited until after his father's funeral before he began experimenting in earnest, exploring possible timelines and their ramifications, searching once more for the skull-faced warriors and ways to prevent their rise to power.

He saw cities rise and fall. He saw a man of ambition and his delusions of grandeur. He saw the power he would seize and the death he would spread across five kingdoms. He saw the skulls march across the land, bathing it in blood. He saw Sekanowari and the darkness that would follow.

That future was as inevitable as death as he pursued other possibilities over the years. No matter what he alternatives he found, Raaku destroyed the world and everything – everyone – that Laafien loved.

He watched futures within futures within futures within futures within futures within futures, but never any events past Laafien's own death.

He saw himself stand beside a king as the end came, a charlatan of hope. He saw himself die in a cell, chained and alone. He saw himself die with a sword in his hand, leading a charge, behind a shield wall, hanged in a tree, decapitated on an executioner's block, starved, beaten, stabbed, strangled.

Then he saw himself beside the man with ambition, leading him to the secret lake, laying the foundations for a city, a nation, an empire, the end. Laafien's death was always the same then – the cell, the chains, the knife – but Sekanowari became shades of shades of shades of shades. The darkness overwhelming. Almost. There was but a flicker of hope in the hurricane. The barest spark in the shadows.

But it was there.

He began to plant seeds of hope as the days marched relentlessly towards Sekanowari. Laafien found four warriors, Huska, Inaren, Mizu and Rizon, and over many nights and whispered words, inspired them to create the Shulka. He was at Gundan when the first stones were laid in the wall.

For one thousand years, he did everything he could to prepare his home for what was to come, through people who would be long dead by the time Sekanowari arrived. Only his older brother, Aasgod, remained at his side throughout, blessed with the same long life as Laafien. Aasgod, who controlled the lightning. Aasgod, who loved his books. Aasgod, a man of beauty, culture and art who had to be turned into a man of steel, war and mercilessness. It was Laafien who suggested to Aasgod that the country's last mages be militarised. It was Laafien who nudged Aasgod towards one day walking with kings and queens.

Leaving Aasgod was one of the hardest things Laafien had ever done. He knew they would never see each other again. Not in the flesh, at least. Aasgod would die in the coming war in one of a million different ways, and Laafien was destined to end his days in the cell by the Red Lake.

Laafien had wanted to confess to his brother about what he'd done and why, to let him know what was coming. But Laafien knew the consequences of those actions, so he stayed silent, said his goodbyes, hugged Aasgod for the last time and left Jia to search for the man who would be a God.

He was a thousand years old, yet he'd witnessed millennia of futures, lost in a storm of what could be, trying to steer the world towards a spit of safety in a sea of destruction.

Laafien walked towards his destiny, into the land of his enemies, guided by his visions, unarmed and alone.

It took eight years to find the boy who was not yet a man.

Raaku was the same age Laafien had been when he'd had his first vision, but they could not have been more different. Raaku had grown up on the wild steppes of Egril, a harsh land that forged cruel souls, where the strongest survived drenched in blood. It didn't require the sight to see the ambition already flourishing within Raaku, already seeking control of his tribe, recording each kill he'd made with a small scar line on his chest. Fourteen years old and he'd already covered one side of his torso with stolen lives. Fourteen years old and he'd made a mound out of the skulls of his enemies for all to see.

He was clever, too, aware that Laafien could give him something no one else could. Of course, the Jian had explored a hundred variations of their meeting before he approached Raaku. He knew what words would get his head cut off and what would win him a place by Raaku's side.

And all paths led to the cell and the chains. There was no escaping that fate, no matter how hard Laafien looked.

But what was a century of imprisonment if Laafien could stop the end of the world? All the deaths he'd caused wouldn't matter if he could change the outcome of Sekanowari.

So Laafien took Raaku to find the Chikara water hidden under the Red Lake, filling his mind with tales of magic and monsters every night, teaching him how a trained army could conquer the world, helping him imagine what a city built in honour of Kage could look like.

Every night he was plagued with visions of what might go wrong if he made the slightest mistake, how centuries of manipulation and guidance could be undone in an instant. After all, the fates wished Raaku to be victorious. Nearly every timeline, nearly every possible path led to Sekanowari and the fall of the Four Gods.

Nearly, but not all. He could see hope. He could see a light, no matter how small the spark. He couldn't give up. He had to be strong.

Still, Laafien cried the night before they found the lake. He tried to remember everything; the way the wind caressed his face, how the stars sparkled overhead and the crickets chirped their late-night chorus. He gazed at the clouds floating past the mountains and watched the ripples glide across the water. Even the way the fire crackled and sparked as they cooked their evening meal was mesmerising.

It was hard to play the part after that, but play it Laafien did.

He let Raaku have his first taste of real power the next day, and he let himself be chained in the cave as a reward.

It was, after all, inevitable.

Raaku didn't think Laafien's words had power, but he was wrong. Words were all Laafien ever had. His words had shaped two empires. His words could perhaps save one.

For more than one hundred years, his words pushed and pulled

Raaku in the direction Laafien wanted, orientating events towards the spark, finding hope. It was so near yet so far.

He had given everything he possessed, devoted every minute of his life since the first time he'd seen the vision of the skull-faced warriors marching across Jia. He'd made it happen so he could stop it from happening.

Now, the world rested on a knife's edge. Raaku on one side, the Mage, the Shulka, the Queen and the Captain on the other.

Sekanowari. Who would win? He still didn't know. He'd never seen any possible future beyond this day, because this was the day Laafien died.

He'd been hopeful, though. He'd seen all the possible defeats of the Egril army become reality. He'd seen Zorique grow into an almost unstoppable force of nature.

Then Raaku had started work on the egg. Laafien had not seen that in any future before. The egg was different – dangerous.

Raaku was going to take it with him to Aisair. He was planning to hatch it there if the battle went against him, but Laafien had no idea what sort of monster lurked inside.

Would it make the difference? Would it win the war for Raaku?

Gods, if only he knew. But he didn't. It was time to die.

The door opened and Raaku entered, dressed in jet-black armour, a scimitar on his hip. 'The end is here, Laafien.'

'I know.' Laafien closed his eyes. He didn't ask about the egg. He realised that, after a lifetime of witnessing every possible future, he didn't want to know. He'd rather die with a glimmer of hope in his heart.

Raaku's sword rasped out of its scabbard.

Laafien bowed his head.

'Goodbye, my friend,' said Raaku, as Laafien knew he would.

Part VI

Sekanowari

89

Tinnstra

Aisair

Dawn. Another day. Maybe their last day. It was fitting, perhaps, that Tinnstra was back in her old rooms in Aisair, where it had all started. She sat by the window, watching the world outside, looking for threats.

Curfew over, people started to appear on the street below, scuttling about, doing whatever they had to do to survive another day – trying to find food, or money to buy food, keeping their heads down so the Skulls didn't notice them. Tinnstra knew the routine well. She'd perfected it back then.

And now she was getting ready to fight Sekanowari. Against the son of a God.

No, Raaku is only a human, changed by Chikara water – just like Zorique and I. Don't forget that.

Still, that was easier said than done. The previous night had scared her. The runes had taken her confidence along with her powers. Gods, if not for Ralasis, she'd have been captured with Zorique.

Zorique lay sleeping in Tinnstra's old bed, and for that Tinnstra was very grateful. Her daughter needed all the rest she could get.

She glanced over at the Meigorian. He was lying on the floor, wrapped up in a blanket. Of course, he was awake and caught her looking at him.

'How are you feeling?' he asked, keeping his voice low.

'Fine.' She almost winced like Ralasis did at the curtness of her answer. It wasn't his fault she felt awkward, that she hated feeling vulnerable. 'I mean ... I'm better, thank you. You saved us last night.'

'The least I could do.' He sat up, rubbed his eyes. 'It was for purely selfish reasons, though. I'd have been dead without you two to save me.'

'Well, no matter your reasons, it was appreciated.'

Ralasis stood up, glanced at the sleeping Zorique, then walked over to join Tinnstra by the window, bringing a chair with him. 'What's the plan? Stay here until we meet with Grace's father?'

Tinnstra nodded. 'It's as good a place as any.'

'Last night ... we were very lucky. It could've easily gone the other way.'

Tinnstra felt her anger flare, but she forced it back down. 'I know.'

'You're an amazing woman, Tinnstra. You know that, right?'

'Ralasis—'

He held up a hand. 'Hear me out, eh?'

'Fine.'

'You are an amazing woman – but sometimes I think you want to fight the world by yourself, and if you do that, we're all going to lose.'

'That's not true,' said Tinnstra, but even she didn't believe her words.

'No? So that wasn't you I chased after the other night? Who I had to beg to join on a suicide mission?'

'I thought I could stop this war.'

'I know. Your heart's in the right place – most of the time. But you need to remember that your only enemy is the Egril. The rest of us – me, Zorique, Aasgod – we're all on your side. You don't need to fight *us*.'

'I don't mean to ... it's just ...' She waved a hand. 'Aasgod ... he ...'

'I know. He's a pain in the neck, and when this is over – and if we're still alive – he can return to the past and the rest of us can all go our separate ways, never to speak again – if that's what you want. But now? Today? You need us as much as we need you.

Together, the four of us have a chance. Alone? We're all dead.'

The breath caught in Tinnstra's throat. 'The four of us?'

'That's right.'

'The Four against the One.' She couldn't believe it. She sat back. 'I'm an idiot.'

Ralasis laughed. 'I wouldn't go that far.'

'No, you don't understand. I had this book on Sekanowari. It was written by an Egril called Kristoff a long time ago.'

'I think I've seen you reading it.'

She shook her head. 'I left it back at the Kotege – I thought it was useless – but it talked about how Champions would come from the people of the Four Gods. I knew Zorique was one. I thought maybe Aasgod was another at first, until I got to know him. I even joked to Zorique that you could be another.'

'Really? That's almost a compliment.'

'I had just slept with you – don't let it go to your head.'

'I must admit people have told me I was Godlike before, but I've never let it go to my head,' said Ralasis with a wink. 'Still, you, Aasgod and Zorique all have powers. I don't. I'm sure whoever the fourth champion is will be a little bit more special than me.'

'And yet, how many times have you saved our lives? How many times have you turned up right when we needed you?'

'Just luck.'

'Perhaps, although my father used to say, "Give me a lucky man to fight beside every time." But you're right, anyway. Together, we have a chance. Alone, we're dead,' said Tinnstra. She reached out and took his hand. 'I promise I won't forget again.'

'Make sure you don't.'

Tinnstra looked over at Zorique, still sleeping. 'I won't let her down again.'

Ralasis followed her gaze. 'Do you think she'll be strong enough by tonight?'

'Let's pray that she is.' Tinnstra was far from sure, though. The girl's magic was normally myriad colours in constant motion around her, yet now she had but the faintest of glows. The vials of Chikara water had been enough to kickstart her powers, but their effects had worn off and Zorique still wasn't what she had been. Maybe the runes around the city walls were stopping her from regaining her full strength.

'For someone who claimed the Gods were a waste of time, you seem to be putting a lot of faith in them now,' said Ralasis.

'When did I say that?'

'That night back in Meigore.'

'Oh.' Tinnstra suddenly realised she was still holding Ralasis' hand – and she didn't want to let go. 'I'm sorry about how I've been. It's just ... everything has gone so wrong since we got here that I became angrier and angrier with myself – and took it out on you and everyone else.'

'It's okay. I understand.' He rubbed his thumb along the back of her hand. 'But don't be so hard on yourself – there isn't a plan in the world that survives first contact with the enemy.'

Tinnstra laughed. 'My father used to say something similar. "Everyone has a plan until they get punched in the face."'

'A wise man.'

'He was a good father, but it was hard being the daughter of a legend.'

'Try being the son of a murderer and a crook.'

'Your father—?'

'Yes. He was quite notorious in Layso society. A man of a certain reputation before he was caught and executed for his crimes.'

'I'm sorry.'

'Why? I didn't think much of him, and he didn't think much of me. When he was hanged, I was better off. I didn't have to listen to his thoughts about how *I* was going to ruin *my* life. The fact of the matter was he should've concentrated on his own problems.'

'That's probably true of all of us.' Tinnstra glanced again at Zorique. 'I'd better go and find us some food and water. We might not get a chance to eat again before tonight.'

'Is that wise?' asked Ralasis. 'The Egril must be looking for us.'

'They're looking for Hanran. They won't see me.' Tinnstra waved the Chosen's mask at the sea captain.

'Be careful all the same,' said the Meigorian, flashing that smile of his. He probably didn't even know he was doing it. In a strange way, it made Tinnstra feel better about things. She was glad Ralasis was with them at the last.

'I'll do my best.' She returned his smile, then slipped the mask on.

She left via the back of the building. Having a Chosen walk out through the front door would attract too much attention, and she didn't need a loose tongue saying the wrong thing to the wrong person. The rear exit led into a narrow alleyway full of debris from ruined lives. She stepped over the shattered bricks, and the splintered planks of wood, and the broken poles, watching the street beyond for Egril. Once, she'd gone hunting down that narrow lane, hoping to catch a rat or two, but most likely any rodents that once called that alley home had been eaten in the time she'd been away.

Not that she intended to bring back rats today. With her stolen uniform, she could requisition anything she wanted without resistance. But Tinnstra had something else she'd always been short of when she lived in Aisair before – money. Enough to pay a fair price for whatever was on sale.

She glanced up at the sliver of sky above and only had to wait a few seconds before she saw Daijaku fly past. Plenty of them.

They'd be looking for the queen – and for whoever had freed her. She hoped Grace had the sense to disappear. It wouldn't take a genius to start searching for the king's concubine after he'd taken a dive out of the window.

The city itself hummed with magic. Tinnstra could sense little blips of red rippling across Aisair. According to Wenna, the Egril had bought in six hundred Chosen to fight Sekanowari. Even a third of that number would cause the allied army problems, and yet, judging by what Tinnstra could sense, she could easily believe there were far more than Wenna's estimate gathered in the city. Far, far more.

Still, the only good thing about that was Tinnstra wouldn't stand out. What was one more Chosen amongst so many? To any Skulls looking, she'd be invisible in her uniform. She stepped out into the main road and the effect on the people around her was immediate. No one made any sudden moves, they just swerved away from her as discreetly as they could. No one looked her way, but all were aware of every move she made, everywhere she walked. A year of Egril occupation had made survivors of them all. The weak had surely been culled by now.

Tinnstra hated the fact that her own people were afraid of her. Of course, it was the uniform they were reacting to, but she knew that she'd changed, too. Was she really any different from the enemy? How many souls had she sent to the Great Darkness so far? How many more would follow?

Gods, even her own soldiers called her Death.

Lost in her thoughts, Tinnstra hadn't realised where she'd wandered. It was only when she saw the all but destroyed building on the corner that everything came back to her.

Ester Street. Once it had been a pretty road full of flower boxes and market stalls. Then the Egril invaded, and beauty was a luxury no one could afford. The corner house became a hiding place for the Hanran until the Daijaku dropped a bomb on it. Tinnstra had watched from a nearby doorway as Skulls dragged the survivors out and into wagons, most likely never to be seen again.

Darus Monsuta had been there, too, watching, enjoying the disaster. That was the first time she'd seen him. She could still remember what it felt like when he smiled at her.

Tinnstra walked on, then stopped where he'd stopped and looked over to where she'd been cowering that day. The shop was empty now, its windows broken. An all too familiar sight in Aisair. The owners had kept the door locked during the attack, despite it being obvious Tinnstra needed help. She couldn't blame them. Back then, she'd have done the same.

Further on, she came to the baker's where she'd used her last few coins to buy a loaf. It'd not been enough, and she'd left owing the baker another ecu. The window was boarded up now, but the door was open and Tinnstra could smell fresh bread inside.

Gods, how long had it been since she'd tasted fresh bread?

She walked in. The man who'd served her back then wasn't there. Instead, a woman stood behind the counter, red-faced, hair tied in a bun, wiping her hands on a dusty apron. She jumped when she saw Tinnstra, but composed herself quickly and bowed. 'Greetings, Chosen,' she said in badly accented Egril.

'Good morning,' replied Tinnstra in Jian.

Hearing her own language spoken by the enemy seemed to shock the woman even more. 'H ... How can I help you?'

'I thought a man used to make the bread here.'

'My ... My husband?' The woman paled.

Tinnstra nodded. 'Yes.'

'He was ... he was a traitor.' The woman all but choked on the words. 'Yes, a traitor. You ... I mean, the authorities ...' She took another gulp of air. 'The authorities arrested him six months ago, they did.' She blinked tears away.

'Oh.' Not long after Tinnstra had bought the bread from him. She knew his arrest had nothing to do with her, but she couldn't help but feel guilty at the news.

'I promise you, my son and I – we didn't know what he was doing. We would've reported him if we did. You have my word. We're loyal. Loyal.' Her hand went to her mouth, but she quickly dropped it again. 'Praise be to Kage,' she said in Egril. 'Praise be to Kage.'

Tinnstra's heart went out to the woman. She wanted to apologise for asking, tell her not to worry, but no Chosen would do that. 'I'd like some bread.'

The woman bowed again, composing herself. 'Certainly. How many loaves would you like?' She glanced quickly back at the counter behind her. 'I only have f ... five ready at the moment. There's more in the oven.'

'One will suffice.'

The woman scurried off, returning a moment later with a cloth-wrapped loaf. She placed it on the counter and bowed a third time.

'Do you have any water?'

'Water?'

'Yes. I need a skin or two of water.'

'Of course, of course. Right away. Right away.' Again, the woman disappeared. She was gone longer this time, but she returned, as promised, with two water skins. 'I'm sorry about the skins ... they're old. I could go next door and see if they have better, if you'd like. I just don't normally ... well, sorry.'

'They're fine,' said Tinnstra. 'How much do I owe you?'

'Nothing, Chosen. It's my pleasure. A gift.' The woman looked truly petrified now, as if her life depended on a conversation she did not understand.

'Here,' said Tinnstra and she placed two staters on the counter. Enough for the bread today and for Tinnstra's past debts. The woman stared at the coins but didn't reach for them. 'Thank you for the bread,' said Tinnstra, turning to leave.

'Your money! Please, take your money. It's a gift, please,' begged the woman, but Tinnstra was already halfway out through the door. She picked up her pace as the woman's cries followed her into the street. The noise had people glancing, however briefly, her way.

She didn't head back to the others straight away. Instead, she took a more circuitous route, taking note of the checkpoints, watching the flight patterns of the Daijaku and anything else that might suggest the Skulls knew where they were hiding.

There were certainly plenty of Skulls on the streets, actively searching Jians as they walked by, but it all appeared random – desperate, in fact.

So they should be. Tonight it will all be over. Raaku will die – or we will.

The latter felt more likely, though. The truth was she didn't think the odds were in her favour anymore. Maybe they never had been. Maybe she'd always been deluded about her chances. Maybe her plan to go to Egril had just been another attempt to run away from what had to be done.

Her hand went to her pouch. Tinnstra didn't even need to open it to check how many vials she had left. She'd looked often enough that morning back in her rooms. There was only the one vial left.

One.

What good would that do? It had taken four just to get Tinnstra and Zorique back on their feet. One barely kept her cravings at bay. One wouldn't get her through the day, let alone in a state to kill Raaku.

Tinnstra stepped into the alleyway behind her home and leaned back against the wall, eye closed.

It was over. They'd lost Sekanowari. Even when the army reached the city, they didn't have the numbers to defeat the regular Skulls, let alone the Chosen and all the other monsters. Without Zorique's full power, without Chikara water, they didn't have the strength to take on Raaku.

All that was left was the dying.

Zorique was awake when she returned to her rooms, her aura brighter but still not what it had been. She was sitting next to Ralasis by the window and her smile as Tinnstra walked through the door was enough to alleviate her mood.

'You look better,' said Tinnstra.

Zorique brushed her hand across her face. Her wounds were not only healed but had almost disappeared. She'd dressed in some of Tinnstra's old clothes and, for a moment, she looked like a reflection of who Tinnstra had once been. Tinnstra could see fear flickering in her daughter's eyes. 'The sleep did me good. Being away from the runes did me even more good.'

Tinnstra walked over and kissed her daughter on the forehead. 'Let's not get captured again, eh?'

'I'll do my best,' said Zorique.

Tinnstra placed the bread and water skins on the table, then removed her mask. Immediately, she felt better, a weight lifted. 'Here. Eat. The bread's fresh from the oven. Not sure how fresh the water is, but it's better than nothing.'

Ralasis fetched some cups from a shelf, blowing in them to get rid of some of the dust.

'Thank you,' said Tinnstra, taking one. She used a splash of water from one of the skins to wash out the rest of the dust. She then filled the cup and passed it to Zorique, who was tearing off a chunk of bread. Tinnstra did the same with the next cup and passed it to Ralasis, before cleaning and filling her own.

'This is so good,' said Zorique with a full mouth. 'I'd forgotten what fresh bread tastes like. It's so soft.'

Ralasis took a bite. 'You're not missing the crunch of weevils?'

'No,' said Zorique, laughing. She glanced at Tinnstra, a mischievous grin forming. 'But I prefer the weevils to your cooking.'

'Tinnstra cooks?' Ralasis chuckled. 'What's her speciality? Roast severed limbs?'

'No one ever taught me,' said Tinnstra with a smile of her own. 'My family had servants to make the meals when I was young, then I was at the Kotege. After that ... bread with weevils was a luxury.'

'What about you, Ralasis?' said Zorique. 'Can you cook?'

'Of course! Every Meigorian man takes great pride in knowing how to make a feast. It's something we take very seriously. Cooking is an act of love.'

'It's more an act of violence for Tinnstra,' said Zorique.

Ralasis clapped his hands. 'Isn't everything? Have I told you about the time—'

'Hey!' said Tinnstra. 'Don't say a word.'

Zorique raised an eyebrow. 'Something you want to tell me, Mother?'

'No.' Tinnstra sat back, enjoying the sound of laughter, savouring the moment more than the bread. Whatever had brought them all together, she was lucky to have Zorique and Ralasis in her life. She was—

Pain unlike anything she had ever experienced before ripped through Tinnstra's brain. She fell off the chair, clutching her head, screaming.

Zorique and Ralasis rushed to her side.

'What's wrong?' said her daughter, cradling Tinnstra in her arms. 'What's happening?'

'Magic. So ... much ... magic.' If Zorique was a rainbow, this was an abyss. It pulsed out from the heart of Aisair, from the palace. It was monstrous, evil, slicing through Tinnstra. 'He's here.'

'Who?' asked Ralasis. 'Who's here?'

'Raaku.'

90

Yas

Arlen's Farm

A night and some of a day had passed since Kenan locked Yas and
Sorin in a wooden cage, with their hands and feet tied. A night
and some of a day with no food and barely a sip of water. A night
and some of a day and there was no one coming to the rescue.
No sign of help from the rest of the villagers, either. Nothing that
gave her any sense that she could get out of this mess alive.

Of all the tight spots Yas had managed to get herself into, this
was the worst. And the last, most likely. She could almost hear
Ma chastising her. 'This is what you get for sticking your nose in
other people's business,' she would've said. 'When are you going
to learn your lesson?'

'Too bloody late,' she whispered. Gods, she wanted to cry.

The cage didn't look like much, just some wooden poles lashed
together with twine, but both Yas and Sorin had tried kicking the
thing apart without success. Turns out the Weeping Men knew a
thing or two about building prisons.

It also didn't help that she'd spent the day watching the bastards packing up and readying to leave Arlen's Farm. Time was
definitely running out before ... what?

The question had been playing on her mind ever since Kenan
ordered them locked up, but she'd not had the courage to ask
Sorin. Now she reckoned there was no avoiding it. 'What are
they going to do to us?' she asked.

Sorin looked up. 'That depends. Nothing good, though.'

'I gathered that much.'

'They might take you as a slave, sell you on – if you're lucky.'

'We both know I'm not. So tell me the bad news.'

'We're both dead.'

'I kinda figured that out, too. Will it be quick?'

Sorin looked away. 'No.'

'Shit.'

When he looked back, there was real fear in his eyes. 'Trouble is ... we're both Weeping Men, and they don't like one of their own crossing them, so Kenan will want to make a spectacle out of us so no one else gets any funny ideas.'

'And?'

'What they do – what they normally do – is called the Eagle.'

'The Eagle?'

'Yeah,' said Sorin. 'They slice your back open, peel away the skin so they can reach in and pull your lungs out and then spread them like bloody wings for all to see.'

'Shit.' Yas wanted to be sick. She wanted to scream.

'I've seen it done a couple of times. It takes a good minute or two for the poor sod to die.'

'From the first cut?'

'From when you see the lungs.'

Yas lifted her bound hands to her face and closed her eyes. Her body started to shake. She wished she hadn't asked. She wished for a lot of things that would never happen. She knew there'd be no rescue, no last-minute reprieve. What a way to die.

When she opened her eyes again, the first thing she saw was the mountain that had been their home for so long, where Ro was hidden. Thank the Four Gods, at least he was safe up there and wouldn't see what happened to her.

Still, she'd have given anything to hug him one last time.

The tears came then. There was no holding them back.

Sorin moved beside her and put his hands on hers. Their heads touched.

'I don't want to die,' she sobbed.

'Me neither.'

She looked up at him through bleary eyes. 'I'm so sorry.'

'There's nothing to be sorry for.'

'There is. I've fucked everything up. For you. For me. For everybody.'

'None of this is your fault. You didn't make Kenan come here.'

'I bloody sent Bros to him to ask for help.'

'All right, that wasn't your best idea. But still, it's not your fault they're bad people.'

'*I'm* supposed to be bad people!'

'Nah, you might not like taking any shit from anyone, but that don't make you bad. Not like this lot.'

Yas sat back against the bars and wiped her face dry with the back of her hands. 'I kind of believed I *was* tough for a while. I kind of liked it, too.'

'That's always the problem. Power feels good, especially for people who've never had any their whole lives – like you and me,' said Sorin.

'How'd you get to be a Weeping Man, then? Through your family?'

'Nah, my father and mother were ordinary. Worked themselves to death every day for scraps, bowing and scraping to anyone who had two coins more than they did. I hated seeing them like that. Couldn't understand why they didn't push back. I mean, my father was a big man. He could handle himself all right. I seen him knock other men down who were twice his size. But he never did anything with it apart from shift sacks and crates for other people down at the docks. I swore I'd never do anything like that – that I wouldn't be like him. Fucking stupid, really.

'Then one of the kids I knew back then started doing odd jobs for the Weeping Men. Nothing heavy, just running shit from here to there, but one job earned him more coin than my father got for a week of hard graft. So, when they started looking for others to help out, I fucking jumped at the chance.'

'Ah,' said Yas.

'I still remember the fights I had with my father about it, the fucking names I called him when he tried to stop me. Then, after I got my first tear, I never went back. Never saw either of them again. I told myself I was ashamed of them – imagine that?

Real truth was I was ashamed of myself. Wasn't until you turned up that I started to recognise the old me – or rather the man I should've been.'

'You've been a big help to me,' said Yas. 'Dean, too.'

Sorin glanced around again. 'I was hoping that daft bastard would turn up and do something.'

'He might yet.'

Sorin chuckled. 'See? You still believe in the best of us.'

'My old ma, she always saw the worst. I reckoned life would be better if I did the opposite to what she thought. Now, maybe, I think she'd just lived long enough to know the truth. The worst is all we get.' Yas sighed. 'I never had the chance to say goodbye to her, either. She died in the bombing of Kiyosun while I was off trying to do the right bloody thing.'

'That's not your fault, either.'

'Maybe. Maybe not. Seems to me all the people I care about get killed while trying to look after me, or help me, or just for knowing me. Sometimes, I really think I'm cursed.'

'Did you really kill all those people in the Council House like they say?'

'Did you know anyone who worked there? Your ma wasn't there, was she?'

'No. No one. Just asking. Figure we've got nothing to do but talk, and I was curious is all.'

'Well then, yeah, I did.' Yas shifted her weight about, trying to get comfortable and failing. 'The Hanran had my little boy and my ma. Said they'd kill them if I didn't do it.'

'A hard choice you had to make.'

'Felt like an easy choice at the time, and it was easy enough doing it, too. A bit of powder here and there. But it weren't easy watching them all die. It's not been easy trying to forget about it, either. I can see them in my mind, clear as day – the fear in their eyes, the gurgles as they choked, the way their faces screwed up as they tried to claw on to life.'

'Fuck. I'm sorry you had to go through that.'

'The worst one – the one that really haunts me – is a woman named Bets. She was the head cook and had been nothing but nice to me since I started there. She was the last to die out of all of them, and the look she gave me ... she knew I'd done it.'

'I still remember my first,' said Sorin. 'Folip, his name was. Used to work with my father. They'd go drinking together now and then. A good man. A family man. Trouble was, he liked to gamble, too. Borrowed money from the Weeping Men and couldn't pay it back.

'First time he didn't have the money, we broke his arm. Stupid thing to do, really, because how the fuck was he supposed to earn any money with one arm? But those were our orders. Folip tried running then, with his family. We caught him by the east gate and that was that. Raab handed me a knife and told me to cut his throat. The man wept and begged and begged. Kept going on about how he'd known me since I was a kid, how he'd been a fool, how he'd change. Then he pissed his pants when I pulled his head back. I looked him in the eyes while I did it, Raab cheering me on from behind. At the time, I thought Folip was a coward. Now? I hope I don't do the same.'

Yas garbbed his arm. 'Shit. Kenan's coming.'

The Weeping Man walked towards them, a slash of yellow teeth showing against his inked skin. Gods, Yas didn't think she'd ever hated anyone more.

'How are my favourite people?' called Kenan as he drew close, spreading his arms out wide as if he was going to give them a hug.

'Go fuck yourself,' spat Yas.

Kenan recoiled in mock distaste. 'Where did you learn such language? And you being a mother and all.'

A chill ran through Yas. Kenan had never seen Ro, and she'd not mentioned she had a son. She kept her mouth shut, scared of making things worse – if that was possible.

Kenan winked at her. 'Did you think I'd not find out? That no one would say anything? Turns out you've got a few enemies – apart from me and my crew, that is.'

Yas stared at him, impotent rage coursing through her. 'Don't.'

'Don't what? You can't threaten me. I can do whatever the fuck I want,' said Kenan. 'That's why I've sent some of my boys to fetch your son and the others from their cave. I wouldn't want your Little Ro to miss his mother's big moment tonight.'

'Don't be a bastard, Kenan,' said Sorin. 'You've got us. There's no need to make it any worse.'

'But I *am* a bastard,' said the Weeping Man with a nasty chuckle. 'You, of all people, should know that. And I want her brat to see when I give his mother wings.'

'Please don't,' said Yas. 'You can do whatever you want to me but leave my boy alone.'

'I'm glad you've found some manners, darling, but it don't work like that. This is about showing everyone else what could happen to them if they try and cross me.' Kenan tilted his head to one side and looked at her out of the corners of his eyes, then grinned. 'It's about getting some revenge for Raab, and if I'm being totally honest with you, it's about having some fun for me, too.'

'You're evil,' said Yas. 'Pure bloody evil.'

Kenan nodded. 'That I am. Now, you make your peace with whatever Gods you got. Because when the sun goes down, the knives are coming out.'

91

Tinnstra

Aisair

Raaku.

Tinnstra could feel him in every inch of her body. His magic. So powerful. Like a stain inside her, his darkness spreading.

Evil. Utter evil.

How could she ever have thought he was just a man? No man could be so ...

She screamed as another wave of agony shot through her.

Zorique said something, but Tinnstra couldn't hear. Couldn't understand. She fell back into her daughter's arms as her mind tried to shatter.

All over so soon. So easily.

'Sekanowari.' Tinnstra spat the word out, her mouth full of froth, her body convulsing. She'd never known pain like it. Sweeping through her. Relentless.

Compared to Raaku, Zorique was but a candle in the wind against his fury.

And Tinnstra? She was nothing.

'Tinnstra!' Her name. Zorique screamed her name over the howling of the world.

Ralasis, by the window, looking scared, said something.

Tinnstra tried to get her mind to work, tried to speak, but the darkness consumed her.

Then Zorique's arm was around her, lifting her up. Ralasis was on the other side, adding his support. Together, they half-carried, half-dragged Tinnstra towards the door as the howling grew louder.

'Help us, Tinnstra,' said Zorique. 'We have to get out of here.'

'I ... I ...' Tinnstra couldn't make her mind work, couldn't push past the pain. Something was wrong. Everything was wrong. 'Wha ... what's happening?'

'Kyoryu are coming.'

Ralasis yanked the door open and they stumbled through just as the downstairs exploded. Zorique dropped Tinnstra and powered up a shield of light on her arm. It crackled and sparked with the effort, despite being barely bigger than a normal shield. A sword appeared in her right hand, burning bright in the darkness of the corridor.

Tinnstra felt the building shake as something big bounded up the stairs. She tried to rise but couldn't get her hands and legs to work.

The howling grew ever louder and then Tinnstra saw it – a Kyoryu, twice the size of any she'd seen before. It vaulted the last few stairs then used its momentum to rebound off the end wall and launch itself at Zorique.

She got her shield up in time to take the worst of the attack and hacked back with her sword. The creature howled and reared up, only to bring its full weight down on Zorique. Again, her shield saved her life, but the creature hooked both its front paws around its edges. Light flared and sparked as it tried to tug the shield away from Zorique.

But it was no ordinary shield. With a thought, it vanished and the Kyoryu fell back, exposing its stomach. Zorique seized the moment and lunged forwards, her sword a blaze of light as it arced down. She slashed it from neck to groin. Blood gushed out, but there was no time to stop. Another creature roared up the stairs and Zorique rushed to meet it.

For one brief moment, Tinnstra and Ralasis were alone on the blood-soaked landing as Zorique took the fight downstairs. The building shook as light met monster, but then a crash came from the roof and they knew they had their own demons to deal with.

They looked up to see sunlight spilling down into the stairwell as something wrenched open the door.

Tinnstra grunted, spat froth from her mouth, tried to rise, failed.

Ralasis pulled her out of the way, then took her sword from its scabbard as he stepped in front of her.

A Daijaku appeared on the stairs, screeching, wings filling the tight space, a Niganntan spear in its hands, its bulbous eyes burning red.

'Shit,' said Ralasis. 'Shit.' He raised his sword and stood his ground.

Tinnstra had to help, had to do something, had to push back the pain. By the Four Gods, she howled as she battled the darkness, searching for the part of her mind that was *her* and not *him*. Sensing magic was her power, not her weakness.

Flame shot up the stairs from below as Zorique battled only the Gods knew what. And more would be coming. The Egril always sent more.

The Daijaku on the landing screeched again and tried to fly at Ralasis. Its wings were too big for the space, cracking against stair and wall as it swung the Niganntan spear at the Meigorian. He slapped it away with his sword, attempted an attack of his own, but wing and claw drove him back until his feet bumped up against Tinnstra's.

I have to help. I have to help. I have to help.

The thoughts ran through her mind. A cry in the hurricane, but she could hear it. Understand it. Tinnstra gritted her teeth and tried to stand one more time.

Ralasis fended off another swipe of the demon's spear. Something howled down below. Zorique cried out.

Gods, this is Sekanowari. No time to be weak.

Tinnstra got to her feet at last, fell back against the wall but somehow stayed upright. She snorted blood from her nose, tried to bury the pain in her head.

The Daijaku's wing slapped Ralasis across the face, sending him sprawling. It saw Tinnstra propped up against the wall and screeched again, ichor flying off its curved beak. Tinnstra reached for the knife at the small of her back and found only an empty scabbard – she'd left the blade in the king's headboard.

The Daijaku thrust its spear at her. Tinnstra veered out of its way, but not quickly enough. Pain flared across her stomach as the blade found her skin. She grabbed the shaft with one hand, yanked it to the side. The creature came with it and she put all her weight into her elbow, driving it into the creature's face.

It shrieked as its eye popped and Tinnstra felt some of the tension leave the spear. She released the shaft, then drew the knife from her wrist-sheath. Claws dug into her back as she drove the knife into the Daijaku's neck. She screamed as she hacked it free, hot blood splattering her face, and stabbed it again and again. She carried on as the demon fell to the ground, welcoming the madness, the fury.

She could still feel Raaku and the pain caused by his magic, but her rage contained it just as it freed her mind.

Covered in Daijaku blood, she left the creature's corpse, snatched up the Niganntan spear and tumbled down the stairs after Zorique.

The entranceway to the building was all but destroyed, with shattered walls and burned floors. Tinnstra jumped over the dead Kyoryu that lay at the bottom of the stairs and landed in the hallway, ready to fight. Ready to kill.

Through the doorway, she saw Zorique in the street battling two more Kyoryu.

I have to help. I have to help.

Tinnstra raced out of the building, howling, Niganntan spear swinging. A Kyoryu turned, snarling, fangs gleaming, but Tinnstra cared not. She put all her strength into the spear as it carved deep into the creature's shoulder and dragged the blade down, taking off the limb. The Kyoryu stumbled and Tinnstra hacked at it again, catching it good and hard in its ribs. It batted a claw at the spear, but Tinnstra held on and thrust it deeper, finding lungs and heart.

A shadow fell over her as she pulled the spear free and she threw herself backwards as a Daijaku swooped down at her. Its talons raked the air where her head had been as she fell. She lashed out with the spear all the same, felt the blade cut flesh. The creature spiralled as one wing went limp and hit the earth hard. Tinnstra rushed after it and struck with the spear as it started to rise.

The Daijaku's head tumbled to the ground.

Tinnstra turned to see Zorique drive her sword through the Kyoryu's heart, but there was no time to celebrate. Skulls appeared at the far end of the street and ran towards them.

'Zorique!' cried Tinnstra. 'We need to get away from here!'

'Where's Ralasis?' Zorique called back.

'Inside.'

'Alive?'

'I don't know.'

'Gods!' She turned back and threw a wall of fire at the Skulls. 'Get him while I—' They both watched the flames wash over the Egril and do no harm.

Zorique thrust more fire towards them, her aura flickering as she drew on whatever reserves of magic she had left, and still the Skulls ran on, untouched by anything she threw at them. They were half a street away now, maybe a hundred of them. Too many to fight.

'We have to go NOW!' Tinnstra grabbed Zorique's arm, yanked her back. She resisted for a second, but then they were both running. They turned right at the end of the street and came face to face with another squad of Skulls.

'*Shirudan*.' Zorique formed a light shield in front of her. '*Oso*.' She sent it flying off – not towards the Skulls but into the building beside them, smashing through its walls with a boom. With its supports gone, the upper floors collapsed into the road, filling the air with dust and debris, crushing the Egril.

Zorique turned and sent another shield spinning into the buildings behind her, bringing them down to block off the Skulls coming from the rear.

Blinded by smoke, choking on dust, Tinnstra grabbed Zorique's hand and they ran into one of still-standing buildings. With her shield, Zorique punched a hole in the wall at the end of the corridor and they raced through into the next building, down another corridor and then out into another street. They could hear shouting from the nearby road and overhead Daijaku swooped and soared looking for them, but for that moment, they were free.

'What about Ralasis?' asked Zorique as they crouched in a doorway.

Tinnstra swallowed, wiped something from her eye. 'We … we leave him. He's either dead or captured. Either way, we can't help him,' said Tinnstra, her voice cracking. 'May the Gods help him, but we … we have to go on.'

Zorique hesitated for a moment, then nodded. 'Where do we go?'

'We go to Kos's house, see if he got word to the others. See if we can get help.'

'Those soldiers – my magic didn't work on them.'

'I know. But you killed them all the same.'

'I can't bring the city down on them all. There were people in those houses. Jians.'

'You don't know that,' said Tinnstra. 'You can't think that.'

'But that's why we're here – to save them.'

'We're here to kill the Skulls and their Emperor.'

Zorique gripped her mother's arm. 'We're here to free Jia.'

'How else do you think we're going to do that? You can't hold back, worrying about casualties. This is Sekanowari. We won't get a second chance.'

'I know,' hissed Zorique through clenched teeth. She slammed her hand against the wall. 'Shit.'

'We can do this.'

'I … I'm not strong enough.'

'Yes, you *are*.' Tinnstra slid her hand into her bag, found the last precious vial, felt the familiar pangs, the need. Gods, she wanted to drink it more than life itself. She pulled it out and showed it to her daughter. Her love. 'Drink this.'

Zorique stared at the vial in Tinnstra's hand. 'How many have you got left?'

'This is the last one.'

'What about you?'

'*You* need the power,' said Tinnstra.

Zorique nodded, took the vial and drank it. Almost immediately, her aura flared back up to its full intensity.

'I'm not going to let them capture me again,' said Zorique.

Tinnstra nodded. 'We fight until the last breath. We'll either win or we'll die – together.'

92

Ralasis

Aisair

The screaming woke him.

Ralasis opened his eyes and spat a mouthful of blood across the floor. His jaw ached from where the Daijaku had slapped him, but thank the Four Gods, it didn't feel broken. The creature lay dead next to him, stabbed countless times. It had to be Tinnstra's work.

She'd saved him. Again.

He pushed himself upright, his body full of pain, and was only a little bit alarmed that there was no sign of Tinnstra or Zorique. The screaming was like something out of a nightmare. It was as if the whole city howled in agony.

Ralasis had to use the wall to get to his feet, then looked over the bannister to the hallway below. A dead Kyoryu lay at the bottom of the stairs and the floor itself was blackened by fire, but there was no sign of Tinnstra and Zorique. The fear in his gut twisted some more.

He staggered back into Tinnstra's old apartment, not willing to admit to himself that he was hoping they'd be there. The place looked twice as big as before, with no one to fill it. Nowhere safe to hide, either.

Ralasis checked the window, careful not to be seen, and immediately ducked his head back.

More dead demons littered the ground outside. Still no sign

of Tinnstra or Zorique, though. But that wasn't what had him worried. He peeked again.

So many Skulls filled the cobbled street, coming his way.

The knot in his gut grew tighter as he watched the Egril. They were running into buildings and dragging Jians out into the street. Scimitars rose and scimitars fell, taking lives with every stroke. Headless corpses were thrown to one side while other Jians were pushed to their knees in the blood of the fallen, all screaming and pleading until steel silenced them.

He looked around for a weapon and only found a rusted eating knife so blunt he could've run it across his own throat without fear of drawing blood.

His Chosen's mask lay on the table, but he discounted putting that back on. He couldn't speak the language or understand it. Without Tinnstra, he'd last five seconds before the Skulls worked out he was a fraud. In fact, he took off the black jacket, too, and hid it under Tinnstra's bed covers. Better to pretend to be Jian than a Chosen. Still, he'd rather not pretend to be anything. The only way to stay alive was to stay out of Egril hands.

By the time he exited onto the corridor, other faces had appeared, peering out from behind their doors, eyes wide with fear. 'Skulls are coming,' he hissed. 'They're killing everyone. Run as fast as you can.'

Ralasis didn't wait to see if they listened. He bounded down the stairs as fast as his tired legs could take him. By the time he reached the ground floor, the Skulls were walking up to the front door. The one leading the party locked eyes with Ralasis and shouted something. Ralasis didn't need to know the language to understand their tone.

But Ralasis was never one for following orders. He spun on his heels and raced the other way, looking for the back door Tinnstra had used earlier. The Skulls followed, judging by the clomp of heavy boots behind him. He didn't look back. He didn't want to see the spear that was going to kill him.

The back door was half-ajar, spilling light into the corridor, a tease of a world outside. Ralasis didn't slow down and led with his shoulder, battering the door open and then half-falling into the alley.

The Skulls shouted some more, but Ralasis ignored them as he jumped over a smashed crate. The remains of a door were propped up against the wall, and Ralasis shoved them behind him as he passed, half-turning as he did so.

The action saved his life.

A spear clattered into the door, thrown by a Skull. A second earlier and Ralasis would've been dead. Both he and the Skull knew it, and so did his two mates. Ralasis stumbled back, then turned and ran, heart racing, tossing behind him every bit of shit he passed.

A spear whistled by his ear and clattered on the ground ten yards ahead. Ralasis' lucky stars were working hard right then, although he couldn't help but feel he was going to push it too far at any moment. With that in mind, he scooped up the fallen spear. Just because it had failed to take his life didn't mean it couldn't save it.

He reached the end of the alley and sprinted onto the next road, a little bit of hope battling against the knot of fear in his gut. Then he saw the collapsed building blocking his path and his hope disappeared. 'Shit!'

There was no going back, so Ralasis started to scramble up the rubble, slipping and stumbling as bricks shifted beneath his feet. Ralasis dug the spear butt into the rocks to steady himself as he climbed, full of fear that the Skulls were still on his tail. He spared a second to look back and was bloody glad he did.

One of the Skulls was almost within grabbing distance of him.

Ralasis spun around, swinging the spear as he fell back onto the rubble. The side of the spear smashed into the Skull's helmet, snapping the shaft on impact, sending the Egril falling sideways off the rubble mountain. Ralasis would've felt good about it if not for the fact he was now weaponless, with the other two Skulls still clambering after him.

He threw the broken shaft at one but the Egril swatted it away. The bastard was obviously feeling bloody sure of himself because he straightened up and drew his scimitar, no doubt grinning behind that stupid mask of his. Grinning right until Ralasis threw a brick in his face.

It hit him smack in the teeth of the Skull mask with the most satisfying crunch. The man toppled back, stiff as a board and arms outstretched – straight into his friend a yard below him. They both went down tumbling and Ralasis wasn't about to waste the opportunity.

He started to climb again, coughing on dust, banging his knees and nicking his hands, but there was nothing on earth that would stop him reaching the summit.

When he caught his first glimpse of the street from above, he nearly cried with relief. Not a single Skull in sight. He just had to clamber down the rubble on the other side and he'd be—

Ralasis threw himself flat when he heard the crack of wings, a second before the Daijaku swooped past. He moaned as claws raked his back, turned as another swooped down on him, talons outstretched. Ralasis grabbed a rock as the Daijaku snatched him up.

Its curved beak screeched in his face as he felt himself lifted off the ground, and all he could do was lash out with the rock. It crunched into the demon's face, but still it flew up.

Panic took over. Ralasis battered the demon again and again, with everything he had, not even sure where he was connecting, not caring, just desperate to hurt the creature.

The Daijaku fought back, digging its claws into Ralasis. He cried out from the sheer bloody agony, but he did not stop. He smashed the rock into the demon again and again and again. He felt a drop as the Daijaku faltered, then another, and then he was free.

And falling.

93

Zorique

Aisair

Zorique and Tinnstra ran down the side of the empty street, chased by a cacophony of nightmare sounds that echoed off the surrounding buildings – the screech of Daijaku, the howls of Kyoryu and the screams of Jians – and Zorique had never felt so helpless. Raaku's monsters were killing her people and, instead of saving them, they were on the run.

If this was Sekanowari, they were losing.

She'd lost her army. She'd lost Ralasis. There was just her and Tinnstra, as it had been in the beginning.

They stuck to the shadows as best they could, using overhanging roofs to hide themselves from sight, but it was painfully slow going. The Daijaku filled the sky, searching for any sign of them. Every other road seemed to be full of Skulls, and then there were the Kyoryu, always threatening to appear.

But it was the screams that had Zorique wincing, feeling an impotent rage. They came from everywhere, as if the whole city was being tortured. Memories of other cities, towns and villages came flooding back. Of Jians murdered for no other reason than being Jian. All that pain and agony and loss – and now the Egril were doing it here, in Aisair, and she had no way of stopping it. Not yet.

At least the Chikara water was starting to work – or Zorique thought it was. She felt on edge, like she couldn't stand still, yet moving, thinking, took her full concentration. She didn't understand how Tinnstra could've drunk so much of the liquid if it made her feel like that. It was awful. She hated it. As if she didn't belong in her own body. But if it brought her magic back ...

She stopped at the corner of a crossroads, tried to catch her breath. She could feel the spark within her growing.

'Are you well?' asked Tinnstra beside her, Niganntan spear in her hand.

'I think so. I—'

The wall erupted, sending Zorique flying. She hit the ground, rolled and was back on her feet in an instant as a Kyoryu leaped through the hole straight at her. She formed her shield on one arm, catching its slashing claws, and materialised a flaming sword in her other hand. She battered the Kyoryu's head away with the shield and lunged forwards to drive the magic blade deep into the creature's heart.

Nearby, Tinnstra shrugged off the rubble that had knocked her down as Daijaku raced towards them. She readied her spear, but there was no need.

'*Kasri!*' With a wave of her hand, Zorique set the swarm of demons on fire. They plummeted down, trailing flame and smoke.

'Well done,' said Tinnstra. 'I'll never get tired of seeing those bastards burn.'

'I'm feeling stronger,' said Zorique. 'I think my power's coming back.'

'I can see that,' said Tinnstra. 'But we'd better keep moving. The Kyoryu can sense it, too. They'll bring the whole army down on us if we're not careful.'

'Let's go.'

As they moved on, Tinnstra used the Niganntan spear as a staff, keeping the weight off her right foot.

'Are you hurt?' asked Zorique.

'It's nothing.'

'But you're limping.'

'I just had a building fall on me,' said Tinnstra, then saw the look on Zorique's face. 'I'm fine. It'll heal in a few minutes.'

They stopped at another crossroads, checked the other streets for sign of Skulls, but the way was clear. Tinnstra ran across the open ground to the safety of more shadows on the other side of the road. Zorique followed, eyes roaming everywhere.

Tinnstra led them down a narrow alley. With walls all but touching their shoulders, the Kyoryu's howls and the Daijaku's screeches sounded ever louder, ever closer. Zorique resisted the urge to power up her shield and sword. The Daijaku would surely spot the flare of light in the darkness. 'How much further?'

'Nearly there,' said Tinnstra as they reached the end of the alley. 'The next road—' She held out her hand, urging Zorique to stop.

She could hear the shouting: Egril voices hollering orders, Jians protesting. She closed her eyes, seeking her magic, needing its reassurance. She felt the spark, burning bright. It would be enough.

Zorique opened her eyes when the screaming started.

'The Skulls are executing Jians,' hissed Tinnstra.

She looked over her mother's shoulder into the street beyond. The Skulls – so many Skulls – had Jians lined up on their knees from one end of the street to the other and, one by one, they were decapitating their prisoners.

'No!' Zorique rushed from the alley, not thinking, her shield and sword flaring to life.

The Skulls turned as she raced to meet them.

She knew without looking that Tinnstra was with her, so she raced straight for the Skull who'd been doing all the decapitations. It was time he got a taste of his own medicine. Half-flying, half-running, she reached him in three heartbeats, her flaming sword already a blur. She struck his stomach without slowing down. The sword passed straight through the Skull and Zorique almost laughed at how easy it had been – except the man was still standing, unhurt and unmarked. Her sword had literally passed through him.

She turned the sword into a fireball and hurled it at the Skull, but she might as well have blown him a kiss for all the harm it did.

'Watch out!' cried Tinnstra as she raced towards them. Zorique threw herself back as another Skull's scimitar slashed down where her head had been. As she fell, she kicked out, striking the Skull's hand, sending his sword flying.

Zorique flipped her legs over her head and landed on her feet, immediately launching an attack of her own. Magic had made things too easy for her, but she'd not spent her life under Maiza's tutelage to forget how to have a proper fight. She drove the heel of her hand up into one Skull's chin, snapping it back and knocking him out. She spun as he fell, avoiding another sword thrust, twisting into a high kick that shattered another Skull's helmet. She stamped down on a fallen Egril's neck, breaking it, then threw herself forwards into a roll, snatching up a discarded scimitar as she jumped back to her feet.

Tinnstra was a whirlwind of death in the Skull ranks, her Niganntan spear slashing almost too fast to see, taking lives with every stroke. The weapon's reach stopped any swords from getting close and Tinnstra was happy to use both the blade and the butt of the spear on her enemies.

But Tinnstra wasn't the only one who knew how to kill. Zorique danced in between the Skulls, darting out with her stolen scimitar just like she'd been taught, seeking the soft parts not protected by their armour, opening throats, slashing across eyes, sinking in under the armpit and slicing hamstrings. Her magic might not work on the Skulls, but her shield worked plenty well against their swords, stopping their blows and blocking their thrusts.

She'd just buried her sword through a Skull's mouth when she heard a cry: 'Watch out!'

She turned, shield up. A Skull was behind her, sword raised, but before he could strike, a man threw himself at the Egril, taking him down in a tangle of limbs. Zorique went to his aid as he fought with the Skull. She grabbed the top of the Egril's helmet and yanked it back, exposing the neck for her sword to do its bloody work.

She flung the dead Skull to one side and helped the Jian up. 'Thank you.'

He nodded, eyes wide. 'Are you the queen?'

'I am.' A Skull came at her then, ending her conversation with the man. She blocked a scimitar with her shield, then twisted away as another lunged at her from the side. The Skull managed to skewer his friend good and proper and then got Zorique's sword as a reward.

Movement near her made her turn, but it was just the Jian who'd helped her. He'd picked up a sword and was battling a Skull. And he wasn't the only one. At least half a dozen others had taken up swords and joined the fight.

The tide was turning. The Skulls were being forced back.

Tinnstra led the charge, her Niganntan spear whirling, screaming insults and challenges. Her strength and the spear's blade were devastatingly effective. Whatever the Skulls had done to counter Zorique's magic, it did nothing against Tinnstra's ferocity.

'For Jia!' shouted Zorique as she moved to Tinnstra's side. 'For Jia!'

The chant was taken up by others as the Skulls retreated, as their bodies fell. Zorique grinned. It felt like she had an army of sorts again. It felt like hope.

Daijaku appeared, drawn by the fighting, and Zorique rose to meet them, her light shining once more. '*Kasri.*'

A cheer went up from the ground as the demons exploded into flame. Zorique took a deep breath before pushing her magic out further, seeking all the demons that flew above the city.

But the Daijaku weren't the only menace that could fly, and the sight of Zorique shining above the city spurred them into the sky.

Chosen. They rose above the rooftops.

Zorique watched, marking their positions, only too aware of the pain their batons could bring – but they would not take her by surprise this time. She was not scared of *them*.

Now she could see them, they could burn like the Daijaku.

'*Kasri.*'

And burn they did. They went up like human candles, their screams echoing around the city.

A baton blast arced across Zorique's path. Zorique turned to see a Chosen on a rooftop, taking aim once more.

Zorique waved her hand. '*Oso.*' The roof ripped apart beneath the Chosen's feet, shredding him in the debris.

More baton blasts shot towards her, a reminder that the city was crawling with Chosen, far more than the ones she'd burned from the sky. The urge to seek them all out was strong within her, but she remembered only too well the price she'd paid the last time she'd gone off on her own. Instead, she dropped down so rooftops and buildings hid her from sight, controlling her breathing. She had to be more than a symbol, more than a weapon. She had to lead.

She landed on the ground. The Skulls were either dead or had fled from the fight. That in itself was a joyous sight, but it was only the start. All around her, the Jians dropped to their knees and bowed – except Tinnstra, of course. Her mother smiled and saluted her all the same.

'Please rise,' said Zorique. 'There is no need for ceremony on the battlefield, not when there is so much more to be done.' She saw the man who'd come to her aid. 'Thank you for joining the fight. We will need each and every one of you before this day is done.'

The Jians slowly climbed to their feet, all eyes fixed on Zorique. She forced herself to remain unmoved by their attention and allowed her aura to shine ever brighter.

Tinnstra walked over, a woman beside her. 'This is Grace. Kos's daughter. She worked for the Hanran in the castle. She was the one who told us you were a prisoner.'

'Thank you for that, Grace,' said Zorique. 'If not for you, I'd still be in that prison.'

The woman bowed. 'Thank you, Your Highness.'

'Please, today's no day for titles, either. Call me Zorique.'

The woman bowed again, her cheeks flushed.

'Grace just told me that her father brought Aasgod, Jax and fifty of our soldiers to the capital this morning,' said Tinnstra.

'They're here? Now?' asked Zorique.

Grace nodded. 'Aye. They're at an inn called the Crook'd Billet.'

'I know the place.' said Tinnstra. 'We rested there once when you were a child, Zorique. It's close by.'

'Let's find them, then,' said Zorique. 'We could do with their help.'

'Grace, where's your father now?' asked Tinnstra.

'I haven't seen him since he got back,' said Grace. 'I was told that he was going to muster the Hanran and then blow the city gates open so your army could enter the city.'

'Good,' said Tinnstra. 'When you see him, tell him to head straight to the Royal Palace. That's where we'll be.'

'I will.'

'Let's get Aasgod and Jax and finish this thing,' said Zorique.

94

Darus

Aisair

Someone pounded on the door to Darus's room. 'General, the Lord Mage has need of you.'

Darus's eyes snapped open. How long had he been out for? 'Give me a minute.' He sat up and immediately put his head in his hands, the lingering pain enough to make even thinking hurt.

His hands. He had *two* hands. His arm – Jax's arm – had grown back while he'd been unconscious. How in Kage's name was he going to explain that? And was that all? Raaku had promised him power – enough to destroy the Jian queen. But apart from the arm, he felt no different.

He pulled his shirt on over his new limb and then shrugged on his coat. He had to hope that would be enough to hide the change until he was ready to strike at the Jians.

Darus pulled the table away from the door and headed out.

Things were in an uproar downstairs. The Jians were all checking weapons and on the verge of moving out. The mage was in the centre, issuing orders, pointing everywhere, looking as out of place as a man could be.

Darus headed for him, stopping ever so briefly when he spotted a bag, open on a table. His heart leaped. Was that the mage's? His little bag of secrets? But no – that bag was slung over Aasgod's shoulder again.

Darus peered inside the bag and smiled. It was almost as good.

A bag full of bombs. He picked one up and slipped it into his pocket, next to his knife. After all, one never knew when such a wonderful little thing might come in handy. No one noticed, or if they did, no one cared. He was, after all, their glorious leader.

'What's going on?' he asked Aasgod.

'The Skulls are killing people in the streets,' said the mage. 'We've got to do something to stop them.'

It was hard keeping the glee from Darus's face. 'Won't that put the rest of our mission in danger? Remember – we're here for a reason.'

'Didn't you hear what I said? They're killing Jians out there,' said Aasgod, going all red-faced and jabbing a finger at the street.

'People die in war,' said Darus, enjoying himself. 'How many people can we save if we rush out and help? A hundred? Two hundred?'

'Just saving one would be worth it,' snapped Aasgod.

'And what if saving that one life costs us yours? Or we lose all fifty of us to save a hundred? Who helps Zorique then? Eh? Who fights Raaku?'

That gave the mage pause. 'We can't let innocent people die.'

'That's why we have to stop the Emperor, not get involved in silly skirmishes. The lives of everyone in Jia are at stake, not just a few here in Aisair.'

'A few?' Aasgod nearly choked on the word. 'There's over seventy thousand people in this city.'

'There you go – the Egril can't possibly kill everyone before we act,' said Darus, as if talking to a simple child.

'But ... but—'

Darus turned his back on the mage. 'Everyone! Stand down! Stand down!'

Everyone stopped what they were doing and turned his way.

'We have a mission. Fighting the Skulls now puts that mission at risk. I know it's awful. There's no one who wants more than I do to go out and kill those responsible, but we can't jeopardise that mission.'

There were groans and mutterings of discontent, but no one objected. Swords clattered on tables and faces fell as the Jians accepted his words like the good little soldiers they were. By Kage, he wanted to laugh.

To think, outside on the streets, their countrymen were being sent to the Great Darkness and this merry little lot weren't doing anything about it. How glorious. He wished he could join in the fun, but watching the men and women around him suffer almost made up for—

The breath caught in his chest.

Zorique was near. He could feel her magic feeding into him. He looked over at the door just as a sentry shouted out. 'The queen! She's here – with Tinnstra!'

A cheer went up as everyone jumped to their feet, full of hope instead of crushing despair. Not what Darus wanted.

Aasgod rushed to the door as Darus slipped his hand into his pocket and felt the orb. The rest were still in the sack on the table. At least a hundred of them.

Perfect.

Darus headed after Aasgod. The mage was already outside. The glow coming off Zorique shone through the gaps in the boarded-up windows drawing everyone's attention, forcing Darus to push his way to the door.

'Get back to what you were doing,' he ordered. 'You've all seen the queen before.' And like sheep, they did as they were told.

He turned to face the room before leaving. A few men looked his way, but most had their heads down, concentrating on other things. This time, he didn't bother to hide his smile.

Death always made Darus so happy.

He pressed his finger against the knife inside his pocket, felt it bite, felt the blood come and smeared it across the surface of the orb. There was a sudden heat against his hand as it activated.

Taking a deep breath, Darus threw the orb towards the table with the sack and then fell back, through the door. Aasgod was with Tinnstra and the queen. Two other Hanran stood guard nearby. They all turned at his sudden appearance.

'Take cover!' he screamed, half-running, half-falling towards them.

Then everything went white.

If there was noise, Darus couldn't hear it. If there was heat, he didn't feel it.

When he opened his eyes, he found himself on his knees inside a cocoon of light with Zorique, Tinnstra and Aasgod. All was safe and quiet. Outside, though, it was chaos. Smoke swirled around them. Debris fell from the sky like rain, pounding a tattoo against the shield, flames licking its sides.

'What *happened*?' said Aasgod.

'One of the men,' said Darus, wide-eyed. 'I saw him take an orb ... there was blood on his hand. He was about to go through the door after you, but I pulled him back. He fell and the orb ... it rolled out of sight.' He looked out at the carnage as the smoke started to drift away, hand over his mouth. Nothing was left of the inn or the men and women who'd been inside. 'Dear Gods, he ... he killed them all. I couldn't save them.'

'It could've been worse,' said Tinnstra. She went to help him but Darus waved her away. 'You saved the queen – again.'

'I should've done more,' replied Darus.

'You did enough,' said Zorique, her voice like honey. 'Thank you.'

'It was nothing, Your Highness.' Being so close to her, being inside her magic, stirred whatever Raaku had done to Darus. He could feel the Emperor's magic leeching at the heathen queen's. He had to concentrate just to speak, just to breathe. 'I promised you my sword and my life.'

'What do we do now?' asked Aasgod.

'We must fight Sekanowari. It is our destiny,' said Tinnstra. She glanced behind her as if looking for someone. 'Let's find Raaku.'

Darus nodded, his mouth clamped shut. He couldn't have planned it better himself.

He couldn't wait to send these fools to the Great Darkness. Everlasting glory would be his.

95

Ange

Aisair

Ange shifted her shoulders, trying to get the shield that she'd slung across her back into a comfortable position. No way was she leaving it behind. She'd given up thinking that long ago. She would've carried ten of them if she could. She was all for anything that kept her alive.

Of course, she was glad she wasn't in one of the teams carrying the bloody tree logs they needed to cross over the trenches they'd been told about. No one looked happy carrying those, but then again, no one was happy about anything.

'I don't like this,' said Danni to prove the point. 'Not at all.'

Ange glanced at him, all red-faced from the long march, his scar more livid than ever. A shade of the confident man she'd met just the day before, and he only knew the half of all the shit going on. 'We'll be all right,' she lied.

'What makes you think that? We ain't got the queen or that one-eyed nutter, and some of the lads said the mage fucked off last night.'

'He did – but he's not left us. He's just gone ahead. Aasgod will be in the city when we get there. He's going to open the gates for us.'

'I'll bloody believe that when I see it.' He hawked a mouthful of phlegm off to the side. 'That don't explain the other two – the queen especially. She's the reason most of us came down south to fight.'

659

'She's still the reason we fight.'

'Some of the lads said she'd been captured – or killed.'

'The lads have been saying a lot,' said Ange.

'When you don't know the truth, the rumours just start up, don't they? People are going to think the worst.'

'Yeah, they do.'

'What do you know? You're tight with the bosses.'

'I don't know nothing,' said Ange, wishing that were true. Dren had thought the world of Jax – he'd given his life because of what Jax taught him – and now that man was a traitor? It didn't make sense, but nothing in the world made sense no more. 'How long do you think to Aisair? We've been traipsing through these woods all day.'

'Nice change of subject,' said Danni. 'Makes me even more worried.'

'Look, I'm not tight with the bosses.' She glanced around, desperate to see someone to rescue her from the conversation. The truth was, she agreed with Danni – he deserved to know what was going on. She'd want to know if she were in his shoes. 'They're all Shulka and I'm ... I'm just a fool who's always in the wrong bloody place.'

'Look around you, Ange. There's no bloody Shulka with us. We're all fools like you who just want to know what's going on.'

'Danni, please ... they told me not to say anything—'

'Fuck. I knew it. There *is* something they're not telling us.' He stopped suddenly and turned on her. 'Tell me, Ange. I deserve to know.'

'Believe me, you don't want to know. I wish *I* didn't.'

'It's too late now.'

Ange looked around, saw others had slowed down their marching as they watched her and Danni. 'At least keep walking,' she hissed. 'I'll tell you, but I'm not shouting it for everyone to hear.'

'All right,' said Danni, dropping his voice again. 'Let's walk and talk.'

Ange glanced around but no one was paying them any attention. Probably had enough of their own shit to worry about. 'The queen's been captured by the Egril. Tinnstra – the one-eyed nutter, as you call her – went to rescue her. That's why Aasgod has gone, too – to help.'

Danni looked at her out of the corner of his eye. 'And that's it?'

'That's it.' Ange didn't think he needed to know about Jax and Moiri. As her father used to say, being too honest never helps. Of course, he was talking about doing the odd bit of thieving, but Ange kind of thought it applied here, too.

'And they'll be waiting for us in Aisair?'

'Yeah, they will.' Well, she bloody well hoped they would be.

At least Danni seemed happy with her answer. Hopefully, Ange hadn't been lying to him about Aasgod and Tinnstra.

They trudged on through the forest, one long, ragged line instead of endless columns, spread over miles. Every now and then they heard fighting as pockets of Skulls were encountered, but there were no significant skirmishes and certainly none near Ange and Dani. Of course, that didn't stop her from worrying about meeting the enemy or endlessly looking for the bastards.

Time and time again, her mind drifted to thoughts of Garo. She wondered where he was, if he'd made it back to Kiyosun yet, or if he was even still alive. Just because he'd fucked off from the main fight, it didn't mean he wouldn't find enough danger on the way back. And knowing Garo, he'd be up to his neck in shit and not realise until it was too late. He needed Ange to keep him alive. And the poor kid with him – the little sod would be going around the twist listening to Garo's moaning.

Not that she would mind listening to him moan just then. She'd even like to have him rub her up the wrong way like he always did. It'd be nice to call him a fool and threaten to thump him one.

All of it would be a damn sight better than what she was doing.

Gods, she hoped she'd get the chance to tell him that.

'Eyes up, lass,' said Danni. 'We're here.'

Ange looked up and saw Danni was right. The trees were thinning out ahead. There was a lot of open ground beyond them, all churned up where the Skulls had ripped the trees out of the ground and dragged them off.

Ange squinted, trying to see further. There was a barrier of some sort – or what was left of it. It looked like someone had a good bonfire with it, because it was mostly black and charred with the odd bit of timber jutting here and there – not to mention the big hole right in the middle of the thing.

As they reached the treeline, Ange got her first view of Aisair. She'd always considered herself a city girl. Born and raised in Kiyosun, she was at her most comfortable on its narrow, crowded streets. But now? Seeing Aisair, she realised she'd never known what a real city was. Kiyosun was a village compared to this. The mass of grey buildings spanned the horizon, with a massive castle towering above it all.

Danni spotted she was gawping. 'Big, isn't it?'

'Big? Looks like the whole world could live there,' said Ange. 'And still have room to spare.'

'Aye, it's a grand old place and no mistake – with some bloody high walls.'

Danni was right about that, too. Skull flags fluttered from east to west and there were plenty of the white-armoured bastards standing about on top. 'How are we going to get past them?'

'This is when we need some magic – or a lot of bombs.'

Ange shivered at the word. Images of Dren dying flashed through her mind, eaten up by whatever was in the Egril orbs. Killed by the Skulls as surely as if they'd shoved a scimitar in his guts. 'We brought a trunk of the bloody things with us from Kiyosun, but I'd rather see Zorique take them apart.'

'Me too, lass.'

'Ange, Danni.' It was Wenna.

'Everything all right?' asked Ange, not sure if she could cope with any more bad news.

'The Hanran in the city have promised to open the gates for us,' said Wenna, 'so be ready for when that happens. In the meantime, I need you to get the logs spread out amongst your teams. When you see the signal, I want you to charge for the walls.'

'What's the signal?' asked Danni.

'Hopefully a big explosion,' said Wenna with a smile.

'Ange was saying we had some bombs of our own,' said Danni. 'Wouldn't mind having a few of those, too.'

Wenna nodded. 'Do you know how they work?'

'I do,' said Ange.

'Okay,' said the Shulka. 'I'll have some sent down to you.'

'What about the queen?' asked Danni, making Ange wince.

Wenna glanced over at her, adding to her discomfort. 'What about her?'

'Where is she?'

Wenna pointed at Aisair. 'Getting ready for the fight in there. You'll see her soon enough.'

Danni pursed his lips. 'A few words from her now would add a bit of steel to everyone.'

'Just try to stay alive, eh? That should be all the incentive you need.' She gave them both a nod. 'I'll see you when the fighting starts.'

They watched Wenna walk off, but Ange's eyes kept getting drawn to Aisair and those big bloody walls.

Maybe a half-hour later, two lads turned up holding a couple of small sacks each. 'You Ange?' one of them asked.

'I am.'

'Wenna said to give you these.' They both held out the sacks.

'Are they what I think they are?' said Danni, chuckling appreciatively. He took one and peered inside. 'Lovely.'

'Don't touch any of them without gloves,' said Ange, still staring at the sack being offered to her.

'You not wanting yours?' said the lad with his arm outstretched.

'Not really,' replied Ange, but she took the sack anyway. Took it with her bare hands and promptly put it down on the ground and stepped back.

The lad looked at her as if she were mad, then shrugged. 'Good luck.'

'What's wrong?' said Danni as the two lads went on their way.

'I bloody hate those things.'

'They're all right as long as you're careful.'

'That's what this lad I knew said. He loved them – he nicked a case of the orbs off the Skulls and blew half of Kiyosun up with them – but the bombs killed him in the end.'

'He blew himself up?'

'Well, yeah, he did actually, but only because he was dying anyway. The magic in those orbs can get you something bad. Makes you as sick as a dog and kills you twice as quick. Last I saw him, he could barely stand, and he was coughing blood and guts up.'

'Lovely.' Danni put down the sack he'd taken. Then he looked at the walls again. Then back at the sack. 'Don't see how we can get away with not using them, though.'

'Wenna said the Hanran will open the doors for us.'

Danni arched an eyebrow. 'Yeah? And how well have our plans gone so far?'

'Like shit.'

'Exactly.'

Ange shook her head. 'I think I preferred you when you were being all encouraging.'

'Maybe it's the effect you have on me.'

'Huh,' said Ange. 'Hadn't thought of it like that. Maybe that's why the last man I partnered with was a right moaning bastard, too.'

'Then again,' said Danni, 'maybe it's the state of the world.'

Ange laughed. 'I hope it's that. I'd hate to think I was—'

The explosion drowned out any words, shaking the very ground and battering the air. They both spun to see a cloud of smoke rise above Aisair like a mushroom.

'What the fuck?' gasped Danni.

A roar answered from the woods around them and soldiers rushed from cover across the open ground.

Both Ange and Danni moved at the same time. She grabbed her shield, drew her sword and charged after the others. A moment later, Danni was with her, iron rod in his hands and his sack of bombs slung over his head and shoulder. Ange's bombs were where she'd left them, in her sack back at the treeline. Gods, she hoped that wasn't going to cost her.

The ground was hard underfoot, full of ruts and rocks

664

threatening to turn her ankle or send her sprawling. She kept going nonetheless, looking for who had logs near her to throw over the trench that was due to appear any second.

The walls grew higher and higher and the number of Skulls watching from the battlements grew larger and the open ground they raced over grew ever wider and more exposed.

She spotted the trench as others waited along its edge for the trees to be dropped in place. Easy targets, thought Ange. Too easy.

Then the logs were down and people started to cross. Still, there was too much bunching for Ange's liking, and she knew nothing about war.

She was good and scared by the time it was her turn. A log that had looked so big when she saw it being carried along was now no more than a foot wide and the drop down was something nasty, with dirt-covered spikes lined up along the bottom of the trench. Having people in front and behind her didn't help, either, wobbling the log more than she would've liked. 'Should've fucking gone with Garo,' she muttered.

She heard cries, too, coming from up and down the line as some poor sods toppled off their logs, but each one was quickly silenced as they landed on the spikes.

When Ange was about halfway across, she saw – or rather *didn't* see – something that scared her even more.

Whatever caused that Godsdamned explosion, it wasn't the signal they'd been waiting for. They shouldn't have charged, because there was no hole in the city walls.

The gates still stood.

Ange and the others had no way into the city. She watched, open-mouthed, as others charged forwards through the gaps in the burned-down barricade and on towards Aisair.

'No,' she whispered. 'Dear Gods, no.'

Then the Chosen opened fire.

96

Wenna

Aisair

'Stop!' screamed Wenna as the army charged from the woods. 'Stop!' She could see that the gates hadn't been destroyed, that the explosion was deeper in the city, but no one else had. Now no one listened.

Thousands of Meigorians and Jians surged forwards, howling war cries.

'Stop! The gates are still up!' She grabbed at bodies as they raced past, but most shrugged themselves free and those that did pause gave her a look that questioned her sanity. 'Stop!'

She watched them go, feeling helpless, feeling out of place, feeling at fault. She was their leader who couldn't lead. She was the one who'd glibly told her soldiers to look for a big explosion instead of developing a real plan of attack.

'The mad fools,' said Nika.

'What do we do?' asked Tavis from beside her.

'The only thing we can do,' said Wenna. 'Go after them and pray for a miracle.'

'I was afraid you were going to say that,' said Tavis. The man drew his sword all the same. Nika and Wenna did likewise. And then they all ran towards certain death.

Wenna fixed her eyes on the gates. Stared at them hard enough to destroy them by sheer force of will alone. But she wasn't Zorique or Aasgod. She wasn't even Tinnstra. She was just a Shulka and the gates still stood, unmoved, as her army ran on.

At least the plan to deal with the trench had worked. By the time Wenna and the others reached it, the leading pack had already dropped the prepared logs over the gap and run over them.

Wenna, Tavis and Nika followed. As Wenna crossed the trench, she saw at least six bodies impaled on the spikes below. Maybe they were the lucky ones.

They reached the burned-out barricade as the first red blasts arced down from the battlements as the Chosen opened fire.

Explosions tore into the ranks. Bodies flew in every direction. Blood, limbs, dirt and debris rained down. It was a slaughter.

'Fall back!' cried Wenna. 'Fall back!'

This time, her cry was taken up by everyone around her and people listened. They turned and rushed back as fast as they could. But still the blasts came, ripping up chunks of earth and wiping out scores of troops. Some blasts were shot high overhead and lashed into the rear ranks stuck on the open ground behind them. The allies were trapped.

'Take cover in the trench,' shouted Wenna. 'Take cover in the trench.' She didn't wait to see if anyone listened but ran herself. A blast smashed into the ground where she'd been standing a second earlier, nearly throwing her off her feet, but somehow she kept going, sliding the last few yards. She dropped over the edge of the trench and nearly impaled herself on a spike. She hugged the dirt as more explosions pounded the ground around her.

Tavis slid down beside her, then Nika was there, Cal, Jen and Ange a bit further down. Plenty of others weren't so lucky in avoiding the spikes in the trench, their screams adding to the cacophony of horror going on around her.

She peeked over the top, saw others still running across the churned-up ground, weaving through the corpses of their comrades. 'Hurry! Down here! Watch out for the fucking spikes!'

Some made it, while too many others didn't. For every one that reached the relative safety of the trench, at least another five died.

Her army cowered in the trench as the red blasts continued to pummel the ground in front of the city walls. It felt as if the assault lasted for ever as Wenna lay there, covering her ears, caked with dirt and blood, choking on smoke. All her hopes of a free Jia lay with the dead. Tears she'd long denied herself now flowed freely.

How had it all gone so wrong? Jia was surely cursed. *She* was cursed. Better she'd died in Meigore than witness this disaster.

She barely noticed when the explosions stopped as her ears were still ringing from the carnage around her. Only the stillness of the ground alerted Wenna to the cessation of the attack. She opened her eyes, blinking away the tears and the smoke.

The first thing she saw was the line of scared faces beside her. Some looked to her, others to the heavens, and a few brave souls looked towards Aisair. Probably all wondering how they were still alive.

Wenna grabbed her water skin with shaking hands, uncorked it and took a gulp, trying to get the taste of smoke and dirt and blood out of her mouth. She wished it was something stronger, enough to make her feel braver, to believe there was still hope. But stale water was all she had.

Someone tapped her on the back. Wenna turned, saw Tavis.

'You okay?' he asked over the roar in her ears.

'No,' she replied, corking the water skin.

'Where are you hurt?'

Wenna shook her head. 'I'm not injured. It's ... it's just ...'

'It's all right. I get it. It's fucking awful. But we're not dead yet. It's not over yet.'

Wenna didn't know whether to laugh or cry. 'Of course it's over. We've got nowhere to go. Most of our army is dead.'

'It's only over if we give up,' hissed Tavis through clenched teeth.

'We've got nowhere to go,' she repeated. 'We attack, we die. We retreat, we die. Soon enough they'll starting raining fire down on us here and we die,' said Wenna. 'It's over.'

'No, it's not. Don't give up on me – on us.'

'What else can we do? If we surrender, they might spare the rest of us.'

'Wenna, no. We are the dead who fight.' Tavis's face contorted in anger as he said the words, but he gave no solutions, offered no way forward.

'Unless we can get past the gates, we don't have a choice.'

'Fuck.'

Wenna turned and climbed up the slope just enough to peer over the top. Corpses littered the blood-soaked ground for at least fifty yards. There was barely anything left of the wooden barricade, certainly nothing to use for cover, before the last stretch of open killing ground between them and the gates.

How long had it been since she'd travelled through them with Royati and Sami, buying their way with chicken and pork? She remembered the gates being big and tall but nothing special. They certainly weren't particularly thick. They'd not been built to stop an invading army from entering the city, after all.

'We got anyone who can throw straight?' she asked, without taking her eyes off the gate.

'I don't know. I can find out,' said Tavis. 'Why?'

'Find someone good enough, maybe they can throw an orb at the gates. Maybe one will be enough to knock them down.'

Tavis stared at the gates. 'Maybe.'

'We do that, we can make a run for it. Some of us might make it through.'

Tavis nodded. 'Better than dying here.'

'Go find me someone.'

'On it.' Tavis slithered down the line, asking questions along the way, getting shakes of the head back. Wenna wondered if he would find anyone. She couldn't blame people for not wanting the job. Not after what they'd just gone through.

Wenna watched the walls. There were plenty of Skulls up there and Chosen, too. Most were watching the ground below, but some were distracted by whatever was going on inside the city. Now her ears were settling, Wenna thought she could hear the sounds of battle from within, mixed with shouts and cries and only the Gods knew what else. Maybe it was Zorique and Tinnstra? Or Aasgod and Kos? Maybe it was Jax, betraying them all.

Probably that.

They were cursed, after all.

Movement caught her eye from the trench. It was Ange weaving her way through the spikes. Wenna watched the young girl approach, all scowls and determination, a shield almost as big as she was on one arm, and tried to remember what she'd been like at that age. Ange was what? Sixteen? Seventeen?

Wenna would've been in her first year at the Kotege, trying so hard to do well. She'd fallen in love with that boy from Clan Huska – what was his name? Gods, it was all so long ago.

Ange slotted into the space that Tavis had vacated. 'Mind if I join you?'

'Good to see you alive,' said Wenna.

'Don't know how I managed it,' said Ange. 'That was some fuck-up.'

'I'm sorry. That was my fault. Telling everyone to charge when they heard a big explosion.'

'Nothing's going right for us, is it?'

'No.' Wenna smiled. 'Still missing that lad of yours?'

'He's not mine. But yeah, I am. I'm glad he's not here, though. If he'd managed to stay alive, he'd be bending my ear off with his moaning.'

'I think he'd be allowed, all things considered.'

Ange peeked over at the gates. 'What's the plan? Wait here till dark and then try and slip away?'

'Not a bad plan,' said Wenna. 'But no.'

Ange screwed her face up again. 'We're not going to attack again, are we?'

'Thought we might.'

'Shit. Wish I'd not asked.'

'Tavis talked me into it. Said some nonsense about not giving up while we were still alive.'

'I never liked that man.' Ange puffed her cheeks out. 'So, what's the plan, then?'

'Find someone brave enough to throw a bomb at the gates, blow them up and then charge in.'

'That's the sort of plan Dren would've come up with – bloody mad.' Ange looked over the ground again. 'Might work. If you can find someone dumb enough to do it.'

'That's always the secret.'

They didn't have to wait long for Tavis to come back with a Meigorian in tow. 'This is Jamie. One of Ralasis' crew. He reckons he can throw an orb from here and hit the gates.'

'Are you sure?' said Wenna in Meigorian.

The man brushed a lock of dark hair away from his face and nodded. 'Yes. I've not seen an orb before, but this man told me they're the size of an apple. If that is the case, then I think so.'

'Show him some bombs,' said Wenna to Tavis.

The Shulka slipped away again, returning a moment later with a small sack. He opened it to reveal the contents – five black orbs. 'Here you go.'

As Jamie went to pick one up, Ange grabbed his wrist. 'You got any cuts?'

The man didn't understand her and looked to Wenna.

'She asked if you have any cuts,' said Wenna in Meigorian. 'Blood activates the explosive within the orbs.'

Jamie inspected his hand. As he turned it, they all saw the red dots that speckled the back of it. 'It's not my blood.'

'Better to be careful,' said Wenna. She picked up her water skin, uncorked it and poured some over Jamie's hand. Ange rubbed at it with her sleeve and the blood was soon gone.

Jamie reached into the bag and took out an orb. Wenna noticed Ange flinch away from it, but she said nothing as the Meigorian weighed the bomb in his hand.

'Heavier than an apple,' he said. 'How long does it take to go off once blood's been applied to it?'

'Ange, how long before it explodes?' Wenna asked.

'Five, maybe six seconds,' said Ange. 'But it feels a lot quicker when you're holding one that's glowing.'

Wenna translated for Jamie. 'Can you do it?'

The Meigorian looked at the gate again. 'I think I'll have to get closer before I throw it.'

'How close?'

'Maybe where the barricade is.'

'They'll see you from the walls.'

'I know.'

'They'll kill you.'

Jamie nodded. 'They might.'

'I can't let you do that.'

Ange was looking from one to the other, not understanding the language, but she was a smart kid. 'What's the matter?'

Wenna told her.

'Shit,' replied Ange. 'But it's our only way out?'

'Yes.'

'Then there's no choice.' She turned to the Meigorian and gave him a nod. 'Good luck,' she said in Jian.

'Thank you,' replied Jamie in bad Jian.

'Tavis, get everyone ready,' said Wenna. 'We go the moment the gates fall. We go fast, straight into the city.'

'Then where?' asked Tavis.

'We head to the royal castle,' said Wenna. 'But it sounds like there's plenty of fighting going on already, so make sure everyone's expecting trouble the moment we're in the city.'

Tavis slipped away to spread the word.

While they waited, Jamie stared at the ground he had to run. His breathing was slow, coming in forced deep breaths, as if he were trying to calm himself.

'You'll be okay,' said Wenna. 'Just be quick and get the hell out of there the moment you've thrown the bomb.'

'I will.' Jamie noticed his hands were shaking so he squeezed them into fists until his knuckles went white. Then he laughed and relaxed. 'I'm nervous.'

'I know,' said Wenna, trying to smile. 'So am I. And I'm not doing the running.'

'If you see the commander – if he's still alive – tell him it was an honour serving with him.'

'You tell him yourself. Start thinking you're not going to make it and you won't.'

Jamie nodded and started breathing deeply once more.

Then Tavis was back and it was time for Jamie to run.

He slipped the bag over his head and shoulder, tested how it felt. 'Too heavy.' He reached in, took out two orbs and placed them on the ground by Wenna's feet. He nodded as if satisfied with the weight, then held out his left hand. 'Who will do the honours?'

'I will,' said Wenna. She nicked his palm at the base of the thumb, not too deep but deep enough. They all watched as a line of red appeared.

Ange suddenly stepped forward and kissed him. 'May the Four Gods look after you,' she said, blushing.

Jamie did some blushing of his own, then started to climb up the side of the trench. He paused a moment at the top, took another deep breath and hauled himself up and out.

By the time Wenna peeked over the lip of the trench, the blasts were raining down from the walls. Jamie was quick, though, zig-zagging his way through the bodies, then across the open ground to the ruins of the barricade.

He disappeared a few times as the explosions threw up dirt and smoke, making Wenna catch her breath, but then there he was – at the barricade. He dropped down behind a post and reached into the bag.

'Come on,' whispered Ange, watching beside Wenna. 'Move!'

Jamie had an orb out, smeared his bloody left hand over it and it started to glow. He stood up, drew his arm back, took aim and—

The Chosen's blast hit him square in the chest, ripping him apart.

A moment later, the bomb went off, destroying whatever was left of him and setting off the other two bombs.

'Shit,' said Ange. She slid back down the slope to the bottom of the trench. Wenna just watched the smoke drift up off Jamie's corpse. They really were cursed.

At least no one charged that time. They all knew that explosion wasn't their signal. They all knew it was a disaster.

Then someone launched themselves past Wenna and sprinted towards the gates.

It was Ange – with a bomb in her hand.

And once more the Chosen's blasts began to fall.

97
Yas

Arlen's Farm

Yas sat in her cage under a blood-red sky and wondered how long she had left to live. 'When the sun goes down, the knives come out,' Kenan had said earlier, and now it had.

The Weeping Men had been busy all afternoon, readying for their farewell party. A pyre had been built in the middle of the village square and more tables set up. The smell of roasting meat had wafted tantalisingly past her and Sorin's noses, but no one had seen fit to give them a cup of water, let alone a bite to eat.

Her mind drifted to Little Ro. She hoped to the Four Gods none of Kenan's mob had found the caves, and that he was safe. Still, someone had talked. If that someone felt inclined to show the Weeping Men how to get to her son, then hoping and praying would be no bloody use to anyone, least of all Yas.

Then again, nothing would be of use to her soon enough.

Two poles had been pounded into the ground an arm's width apart, with hooped ropes fixed to the top of each.

'They'll take us up, one at a time, and make us stand between them,' said Sorin. He was slumped in the corner of the cage and had barely spoken since Kenan had been around to see them. 'Our hands go through the ropes, and when we're good and secured, they'll start cutting.'

'By the Gods,' said Yas. Just the thought of it made her want to throw up. 'What sick bastard came up with that?'

Sorin chuckled. It wasn't a happy sound. 'Never bothered to ask myself.'

'Not that it matters anyway,' said Yas.

People started to arrive. The Weeping Men sat at the tables and helped themselves to food and drink while the villagers were all herded together on the other side of the square. Yas looked for her son amongst the gathering crowd, but thankfully there was no sign of him. She spotted Mayes, Sala, Anan and Venon, all looking scared and uncomfortable.

Then she saw another face she recognised and stiffened. Yas couldn't believe it.

Simone was there, amongst the villagers. Her eyes locked on Yas's and she gave the slightest of nods.

'Fuck,' muttered Yas.

'What?' asked Sorin.

'Simone's here,' whispered Yas. 'She just gave me a nod.'

'A nod? What sort of nod? A "we're here to rescue you" nod or an "I've come to watch you die" sort of nod?'

'I don't fucking know,' said Yas. 'The way my luck's been running I doubt it's good news for us.'

Sorin sat up, craning his neck for a better look. 'She got others with her? She brought the Meigorians?'

'I don't *know*,' she hissed. 'Now calm down before every Weeping Man here starts to wonder what's got you so excited.'

Sorin sat back, but he still kept looking. Yas couldn't really tell him off – she was doing the same. She couldn't help it. Seeing Simone had given her the faintest of hopes where there had been none. Was she there to rescue Yas, or was she there to see her die? It said everything that Yas didn't know which.

By the Four Gods, she'd really fucked up everything.

One of the Weeping Men lit the bonfire they'd built. It went up quickly, flames leaping from one batch of kindling to another before taking to the thicker logs, and the blaze got a cheer from the rest of Kenan's men.

'Yas. Sorin. Don't turn around,' whispered Dean from behind them.

'Where have you been, you bastard?' said Sorin.

'Trying my best not to end up in here with you,' replied Dean.

'They've been watching me, waiting for any sign I might not be loyal.'

Yas kept still, eyes fixed on the square. 'But you're here now, eh? With good news, I hope.'

'Got knives for you,' said Dean.

'That it?' said Yas. 'I saw Simone in the crowd.'

'I haven't been able to get down to the beach to speak to her.' There was a scrape of metal on wood and Yas felt cold steel against her fingertips. 'Take these,' said Dean. 'Be quick. You've not got much time.'

'Thanks,' said Yas, appreciating the risk the man was taking. She couldn't help but wish it was more.

'Good luck, Chief,' said Dean and then he was gone.

Yas looked down, saw the two knives Dean had left behind. Hefty hunter's blades, they were, and sharp-looking, too. 'Cut my hands free,' she said to Sorin.

It was clumsy work, but the knife did its job without Sorin drawing blood. It wasn't much, but Yas was certainly happier with her hands free and holding a sharp knife.

'So, what do we do now?' said Sorin as Yas returned the favour.

'The only thing we can do,' said Yas, glancing over at the gathering crowd. 'Get out and run.'

'Can't argue with that.'

They cut the ropes around their ankles next. The day and a half she'd spent tied up had left Yas with welts and cuts and raw skin around her ankles and wrists, but she could live with that – it was her lungs she couldn't live without.

All that was left then was to hack their way out of the cage. 'Keep watch,' said Sorin as he started cutting away at the twine.

'Be quick.'

He gave her a look that said she was saying the bleeding obvious, and then got back to cutting.

Yas turned her attention to the crowd and immediately wished she hadn't. Kenan was standing a few yards away, watching with that bloody awful grin of his plastered across his face. 'Shit.'

'Yas! Sorin!' Kenan called out, loud enough for the whole bloody village to hear. He spread his arms wide. 'You're not trying to leave us, are you? The night's barely begun and you're our guests of honour.'

'Why don't you just fuck off, eh? Give us something to celebrate.' Yas held up her knife in front of her. 'Keep bloody cutting,' she hissed out of the corner of her mouth to Sorin. A pole popped loose in reply.

'Ooh, who gave you a knife, Yas? Someone been naughty?' Kenan winked. He clicked his fingers and two of his men dragged a third out from the crowd and dumped him in front of Kenan. It was Dean.

He tried to run, but barely got three yards before he was dragged back. This time the Weeping Men held his arms.

'Hey, you evil bastard,' shouted Yas. 'Let him go.' She moved, blocking Sorin from sight. Hopefully that would be enough to stop Kenan from noticing the hole Sorin was making. Still, she needed all his attention on her. 'It wasn't him.'

'It wasn't him,' mimicked Kenan. 'Should I take your word for it, eh? Because you wouldn't lie to me, would you, Yas?'

'I'm telling you the truth.'

Another pole fell from the cage. 'One more and we can get out,' whispered Sorin.

'Why don't I believe you?' said Kenan, producing a knife of his own.

'Don't do it, Kenan,' said Yas, but she knew she was wasting her words.

Kenan pulled back Dean's head, exposing his throat.

'I didn't do anything,' said Dean. 'I'd never betray you.'

'I always know when someone's lying to me,' said Kenan. He looked around, knife held high. 'Watch, all of you. Dean here won't be the last to die tonight, but at least he'll die quick. Unlike the two in the cage over there. They'll be going out screaming the bloody heavens down. Now, I promise you, anyone else who gets any ideas about crossing the Weeping Men and helping those pieces of shit will join them in their suffering. Got it?'

Another pole fell from the cage. 'We can get out,' said Sorin.

Yas turned her back on Dean and Kenan. She didn't need to see another friend die.

98

Ralasis

Ralasis felt hands on him, pulling him. He fought back, swinging wildly, barely conscious. Pain screamed from his left arm when he tried to move it and he howled from the agony.

'No, no. We're on your side,' said a man in Jian.

'We need to be quick,' said a woman. 'The Skulls are coming.'

Ralasis blinked his eyes open, tried to focus. A bald man and a woman had him upright between them, a third man covering them with what looked like a home-made spear in his hands. They dragged him down the pile of rubble the Daijaku had snatched him from, each jolt sending white-hot pain through Ralasis' arm.

'My arm,' he managed to say.

'I think it's broken,' said the man by his side. 'We can look at it when we're safe.'

'The Skulls are killing everyone,' said the woman. 'Nowhere's safe.'

'They're doing what?' said Ralasis.

'Killing everyone,' said the man with the spear as they reached the flat ground of the street. 'Dragging people out of their houses and cutting their heads off right there.'

'By the Four Gods.' Ralasis found his feet as he tried to clear his head. 'What are your names?'

'I'm Modi,' said the man with the spear.

'Lisa,' said the woman, 'and this is Watt.' The other man nodded.

'Thank you ... for saving me,' said Ralasis. Something wet ran into his eye. When he wiped it clear, he saw his blood smeared on the back of his hand. He traced a cut across half his forehead with his fingers.

'We're not going to leave anyone to die if we can help it,' said Modi.

'We need to get away from here,' said Lisa. 'The Skulls will be back soon enough – and in greater numbers.'

'Let me do something for his arm first,' said Watt.

'Get on with it, then,' said Lisa. 'Otherwise we'll be here all night.'

'I'll keep watch,' said Modi, clambering back up the rubble.

'Don't mind them,' said Watt as he delved into a bag on his hip. From it, he produced some cloth cut up into bandages. 'If I had time, I'd put a proper splint on you, but this'll have to do until later.'

Ralasis winced as Watt placed his broken arm in a sling and tied the cloth around his neck. The arm was already an ugly shade of purple, but at least the bone hadn't pierced the skin. 'Thank you.'

Watt and his two friends weren't the only ones gathered in the street. A good hundred or so had come out of their homes. Some were ready to fight with makeshift weapons, everything from kitchen knives to broomsticks and chair legs. Others were ready for flight with bags and belongings in their hands and kids clinging to them.

All of them looked scared.

An explosion went off, shaking the very ground, but it wasn't close by. He didn't think so, at least – if it had been, they'd all be dead.

A second later, a mushroom-shaped cloud of dust billowed up. It was followed by more cracks further out – baton blasts. Lots of them. Smaller explosions, too. Orbs.

'It's getting bad,' said Lisa. 'You done playing doctor?'

Watt nodded. 'Done for now, anyways.'

'The army's here,' said Ralasis.

'The what?' said Lisa.

'The noise. The fighting. The Jian army's here to liberate Aisair.'

'You're no Jian,' said Watt.

'I'm Meigorian. I came here with your queen, Zorique, and her army. We've come to free Jia,' said Ralasis. 'That's why the Skulls are killing everyone. That's why there's all this fighting.'

'Don't seem like the Skulls are losing,' said Modi from the top of the rubble.

Ralasis looked up at him. 'That's why we have to help.'

'We don't have to do anything,' said Lisa. 'Apart from stay alive. And fighting isn't going to help much in that regard. Better we hide.'

'No!' said Ralasis, raising his voice as he staggered into the middle of the street. 'We have to help! We have to fight.' All eyes were on him as more explosions went off, rattling windows. 'We can put an end to the Skulls once and for all if you'll join me and join your queen's army.'

'You can barely stand, let alone fight,' said Lisa. 'We have to run.'

'Where to?' said Ralasis. 'There is nowhere to run. This is Sekanowari. It's happening now. We either fight together and win together or we can run and die alone.'

'We're not Shulka,' called out a man from the crowd.

'No, you're not. But you're Jians, every single one of you. The Skulls can kill you all one by one but, if you join together – join me – then we can kill them instead. We can free this city, this country.'

'We've got kids to think about,' shouted out another woman, a boy and girl hiding behind her dress.

'And the best way to keep them safe is for those of you who can fight to come with me. We'll never get an opportunity like this again. To decide now, while we can, to live or die. Because those are your choices.'

'I'll fight,' said Modi, holding his home-made spear. 'Skulls have already killed everyone I love. I've got nothing to lose.'

'I'll fight, too,' said a woman with a meat cleaver clutched in her fist.

'Good. Good,' said Ralasis. 'Who else?'

Before anyone could answer, Daijaku screeched overhead, making everyone cower.

'How can we fight them?' cried a white-haired man.

A golden light appeared over the rooftops in answer.

Zorique.

Ralasis was as entranced as everyone else as she waved a hand after the demons and they burst into flames.

Baton blasts shot into the sky, seeking her, but she was gone as quickly as she had appeared.

'That's your queen,' said Ralasis. 'That's Zorique. Let her deal with the demons. We'll deal with the Skulls.'

Someone cheered, then others joined in, and just like that, Ralasis had an army of his own once more. Hopefully one he wasn't going to lead to their deaths. He glanced down at his left arm and winced at the sight of the unnatural bend in the middle of his forearm. Truth was they would probably all get killed. Maybe the woman was right. Maybe the sensible thing to do was run and hide.

Shame Ralasis had never done the sensible thing in his life.

99

Ange

Aisair

Ange ran towards the gates with a bomb in her hand. Her heart hammered away, blood pounding through her veins, as she sprinted over the barren ground. Only the Gods knew what she was doing – she certainly had no clue. One minute she'd been cowering in the trench, watching that poor sod of a Meigorian get killed, thinking it was all over, and then she'd snatched up a bomb and she was on her way.

Sure, the Meigorian had reminded her of Dren, with the same sort of eyes and a smile that knew how to break hearts. A suicide run was exactly what Dren would've done – what he did do – so watching that lad die was like watching Dren die all over again. Not that she'd actually seen Dren die. Except in her dreams.

So maybe that's why she'd done it – for Dren. But she also knew they were all fucked if the gates didn't fall. No one was going to walk away from that mess. So maybe that was why. Maybe she was just stupid.

It was a long run, now she was doing it. Should she start weaving? Make it hard for the Chosen to guess where she was going to run? Or would that slow her down? Better to be fast. Too fast for them? Were they even firing those fucking blasts at her?

The thoughts rattled through her mind as quickly as her lungs heaved air in and out, burning her throat. The orb seemed to change shape in her hand, too, getting bigger and slipperier.

Chances were she'd drop the fucking thing a heartbeat before the Chosen killed her.

No glory for Ange. Just a big bloody hole and a pile of ash for being so stupid.

What was she doing?

Should have gone with Garo. Stayed safe with him.

She heard a crack. Knew instantly what it was. She swerved right a heartbeat before the ground exploded to her left – where she would've been. Fucking lucky.

Another crack. She veered left, nearly tripping herself up in the process, and the ground blew up to her right. Two times lucky, three times what?

She kept running, her mouth full of smoke and dust, head down, sprinting straight, as scared as she could ever remember being, trying to find speed in her legs that she wasn't sure she'd ever had.

There were more cracks. More explosions. One sent her flying through the air and dumped her on the ground so hard that she bit her tongue and forgot how to breathe. The orb went flying, too, straight out of her stupid, sweat-slick hand. She watched it bounce as she failed to do so and fixed her eyes on it as she willed herself up and somehow got running again.

Ange thought she heard cheering from behind her. Heard her name. Probably Wenna cursing her. With good reason.

She snatched up the bomb, glad she hadn't cut herself with all the stumbling and falling and nearly getting blown up. It would be just her luck to blow herself up when she was almost at the gates.

But was she? She was closer – sure – but it was hard to tell how close with the fucking world blowing up around her.

Close enough to throw the bloody thing? What if she tried and missed? She couldn't let everyone down, couldn't die for nothing.

Dren didn't die for nothing.

Another explosion and another and another and another.

How the hell was she still alive? She should've been dead a hundred times.

Ange went down again, cracked her head on a rock, saw stars amongst the smoke. She still had the bomb, though. That was something. Pressed tight up against her chest, holding it like a baby. All its bad magic probably leaking into her like it did Dren, killing her tomorrow if the Chosen didn't kill her today.

She got up, started running, pain shooting through her feet with every step. Maybe she was limping more than running.

The gates *were* close now. A few more yards and she could bloody touch them.

Close enough to throw the fucking thing. Just needed to set it going. Needed blood for that. Luckily, she had loads. A mouthful at least from where she'd bitten her tongue. She dropped to her knees and spat every drop of it over the black orb.

It lit up straight away, swirling mad, all its evil set to work just like that. Death in a ball.

Ange threw it at the gates, watched it bounce against the wood then drop to the ground a foot away.

Close enough. Close enough to kill her.

Fuck.

100

Wenna

'Run, Ange, run!' screamed Wenna as she watched the girl sprint through the barrage of Chosen blasts. A bomb in her hand.

One orb was left lying on the ground at Wenna's feet. She picked it up and placed it in the bag on her hip. She didn't know why, except for the old Shulka saying that it was better to have a weapon and not need it than need a weapon and not have it.

'She's going to die,' said Tavis, staring wide-eyed at the running girl.

'No, she's not,' said Nika.

'Run!' The shout was taken up down the line of the trench as they all watched.

Wenna held her breath when Ange was close enough to throw the bomb, but the girl just kept running. 'What's she doing?' she said to no one in particular. 'Why doesn't she throw the bloody thing?'

'Throw it!' shouted Tavis.

They lost sight of her then as smoke and dirt swirled around and the Chosen continued to bombard the open ground. Ange had to be dead. There was no way she could've survived that barrage. There was—

'She's at the gate,' shouted Tavis as the smoke cleared. And there she was. She'd made it. By some bloody miracle, she'd made it.

They watched her throw the bomb. They all saw it hit the gate. They all saw Ange dive to the side.

The orb exploded. There was a flash of light, a roar of noise, more smoke, more debris, more dirt flying.

Most likely Ange dead with it.

Still the Chosen rained their blasts on the ravaged ground near the walls.

'The gate? Is the gate down?' she shouted to Tavis.

The man peered over the edge of the trench. 'I can't see. I … yes! Yes, it is!'

Wenna could see it, too – a hole had been punched straight through the centre of the gates. Big enough for at least six or seven people to get through. Big enough for her army. She drew both her swords and stood up. 'Let's go! The gates to Aisair are OPEN!' Tavis rose with her, Nika, too. Others followed. The movement rippled up and down the line. This was it. She pointed a sword at the ruined gate. 'CHARGE!'

With her command ringing in her ears, Wenna clambered over the top and ran with everything she had. She didn't look to see who followed, but she could sense the army moving with her out of the corner of her eye and felt relief that, no matter what happened next, she would not die alone.

Others were faster than her and Wenna found herself within a mass of bodies, being pulled along, shoulder to shoulder, the crush growing tighter as they all veered towards the same hole in the gates.

And still the Chosen fired down. There were no wasted shots now. Every blast killed more of her army.

The ground exploded all around Wenna as she ran. Blood and guts and body parts flew in every direction. Screams filled the air. The injured begged and pleaded for help from their friends, their mothers and the Gods. The dead just got in the way.

There were too many people around Wenna to dodge and swerve from the Chosen's blasts like Ange had done. It was all down to luck now. Luck and the speed in her legs. 'Keep going!' she cried with what little air she had in her lungs. 'We're nearly there.'

She caught sight of Tavis a second before an explosion sent him to Xin's kingdom. She fought back a sob, fixed her eyes on the damn hole in the gate and forced her legs to keep moving.

'For Jia! For Jia!' Wenna shouted for herself as much as for the people around her – not that anyone could hear her over the carnage.

The gate was close now. She could see the city on the other side and there were still enough of her army around her, enough to make a difference. Enough to—

White shapes appeared at the breach. Skulls sent to stop the Jians. They poured through the opening, scimitars drawn.

Wenna was actually glad to see them. They were foes she could fight. She howled as she threw herself at them, swords swinging, rage and desperation fuelling her, lost in the madness of it all.

Her army came with her – what was left of it – smashing into the Skulls. There was no finesse to the fighting, no form or discipline. Wenna hacked, slashed, parried and thrust, attacking anything in white, forcing her way forwards, towards that bloody gate.

Ange's friend Danni appeared by her side, swinging a metal rod that cracked helmets and broke bones, his scarred face all red and contorted. Nika was there, too, screaming in fury, her sword hand darting again and again into the melee.

Bodies pushed from all sides, lifting Wenna off the ground, carrying her forwards then back. Blood flew in every direction, covering her hands, her face, getting in her mouth and eyes. Still she stabbed at the Skulls, fighting with everything she had to gain another inch towards the breach. Her swords were red and her hands ached, but she willed herself on, praying to the Gods to protect her as she killed another white-armoured bastard that crossed her path.

Wenna felt a jolt in her side as a sword was turned by her breastplate, then felt another as it tried to find a way into her guts. She smashed down with her sword pommel on a Skull's mask, splintering it in two, then pounded it down again into the man's face, breaking bone. He fell with the third strike and became just something to be trampled underfoot.

Another sword found her cheek, a quick kiss of steel. Wenna jerked her head back, not wanting to lose her eye, and cracked her skull against the person next to her on the other side. Something stung her right hand and she dropped the sword. Panic flared through her battle-crazed mind, fearing she'd lost her fingers with it, but they were still attached and working, all black and red, so she yanked back a Skull's helmet and rammed her other sword into his neck.

More Skulls flooded through the breach, adding their weight to their brothers in the front lines, and the push forward quickly turned into a push back. The breech that had been so close retreated from Wenna.

War's favour, ever fickle, left the Jians. Wenna could sense defeat waiting for them now. Others could, too – obvious in the way bodies shifted and heads turned, looking for ways out rather than ways forward.

'No!' cried Wenna. She tried to force her way towards the breach, but her legs weren't enough. Her strength was lacking. 'No!'

And more Skulls came through the gate.

No. She couldn't let it end like this. She wouldn't. Not after everything they'd been through, the lives lost.

Then she remembered the bomb in her bag.

Wenna thrust her hand down, felt for the bag on her hip. Such a simple task made all but impossible by the bodies squeezed tight against her and the Skulls trying to kill her. She fought with the sword in her left hand as her bloody fingers delved into the bag and found the orb.

Wenna knew the bomb was activated and the more blood, the faster the detonation. She had to be quick. She had to be—

The front of a Skull helmet smashed into her mouth and nose. She spat blood in the Egril's face, then slashed at him with her sword. She didn't hurt him, but it gave her a second's precious room. She pulled her arm out of the press, saw the orb glowing bright, burning hot and knew she was all out of time.

Wenna threw it as best she could, straight at the breach, straight at the Skulls pouring through.

She was grateful for the press of bodies around her then, grateful for the enemy that were trying to kill her. *Those* Skulls took the brunt of the blast. *They* died as it washed over them with all its fury.

The bomb did more than that, too. Ange had managed to create a breach in the gates, but Wenna's bomb obliterated what was left. The gates were no more than splinters and half the walls around them were missing, too.

'For Jia!' cried Wenna, pushing the dead bodies away from her. Some Skulls had survived, but none were capable of offering any real resistance. A nobler enemy might have shown them mercy, but Wenna was not that person. 'Kill them all! Kill them all!'

It didn't matter if the Skulls still held weapons or were on their hands and knees trying to crawl away.

'For Jia!' she cried as she stabbed men in the back.

'For Jia!' she screamed as she cut the throats of Skulls begging for mercy. Wenna slaughtered any Egril within her reach and was overjoyed to see her army doing the same.

Then they were through the gate and into Aisair. More dead Skulls waited for them there, killed by the bomb's blast, but there were plenty more living Skulls waiting for her.

Plenty more to kill.

'For Jia!' she howled as she charged towards the enemy.

IOI

Yas

Arlen's Farm

Yas had her back to Kenan as Sorin jumped from the cage, but she heard the thunk all the same. Like an axe into wood.

Then everyone started screaming.

She turned, saw the arrow jutting from Kenan's forehead as he tumbled to one side. Dean was looking all around, confused to still be alive, then he was on his feet and moving. A Weeping Man lunged to intercept him but an arrow in the back stopped him good enough.

People started running in every direction as the rest of the Weeping Men sprang up from their tables, drawing weapons, then more arrows flew in before many had taken even two steps. Over a dozen fell dead before the others scattered.

'Come on!' hissed Sorin. 'Let's get out of there. Quick.'

Yas tried to move, but she couldn't take her eyes off what was happening. Meigorians appeared, brandishing swords, and charged in. Even amidst the chaos, Yas could see there weren't enough of them to claim certain victory.

'Come on, Yas,' repeated Sorin, but this time he reached back into the cage and gave her arm a yank.

'All right,' she said, allowing herself to be pulled through the gap in the bars. Sorin helped lower her to the ground as the sword song rang across the square, along with a chorus of screams.

'This way.' Sorin kept low, moving around the back of the cage, heading away from the fight and towards the rows of homes.

'No,' said Yas. She stopped and stood up, hand tight on the knife she'd been given.

'What do you mean, "no"?' said Sorin.

'The Meigorians came to fight for us when we didn't deserve it,' said Yas. 'I can't run away and leave them to it.'

'Of course you bloody can,' said Sorin. 'It's called staying alive.'

'You go. I can't.'

'Think of your son, Yas. He's waiting for you up in that mountain.'

'Tell him I loved him if I don't make it back.'

'Yas, for fuck's—'

But Yas wasn't listening. She knew it was mad, knew it was the wrong bloody thing to do, but she ran the other way, towards the square, towards the fighting.

A Weeping Man appeared in front of her, screaming and cursing, an axe in his hand. She didn't know if he meant to attack her or just wanted her out the way, but she stabbed him all the same. More than once. In and out, again and again, just like when she'd killed Raab.

Better to be sure, after all.

She stepped over the body and moved into the square. There was fighting everywhere. A jumble of bodies as Meigorians tussled with Weeping Men. Some were one-on-one duels while others involved clusters from either side facing off against each other.

Villagers watched, eyes wide, hiding behind overturned tables or sheltering behind barrels. Mayes, Sala, Anan and Venon were there, and Yas spat a curse of their own. They should have been helping, too.

'Come on!' she screamed, waving her bloody knife. 'They're fighting to protect your homes!'

A Meigorian and a Weeping Man, locked in a tussle, each clasping the other man's sword arm, staggered her way. The moment the Weeping Man's back was facing her, Yas stepped in and drove her knife into the man's side.

She moved on, slipping into the fray, looking for more backs to stab. Hasan would've complained about the lack of honour in striking from behind, but no one died from shame as far as

Yas knew, and attempting a straight-up fight would only get her killed.

She moved quickly. If she couldn't get the back or side, she sliced hamstrings instead – anything that took a Weeping Man out of the fight.

Someone appeared beside her. She spun, ready to lash out, and saw that it was Sorin come to join her. He'd picked up a cleaver from somewhere and took on his foes with a gusto Yas couldn't match.

Then there were others, too – Venon and Anan leading the way. All come to join in now the tide had turned. All eager to get some blood on their hands now there was less chance to spill their own.

Yas didn't blame them. Truth was she'd rather not have any blood on her, same way she'd never wanted the tears on her cheek. Trouble was ... life didn't give a shit about anyone's wishes or wants.

By the end of it, most of the Weeping Men were dead. Fewer than twenty were rounded up as prisoners by the Meigorians.

Simone was with her men and gave Yas one of her nods as she approached.

'Thank you,' said Yas. 'We owe you all more than we can ever repay.'

'Sorry we left it so late, but some took more persuading than others to get them to agree to help,' replied Simone.

'Yeah, well, can't say I blame them,' said Yas. 'It's not like I made them feel too welcome. Sorry – I was a right shit.'

'We all make mistakes.'

'Hopefully, I learn from them, too. If any of the Meigorians want to move up to the village, they can. They've bled for this land twice now – it's as much theirs as ours.'

Simone nodded. 'Some might take you up on that, but most of them are still planning on going home soon. You heard any news from the north yet?'

'No,' said Yas. 'Not a word.'

They shared a look then. Both knew no news was bad news.

'What about the prisoners?' asked Simone instead.

Yas glanced over at the sorry bunch. They didn't look so tough now, on their knees, hands tied, a good few cuts and bruises shared between them. 'I kinda wish we didn't have any.'

'My men aren't murderers,' said Simone. 'They all surrendered and asked for mercy.'

'Like they showed us?' Yas took a breath, rubbed her face, then saw the blood already on her hands – on her. There was too much of it. She didn't need more. 'Come on.'

She walked over to the prisoners, aware that Dean and Sorin had fallen into place behind her. Others came too, her little council of Mayes, Sala, Anan and Venon amongst them. Even Rena was there, not looking like she wanted to kill Yas for once – that was progress, at least. All watching to see what she'd do next.

Yas raised a hand and a hush fell over the villagers. 'My friends, thanks to the Meigorians yet again, our homes are ours once more. We can sleep this night without fearing for our lives. We owe them all a debt we can never repay.'

A cheer went up, and Yas let everyone enjoy the moment before raising her hand once more. 'I've said to Simone already that any Meigorian who wishes to can build a home here with us in our village. It was my mistake not inviting them in the first place, and I hope you all agree they have earned a place here.'

Again, everyone cheered, louder this time. Yas only hoped they meant it.

'It's time I learned from all my mistakes,' said Yas. 'I never wanted to be in charge, but I must admit I liked it. Perhaps too much. And I relied on the tears on my cheek and the men at my back to get my own way. For that, I'm sorry. It was wrong of me. And because of me, the Weeping Men turned up and more of us suffered and some of us died.'

There were no cheers now. Just solemn faces staring at Yas.

'Simone has asked me what we're going to do with these prisoners. If we were Shulka, we'd put them to the sword without question. If the positions were reversed and it was the Weeping Men deciding our fates ... well, we'd all be dead. If we were Skulls, we'd be building gallows right this very moment to string them up. But seems to me, the old ways haven't done us much good.'

'We can't let them go,' shouted someone.

'They raped us,' called out a woman.

'Some did, but not all of them,' said Yas. 'If you want to punish anyone who's a Weeping Man, then you might as well lock me, Dean and Sorin up with them because we've all got tears on our cheeks, too.'

'You saved us,' said a man.

Yas shook her head. 'Nah, Simone and the Meigorians did that. Not me.'

'What do you want to do with them, then?' asked Venon.

'It's not up to me,' said Yas. 'It's up to you. I'm not going to be in charge anymore. You can all pick a new leader or have a council to look after things. You can make the hard choices, starting with this lot.'

'What are you going to do?' asked Mayes.

'Me? I'm going to climb up that mountain, see my boy, give him a hug and tell him I love him,' said Yas.

'You want us to come with you?' asked Sorin.

'I'm okay,' said Yas. 'You stay here. Have your say in what happens next. And Dean?'

'Yeah, Chief?'

She held out the bloody knife. 'Thanks for lending this to me. Much appreciated.'

Dean looked at the knife. 'You can keep it if you want.'

Yas shook her head. 'I'm just a mother. I need my son. That's all.'

102

Raaku

'Sekanowari,' said Raaku with a smile. He stood on a balcony
of the royal palace, looking over the city as war tore through
it. Loyal Vallia was beside him, his four guardians behind them.
'When we have won the day, raze whatever is left of this heathen
hellhole to the ground.'

'Yes, Your Majesty,' said Vallia. Despite being covered by
armour, he knew Vallia's skin was painted with runes. He could
feel them interfering with his powers, but he did not ask her
to step away. Raaku was still more than enough for whatever
challenged him today. For he was the son of the mighty Kage,
and all was as it was destined to be.

Raaku had been taken to the balcony in the royal suites the
moment he'd arrived. The sounds of Jians being sent to the Great
Darkness drifted up from the streets, a delightful murmur, hinting
at what was to come. Too long had Raaku been away from the
battlefield, too long since he'd personally directed his faithful
soldiers in doing his father's work.

He'd seen the heathen queen over the course of the morning,
flying above the rooftops, burning his Daijaku from the skies, but
quickly scurrying down out of sight. Nevertheless, her progress
towards the palace had been easy to track as she'd brought half
the city down around her in her efforts to defeat his men. It was
all so very desperate.

There'd been lightning, too, from the mage. From Laafien's

brother. The man was doing damage, but Raaku was not impressed. Laafien had possessed power – not this upstart.

Laafien. His body would've been disposed of by now. Perhaps fed to the young Daijaku. Strange that Raaku felt a sense of ... loss at the man's death. Laafien had been beside Raaku for over a hundred years as he'd carved the world in Kage's image. Laafien who'd been sent by Kage to ensure victory in Sekanowari. Perhaps he should've let the man live to witness this moment. Instead, Laafien would watch the souls flood into the Great Darkness and know Raaku had sent them. He would, at least, be reunited with his brother there.

'Any sign of the fourth champion?' asked Raaku.

'No, Your Majesty,' replied Vallia. 'There was a man with the Shulka when they rescued the queen, but he displayed no powers.'

Something exploded to the east, sending a mushroom-shaped cloud into the air. There was no way of telling who had set it off or gained as a result of it.

More explosions went up across the city and messages reached them that the main city gates had been breached by the heathen army.

Vallia glanced up at him. 'If you'd rather return to Kagestan, Your Majesty, I can send word to you there once we are victorious.'

Raaku watched the fires and the smoke. He listened to the shouts and cries, the clash of swords, that song of war he'd missed so much. 'You doubt we will win.'

'No, Your Majesty. Not at all. It's just—'

'They will not win, Commander.'

'Forgive me, Your Majesty.' Vallia bowed her head.

'I have told you from the beginning that the final battle will be here. Everything is as it was meant to be. The False Gods' champions will converge on the palace. They will sense victory, despite the bloodshed and the lives lost. Death will stand amongst them and they will think Sekanowari is theirs.

'But remember, False Gods give false hope. We serve the one true God, the mighty Kage, and the day will belong to him.'

696

'Yes, Your Majesty,' said Vallia, strength returning to her voice.

'The Tonin are in position?'

'They are, Your Majesty.'

'And the orb is guarded?'

'Yes, Your Majesty. Members of the First Legion stand sentry over it in the throne room. No one will get near it.'

'And the prisoners?'

'As you ordered, Sire. We have a hundred Jians bound in a circle around the egg.'

Raaku smiled. 'Then we wait, like the spider for the flies.'

103

Tinnstra

Aisair

Tinnstra concentrated on fighting. It was all she could do. She almost didn't need to think about it. Her body, trained over fifteen long years, knew how to kill. The Niganntan spear already felt a part of her as she whirled it from foe to foe, dealing death with the blade and the butt. She'd picked up a new sword on the way. There was no way she'd be caught weaponless again.

Not now *he* was there.

Raaku. She could almost feel him watching her.

His presence filled her mind. A crushing darkness sitting in her head like a cancer, pounding away, growing stronger with every step they took towards the royal palace.

The only thing that stopped Tinnstra from collapsing in agony was the light she sensed from Zorique and, to a lesser degree, Aasgod. What once caused her crippling pain pushed against Raaku's magic, preventing it from consuming her. The irony wasn't lost on Tinnstra that the two people she'd abandoned turned out to be the two she needed most.

The three of them and Jax moved street by street towards the royal palace. She should feel hopeful, but she couldn't help but feel Ralasis' absence all the more. He was the fourth champion – she was sure of that now – but he was probably dead. Killed being a hero, the bloody fool. So, what did that mean for their cause?

She couldn't believe it was over.

Raaku's forces rushed to stop them, but all the Egril managed to do was die. Even the Skulls who were immune to Zorique's magic couldn't survive having a building dropped on them, or the street beneath their feet throwing them a hundred feet into the air.

And those that did manage to get close? Tinnstra was there, ready to send their souls back to the Great Darkness. She stained the streets red with their blood. Bodies tumbled left and right, cleaved from shoulder to groin, from hip to hip, from head to arse.

Tinnstra didn't care how she killed them.

She didn't care how many she had to kill.

She would fight until the last Skull had died.

Zorique fought beside her, using an Egril scimitar when she couldn't use her powers, her technique calm and precise. She struck at the Skulls' vulnerable spots, wasting no energy, darting in and out of attacks, leaving no threat alive.

Jax and Aasgod brought up the rear, the one-armed Shulka protecting the mage. After all, Aasgod was no good in the close-quarter fighting.

And behind them, a force off their own followed; men and women, armed with scavenged or improvised weapons, drawn by the freedom that the four champions promised, rushed out of their homes and from behind their barricades.

'Aasgod! Chosen!' shouted Tinnstra as two black-clad figures flew towards them.

'I see them!' the mage shouted back. Lightning shot out a heartbeat later and struck the two figures.

The Chosen weren't protected from Aasgod's magic like the Skulls were. Perhaps it stopped their own powers from working as well as Zorique's and Aasgod's, but the why didn't really matter. It was enough that the Chosen died.

And die they did, tumbling from the sky, burning as they fell.

More appeared on a rooftop. Six of them, bringing their batons to bear. Lightning arced out, destroying half the roof as well as their enemies.

After that, Tinnstra lost sight of who Aasgod targeted, but again and again he lashed out, his magic crackling through the air. He held nothing back. He showed no mercy.

And even then, in the chaos of her mind, Tinnstra still thought about the Chikara water he must have. Even over the raging battle, she could still hear it whispering to her with promises of much-needed strength, perhaps even relief from Raaku's presence. But there was no time to ask for some. No time to take some. She just let the pain drive her on. She knew there was only one way she would find peace that day.

A Skull rushed at her and Tinnstra thrust her Niganntan spear to meet him. It ripped through his open mouth and burst out of the back of his skull before she whipped it in reverse and cracked the butt into another man's knee, felling him.

She left him lying on the ground for Jax to kill and moved on to the next Skull. She wasn't sure how good the one-armed general would be in a straight fight, but she trusted him enough to deal with the stragglers she left alive, while protecting the mage and watching her and Zorique's backs.

Tinnstra howled at the pressure in her head as she shoved her spear through a Skull's chest. Another hacked down at her, aiming for her hands, but she jerked back, releasing her hold on the spear. The scimitar chopped through the shaft, throwing the Skull off balance and leaving him open to a counterstrike.

Tinnstra drew her own sword, spinning as she did so, and took the man's head clean from his shoulders. As his body fell, spraying blood everywhere, Tinnstra pulled the rest of her spear from the other Skull's body. Even with half of it missing, its blade still made a fine weapon. And with that in one hand and the scimitar in the other, Tinnstra strode on. 'Blood I will give you, O Great One. Lives I will send you. My body is your weapon. My life, your gift,' she snarled, enjoying the irony that Raaku had made her into the killer she was as much as anyone. His God had shaped her life more than her own had.

The castle loomed ahead, towering over Aisair's old town, the magic-made buildings that had once been the pride of Jia.

'Keep your eyes open,' she called out. 'There has to be a trap or something waiting for us. It can't be this easy.'

'Easy?' said Aasgod, wiping sweat from his forehead. 'There's nothing easy about this.'

'The Skulls mean nothing,' said Tinnstra. 'They're just fodder to wear us down.'

'Their lives are gifts to Kage,' said Jax, almost to himself. Then looked up and caught Tinnstra's eye. He smiled as if he was in on some private joke. Had he heard her prayer? Had he—

The darkness pulsed in Tinnstra's mind, making her wince. Raaku's magic felt ever closer. A vice crushing her thoughts. She snorted snot from her nose and was alarmed to see it was red with blood.

'Are you all right?' asked Zorique.

'Never better,' lied Tinnstra. But what did the truth matter? *I just have to stay alive long enough to see this done. That's all.*

Aasgod shot more lightning at another rooftop as Zorique threw up a shield to protect the four of them from baton fire in return. His lightning flashed across the sky and the rooftop ceased to be. Rubble rained down, blocking the road, but Zorique used her shield to sweep a pathway clear. 'Keep moving,' she cried, and they charged through the dust and the smoke.

A smattering of Skulls – maybe two dozen – were at the far end of the road, armed with scimitars and spears. They waited, shifting from foot to foot as the Jians ran towards them.

The Skulls should've run. Perhaps they wanted to, but Zorique scooped up rubble with her magic and flung it at the Egril before they could do anything. The rocks flew with devastating speed, striking heads and chests, knocking down Skulls. And then Tinnstra waded into that chaos, *her* sword and *her* spear sending lives to Kage with every flick of her wrist.

Zorique was beside her, the epitome of a Shulka, showing no mercy. Maiza would've been proud of her form and technique. Tinnstra certainly was. Zorique burned with all Jia's hope.

The last few Skulls turned and fled. Tinnstra hurled her broken spear through the back of one, but the others reached the end of the street and disappeared around the corner.

Into the Grand Avenue. Sun streaked down it, drawing them on. Now their target was so close, the urge to rush after the

Skulls was immense. But Tinnstra stopped as she reached the last building and signalled the others to do likewise. Only a fool would run on without checking what waited for them.

Tinnstra pressed her back to the wall, gulping air down her raw throat. Zorique slotted into place beside her, then Jax, while Aasgod watched their rear. Further down the street, there had to be two or three hundred Jians waiting to see what they did next.

Dropping into a crouch, Tinnstra peered around the corner of the building.

Rows of Skulls filled the Grand Avenue from one side to the other, blocking their way. But not too many. Not enough to stop them reaching the palace.

But once they got there? Whatever waited inside was the real challenge.

She could feel Raaku, so close now that his darkness all but overwhelmed her mind. Even Zorique's presence was dimmed in her thoughts compared to his power. No doubt he was watching from some vantage point. How many warriors did he have waiting inside that building? How many Skulls and Chosen and Kojin?

Does it matter? I've promised to kill them all. 'God or man, Death calls for you,' she whispered to herself.

'Look!' said Zorique, pointing past Tinnstra to the other side of the Grand Avenue. 'Ralasis!'

Tinnstra's head snapped right, a grin spreading across her face.

She didn't think much could surprise her anymore, but Ralasis never ceased to do so. Because there he was. Still alive!

The Meigorian was approaching the Grand Avenue down the opposite road. His head was bandaged, his arm in a sling, but the man was alive – and he had found an army of his own, just as ragtag as Tinnstra's.

Ralasis saw her, too, and waved with his good arm.

'Maybe the Gods *are* with us,' muttered Tinnstra as she waved back.

Jax giggled behind her. It was a frightening sound.

Tinnstra turned, hand tightening on her sword hilt.

Jax looked like a different person, his eyes glinting, that smile back on his face, sword in one hand, knife in the other, a red aura of magic radiating all around him.

A Chosen's aura.

'No,' said Tinnstra, her sword arm moving.

'Yes,' said Jax, and he drove his knife into Zorique's back.

104

Darus

The time for waiting was over. Darus had to act now.

While everyone's attention was elsewhere, he shrugged off his coat and loosened his shirt so he could slip his newly grown arm through the sleeve. By the time he caught up with the others, he had a sword in one hand and his knife in the other, and not one person noticed. By Kage, he could've laughed.

Tinnstra had her one eye peering around the corner of the building. Zorique was next to her, watching the skies and the rooftops. And Aasgod? He, too, was searching for danger from above. He didn't see that it was right next to him. For a heartbeat, Darus was tempted to kill Aasgod first. After all, the man deserved to die – but one must have priorities. Zorique first, then the mage.

Darus slipped in beside the heathen queen, heart racing with his growing excitement.

So much so, he giggled. Couldn't stop himself.

Tinnstra turned around, looking all worried, seeing him properly for the first time. She raised her sword as if that could stop him.

He smiled as he rammed his knife into the heathen queen's side, good and hard.

By Kage's might, how she screamed.

How she—

Magic rushed along his arm from Zorique. It was like a flood, shocking his system. He cried out, maybe even screamed himself as light burned off him and the queen.

Tinnstra screamed as well as she slashed at him with her sword and broken spear, but her weapons sparked off the light around him. Again and again she hacked away, howling with rage, but the shield held.

Even Aasgod was trying to force himself through the light, trying to reach Zorique. Lightning crackled around his hands, but he was as impotent as the Shulka. Darus would've laughed if it wasn't for the pain.

It was killing him.

He had to let go of the knife in Zorique's side – break the connection. He had to—

Something exploded and Darus was smashed off his feet and flung across the road. He crashed into a building, through the wall, bricks and dirt and dust and debris swirling around him, carving a chunk out of the ground. When he came to a stop, he had one heartbeat to look up and realise he was still alive and still glowing, and then the whole building collapsed on top of him.

A whole building should've killed him.

And yet still he lived.

Still his body burned with the light siphoned off the heathen queen. Like Raaku had designed. Like Raaku had wanted.

105

Zorique

Aisair

Zorique wasn't sure if she was dead. She knew she wasn't alive. Not in the way she had been. Where there had been a world, now there was just light – pure, bright and all-encompassing. As if it was the sea and she was just a speck in it. Or her thoughts were. That was all that seemed to remain of what she once was.

Just thoughts.

Lost in the light.

Zorique felt at peace. That she did know. Now that the pain was gone, along with the anger and the fear and the hate and the sorrow. Now that the fighting was over.

But was it?

Was she dead?

Was this Xin's kingdom? Or was she travelling there, carried on a river of light?

Not the Great Darkness, though. It was far from that. The Great Light.

Would she see her parents again? Her brother? Would they be waiting for her? It was so long since she had last seen them. So long that she could barely remember their faces.

Other things were still sharp in her memory – like the way she felt in her father's arms when he carried her from her bed each morning, or the way her mother made her laugh. Emotions she treasured and wished she could repeat.

706

And what about Anama and Maiza? Would she see them? Would they be proud?

She'd failed, after all. Failed them. Failed her mother. She'd been their last hope. A fool's hope.

Zorique hadn't been a true queen. She'd been no one's saviour. She'd just followed a trail of the dead until she, too, had died.

But was she dead?

If she wasn't ... if she was just ... what? Unconscious? Injured? Dying but not yet dead?

Jax had stabbed her. She'd felt it like a punch to her ribs, seen the knife, and she'd seen ... the light as it'd poured out of her into him, felt it dragged and clawed and stolen from her.

It felt like death.

106

Wenna

Aisair

Wenna moved quickly through the city. She had ten thousand soldiers with her after all, and the Skulls fell before their swords.

'To the palace,' she hollered over the steel storm. 'To the palace!' By the Gods, she hoped she got there before that traitor Jax could do any more damage.

She led from the front, forging a path down the main thorough-fare from the city gates to the palace, bloody sword in hand. Her eyes roamed everywhere, watching the skies for Daijaku and the rooftops for Chosen and the streets for Skulls. Now they were close, Wenna wasn't going to let anything stop her.

The narrow streets helped their advance, limiting the op-portunities for the Skulls to counterattack and restricting their numbers when they did. Each time the Egril launched an assault, the allies swarmed over them and left only the dead in their wake. It felt glorious.

They'd reached the start of the Grand Avenue, the palace still at least a mile away, when light shot into the sky. It was the width of a building and roared up mile after mile to the very heavens.

Only one person was capable of producing a beacon like that, as far as Wenna knew – Zorique.

She started to run. There was no time to waste. Not even to give any orders.

She wasn't alone. Her army came with her. Their feet thundered along as they charged, the weight of bodies tight around her.

When they were nearly halfway to the palace, she saw Ralasis first and then, beyond him, a horde of Skulls racing to meet them.

'For Jia! For Jia!' she howled.

And then the two armies met in a crunch of bone and steel, of hate and fury.

Wenna collided with a Skull, knocked him down with the force of her charge and nearly went over with him. Somehow, though, she stayed on her feet. Maybe someone had helped her. She had no idea, already swinging at the next white-armoured body in her way. Her blade skittered off the man's breastplate but got a chunk of another's thigh. Her opponent drew his scimitar back so Wenna punched him in the face, knocking him away and buying enough time to bring her own sword around once more.

Someone else's blade took the Skull through the throat before she could strike, though. Wenna found herself pressed up tight against another Skull, so close she could see his blue eyes staring at her, feel his breath hot on her cheek. There was no room to swing a sword, not packed up tight like that. So she dropped it, wriggled her hand around, found a knife, hoping the Skull wasn't doing the same thing, hoping she could kill him before he killed her.

The Skull snarled in her face as she pulled her knife free, wriggled her arm back up, all the while swaying backwards and forwards with the press. It was a battle in itself just to work her hand under the Skull's arm. He knew what she was doing, did his best to clamp his arm over her hand, stop it moving, stop her blade from finding the weak spot, the gap in his armour between chest and arm.

The Skull snapped his head forwards, butting Wenna with his helmet, drawing blood, but she kept going, kept pushing the knife up, feeling its tip trace the scales of his armour. Then she felt it bump free of resistance, saw in the Skull's eyes that he felt it, too, and Wenna pushed the knife in with all her might, screaming as it punctured flesh, screaming as the Skull screamed back, screaming as she saw the light go from his eyes and the strength left his legs.

Only the press of bodies kept the Skull upright as Wenna gulped air and thanked the Four Gods for keeping her alive. All around her, everyone was shouting, cursing, swearing, calling on their Gods for protection, salvation, destruction. Spit and sweat and tears and blood flew in every direction. People stabbed and hacked, gouged and wrestled as they struggled to stay alive.

Wenna pulled her knife free and, for one more moment, the dead Skull stayed pressed up against her, then he slipped down and she had to fight once more. She reached over the back of one of her soldiers and thrust the knife into the eye of the Skull he was battling. Out came the knife again and she stabbed another Skull in the neck. Out again and in again, Wenna moved quickly, being the difference in individual struggles, cutting throats and taking lives.

Slowly, space appeared around her. Room to swing a sword. She picked up a Shulka blade off one of the dead. No one she recognised, but it was someone's son, someone's loved one. Another life given for Jia.

'For Jia!' she screamed, thrusting the sword in the air, aware that every inch of her was covered in blood. 'For Jia!'

It was taken up by others around her. They could all feel it, the way the tide was turning, the press against them weakening.

This was going to be their day.

Then the ground began to shake.

107

Tinnstra

Tinnstra cradled Zorique's body as the fighting continued around her. Her daughter wasn't dead, not yet, but Tinnstra wasn't sure she was alive, either.

It had all happened so suddenly. Jax had stabbed her. Light had flooded out of her wound and into Jax, enveloping them both – protecting the bastard from Tinnstra's blows – before Zorique's magic erupted from her with a force that had sent them all flying.

When Tinnstra could see again, Zorique was lying on the on the ground, not moving but still glowing. She'd crawled over to her daughter and pulled Zorique into her lap, tears falling, and she'd prayed and prayed that Xin hadn't taken her.

Jia needed Zorique.

Tinnstra needed her.

She looked up at Aasgod. 'Do something!'

'I ... I ... I don't know ...' said the mage, eyes wide.

Fighting broke out around her as the Skulls clashed with the Jians, and all Tinnstra could do was hold on to Zorique, protecting her daughter, her queen, with her own body.

'Please don't die,' she whispered. 'Don't die. Not now. Not now.'

She barely heard the people's cries around her, nor the clash of swords. Tinnstra's whole being was focused on Zorique, looking for any sign that her daughter would wake up.

'Your magic is strong. I can see it swirling inside you. So many colours. So bright,' said Tinnstra into Zorique's ear. 'It used to hurt me, especially at the beginning. But now I see the beauty of it, its power to do good, and that comes from you, my beautiful girl, my love. Even in this mad, horrible world, you've not let the darkness get to you. Not like I have. You've stayed strong. You've always done the right thing, because you wanted to be better. Not like me. I became like the very people I hated, and I'm so sorry for that. Especially for hurting you and letting you down. I got lost in the darkness. Stupid, really. I should've seen what to do simply by watching you. I should've followed your example.'

She was so wrapped up in Zorique, Tinnstra almost didn't notice the first tremor, and the rumble was all but lost in the fury of the battle around her. But the tremors grew, and people were thrown this way and that.

A rumble came from the building that had collapsed on the traitor, Jax, drawing Tinnstra's eye away from her daughter. Bricks and shattered stones started to shift. A wooden beam so large that it would've taken ten men to move slipped from the top of the rubble and rolled down to the street. More rocks followed. Big slabs of stone flew clear, as if some monster burrowed its way beneath it.

Of course. The Egril never stop.

Tinnstra got to her feet and hauled Zorique to the side of the street, looking around for anyone she recognised. Aasgod's lightning shot out from amongst the melee, but he was too far away to be of use.

And still the ground shook and the rubble shifted in that demolished building as whatever was buried there got closer to freeing itself.

'Tinnstra! You're alive!' It was Ralasis, arm bandaged, head bandaged and hurt all over. 'Zorique! Is she—'

'Alive – I think,' said Tinnstra.

'Thank the Gods.' He crouched down beside Zorique.

'I need you to protect her, Ralasis,' said Tinnstra. 'Don't let anyone hurt her.'

'I won't – but where are you—'

His words were drowned out by the last of the rubble falling clear. Even the fighting stopped as Egril, Jian and Meigorian alike stopped to watch what emerged, for no one had ever seen the like.

The monster was bigger than a Kojin in every sense. Purple-skinned and bulging muscle, the creature barely looked like the man it had once been. It roared at the world around it, naked and angry, small eyes shining with hatred and pulsing with red magic. It was one of Raaku's creations.

Even so, Tinnstra recognised who he had once been, despite his size and his two bloody arms.

It was Jax.

Jax the traitor.

Jax the murderer.

'Keep Zorique alive,' she told Ralasis one more time as she picked up a fallen Egril spear. It wasn't as long as its Niganntan counterpart, but its reach was longer than her sword's.

Jax roared again. Then he leaped from the pile of rubble into the soldiers on the street and began killing. He didn't need any weapons. He just swung those massive arms of his and sent broken men and women flying. He didn't care who he slaughtered. Skulls were pulverised along with Jians and Meigorians.

Jax snatched one man up from the ground and ripped him in two, showering the street with his blood. By the Four Gods, he was laughing as he did it.

Others started to react at last. Spears flew up at the monster, and Jax batted all but one away. A lone spear pierced his forearm. Blood trickled from the wound as he wrenched the spear free, and there was something else, too.

Sparks of light.

Zorique's light. Her magic.

The traitor had stolen it.

Well, Tinnstra would get it back.

She moved forwards, clutching her spear, watching the monster as he wreaked havoc all around him. His fists shattered bodies and he swatted away any who dared come too close. All the Jian and Meigorian forces were reduced to throwing spears and rocks – none of which were slowing Jax down.

'Circle him,' shouted Tinnstra. 'And stay out of his reach!' The tactic had worked on the Kojin and it would work on Jax.

Jax's head snapped around at the sound of her voice. His eyes widened as he saw her. 'You!' The word was barely decipherable, almost lost in the rumble of his voice. But Tinnstra got the meaning well enough.

She pointed her spear at the monster. 'Jax!'

'No!' he growled. 'Monsuta!'

Tinnstra froze. Monsuta was the Chosen who'd chased her and Zorique across Jia, who'd tortured Jax. She'd seen him die. 'Impossible,' she breathed.

'Monsuta! Monsuta!' He bounded forwards, moving quicker than Tinnstra thought possible for something that big, and his giant hand lunged at her.

Tinnstra danced back and slashed her spear across the creature's palm for good measure, drawing a line of blood. Sparks of Zorique's magic escaped with it.

'Monsuta!' The monster's fist smashed down, shattering the ground where Tinnstra had been a second before. She moved to her right, aware of how close they were to Zorique, and Tinnstra didn't want Jax or Monsuta or whoever it was hurting her.

'I'm going to kill you,' she called out and the monster slapped both his hands together in reply, trying to squash her like a fly between them.

A few of the soldiers behind the creature darted forwards and thrust swords and spears into his back. Like they'd done with the Kojin.

But Jax wasn't just bigger than a Kojin, he was faster, too. He spun around quicker than they could move out of his way. One swipe of his arm pulverised three of them. The rest only just managed to move clear in time.

The monster had his back to Tinnstra now, and that was an opportunity she wasn't going to waste. She shot forwards and rammed her spear into Jax's bare arse. She didn't bother trying to hold on to the shaft but danced back as quickly as she had attacked.

Jax roared as he pulled the spear free and came for Tinnstra again. She retreated, drawing her sword as she did so. She made sure he could see her smile, demanding his attention, his focus, because Wenna was leading another group to attack him from behind.

The two Shulka locked eyes momentarily and Wenna gave a nod. The woman knew what had to be done.

'Come on, then!' Tinnstra shouted, waving her sword at Jax. 'Here I am, big man.'

Jax howled in fury and raised a fist to attack. Wenna surged forwards, then Jax stopped, suddenly. He turned as Wenna and the others were about to strike. His fists were a blur. There was a sickening sound of bones snapping, the pulp of bodies pummelled. People fell. No one got up.

'No!' screamed Tinnstra. She ran at Jax.

The monster turned. His fists rose above his head, blood dripping off his fingers, teeth bared. 'Monsuta!'

Tinnstra dropped as his fists came down, sliding past the monster's blows, between his legs, sword moving, turning with it, putting all her might, all her hate into her strike. The sword bit deep into the back of Jax's ankle, severing the tendon in a gush of blood, spilling more of his precious stolen magic.

Tinnstra rolled to the side and struck again, hacking into the bottom of Jax's knee, then sprinted out of the way again.

The monster was still on his feet, though he wasn't going anywhere in a hurry. But slow wasn't dead. She ducked a fist but not the elbow that followed it. Even a glancing blow felt like she'd been hit by a mountain. She went sprawling, head dizzy, her mouth full of blood.

Luckily, Jax had to drag a limp leg to come after her and that gave Tinnstra enough to time to get back up. She spat blood and gave the monster another grin as her fingers opened the pouch on her belt. 'You'll have to do more than that to stop me killing you.'

Jax reared up like before, bellowing like a mad bull, fists rising above his head.

Leaving his chest a massive target.

She hurled the throwing stars in quick succession. All four sank into Jax's flesh. Each one coated with enough poison to kill a normal man. Jax didn't seem to notice them as he smashed her halfway across the street.

Tinnstra groaned, clutching her ribs with one hand, feeling for her sword with the other. The ground shook as Jax lurched towards her. Other soldiers rushed in, but they fell before the monster.

Jax grabbed a Hanran with a spear and ripped the man in two. He threw the body parts at Tinnstra, covering her in blood as she ducked out of the way.

It hurt to breathe as she staggered to her feet, her hands weaponless. She looked up as a shadow loomed over her.

Jax.

His fist slammed into her again, sending her flying. Tinnstra bounced on the road, battering her head even more. The world spun as she sat up, then she puked blood over the ground.

Anger welled within her. This wasn't going to be the end. Not after everything she'd been through, not after everything she'd sacrificed. Not after what he'd done to Zorique.

Tinnstra saw a sword lying on the ground next to a dead Shulka. She scrambled for it as Jax lurched towards her. Time slowed. She had to get the weapon before he got her.

'Monsuta!' bellowed Jax.

Tinnstra threw herself towards the sword, sensing the monster's shadow falling over her. She stretched out, fingers splayed, skidding on the stone.

Tinnstra snatched up the sword a second before Jax's fist came down. She rolled to the side as she felt the ground shake, turned and jabbed up as another fist hurtled towards her. The blade took a chunk out of a finger and did just enough to deflect the blow from killing her.

As Jax reared up again, Tinnstra shot forwards as quick as she could and buried her sword into his gut. Blood and magic leaked from the wound but the damn monster still didn't fall.

'Monsuta!' he screamed, lashing out with his fist, but Tinnstra was already moving again, slashing at his arm as she went. He stumbled after her, chasing her as she hacked at his ribs, then slipped under an arm to chop into his back.

Tinnstra found strength with each wound she inflicted as the magic in her worked on her injuries. She was like a wasp, stinging here and there, avoiding Jax's flailing arms, leaving her bloody marks across his body, watching the magic leak from his grotesque hulk.

She could see him slowing down, her sword work and her poison doing their task.

Still he howled, 'Monsuta! Monsuta!'

As if she gave a fuck.

She sliced the hamstring on his good leg and down he went. He clawed at the dirt, trying to rise, but Tinnstra climbed up his back, stabbing him as she went. When she reached his head, she yanked his hair back. 'I hope this is the last time I have to kill you,' she whispered in his ear and rammed her sword through his temple, up to the hilt.

A cheer went up as Jax fell, but Tinnstra didn't feel like joining in. She ran over to Ralasis and Zorique. Aasgod was with them as well. Zorique still lay unmoving, still glowing. 'Is she ... ?'

'She's alive,' said the mage. 'And the wound's healed.'

'What?' Tinnstra checked for herself, saw no mark, not even a scar. 'How's that possible?'

'I don't know,' said Aasgod. 'It happened as you fought that monster.'

'That monster was Jax,' said Tinnstra.

'The one-armed general?' asked Ralasis.

'The very same. He siphoned off Zorique's magic when he stabbed her.' Tinnstra looked back down at her daughter. 'Is she going to wake up?'

'I don't know,' said Aasgod.

'What about giving her Chikara water?'

'It might help, but it might kill her, too,' said Aasgod.

'Shit,' said Tinnstra. She looked around, saw hundreds of faces watching, waiting for orders now the Skulls lay dead around them. Then her gaze fell on a clump of bodies and Tinnstra was running again.

They lay on the spot where Wenna had fallen. When Tinnstra reached them, the sight nearly made her sick. There was a tangle of limbs and blood where Jax had pummelled them together, and not one still looked as the Gods had intended.

Tinnstra had to move someone's arm to find Wenna's face. She felt for a pulse and, by some miracle, found the faintest trace of one still beating. 'Wenna. Can you hear me?'

Wenna coughed and her swollen eyes flickered but didn't open. 'Tinn ... stra?'

'It's me.' She wiped some blood from Wenna's forehead, not that it made any difference.

'Jax. Is ... is he ... dead?'

'He is.'

'Good.' She coughed blood. 'Killed Hasan ... killed ... killed your ... m ... mother.'

The words stabbed at Tinnstra's heart. More people she'd loved, lost to the Godsdamned war. 'It's okay. You don't have to say any more. I'll get someone to help you.'

But Wenna didn't hear her. She was dead, too.

Tinnstra stood.

'Everyone, listen up!' she called out. 'Make sure you have plenty of weapons to hand, because it's time to end this war. It's time we took our palace back! It's time we took our country back!'

'For Jia!' someone cried.

'For Jia!' a man called out.

'For Jia! For Jia! For Jia! For Jia!' The cry was taken up all around her by everyone. It echoed around the boulevard, loud enough for even Raaku to hear.

'How much Chikara water have you got left?' she asked Aasgod.

The mage looked in his bag. 'Three vials.'

Gods, she wanted one. She wanted all of them. She needed the water's power.

She ...

'Here. Take it.' Aasgod held one out to her. No need for her to ask. No need to argue. No need to steal. Tinnstra stared at it, desperate and longing for its bitter taste and the rush that followed. She wanted it more than she thought possible. She reached out with bloody fingers, not thinking about it. She snatched it out of Aasgod's hand, already reaching for the stopper. Then she saw Zorique watching her. Her beautiful girl.

'No,' she said instead. 'Zorique might need it. You might need it. I don't.'

'Are you sure?'

'Yes.' She handed it back and her hand had never felt so empty. Aasgod slipped the vial into his bag.

And Tinnstra felt calm. Confident. In control. Raaku's darkness filled her mind, drowning out all the magic around her. Even Aasgod and Zorique were whispers compared to that monster's presence. But instead of letting it overwhelm her, she focused on it, locking it in place.

'Protect the queen,' she told Ralasis and Aasgod. 'I'm going to kill an Emperor.'

Ralasis said something, but Tinnstra didn't hear him. A screech they knew only too well silenced his words. It came from buildings all around them.

It was the sound of Tonin opening gates.

So many gates.

108

Vallia

Vallia listened to the Tonin open the gates. She watched as more soldiers poured forth to fight the heathen army and could not help but wonder if it was all too little, too late.

To think she'd once called herself Vallia the Victorious. By Kage, she had been so proud of that title. She'd worn it with an air of invincibility, with arrogance. Such hubris.

Jia had shown Vallia the folly of such thoughts. Now she was Vallia the Defeated. Vallia the Routed.

Now, she'd watched her soldiers, with their superior armour, weaponry and training, fight a rabble until the last man died. She'd watched Raaku's monster emerge from the rubble of a building and lay waste to all around it, until it, too, was killed. Bile burned in her stomach as the heathen army roared its success and then turned its attention towards the palace. Towards her Emperor.

And Vallia the Defeated couldn't help but think she was about to lose again.

They were thoughts unlike any she'd ever had. Doubts that she'd never felt before. She wished she could strike them from her mind, but they only seemed to multiply the longer she watched the battle below.

But perhaps Raaku's plan had worked. There had been no sign of the heathen queen since the burst of light, after all. No sign of the mage and his lightning. Perhaps the Shulka had killed the monster, perhaps not. Perhaps she lay dead or wounded with so many others.

Perhaps all of the False Gods' champions had fallen.

Perhaps.

She said nothing, of course. Raaku was standing next to her, watching the very same things she did. He watched, unmoved, as the son of Kage should be. To question his tactics would be to question her faith in Kage himself.

Perhaps she was just tired. It had been a long and bloody journey to this point, to this Last War. Soon, it would all be over. Soon, they would reach the end.

Victory would be theirs.

Perhaps.

Vallia looked down on the rabble in the boulevard. Were they really that powerful? And as she thought of the defeats they'd inflicted on her over the last few months, she knew the answer was yes. The fact there wasn't any sign of the queen, the mage, the Shulka or the mysterious fourth champion didn't make her feel any better. They'd survived everything she'd thrown at them, and now they were here.

'I wish to see the orb,' said Raaku. He turned without waiting for her to answer and headed for the door. Vallia took one last glance at the disaster below and then followed.

They headed down the stairs, with Raaku's guards a few steps behind. The inside of the castle was eerily quiet now that all the administrators and servants were confined to quarters, and they could only hear an echo of the battle outside.

Raaku moved quickly through the central hall to the throne room. He pushed open the large double doors as if they weighed nothing.

The throne room had long been stripped of its gaudy Jian pretensions. Only the stained-glass windows along the walls remained, as well as the shattered remnants of the old throne piled high at the far end.

Now, the dark-shelled egg stood in the centre of the room. In a circle around it, on their knees, hands bound behind their backs, were one hundred Jian prisoners. Behind them were twenty soldiers from the First Legion, members of Raaku's original tribe, with their red armour and demon masks.

They bowed as Raaku entered the chamber, but he ignored them and walked straight to the orb, running his hands over its surface. At one point, Raaku sent a pulse of magic through the shell and Vallia thought she saw a liquid inside react.

As Vallia waited for her Emperor, she heard the shriek of Tonin gates opening from outside. Soon, the last of the Empire's might would be thrown at the heathens and, by Kage, she hoped it would be enough. She wanted to go outside and be with her army. If this was to be the Last War, she wanted to fight with them. She wanted to win or die with them. Instead, she was watching Raaku tend to an orb containing only he knew what.

She ran her thumb up and down the hilt of her sword as she remembered her words to Torvi: 'If all seems lost, then Raaku will be here by our sides, and no mere mortal can defeat the son of Kage, no matter what powers the False Gods have gifted them.' She'd believed it then, but did she still? Was she so weak that a few battles going against her could shake her faith? She should take her own life just for thinking—

'Is that the sword I gave you?' said Raaku, his voice almost gentle, almost ... fatherly. His back was still to her, his attention focused on the orb.

Vallia glanced down at the scimitar on her hip, as if to check – not that there was any need. 'Yes. It is my most treasured possession.'

'Have you kept the blade sharp?'

She thought of Illius. 'Yes, Your Majesty.'

Raaku turned to face her.

'Then let us go down below and fight this Last War together, as we did when we were younger. Let us spill blood and take lives like my father commands.'

It was as if he had read her thoughts. Had he? Had Raaku seen her doubts? Vallia took a step back. 'I will go gladly, Your Majesty, but there is no need for you to join me. Stay here and await news of the victory we will win for you and for mighty Kage.'

Raaku smiled. 'Dear Vallia, still you fear. Still you doubt. Sekanowari will not be won by staying away from the battle. My father demands blood and souls. I will give both to him.'

Vallia bowed her head. 'Yes, Your Majesty.'

'The rest of you wait here,' said Raaku, drawing his sword. 'Be ready to execute the prisoners on my orders. The orb will need blood if I am to use it.'

Vallia wanted to ask what was inside, but she dared not. It was not her place.

Again, Raaku fixed his gaze on her. 'We will have victory, Commander. In this world or the next.'

109

The Queen and The Shulka

Aisair

Zorique heard the screech. Even lost in the light, far from the world, she heard it. Somewhere, a Tonin was opening a gate, forcing one place together with another.

It didn't seem right, somehow. If she was dead, that is. To have her peace shattered by that ungodly howl.

She reached out with her senses and found its source, then found another and another and another. She traced the magic, watched it connect to faraway places, watched it and understood it. The Tonin's tricks were not unlike the gates the Jians had once used, like she had used. She knew how that worked. She knew how to control it, how to stop it.

And, of course, the fact she could sense all that meant one other thing.

I am alive.

All Zorique had to do was find her way back through the light. Back to the world. Back to Tinnstra and her people. Back to where she was needed.

No. She couldn't leave the light.

Unless …

She was the light, and the light was her.

'To the palace!' screamed Tinnstra. 'Free Jia!'

She set off at a sprint, the screech of the Tonin's gates filling her ears. She was relieved the others followed. If they weren't quick, it would be too late. Too late for everything. Her senses picked out fifteen of the damn creatures up and down the boulevard. Too many for her to try and stop by herself. Perhaps too many for Zorique if she'd been ... No, Tinnstra couldn't bring herself to even think that. Her daughter wasn't dead. Not yet.

Still ... fifteen Tonin. The Egril could flood the Grand Avenue with every type of monster with that many gates open. It would be easy to kill everyone. To slaughter every last Jian.

She ran as fast as she could, chased by the scream of the Tonin's magic. She just had to get to Raaku and put an end to all of this.

By all the Gods, she wished she'd drunk the Chikara water when she'd had the chance. She could've done with its strength and energy now.

Then she saw the Skulls come pouring out of buildings on either side of the avenue. So many Skulls.

'For Jia!' Tinnstra cried once more – not that anyone could hear her over the Tonin's howls. Any hesitancy on her part and she knew her army would break, so she charged straight at the enemy, sword raised in the air, dragging her army with her by sheer force of will.

The gap closed between the two forces. One hundred yards, seventy-five, fifty. Tinnstra locked eyes on the man she was going to kill first, her arm already moving.

'For Jia!' she screamed with fifteen yards to go.

Ten yards. Eight. Seven.

Everything slowed in Tinnstra's mind as she turned her body to add weight to her sword stroke, aware of everyone around her, of the Skulls in front, anticipating the impact, already looking for the next target and ...

Her sword took the Skull across the gut, slicing through his armoured plates, finding flesh, biting deep. Tinnstra dragged the blade free, her axe in motion. She hacked into the next Skull's mask, splitting it in two, right between the eyes. She brought her sword up and over and down through another Skull's arm, turned and rammed her axe between another's legs.

On she went, wading deeper into the Egril ranks, sending soul after soul back to the Great Darkness.

Her army followed, bellowing their rage, fighting with all their hearts. 'For Jia!' they cried. 'For Jia!'

Of course, the Egril wouldn't just send humans against her army. More Daijaku appeared, flying over the melee, glowing red orbs in their hands.

'Shit,' whispered Tinnstra as the bombs fell.

Explosions rocked one end of the Grand Avenue to the other, killing Jian, Meigorian and Skull indiscriminately.

Tinnstra snatched up a spear from a fallen soldier, hurled it at a Daijaku, but there were so many she hardly needed to aim. The spear arced up and she saw it pierce a Daijaku's chest. The demon fell, but what was one taken from a swarm?

And still the Tonin's magic screamed.

Kojin came next. Blue monsters stomping into their midst. Clubs thrashing through her soldiers, sending bodies flying into the air.

Finally, through the gates came the Chosen. They were little red dots of magic in her mind before she saw their magic at work and their baton blasts burning through the air.

Even Tinnstra's charge faltered in the face of all those monsters. She had brought the men and women of Aisair to fight, and Raaku had brought every horror of his Empire.

Such was the Egril way. Such was Sekanowari.

Raaku was moving, too. He was drawing closer, coming to join the battle, to see their end first-hand.

For a moment, Tinnstra felt like the girl she had once been at the Kotege. Overwhelmed and petrified. Around her, people turned and ran in every direction. Running anywhere to escape the death Raaku had brought.

It was over.

No. No, it's not. Not while I still breathe.

Tinnstra tightened her grip on her sword and her axe, and she did the only thing she knew how to do. She killed and she killed and she killed, moving ever closer to the palace, one dead Skull at a time.

She held nothing back, showed no mercy, as she fought her way towards the darkness.

A Chosen came at her, his baton humming with power, his aura pulsing with Egril magic.

Tinnstra crouched low, sword and axe ready and waiting.

The baton swung towards her, crackling, charge building. She threw herself forwards into a roll, coming up quick and vicious. Her axe took the hand that held the baton. Her sword sank into the man's throat.

She leaned in, close enough to kiss. 'Off to Kage you go.'

Another crackle.

She spun, the Chosen still impaled on her sword a good enough shield as the baton blast hit the corpse, turning it to ash. Tinnstra lunged through the soot, giving the other Chosen no time to recharge his weapon, her axe swinging. The hooked blade found the man's neck and cleaved deep. Blood splattered over her face as she yanked her weapon free and moved on, fighting by instinct, relying on all six senses to murder any enemy within her reach.

But then, a spark flared in her mind, achingly familiar.

From behind her.

She turned to look and nearly got a sword through her chest because of it.

Fool. Don't let your mind wander. Not now.

She caught the scimitar with the hook of her axe, pulled it to one side and rammed her sword into the Skull.

On she fought, aware that the spark at the back of her mind was growing, too. Becoming a flame, becoming . . .

Zorique opened her eyes.

She lay on the ground, her whole body glowing. No, more than that. She was made entirely of light. She could feel it running through her veins, pumping through her heart, filling her lungs, binding her together, giving her strength, giving her power. Making her more than what she had once been. More than what she'd thought possible.

Aasgod stood over her, firing his lightning in every direction. Ralasis was nearby, too, one arm in a sling, battling with a Skull.

No one noticed when she sat up, because everyone was fighting for their lives. Daijaku filled the sky, dropping bombs

727

or swooping down with their Niganntan spears. Skulls poured out of nearby buildings, grouped together like white-armoured battering rams as they piled into her army's ranks. Chosen baton blasts ripped through the air from one side of the boulevard to the other as Kojin stomped everywhere, swinging their clubs around, while Zorique heard the howls of Kyoryu even over the screech of the Tonin's gates. And beyond them? She could sense even more monsters waiting to pour through.

'No.' She stood up.

Aasgod, startled, took a step back. 'Zorique? Are you—'

'Wait.' She had to close the gates first. She fixed them all in her mind. Fifteen of them around the boulevard, connected like roads through space to fifteen Tonin elsewhere.

She took off, glowing bright, building speed. The first Tonin was in the building straight ahead, a grand mansion fitting its prime position on the Grand Avenue.

'*Shirudan.*' Her shield flared to life as baton blasts arced her way. Of course they'd concentrate on her, now. It was her they wanted dead most of all. Well, let them try.

Zorique crashed into the heart of the building at full speed and erupted out of the other side in a shower of brick and stone. As she turned, the building was already collapsing, burying everyone inside it. That was one way to shut a Tonin's gate. Dirt and dust billowed out, but Zorique was untouched within her shield, shining like a beacon in the smoke.

Daijaku swarmed towards her, clutching bombs and spears, but they were no more than a nuisance.

'*Kasri.*'

The ones nearest her burst into flames, little pops of fire that turned the demons into ash. She pushed her magic out, sweeping over the top of the battle in the street, taking all the Daijaku out of the fight. Chosen fell, too, those in the air burning just as easily as the winged demons.

She flew on, smashing through one building after another, demolishing anything that housed a Tonin. Chosen energy blasts chased after her, but she was too fast a target for them to hit.

From town house to mansion, she silenced the Tonin and closed their gates.

Tinnstra watched her daughter close the Tonin's gates, one by one. And by the Four Gods, the way she glowed in Tinnstra's mind – suddenly Raaku's darkness wasn't overwhelming. Her daughter's magic shone a hundred times – no, a thousand times brighter than before.

Could Raaku sense that? Did he know what he now faced? Did he still feel his father's might? Or was he shitting himself with fear?

Tinnstra damn well hoped he was.

The sight of her daughter didn't just lift Tinnstra's spirits. As the Daijaku and Chosen fell from the sky, her army on the ground was transformed. Despair switched to hope.

A cry echoed across the boulevard. 'Zorique! Zorique! Zorique!'

Tinnstra spat blood and smiled. Zorique changed everything. 'For Jia!' she cried as she slew another Skull. 'For Zorique!'

How far to the palace? How far to Raaku? She could feel him moving ever closer. Then she heard the screams from the far end of the boulevard, and she knew the Emperor had left the palace.

Zorique flew through the falling rubble and back over the boulevard. Ten gates had fallen so far. Five left.

She flipped in mid-air, changing direction, aiming for the next gate.

A blast of magic hit her, shattering her shield, and she fell from the sky. '*Shirudan*,' she gasped, reactivating it a second before she smashed into the ground. She stood up, dazed, saw that she'd left a crater in the road and Jians and Meigorians lay dead around her.

Anger swept through her. She knew it had been Raaku's magic that had struck her down. Raaku who had caused so many to die.

She had to end this war.

Howls and screams drew Zorique's attention. She turned to see at least two dozen Kyoryu racing towards her, clawing through anyone in their way.

Zorique held out a hand. She could see all their magic now, see the spells that had made them and knew how to undo them. '*Teishon.*'

Stop. A word of power taught to her long ago by Anama. A word that had been just a word until now.

The Kyoryu froze mid-stride, mid-carnage.

Zorique walked towards them, her powers reading them like books. The Kyoryu were savage monsters but, long ago, they had been human once, taken from their parents to be twisted and warped by Raaku. She could feel their anger and pain. Their hate. That was Kage's gift to them.

What was it the Egril said? Pain was good?

They were wrong about that, as they were wrong about so many things.

At least Zorique could put an end to the Kyoryu's suffering. May they find peace at long last.

'*Kasri.*' Zorique spoke the word and the demons burned.

'Zorique!' It was Aasgod. Loyal Aasgod. He sprinted towards her, his own power all but doused after all the fighting. He clasped a vial of Chikara water in his hand, but he didn't need it. Not now.

Zorique raised her hand. '*Nosou.*'

Heal.

Light pulsed through him, stopping him in his tracks. Charging him with all the magic he would need. Even the nicks and cuts all over his body healed, and his exhaustion vanished.

'How did you do that?' he gasped.

'By the Four Gods, who cares?' said Ralasis. 'Can you do that to me?'

'Of course.' She touched his broken arm, moving the light across it. Ralasis gasped as the bones shifted together, then fused once more.

'How did you do that?' asked Aasgod again.

'With the light.' Zorique looked around. Fighting was still going on. Raaku was waiting. There was still much to do. 'Where's Tinnstra?'

'She's gone to kill Raaku,' said Aasgod.

'She can't defeat him by herself,' said Zorique. 'We must find her.'

The battle changed. At times, Tinnstra had felt like she was going to drown under the weight of Egril around her. She'd lashed out at anything in white without time to think or catch her breath. But now? There were spaces around her, pauses in the melee to gulp air into her burning lungs and opportunities to look for her next target.

It wasn't because the allied forces were winning or that there were fewer Egril to fight. Rather that they were being drawn away from the main body of the battle, towards Zorique. Her light drew the darkness.

Suddenly, Tinnstra could see a path open up to the palace.

To Raaku. She could feel him. So close now. She knew the screams she heard came from his work.

She started to run once more, sword and axe carving down anyone foolish enough to get in her way. She had a monster to kill.

Zorique made her way through the battle, with Aasgod and Ralasis following close behind. As she moved, she expanded her light, letting it pass over friend and foe alike, understanding them, judging them.

Skulls fell by the dozen. They were irredeemable, after all, and a price had to be paid for the lives they'd stolen. Those that were warded against her magic were left as isolated targets for her army to strike down with good old-fashioned steel.

She was the heart of the battle now. Her own soldiers surged after her, chanting her name. Some of the enemy – the more human of the Egril – tried to run. The others – the monsters and the Chosen – turned to confront her.

Kojin roared their fury, swinging their blood-caked clubs at the sky – for all the good it did them. Zorique sent bolts of light through their hearts and the ground shook as they tumbled to the ground.

The Chosen, however, did not die so easily.

There were hundreds of them. Some flew towards her, batons already blazing. Others fired from the ground. Red light burst around her as their blasts battered her shield. Once, not so long ago, it had hurt her when they attacked her like that.

But she was different then. Now, she was the light. Now, their magic was as dangerous as rain.

She reached out, searching for the Chosen, sensing their powers. Zealots one and all, they had been changed by the blood-soaked Chikara waters under Raaku's castle like all his creations.

It mattered not. If Raaku was the great maker, she was the unmaker.

'Hasik.' Change. She said it in a whisper, and the word hit them like a hurricane. Those who could fly now could not. Those who had fired their batons or burned people alive or shattered Jians with ice or controlled the innocent with their minds now could not. She ripped their magic from them and set it free on the wind.

Now, the Chosen could face her army, human to human.

Only their master remained.

Raaku.

Tinnstra cut a Skull down, and there he was.

Raaku. Two hundred yards away, surrounded by the dead. Black magic swirled around him in a maelstrom as he carved down anyone within reach of his sword. A simple grey mask covered his face, black armour his body. He was evil personified.

There were others with him, too. Four giants in red armour and devil masks, as adept at murder as their master, and a woman, dressed like Raaku in black, her scimitar just as deadly.

No Jian wanted to fight them, but there was nowhere for them to run.

'Get out of my way!' shouted Tinnstra. 'Let me through.' She pushed bodies aside, trying to force her way towards the Emperor.

She was one hundred yards away when the woman saw her.

'The Shulka!' she cried, pointing her sword at Tinnstra. One of the giants broke away from the others and charged towards her, blood dripping off his sword.

110

The Last War

Aisair

It was chaos and Ralasis was caught in its heart, doing his best not to get killed as he raced after Zorique. She led the charge to Raaku, shining like the sun amidst the blood, death and mayhem, giving hope to all who followed. They chanted her name as they fought their way to freedom, killing the few Skulls she left alive in her wake.

Since Zorique had come back to life, her magic was more than a match for anything the Egril threw at them. She waved her hand and another building collapsed, closing a gate and cutting off more Skull reinforcements. Daijaku appeared from another gate and simply burst into flames. And all the while, Zorique's face remained impassive, as if she was above it all – the fear, the terror, the hate and the anger that everyone else felt.

She looked like a God.

Even Aasgod was fighting like a different man since Zorique sent her light through him. His lightning scorched the very air as he threw it, taking out Egril before they even had a chance to pose a threat. He'd picked up a few new tricks, too, crushing Skulls in on themselves and throwing others halfway across the boulevard.

The question, though, was what was Ralasis doing by their side? Even Tinnstra had abilities far beyond any normal human's.

He was just a man in a battle between Gods. A fool with a sword, running towards certain death.

If he had any sense, he'd step back and leave the fighting to the others.

Even as she killed Jian after Jian, Vallia knew they were losing the battle on the street. She was too experienced to lie to herself. She'd seen Raaku throw all his magic at the heathen queen, knocking her from the sky, but a few moments later she was on her feet again and leading her army towards them.

Shining so bright, working her magic.

Those soldiers that hadn't been warded collapsed dead on the ground, their devotion to the Emperor and Kage no protection against whatever magic she cast. Even the Kojin had fallen without getting close to her.

Now only two Tonin still had their gates open, bringing more soldiers to fight. One of those was in the palace behind her, and if that creature fell, there would be no escape back to Kagestan for the Emperor.

She spotted Torvi to her right. The woman looked lost, staring at her hands as if they were no longer there. 'Torvi!' she called. 'What's wrong?'

The woman looked up, her eyes wide with fear. 'My power … it's gone.'

'Go back to the palace,' said Vallia. 'Move the Tonin to the dungeons. Make sure it's safe there and ready to open a gate back to Kagestan. Do you understand?'

The Chosen nodded.

'Good. Now go!' Vallia had to duck as a Jian with a scarred face swung a metal pole at her head. Her sword took his arm first, then his head.

Still, there were plenty more of the bastards coming their way. And that girl, shining bright, not caring that it made her a target, because Vallia had nothing to throw at her that could do her harm.

Even the Emperor hadn't tried to kill her since that first attempt.

Then another heathen caught her eye and Vallia recognised her immediately. 'The Shulka!' she cried, pointing her sword at the one-eyed woman.

One of Raaku's guardians turned towards her in an instant.

The giant in the red armour rushed towards Tinnstra, slashing his monstrous sword left and right to cleave any Jian in his way.

Tinnstra stood her ground, axe and sword ready, watching the beast, searching for a weakness – and finding none. Tinnstra's speed and strength had enabled her to deal with a normal Skull, but her weapons suddenly felt very small in her hands in comparison to her opponent. Maybe she could drive her sword through his chest plate, but would it be a killing blow? She doubted that.

A shadow fell over her as the giant reached her. She threw herself backwards as his sword sliced through the air at a speed she barely believed possible. Tinnstra felt a nick on her leg that told her she had to be quicker. She rolled as the sword carved a lump out of the ground and then dived as it chased after her.

She threw her axe at the bastard's face, trying to buy some space, but the giant hacked the weapon from the air and sent it clattering into the rubble. Tinnstra was back on her feet, though, so that was something. Even if it only meant she could keep her eye on the giant as he forced her to retreat again and again, herding her further away from Raaku.

A rock sailed over and hit the giant in the side of the head, stopping his pursuit for a moment to look for who'd thrown it. As he did so, another brick struck him from behind. And another.

'Stone him!' shouted Tinnstra, grabbing a rock herself. She threw it with every ounce of her strength. The giant swung back to face her and the rock smashed into his demon mask. Shards fell away, revealing the bloodied face of a very angry man. 'He's only human. Stone him!'

More rocks of every shape and size flew from every direction. The giant tried to ignore them, tried to march towards Tinnstra, but for every step he took, bricks and stones forced him back another two.

A man staggered up behind the giant, a large boulder held above his head, but the giant spun around before he could throw it, slicing him in two. But it wasn't enough to stop the barrage from the Jians around him.

The giant dropped his sword, tried to swat at the bricks with flailing arms, but on and on they came, striking him in the face, the arms, the chest, the back. There was nowhere to escape them. He staggered forwards, swaying like a drunk. A Jian ran at him, a spear in his hand. The giant waved an arm in his direction but he hit nothing, and the Jian thrust the spear into his eye.

The mob fell on the giant, all eager to kill him many more times now that he was dead.

Tinnstra looked towards the palace, towards Raaku, and saw that Zorique had reached him before her. Her light blazed against his darkness in Tinnstra's mind and she didn't know which was stronger.

No time to waste. She started to run.

Ralasis stared at Raaku in utter horror. Even after all the monstrosities he'd witnessed over the past months, nothing had prepared him for the man – the God – before him. Raaku stood on a mound of corpses, drenched in blood, holding a sword the length of a normal man's height. Evil emanated off him, and Ralasis had no idea how he didn't piss his pants there and then.

Three red-armoured giants killed anyone foolish enough to get close, and there was a woman, too, shouting orders and directing the Skulls as they came pouring out of the palace to join the fray.

'Get Raaku,' shouted Aasgod. 'I'll deal with these bastards.' For one dreadful moment, Ralasis thought the mage was talking to him, but then Zorique launched herself at the Emperor. She burned as she flew straight at him. But Raaku wove a pattern with his hands and a wall of black light smashed her into the ground.

By the Four Gods, it had been like swatting a fly.

Then Ralasis had to cover his eyes as Aasgod sent bolt after bolt of lightning into the charging Skulls. Men screamed and men died as the smell of charred flesh wafted over the battlefield. Then a red-armoured giant had Aasgod retreating, before a gesture of his hand crumpled the man's armour on itself.

Zorique was back on her feet and sent a torrent of fire at Raaku, but again he formed another shield of black light. The flames roared against it, but Ralasis could see they were having no effect.

Nothing was going to harm that monster.

'Your Majesty!' screamed Vallia over the clash of magic. 'You have to retreat! We're going to be overrun. If we lose the palace, it's over.'

She didn't think the Emperor had heard her as he used his shield to stop the heathen queen's attack. Then his head snapped towards her. His eyes crackled with red magic, and may Kage forgive her, more than a touch of madness. For a moment, she thought he was going to strike her down for even voicing her fears, but instead, he nodded.

'Thank you, Commander. My father will reward you well for your service.'

'The Tonin is in the dungeons. It is ready to take you to Kagestan.'

Raaku shook his head. 'I go to the orb first.' He stood, still under the heathen queen's barrage, but his eyes were on Vallia. 'You are warded against the girl's magic?'

'Yes.'

'Kill her.'

Vallia nodded. 'My body is your weapon. My life, your gift.'

With the sword Raaku had given her in her hand, Vallia charged towards the heathen queen.

Everything Zorique threw at Raaku, he countered. She tried to read his powers so she could undo them, but the man was impenetrable. She had to shift from attack to defence heartbeat by heartbeat as he countered her with raw aggression.

Even so, she sensed the battle around the palace and in the boulevard was turning in her army's favour. Another Tonin had fallen, killed by Jian and Meigorian steel. Only one remained – the Tonin in the palace – but that was enough for more re-inforcements to flood out to confront her army.

Aasgod was by her side, casting lightning at the Skulls racing towards them. Brave Ralasis was there, too, fighting with steel and heart, but there was no sign of her mother. By the Gods, she hoped Tinnstra was still alive.

Suddenly, she felt Raaku's magic shift, expand. She moved with it, balancing her light against his darkness. The air rippled with fury as the weight of a mountain fell on her. She gritted her teeth and pushed back, arms shaking, knees all but buckling. Her own powers suddenly didn't feel endless. She could sense their limits fast approaching.

A woman in black armour and black mask ran at Zorique, sword raised. Zorique recognised her. It was Vallia, her jailer and torturer. She thrust a blast of light at the Egril general, but it fizzled against the woman's armour.

Aasgod saw her, too, but his lightning was just as ineffective. The woman was warded against them.

Unarmed, Zorique had to retreat as the woman's sword slashed down. She conjured another smaller shield to deflect the blow, but it was weak – too weak. It shattered when the blade struck it.

Raaku must've sensed her concentration waver, because he pushed out once more with an explosion of brute force. Zorique staggered, her shields failing, blinding pain shooting through her mind. Blood ran from her nose as she tried to gather her wits.

Vallia rushed at her, her sword a blur. Zorique threw fire at the Egril as she fell, but Vallia waded through the flames unscathed.

The black-armoured woman lifted her sword over her head for a killing blow.

Ralasis saw Zorique go down under the Egril woman's attack. Time slowed as he ran to help. Each footfall took a lifetime as the Egril loomed over Zorique, sword already in motion. Gods, he wasn't going to close the gap in time – but he had to. Had to do something.

He threw himself forwards, turning as he did so, and clattered into the Egril's legs. They both went down in a tangle of limbs and he felt the sharp bite of steel on his back.

He swung an elbow as he tried to kick himself free, smacked the woman in the jaw, but her hand found his face. She clawed at him, trying to find purchase in something – his nose, his mouth

– pulling his head back. He elbowed her again, but she wriggled behind him, legs scissored around his waist, squeezing him tight. He tried to yank her hand away, tried to bite down on her fingers, but she pulled and squeezed and Gods, she was strong. Stronger than him. And she knew how to fight, to kill. He saw her sword come around, point turning towards his chest.

Ralasis grabbed her arm, locking his elbow, needing to keep that blade from impaling him. The woman's other hand moved from his mouth to his nose, back towards his eyes.

Fear gripped him by the balls. He was going to end up blind and dead if he didn't do something.

He smashed his head back into the woman's mask, heard it crack, heard a grunt of pain, so he did it again. He howled in agony, eyes squeezed shut against her fingers, and rammed his head back a third time, a fourth time.

He heard a thunk, felt blood splatter across his neck and cheek, felt the woman go limp beneath him, the pressure around his waist disappear, the hand on his face fall away.

'Get up,' said a voice he knew only too well. He opened his eyes, saw Tinnstra standing over him.

'You saved me,' he croaked, rolling off the Egril woman.

'You've saved me enough times,' said Tinnstra. She bent down and yanked an axe out of the woman's skull.

'Raaku's gone back to the palace,' said Aasgod.

'Zorique? Is she …' asked Ralasis, still lying on the ground.

'I'm fine,' said the girl, stepping into view.

'Come on, then,' said Tinnstra. 'Let's finish this.'

By the time Ralasis was back on his feet, the others were already running.

He's not a God, just a man – and all men die.

The words ran through Tinnstra's head as they raced into the palace. They gave her small hope against the power she'd witnessed – the power she felt in her mind – but they were all she had to keep herself going.

Skulls rushed to intercept them, but they fell like leaves in the wind against Zorique's and Aasgod's magic.

'He's in the throne room,' shouted Tinnstra.

Their feet echoed down the long hallway as they ran past the Egril flags and statues of Kage and Raaku, past the dead Skulls.

Raaku's last two giant guardians stood before the doors to the throne room, barring the way. Screams from inside rang out. So many screams. *What's he doing in there?*

Zorique could see Raaku's magic flowing through them, giving them strength and power. But not enough to stop her. She thrust her hand forwards and the giants were thrown off their feet, smashing through the oak doors behind them, falling dead on the other side.

In the throne room, Tinnstra could see more demon-masked soldiers killing Jians on their knees and, past them, was Raaku. He stood by a giant orb, his magic pulsating into it. Inside red liquid swirled, gaining speed.

They rushed through the door. Raaku's soldiers turned to face them. The blood from the dead at their feet pooled around the orb. They were all unwarded in this place of magic.

Light and lightning lashed out, striking them down.

Only Raaku remained. He turned to face them, covered in blood, and laughed.

'In a few minutes, it will all be over,' he said, his voice booming in the cavernous space. 'And I have won Sekanowari.'

Tinnstra stared at the orb. Dear Gods, she'd seen something like that before. Seen enough people die by something similar. Something smaller.

'It's a bomb. A giant bomb,' she said.

III

Tinnstra

Aisair

Everyone moved at once.

Raaku fired black energy from his hands. Zorique cast a shield of light to catch the brunt of the blast, but it shattered on impact and Raaku's magic smashed her and Aasgod across the room.

Ralasis and Tinnstra both charged at the madman, screaming as they went. The Meigorian was closer, reached the Emperor first. He swung his sword up and over, but Raaku backhanded him before the blade got close. Ralasis was sent sprawling across the floor and didn't move.

Tinnstra jumped, propelled by her enhanced muscles, sword and axe aimed at the giant monster's heart and neck. Raaku snatched her from the air, his hand tight around her neck. Her weapons clattered to the ground as he crushed her throat.

Words written in a book a millennium ago flashed through Tinnstra's mind. *The Four against the One. Death comes for all that live. The Great Darkness waiting. The Light fading. Hope lost.*

She'd thought that she was Death, the killer that would slay a God. But she'd been a fool. It had always been Raaku.

As her vision dimmed, she watched the red liquid inside the orb swirl ever faster. 'How many people are you going to kill?' she croaked.

'Everyone.' Raaku grinned. 'The whole world will join my father and I in the Great Darkness.'

Then Tinnstra found herself falling free as a blur of light

smashed into Raaku. She hit the ground hard, but she forced herself up, spitting blood, as she saw her daughter burning bright, landing blow after blow on the Egril Emperor. He was over twice her size, but Zorique was relentless. She smashed fists full of fire down on the monster, pounding him into the ground.

Tinnstra snatched up her weapons, but before she could take a step to help, Raaku floored Zorique with a single punch. That was all it took.

'NO!' screamed Tinnstra as she started to run.

Lightning flashed past her, striking Raaku as he staggered to his feet, his mask cracked and falling off. It latched on to him, dancing around his body, lighting up his bones, forcing him back to his knees and, by the Four Gods, it made him scream.

He's not a God, just a man – and all men die.

His flesh burning, Raaku got to his feet and staggered towards Aasgod. Black energy mingled with the mage's lightning, forcing its own way back along Aasgod's magic. Raaku dragged his feet, gaining strength with every step, standing taller, until the lightning flickered out around him and it was Aasgod's turn to scream. Raaku's black energy had found him.

Tinnstra dropped her sword and fumbled at the pouch on her hip, pulling a throwing star free – a throwing star with poisoned tips. She hurled it with all her might, had a second following it while the first was still in the air.

Raaku jerked back as both struck home. He turned to face her, roaring with rage, one star sticking out of his eye and another in his neck.

'Serves you right,' spat Tinnstra as he pulled them free and threw them to the ground. 'An eye for a fucking eye.'

Raaku charged her. Tinnstra shifted her axe to her right hand and swung as he crashed into her, burying it in his side. It was like being hit by a mountain. All the air went from her lungs as her ribs broke, but she kept hold of her axe and hacked again at Raaku a split second before they hit the ground.

She coughed blood as Raaku climbed back to his feet. 'Stupid woman.' He stamped on Tinnstra's thigh, shattering the bone. She screamed, spittle and blood flying everywhere. She swung the axe again, but she had no strength left. He caught her arm easily and snapped it to one side. She screamed and she cried, staring at Raaku with all her hate. It couldn't end like this.

He laughed through bloody lips of his own. 'I'm not going to kill you. I want you alive until the very last moment. You'll see the orb explode. You'll die with everyone else in this city and you'll know that the orb's poison will blow across the world, sending generation after generation into the Great Darkness.'

'You'll be dead, too.'

He leaned closer. 'I'll be with my father.'

'Then fucking die!' shouted Ralasis.

Raaku turned as the Meigorian's sword cleaved him between the eyes. The Egril Emperor staggered back, pushing Ralasis to one side. Slowly, he seized the hilt of the sword and pulled it free. Raaku swayed on his feet, his one eye fixed on the blood dripping from Ralasis' sword. 'How ... did ... you ... do ... that?'

He had time to stagger once more, then Raaku fell to the ground.

Dead.

'Just a man,' Tinnstra said, coughing, but his death gave her little satisfaction. She turned to look at the orb. The red liquid was a storm inside, burning with its evil. 'Ralasis.' It hurt to call out, but she needed the Meigorian one more time. 'Ralasis.'

'I'm here.' He crawled to her side.

'Zorique has to stop the bomb.'

Ralasis glanced to his left. 'I don't think she's alive.'

Tinnstra closed her eye and let her senses open. Light shimmered around her daughter's body. 'She's alive.' She grasped Ralasis' arm, squeezed it. 'See if ... Aasgod has ... some Chikara water left. Whatever he has, pour it into Zorique's mouth. It'll wake her up.'

'Okay,' said Ralasis. 'Don't die on me while I do this.'

'We're ... all dead ... if you don't.'

'Shit.' Ralasis staggered to his feet and limped out of Tinnstra's sight. She watched the orb swirl as she listened to him scrambling inside Aasgod's bag. 'One's broken, but there's two more. They're ... they're fine.'

'Give them to Zorique,' said Tinnstra. 'Like I did ... in the castle.'

She heard him shuffle over to where Zorique lay.

'I can't feel a pulse,' said Ralasis. 'She's dead.'

'No ... no, she isn't. Give her the bloody water.'

'I am. I am.'

Tinnstra closed her eye again as pain wracked her body. It was hard to breathe, and she felt like she was choking on blood. A rib must've punctured her lung. She concentrated on Zorique's light, watched it flicker like a candle in the wind. 'Come on, my love. This is why ... we trained. We fight ... until the last.'

'Let me help,' said Aasgod.

Tinnstra smiled. Somehow the mage was still alive. She heard the crackle of lightning and Zorique screamed.

112

Zorique

Zorique sat bolt upright, lightning crackling around her. Aasgod and Ralasis fell back. 'You're alive,' said the mage.

She looked around, saw Raaku dead, saw her mother lying near him, bloody and broken. 'Tinnstra!'

'She can wait,' said Ralasis. 'You have to stop the bomb.'

'Shit.' Zorique climbed to her feet. 'Just keep my mother alive until I get back.'

She walked over to the bomb, reaching out with her magic, feeling the furious darkness within, sensing its origin and manufacture in the red waters under Raaku's castle.

Zorique placed both hands on the shell. Its vibrations rattled through her, telling her there wasn't much time.

'It's not just a bomb,' called out Tinnstra. 'Raaku ... he said its poisons will kill everyone they touch for generations.'

'Save your strength, Tinn,' said Zorique. She sent pulses of light into the orb, trying to slow the liquids down, break apart what Raaku had created. 'If Raaku was the great maker, I am the unmaker,' she whispered.

But the liquid didn't want to stop. It evaded her as she tried to corral it. It pushed back as she tried to stop it.

Aasgod staggered to her side. 'Can ... can I help?'

'I don't know,' she replied as sweat dripped off her brow. 'I'm slowing it down, but it's resisting everything I try. It's as if its alive.'

'Can you stop it?'

Zorique ran more light through the orb, trying to draw the heat from it, cool its fury, but she knew the truth. 'No.'

'Can we destroy it somehow?'

'We break the shell, it'll explode.'

'What about burying it? Collapse the palace on top of it?'

'I don't think that will stop it.'

Aasgod took a breath. 'What about your shields?'

'No.'

'Then it's over. We've lost.'

'No.' Zorique wasn't giving up. There had to be a way. She had to get it away.

She looked up. Of course. The sky.

'Tell Tinnstra I love her,' she said in a whisper. 'And watch out.'

'What are you—'

Zorique wrapped the orb in a shield and took off, shooting up, smashing through the ceiling, up through three more floors, then out through the roof into the blue sky.

Up she went. One, two, three, four miles. Higher than she'd ever flown. She glanced down and saw a carpet of green beneath her, Aisair no more than a brown dot.

Was this high enough? The cold attacked her skin and froze her blood. She gasped for air and found none.

The orb shook as if aware of what she was planning, desperate to be free of her, eager to kill the world. Cracks appeared along its surface. Tiny lines rushing to meet each other and spread across the shell.

Still Zorique flew on, eyes fixed on the heavens, until there were only stars.

'*Oso*,' she gasped with what was left in her lungs.

Push.

The orb flew on, the liquid free of Zorique's control, swirling, swirling ever faster, glowing red, light spilling from a multitude of cracks. Up into the heavens. Far from anyone it could harm.

She'd done it.

Zorique shot back to earth as the orb exploded.

113

Tinnstra

Aisair

Tinnstra was pretty sure she was dying. Every breath sent a stabbing pain through her chest, and she had to cough up blood to stop herself from choking. Her arm and leg were in ruins. Most likely her spine as well.

It had been worth it, though. They'd done what they had set out to do. Let Raaku explain to his father in the Great Darkness how he lost Sekanowari.

Tinnstra closed her good eye and watched Zorique's light fill her mind as her daughter flew back to Aisair. By all the Gods, she was so beautiful. She'd never once given up or run away, no matter how great a weight was put on her shoulders. How far she'd come from that frightened little girl, hiding behind Aasgod in a basement. Tinnstra couldn't have been prouder, nor love her more.

She only hoped she lived long enough to tell Zorique that.

Outside, her army chanted her name as they rejoiced in victory. Soon, the whole country – the whole world – would join in.

'Tinnstra!' said Ralasis. 'Stay with me.'

She opened her eye, saw the Meigorian leaning over her, fear on his face. 'I'm not ... going anywhere.'

'I mean don't die.'

'I don't think ... I have ... any choice about ... that.' Tinnstra coughed up some more blood.

'You've never done what was expected of you, so don't start now, damn it.'

747

'Why ... why do you care?'

'I've always bloody cared.'

'I thought I ... I was just another girl ... in a port to you.'

Ralasis leaned in closer and she saw the tears in his eyes. 'You could never be that.'

'Huh.' Tinnstra tried to breathe, coughed blood instead, shards of pain chasing after. 'Fuck.'

'Hold on,' whispered Ralasis, but Tinnstra was too tired to listen. Her eye fluttered shut and she let Zorique's light distract her from all the pain. It was easy to get lost in, to feel safe in.

Strange to think it once hurt her, that she ran from Zorique's light as she'd run from everything else.

Strange to think she'd been so scared of dying.

It felt right now.

The way it should be.

Lost in the light.

No Great Darkness.

Only light.

They'd won.

'Tinn?' Zorique's voice drifted by.

Her beautiful girl. Her love.

It's good to hear her voice at the end.

Hear love.

Feel love.

It's all I want.

All I need.

114

Zorique

Aisair

'Don't die on me.' Zorique knelt over her mother's body, sending pulses of light through her, doing everything she could to keep her alive while she fixed Tinnstra's injuries.

But this wasn't just a case of mending a broken arm or healing some nicks and cuts. Tinnstra had multiple injuries, most of which would kill her on their own: a fractured skull; swelling in the brain; a crushed vertebra in her neck; crushed trachea; broken ribs – two of which had punctured her right lung; a ruptured spleen; a shattered arm; severed tendons; a dislocated elbow; a fractured lower spine; a broken pelvis; a shattered femur. And on and on it went.

Maiza and Anama had both taught her anatomy when she was younger, so she could heal wounds and be a better killer.

She was vaguely aware of others – her army – entering the throne room, but Aasgod kept them back and ordered them to find the remaining Skulls or Chosen. Tinnstra would've told her to stop wasting time trying to heal her and get on with the job.

But then Tinnstra never gave up on her, and she would definitely have ignored her own advice had their positions been reversed.

So Zorique didn't give up.

She worked on, concentrating on Tinnstra's head and lungs, shifting bone, slotting it back into place, fusing it, mending tears and rips and punctures.

749

Ralasis sat on Tinnstra's other side, holding her hand. Zorique knew the Meigorian liked Tinnstra, but he looked devastated by what was happening.

'Can you fix her?' he asked.

'I'm trying, but she's got so many injuries. She's slipping away from me,' said Zorique.

'Come on, Tinnstra,' said Ralasis. 'Don't give up. Not now. You're a fighter. You're the best Godsdamned fighter there ever was. Don't bloody give up now that we've won.'

Zorique worked on. Reconstructing Tinnstra's spleen, helping her blood be reabsorbed, reducing the pressure from swellings, slotting bones together – but none of it seemed enough. She could feel Tinnstra fading. As if she didn't want to come back.

Could Zorique blame her? She, more than anyone, had earned the right to be at peace. Was Zorique being selfish trying to bring her back to the world?

Maybe.

But Zorique couldn't stand the thought of losing Tinnstra. Her mother was all she had left. The only person who didn't look at her like she was something other than herself. Not a queen, not a God. Just Zorique – and she needed that.

And Tinnstra deserved a life that wasn't a constant battle. She deserved a chance to be happy, to be herself and not the Shulka or Zorique's guardian.

So Zorique worked on. Mending, fixing, healing. She sent wave after wave of magic through Tinnstra, scanning her from top to bottom, dealing with every injury. Tinnstra's ruined eye was the only thing she couldn't fix. That damage happened too long ago to repair.

But still Tinnstra didn't wake.

'Come on, Tinn,' she whispered in her mother's ear. 'Come back to us. You're all fixed. Almost as good as new. Time to wake up. Come back to the people who love you.'

Still Tinnstra didn't move.

'Do you want me to try?' said Aasgod. 'My lightning worked on you.'

'This is different,' said Zorique, looking up. 'I've healed her body. Her heart is beating, her lungs working. She should wake up.'

'Then why doesn't she?' asked Ralasis. 'What if you've missed something?'

'I haven't missed anything,' said Zorique. 'It's as if she doesn't want to wake up.'

'Can you blame me?' croaked Tinnstra. 'With the three of you bickering over me?'

'Tinn!' cried Zorique.

Her mother still had her eye shut, but she tried a smile. 'Please – some peace and quiet.'

'Thank the Gods,' said Ralasis, crying freely. 'You're alive.'

'No, thank my beautiful daughter,' said Tinnstra. She finally opened her eye and looked straight at Zorique. 'You saved me, and you saved the world. Not bad, eh?'

'I had a bit of help,' said Zorique, fighting back tears of her own. 'You and Ralasis managed to kill a God.'

Tinnstra shook her head ever so slowly. 'He was no God. Just a man.'

Two months later

115

Ange

Arlen's Farm

Ange burst into tears when she saw the village at Arlen's Farm for the first time. She'd cried a lot on her journey back with the Meigorian army, but this was the first time she'd done it because she was happy. It wasn't the home she'd left, but she was glad it was the home she found. Gods, it looked so normal.

Someone had started ringing a bell when the column was still a few miles out and a crowd had come to investigate who they were. Word had been sent back to the village that they were no threat, and a very welcome committee had lined up to wave them all in.

There were more than a few familiar faces amongst them, bringing on more tears. Timy and Daxam, old woman Sala, big Anan. Gods, there were plenty of kids running around, shouting and cheering. Some were even laughing. How long had it been since she'd heard that?

But she didn't see the one face she was looking for, and that cut into the joy something bad. That stupid fool, Garo. He'd better be there. She'd been searching for him all the way back, after all, and not found him. If he wasn't at Arlen's Farm, she didn't know where else to look. It would be bloody typical of him not to do what he was supposed to do and go somewhere completely new, somewhere she'd never find him.

She hoped that was what he'd done, and not gone and got himself killed because Ange wasn't there to watch his back. She didn't want to think that, so, of course, she did.

Then again, what would he think if he saw her, looking the way she did? The bomb had done some pretty nasty damage to her face when it went off, sprinkling her right side with rocks and shrapnel. One chunk had even left a nasty groove in the back of her head. Lucky to be alive, they said, when they dug her out of the mess of bodies at the front gate.

Naturally, she'd got an infection in all the wounds, to add to matters. Only to be expected after lying in all that mud, blood and filth for so long. None of it had done her looks any favours, but there were plenty worse off than her. Plenty that had ended up dead or missing an arm or a leg or two.

At least Ange was walking and talking, lucky to be alive. Not like them.

That didn't make her lot any easier to deal with, though. She …

She saw him. Standing with Linx in front. Alive and smiling. Bloody Garo.

Ange threw her kit to the ground and ran over to Garo. Linx had the good sense to get out of the way as she jumped into Garo's arms and wrapped her legs around him.

'Ange,' said Garo, but she didn't give him a chance to say any more than that, because then she was kissing him.

When they broke apart, Garo pulled his head back so he could get a proper look at her. 'Why are you crying?'

'Bloody hell, Garo. I come back with my face in bloody ruins, and all you can say is "why are you crying"?'

He studied her face again. Grinned. 'You look all right to me.' Then he was kissing her back, and everything was good in the world, at last.

116

Yas

Arlen's Farm

They threw a feast that night, celebrating the returning soldiers and saying a few goodbyes, too. The injured Meigorians had been busy while their countrymen fought their way to victory, and they'd repaired enough of their ships to be able to sail home as soon as everyone was ready. There'd be a few Jians going back with them, too, hearts lost to the country's saviours, and more than a few Meigorians staying behind for the same reason. After everything they'd all been through together, even Yas had to admit she'd be sad to see most of them go.

She sat at one of the long tables with Ro next to her, watching everyone else have a good time, thinking once more about who wasn't there.

Yas had stood with everyone else, waving the column in, but she'd only been looking for one person – Hasan. But even as she watched, she'd known he wasn't going to be there. Life didn't work that way for her. The men she liked didn't last long: her husband, Rossi, Gris, Caster ... and now Hasan.

'Just you and me, eh?' she said, rubbing Little Ro's head. 'Just you and me.'

'Mind if I join you?'

Yas looked up to see Ange standing beside her. 'Sure. I'm not great company, though.'

'Not many of us are these days,' said Ange, sitting down beside Yas.

'You looked pretty happy earlier. Garo certainly looked like he'd won at life.'

That got a smile. 'Yeah, well, he has and I'm happy about that. Trouble is, I end up feeling guilty about being happy, which kinda takes the fun out of it a bit.'

'Why's that, then?'

'Somehow it doesn't feel right to still be alive when so many others aren't.'

Yas turned the girl's face so she could get a good look at her scars. 'Seems to me you came close enough to dying that you shouldn't worry about that now. You've earned it.'

'I know that, but it still don't change how I feel.'

'Give it time, love. It's early days.'

'How are you doing?'

'Surviving. Not much more than that. I'm glad the war's over, though. Glad we won.'

'I'm sorry about Hasan. He was a good man. Always treated me right.'

'Yeah, he did that.'

A silence fell between the two women that wasn't uncomfortable. Both of them giving room to the ghosts that would always be with them. 'I was surprised when I heard you gave up being the boss,' said Ange eventually. 'You were good at it.'

Yas shrugged. 'Maybe. Maybe not. I think I liked it a bit too much. Got sloppy. Thought I was something I wasn't. People died because of that.' She tilted her head towards the dancing crowd. Simone was twirling around with the Meigorian she'd fallen for. 'Simone does a better job of it – or most people seem to think so. She certainly doesn't need a couple of gangsters walking around behind her to get people to do what she asks.'

'I noticed you don't have your two shadows lurking around.'

'Despite the tears, I'm no Weeping Man. I'm just Yas now, Little Ro's mother. I'm good at that. Keep myself to myself, like my old ma used to tell me to do. Seems to be working.'

'Ah.' Ange winced. 'You might not be wanting this, then.' She reached into her jacket and pulled out an envelope. It had a fancy wax seal on the back.

Yas didn't make any attempt to take it off Ange. 'What's that?'

'A letter.'

'No shit. Who's it from?'

Ange placed it on the table in front of Yas. 'From the queen herself. Zorique.'

'What's it say?'

'Read it and find out.'

'I'm not sure I want to.'

'Bloody hell, Yas. It's good news. Well, I think it is. It's certainly not anything bad.'

'So tell me what it says.'

'I haven't read it. It's sealed.'

'I can see that,' said Yas. 'But you know what it says.'

Ange shook her head. 'The queen is setting up a government to help her get things back on their feet. She wants ordinary people who know what's what to be in it. She wants you to be a part of it.'

'Fuck off.'

'The Gods' honest truth. Seems Hasan spent most of the journey north telling her how good you are at running things. He must've been convincing.'

Yas picked up the letter with shaking hands and broke the seal, convinced Ange had got it wrong. But it turned out she hadn't. It was an invitation to join the queen in Aisair, be a part of a government 'of the people'. 'What about the Shulka?'

'Tinnstra's going to rebuild them, but no one wants them to be like they once were. Not lording it over us. Not made up of people only from certain families.' Ange laughed. 'She even asked me if I wanted to be one, but I said no. Done enough fighting.' She looked back over at the others. 'Thought I'd see if that big dumb lump had made it back alive, so I could tell him he isn't so bad after all.'

Yas folded the letter back up. 'Sounds like a good decision.'

'Yeah. What about you? You going to take her up on it?'

Yas smiled. 'Certainly something to think about.'

'I'll leave you to your thoughts, then.' Ange stood up. 'I'll see you around, Yas.'

Yas watched her disappear into the crowd, then she turned back to Little Ro. 'Who would've thought it, eh? Your old ma invited to the capital by the queen. To be someone important. Maybe even do some good.'

Someone put two bowls of stew down in front of them.

'Thank you,' said Yas, not looking up. The food smelled wonderful, and she was suddenly very hungry. She scooped up a spoonful and fed it to Little Ro. He must've been hungry, too, because he gulped it down. Yas sneaked herself a couple of mouthfuls as she fed her son, and she was glad she did. The stew was full of flavour.

'You enjoying that?' said a woman from behind her.

Yas looked up, suddenly afraid.

It was Rena. 'I made that special, just for the two of you.'

117

Zorique

Layso

It took only a few hours to fly Aasgod back to Meigore. Zorique kept her light as dimmed as she could but enough people still saw her fly over Layso, even though they'd arrived just before daybreak. She could hear the shouts and the cries as she passed over the rooftops, all so full of joy.

'I don't think I'll ever get used to it,' she said, more to herself than to Aasgod.

'What's that?'

'Happiness. Even though the war is over, it still sounds strange.'

'Give it time. It's still raw for all of us.'

Zorique lowered them both down in the grounds of the embassy and immediately staff ran out to meet them. The building was looking far better than when they'd left however many months ago.

The servants, two men and three women, fell to their knees before them and bowed.

'Please,' said Zorique, her cheeks colouring. 'There's no need for that. Please rise.'

The servants did so gingerly, but none would meet her eye.

'We didn't know you were visiting, Your Majesty,' said an older woman with grey hair tied in a bun. 'I'm sorry, but nothing has been made ready for you.'

'Don't worry,' said Zorique. 'We're only going to be here for a—'

Noise drew her attention to the street. A crowd of Meigorians were starting to gather. Word had spread quickly.

'Let's go in,' said Aasgod.

The servants followed them inside and closed the main doors behind them.

'Do we have guards for the gate?' asked Zorique.

'Yes, Your Majesty,' said one of the men. He was missing an arm and, for a brief moment, memories of Jax made Zorique shudder.

'Good. See that we're not disturbed,' said Zorique. 'We will be downstairs.'

'Yes, Your Majesty,' said the man. 'Shall we prepare breakfast for you both?'

'Just for me,' said Zorique, glancing at Aasgod. 'I'll be back up in a few moments.'

Aasgod and Zorique headed down to the basement. The bodies and the blood were long gone, leaving behind a sorrow in the air. However, when Zorique stepped into the chamber, she gasped. She could see the magic running through the walls, the road maps to places far and near. Where once there had been mystery, now there was knowledge.

The room lit up in response to her presence. Green light danced from ward to ward, powering the gate.

'Are you sure about this?' she asked Aasgod.

'I can't stay,' said the mage. 'No matter how much I want to. I should never have been here in the first place.'

Zorique smiled. 'Tinnstra was rather persuasive.'

'She kidnapped me.'

'Only the first time.'

'True. The second time was all me.' Aasgod sighed. 'I would prefer to stay and help you – you know that, don't you?'

'Of course. I'll be sad to see you go. Your advice has been invaluable. We wouldn't have won the war without you.'

'I think you would've,' said Aasgod. He looked around the chamber. 'Shall we go?'

'*Aitas.*'

Zorique controlled the transition this time. There was no

violent spinning, no sensation of the world being ripped apart – just a flash of green light and they were in a different place in a different time.

Back in Aisair in the past, at the remains of the villa where she'd grown up.

It was snowing outside and Zorique could see the remnants of the funeral pyre she'd built for Anama and Maiza under the snow.

'Looks like nothing's changed since I left,' said Aasgod, staring out over the garden.

'It hasn't,' said Zorique. 'You only travelled to the future with me an hour ago.'

'But that's impossible. Time passes in both locations.'

'That's how *you* set it up,' said Zorique. 'But I can see the magic that lies underneath, and I made it work differently. Now almost no time has passed. Your life awaits you. Go and live it for all of us.'

'I don't know if I can do that. I have so much to do, so much to prepare,' said Aasgod. 'Now I know how we win Sekanowari—'

Zorique held up a hand. 'That's knowledge you shouldn't have.'

'But I can't forget what I know. I—'

'I can help you with that,' said Zorique.

Aasgod stared at her, mouth open. He tried to speak but words failed him.

Zorique smiled. 'It will be for the best.'

'I'll miss you,' said the mage, a tear forming in his eye. 'You are a credit to all your mothers.'

'I'll miss you more,' said Zorique. She reached out and touched the side of his head. '*Wasuran.*' Light pulsed through the mage's brain.

'I don't feel any different,' said Aasgod, smiling. 'I still remember everything.'

'You won't by the time you get home,' said Zorique. She kissed the mage on the cheek. 'May the Four Gods watch over you.'

'Goodbye, My Queen.' Aasgod squeezed her hand and then

stepped out into the garden, immediately wrapping his arms around himself. 'It's cold.'

Zorique waved one last time. '*Aitas.*'

118

Tinnstra

The Kotege

'Why are we here again?' asked Ralasis.

'You'll see,' said Tinnstra, stepping through a hole in the Kotege's walls. The place was even more of a ruin than the last time she'd been there. Maybe they'd rebuild it. They'd need somewhere to teach the next generation of Shulka, after all.

'When you asked the queen for some time to go away,' said Ralasis, 'I was hoping for somewhere a touch more ... romantic.'

Tinnstra laughed. 'The Kotege not good enough for the Meigorian commander? The finest Shulka children were taught here.'

'Well, I'm not a child, and I'd prefer somewhere with a well-stocked wine cellar and a comfortable bed.'

'If you're a good boy, I'll let you have some of the wine I've got in my bag.'

'As long as it's not that Chikara water you used to drink.'

Tinnstra stopped in her tracks. She knew Ralasis didn't mean it, but it cut a little too close to the bone. 'I don't drink that anymore,' she said, almost to herself.

'I'm sorry,' said Ralasis. 'Bad joke.'

Tinnstra ran her hand up Ralasis' arm. 'Nothing to apologise for – and you'll be pleased to hear that I have a Meigorian white wine to go with our dinner tonight.'

'Now you're talking.'

They walked on through the empty building and up the stairs, while Tinnstra tried not to think about Chikara water and its bitter taste and the rush that came with it. She'd not drunk any since the battle for the city, not that there was any left to drink. She liked to think it was her choice, that she didn't miss it. She certainly didn't *need* it like she once had. Whatever Zorique had done to heal Tinnstra's injuries, it had put paid to that urge. Sometimes, though, she remembered what it was like, back when it was good and not necessary. She did miss that, if she was being honest with herself.

They walked down the corridor, past empty rooms.

'I seem to remember being here before,' said Ralasis.

'Hopefully this time will be more enjoyable.' Tinnstra stopped outside the room she'd used before they'd left for Aisair. 'I hope everything's still here.'

She pushed open the door and smiled. Everything was as she'd left it. She walked in and picked up her axe from the bed, enjoying the feel of it in her hand.

'Please tell me we didn't come all this way to pick up your favourite axe?' said Ralasis.

'It's a good axe.'

He raised an eyebrow. 'It's an axe.'

'Here – hold it for me.' She passed the weapon to him and then started to rummage through the pile of old clothes she'd left in the corner. 'Here it is.' She held up the map she'd stolen, so very long ago.

Ralasis' eyes went wide. 'Is that ...'

'The map.' Tinnstra unfolded it across the bed. 'Your map. I promised it to you after Jia was safe, didn't I?'

Ralasis was grinning from ear to ear, giving the map his full attention. 'You did.'

'You deserve it.'

'There's a piece missing,' said the Meigorian, pointing to the hole in the top-right corner.

'I cut out Egril,' said Tinnstra. 'I didn't think you'd mind.'

'I can think of better places to go.' He looked up. 'Places *we* could go.'

'Are you asking me on another adventure, Commander?' Tinnstra stepped closer, so their bodies touched.

'I think you asked me last time.'

'I seem to remember you inviting yourself.'

'I can be pushy like that.'

'The world *did* need saving.'

He kissed her. 'And save it we did.'

'*You* killed Raaku. Quite the claim to fame.' Tinnstra kissed him back.

'I don't need any more fame.' He looked up, almost shyly. 'So? Will you come with me?'

'Zorique has rebuilt the defences at Gundan. The government is in the process of being set up. I think I could disappear for a while with you.'

'Thank the Four Gods for that,' said Ralasis, pulling her down onto the bed. The map crunched beneath them. 'I thought you'd make me beg, for a moment.'

'I still might,' said Tinnstra.

'Promises, promises.'

Acknowledgements

Writing this book during a pandemic wasn't easy. Everything else life decided to throw at me made it even harder. There were times when I thought I'd never finish it. Then, somehow, it was done. Sekanowari had been fought. Victory achieved. And I couldn't be happier with how it turned out.

However, there was a massive team that made that victory possible. My name may be on the cover but I had the very best people supporting me without whom there would be no book.

Thank you to the team at Gollancz. Tomas Almeida, Will O'Mullane, Marcus Gipps, and Gillian Redfearn are all incredible people. However, special thanks must go to my editor, Brendan Durkin. I've loved working with him more than I can adequately put into words (I'm open to suggestions). His insights are always spot on and his patience with me during the writing of this book was quite legendary.

I have been extremely blessed to have Lisa Rodgers, the world's finest copyeditor, work on all my books. (I promise next time I will count better.)

Cheers to Jeremy Szal, for organising writers' drinks across 5 time zones and being willing to have a beer at 6am. (I hope you enjoyed how I killed you off.)

The books of my fellow authors Nick Martell, Brian Naslund, Justin Call, and David Wragg. Kept me entertained and inspired. Their virtual company kept me sane.

The book community is made up of truly wonderful people who do so much simply because they love books. I really appreciate everyone who has supported my books over the past few years and said such nice things, including Novel Notions, The Chronicler, Starlit Books, Bibliophile Book Club, The Book In Hand, Benny Books, Peter The Swordsmith, Under The Radar SFF Books, Fantasy Book Nerd, Nick Borrelli, David Walters, Jennifer Stebing, Timy Takács, and Adrian at Grimdark Magazine. They are all top people who do so much for the industry.

A special shout out must go to Filip Magnus. He reminded me of a character that I'd forgotten about and made this book something very different from what it was.

To the Fantasy Cabal. You know who you are. You know what you did. I shall say no more.

Thanks as ever to Mark Stay and Mark Desvaux and all the BXP team.

Mad respect to Nikki and Kevin. Wow. You have the biggest hearts and the most incredible talent. Whether it's in the booth or down at the farm, you kill it always.

Finally, the people I owe everything to:

My father, Arthur. COVID might've kept us apart during a time we really needed to be with each other but our chats will always be the highlight of my day. You are the best.

My sister, Suzie, and Mike. Thanks for being there when I couldn't. It made all the difference.

My son, Dylan. You are incredible. (Sorry about all the swear words in my books.)

My daughter, Zoe. Keep marching to the beat of your own drum (but try not to wreck the furniture).

My wife, Tinnie. What can I say? Your love and support makes everything possible. Even when I'm being grumpy, I know I am a very lucky man to have you in my life.

Love is all, now more than ever.

Credits

Mike Shackle and Gollancz would like to thank everyone at Orion who worked on the publication of *Until the Last*.

Agent
Alexander Cochran

Editor
Brendan Durkin

Copy-editor
Lisa Rogers

Proofreader
Alex Davies

Editorial Management
Áine Feeney
Jane Hughes
Charlie Panayiotou
Tamara Morriss
Claire Boyle

Audio
Paul Stark
Jake Alderson
Georgina Cutler

Contracts
Anne Goddard
Ellie Bowker
Humayra Ahmed

Design
Nick Shah
Tomás Almeida
Joanna Ridley
Helen Ewing

Finance
Nick Gibson
Jasdip Nandra
Elizabeth Beaumont
Ibukun Ademefun
Afeera Ahmed
Sue Baker
Tom Costello

Inventory
Jo Jacobs
Dan Stevens